Secrets

Volumes 3 and 4

❧

The Best in Women's Sensual Fiction

Secrets

Volumes 3 and 4

The Best in Women's Sensual Fiction

Red Sage Publishing, Inc.

Red Sage Publishing
P.O. Box 4844
Seminole, FL 33775

Contents

Volume 3

Volume 4

Contents

Secrets

Volume 3

The Spy Who Loved Me

❧

by Jeanie Cesarini

To my reader:
Wouldn't it be a wonderful world if all undercover work ended with a happily ever after?

Decisions. Decisions.

Special Agent Paige Ellison froze in the open doorway. Inside the cramped dressing room, a man came to his feet, his broad frame stealing the air. Her hand itched to grab a weapon that should have been within easy reach, her fingers burned to feel the comfortable weight of a gun in her hand. But Paige didn't need a weapon. This time. She recognized her unexpected guest.

Her pulse steadied its rapid-fire tempo. After two years of living undercover among scum, she should have been used to the clandestine meetings, the subterfuge, the backstabbing, the corruption that clung to these people like stale sweat.

But she wasn't used to them. Not yet. Not ever.

"What do you want?" She hoped he would interpret her terseness as annoyance when a nervous sweat was already beading her brow. This man was no ordinary thug—he was Lewis Goddard's right-hand man.

"The boss wants to see you. Now."

Paige didn't hesitate, just nodded her consent and followed him out the door.

Lewis Goddard wanted to see her. She wondered if this was the opportunity she had been waiting for. Waiting forever it seemed. Day after lonely day living among criminals and assuming an identity not her own. Something important must have happened, because if Goddard had made her cover, she'd be dead by now.

Smoothing the fringe of her hem as the elevator shot toward the penthouse, she wished there had been time to change her dance costume. The beaded fabric suddenly hung heavy on her shoulders, the plumage of her headpiece cumbersome and awkward even though it forced the bodyguard to keep his distance in the elevator.

Her heart accelerated as the doors hissed open and she was directed through a reception area furnished in a tasteful contemporary style that contrasted dramatically with the opulence of Goddard's casino.

But Paige had no time to admire the details of this inner sanctum before the bodyguard swept her through the office doors and left her facing one of the most wanted criminals of the nineties.

Lewis Goddard.

She had never been formally introduced. He spent most of his time on a private island in the Pacific or jet-setting around the world. She had only seen pictures of him in the FBI dossiers and glimpses through his crowded casino.

A striking man with jet black hair and fair skin, he was tall, leaner rather than muscular, but not without a raw-boned strength. Women found him attractive, but Paige couldn't get past the iciness emanating from him. The flat gleam in his eyes made her wonder if he had a soul.

Yet she was surprised. He seemed smaller, only man-sized compared to the monster proportions he had assumed in her mind. Goddard was just a man, she reminded herself. Even the most heinous mass murderers and serial killers throughout history had only been human.

He motioned her toward the desk. "Thank you for coming, Paige." Despite the words, his voice conveyed no appreciation.

Coming to his feet, he extended a hand across the desk, and Paige forced herself to respond calmly, even though it struck her as horribly incongruous they should be conducting business like two normal people when nothing about this situation was normal. She slid her palm into his, willing herself not to recoil from his granite-like grip. A grip that reminded her of touching a gravestone.

"What can I do for you, Mr. Goddard?"

His midnight gaze pierced the distance between them, assessing her appearance in a single glance, but Paige felt every inch of his perusal as though time moved in slow motion. The cool air shimmered along her bare neck, her breasts suddenly much too exposed above a costume that seemed to shrink beneath his gaze.

She felt the whisper of feathers against her skin as her shoulders rose and fell with each tight breath. The beaded fabric molded every curve of her body, and she read the appraisal in his gaze, as though he was calculating her worth to him.

He withdrew his hand. "I caught your show tonight and wanted to meet you personally."

"I hope you were pleased."

He didn't respond, just circled the desk in a few long strides and positioned himself half-sitting before her. She resisted the urge to step back and met his gaze instead.

"You've been working for me for almost two years now. Isn't that right, Paige?"

She nodded. Of course he would have done his homework. Goddard made it a point of knowing everything about his employees.

"You were hired in my LA club, dance rotations there and in the casino, too. Something not many of the girls get a chance to do. Why, do you think?"

"Luck, Mr. Goddard," she replied easily. "I was at the right place at the right time." Luck had definitely brought her here, and Paige was damned near positive all of it was bad.

"That's not what I heard." He flashed a thin smile, showing a row of straight white teeth. "Had to do with your dancing ability and willingness to help out, I believe."

Paige forced herself to return his smile. Every single gesture mattered. She wasn't sure what he was auditioning her for, but this was an audition if ever she saw one.

"Mr. Corvasce was short a dancer for the New Year's show and didn't have time to train someone here in Vegas." The humble approach was her best bet. Goddard was used to women coming on to him, but Paige knew conventional sex didn't interest him.

"I studied dance professionally for several years and learn the routines quickly."

"You were well-received, I understand."

"As I said, I've been lucky." Leaning back, Goddard studied her openly, his brow creased as if trying to read her mind. It took a Herculean effort not to flinch beneath that stare, especially when she was on the most humiliating form of display.

Despite all the glitter and plumage and make-up, Paige felt naked and hoped he mistook the goose flesh on her arms for anticipation and not the revulsion it was. "That's very kind of him to mention. But I don't have any ties to LA, no family or anything, so it's easy for me to fly to the casino at a moment's notice."

He braced his arms on the desk and leaned toward her until she couldn't draw a breath without the scent of Opium filling her nostrils. "I believe loyalty should be rewarded. Have you been rewarded for your loyalty, Paige?"

"Absolutely. Not only has Mr. Corvasce allowed me to work here and earn the casino's wages, he's given me the chance to headline the chorus show several times already."

Goddard didn't respond, and despite the air conditioned coolness, a trickle of sweat slipped between her shoulder blades. She held his gaze, hoping she hadn't blown it. Her entire demeanor was accommodating, as though she would never dream of displeasing him, yet she didn't want to come off like a wimp either.

But nothing flickered in those cold black eyes, no sense of encouragement, no emotion whatsoever. Just flat, dead eyes. This man was more dangerous than even his dossier had prepared her for. Warning bells rang inside her head, but Paige had no choice—she must get him to reveal himself, to trust her.

This was first contact, and it frustrated her to no end that while she knew everything about Lewis Goddard, knew his every sin intimately, she couldn't interpret his simplest expression. No FBI file could tell her what he was thinking.

"I've been quite pleased with the direction my career has taken since coming to work for Goddard Enterprises." She may as well toss out the hook and see if he bit. He had asked her up here for a reason, and she was tired of waiting. "I hope I can continue to prove myself as valuable."

Goddard pushed away from the desk and stood before her, so close she noticed the fine threading of his Italian jacket. "I gather it's not your ultimate career goal to be a chorus girl." Laughter softened the edge of his words, and Paige knew she was winning him over.

"I plan to become an entertainer." The lie rolled off her tongue with just the right blend of desperation and guile that it was spooky. She'd been living this lie for so long she was almost buying her own cover.

"Perhaps I can help you." He swept the turquoise feather from her cheek with a flick of his long finger. "Do you know I make movies, Paige?"

Movies? Her heart began to thump madly, and she struggled to keep her hands from fidgeting. "Yes," she answered simply. Now was not the time to get squeamish.

His finger trailed along her cheekbone, so softly she was certain she had imagined it until he cupped her chin and tipped her face upward. "What have you heard?" There was no mistaking the silken threat in the question.

"That you make . . . special movies." Special wasn't the ideal word to describe Goddard's porno flicks, but it was the only one she could think of when his hot breath fanned her face.

Besides, he didn't produce pornography in the conventional sense. Goddard's films were not for public distribution. He catered to a very wealthy, very depraved crowd.

"They are special, Paige. And I want you to star in one."

Her throat suddenly went dry, and she couldn't seem to draw a decent breath. "A . . . a movie?"

"I have a delightful screenplay. A collection of vignettes about sex through the centuries." He took her hand and let it rest gently within his. Such a gentle touch, a deceptive touch, because what he offered was death.

"Why me?" She inhaled deeply, a spark of fury making her fingers itch to gouge his skin.

"I'm not interested in teenagers. I want a woman for this role." His grip tightened ever-so-slightly. "I want you."

Her mind raced. She had known the case might ultimately lead to this, but had hoped, no, prayed she would find some other way to penetrate his "inner circle." She needed a moment to think, to control wayward emotions before she ruined everything.

Withdrawing her hand, she took a step back and fanned herself for effect. "I am completely overwhelmed by this opportunity, Mr. Goddard." She restrained the tremor in her voice. "I need a moment. Please, tell me about the movie."

Apparently satisfied with her response, he smiled and reached across the desk. "I have a copy of the script right here." He passed her a spiral bound sheath of papers. "I film on my island. I'm almost ready to start production."

This was the chance she had been waiting for. "Your island?" she repeated as casually as possible, flipping through the pages even though her palms were sweating and she couldn't dry them on the beaded costume.

"I have a studio there." He eyed the script as she let it flutter closed. "I understand you have some experience as an exotic dancer."

The FBI had provided her with a background that would fit in with Goddard and his ilk. She nodded. "I did a stint a few years back."

"But no nude film work?"

"I'm afraid not."

He dismissed the problem with a shrug. "Doesn't matter. We'll begin rehearsals immediately. You will leave for the island tonight." The statement was a command.

Tonight?

"I have an apartment. Some bills to pay. I'll have to make some arrangements, but it will only take—"

"I'll send someone to take care of everything." His hands cupped her bare shoulders, and he leaned down to meet her eye to eye. "If you accept my offer, you are to concern yourself with nothing but this script. I demand excellence from my actors." His voice swelled with pride. Paige felt sick.

"But before you agree," he continued, "I want you to understand what I mean by excellence. I have a very special method of rehearsing. You'll have an entire wing of my house where you can get to know your co-star intimately. You can absorb yourselves in your roles without all the distractions of the set. It's a technique I have found works brilliantly."

He sounded so logical, but her stomach clenched tight with dread. Rehearse? Sent to the west wing to perform sex with a stranger. While Lewis Goddard watched.

The man was a voyeur, the rehearsals nothing more than a private peep show.

His unsuspecting actors didn't realize they were being watched—or that they would be murdered in the final scene of the script. Goddard made snuff films. One actor died on screen. The other actor died as soon as the cameras stopped rolling. "Do you have any questions?" His dark eyes bored into her.

Panic made her voice lodge in her throat. She could not do this. Paige had thought she could handle this assignment, but she wouldn't perform for this monster. There had to be another way to gain access to his island.

There was no other way. It had taken almost two years to find this one. Time spent taking baby steps when she needed to be sprinting. Since she had gone undercover, Goddard had claimed two more lives. More names added to the FBI's list of victims.

But fear scattered their names like leaves in the wind, and Paige suddenly knew that going head to head with this sick bastard wouldn't make any difference. She would just end up dead like everyone else who got involved with him. She had to get a hold of her contact and get an exit code. Now.

"I believe you'll like your co-star. Quite an impressive gentleman," Goddard said, his scowl letting her know he was conscious of her indecision. "A bit older than you, but I believe you'll be exceptional together."

"Older?" she ground out.

Goddard laughed, such a blend of arrogance and lack of conscience that a chill raced through her. "I cater to a very exclusive clientele, Paige. I work with actors and actresses of all ages."

All ages.

Fear roiled inside her like brushfire—the very same fear Goddard's victims surely felt before they were murdered.

Suddenly images of those people imprinted on the backs of her eyelids. She had seen the aftermath of his work before. She remembered their names and her own horror and rage. One of his stars had been a beautiful fifteen-year-old girl, who was bright, full of life and potential.

Shelby.

As a volunteer for a community service program in college, Paige had been assigned to help Shelby through her first traumatic years in the state foster care system. But Paige's friendship and nurturing hadn't been enough to save the young girl from the lure of Goddard's venom, disguised as it was as a ladder to the stars.

Now Shelby was in Witness Protection while the FBI built a solid case against him. When she should have been making friends and going to proms like a normal teenager, she was running from city to city, scared to death of Goddard's vengeance because she had fled after her co-star had been murdered. Now Paige had a chance to give Shelby back her life. A chance to demand justice.

Could she walk away?

The answer tore through her like a gunshot. No. Her job would not be finished until this bastard stood before a jury.

If she had to play the porn star for his benefit, then so be it. Whatever it took to get on that island and retrieve a copy of Shelby's film and proof the other victims had been there—because even with eyewitness testimony, Paige had to have concrete evidence for a murder conviction. She would settle for nothing less.

"Are you having reservations?" Goddard asked. "If you don't think you're up to this, I have to know now. Once we begin filming—"

"This is a marvelous opportunity, Mr. Goddard. You are so well connected in the industry. All the exposure I'll get . . . I'm just a bit overwhelmed," she explained, determined to control her raging emotions, to lead this man into her trap.

"Good. Before we go, you can write your instructions down. Right now we need to discuss business. I want to see what I'm dealing with." He motioned to her costume with an impatient flick of his hand. "Undress."

Every fiber of her being cried out to lunge for him, to smash his skull with his own crystal paperweight and drop him where he stood. But she wouldn't. The need to put him behind bars tempered her hate and strengthened her resolve. She reached for the hook that held the costume secure.

The breath seemed to freeze in her lungs, and Paige could not suppress a shiver. The weight of the beaded fabric fell away as the zipper separated, the chilly air piercing her skin like pinpricks. Garters and shimmery hose slipped to her ankles, leaving her exposed. Vulnerable.

Goddard's black gaze raked over her. He had seen her on stage before, but appraised her with the practiced eyes of a professional. With the eyes of a man who thrived on power. On watching.

His mouth compressed into a straight line, and his nostrils flared.

Raw carnality rolled off him in palpable waves, blasting her with the force of his hunger. The air grew thick, cloying, and she fixed her sight on the glittering skyline through the windows, refusing to give in to the revulsion pumping through her veins with each beat of her heart.

Burying every shred of emotion deep inside, Paige stood naked before him, head high. She would not let Lewis Goddard destroy her, too. She would bury her feelings deep inside, protect herself, so when this game was over, her heart wouldn't be a hollow cavern in her chest. She would win her case and then enjoy the peace of knowing justice had been done.

But tonight was only the beginning. Tomorrow she would have to submit to a stranger's touch.

Ace in the Hole

Special Agent Christopher Sharp unstrapped the chamois roll hanging around his hips and slid it from beneath his running shorts. Weighing the familiar heaviness in his palm, he outlined his "tools of the trade" through the soft leather. The weatherproof roll definitely wasn't much by way of bureau-issue gadgets, but it just might come in handy when the time came to escape the island.

Wedging his fingers in the crevice of the rockface, he grappled for purchase on the rugged slope and shifted a stone enough to create a hiding hole behind it. Shoving the roll inside, he set the stone back in place with a satisfied grunt. His ace in the hole. He never left home without one. Damn good thing, too, since he had been in Goddard's lair less than twenty-four hours and this case had already taken an unexpected turn.

Caught with his pants down.

The phrase played over and over in his head with irritating regularity. He had been caught—both literally and figuratively. After months of arranging the perfect legend and living his cover, Christopher had auditioned for the male lead in Goddard's upcoming snuff film and won the role.

His first surprise came when he hadn't been given a chance to pack a toothbrush before flying to this island fortress. Goddard had preached some crap about "taking care" of his actors, but Christopher recognized it for the security measure it was.

And should have anticipated it.

Lewis Goddard hadn't eluded the nation's top law enforcement agencies without being cautious. Miscalculations like this had gotten agents killed. He could only claim preoccupation. In his impatience to see Paige, he hadn't been using his head.

Sweat trickled down his brow, and he wiped it away while visually marking the twisted clump of tree roots in relation to the rock his tools lay under. He scrambled down the slope to the beach. Paige's contact could put him back in touch with his own. He would get harassed royally when he returned to Washington, but if that was the worst of it, he would consider himself lucky.

Resuming the pace of his run, Christopher breathed deeply of the sea air as the Pacific wind cooled the sun pounding on his bare shoulders. Goddard was expected any time now. Paige would be with him. He couldn't suppress his anticipation at the thought of seeing her again.

She had captured his heart when she was his student at Quantico. Strict regulations and personal honor had forbidden him from pursuing her then, but he couldn't forget her. She lurked in the darkest reaches of his mind, the memory of her full lips turning upward in an easy smile, a vision of her lithe dancer's body gleaming with perspiration as she scrambled over iron corrugated walls and rope bridges. After her training at the Academy, she had left sporting a gold badge. He had gone back into the field. And the game of cat and mouse had begun.

What a game it was. Every time he maneuvered them together—a stint in Washington or some quickie surveillance assignment or, hell, even a layover in some remote field office—Paige managed to slip through his fingers, leaving him a little more fascinated. A little more frustrated. She rebuffed him. Rejected him. Almost made him believe she didn't want anything to do with him.

Almost.

Even though she routinely denied that sparks flew between them, those beautiful sapphire eyes didn't lie. The way she had melted in his arms when he kissed her in Montana told another story. Paige wanted him as much as he wanted her.

Now the chase was over. They were stuck together on an island where she couldn't get away. He would finally discover why she fought the passion between them and learn to respect her resistance. Or wear away her every last defense. But this time she wouldn't get away.

Christopher drew a deep breath and slowed his pace as the footpath gave way to craggy cliffs. Taking care with each step, he considered the role he played. The role Paige played. What they must do to stay alive in Goddard's world.

Sex.

Everything he had ever fantasized about was detailed in a script, and his heart raced just thinking about it.

True, the intimacy he had always imagined was not a part of this scenario. They would be performing for Goddard's benefit. And they would be murdered after filming.

That grisly thought dragged him back to reality.

Below, waves exploded against the cliffs in a violent dance, reminding Christopher of those who never made it beyond that churning current, their lives ended in a host of inventive, grotesque ways to pleasure a sick audience. Lewis Goddard was an animal and meeting the man hadn't changed Christopher's opinion.

He still marveled that Paige had actually taken this case. She had always fought so hard against the chauvinism that had haunted the FBI since the days of Hoover and his G-men. Yet this assignment forced her to face the worst of sexual crimes, to use every feminine wile created since the dawn of man. Totally against her "if he can do it, I can blow him away" mentality. She had barreled through the Academy with brains and physical prowess, yet here she was wielding her femininity like a sword to carve her way through Goddard's camp.

All to protect a witness? He wondered.

The cliffs beveled into a rolling grade as he approached the harbor. An increase in activity along the docks alerted him to the new arrivals. Christopher kept his pace as the marina came into view but couldn't slow the pounding of his heart when he saw Goddard's powerboat occupying a previously empty slip.

Paige had arrived.

He had barely dried the sweat from his face when one of the marina attendants met him at the bottom of the cliff.

"I was just about to come looking for you," the attendant said with a gravity that suggested he was announcing the end of the Cold War. "Mr. Goddard is in. He wants to see you up at the house."

A twenty-five-thousand-square-foot showpiece designed to impress, Goddard's house served its function admirably. From its lofty perch on a cliff, the house eclipsed a sheltered harbor. White-stone walls glinted in the sunlight with a brilliance that drew the eye, a sprawling angel with wings spread in a protective embrace over the island. How deceptive appearances could be.

Composing himself as he wove through the halls toward the west wing, Christopher had no success at curbing the sudden rush of adrenaline that powered his footsteps into a barely dignified trot.

He found them in the library discussing the script. "Good morning, Christopher." Lewis Goddard came to his feet behind the desk and motioned toward the woman who stood and turned toward him. "I want you to meet your lovely co-star, Paige. Isn't she everything I said she'd be?"

Christopher still recognized the idealistic young rookie in the exquisite woman before him. The lines of her body were long, fluid, beneath the casual silk pantsuit she wore. The delicate fabric revealed more than it concealed, emphasizing the fullness of her breasts, the slim curves of her waist and the incredible length of her legs. Images of those legs twined with his threaded through his imagination, and blood pounded through his body.

Her auburn hair fell in a riot around her shoulders, its length a silent tribute to the time that had passed between their meetings. God, just the sight of her was like gasping much needed air. How had he survived from one breath to the next?

The slight parting of her lips drew his gaze to her face, to the dimples that peeked at the corners of her mouth, to the smooth cheeks blushing in shades of peach and cream, to the thick fringe of lashes silhouetting eyes bright with sapphire lights.

Deep inside, he had hoped Paige would be pleased to see him, at the very least relieved her co-star was not a stranger. A lot to hope for, he knew, but hope sprang eternal. Yet in all his imaginings, Christopher had never expected to be greeted by the surprise that flashed across her face now.

She stared at him, eyes wide, posture rigid. She was not pleased to see him. But her shock was even more of a blow. The worst had happened—Paige had lost touch with her contact, too, or she would have known to expect him.

Renewed Acquaintances

What in hell was he doing here?

Paige could only stare. The breath had solidified in her throat, and she could scarcely swallow, let alone breathe. Why hadn't the bureau warned her? She would have insisted they find another agent. Any other agent!

Christopher faced her with a warning glint in his deep chocolate eyes. Years melted away, and she was instantly transported back to the role of student. Christopher Sharp was in charge, always in control of himself and everyone around him. The "iron spy" they had called him at Quantico, an appellation that summed up the man to a T.

He had forged himself an almost legendary reputation within the bureau as an internal spy—a man who specialized in undercover operations reminiscent of those immortalized by the CIA. He was called in to deal with heavy hitters like Cosa Nostra, industrial espionage and crime rings the caliber of Lewis Goddard's. Word had it that he was a chameleon with a knack for bringing the bad guys down. Paige knew better. The iron spy was a power junkie who liked playing the odds.

And now he was here.

Plastering a smile on her face, she extended her hand, and he caught it within his, gaze raking over her in one bold stroke.

"She is everything you said." He brought her hand to his mouth and pressed a kiss to the center of her palm, his lips rough velvet, his breath a warm puff against her skin.

A wave of desire that betrayed every shred of her reason spiraled straight to the pit of her stomach. Damn!

"A pleasure," she replied, her throat barely forming a whisper. She withdrew her hand, needing distance between them, needing to collect her thoughts before she blew this whole meeting and got them killed.

"I knew sparks would fly between you two," Goddard announced, sounding so pleased Paige wanted to kick him. She schooled her emotions and faced the one agent in all the world she did not want to see.

"This is Christopher," Goddard announced, obviously in the throes of some ego trip at the sight of them together. "You two will get to know each other very well in the next few weeks."

Paige swallowed hard. If that wasn't the understatement of the century.

Christopher smiled a roguish smile. "I believe the pleasure will be all mine."

No doubt!

Goddard laughed, and the sound grated along her nerve endings. "We've been going over the script, Christopher. Grab a chair. There are a few things I want you to keep in mind during rehearsals."

Goddard circled the desk while Christopher took the seat beside her. His nearness sent a shimmer along her spine and brought to mind all the lurid details of the script she had been discussing with such calm detachment.

Damn, but the man was gorgeous! The last time she had seen him, his deep golden hair had been cropped close in a style that emphasized the rugged line of his jaw, the strong shape of his head. Now it was long—longer than she had ever seen it. Rebellious waves escaped the clip at his nape, sculpturing his face like a tawny mane.

With his broad, high cheekbones and deep-set eyes, he reminded her of a lion. King of the jungle. King of wherever he was. There was a predatory air about him, about the erotic fullness of his mouth, about the plated muscles that shifted with sleek grace as he reached for the script, about his sheer size that made him overshadow everything in his presence. Including her.

How could she work this case with him? Just looking at him bombarded her with that familiar melange of emotions she struggled with every time she saw him. Christopher Sharp the mentor. The slave-driver. The predator.

The man who wouldn't take no for an answer. Like the time he had kissed her in that Montana field station. She had melted in his arms then, confirming her denial of him meant nothing beneath the potency of his maleness.

God, how embarrassing—she still cringed at the memory.

And just when she thought her fascination with him was finally under control, he showed up again to prove her wrong.

Oh, so wrong.

Perhaps her hot/cold response to him wasn't so surprising. The male domination thing had been an issue her entire life. Her father had controlled her mother, had controlled her for far too long.

"Paige, you'll study dance because it's cultured . . . Paige, you will not go to the prom with that motorcycle-riding dope head, you will go with the boy in the Baccalaureate program . . . Paige, you'll go to med school,

specialize in cardiology like me . . . Paige, you'll date this resident. He's a fine man with a promising future. . . ."

No. Paige wouldn't.

Paige was finished being controlled. She was becoming a federal agent—a career she found interesting. A career that allowed her to exercise some control of her own.

But with visions of G-men dancing in her head, Paige had found Christopher Sharp, instead. Exactly the type of man she needed to stay away from. A man with a need to control.

He had manipulated her completely during training, forced her to surrender to his tutelage so he could mold her into the perfect agent. A perfect "spy" like him. Through the years since Quantico, she had blessed him for it. And cursed him every time her convoluted sense of duty made her accept an assignment like this.

And this one was certainly proving to be a winner. She had just about convinced herself that performing sex with a stranger while Goddard watched would be worth it just to put the sick bastard away. Besides, after Goddard went before a judge, she would never see her co-star again.

But Christopher Sharp wouldn't disappear. She hadn't been able to get him out of her mind before. She'd never get rid of him now.

As if that wasn't bad enough, the heavy-lidded look in his eyes made her tingle, made her think about how his strong hands would feel on her body.

"This rehearsal is not about learning your lines," Goddard said, tapping a manicured nail on the desktop and dragging her back to attention. "It's about arousal and sex. I want tension between you. The script is a build up toward a climactic finish, and it won't work if you are indifferent to each other."

Climactic finish. Paige suppressed a shiver. Murder was more like it. Dread knifed through the edges of her calm. She wondered who was scripted to die, yet it didn't really matter. Whoever didn't die on film would die as soon as Goddard yelled, "Cut."

But unlike the other actors, Paige knew this was a snuff film. What she didn't know was how Goddard could sit there so coldly, so blatantly unaffected, while playing god with their lives.

Sick bastard.

"I'll answer any questions that come up, but I want your rehearsals to remain unstructured," he continued. "Stick loosely to the script, but remember that this time is for you to interact, to find out what turns you on. When we do start filming, I expect chemistry. I want your sex to be much more than an act." He formed the words carefully, as if savoring the idea of seeing them together.

Christopher stiffened beside her, so subtly she might not have noticed had she not known him. But she recognized the way his fingers flexed as if he was having trouble keeping his fists to himself.

The iron spy.

He was a miracle in self control. While she could barely suppress the urge to lock her hands around this pervert's throat, she marveled at Christopher's restraint when Goddard gave them a tour through the luxurious stage that was the west wing.

He had designed every room with a carnal purpose. Her gaze traveled over the lay-out, spacious and open, with no walls to obstruct the surveillance equipment concealed in the ornate wainscoting. The furniture provided a staged panorama so exact she could easily pinpoint the camera's positions.

They toured room after room—an enormous kitchen where she found five separate surfaces to make love on at first glance, a study with a huge fireplace and a real bearskin rug, an opulent indoor spa she could easily envision as a mystical spring—with Goddard playing both tour guide and director.

Christopher's jaw was set, his gaze fixed beneath burnished brows, as they listened to Goddard's lurid suggestions. She walked along at his side, acutely aware of his presence, but he only remarked upon the rooms, paying no particular attention to her, as though they were indeed the strangers they pretended to be.

"You can rehearse your striptease in this dance studio." Goddard rested a long-fingered hand on the bar that circled the room and cast her a penetrating glance as though her clothes would start melting off of their own volition. "I want classy, not slutty. Think Gypsy Rose Lee or Tempest Storm, not some strung-out thrash from the Mons."

Paige only nodded, eyes darting to the corners of the room. No cameras in here. The entire studio was walled in observation mirrors.

As if those mirrors reflected her vulnerability, Christopher placed a hand on her shoulder, his touch firm but gentle. She met his gaze, wondering how much her eyes revealed. Did he know that the very idea of dancing for him made excitement clench low in her belly?

A smile curved his full mouth and sparkled in his eyes. He knew all right. And with every step, her pulse increased in tempo until it slammed through her veins like a tidal wave. But the enormity of their situation didn't really strike home until she stepped into her suite and realized it was Christopher's, too.

His robe lay across the bed like he had discarded it carelessly before his morning run. Personal items sat askew on the dresser, a bottle of Calvin Klein's Escape, a sweat band from some work-out session that had been left to dry in a heap.

On the floor sat a pair of well-worn topsiders, slipped off and forgotten, but marking his presence in the room. His room. Her room. The room they would make love in. A knot formed in her throat. This was a scene from her worst nightmare. Her most secret fantasy. Her eyes kept darting back to the bed. She shivered.

"You've got all kinds of toys here." Goddard cracked open a night table drawer and revealed an assortment of sexual paraphernalia. Twisted silk ropes in a variety of sizes. A double-headed vibrator. A whip.

His excitement was almost tangible, transforming the room into a high-tech sexual chamber. His pale fingers trembled slightly when he held up a set of handcuffs. The sudden silence pulsed in her ears. "I want much more than a performance."

Paige cast a surreptitious glance at Christopher and had no trouble at all envisioning his powerfully built body clad in leather and furs, his sensuality potent as he played the role of medieval chieftain.

Whatever had possessed her to accept this assignment?

"The days are for rehearsing, but the nights are yours," Goddard told them. He slid the drawer closed and stepped off the platform that made the bed the visual focus of the room. "Enjoy my hospitality. Let me know how you are progressing." He clasped Christopher's hand and then pressed a kiss to her cheek. "Make it good. You are part of my team now, and I only work with the best."

Paige watched him retreat, anxiety spiking each breath. She jumped when the door slammed shut behind him, leaving her alone with Christopher.

Before she had a chance to swallow a calming gulp of air, Christopher's hand clamped around her wrist and she was propelled into motion.

"Come on," he ordered, not bothering to glance back as he dragged her across the suite. "I need to shower, and you're coming with me."

Paige came to an abrupt halt that was less a show of resistance than surprise. Either way, she forced him to stop in mid-stride. "Excuse me?"

That chocolate gaze snared hers, and there was no mistaking the intensity of his mood. "I said let's go."

She recognized his tone from the Academy. Once she had obeyed him with no questions asked. Never again. "I have no intention of showering with you." She fixed him with a glare that would have caused anyone else to think twice. Anyone except Christopher.

He only exhaled sharply, a breathy burst that clearly conveyed his annoyance. Paige didn't care. Better he learn right here and now that her days of obeisance were over.

Before she could tell whether or not he got the point, his arms lashed around her and he hoisted her over his shoulder as easily as he shrugged on body armor. "I have no intention of starting rehearsals without a shower. Call it a quirk of mine, but I can't perform until I know we're both squeaky clean."

Of all the . . . Paige struck at him with her fists, but he only grunted and tightened his grip. Marching through the doorway leading into the bathroom's spacious outer area, he wedged her through another doorway toward the spa. She eyed her retreating reflection in the mirrors as dispassionately as the sterile surroundings. Her attempts to resist were futile. She stopped struggling when they emerged in a sort of a mini spa with a Jacuzzi tub and glass-enclosed shower. He kicked the door shut behind them.

Without a word, he let her slide to the floor, her breasts riding the length of his hard chest, her abdomen rounding the arch of a very noticeable bulge between his legs. The tightness in her belly twisted into a knot. He was excited by her? The iron spy couldn't possibly suffer from something as base as arousal. That would suggest a loss of control, and Christopher Sharp never lost control.

The very idea contradicted everything she knew about him, and Paige wasn't at all sure she wanted to deal with any more surprises today. Not when she was facing the most important case of her career. Not when Shelby's future—not to mention her own and Christopher's—rode on nailing Goddard with a charge that would stick.

She pulled away, and he released his grip so suddenly that she staggered back a full step. Turning his back to her, Christopher flicked on the light switch then turned the shower on full blast.

"Undress." He pulled the rumpled shirt over his head, and her gaze stuck on his broad chest with its thick muscles and tawny hair trailing down his stomach into a slim line at his navel.

He radiated sensuality, as though his bronzed body had been created for the sole purpose of pleasure. Her pulse throbbed in her temples as she took in every hollow and ridge of that muscular physique, so strong, powerful—not the raw-boned strength of a boy, but the solid, sun-hardened strength of a man.

Paige blinked once, twice. The skimpy running shorts only emphasized his size, making him appear more erotic than sheer nakedness would allow.

"I have no intention of . . ." the protest died in her throat as he pushed the shorts over his hips and kicked them away.

His thick sex sprang out from a thatch of lionine fur, and Paige could only stare. He was hard. And enormous. Blood pulsed through a network of veins toward a wide smooth head that pointedly accused her of being responsible for its current state.

"Everything meets with your approval, I hope." His throaty laughter resounded above the steady pulse of water, shocking her from her unwitting inspection.

Fire erupted in her cheeks, and she turned her back to him. Desire simply had no place in her thoughts right now. She should make another attempt to escape, but his sheer masculine presence rooted her to the spot. To reach the door she would have to face him, and she just couldn't do that. Not when her face would reveal how much he affected her.

"Don't get prissy on me now, Paige." His laughter echoed in her ears.

Before she could think up an adequate defense, his hands were on her. She whirled to resist and met his nakedness head on like a train. A dizzying current soared through her as he wrestled the thin blouse over her head, his size an advantage she simply couldn't overcome. Not when all rational thought fled. Not when her gaze seemed locked onto the sight of his broad hands sliding the silky pants over her hips and down her legs, leaving her standing before him in nothing more than a sheer bodysuit.

She heard his breath catch, and the sound snapped her out of her daze. "Christopher, stop!" she commanded, but her voice betrayed her, the words tumbling from her lips in a garbled rush.

He had no intention of listening anyway and pulled her hard against him, his touch hot, potent, as he peeled the bodysuit away.

Her reaction was instant.

Desire speared straight between her legs, and her imagination conjured all sorts of ways to indulge the sensation. Just an inch or two more, just the simplest of motions, and those hot fingers would stroke her, caress the tender skin that ached with the promise of his touch.

"God," he whispered as his hand skimmed her bare flesh and pushed the bodysuit down her legs.

She swallowed back a moan, exhilarated he was so similarly affected. Steam billowed from the shower stall in amorphous clouds, glossing her skin with hot silk and slicking their bodies together with moist suction. She wanted him to touch her. Desperately. The need was so sudden, she couldn't make sense of anything except his body pressed against her.

Christopher growled, a throaty male sound, and his mouth found hers, tasting, causing the most delicious deluge of pleasure to pour through her. A sigh slipped from her lips. Christopher caught the sound, sharing the strength of his attraction, making her realize just how much she wanted him.

With each greedy taste of his lips, with each demanding thrust of his tongue, he wrung the most heady responses from her. She had never reacted like this to a man.

But then Christopher Sharp was no ordinary man.

He had been her instructor, had held her future within his grasp. From the way she dressed to the way she handled a gun, she had tried to please him.

As always, he was unmerciful. He had driven her past all perceived boundaries until she had discovered that no limits existed between them. He would make her sample passion the same way. Unless she stopped him.

She would not get caught in this power struggle. Not after finally escaping a lifetime of dictates and commands. Not after she had grown accustomed to calling the shots. Christopher threatened her fiercely-won independence. Everything had to be his way. Always. Paige would fight.

But even as her mind made the vow, her will seemed to melt. Their flesh molded together as one, and she abandoned all pretense of resistance, wanting to touch him, to feel the play of muscles beneath her fingertips. Slipping her hands between them, she smoothed her palms over his chest, exploring the raspiness of hair cushioning the muscles below.

Christopher had won. Again.

The heavy languor of desire lapped through her veins like hot wine. And he knew. Oh, yes, he knew, just like he had always known her every strength, her every weakness, her every thought. And as always, he pressed his advantage to tip the scales into his favor.

She struggled to remain standing when his thigh found a welcoming niche between hers. No matter how hard she willed herself not to, she rode that length of hard muscle, the ache inside propelling her into motion along his flesh.

Her hand slid down the arc of his waist, over the trim line of his hip, drawn toward his tantalizing maleness. Her fingertips skimmed the ruff of hair at its base, her palm cupping him until a throaty groan echoed between them.

Ah, a flash of triumph. She savored the sound of his reaction, savored the sensation as that hot shaft jumped in her hand.

Christopher Sharp never could handle defeat, and Paige knew it. He tore his mouth from hers with a growl, a sound so raw, so primitive she almost took a step back. Her hand fell clumsily to her side.

Without a word he dragged her into the shower and stood beneath the spray, eyes closed, breaths coming in ragged gasps. The echo of his touch faded as she watched his struggle, knowing he fought his desire for her.

The iron spy had lost control.

So had she. Passion turned resolve to water, and she leaned against the wall, pushing hair out of her face, dignity dissolving in the sensuality of the moment. How could she have liquefied in his arms as if starved for his touch? Paige knew the answer even as the question formed in her mind.

She had spent her whole life seeking approval. First her father's and then Christopher's. Ice skated across her nerve endings despite the steamy heat of the shower.

"You're out of touch." He glared at her.

She brought her finger to her lips in a plea for silence, shocked by his lack of caution.

"There's no surveillance in here." He dismissed her concern with a scowl. "I checked out the place last night. That's why we're in here."

"Are you sure?"

His tawny brows shot upward. "Of course."

Well, she didn't take chances. He had taught her that. "I guess it's a good thing we have a place to talk. Now that you're here."

Christopher snorted. "Goddard apparently thinks we deserve some privacy in the bathroom. And inside the closets." He leaned into the spray to grab a bar of soap from a niche on the back wall.

"Cordial host, eh?" Paige tightened her arms across her chest. He would read the defensive gesture for what it was, she knew, but couldn't stop herself from reacting. She was defensive. Christopher might be back in control again, might be able to dismiss what had passed between them so easily, but she was standing within arm's reach, bare-assed, her body still trembling with the memory of his kiss.

"You're out of touch." A frown drew his brow together as he pinned her with a stare.

"How did you know?" she whispered.

He worked a lather over his chest. Water sluiced over him, and his muscles shifted and glowed beneath rivulets of soap. Bubbles cascaded down his body, playing along the trim lines of his waist, into the hair surrounding his sex, down the muscular hardness of his thighs. His body gleamed like bronze under the rush of water. She couldn't manage more than a blink when he said, "You'd have expected me otherwise."

She hadn't expected him. Not in a million years.

"You came here knowing you were out of touch with the bureau." His words were an accusation. "What in hell were you thinking?"

His nakedness may have made it difficult to think, but his indignation sparked her temper.

"That should be obvious." She erupted from her daze, ignoring the muscles that glinted beneath the bubbles. "I was unwilling to blow this chance just because Goddard threw me a curve."

"A curve?" Christopher shook his head, incredulous, sending water droplets spattering.

Paige hugged her arms around her as much to shield herself from the spray as to protect herself from his relentless stare. "I know it wasn't procedurally correct—"

"Procedurally correct," he repeated, his soapy fingers grasping her chin and jerking her face upward. "I don't give a damn about procedure. This man makes snuff films. Your life is at risk."

She wanted to point out that his life was also in danger, but something in his face, some emotion she didn't recognize, made her hold back.

Her voice dropped to a whisper, and she asked, sweetly, a concession to whatever sentiment the iron spy had let slip, "You'll put me back in touch with my contact, won't you?"

Christopher's hand fell away, leaving a bubbly trail in its wake. A scowl shadowed those warm eyes, gathering like cloud cover before a summer storm. Had Paige not known better, she would have thought he looked . . . well, sheepish.

Christopher surprised her by drawing a deep breath. "I'm out of touch, too."

She should have mercy on him, knowing as she did how difficult his admission must be, but even after all these years, there was still a rookie inside who demanded justice.

When the urge to laugh struck, it struck hard. She managed to swallow most of it back, but the sarcasm was there, biting, tangy. Whoever said revenge was sweet?

"Explain something to me, Christopher. Why are you here if you're out of touch?"

If he could have devoured her in one bite, he would have. "I assumed I could get back in touch through you."

"That'll teach you to assume."

Oops! The man had no humor whatsoever, she remembered too late when his hands locked onto her shoulders. He shook her. Hard. "Paige, this is serious. You know Goddard's dossier even better than I do. This mission is out of control."

She tried to shrug away, irritated when she couldn't shake off his wet grip. "What are you suggesting?"

"Abort." The command echoed through the shower stall with eerie finality.

"Abort?" she blurted out and immediately lowered her voice to a strained whisper. Even if there wasn't any surveillance equipment in the bathroom, Goddard's cronies could be lurking behind closed doors.

"I've worked for two years getting Goddard to invite me here."

Christopher ran impatient fingers through his long hair and pushed the dripping strands back from his face. "I cannot approve this, Paige. We're of no use to the bureau dead."

Could she possibly make him understand? One glance at the unyielding set of his jaw told her that any attempt to reason would be useless.

Paige did the next best thing—took the offense. Thumping him hard on the chest with an outstretched hand, she growled, "Listen, buddy, you may be the senior agent here, but this is my case. If you want to abort, that's your call. Swim back to the mainland for all I care." She snapped the shower door open with such force the glass rattled in its casing. "Just don't jeopardize my cover."

Paige left the bathroom without looking back.

Put Your Money Where Your Mouth Is

Christopher reappeared in the suite dressed to watch a striptease. "Have you spent much time going over the script?" he asked, heading toward the dresser and running a comb through his damp hair.

He had apparently decided not to swim for shore, but his expression told Paige he wasn't thrilled about it.

Neither was she. His mention of the script and its explicit sexual scenarios reminded her of exactly what she was expected to do with him.

"Enough." More than enough.

She had spent the better part of her career dodging Christopher and his *chance* meetings. Avoiding the man and the emotions he aroused inside her. Refusing to give in to feelings that made her vulnerable.

His gaze caught hers in the mirror as if he knew her innermost secrets. Sensed her hesitation. "Are you ready to put your money where your mouth is?" She couldn't miss the challenge reflected in that deep gaze.

Ready? Now that was another question entirely. Christopher Sharp was here to have sex with her. Lewis Goddard would be watching. An icy fist hammered at whatever courage she had mistakenly thought she possessed. Paige was not ready.

She nodded anyway.

"You certainly dressed for a striptease." He cast a wry glance at the full leotard she wore.

Everything except her toes, heels and hands was covered, and she had thrown on a sheer skirt that fell to mid-calf for good measure. Not the easiest costume to strip out of, but one that kept her sufficiently clothed as she battled this overwhelming sense of vulnerability. "I was cold."

A smile twitched at the corners of his mouth, and she dug the crescents of her nails into her palms to resist the urge to slap him.

"You still want to start with the striptease?"

"Rehearsing the scenes sequentially seemed like a novel idea," she remarked dryly.

The striptease was the first vignette. She was expected to slither around a pole and have sex with Christopher—while Goddard watched from behind observation mirrors. She understood what she had to do, and this vignette had seemed tame compared to the submission and bondage in the rest of the script. Now she wasn't so sure.

"Shall we, then?" Christopher grabbed the script off the coffee table and offered his arm in a gentlemanly fashion.

She ignored him and sailed through the door.

Hogan's Alley hadn't prepared her for an eventuality like this one. Shoot outs—yes. Hostage negotiations—yes. But never had any courses or subsequent work experiences explained how to make sex with Christopher a casual experience.

Her throat constricted, and she padded down the carpeted hallway beside him in silence. He appeared much larger than life in the light cotton sweats that emphasized the muscular length of his legs, the loose-fitting tee that didn't quite cover his taut stomach.

She never dreamed he would take on a case like this one. Suddenly he no longer resembled her brusque instructor from the Academy. The man who had trained the next generation of "spies" for the FBI. This man was a stranger.

The dance studio was equipped with all the modern conveniences, including a stripper's pole. An image of herself hanging onto it, breasts jiggling and hips undulating while Christopher watched, made her stomach flip-flop precariously. And all those mirrors. Goddard was back there somewhere waiting for the show to begin. Watching.

Christopher tossed the script on to a shelf above the sound system and began flipping through CDs. "Anything in particular? There's quite a selection here."

Paige shook her head, not trusting herself to speak. He chose a piece with a two-second beat, perfect for warming up, but she stood frozen in the doorway, unable to move, risking everything with an amateurish display of nerves.

God help her, she couldn't do this.

"Paige, are you ready?"

No! She wanted to cry out, but swallowed the protest on the edge of a strangled breath when she lifted her gaze and met chocolate eyes warm with understanding.

He strode purposefully toward her, and suddenly she wasn't alone. As he clasped her hand firmly and led her into the center of the room, fear eased its garrote.

"Come on, Gypsy. I'm looking forward to a show."

No doubt. Paige sank to the floor and closed her eyes, letting his nearness flow through her. He squeezed her hand in quiet reassurance.

Inhaling deeply, she focused on her body, on muscles tight with tension, trying to forget that somewhere behind those mirrors lurked a man who killed for a sexual thrill.

But Paige would do her job. She might have to rehearse, but this was the last rehearsal Lewis Goddard would watch.

Arching her back, she flexed to isolate specific muscles through her body and gradually built up a rhythm, letting the music soothe away her stiffness, working each muscle sequentially from her ankles to her toes, searching desperately for some corner of her heart where her emotions could hide.

But mingled with dread was an intense awareness of Christopher, of his breathing in deep even bursts, over-riding her own tempo. Her awareness of Goddard became overshadowed by the man physically beside her.

She opened her eyes. Christopher sat nearby, arm draped casually across his knees as he watched her with the very concentration she lacked. Paige redoubled her efforts. This entire charade wouldn't work unless she got a grip on herself. Christopher's appearance may have upset her plans, but she had to focus.

Much easier said than done.

She found her gaze drawn again and again to his reflection. Her every movement revealed a new glimpse of his body: the strong lines of his thighs, the supple curve of his hips, the rippled length of his torso, the bold sweep of his back.

Spellbound by the sight, she rose to dance a sequence in an effort to distract herself. Relevé, plié, parallel, arabesque. Every motion became a study in unity, arms cascading in smooth glides, her body dipping and swaying in time with the music.

Panic melted beneath a warmth that suffused her entire body and made her muscles glow. She danced close to him, but never touched, only their reflections revealing how perfectly matched they were. His powerful body contrasted boldly with her lithe grace. The gleam of artificial light illuminated the golden highlights in his wavy hair, the bronze of his skin.

She was fire to his light, and Paige knew why Goddard had cast them together. If nothing else, the lecher had an eye for the aesthetic. A fleeting image formed in her mind of a lion chasing a gazelle across a sun-burned plain, and she recognized Christopher as the lion. He was the predator and she the prey. Always.

How she had avoided getting caught, instinctively knowing what her response to him would be. But now she was trapped. Desperation raged inside. She must finally face these feelings he aroused in her.

His gaze challenged her to take pleasure in the dance. In him. She wanted to resist, prove herself immune to his virility, but found herself kneeling beside him, reaching out to touch him instead.

Reality retreated to the fringes of her consciousness and filled her with sensation, the pulsing heat of his skin beneath her fingertips, the gravelly sound of his voice when he asked, "Do you hesitate because of me or the script?"

"You," she confessed.

His smile was warm, satisfied. "I don't care how I catch you, Paige. Just as long as I do."

"I know." And she did. That's why she had always run. He possessed the power to consume her. To reduce her to ashes with the heat of his flame. "You're too arrogant for your own good."

"Or for yours?" He reached up and stroked the curve of her cheek. And just like in the shower, her body sang in response to his touch.

"I've no doubt I'll suffer." She swayed against him, feeling his coiled strength, the desire in his smile as he stared into her face. Music surrounded her. Inhibitions melted beneath his touch, leaving behind only the thrill of the moment.

"This isn't suffering," he murmured against her ear. "Not by a long shot."

Paige had known it wouldn't be. Whether her hand was connecting with his cheek in anger or stroking that magnificent body in a lover's caress, touching Christopher meant losing herself in the blaze of his passion.

She shouldn't surrender so easily. Even though they were bound together by the unwritten laws of deep cover, she should simply do her job. Detach. Show him he wasn't affecting her.

But he was. Oh, how he was affecting her. Somehow the knowledge of Goddard's presence lurking behind their reflections only spurred her need to touch this living, breathing man.

Her fingers stroked the length of his forearm, eager to indulge this fascination she had denied herself for so long. And when she did, Paige realized she wasn't the only one on fire. The iron spy wanted her as much as she did him.

With her hand tightly in his, she dragged him to his feet. Swaying in time with the music, she parted her legs until her thighs straddled the strong muscles of his. She arched backward in a spine-melting curl, trusting the hand he clasped securely around hers, and glided suggestively against his thigh.

His eyes widened just enough to betray his surprise, and she was rewarded by his quick intake of breath.

Paige laughed, delighted by his response and feeling a rush of wicked excitement. "You like that."

Those warm brown eyes glowed. "Audience participation, is it?"

Paige only smiled. Balancing herself on the balls of her feet, she drew herself upright in a fluid motion, and brushed her hand lightly across his jaw.

Christopher shivered, and she was delighted by his response. She had been so busy avoiding him that she hadn't realized how much power his attraction gave her. Or given any thought to what she could do with that power.

But this was Christopher Sharp, and he would give as good as he got. With a quick maneuver, he circled her until her back came hard against his chest. Suddenly she faced the mirror with full view of the bold hand he traced along the curve of her breast. The length of his maleness swelled against her as if it had a life and voice all its own.

Tease me, will you?

His palm cupped her breast for the barest of instants, but long enough for her nipple to pucker through the spandex. His deep chuckle was a warm burst against her ear, making hairs flutter against her face and her stomach somersault with tension.

Glancing in the mirror, he said, "We look good together." The approval in his voice flowed through her like a drug. "I knew we would."

His eyes were heavy-lidded with promise, and though he held her pinned, his grip barely mattered because it was the sight of their reflection that held her transfixed.

Mirrors were said to capture the soul, and if that myth was born of truth, then the creature who stared back, mouth parted slightly and hips swaying in time with the music, must be her dark twin. Surely she couldn't be this aroused with Goddard so close. She could almost feel his dead black eyes upon her, caressing her just as surely as Christopher's hands traced the curve of her waist.

She should feel revulsion. Or outrage. Or fear. But there was something erotic about the sight of those strong hands on her body . . . something compelling about the danger of Goddard's presence.

Blood pulsed through her veins. A feeling, not unlike the high she got during a bust, sparked a heat inside.

"I want you to dance for me." Christopher nibbled on her earlobe, sending little shivers of pleasure darting outward and surprising her with the intensity of the sensation.

His tawny head burrowed in the curve of her neck, and the sight made her realize just how thoroughly she was enjoying this game. The situation was so tantalizing.

Forbidden.

The iron spy looked literally wrought from metal as he watched her arch sideways in a deep stretching curve, the skirt parting like sheer wings to reveal her leotard-clad body. Tugging the bow at her waist, she let the skirt slither to the floor, then pushed it aside with a toe.

Christopher looked like he was about to pounce.

"Indulge yourself," his hungry expression seemed to say, "Indulge me."

The arousal in his face urged her on, sparked her appetite for control. Paige slipped away from him and covered the distance to the pole in one well-executed leap. Her hand met the solid metal with a resounding ring, and she pivoted, turning her back to him and catching his gaze in the mirror.

With an easy swaying motion, she shrugged the bodice off her shoulders, coaxing down the spandex sleeves. Baring one lacy bra strap then the other. One bare arm. Then the other. Until the leotard clung to her breasts precariously, and the promise of disaster was only a deep breath away.

Stretching back against the pole like a cat, she arched her body in a long motion. One shrug, and the spandex snapped over the swell of her breasts and rolled down her ribs. A flash of white lace caught her eye in the mirror, and she almost laughed at how virginal her choice of intimate apparel appeared given the twisted dynamics of the situation.

"Are you a white lace man?" she asked huskily and spun around, separating her thighs and straddling the pole.

The bulge in his pants was his only reply. His need would translate into skillful hands on her body, Paige knew, but she was not ready to relinquish this power she had over him. Some quirky inner voice urged her to push him beyond endurance. To test him, test his limits, define new boundaries just like he had done to her at the Academy.

As she lifted her hand to her head in an exaggerated motion, his gaze followed. She felt beautiful, daring, in the face of his desire, and his reaction to her dance acted like wildfire on her senses. Shaking her hair free, she let it tumble down her back, glad she had grown it long when Christopher's gaze grew hot and desperate and his magnificent body grew taut.

She laughed again, not only because he was chomping at the bit, but because Fate had played such an ironic little game. What she had expected to be a denigrating and mechanical sex act had become a fever singeing her blood. She had never known such desire. Her body vibrated with excitement, made her ache, electrified her with the thrill of danger.

Her movements took on new purpose as she arced and curled around the pole. Closing her eyes to the sight of them reflected in triplicate, she absorbed the music into her dance, reveled in the knowledge of Christopher's hunger. Her body burned, the lack of visual stimuli exaggerating other senses, making her aware of the men who watched her.

Fire ignited her imagination. Watched. Wanted. With one skillful twist, she released the clasp of her bra and rolled her body forward, knowing Christopher's gaze locked on her, not her reflection, as the bra straps danced a slow glide down her arms.

The bra slipped from her fingertips. Her nipples grew diamond hard as the air grazed her skin. Drawing up full length against the pole, she anchored herself against it, pressing her breasts together, unable to suppress a shiver as the cool metal caressed her hot skin, naked, brazen.

Paige opened her eyes to see the effect of her boldness on Christopher. What she saw made her insides melt.

He was on fire. Pressing the discarded bra to his lips, he caressed her with eyes glowing from passion. She ached to reach out and touch him, to give in to the sizzling attraction that arced through the air between them.

"Do you want to touch me?" Her words were a whisper above the silvery strains of music.

He shook his head, golden hair flying in halo around that rugged face, a wry smile touching his lips. "No, Paige." His voice was thick. "I want to flip you over that bar and take you."

She bet he would. Whoever said power was a drug hadn't been kidding. Christopher struggled visibly for control. Executing a series of hip spirals that brought her around the pole, Paige thrust her breasts proudly before him and was rewarded when a violent shudder rocked his powerful body.

He spanned the distance between them in a whipcord motion. In the space of a heartbeat, the balance of power shifted. His hands locked onto her hips, and when she pulled away, the solid length of the pole blocked her escape.

"Christopher, don't—"

"I'm participating," he gritted the words out between clenched teeth and hooked his fingers into the wad of fabric around her waist.

Exhaling an audible sigh, he rolled the leotard in a slow glide over her hips, leaving her clad in nothing more than a G-string. His teeth followed in the wake of his hands, nipping a trail of teasing bites along her sensitive flesh.

She should push him away—God knew she wanted to—but could only manage to smother a moan as his tongue outlined the triangle of lace that promised so much more than it concealed. Pleasure erupted when his warm breath streamed over her aching sex. The reflection of his tawny head between her legs seared away any lingering shreds of resistance.

He snatched the control from her as easily as snapping his fingers. She should have fought harder, should resent him at the very least, but anger exploded in a flash of sensation. She writhed her hips, unable to resist the velvet lure of his tongue.

With one quick stroke, Christopher tore away the intrusive scrap of fabric and found her tiny bud. With his strong hands clasped on her buttocks, he drew her closer, edging her thighs apart, assaulting her body until she moaned aloud, desire throbbing in time with the beat of her heart.

His tongue dipped inside her, and she leaned back against the pole, suddenly grateful for its support as the strength drained from her legs and reality spiraled into a burning awareness of him. Of those delicious thrusts that mimicked the most primitive loveplay.

His tongue flicked inside her with precise rhythm, lifting her onto a crest of arousal that made her squirm. She buried her fingers into his hair and pulled him closer, eager . . . no, desperate to scale the heights of this sensation.

He drew her clit into his mouth, drawing on that tiny nub and making her whimper with the strength of her need. One gentle nip would hurl her over the edge. One tender bite would pitch her into a blaze of ecstasy.

But Christopher had other ideas. His mouth brushed the fine cover of hairs that veiled her sex, then raked a path down the inside of her thigh, leaving her gasping, thrumming with unfulfilled need. He drew the leotard down the sweep of her legs, raining a hail of little kisses on her toes as he drew the leggings over one foot then the other until she stood before him naked.

Vulnerable.

A flash of reason pierced the delicious fog clouding her brain. Christopher had always been in control. Always the one to call the shots. No matter what she wanted.

Right now she wanted him. For once he was going to listen.

In a liquid glide, she dropped to her knees, straddling him like a lap dancer, her breasts full in his face, body yearning for his touch, soul aching with the need to dominate.

He exhaled in a low whoosh and sank back onto his heels. His hard thighs dug into hers. She wove her fingers into his hair and tilted his face to hers.

"You think we're going to do this your way, do you?" she asked, riding the thick length of erection that swelled beneath his sweats.

Christopher slanted her a curious glance. "I'm open to suggestions."

And suggest she did. With her nipple nudging at those full lips.

His hot mouth enveloped her, his deep chuckle sending a warm gust of air across her skin. His hands reached up to cup her breasts, strong hands kneading her as his tongue began a hot dance.

Her hips never slowed the erotic rhythm she set, lightly caressing his erection, then riding that thick length as though she planned to take him inside her with the next stroke.

The mirrors became their erotic theater as his dark hands traveled the outside of her thighs and cupped the pale roundness of her buttocks. She swayed against him, inspired by the music and spellbound by the play of muscles along his broad back, by the sight of his tawny head as he laved such delicious attention on her breasts. Her nipples darkened to ruby and swelled with desire. The moisture from his tongue flashed against her skin. Rolling her head forward, Paige veiled them beneath the fall of her hair, a frail attempt at privacy against their reflection. Against their audience.

"Sweet Christ, you make me hot." Christopher outlined her legs with a firm grip.

"I know." She ground her hips down, savoring this power over him.

His arousal pulsed against her. He slid a hand between their bodies, and suddenly that erection was filling her, stretching her moist flesh until she melted against him with a sob.

Christopher locked his arm around her waist and withdrew, then slid back inside with one smooth stroke. The expression on his face was of such pure maleness, such pure aggressor, that she wanted to scream. His touch was so much more than she had ever imagined, yet exactly what she had always feared. Surrender.

She fought it. With every ounce of her determination, Paige resisted his power to ravage her will. Even as his palm cupped her mound, rubbing with such sweet pressure, the explosion upon her, imminent, unstoppable. She rode the sensation, rode him, trapped in the midst of an inferno that scorched her pride. She moaned, resisting with every shred of strength she possessed and rocking against him with a passionate demand of her own.

She met his every thrust with a rhythm that stole her breath. A violent shudder rocked his powerful body, a groan slipping from his lips and telling her just how close he was to the edge. Bracing her arms around his neck as leverage, she arched against him, determined to take him with her.

Trailing her mouth along his brow, her tongue grazed his temple, the shell of his ear. "You're coming with me," she whispered, swaying against him to emphasize her words.

Christopher rammed deep inside with enough force to make her gasp. "Is this suffering?" She could see the male triumph smolder in his gaze as she reached the first gasping climax.

To deny the effect of their passion would make her a liar, so she let her body answer. Abandoning herself to sensation, she coaxed his orgasm with her throbbing flesh.

Time fell away as he exploded, the sound of his surrender as sweet as her own. This man was everything she had ever imagined. The reality was so much more than the fantasy. As the blaze faded to embers, Paige knew their sex had set the precedent. She had fought with him for control, had tasted the power of his response and discovered an appetite for Christopher Sharp much larger than their circumstances. Much larger than Lewis Goddard.

Paige had more control than she ever realized and over the next few days, she would have a chance to explore it.

To explore Christopher.

Dragging herself from the glorious haze of contentment, she covered his mouth possessively and whispered against his lips, "I was wrong. I won't be the one suffering after all."

Let the Games Begin

Suffering? Now here was something Christopher hadn't considered. After years of chasing Paige, he had finally caught her, but instead of indulging in that victory, indulging in her, he had to share her with a pervert. He was not thrilled with the situation and considered the effects on their developing relationship. Not good.

They returned to the living room in silence. Paige headed toward the couch while he made his way to the bar. He needed a drink. Eyeing the Johnny Walker covetously, he chose a bottle of wine from the rack instead. Dinner was in an hour. He would need a clear head to deal with Goddard, and there was nothing clear about his head right now. Or his body.

Every nerve ending echoed with a heady combination of satisfaction and discontent. Paige was a fever raging in his blood, and having her only made him want more. They should be lying in bed right now, basking in the afterglow without Goddard's prying eyes, yet they were forced to work, to apprehend their very sick, and very dangerous, host.

"Come down is a real bitch." He held up the bottle for Paige's approval. "Want some?"

"Please."

Decanting the merlot into two crystal glasses, Christopher deposited one on the coffee table next to her. "Well, I don't think chemistry is going to be a problem between us."

Paige cast him a sidelong glance. "Doesn't seem to be." She stretched languorously and sank down onto the leather sofa. A fresh stab of arousal sliced through him. He wanted her again. Here and now.

"You said you'd read the whole script," she commented, and with his confirming nod, asked, "Are you going to have a problem with the next vignette?"

"A problem?" He watched her, glass poised at his lips, curious. The second scenario had Paige playing the part of a Celtic priestess and he a Roman slave. "Why do you ask?"

She spared him a shrug, a gentle motion that lifted the hair from her shoulders and made the auburn tresses spark beneath the light. "I just gathered from our rehearsal that you like to be in control. I thought maybe letting me take charge might not be . . . comfortable for you."

Control. Was it his imagination or did he detect a hint of resentment in her voice? She stretched her legs out on the coffee table and pointed her toes. She sipped her wine. Every gesture casual at first glance. Too casual.

Now here was a twist he hadn't expected.

Christopher was still puzzling over Paige's allusion to his need for control when they went to dinner. Despite her offhand demeanor, this was obviously an issue, and he mentally retraced the steps of their relationship, searching for a time he had incurred offense. No specific incident came to mind—if he didn't count chasing her through the years since the Academy.

"Please sit down." Goddard motioned to the exquisitely-laid table with a broad sweep of his hand, inviting them into the dining room. "You are my only guests this evening. I want to know how rehearsal went today."

It appeared he had gone through a great deal of trouble to impress them, and Christopher wondered if that generosity translated into approval with their performance.

"You two seem to be hitting it off very well." Goddard lifted his champagne flute in silent toast. "Like soul mates."

Had their performance been too convincing?

Christopher detected the suspicion in Goddard's voice, and his first impulse was to reassure. But something, perhaps Paige's earlier comment about control, made him hesitate, and she slipped into the void.

"I simply have to tell you, Mr. Goddard," she said. "I had my concerns when you first introduced me to Christopher. But after we began to work, I could see why you cast us together." She affected the right tone of feigned awe and humble embarrassment. "We just sort of . . . clicked."

Goddard bought it, and Christopher couldn't help but wonder how much Paige's lap dance had to do with it.

"Clicked? Tell me about it." His tone conveyed only marginal interest, but those hooded eyes roamed over her with the intensity of a laser.

Paige toyed with the edge of her napkin. "We have chemistry," she said simply. "It made all the difference in our performance."

"Good. Good. Some consider my method of rehearsing unconventional, but I've had great success with it." Goddard leaned back in his chair like a king perched on a throne. "I'm not looking for a crude parody of the sex act. Emotions make my films unique, make each couple unique. Conflict brings my movies to life."

"Unconventional or not, your method works." Paige laughed, a sultry sound, as if amused by the whole world. "I was certainly in for a few surprises—emotional and instinctual." She flipped on that feminine charm like a light switch, and Christopher gritted his teeth when their host took the bait.

"Surprises, Paige? Tell me." Resting his elbows on the table, Goddard leaned toward her, like they were two lovers alone in the candlelit room.

Christopher marveled at how quickly Paige turned around this potentially disastrous situation and wondered what Hoover's objection had been. Female agents certainly had a few more tools in their arsenal than their male counterparts.

She looked like an enchantress in a copper-colored sheath that shimmered around every luscious curve. And when she gifted Goddard with a smile, her pink tongue darted out to moisten her lower lip in a sensual display that made Christopher shift uncomfortably in the chair.

The gesture wasn't lost on Goddard, either. His Adam's apple bobbed the length of his throat. Christopher visualized ramming his fist into it.

"At first I thought Christopher was a bit . . . mature." Paige shook her head, sending a cascade of wild red waves tumbling over her shoulders. "But I was mistaken, Mr. Goddard, and commend your expertise in these matters."

Ouch! Christopher wanted to kick her under the table. Goddard stroked her hand, and a dagger of fury carved another notch in his composure.

"How could you know?" Goddard asked, that pitiful excuse for a mustache twitching like rabbit whiskers when he smiled. "Even though you have worked in my casino, I've been inattentive. But that's behind us now. We have a movie to make." He turned an inviting gaze on Christopher as if welcoming him into some bizarre kind of club.

Christopher forced a smile to his lips, slightly queasy at the look of almost desperate desire on Goddard's face. A vision of Goddard jerking off behind the dance studio mirror flashed in his mind, and for the first time in fifteen years, Christopher questioned all he had sacrificed for the bureau. Putting his life at risk was one thing, but this case went beyond the norm. Christopher had just been inducted by the secret society of voyeurs.

Spreading his arms in a magnanimous gesture that encompassed them both, Goddard said, "What matters now is your rehearsal. Without a solid foundation for your performance, I can't film. So as long as you are both pleased with each other. . . ."

"The bear turned out to be a lion," Paige said with a suggestive half-smile, and Christopher swore he heard her growl.

Goddard laughed. "And you, Christopher?"

With his pride still stinging from Paige's reference to age, Christopher caught her hand and brought it to his lips. "While I'm grateful I proved myself worthy, I never questioned the lady's talents. But I am interested in your expectations for the second vignette."

Goddard picked up his knife and sliced into the veal. "Submission, Christopher. Think submission."

❧

"I wonder if he's still suspicious?" Paige asked in a low whisper as she circled the deserted pool.

Christopher felt a surge of male pride in her abilities. "You did a thorough job of turning him around."

"Hmm," was her only reply.

The moonlight silhouetted her graceful form against the black water, and with her head bowed as if in deep thought, she looked like a siren emerged from the deep. He wondered if she could sing.

The pool brought to mind the indoor spa in the west wing that would double as a mystical spring during their next rehearsal.

"Having second thoughts about tomorrow?"

"No." She glared up at him. Starlight caught her lashes and made them glint like embers. "But I think we should take the 'boss' up on his very generous offer of hospitality tonight."

Christopher knew what she was saying—they needed to get a lock on their position. "We're in Goddard's camp with no reconnaissance. I think we should—"

"—determine the security of the area," Paige informed him in a tone that might have intimidated a less experienced agent.

He was not a less experienced agent. But he did understand the necessity of working together and forced back a sharp reply to keep the peace. Besides, he had been about to suggest the same approach. He had trained Paige, after all.

"We need to decide how to get around the security," he said. "I want to determine the sequence and the timing of the sweeps. I know where the cameras are in the west wing, but we need to be able to move around the mansion."

"Let's just run with the porn star routine." She stopped in mid-stride and turned to face him, her skin fair beneath the starlight. "Everyone expects us to be rehearsing the script, so let's give them what they expect."

He fought the urge to run his fingers along her creamy cheek. "In English, please."

"Goddard wants us to get to know each other, right? So no one will notice if we're so busy getting to know each other that we turn up in places where we shouldn't be," she explained as if he was an imbecile.

Christopher scowled. "You want us to march through the halls groping each other? What the hell is that supposed to accomplish?"

"Not groping. Investigating." She shook her head emphatically. "We only grope if someone catches us." She lay a slender hand on his arm, and his blood quickened. "This'll work, Christopher. Trust me."

She gifted him with a smile that brought to mind her display of mind-boggling femininity at dinner. She had definitely calmed the beast there. "Let's give it a shot then, my dear."

With their arms wrapped around each other like new lovers, they marked every room as they toured the house. Goddard's offices surrounded an impressive foyer while his private rooms comprised the east wing with a magnificent view of the bluff. The security office and guest rooms were located in the rear of the house with the production studio in a separate building entirely, reminiscent of a larger scale lot back on the mainland.

Paige's technique was put to the test when they stumbled across a security guard. "Put your hand under my dress," she hissed as a door cracked open a few feet away.

She fell back against the wall. Christopher didn't have time to ask whether she meant underneath her hem or down the bodice before her lips locked onto his like a vice. His tongue met hers in an excited frenzy while he decided on the hem and a chance to cop a feel of her extraordinary ass.

His hand slid up her leg to discover thigh-high stockings and no panties. His fingers locked on to the satiny curve of her buttock just as a uniformed security guard stepped into the hallway.

"Oh." The guard came to an abrupt halt.

Paige pulled out of Christopher's arms. "Excuse us, officer," she gasped in her best bedroom voice, and the guard's chest puffed visibly at the way Paige stressed the title.

His roving gaze took in her every luscious inch as she smoothed the skimpy dress back into place. He apparently liked what he saw. Christopher could just imagine what was going through his mind, and his fingers itched to turn that leer into a toothless maw.

The guard didn't stand a chance when Paige turned those sultry blue eyes on him. "This is so embarrassing. Is it okay to be here?" She giggled. "Except I don't really know where 'here' is. Do you, Christopher?"

Christopher shook his head, but met the guard's gaze with a glare that clearly said "no trespassing."

"This is Mr. Goddard's shooting range, miss," the guard supplied with an indulgent smile before breezing past.

"He was only carrying a standard-issue," Paige whispered once the guard was out of earshot. "I bet the weapon room is inside."

That was Christopher's guess, too, but he couldn't seem to form the thought into words. His blood pounded. Straight to his crotch. It was no wonder Paige had managed this assignment. Not only did she have a quick mind and steely composure, if she ever got burned out on being an agent, she would make a helluva actress.

But he didn't see that happening. One thing he had learned about Paige over the past twelve hours—she was a junkie for her work. She wouldn't forget Lewis Goddard until he sat in a cell. Christopher had suffered from the same addiction long enough to recognize the symptoms.

While persistence was one thing, the security office was another entirely. Manned by a single guard, the room boasted enough surveillance equipment to make even a federal agent envious. Nevertheless, it was going to be impossible to find out exactly which areas of the mansion and grounds were under observation without luring the guard out of the room—a guard who looked more like a professional power lifter than security personnel. Like nothing short of an explosion would dislodge him from that chair.

Or a bomb named Paige.

She assessed the layout of the corridor with a practiced eye. Slipping the slingback from her foot, she snapped the heel off with one easy stroke, then gazed up at him with liquid eyes. "Darn, my shoe broke."

Christopher frowned. Chalk another one up from her feminine arsenal. "Think you can lure him out?"

"Can't say. He looks pretty hard core, but stay close just in case."

She leaned up on tiptoes and pressed a soft kiss to his cheek. "I need evidence for trial. A film starring Shelby Moran."

She disappeared around the corner, leaving him standing there with his jaw slack and his cheek tingling.

A sharp knock resonated through the corridor, and suddenly he heard Paige say, "Excuse me, officer. I have a problem and wondered if you could help."

Her voice faded, and Christopher inhaled deeply, trying to dispel the effects of Paige's touch. The woman had a way of shooting his composure straight to hell.

When she re-emerged five minutes later, the power lifter was by her side with her shoe in his hand.

"We'll have to be fast. I can't be gone long."

"I really appreciate your help, Jerry."

The way she oozed the man's name made Christopher gnash his teeth, but in seconds they had rounded the opposite corner and were out of sight. Now was his chance.

A burst of adrenaline saw him sailing toward the room, pausing only to make certain no one watched him enter. The room was a high-tech paradise. Monitors flashed images of the house on a dozen screens while recording devices blipped and droned as images changed.

Lewis Goddard was a Peeping Tom of the finest water. But even cutting-edge surveillance equipment could be avoided by knowing when the cameras were sweeping and where.

Now Christopher did.

Paige had charged him with locating evidence for trial, and the two rooms adjoining the security office provided a bonanza. Within minutes, Christopher had completed his mission. And confirmed the arsenal was connected to the shooting range. And discovered safe zones in and around the house. Not bad for a few minutes of work.

Just as the muted sound of footsteps sounded around the corner, he slipped out of the room and headed back toward the west wing.

"Christopher, is that you?" Paige chimed out after he pulled the door closed. "I'm in the bedroom."

He found her in the closet. "As long as you're here," she said, "would you mind giving me an opinion on this outfit I'm wearing for rehearsal tomorrow. Is it Celtic priestess enough?"

"Will you model it for me?"

"Maybe."

She greeted him with a delighted smile. She was half-dressed and beaming and obviously no worse for the wear. The tension ebbed from him in a rush. Christopher hadn't realized it, but he had been worried about her.

"How'd it go?"

Unable to drag his gaze from the copper sheath slipping from her shoulders and journeying down every slender curve, he fumbled to free the video cassette from his waistband. "Is this what you're looking for?"

She took the tape, eyes darting from the video cassette back to his face. Satisfaction surged through him when delight wreathed her features.

"This is it! Will he miss it?"

"Not unless we're profoundly unlucky. He keeps the films in a room adjoining security. I left a bogus in its place."

He had recognized the names on the tape. Paige's witness and her murdered co-star. "So what's next?"

"I want to access his computer. But first, I've got to conceal this somewhere secure." She gave a short laugh. "As if there's any safe place on this island."

He was inclined to agree, but could not form the thought into words before she slipped the sheath down from her hips and stood before him clad in only a black bra so sheer he could see the outline of her nipples. And thigh-high stockings. She didn't wear any panties, he knew, and his gaze dropped to the fringe of auburn hair between her legs where he'd spent such a delightful time earlier.

He swallowed hard. Technically, he'd seen her in less, but his blood was already pumping.

"I can't believe you got him to leave his post," Christopher commented in an effort to distract himself. He unbuttoned his shirt and found his fingers stiff and uncooperative.

She slipped off her shoe and winked. "Works every time."

"Yeah, but—"

"Unfortunately—or fortunately in our case—a great deal of men don't take women seriously." She pursed her lips in a flirty pout. "I can usually pass without being seen as much of a threat."

Paige was a threat. Maybe Goddard and his men were too stupid to realize it, but she was certainly wreaking havoc on his peace of mind. She slipped the video cassette into the thigh-high hem of her stocking and pulled a leaf green negligee around her.

"Is this Celtic priestess enough?"

He nodded, fighting an overwhelming urge to drag her down to the floor and make love to her. "Listen, Paige," he said, determined to get the information out before he made a complete ass of himself. "The sequences are rotating every four minutes. The cameras linked to the west wing are turned off, so I figure Goddard is monitoring privately." She had unfastened her bra and slipped it through the sleeves of her negligee. The sight of her breasts swaying beneath the silk even more erotic than if she'd just removed the bra in plain view. He bit back a groan.

"That will give us an edge in finding a way off this island."

Christopher should say something, but no reply came to mind. He shrugged off his shirt instead.

"I'm going to hide this in the bathroom." Her gaze trailed to his bare chest, and a slow smile curved her lips. "Behind the tank, I think."

"Good idea."

"Thank you." She reached up on tiptoes and pressed a kiss to his mouth before brushing past and leaving him alone in the closet. A flush of pleasure stole through his cheeks, and he whispered after her, "No problem."

The Tables Turn

The indoor spa where they would perform the second vignette boasted a pool, a Jacuzzi and a resident priestess named Paige. Christopher found her swimming and paused in the entry to enjoy the view.

Red hair billowed around her like a silken cloud, flowing outward as she glided through the water. His first impulse was to dive in and find out for himself if she was really as naked as she appeared, but he checked the urge, reminded of her concerns about his ability to relinquish control.

The script called for him to submit, and he had every intention of doing so. But the idea of becoming a sex slave to a woman who held a grudge made his gut clench tight as a fist.

Somehow he had misread the warning signs at the Academy. Their battle of wills had been part of his initial attraction to Paige, but the parameters of their relationship had been clearly defined.

He was in charge.

But Paige was a leader, too, and while he had recognized that, he had handled her like all his other students, not like a leader in training.

Now she was a seasoned agent with a grudge. He could tell by the way she emerged from the water, dripping, the glint in her eyes promising retribution.

Hindsight was a bitch.

The bikini she wore barely deserved the name—the sheer triangles were a color remarkably similar to her skin, and he could see right through them to her lush ruby nipples and auburn mons.

Drying herself in long gliding strokes, she lifted one leg then the other, revealing tantalizing glimpses of that dewy juncture between her thighs.

Great. Another show.

Dropping the towel, she slipped into a sheer silk negligee that molded her slender curves like a leafy green veil. He could barely draw a breath.

She motioned him to a lounge chair with a seductive smile. "Care to join me?" She might as well have asked, "Any last words?"

He groaned aloud.

"This control thing is going to be an issue, isn't it?" She looked delighted by the prospect.

He sat down but couldn't seem to bend the steel rod that had taken up residence in his spine. "Not at all. I have a good idea of how to play this from the script." He would behave like a vanquished Roman slave and let the conqueror take his body. It was just a matter of . . . submission.

Goddard's command echoed in his head and must have been reflected in his face because Paige smiled and said, "Liar."

He shrugged. "I know my job."

"That's good. Slave." She kneeled on the chair beside him and unbuttoned his shirt, starting at the collar and working her way down toward his waist. "Now submit."

As her fingertips trailed along his bare chest, any thoughts of resistance splintered.

"Mr. Goddard has been very specific about how he wants this scene performed," her whisper gusted along that sensitive area between his neck and shoulder.

"I understand what he wants."

Paige pulled the shirt from his arms and tossed it into a heap on the floor. Sliding from the lounge chair, she knelt before him. "Good. Then you know what I want, too."

Vengeance. That's what this was all about.

The top of her head ended at the middle of his chest, and he stared down at the rich sweep of auburn with a mixture of excitement and dread. Her fresh herbal scent assaulted his senses, filled his mind with hot images of what it would feel like to plunge deep inside her, to stop playing these games and just make love to her. Without a script. Without an audience.

Her fingers slid into his waistband. "Stand up," she commanded in a throaty whisper.

Christopher obeyed. She tugged the drawstring pants down his legs, and he stepped out of them. Suddenly the humid air of the spa felt cloying, heavy.

Her gaze locked onto his purposefully, and she ran her hand the length of his semi-erect cock. Christopher shuddered.

"You're so stiff."

He got even stiffer and struggled to stand still as her hands glided upward over his stomach then circled around to his buttocks, her fingers exploring every inch of skin along the way.

"Way too stiff," she admonished, moist lips forming a petulant little moue. "Lie down, and I'll give you a massage."

He sank down into the cushions with a groan. Anything to put some distance between them.

But distance wasn't part of the script, and Christopher barely had time to draw a deep breath before Paige returned with a bottle from a nearby shelf and knelt beside him. After brushing his ponytail aside, she applied a palmful of warm liquid to his shoulders.

She was more skilled than he would have imagined. Working her hands in deep circular sweeps, she isolated each muscle and dissolved the tension that had mounted since awakening this morning. Her fingers probed the corded length of his neck and caressed the line of his jaw.

"How does this feel?" she asked, her question a breathy whisper against his ear.

"Mmm," was all he could manage.

While his mind worked just fine, control of his body seemed to be leaving in a hurry. He had to stay on his guard. Goddard lurked at the other end of a surveillance camera, and Paige herself had a less than trustworthy gleam in her eyes. Yet despite his best efforts, the jets from the spa and the rhythmic bubbling of the pool filter lulled him into a state of quasi-awareness. He closed his eyes and surrendered to the smooth strokes of her hands, to the languor flowing like a hot tide through his body.

Her hands traveled the length of his spine, swirling off in little side trips to massage the muscles of his back. Her touch was deep and even, and he gradually became aware of the subtle difference in the way she moved. Only her hands had been a presence before, but now he could feel the warmth of her body as she swayed close. The negligee whispered against him, and he imagined what tantalizing part of her lay below the diaphanous fabric. Her thighs. Her hips. Her breasts.

"You've got the most wonderful ass," she told him, penetrating the fog that rendered him immobile. "I like to touch you here." Her palms slid over his buttocks, and she massaged the lotion into his skin with strong strokes.

Her throaty murmur made desire spiral through the spell of relaxation she wove over him. Veiled skin brushed against him. Her thigh. "And here." Her finger traced the outline of his cleft, parting that sensitive skin just the barest amount.

His body shuddered in response to the intimacy of her touch, and she dipped low over him, pressing against his buttocks. Breasts definitely.

Continuing her journey down his legs, her fingers sailed along his calves, and he thanked whoever wrote the script when she lavished attention on his feet.

"Turn over."

Easier said than done. His muscles had turned to molten lava and moved about as well. With a supreme effort of will that half dragged him from his stupor, he managed. Only now there was no disguising the effect she had on him. The true extent of his desire displayed itself with all the subtlety of a lighthouse.

Paige noticed. A smile tipped the corners of those luscious lips. "I'm glad you're enjoying my massage."

Her gaze melted along his body, and he felt his nakedness as keenly as her amusement. She was enjoying this game much too much for peace of mind. So was he. Slavery didn't feel quite so repulsive with a beautiful woman paying homage to his body.

She rose above him in a graceful motion and straddled his hips. The breath caught in his throat as her thighs trapped him in a velvet vice while she poured more liquid into her palm and began a slow, swirling assault on his senses.

The filmy drape that covered her taunted him with glimpses of the slim curves below, making him itch to drag her full length against him. He checked the urge. This was her game. Goddard's game. He wouldn't give them the satisfaction of losing control.

He would submit if it killed him.

It just might. Only Paige had the ability to shatter his discipline and splinter any thoughts of restraint. She was a siren luring him into a spell, promising him pleasure only she could provide.

His control slipped a little more.

Her hips began a sinuous glide along the length of his erection. Her own heat radiated through the sheer veil that separated them, spurring the flood inside into a downpour. His hips ground against her in purely instinctual need, and he fought the undertow of desire that threatened to drag him away.

Her mouth branded a trail along his shoulder, the pressure of her hips growing more insistent as she moistened the nubby skin around his nipple with a slow stroke of her tongue. Her lips pursed sensuously, and a puff of warm breath cascaded over him.

"No matter how much you want me, Christopher, you can't lose control. Your only thought is to please me, and it pleases me to watch you surrender."

He should say something to diffuse her power, something to temper the edge of superiority from her voice, but speech was quite beyond him at the moment.

He tried not to thrust against her when she slid down his body, the soft fullness of her breasts surrounding his erection. He exhaled in a sound that was neither gasp nor groan, and his hands slipped around her of their own accord.

"I didn't give you permission to touch me," she warned, teeth locking onto the tender skin of a nipple and stopping him short.

Submission.

His hands dropped to his sides, aching to touch her, not daring.

Paige had been right. giving up control did not come easily. He liked the power of command, and if he hadn't realized it before, he was quickly discovering how that need transcended his job and extended into other areas of his life.

Especially sex.

Where Paige had once been the student and he the teacher, the tables had turned. Today's lesson was about relinquishing control.

And his one transgression cost much. With a wicked glint in her eyes, Paige set out to prove how easily he would fail. With what was left of his will, Christopher vowed to resist. He tucked his hands beneath him as she fitted her long body between his legs until her face was level with his cock.

"You are my slave now, Christopher." Her voice was deceptively gentle, but the hand that cupped his balls was firm, out to prove a point. "You are not permitted to lose control. Not until I say."

When she laughed, a chiming sound that made his blood boil, his heart forged in his chest. She never even glanced up, just kept her gaze locked on his traitorous cock as it swelled and jumped beneath her touch.

"He likes me." Her hand ran the length of his shaft to emphasize the words. "And you know what? I like him too." She pressed a soft kiss to the tip, and his hips bucked sharply in reply.

Christopher closed his eyes, could do nothing else. The sound of her voice, deep with desire, carried him away on the edge of a fantasy as her mouth and fingers played a tantalizing game with his body.

"He is beautiful." Her tongue circled the head in a slow glide, her warm breath pulsing against his sensitive skin in airy bursts. "I never dreamed you had him hidden away. He's so smooth." She traced the outline of a vein with a light brush of her fingertip. "Like hot satin. And so thick." Her hand caressed the full length of him. "And so very long."

Christopher's eyes flew open, and he bit down hard to keep from yelling out.

Paige stroked him until a pearlized drop appeared at the head. She brushed away the moisture with her mouth, and when she finally met his gaze, it was with her long red hair tumbling across his thighs and his come gleaming on those luscious lips.

He was going to die. A maelstrom surged through his body, his blood mounting in a familiar torrent that was going to hurl him over the edge and send him crashing into a thousand pieces.

Until Paige clamped her hand around him, effectively cutting off the sensation and making him arch against her in frustration.

"Come, slave." She slid off the lounge chair and out of reach before he even caught his breath. "Let's get in the pool. Looks like you could use some cooling off."

"Arrgh!" He was going to strangle her. Just as soon as he could move again. He could barely sit up, let alone walk, and it didn't really matter because she was already gone, way out of reach.

Covering the distance to the pool in a few graceful strides, she unfastened the negligee and let it slip from her shoulders. The breath he had fought so hard to draw locked in his throat at the sight. His gaze fixed on her breasts, lush nipples outlined through sheer fabric, beckoning him, making him tingle with the memory of how his cock had felt buried between them. How her long, firm body had felt draped across his.

She was an earthy, natural beauty. A born Celtic queen with her high firm breasts, the slender arch of her waist yielding to a graceful sweep of hips. And her legs. Those incredibly long legs made him yearn to sink between them, feel them lock around his neck and pull him toward her hot wet sex. . . .

This was torture in its purest form. His knees were weak as he tried to stand and his temper justifiably blistering when he thought of Goddard and his video monitor enjoying the sight of her beautiful body, watching their intimate game.

Temper diverted him from his own agony enough to make it to his feet, but the cold hard facts of their situation were nothing short of depressing. This was no way to begin a relationship, and there was no doubt in his mind a relationship was happening between them. What he felt was so much more than work, so much more than sex. Paige must surely feel it, too. And if she didn't, well, there was still enough time to convince her.

If he survived this damned rehearsal. Which was unlikely, he decided, as he watched Paige enter the pool. One lingering step at a time. Gifting him with several breathless moments to appreciate every liquid curve of her body before the water swallowed her up.

She paused at the bottom step, water lapping around her waist, full curves of her breasts showcased as she lifted her arms and shook out that glorious mane of hair.

"Think sacred spring. Very cold spring." She shivered, nipples gathering to erect peaks through the flesh-colored fabric. Christopher found his spirits rising at the thought of her own torture.

"If you can catch me, slave, I'll reward you with a kiss."

The challenge in her voice propelled him over the edge. He dove into the opposite end of the pool, the shock of cold water dousing the flame in his groin to a more tolerable level. With long hard strokes designed to shake off his excitement, he swam across the pool, but when he emerged, lungs bursting and body tight with tension, Paige had already begun her flight. She led him a merry chase through the water, pale glimpses of her legs beckoning just beyond reach as she swam ahead like a mermaid.

"Catch me, slave," she dared, and he could not resist her challenge even though the game only whetted his barely-controlled appetite. The contrast of cold water to the heat of his arousal incited a hunger deeper than anything he had ever known. The desire to catch her, to master her, consumed him until his single thought was no more than the need to feel her wrapped around him, to sink deep inside her and wring one draining climax after another from her body. Hunger fueled his strokes until Paige's quick, darting movements through the water could no longer evade him.

He captured her by the stairs.

"Reward me," he said, body throbbing with unfulfilled need.

She writhed against him in an erotic dance, her laughter ringing in his ears. She almost escaped. But the game was wearing on him, so he pressed her back into the handrail and used his body as anchor.

Instead of resisting, she arched sinuously, letting the buoyancy of the water lift her until she clamped her thighs around his cock. The moist suction coaxed him back to full hardness and cost him whatever advantage the cold swim had gained.

Her hands glided around his waist, upward along his back, sending trails of pleasure in their wake. She smoothed the dripping hairs from his face and gazed at him with a sultry smile. "A kiss. Isn't that what I promised?"

Her mouth latched onto his, devouring him, spiking a need so sharp he could only groan against those luscious lips and hang onto the handrail for balance.

She molded into the curve of his body, breasts swelling against his chest. He thrust his tongue into her mouth, unable to resist no matter what the script said.

"You are a bad slave." She tried to pull away.

"I'm not bad," he ground out against her lips. "I just haven't gotten the hang of this yet." It was suddenly important that she know he could.

"I don't know," she whispered, abandoning resistance as her tongue traced his teeth and her legs slithered along his. She locked them around his waist, poising herself open and ready above his sex. "All you want is control." She ground herself against him, teasing him ruthlessly.

Control was nothing more than an illusion and what she asked was beyond his ability. She wanted submission, and he cursed his job, his own need to be in charge and most of all this damned script that seemed to anticipate just how to push him to the edge.

"Paige. . . ." His words came out a thready whisper, and his cock surged against her in a blind need for fulfillment.

"What, slave?" She laughed against his mouth, sucking on his lower lip, her arms tightening around him when he tried to back away. "You want more practice?" Her hips rolled against him, driving down another glorious, agonizing inch. "Resist me."

To hell with the script!

A bolt of pleasure impaled him, and all his good intentions fled on a wave of need so strong he could do nothing but submit to instinct. His hand slid from the rail, the water cushioning them as he fell back against the wall, and drove inside her in one thrust.

Paige gasped aloud in a strangled sound that afforded him no small amount of satisfaction. She arched back wildly and grabbed the handrail for purchase. He used her position to his advantage and pounded into her again. And again. His hands slipped down to grasp her buttocks and pull her closer.

But letting go of the handrail had been a mistake. Suddenly she was free, lifting off him, and before her escape even registered in his brain, he was alone again, aching . . .

"Damn it!" He lunged for her.

Paige realized her miscalculation by the time she reached the lounge chair. Like a dripping giant, Christopher loomed above her, teeth clamped, droplets of water spraying off him as he wrestled her onto her back. She struggled, fighting him in a fashion that wouldn't alert Goddard to her physical training. But without her defense skills, levering him off was impossible. He was far too strong. Far too gone.

"Slave, you could die for this offense," she said, hoping to jolt him back to sanity with a reminder that one of them was scheduled to die in the final scene of the script.

His eyes widened, and sanity returned on the edge of a breath. He paused long enough for her to caress his cheek and promise, "Unless I give you permission." She lifted her lips to his. "Why don't you kiss me now. Touch me."

Suspicion honed his features to a sharp edge, and she seized the moment to spread her legs and prove herself. He drew a sharp breath, and his powerful hips sank between her thighs. His mouth dipped slowly toward hers.

Wrapping her arms around his neck, Paige lifted her lips to his, feeling the trap just as surely as he did. What was this feeling . . . this turmoil? She had started out wanting to drive him crazy, to shatter his iron control, but now all she could think about was making love. Feeling that magnificent erection pulse deep inside her.

The warm weight of his body pressed her into the cushions, spiking desire into a stab of longing so fierce, she could only surrender. She recognized the feeling, the rush of excitement that drove away reason, good judgment and common sense—everything except what was happening between them. Except the reality that Goddard was watching and there really was no choice.

Giving in to the sensation, she explored every hollow and ridge of Christopher's strong back, his waist, his buttocks, and they kissed slowly, deeply, desire melding them together like two halves of a whole.

She had never wanted like this before. Shouldn't want a man who could dominate her so completely. She lost herself to him, irrevocably, irretrievably. But how could she resist?

She couldn't. Not when Christopher arched above her, tasting her breast with soft nips and bites. She sighed, knowing they were caught up in the performance just as surely as Goddard was, not caring. Nothing mattered but the feel of his wet body and the hand that traveled a fiery path along her waist, rounded the curve of her hip. She arched against him, the moan that slid from her lips involuntary.

Taking his erection in hand, Christopher rubbed the head against her sensitive opening, mimicking the tactics she had used on him in the pool.

"What do you want?"

That he could even ask the question amazed her. Gazing into his face, she was touched by the frown that creased his brow, by the strands of wet hair clinging to his skin, but it was the mixture of resentment and vulnerability in his expression that captured her heart, the effort she saw in those deep chocolate eyes that told her how much he struggled to play this game.

Desire warred inside, confusion eddying like a torrent, eroding her will, yet at the same time strengthening her resolve. He still didn't understand how much she feared his domination. She hadn't understood herself until this instant. She would not be trapped by a man who wielded such power over her—the power to make her lose herself in him.

She needed to run, to regroup, but Goddard's script demanded she give herself to Christopher.

Her body. Not her soul.

Even if they had sex, she would use her professional training to detach, to keep her emotional distance and shield her heart from this man.

"Pleasure me, slave."

As his hands clamped around her hips and pulled her hungrily toward him, Paige realized distance was only an illusion.

"God, I am so hot for you," he ground out, filling her in one endless glide, pressing her into the cushions. She shuddered at the strength of his thrust, body throbbing as he rammed into her, hips rolling, drawing his thick heat even deeper.

"Oooh, yes." She threaded her hands into his hair and dragged his face toward hers as emotional distance crumbled.

Everything but the wine-sweet taste of his mouth faded away. She nibbled his lips in erotic bites, tongue plunging into his mouth while his powerful body melded with hers and proved they were meant to be together.

As equals.

"Roll over," she whispered, hands gliding over his muscled chest, urging him to comply.

He scowled. "I suppose a slave has no choice."

"No choice at all."

He obeyed.

Scooping her against him, he carried her over in one strong motion, never letting their bodies break contact as he settled back into the cushions.

"Mmm. You obey well." His submission excited her. Arching her back, she rose above him, reveling in her new position of power and taking stock of the man who lay spread out beneath her. Inside her.

God, he was gorgeous.

His tanned chest and broad shoulders spanned the width of the chair. Long golden strands of unbound hair wrapped around his neck. His skin gleamed from the water that dripped off her hair as she swayed above him, withdrawing almost full length, then driving down onto his thick shaft in one sleek stroke.

He rocked against her, and a moan slid from his lips. His hands cruised along her waist and cupped her breasts, rolling the nipples until she cried out. The time for control was past.

Throwing back her head, she rode him, urgency spurring long slick glides into frenzied thrusts. The sounds of their passion resonated through the liquid stillness of the spa. Resounded along every nerve ending in her heated body. Christopher was hers.

His hands slid from her breasts, twining into her hair, resisting her movements. "Paige, enough," he gasped. "I'm so hot . . . I won't last—"

She laughed, a throaty sound that echoed her pleasure. "You do what I say, slave." She drove down on him to accentuate her point. "And I say . . . now."

Reality came crashing down as his gaze locked onto hers, his eyes glowing with an intensity that pitched her over the edge. She drowned in the need she saw there, the understanding that he wanted her— enough to bend his iron will to please her.

She had asked for control, and he would give it. His shoulders tensed, and the set of his mouth grew determined. And though she knew he wanted to turn the tables and command the moment as his, he would yield to her desire.

She desired him now—and took him with deep eager strokes that melted what was left of restraint.

Nothing mattered beyond the ecstasy that gripped her, pulsing like a molten wave with every heartbeat, and that Christopher came with her, unbridled and unbidden, his low growl of release thundering through the room like a lion's roar.

∞⋇⋲

Submission was not in the same category as defeat, but Paige wouldn't have known it by the way Christopher was acting. "I don't want to make the orgasm sounds," she hissed beneath her breath. "You make them."

Their gazes locked. An ocean breeze tossed stray hairs around his face, making the strands glint like gold in the porch light. "I can't hack into his computer, moan and thrash wildly at the same time."

Halting at the top of the portico, she faced him, not ready to enter the house where they would be picked up on audio. "I still don't understand why you get to hack into his system." She sounded like a sulky child and didn't care.

"I'll get past his security codes quicker." If he could have clamped her head between his jaws and bit it off, he would have. "Now stop arguing and help me figure out how to get past the surveillance camera."

"My, my. Someone's got quite a case of the grumpies," she pointed out, knowing she shouldn't tease him, but unable to resist. "Didn't the sex agree with you?"

The tiny gold flecks in his eyes glowed beneath the lanterns flanking both sides of the door, and she felt that familiar swooping sensation in her belly.

"The sex agreed with me just fine."

Humph! The man didn't do submission very well. No surprise there. "I suppose we could hang onto each other and act as if we're looking for a place to screw," she suggested, yielding the first inch. "The camera only covers the doorway. Once we're inside we'll be out of range."

"As long as you make enough noise to hide the sounds of me clicking away at the keyboard."

"All right." She sighed and grasped the door handle. "I'll make the orgasm sounds."

It was the least she could do after watching him struggle through dinner. Goddard had shot questions at them all during the meal. Such intimate questions that if she hadn't already known he had been watching, she would have suspected.

But Christopher had born the brunt of Goddard's inquisition by being forced to explain—in graphic detail—just how it felt to be taken. A fact that hadn't sweetened his disposition. She would have mercy on him. This time.

They crossed the foyer in a few quick strides.

"All right, Christopher. All right," she said loudly for the benefit of Jerry the security man on the opposite end of the camera. "I'm horny, too. Come on, it doesn't look like anyone's in here." She cracked open the office door and began unbuttoning her blouse as they passed through the camera's range.

Christopher closed the door behind them and looked around. "This will work, babe. I'll do you right on the desk."

Facing him in sultry invitation, she simpered, "Oh, yes. Do me right here."

Christopher smiled for the first time all night.

After a few minutes, Paige fell into sort of an erotic tempo: breathless gasp, throaty moan, strangled whimper, satisfied sigh. Christopher occasionally piped in with a grunt and groan to add to the authenticity of their performance and cover up the assorted blips and beeps of the computer.

He looked supremely amused, as though her debasement was divine justice for the way she had ordered him around today. Paige only smiled, determined to maintain her dignity, and moaned louder.

"Oh, yes, Christopher. Right there. Mmm, that feels good." She enjoyed a brief moment of triumph as he struggled visibly not to laugh aloud.

But he got his revenge by taking forever to download the files she needed onto a disk. Her throat ached. The sounds of her own moans echoed in her head like some catchy tune stuck in playback.

She could have hacked into Goddard's files faster than this, and Jerry the security guard could have masturbated himself to orgasm two, maybe three times by now.

Suddenly the light below the doorway flickered. She spun toward Christopher and signaled him with a nod. Smashing his palm against the surge board, he shut down the entire system and stuffed the disk in his sock.

The key rattled in the lock. Paige flipped herself over the desk, hoisted her skirt up and pointed her bare bottom at him. "Quick," she whispered. "Pretend you're doing something."

"Your wish, my dear." Christopher rounded the desk and came to stand behind her just as the door cracked open.

Jerry got what he thought was quite an eyeful before backing out of the room. "Would you mind taking it back to the west wing."

"No problem." Christopher tightened his grip on her hips and rubbed what was turning into a prime erection against her bottom. "God, I can't get enough of you."

Paige should be flattered, but somehow he just didn't sound pleased.

Paybacks are . . .

The final scene of the script. The Medieval chieftain vignette where she or Christopher would die during filming. As far as Paige was concerned, it didn't take a rocket scientist to figure out who. While her character seemed the obvious choice, her money was on the maiden slitting the chieftain's throat in a surprise plot twist.

But this was only a rehearsal, and she had no intention of sticking around for filming. She had the evidence she needed and would have been out of here last night if Goddard hadn't sent his personal powerboat back to the mainland. She wanted to avoid this last rehearsal so much she had been tempted to take another boat. But that would have been pure insanity. Goddard's security had state of the art powerboats that she and Christopher couldn't get near.

If they were going to leave, it would have to be on a boat just as powerful, and that meant Goddard's. Hopefully it would be back on the island by nightfall. But until then there was this barbaric little scene to deal with. And one undercover agent who had been in a very foul mood for the past twenty-four hours—ever since she had taken him against his will during the Celtic priestess vignette.

The door slammed shut with such ominous finality that Paige cringed. She was not looking forward to this. Christopher stalked across their suite like a wild animal, the hard lines etched around his mouth lending him a feral look. Unbound, his hair fell to his shoulders and accentuated his rugged features so that even civilized clothing didn't tame his appearance.

Medieval chieftain, definitely.

Perhaps she had been a bit short-sighted to make jokes last night in the office.

"Lay down, Paige. Supine." His command bolted through the air like a gunshot.

She skittered toward the bed without argument. Not so much in response to the steely threat as to clear out of his oncoming path. But in a move reminiscent of how deftly he had taught her to fight at the Academy, Christopher pounced on her, seized both her wrists in a stranglehold the instant she came down on the mattress.

He ripped the front of her dress in one clean stroke. Buttons flew in all directions, bouncing off his chest and scattering onto the bed, even pelting her on the cheek. The dress parted, hanging by only two thin straps and baring her to his gaze.

"What in hell are you doing?" She stared into the hard lines of his face, recognizing his need to dominate. Her heart throbbed in time with her pulse.

With the advantage of strength on his side, Christopher flipped her easily. She fought back, twisting wildly and trying to break his hold. He just laughed and sat on her thighs, loosening his grip only long enough to free her from the sundress.

"Are you crazy?" she yelled, feet scrambling against the satin comforter for purchase while she tried to buck him off. He jerked her arms over her head so roughly that she cried out.

"No. Horny." Silken ropes threaded her wrists, and Christopher ignored her struggles and imprisoned her to a notch on the headboard. "Didn't your mother ever tell you paybacks are a real bitch?"

Surprise squeezed the air from her lungs. He couldn't restrain her. Not with Goddard watching. It was a terrible risk. If Goddard decided to take advantage of the moment, she would be at his mercy. Was at Christopher's mercy.

She was in deep trouble.

"Christopher, please . . ." the plea lodged in her throat as he wrapped his hand in her hair and lifted her head until she could see him.

"Now it's your turn to submit, Paige." He loomed above with a hard smile. "I'm the Medieval warlord. You are the captive." He gestured around him with a large hand. "And this is my castle. You are mine. No one will come to your rescue." Despite the almost overwhelming urge to fight him, anxiety, or perhaps anticipation, sent a frisson zipping through her.

Especially when he loosened his hold, brought his knees around her waist and hunched over her. His hair fell across her cheek. His mouth brushed her ear, and he said in a voice as low and thick as cashmere, "Now spread your legs before I tie them, too."

A ripple of erotic excitement shimmered like a hot breath along her skin when his hand slipped between her thighs and urged her compliance.

She wanted to resist but knew by the coiled strength of his movements, the fury radiating off him, that she would be far better off conceding this battle. She hesitated only an instant before letting her legs fall apart.

He laughed, a triumphant sound that made her gnash her teeth. He was going to make her pay. And with her arms bound to this bed, there wasn't a damn thing she could do about it. She had unwittingly helped him, in fact, by dressing to entice, to brandish her sensual power like a sword.

A double-edged one, she realized a bit too late.

Had she dressed like a Quaker, she would not be lying here now with a bare bottom and thigh-high stockings, her pretty pink sundress laying forgotten on the floor.

Sliding off her, Christopher came to his feet and stripped, never once taking his eyes from her until he was naked. Bold. Powerful.

Twinges of appreciation trembled deep inside. God, just the sight of him made the blood rush in her ears. That warrior's grace and size made him move with the supple savagery of a cat. Every muscle limber. Every movement predatory. His very fierceness excited her, and she couldn't help but wonder what it would be like to have the freedom of exploring that beautiful body at her leisure. To wake up beside him every morning. To become a part of his life.

There was a whole lot more at stake here than her pride—somehow her heart had gotten caught up in the game. Christopher had all the control—again. And his smile told her he planned to use it. She twisted away.

"Resistance, Paige." His laughter filled her senses, spurred her will to resist. "There's nowhere to hide."

That was beside the point. She wasn't going down without a fight.

"Damn you," she hissed and scrabbled away when he sat down on the edge of the bed, eyeing her in calm amusement.

"Submission isn't so easy when you're the one submitting, is it?" He arched a tawny brow. "What do you think?"

"Arrgh!" Her toes touched the carpeted floor. Her arms were about to break and her upper body wasn't budging, but she still fought. Fought the control he had over her. Fought the impulse to submit.

"This doesn't have to be difficult, Paige. Just admit you want me— that you've always wanted me—and I'll let you go."

Yeah, right. Leave her heart bleeding on the bedspread. She saw that happening sometime before hell froze over. "Don't hold your breath."

Christopher shook his head in mock sadness. "That was my one and only offer."

He lunged. His hand clamped around her knee and dragged her back onto the bed.

"Get your hands off me, you . . . animal."

He cast her a roguish grin. "Animal, is it?" His hand seared a path up her thigh, rounding the curve of her bottom and stoking the spark deep inside.

"Fuck you, Christopher."

"No, Paige. I'm going to fuck you."

She gritted her teeth against a moan, refusing to give him the satisfaction of a response.

Those gold-flecked eyes glowed. Her refusal only steeled his determination. "Guess I'll have to move on to alternate plan B."

Premeditated revenge. The man was a maniac. Burying her face in the pillow to hide from the sound of his laughter, she quickly discovered plan B was going to be much harder to resist.

Suddenly his mouth was on her skin, strong hands lifting her hips upward, lips and tongue making her writhe against a bolt of pleasure so strong she could not defend herself long in the face of such an erotic assault.

"Still resisting?" His breath breezed in hot bursts along her bottom, and she emitted the most pathetic whimper when he forced her to submit to the series of love bites that jolted every nerve in her body.

She was drowning in sensation, drowning in him. He knew how to unleash this urgency inside her, to make her need him as surely as she needed air to breathe. On some level she had known all along, had run from him, fought him. But he had her now. There was no escape.

His mouth trailed up her hip and along her waist. His powerful body covered hers, cradled her possessively, pressed her shoulders into the mattress and left her bottom bare to his touch.

Her arms were going to break. Her neck was already numb, or so she thought. Until he buried his face in her hair.

"You've been a bitch, Paige." His accusation blasted hot against her ear, sending electric tendrils thundering through her. "And now you're going to pay." His hand dipped between her legs.

The breath locked in her lungs. Submission. He wanted her to lose control like he had. And as his thumb centered on that tiny pebble of desire and massaged it with spiraling strokes, Paige knew she would.

"I'm not nearly as selfish as you," he assured her. "I'm not going to tease you. That was your game. I want to feel you respond to my touch, hear you beg me to take you, convince you that no one can make you want like I do."

Her only response was a low moan as his finger slipped deep inside.

"You like that." His words were a statement because no question existed.

Feeling her own moisture surround him as his finger glided in and out, she resisted the urge to arch into his touch and clamped her lips shut against the plea for him to take her. She knew his game and was powerless to resist. He would not stop until she faced the jagged reality of her desire.

One finger suddenly became two, thrusting deep inside, and Paige writhed beneath him, helpless against the onslaught of sensation. Arousal soared through her, lifting her higher and higher until a shudder of the purest pleasure rocked her very soul, and she gasped aloud.

"Feels good doesn't it?"

She burrowed her head in the pillows, willing to asphyxiate if she could just escape the masculine triumph in his voice.

"Don't bother to deny it. Your body tells me everything I need to know." He dug his fingers in a little deeper to prove the point.

A strangled moan slipped from her lips as another stab of pleasure pierced the fading echoes of her climax. With a laugh, he withdrew. Paige sucked in deep gulps of air when he lifted off her.

Christopher leaned over the edge of the bed, and she heard the rustle of clothing as he rifled through his pockets. "I'm sure a tactical blade would be much more impressive, but the first rule of scouting is to utilize what's at hand."

Paige felt the small blade against her skin before she actually saw it. Craning her neck, she caught a glimpse of a Swiss Army knife.

"I don't suppose an apology would do it," she asked, surprised by the catch in her voice. By her excitement.

"Afraid not, my dear. Had your chance." He cut her bra with precise strokes. The pink silk shredded easily and fell away. "Now I want my pound of flesh. Literally."

His erection fitted between her legs, hard, probing, while his hands circled her, cupping her breasts in his palms. He tugged at her nipples, twisting, pulling, until passion mounted again, and she arced back, unable to resist his insistent pressure against her.

"You're going to . . . torture me." Of course he would. As far as he was concerned, it would be no less than she deserved.

"Not torture, Paige, pleasure." His throaty voice revealed his own excitement. "I want you to admit what is happening between us."

What was happening between them? It was much more than sex. Christopher was ruthless enough to throw the truth in her face. He had known all along what she was now only realizing—their power struggle was only the result of feelings between them. Feelings she had denied since the Academy.

Paige couldn't deny any longer.

Even now the tangle of emotion unraveled inside, obliterated protest and reason. She wanted to indulge her feelings, indulge her desires. Control didn't matter when he touched her like this, invaded her senses and made her feel . . . wanted.

But Christopher would accept nothing less than her complete surrender. Determination steeled his touch, fueled his battle for dominance.

"Christopher. . . ." His name came out a plea, but Paige no longer cared.

"Tell me what you want, Paige. I want to hear you say it." The smooth head of his erection nudged her, stretched her, urged her to give up the fight.

"I want you . . . inside me," she rasped, wanting him more than she had ever wanted anything. "Now."

With a low roar that conveyed just how tenuous his own restraint had been, he rammed inside her with one forceful stroke.

Long-denied passion ignited as their bodies came together. Paige had known . . . had feared her response to him, knowing that the instant Christopher caught her she would be powerless to hold anything back.

She gave herself to him, willingly.

And he proved to her just how much she wanted him. He used his body like a weapon, giving no quarter, no mercy, thrusting deep only to withdraw, making her arch greedily toward him, desperate to be surrounded by his male strength as he cradled her with his body.

His chest grazed her back, his hips rocked against her as he plunged back in. She moaned aloud, submitted to the knowledge that this battle was not for power alone, but to make her acknowledge the truth. He had proven what she had been unwilling to admit all along. She wanted him, had always wanted him.

Paige realized for the first time that she didn't mind. She trusted Christopher, and trust changed everything. The desire she had fought since the beginning did not weaken her, but made her strong. He was her other half, a kindred spirit, a soul mate. Together they blazed—not only as agents, but as lovers. A team.

The flames licked higher inside, flaring, consuming, as he took her with long hot strokes until Goddard's presence vanished in a haze of urgent need. Until the world shattered in the face of ecstasy between them. Until they came together as one.

Christopher dragged himself off her and roused enough from the thick haze of passion to untie her wrists. Rolling onto her side, Paige gifted him with a sleepy smile before her lashes fluttered closed. The warmth of contentment washed through him, and he pulled her into his embrace, arranging the comforter to cover their nakedness. He wanted a momentary respite from Goddard's view, peace from the conflict that raged between them.

Paige purred as her long body unfolded against his, every pliant inch conveying satisfaction, glorious submission. Christopher massaged her arms, abashed he had restrained her—that he had needed to—but pleased she had finally stopped fighting what was happening between them.

Would she be back in force once recovered from the effects of their lovemaking? He had dragged unwilling responses from her sweet body and forced her to admit to a truth she had resisted for so long.

A truth that had become more complicated during the past few days. What had started as a purely physical attraction and grown into an obsession had become something so much more. She felt so good in his arms he did not want to let her go. Ever. With a groan, Christopher buried his face in that cloud of fragrant hair. What did he feel . . . love?

He had expected the passion and the excitement, but not the longing. They had enough evidence for a conviction—now all they needed was a boat. And then what? Once debriefed, they would be free to go their separate ways, meeting again only to testify in court. Could Christopher let her go, give her months, maybe even a year to rationalize what had happened between them? Or to forget?

A burst of angry denial made his gut clench tight. He ran a hand along her shapely arm, savoring the softness of her skin, the way her breasts molded against his chest. A deep, abiding hunger for her aroused him again, a slow wave of desire that would take a lifetime to satisfy. Christopher wouldn't let her go. Not just because Paige was too stubborn to admit what was happening between them.

Or too scared.

The thought struck him without warning, but once it formed, he knew he had found the missing link. All the pieces fell into place, her avoidance of him, her resentment when he finally caught her. Suddenly Christopher understood.

Paige was scared to fall in love.

What an idiot! He had been seducing her all wrong. Bold pursuit had only strengthened her resistance. Instead of demanding her surrender, she had to come willingly, had to trust him with her heart.

But Christopher didn't see that happening, not after he had forced her submission so completely, had made her beg for him. Even if she did glow in his arms right now. Even if she did snuggle against him like a woman in love. Paige would wake up. And when she did, revenge would be the uppermost thought in her mind.

A Heart to Heart

"We begin filming tomorrow," Goddard informed them at dinner. "The set is ready. The crew is ready. You are ready."

Paige wondered what would be the best way to respond to this announcement since she wasn't supposed to know he had been watching their rehearsals. Goddard was smiling expectantly, but she just couldn't bring herself to reply.

"We are ready," Christopher agreed, setting the fork down and meeting Goddard's gaze in a steady bit of acting that impressed even her. "We had an exceptional rehearsal today. I don't think we can get much better in the chemistry department, but we should spend some time reviewing our lines tonight." He glanced over at her for reinforcement. "What do you think, Paige?"

"We should." She set the wineglass down, hoping Goddard bought the excuse and didn't make them linger after dinner.

"Well, then," Goddard granted her fondest wish, "let's finish our meal so you can be on your way."

Paige went back to pushing beef tips around on her plate. Was it the impending filming or Christopher's lovemaking that had chased her appetite away? She had no intention of filming—she was leaving this island tonight if she had to swim—so it must be Christopher. The one man on the planet who was everything she shouldn't want. But did. Her stomach churned.

She was ready to sprint back to the west wing by the time the last swirl of cognac disappeared and Goddard released them to practice. But Christopher had another sort of running in mind.

"I missed my daily jog this morning and want to get it in before we go over the lines," he explained while leaving the dining room. "Come with me."

Paige only nodded. They still needed to find out if the boat had returned, and perhaps the exercise would help her diffuse the overwhelming sense of dread that came along with the understanding that she wouldn't be happy without Christopher in her life.

After a quick change, she found herself keeping the pace he set around the island. The night was moonless, the sky clear. A velvet blanket pinpricked with stars glistened above the endless expanse of black water, gilded the rocky terrain in silver lace. A cool night wind piped along with the rhythm of the pounding surf, filling her nostrils with the sea and driving home just how alone they were on this island.

A familiar sense of isolation gnawed at the edges of her mood. A feeling born of undercover work. A feeling Paige had learned intimately during the past two years. She was cut off from the mainland, her contact and the bureau.

But now she had Christopher.

And all these damn feelings that came with him. Even as she watched him stop beneath a twisted tree, her heart squeezed painfully in her chest, as much from the run as from the gloominess of her thoughts. Turning her back on the ocean, she faced the only man who could chase the solitude away.

"It's time for a little heart to heart, Paige," he said, sinking down in the grass and leaning back against the tree. "Why did you accept this assignment?"

His white T-shirt and shorts glowed in the darkness, but she could barely make out his features as he stared at the ocean, silent, back straight as if facing demons similar to her own.

"What does it matter?" Her question was a lost whisper in the night.

"It matters to me."

She glanced at him, surprised. There wasn't a command in his voice, or pride, or anger, just a simple statement of fact that she hadn't expected. Shrugging, she paced beneath the starlight, unsure where he was going with this conversation and not in the mood to play mother confessor.

"What difference does it make, Christopher?" she snapped, unable to level the annoyance in her voice. She had played the whore to catch Goddard. The end justified the means. It was that simple.

He wasn't buying it. "I watched you fight to be treated as an equal at the Academy. You were quite vocal about the 'Hooverish' mentality."

For the first time in their acquaintance, J. Edgar Hoover's name rolled off his tongue like an accusation. "Hey, without Hoover the FBI wouldn't be what it is today," she echoed his often-voiced sentiment.

Christopher smiled, a gesture that had the ability to coil her insides into knots, but he didn't respond to her jibe. "This assignment is one of the most discriminatory I've ever come across." He ran his fingers through his hair and shook his head. "You must have had a reason."

His disapproving tone sparked her anger. She whirled on him, ready for battle. "You accepted this assignment, too. If it's so damn distasteful, why are you here?"

"I had a reason."

Oh, that made all the difference, she supposed. Hands propped on her hips, she demanded, "Which was?"

"You."

Whatever Paige had expected, that wasn't it. "What do I have to do with it?"

"I've been chasing after you for the past eight years." He choked back a laugh. "And you still don't get it."

She could only stare at him, anger snuffed out and a tiny flicker of hope sparking to life at the exasperation she saw in his face.

"I accepted this assignment so I could work with you." He hitched an arm across his knee and met her gaze steadily. "If you haven't noticed, I've been turning up like a bad penny ever since you left the Academy."

"Oh, I've noticed all right," she informed him haughtily, determined to keep him at arm's length. "If you didn't notice, I kept running away."

"Why?" His question was a raspy whisper, betraying just how much he wanted an answer and twisting her resolve into a knot in the process.

Admit to the iron spy that she was scared he would take over her life, interfere with her career and swallow her whole? Not in this lifetime.

"You were a tyrant," she accused, a last ditch effort to resist. "I could never please you. Nothing was good enough. You demanded more from me because I was a woman."

"Not because you were a woman, Paige." His earnestness shimmered through her remaining defenses. "Because I knew you could be the best."

She heard the words, saw the sentiment mirrored in his face, and the icy edge of fear thawed.

Christopher believed in her.

And if he still believed in her after all these years, could she take a chance on him?

The truth suddenly loomed before her, and for the first time, Paige took a hard look. Christopher may be bossy and demanding, but he had never tried to destroy who she was in favor of who he wanted her to be. He had trained her, supported her, helped her realize her potential. There must be some middle ground to this control issue. Could they find it?

"I was right," Christopher announced without the slightest attempt at modesty. "You are the best. Agent and woman."

Starlight played like silver strands on his face, and she couldn't resist the urge to touch him. Her hand followed the arch of his neck to stroke a stubbled cheek. "I lose myself in you."

His fingers snagged her chin. "You're supposed to feel that way when you're in love," he said with an eagerness that humbled her. "I lose myself in you, too."

The tightness in her chest eased. Shadows receded and left a glowing ache in their wake. She leaned into his touch, answering the silent need of their bodies even as she wondered if they could really learn to compromise.

"Love?" she repeated, afraid to believe yet daring to hope.

His lips found hers, and he whispered on the edge of a kiss, "Do you really have to ask?"

A lump swelled in her throat.

"We are good together." His hand threaded through her hair, his belief in her so sincere, so sweet. She had let fear blind her to the love of a wonderful man who thought she was worth fighting for. Worth waiting for. Sure Christopher was a tough act to follow, but with him by her side, she could accomplish anything.

Her mouth parted beneath the gentle pressure of his, and Paige answered him with all the emotion that bubbled inside, willing to risk anything for a chance at tomorrow.

Christopher would settle for nothing less than a lifetime. Paige was his, and he undressed her beneath the brilliance of the stars, bathed in the ocean's sultry breeze. Alone. With no eyes except his.

His mouth never left hers as he lowered her to the ground. Every graze of his lips on her skin, every caress of his hands along the curves and hollows of her body expressed his longing, his love. Every touch was designed to lift her onto a wave of passion as strong as his own, designed to answer her every sigh, to satisfy her every shiver.

She clung to him, willing, trusting as he loved her with a long lush rhythm. He didn't take. She didn't submit. They just loved. Together.

He had never suspected such joy could exist in her response. Never knew that such tiny gasps of pleasure could sound like music. Or how much he wanted to charm those sweet sounds from her lips.

With his every breath, he devoted himself to pleasuring her. He cherished every sensation, every sigh of rapture until he felt the first vibration of her ecstasy. Unable to hold back, he rose with her, overcome by a need so powerful, so consuming, that he would never be sated until they had shared their lives together.

He gazed down into her face, both amazed and touched by the tenderness that softened her features, the tears that welled in her eyes.

She started to cry, first small little sounds and then big gulping sobs that rocked her entire body. Christopher held her close and kissed the tears from her cheeks.

"I love you, Paige."

"I know." She smiled through her tears with such happiness that he experienced an inner contentment stronger than anything he had ever known.

Rolling onto his back, he pulled her on top of him and snuggled her against his chest. He would never let go. From the beginning, he had known they were destined to be together. She was finally his.

But first he had to get her off this island. "We have to see if the boat's back."

"I'll swim if it isn't." A shudder rocked her body, and he pulled the T-shirt over her shoulders, covering her against the night air. "I can't perform on film."

"Not with what Goddard has planned for the last scene." He didn't remind her that they had already performed for the surveillance cameras.

"Do you think Goddard plans to kill you or me?"

"Both." He used his lips to soothe away the frown line between her brows. They were out of here. Tonight.

"I know that." She turned a soft smile on him. "I was talking about in the script."

"I think the warlord will get too rough with his beautiful captive."

She cuddled against him, and he held her tighter. "I thought so, too, but then I decided the script needed a plot twist."

"Are you going to pull a knife out from under the pillow?"

"The minute you start to come." Her wicked smile made his pulse pound.

He popped her bare bottom with an open hand and made her jump. "Our days of performing for an audience are over, my dear." Even if he had to make sure Goddard never saw the inside of a courtroom. "I've got a few ideas about getting off this island."

"Me, too." She writhed against him, and he couldn't resist kissing her passion-swollen mouth.

"We're a team. Remember?" The thought sent a rush of excitement through him about the future. Their future.

"Yeah. I remember."

"Come on, then. Let's get dressed." He pulled her to her feet, chuckling at her groan of protest. "I've got something to show you."

"This had better be good," she cautioned, visibly shaking off her languor. "I would have enjoyed a few more minutes basking in the afterglow."

"Just as soon as our job is done." Christopher laughed, refusing to even consider the danger that lay ahead. What he had to show her was good. Useful, at the very least.

Paige agreed. There was no mistaking her whoop of delight when he dug up his tools. He unrolled the chamois binding and peered at the items inside with a mixture of relief and satisfaction. His gun. His knife. His lock pick. His good luck baseball cap.

"This is big enough to store the videotape and the disks." Paige caressed the waterproof leather and gazed up at him with a smile. "Just in case we end up swimming back to the mainland."

He couldn't help the rush of raw pride at her pleasure. "It comes in handy."

"There really is a God." She lifted up on tip toes and pressed a soft kiss to his cheek. "And he sent me you."

Contentment blew through his veins like a power surge, leaving him awed in the face of her love. This singular moment would be etched in his mind forever. The amazement in her eyes. The way that look made him feel as if he could conquer the world.

"Let's go, my dear." Christopher strapped the pack around his waist and concealed it beneath his running shorts. "I'm suddenly eager to put debriefing behind me and request a well-deserved vacation." Tugging on his baseball cap, he led her back toward the house.

"My thoughts exactly." Paige laughed, and the sound rippled through him.

The Moment of Truth

Lewis Goddard had other ideas. The excitement of the boat's return shriveled when they arrived back at the marina and an attendant told them, "The boss wants to see the lady in his office right away."

"I'm on my way," Paige said with a smile, but the instant they were out of earshot, she whispered, "Something's up. Would you stay close?"

"Of course." Christopher didn't ask how she knew. He had learned long ago to trust an agent's instincts.

She took a deep breath when they entered the house, wariness sharpening her sapphire gaze to jewel-like hardness. "I could be worrying needlessly—"

"I'll be right here." He dropped a reassuring kiss on the top of her head and disappeared into the shadows of a leafy ficus.

Christopher watched as she pulled her composure around her like a cloak, becoming the bold actress he had become so intimately acquainted with during the past few days. She sailed into the office with confident strides.

"Out for a run, Paige?" Goddard's eel-slick voice echoed through the confines of the marble foyer. "With Christopher? I have some questions I think you might be able to help me with. Get the door and come sit down."

The door swung closed behind her, but didn't click shut.

Goddard's questions could be nothing more than curiosities about their upcoming performance, but something was lifting the hairs on the back of his neck, sending those little adrenaline alarms firing through him. Freeing the gun from his tool pack, Christopher secured it in his waistband and slipped from the shadows to eavesdrop by the cracked door.

Goddard's voice faded to a low rumble as he settled behind the desk, ". . . all these cutting edge security features on my computer . . . imagine my surprise when I discovered . . . doesn't make sense unless the system was expertly bypassed."

Paige hadn't been worrying needlessly. Christopher had gotten past all of Goddard's securities, but it sounded like he might have triggered something else. His hopes sank.

Paige sat in a chair before the desk, and her voice carried through the door.

"Well, yes, Mr. Goddard," she was saying, "we were in here last night . . . an unexpected detour." He could hear the blush in her voice and smiled despite himself. "But we didn't touch anything." She paused for a moment and then admitted, "Wait. I did flip the surge board on. I accidentally hit the switch while Christopher and I were otherwise . . . engaged. But I turned it off as soon as I realized what I'd done."

Damn. He hadn't missed one of the securities, but some innocuous program that logged whenever the computer was shut down improperly and the scan disk erased free space on the hard drive.

Paige's cover was good. He reminded himself to give her a kiss for her cleverness and waited in the throbbing silence to see if Goddard bought it.

"I know you and Christopher have grown close, Paige." Goddard's voice grew clearer, louder, as though he was moving around the desk. "With the rehearsals, that's to be expected. But you've been my employee long enough to know I expect loyalty from my people. Don't let your emotions cloud your judgment. I'm going to ask you only once— did Christopher access my computer?"

Looked like cleverness wasn't going to get it this time. Christopher adjusted the rim of his baseball cap, then reached for his gun. The instant he entered the room, security would be alerted, and they would have visitors. But he wasn't about to play games with Paige's life. They had a future to share—together.

Paige didn't believe Goddard had blown her cover. Yet. He thought she was protecting Christopher, apparently hadn't figured out they were working together.

"Mr. Goddard, I would never dream of betraying your trust," she told him, meeting his gaze with a look of what she hoped was quiet desperation. "Not for anyone. You've done so much—"

"I wish it was that simple." He half sat on the desk, towering above her with his deceptively casual posture. "I'm concerned Christopher may not be who he claims. That he may be misleading us."

He must think she was really stupid, but there was nothing stupid about the wicked .44 Magnum he pulled out of his desk drawer.

"Wh-what are you going to do?" she stammered, affecting a nervousness that wasn't all an act.

Goddard hefted the gun in his palm, turned it over for effect and stared at it thoughtfully. "That depends entirely on you. Are you going to answer—"

The door exploded against the wall, and Paige spun around as Christopher burst into the room. The breath caught in her throat when she saw him, broad shoulders filling the doorway, tawny hair swirling around that strong face, the emotion in his eyes reflecting such a violent blend of love and rage that her heart swelled in her chest.

Hurling herself from the chair, she almost broke away, but Goddard's arm snaked around her neck and cut off her escape. With the revolver aimed at her temple, he dragged her against him like a human shield. She met Christopher's murderous stare with a wry grin.

A hostage. Christ, she'd never live this down.

"All right, James Bond," Goddard warned, pressing the gun barrel into her skin so hard she winced. "One more step and her brains will be painting a fresco on my wall. Now why don't you tell me who you really are."

Compared to Goddard's revolver, Christopher's bureau-issue 9mm looked deceptively small, and an image of blood and guts flashed through her mind. Fury hardened Christopher's features. She could almost feel the determination radiating off him, and a zing of hot assurance sliced through her. They had played out this scenario back at the Academy. They could play it again. She winked and hoped Christopher remembered.

He did. She saw the flicker of acknowledgment in his eyes as he held his gun trained on Goddard's forehead. "I'm Special Agent Christopher Sharp with the Federal Bureau of Investigation." Paige couldn't drag her gaze from the sight of him, so masculine, so powerful. Or quell her surge of pride at his announcement. "You're under arrest."

"FBI?" Goddard laughed, to all appearances amused, but Paige felt his body tense. "Shit, Christopher. I should have known you were too good to be true. Did the FBI train you especially for this job? You were quite a natural."

Fury struck hard. Paige fought the urge to bite a chunk out of Goddard's arm and focused on Christopher instead. His eyes had narrowed to slits. As he read Goddard his rights, the muscle in his jaw flexed wildly. The effort was costing him, too.

"So," Goddard asked conversationally, "what are you arresting me for?"

Christopher never wavered. "Murder one among other things."

"Murder!" Goddard leaned back against the desk, catching Paige hard around the throat and pulling her with him. "Now that's a nasty accusation. Who?"

Goddard wasn't really worried yet, Paige knew, he was more concerned with fishing out whatever information he could. The criminal mind was so predictable.

Christopher led him right down the garden path. "You're a suspect in seven deaths related to your pornography ring."

"Pornography?" Goddard cringed in mock horror. "I like to think of it as art erotica. You should know that—you're starring in my latest film." He sighed dramatically, but Paige felt the first traces of fear roll off him like sweat.

"I suppose this means I'll have to recast your role." He rested his chin on her head and inhaled deeply. "A damn shame. You two were magic together."

Christopher stared down the length of the gun barrel, his voice as steady as the gun he held, his fury exhilarating to watch. "You won't be recasting our roles. I'm closing this production down. Permanently."

"You can prove these charges?" Goddard's arm tightened, and Paige struggled to appear calm, not to distract Christopher even though she couldn't breathe.

The iron spy never wavered. "Look around you. You're not exactly hiding anything here."

"Circumstantial. You can't connect those deaths to me, and anything incriminating will disappear within the hour. So how does any of this translate into murder one?" The gun bit into her skin, but Paige felt his hand tremble. They had his attention now.

"I'd have your lawyer pack more than an overnight bag—"

"It's that goddamn kid, isn't it?" Goddard shouted. His body arched tight as a bowstring, but he eased his grip on her throat just a bit. "You've got her, don't you?"

"He's telling the truth?" Paige choked out, gulping air. Opportunities like this didn't come along often, and she wouldn't have missed it for the world. "You murdered those people?"

"Yes." The defiant hiss echoed in her ear. "And you're about to witness another murder." Goddard jerked to his feet, taking her with him.

Paige knocked the gun from his hand and drove her elbow into his stomach. He had barely managed a gasp before she broke free and spun around, ramming the heel of her palm into his face.

Goddard staggered back, but the desk trapped him, and before the revolver hit the carpeted floor, Christopher held him around the throat, gun pressed against his head. "Don't move."

Goddard didn't.

"Please tell me the audio picked this up." Paige stared up at the video camera pointed uselessly toward the door. An audio tape of Goddard's confession would clinch her case.

"Doesn't matter." Christopher rolled his eyes toward the cap on his head. "I've got it all on videotape."

"A microvideo camera?" she burst out, afraid to hope he had a tiny recording device concealed in the emblem of his baseball cap.

That sensual mouth curled into the most radiant of smiles. "I never leave home without it."

"I love you." She blew him a kiss.

"I know."

"You're making a mistake, Paige," Goddard spat out. A desperate attempt by a man who still didn't grasp the whole picture. A man who was scared. "You agreed to star in my film, knowing what it was. You're an accomplice. What do you think the FBI will do to you?"

"Give me a vacation, I hope." Paige grabbed the revolver and cocked the cylinder to check the chambers. Loaded. She caught his gaze and smiled. "At full pay."

Goddard's face went blank.

"Full pay?" Christopher snorted, poking the gun barrel into Goddard's temple to emphasize the point. "I don't think they'll be that grateful."

Goddard's skin took on a decidedly greenish cast, and she could almost see the light bulb flicker above his head as full impact of their words hit. Paige couldn't stop the laughter that burst from her lips. "Should've checked my references."

Crossing the room, she kicked the door open and aimed the revolver at Jerry the security guard who struggled to keep his balance on the other side.

"Drop the weapon and get down on the floor. Now."

"See if he's got cuffs," Christopher suggested.

He did, and in the space of a heartbeat, he was wearing them.

Paige burst through the doorway and searched the foyer for any of Jerry's friends. "It's clear." She motioned Christopher out.

"You'll never make it off this island." Goddard warned with a show of bravado as Christopher dragged him through the door. "Do you honestly think I don't have this covered? My men know what to do if anything happens to me."

"Thanks for the warning, but I don't think they'll risk your life while I'm holding a gun to your head." Christopher called his bluff, and one turn into the west wing proved he was right.

A trio of Goddard's men waited, guns trained and ready, surprise registering on their faces when they saw their boss's predicament.

"Mr. Goddard, what—"

"Don't even think about it, gentlemen, or he's a dead man," Christopher cautioned.

Paige covered him, knowing he covered her, feeling a sweet edge to the rush of danger because Christopher was here. He loved her and would protect her. She'd do the same for him.

They sailed past Goddard's men into their suite. She slammed the door shut behind them and threw the lock.

With one powerful blow, Christopher cold-cocked Goddard. "Ouch. Bet that hurt." But he didn't look the least bit repentant as Goddard crumbled to the floor in a flaccid heap. Aiming his gun at the door, he glanced over his shoulder and said, "Go get the disks and the tape. Bring the handcuffs from the bedroom, too."

"There's no other way to do this except out the back door," Christopher said when she returned. "We have to get to the marina."

"They'll be waiting for us."

"We'll protect each other." His face was radiant, and she felt the warmth of his love flow through her.

A smile touched her lips as he bent to hoist Goddard over his shoulder. The running shorts hugged the sexy curve of his bottom. It would be an absolute tragedy to risk that magnificent ass. "Perhaps they'll think twice before they shoot since we've got him."

They did. No one did more than make threats when they left the west wing and headed down the narrow hallway. Even with all the doorways and turns, when Goddard's men had the home team advantage, they did not interfere. Either Goddard had been quite explicit about procedure in the event he was taken hostage, or the team was a trifle shy without the coach.

Christopher led them into Goddard's private apartment and positioned himself in the doorway, gun poised dramatically at Goddard's temple. "Check out the other rooms."

"They're clear." Paige locked the surrounding doors, securing the room. She didn't need any prompting to locate their own surveillance tapes and ran across an assault rifle in her search.

Tossing the tapes into a knapsack, she slipped it and the rifle over her shoulder.

"Hey, Rambo, got our tapes?"

The laughter in his voice jolted her into a quick smile. She patted the pouch. "Wouldn't want anyone to get a hold of these."

"My thoughts exactly."

She covered the distance between them in a few quick strides. Pointedly ignoring Goddard, she brought her fingers to his hair, gliding through the tawny strands in a lover's caress. "You really don't miss a trick, do you?"

"I hate loose ends." A frown creased his brow. She saw the failure flash in his eyes and knew his pride was all tangled up in that little twist of fate. "But I should have known about the scan disk—"

She shrugged, not wanting him to dwell on one oversight when she could never have caught Goddard without him. "You're pretty great, Christopher, but you're not like . . . Hoover, or something."

"Oh, I'm not, am I?"

She couldn't resist pressing a kiss to that luscious mouth. "You're the man I love. That's even better."

His deep chuckle gusted against her lips. "Works for me."

Paige resisted the impulse to pull him deeper into her kiss. Love was grand, she decided, but that didn't change the fact that they weren't home free yet. Taking a step back, she ruffled Goddard's hair. "Do you think he was serious about this stuff disappearing before anyone can get back with a warrant?"

"Perhaps. But we have what we need. Anything else is gravy."

He was right. Wouldn't do to get greedy now. Not when they still had to make the marina.

"Here we go." She pulled aside the drapery to reveal a wide angle view of the lighted pool and the marina beyond. "His bedroom connects. Just like you said."

"Let's go." He shifted Goddard's inert form higher onto his shoulder. "He weighs a ton."

"And smells bad, too."

A wall of glass doors opened out onto the pool from Goddard's bedroom, providing both the clearest route to the marina and the show of resistance awaiting them. Even through the shadows of the floodlights, she could make out half a dozen men surrounding the dock, armed with enough hardware to take over a small country.

"I'm going out shooting." Paige shoved the revolver into her waistband and grabbed the rifle. She lifted the weapon to survey the left side of the breech casing and flipped the control selector to burst. "Let's hope they want Goddard alive to sign their paychecks."

Christopher nodded, but she could see the apprehension stiffen his spine as he gazed out the window.

"You ready to wrap this up?" she asked lightly, hoping to reassure him.

The hot gaze he turned on her heated her blood. "Let's go, my dear." Paige yanked back the verticals and threw open the door. "You're aiming those guns at two federal agents," she shouted, "back off. Now!" Firing the first salvo onto the ground close to the bad guys, she sent them scrabbling for cover in all directions.

With Christopher on her heels, she took off toward the pool, firing a new burst each time a head popped up over some makeshift barricade.

Paige snagged keys from the boathouse and headed for Goddard's powerboat. Not only was it light and fast enough to compete with the security vessels, it was equipped with enough radio equipment to put them in touch with the mainland.

She leaped in, covering Christopher's back as he dumped Goddard unceremoniously onto the deck.

"Well done, my dear." His dark eyes sparkled, and Paige recognized the gleam of excitement, the flash of triumph.

"I learned from the best." There was nothing like a good escape to get the blood flowing.

Christopher laughed, but she could see him glow beneath the compliment. She untied the boat from the dock while he shoved Goddard into the cramped storage compartment under the bow, leaving the door open for air. They wouldn't have to worry about his safety, and handcuffed, he wouldn't be able to get out without drawing their notice.

Christopher started the engine and within minutes, the bright lights of Goddard's sanctuary faded into the night as they gained the freedom of the Pacific.

He stood at the wheel, wind whipping the tawny hair away from his face, the spray of salt water glistening on his skin. Paige's heart did a somersault in her chest. She wanted to hug him, to feel those strong arms around her.

"Activate the homing device and give me the videotapes," Christopher said, and she settled for the gaze that caressed her instead.

Paige tossed him the backpack, then set up a signal that would alert the mainland field office to their location. She took stock of her meager weapon store. Within seconds, several boats filled with Goddard's men shot out from the harbor. It wouldn't be long before they were within firing range.

"We'll make new memories," Christopher shouted, his voice carrying over the roar of the engine.

"What?" Paige rested the rifle in her lap and glanced up at him, just as he tossed a videotape overboard.

"The Celtic priestess skit," he explained with a grimace. "I couldn't stand to watch myself suffer the agonies of the damned. It's still too vivid in my mind. But the Medieval scene." He held up another tape. "Wouldn't the boys back in Washington just love this. I know for a fact you are more than one agent's fantasy." His wicked grin made a little trickle of apprehension skitter through her. "What do you think?"

He couldn't be serious, could he?

"Toss it," she said, and to her relief, he did.

"The striptease. My personal favorite." Turning the last tape over in his hand, he glanced at it, his grin softening into a fond smile. "You will dance for me again, won't you?"

No loose ends. Of course he would have to ask, flex those control muscles he was so fond of using. That was just Christopher. The man she loved.

"Anytime." She had never meant anything more in her life.

"How about on our wedding night?"

Wedding night?

"What?" Her jaw went slack, and she could only stare at him. Until the first shot screamed past her head.

Christopher slid onto his knees and hunched low over the steering wheel, while Paige aimed the rifle and fired at the headlights that sliced through the darkness, unable to make out individual figures.

"What are you talking about?"

"Our wedding night," he repeated. "You know, the night of our wedding." He cocked the wheel one-handed and the boat veered starboard so sharply that Goddard's head clunked solidly against the fiberglass door frame. "Marry me, Paige."

"You want to get married?" The idea finally started to sink in, but emotion hadn't pierced her shock yet.

"Yeah, we can work together."

Paige dropped close to the deck and reloaded, shock finally dissolving into a wave of exasperated surprise. "I can't believe you're proposing to me while we're trying to escape." Her voice rode the crest of an explosion as she discharged the final burst. Tossing aside the rifle, Paige rolled toward the bow, grateful for the expert way he handled the boat. "We'll probably never make the mainland alive."

Christopher slapped his 9mm into the palm of her hand with enough force to make her skin tingle. "Incentive. We have to escape, so you can shop for a wedding gown." He dangled the striptease tape in front of her. "Do I have an affirmative?"

"That's blackmail, Sharp."

He nodded gleefully, and happiness swirled inside her. Who would have ever guessed the assignment from hell would lead to the love of her life?

"You have an affirmative." The last tape disappeared in the churning waves, and the smile she gave him echoed all the love in her heart.

He reached for the radio transmitter. "United States Coast Guard. This is Special Agent Christopher Sharp with the FBI requesting assistance." She heard the impatience in his voice and couldn't hold back a chuckle when he said, "And make it snappy, will you? I have a wedding to attend."

Damned control freak. He even bossed the Coast Guard around. Bracing her wrists on the gunwale, Paige pulled the trigger with a satisfied sigh. Life was grand.

Love Undercover

❧

by B. J. McCall

To my reader:

The truly rugged individualist, no matter what his day job, is usually a cowboy at heart.

And what woman doesn't want a cowboy . . .

Chapter One

"I hate meetings," Detective Wes Cooper muttered to his best friend and partner, Tom Jenkins. Just thinking about sitting through another squad meeting with his sexy new boss reminded Wes of his eighth grade year in Miss Hollister's English literature class. Captivated by the beautiful redhead, he'd experienced several embarrassing classroom moments. At thirty-seven, a public erection wasn't likely, but it was damn hard to concentrate on the Lieutenant's comments when all Wes could think about was giving her a slow, intense strip search.

Tom checked his watch. "The Lieutenant's running late. Maybe she'll cancel."

"I can only hope." Wes shifted his gaze once again to the standard beige colored corridor visible through the glass-fronted conference room. When he spied his boss, dressed in a dark blue suit, threading her way past uniformed officers, lawyers, and assorted police personnel toward the conference room, Wes almost groaned.

On any other woman, a suit did little to compliment the body, but on Lt. Forbes an ordinary straight skirt and a double-breasted jacket took on a whole new dimension. No matter how hard he tried, and he had, Wes couldn't ignore the curves filling out the fine blue wool.

How many times had he chastised himself for looking?

Covertly, he'd watch the graceful, fluid swing of the Lieutenant's rounded backside as she navigated the crowded, narrow precinct corridors. Her long, slender legs captivated him.

At night, in his dreams, she walked naked.

If he had to have a female boss, why did she have to be so damned sexy looking? And a green-eyed redhead to boot?

Like Wes, Tom's gaze was fixed on the new Lieutenant. "The Captain says the boss has a master's degree. I understand she took a bunch of classes at the FBI school."

"Just my luck," Wes replied, thinking again of the sexy, unobtainable Miss Hollister who'd undoubtedly been responsible for his penchant for redheads. He glanced at Tom. "She'll probably want to teach the burglars to read Milton."

"Who's Milton?"

"Never mind." Wes placed one booted foot on the unoccupied chair next to his as the Lieutenant entered the conference room and brushed past him. For a split second her tush was a mere inch from his face. A hint of flowery perfume lingered in her wake.

Wes could just kill the Captain for hiring a female who put his male senses on full alert every time he saw her.

Amanda sorted out her prepared notes, then began. She was tempted to ask Wes Cooper to remove his booted foot from the chair directly to her immediate left, but as usual he sat there, his unsettling blue gaze fastened on her.

Fearless and cool when it counted, the good looking detective was too provocative for Amanda to ignore.

His startling silver-blue eyes enchanted her. His western style of dress and long-legged swagger had captured Amanda's attention and fueled her imagination. Whenever he was near, her concentration suffered, making her uncomfortably aware of how long it had been since she'd felt the caress of a lover's hands on her bare skin, the lustful brush of lips across her breasts or the heated thrust of an erection between her legs.

Her pulsed raced and her thighs tightened at the sensual and erotic images. Just looking at him, her temperature climbed and her underwear felt hot and tight.

Without taking his eyes off of her, Cooper said something to Jenkins in that low, sexy drawl. Amanda had no idea what he'd said. Her attention was focused on his mouth. Her tongue slid across her lower lip. She wanted to taste him, to feel his firm lips easing the pressure of her taut nipples.

Her hands clenched the podium. Her gaze dropped to the bulge enhanced by his tight jeans. Could he justify that delicious swagger?

Someone asked her a direct question, snapping Amanda's attention back to the meeting. She cleared her throat, glanced at her notes and asked for case updates.

As the reports droned on, Amanda swore silently. She'd never faced this predicament. She'd never fantasized about a co-worker before. A set of tight buns would catch her eye, but never had she experienced such plaguing erotic fantasies. Unfortunately, fantasize was all she could do. After a few costly sexual harassment suits, the department had made it clear any sexual contact between supervisors and subordinates, even consensual contact, was forbidden.

She'd never been tempted by the forbidden before. Until now.

Amanda liked cowboys. Raised on a working Arizona ranch, Cooper was the living manifestation of her cowboy fantasies, and an undeniable temptation.

There was something about tight jeans and leather chaps which drew her to western movies and rodeos. At night, alone in her bed, she read western romances.

Last night Cooper had saved her from a group of desperados. His gaze had been heated as he'd removed her torn dress, lace-trimmed chemise and drawers, and taken the only reward she had to offer so gallant a hero. Amanda's gaze slid from the podium back to Cooper. She could recall the feel of his hands on her body, his mouth on her breasts. They'd made love out in the open, beneath a blazing sun. The dream had been so vivid, Amanda tingled at the memory of their entwined bodies brushed by a hot desert wind.

Cooper's eyes narrowed.

Realizing she'd been thinking about making love to Cooper instead of listening to the detectives' case updates, Amanda forced her errant thoughts back to her main reason for calling the meeting.

She was about to speak when Cooper beat her to the punch.

"What about the strip joint robberies?"

"I was getting to that," Amanda said, meeting his intense blue gaze. "We're going undercover."

A few of the guys whooped. As she suspected this was one assignment they'd all jump on. Cooper stared right at her. His eyes widened. "We?"

She wanted to lean close to him and answer his question in minute detail, instead Amanda forced her gaze to focus on the rest of the squad. "I've arranged for teams of two to work in six clubs, Thursdays through Saturdays, for the next month. Hope you like overtime, Detective Cooper," she said, cognizant that his gaze had remained firmly on her.

Whenever he was in the room, within the scope of her vision, she felt drawn to him. No matter how many times she forced herself to look away, she was aware of him. At times, when their gazes locked across the room, she'd had to remind herself to breathe.

He excited her. He scared the hell out of her. If Cooper ever touched her, she wasn't sure she could resist.

"I do, Lieutenant," he spoke in an affected drawl. "Sitting around watching ladies shake their fannies—"

"You won't be a customer, Detective. You'll have to work this one." Amanda enjoyed the skeptical look Cooper gave her. "You're the new bouncer at the Prickly Cactus. All that country music should make you feel right at home."

Amanda waited as Cooper took some good-natured ribbing from the other detectives. When he looked her straight in the eye and grinned, she remembered he'd grinned in her dream. Right before he pulled her, naked and willing, into his arms.

"I hope you don't expect Tom to dance," Cooper drawled.

The detectives' laughter skittered about the room. "That's my job, Detective. And I'll be doing it at the Prickly Cactus. Tom's assigned to the Bosom Buddies."

The room went silent. So silent Amanda worried he could hear her thundering heart as she waited for his reaction. Every hair on her body stood on end when she looked into Cooper's silver-blue eyes.

He's imagining me naked.

The thought ricocheted in her brain, the image of herself peeling down to a tiny bra and G string in front of Cooper. Her cheeks burned along with another portion of her anatomy.

An odd look crossed Cooper's face. "You're joking."

"The robbers are quick and efficient. They know our response time. Undercover is the only way."

One corner of Cooper's mouth twitched. "And where will you hide your badge and gun?" Cooper asked. His gaze was centered on her chest.

Amanda ignored his teasing remark. The guys in vice had needled her until she'd nailed more johns in a street walker sting than any of her female colleagues. So far she hadn't met one female officer who'd hidden her gun in her bra.

"I believe an undercover sting will solve these robberies. The Captain agrees."

Cooper's gaze slid from her face to travel the length of her body. He remained silent, but his cool expression told her he didn't believe she was up to the task, as a cop or a woman. In fact, he looked annoyed. When he finally raised his eyes, Amanda greeted him with a glare which dared him to object. He did. "Wouldn't Barbara Bates . . . she's worked vice—"

"Officer Bates is assigned to the Bosom Buddy with Tom," Amanda snapped. She understood why Cooper would prefer to be paired with Bates. The woman must be a 38 double D, and gossip had it the two officers were more than friendly when off-duty.

A couple of the guys slapped Detective Jenkins on the back, but Cooper kept his attention focused on her. "Tom's married. Wouldn't it be better—"

"Detective Jenkins, do you have an objection to your assignment?" As Amanda expected, Tom Jenkins gave her a negative response. She read off the rest of the teams and where they would work. "If there's nothing else," she said, looking at Cooper. To her relief he remained silent. "I'll expect all of you to remember that during this operation you are still on duty and your behavior must be exemplary."

After she dismissed the group, Amanda picked up her notes and walked out of the room. All the way back to her office, she felt Cooper's cool blue gaze centered on her back. She'd be damned if she'd dream about him tonight.

Without the stage lights and music on, the Prickly Cactus reminded Wes of a big black box. The walls were dark gray and the carpet, a dull black and burgundy pattern, managed to hide the cigarette burns. Except for the neon cactus centered on the wall, even the oak wood bar looked dull to Wes. But when the show began and the near-naked girls gyrated beneath colorful lights to deafening music, no one would give a damn.

As the bouncer, Wes had access to the dressing rooms behind the stage. He wanted to go backstage and say hello, but he was quite sure the Lieutenant wouldn't like it.

Instead he sat at the bar, nursed a diet cola and wondered why the hell she'd chosen him to be her partner. Did she have any idea how much she turned him on? Whenever he looked into her green eyes, he could swear he felt a connection. Wes shook his head and swore. Assignments like this were tough enough, but watching the sexy Lieutenant dance half naked all night, then going home alone would be hell. Working with Bates would have been a cakewalk.

He couldn't remember the last time he'd been tempted to jack-off. Maybe he just liked redheaded, authoritarian females. Wes chuckled. He bet the department psychiatrist would have a field day with that one.

The lights went down around six and Wes took his place by the door. The customers, mostly businessmen working in the financial district, began to fill the place. Guys in three-piece suits usually pulled out a credit card, instead of a gun, when they got out of line. Wes liked suits.

When the lights on the stage began to pulse, Wes, along with every other guy in the room, fastened his gaze on the beaded curtains at the far end of the narrow stage. Wes realized he didn't care about the other dancers. He was waiting for *her*.

Since the Lieutenant had joined the squad, she'd worn her hair up in a tight twist. Wes's fingers had itched to remove every pin, just to see how far that mass of red hair would cascade down her back. Tonight his fantasy would become a reality. His pulse jumped as the beaded curtain separated. A lush blonde in a red sequined cowboy hat, vest, and tight, red shorts pranced onto the stage.

Disappointed, Wes turned his attention to the crowd. He'd bet his weekly paycheck that half the customers were married and their wives had no idea they were here spending five bucks for a beer and leering at girls. Chuckling at his holier-than-thou attitude, Wes walked over to the bar and ordered a cup of coffee.

Backstage, Amanda stood before a full length mirror. She tugged the green spangled demi-cup bra down, but that only forced her breasts higher. How would she ever dance with her knees trembling and her stomach doing flip-flops?

"Come on, honey, giv'em a shake."

Amanda looked over her shoulder at her advisor. Lucy Morals, also-known-as Lucy Morales, was the star act at the Cactus. An exotic mixture of several nationalities, Lucy had to be the best looking woman in the business. Her eyes were big and dark, her thick brown hair so long it grazed her butt when she walked.

"The first night's always the hardest," Lucy said as she adjusted her gold sequined bra over a set of pasties. Her bra in place, Lucy demonstrated. Her shoulders barely moved, but her large breasts bounced, jiggled and shifted side-to-side. "The guys love it. Especially if you put'em right in their faces."

"I don't think I can do that," Amanda croaked. Performing before her closet door mirror in her own bedroom was entirely different from what faced her out front. She heard the hooting, hollering and whistling from the men when Candy Redd stepped on stage. Lucy said it was a good crowd for a Thursday.

"You got a boyfriend, honey?" Lucy asked.

Amanda shook her head and fiddled with the fringe of her extremely short skirt. She shifted her hips trying to get comfortable with the narrow strip of material covering her. She'd never worn a thong bikini before.

"Maybe a guy you got the hots for?"

Without responding, Amanda tried Lucy's move. In comparison she looked pitiful. "Guess it works better if you're larger."

"It works better if you're into it," Lucy remarked. "Just pretend one of those guys is Tom Cruise or whoever. Dance for him and let it go."

The image of Wes Cooper in nothing but a pair of jeans leaped to mind. Amanda tried again. It worked.

"Tom Cruise will do it every time," Lucy said. She cocked her head as the music ended. "You're on, honey."

Amanda ran from the dressing room and up the narrow stairs leading to the beaded curtain. Her stomach lurched. If she barfed on stage, she'd never live it down. Candy bounced through the curtain, and said, "It's all yours, Blaze."

As "Achy, Breaky Heart" began to play, she stepped through the beaded curtain. Thankful for the bright lights, Amanda couldn't see the men, but she could hear their whistles and shouts. An "ohhhhhh, baby," and a "give it to me sweetheart," collided in the babble.

She forced a smile.

Concentrating on the music, she dipped and wiggled, but Amanda knew she wasn't giving the crowd what they wanted. Her arms and legs felt stiff and awkward, and her heart was a thundering lump which her brain couldn't seem to control.

Then suddenly the front door opened and two guys walked in and disappeared into the blackness. In that brief slash of light from the marquee outside, she glimpsed Cooper. Staring in his direction, she forgot the men surrounding the narrow stage. Their shouts no longer registered. Only the music, her body, and Wes Cooper remained.

She imagined a bare-chested Cooper watching her, and suddenly her body discovered a sexy rhythm all its own. Her legs and hips began to move and her forced smile transformed into a sensual pout. In time with the backbeat, Amanda rolled her hips. When she thrust her pelvis forward, shrill whistles nearly drowned out the music. She whipped open her vest, then let it slip down her arms a few inches at a time. Twirling the shiny scrap of fabric like a lasso, she danced to the end of the stage. Resisting the urge to fling the discarded vest in Cooper's direction, she tossed it over her shoulder. When she bent low and jiggled her breasts, the crowd roared. Knowing somewhere in the darkness Cooper's silver-blue gaze was fastened on her sent a fiery rush of heat pulsing through Amanda's veins. She turned around and let go with a slow, raunchy grind which felt so good she repeated the move several times.

Ignoring the whistling audience, Amanda kept her focus above the men's faces. She danced only for her blue-eyed cowboy.

As she whipped off her short skirt, she looked toward the front door and imagined herself popping open the buttons of his tight jeans one-at-a-time.

As each button gave way, her bump-and-grind became slower, deeper, and decidedly more sensual. Keeping her gaze in Cooper's direction, she gave him a wouldn't-you-like-to-touch-them jiggle. The crowd yelled and stomped their feet.

Amanda turned away from the crowd and thrust her near-naked hips from side-to-side. In slow, sensual swings she imagined Cooper running his long calloused fingers along the length of her legs, across her belly and finally cupping her breasts. Heat pulsed throughout her body, her breasts tightened, and she throbbed with a fiery heat between her legs.

Right in your face, Cooper.

The men cheered, but Amanda didn't care. She focused on Cooper's silent challenge of her abilities and went into her finale.

With her back to the crowd, she stood with her legs braced apart and pulled off her white hat. She felt the weight of her hair fall as it tumbled down her back. The men yelled louder. She strutted along the edge of the stage and the yahoos showed their appreciation, slipping bills beneath the garter on her right thigh. She endured the lewd comments and suggestive gestures, and made one more pass across the stage, but Detective Cooper never left his post by the door.

By the end of the night, Amanda's legs ached from dancing in high-heeled cowboy boots. Her knees had almost buckled during the last set. Too tired to change, she pulled off her boots, then flopped down on a narrow cot in the dressing room.

Candy Redd had already left. As Lucy tucked her black tee shirt into her jeans, she said, "Ya done good, Blaze."

"Thanks. At least I didn't throw up on anyone."

"I've known girls who have. Really pisses off the boss." At the door, Lucy hesitated. "Go home and soak in a hot bath. It helps."

Amanda rolled off the cot to her feet. Her knees protested. She hoped she never heard "Achy Breaky Heart" again.

She'd just unclasped her spangled bra when the door swung open. A draft of cold air poured into the heated dressing room and fanned her bare skin. Clasping the loose bra to her chest, Amanda spun around. Cooper leaned against the door jamb.

"Is there something you want, Detective?"

That cool blue gaze slowly slid over her. "Good show, Lieutenant. Especially that little finale you do. You had 'em comin' in their pants."

"Tips weren't bad either." Holding his gaze, Amanda carefully refastened her bra, then glanced down at the lacy black garter circling her thigh. A wad of bills protruded from it like an open fan. "With six of us dancing, the widows and orphans fund should have a banner month."

Cooper grinned then eased his big male frame away from the door and toward Amanda. For a split second she knew how it felt to have the Duke coming at you. Cooper'd even mastered the easily recognizable shoulder-swing. Resisting the urge to step back, Amanda planted her bare feet.

"Then let me give you some advice," Cooper said, pulling a bill out of his pocket and tucking it right down the front of her G string. His warm fingertips grazed over her curls. "Real strippers give the boys a little thrill."

She grabbed his arm. Although the contact was pure reflex, awareness of the corded strength of his forearm and the power he was capable of unleashing held her spellbound. She wished she could uncurl her fingers and let him know she welcomed his touch. He didn't move his hand. His fingertips remained pressed to her bare flesh as she fought hard for control. In a voice she hardly recognized, she said, "You forget yourself, Cooper."

"That's a fifty," he said, removing his hand. "The guy's name is Harold."

"And?" Amanda asked as Cooper turned and sauntered to the door. She could still feel the warm imprint of his hand.

"He wanted to know if you were available after hours," he said quietly, not looking at her.

Amanda smiled as her flesh cooled. "Looks like I can handle it, doesn't it, Detective? At least he doesn't suspect I'm a cop."

Cooper started to close the dressing room door, but Amanda's curiosity had been piqued. She knew she shouldn't, but she wanted him to stay. "What did you tell Harold?"

Cooper glanced over his shoulder and gave her a level stare. "I told the bastard you were my woman."

His woman. Before Amanda could respond, the door closed and she was left alone with her racing pulse and wilder imagination. Had the detective somehow felt her vibes? Did he suspect she'd danced for him?

Amanda collected the bills from her garter and stuffed them in her bag next to her badge. The shiny metal brought a welcome flash of common sense. His little demonstration had been nothing more than an attempt to provoke her. When she'd worked vice, one of the guys had insisted on trying to adjust her push-up bra on a nightly basis. Instead of getting upset, she'd slapped his hands away and laughed. Eventually she'd been treated as one of the team.

The sexy detective was just yanking her chain.

Her pulse back to normal and her imagination in check, Amanda dressed in a pair of comfortable sweats, grabbed her duffle bag and exited the back door of the Prickly Cactus. She scanned the partially lit parking lot and headed for her car. On the opposite side of the small lot, the driver's door of a Jeep opened and Cooper stepped out. *Now what did he want?* She tossed her duffle bag in the back seat, then leaned against her red Firebird, waiting.

She sensed motion in the luxury sedan parked opposite her car. Dragging her gaze away from Cooper, Amanda glanced at the sedan. In the faint light she made out a bobbing head of blonde hair and a white shirt in the sedan's back seat.

"That's not very ladylike," Cooper whispered. His breath fanned her cheek.

Aware of how close Cooper was, Amanda turned. His big hands firmly clutched her hips. She wanted to press her body to his and feel the hard muscles hinted at beneath his shirt and the strength in his thighs. If he had been a bouncer and not her subordinate, she'd take him home, now, this very minute, and spend the night naked in his arms.

Reluctantly she pushed him away.

"Don't go blowing our cover, Lieutenant," he whispered as his fingers fanned out over her backside and his thumbs fastened onto her waist.

She had imagined so many times how it would feel to be in his arms. Amanda forced herself to relax. At least she could satisfy some of her curiosity. "Then don't call me Lieutenant."

He moved closer. So close she could sense how they'd fit together. "Okay, Mandy."

At his use of her family nickname, an odd sense of familiarity slid up Amanda's spine. She liked the way he said it, low and sexy. "The name's Blaze around here," she reminded him.

Cooper eased her back against the car. His fingers slid beneath the waistband of her sweats. "Why don't we just let Candy finish, then we can talk?"

A sense of foreboding slid along her spine. She should push his hands away, now, but his fingers felt good on her warm flesh. Too good to resist. Staying in Blaze's character, Amanda kept her voice low and a little sultry. "Is she doin' what I think she's doin'?" she asked.

"Uhmmm. And from the looks of it," Cooper whispered, leaning into her to peek over the car roof, "she's almost finished."

"I guess we can't bust her." Amanda tried to block the image of two naked bodies locked in climax. She was much too aware of the warm male body pressing her own against the Firebird's cold metal, the strong hands sliding over the rounded curve of her buttocks and the sensual kneading of fingers into her flesh.

Just this once, she wanted to abandon all the rules, to give into the fire her dancing had ignited. Her skin burned. Her sweats felt hot and confining.

She'd fantasized how his lips would feel, hot, demanding, intoxicating. She wished Cooper would kiss her now, fulfill her dreams or dispel them forever.

"Kiss me," Cooper ordered in a husky whisper.

"What?" Had he read her mind?

"I said kiss me."

I can't. He shouldn't. I'm his boss. Reality dissolved the moment Wes Cooper's mouth covered hers.

Either the detective was the best kisser on earth or it had been too damn long since she'd been kissed. Latching onto the latter as the reasonable explanation, she kissed him back. His lips moved over hers as if he knew exactly what she needed. Vaguely she heard a car door open, a woman's giggle, the rustle of clothes. Then there was only the heated rush of her own blood.

Cooper turned them both and leaned against her car. His hands cupped her backside while his fingertips massaged the cleft of her buttocks, pulling her tightly against his obviously thickening shaft. Reality blinked. This was going too far, beyond duty, beyond the job. His probing tongue filled her mouth. His powerful erection pressed her belly.

Fantasy became hard reality. He shifted and bared her to the thighs and Amanda was powerless to protest. Cool air struck her hot skin and her hotter sex as he dragged her sweats lower. The hard promise of his erection rubbed her sensitive mound. Her sex pulsed in eager anticipation.

Cooper's kiss deepened. Amanda felt herself spiraling down, down into a lush vortex of sensation. She strained to seal her body to his. She wanted him. Wanted him inside her. Nothing else mattered. No one else existed.

She thrust against the bulge in his jeans. So close. Sensation rippled through her.

His hand slid between their bodies, his finger slipped between her slick folds, penetrating her heated sex. The intimate contact sent warning bells, ominous as police sirens, off in her head.

She broke the kiss and pushed his hand away.

Wes's deep chuckle barely registered. Suddenly, she was turned and forced against the vehicle, a suspect under control. Instead of the cold steel of handcuffs binding her wrists, she felt Wes's hands, hot and greedy, sliding beneath her sweatshirt, grasping her breasts.

She gasped for air, wanting, needing to protest this assault, this terrible breach of conduct, but his hands began a fierce massage across her needy breasts, his hard erection pressed into her buttocks, forcing her bared belly against the cold metal car, and her protest transformed into a small, whimpering cry.

His lips closed over her left earlobe, suckling, drawing on the sensitive bit of flesh. His fingers rolled and tugged her turgid nipples until pleasure flamed, deep inside her womb, and drenched her sex with undeniable need.

He eased his hold. His tongue teased the tender flesh beneath her ear, and delicately, tenderly, he brushed his big hands over her swollen breasts. His rough palms skimmed her hardened nipples, tantalized her heated skin, driving her mad with desire.

He dropped to his haunches, and his hands slid down her torso, over her hips to clutch her thighs. Long fingers slid between her legs. Hot and damp, she responded to his skilled probing of her swollen folds.

His tongue flicked over the rounded curve of her hip, teased her buttocks, lingered on the sensitive flesh at the crease of each thigh, then slowly meandered to the spot where her skin parted into the distinct globes of her buttocks.

Moaning, lost in pleasure, Amanda leaned against the car and widened her stance. His long fingers slipped inside her. Hot and demanding. Slow and deep. Her muscles flexed wildly, rhythmically, wanting more. Wanting him.

She arched as his tongue licked the small of her back, then explored the valley between her buttocks, and shuddered at the fiery path descending between her legs. The rush of heated blood drummed out the warning bells ringing furiously in some small neglected corner of her brain.

Desire controlled her. Desire and need and wild sensation. She pumped against his demanding fingers, reaching, wanting, then crying out as suddenly he withdrew his hand. In one swift movement, he turned her around, pushed her legs apart and covered her hot, demanding clit with his tongue. Gently, so gently, sipping her desire.

"Please," she whimpered, thrusting her hips forward, surging against his mouth, then crying out in frustration as he pulled away and pushed himself upright.

She grasped the thick bulge stretching his jeans, daring him. He sucked in his breath, and cupped her face in his huge hands.

She squeezed his erection, gently.

He kissed her hard, not gently at all, plundering her mouth.

She fumbled at his belt, then tore at the buttons of his jeans and tugged at his briefs, desperate to free his swollen shaft and guide it between her legs.

He grasped her hips and broke the kiss, then placed her arms around his neck. "Not inside, not here," he gasped, drawing deep gulps of air. "Just ride it."

Lush and wet, back-and-forth over the hard ridge of his length, she followed his command. He was thick, long, hard. She needed this. She needed this forever. Rivers of naked desire, long-denied, raged through her body.

Desire demanding satisfaction.

She was horribly aware of how tight she held him, of how good his flesh felt, hard against hers. Her whole body burned at the searing contact. Seeking, needing, release; she rode him, used him for her own pleasure.

Lost. She was lost in heat, growing hotter, wetter. Waves of heat, centered between her legs, exploding in cataclysmic release. Racking her body, drawing a strangled cry of satisfaction from between numbed lips.

Her body still trembled when Cooper whispered, "Let's go home, Mandy. I need to be inside you."

The impact of his words registered like a wave of cold water. *Oh God*. What had she done? Her lips felt swollen and raw. Her arms hung loosely about his neck. His hands still rested on her bare hips and his hard length throbbed between her clenched thighs. She ached for more. Ached for him to fill her. She drew in a breath of cool air and all her senses slammed back to earth. To the public parking lot behind the Prickly Cactus. To her employee with his hard cock between her thighs.

She'd lost control. She never, ever lost control. "That's a negative, Detective." She sounded far cooler than she felt.

Without a word, he separated their bodies. A rush of cool air filled the space between them and brushed her tender sex like a lover's caress.

She'd actually climaxed, her pleasure had flowed wet and hot over his hard flesh, over his still erect penis. She pulled up her sweats and turned away.

The luxury sedan was gone.

When had that happened?

How long had she and Cooper kissed? How long . . . ?

She sucked air into her strained lungs and exhaled, struggling to control her racing heartrate. Cooper remained relaxed and seemingly unaffected. If he was going to act like nothing had happened, so could she. Damn him!

"What did you want to talk about?" she managed.

"While you're pretending to be my woman, I'm going to pick you up and drive you home."

At the thought of him driving her home and kissing her goodnight on her doorstep, Amanda's body caught fire. The temptation of Wes so near her bedroom was too much. "That's not necessary, Detective Cooper."

"What if some guy corners you out here and decides to do what I just did?"

"That's not likely. I don't . . . kiss strangers."

"The hell it isn't. I don't want our cover blown because you have to pull a badge one night when some clown you've turned on follows you home. It happens. And Candy's side business doesn't discourage it."

"I've handled horny guys before," she snapped.

"How? By kissing them senseless?"

Despite the teasing nature of his words, Cooper's voice had a delicious silky texture. She felt his large hands settle on her shoulders. She waited for him, longed for him to kiss her again. He didn't, but his hands rubbed her upper arms. She was tempted to move his hands to her breasts.

"We're partners." His tone shifted, reminding Amanda of her duty. "If I felt Tom was in danger I'd cover him."

Turning around to face him, Amanda asked, "Do you kiss Tom?"

Cooper lifted his hand and cupped her chin. His thumb slid over her lower lip. "Naw, we usually just settle for a hand shake."

"Don't you think we should?"

"We're supposed to be lovers," he said as he fastened the top button of his jeans. "Besides you needed—."

Cooper's head snapped to the right. Out of the corner of her eye, Amanda noticed the back door of the Prickly Cactus had opened. It was the bartender. He muttered a goodnight and headed for his pickup.

"Get in," Cooper said as he opened her car door. "I'll follow you home."

Seizing the opportunity to end their conversation and her completely unprofessional behavior, Amanda slid into the driver's seat. Without waiting for Cooper to return to his Jeep, she started the Firebird's engine.

As she pulled out of the parking lot, Amanda remembered Cooper's half finished statement. Just what did he think she needed? Him? What else could he think after what just happened?

Face it, Amanda, you want him. Want him so much. Too much.

The fierce reality of desire scared her. Amanda gripped the wheel and glanced at her rear-view mirror. A pair of headlights greeted her. When she turned right, so did the vehicle following her. Amanda stepped on the accelerator.

All kinds of sirens went off in her head. She drove like a madwoman. When she turned onto her street, she couldn't remember how she got there, as if the drive home had taken seconds instead of the usual twenty-five minutes.

Approaching her house, she pressed the button on the remote control resting on her dash. When her garage door began to rise, Amanda slowed her Firebird and timed her entrance. Once inside her garage, she punched the remote.

The detective's black Cherokee pulled up just as the door began to descend. Amanda waved her hand in dismissal then rushed upstairs into the safety of her home. When she heard the Jeep slowly drive away, she groaned. If Cooper had gotten his way, she had little doubt they wouldn't have settled for a handshake.

They'd be stripping off their clothes and screwing their brains out.

And tomorrow, while she'd spend the day regretting her lack of control and worrying about her suitability as a supervisor and lieutenant, Cooper would probably be swaggering through the precinct with a grin on his face.

The solution was simple. Cooper would not pick her up and escort her home. She was the boss and she would act like the responsible person she'd been prior to laying eyes on his taut buns and broad shoulders. And there would be no more sensual interludes in dark parking lots.

Tomorrow night she'd dance, but Cooper would never know she danced for him.

Chapter Two

At the sound of knuckles tapping on her office door, Amanda felt the same odd rush she'd identified with a dangerous situation. Not quite as intense, but definitely there. That odd mixture of alarm and exhilaration fueled by adrenaline right before she drew her weapon or entered a strange building in search of a suspect. The muscles of her arms, legs, abdomen and back clenched. When the door opened and Officer Bates's blonde head appeared, Amanda felt relieved, yet disappointed. She leaned back in her chair, feigning a humdrum posture she did not feel.

"Morning, Lieutenant. Do you have a minute?"

"Sure," Amanda responded, willing her heart to downshift. "How did it go last night?"

As the blonde officer closed the door, Amanda felt a tinge of jealousy. With her thread-bare jeans molded to her generous hips and her red knit top clinging to her double D's, Bates reminded Amanda of Dolly Parton.

"I was terrified during my first set," Bates said as she slipped into a guest chair.

If Cooper hadn't been in the audience, Amanda wasn't sure she could have gotten through the evening either. But he had been and Amanda had to admit, if only to herself, she'd loved dancing for him. It was a turn on.

So much of a turn on, they'd practically had sex in a public parking lot.

"Embarrassing for you, too," Bates said. "I'm sure my face got as red as yours is now."

Amanda's cheeks burned. She knew they were a bright pink, but not for the reason Bates thought.

"Guys have stared at me all my life," Bates continued. "I grew breasts in sixth grade. But last night . . . that was way different."

"Do you wish to be relieved of this assignment?" Amanda asked, glad to latch onto something that had to do with police work and not Wes Cooper.

"No, I can handle it. I volunteered because I'd like to be considered for detective. I'm studying hard and my exam scores are improving. I've helped the guys over in vice, but they . . ."

Before Amanda could respond, Bates jumped to her feet causing her large breasts to sway. What would Cooper have done last night if he'd spent the evening watching Bates dance?

"I'm sorry, Lieutenant. I'm nervous as a cat. I want to advance. Lt. Marks . . . he wouldn't take me seriously."

"A few of the men didn't think I had what it takes. Some still don't, but I like proving them wrong."

Officer Bates smiled. "So do I."

"This assignment is important. Do well and I'll make sure to note it in my report."

Bates hurried out of the office. A second later she popped her head back inside the door. "Wes said you were really nice. When he told me how well you did last night, I knew I could tough it out."

Since it was nine in the morning, just when had Wes told Bates about her performance? No matter how tempted, Amanda wasn't about to ask. She stared at the closed door. The unwanted image of Cooper and Bates naked and making love came to mind. Cooper's big hands sprawled all over those double D's.

"Damn him." Amanda grabbed the top five file folders off the stack on her desk. The folders, at least one-inch thick each, were the most difficult cases in her section. With the folders tucked securely in her arms, she marched out of her office, across the corridor and into the vacant squad room. Despite the hefty stack of case files on Cooper's desk, Amanda dropped the five folders dead center. "That should keep you busy," she muttered under her breath.

❦

Wes eyed the stack of file folders on his desk which hadn't been there five minutes ago. He put down the double espresso he'd just purchased, flipped through the files, and grinned.

So he had gotten under her skin last night. Good. After she'd spent the evening turning him on, he'd hoped she'd live up to her hair color. He liked feisty redheads. Going toe-to-toe, then one-on-one and trying not to get burned.

Mandy was feisty plus some. Last night he'd gone home and straight into a cold shower. It had worked until he'd flipped on the radio as he crawled into bed. When "Achy Breaky Heart" came on, Wes had nearly lost his mind. He'd envisioned Mandy's dance all over again. In dreamlike slow motion, he recalled her hair falling down her back, swaying with the gyration of her hips. He felt achy breaky all right, but it wasn't his heart that was ready to break.

He hadn't slept a wink last night.

Tired and horny, he'd dragged his ass out of bed and into the precinct. Most of the squad hadn't shown yet, but Wes prided himself on the number of cases he solved. His numbers were the best. Rumor had it Amanda Forbes was just as obsessive.

Wes worked hard and he played to win. After watching Mandy climax during mere foreplay, he had no doubt she would be his.

He drained his double espresso and left the squad room.

Wes knocked once, then pushed open her office door. His gaze swept the room and riveted on Mandy's navy clad backside. After last night, watching it swing and wiggle, then holding it in his hands, he'd recognize the Lieutenant anywhere. A smile curled his lips. On hands and knees, with her skirt hiked high on her thighs exposing a generous amount of leg, his boss was more fetching than ever.

Ahhh, how he loved that position.

The thought of Mandy, naked, taking him . . .

He closed the door. Her head popped up and her mouth dropped open. Despite her conservative hair style and suit, those kissable lips and long legs were far too sexy for a lieutenant. Wes crossed his arms and leaned against the door as he watched her scramble to her feet and straighten her skirt.

"You should do that on stage."

"What?"

Her cheeks flushed pink. Maybe she was embarrassed to be caught crawling around on the floor, but maybe she knew he was thinking about the two of them. Both on their knees, his hands holding her bare backside. . . .

"On your hands and knees," he managed. "Your tips would double."

Her cheeks went from pink to crimson. So she did know what he was thinking.

She dropped back into her chair, but her gaze never left his face. "Is there something you wanted?"

He pushed away from the door and closed the short distance to her desk in two strides. "You bet," he said, placing his hands on the papers strewn across her desk, and leaning toward her. "I want to know why you broke every posted speed limit last night? Are you trying to kill yourself or just take out any unfortunate motorists who might have gotten in your way?"

She glared at him, but she didn't speak. He expected her to order him out of her office. With a stroke of the pen, she could change his assignment. She'd already given him five new cases, but for some reason she'd picked him as her undercover partner.

"We're partners," he said, leveling his tone. "We're suppose to watch each other's back, remember?"

"I doubt you escort your male partners home."

"I would if they'd spent the evening dancing naked."

She pushed herself to her feet. "I wasn't naked."

Toe-to-toe. Wes dropped his voice to a hoarse whisper. "Every man in that place wanted you naked. Don't you understand what you do on that stage? Every guy has a fantasy. And once in a while we get lucky. There it is before our very eyes. Promising everything. Giving nothing."

"That's ridiculous. I was just dancing."

Wes might have believed her if she wasn't looking at him like she wanted him. Her body was rigid, her voice pushing strident, but her eyes were a lush, brilliant green. Wanting.

"Who are you dancing for, Mandy?"

"No one." Her voice caught. "You have no right to question—"

"You liked it. You liked every minute of it. It's like making love. You know when your partner—"

"What does this have to do with making love?"

"When you're up there, you're doin' it. It may all be in your mind, but I felt it. Every guy in the place felt it."

Matching his position, she put her hands on her desk and leaned forward. "I've always excelled undercover. I'm good at it."

One-on-one. Her face was inches from his. Her sweet lips only a movement away. If they were anywhere else he'd kiss her, then he'd pull her to the floor. . . .

"I'll pick you up at five."

"I don't need a keeper, Detective. You will report at six."

"You may be the boss, but you're my partner. Safety comes first. Don't make me go to the Captain."

"I can remove you from this operation."

"Then do it, but make sure you tell the Captain the truth."

"And what is the truth, Detective?"

"You're worried about last night. What happened. Apparently what you do on that stage affects you as much as me. If you need to blow off a little steam, who better than your partner?"

"You're out of line, Cooper."

That was true. She made him feel wild and reckless. He didn't give a damn she was his boss. He wanted her. He wanted her beautiful bum slapping his belly. He wanted to lick his sweat off her bare skin. "And *you* are the hottest thing I've ever seen on stage. So, I will pick you up and see you safely home 'cause no one messes with my wo . . . partner."

She opened her mouth to speak, but Wes leaned closer. She stood her ground. "I excel at being a partner. I know more about Tom than his wife will ever know. I'm loyal. As loyal to my partner as I would be to a wife."

Her lips trembled slightly. She pushed out a breath. It felt hot against his skin. She said nothing. Wes had to force himself to move back before he caught her next breath with his own and the fine edge of his control disintegrated. Without waiting for a response, he left her office and closed the door firmly behind him.

❧

Amanda dropped back into her chair and stared at the closed door. She could swear he'd almost said his woman instead of his partner? Wife? Had he actually used the forbidden word? She didn't think guys like Cooper dared lest they be stricken.

And that crack about blowing off steam!

Who are you dancing for? You're the hottest thing . . . . You liked it.

She licked her lips. Cooper had wanted to kiss her. Wanted to push her to the floor and take her. Her whole body had tightened in anticipation. Even now her breasts felt full. She was wet with desire. Thank God he'd come to his senses.

It was as if he could see into her heart and mind. As if he knew exactly how to feed all her hungers. She did like dancing and stripping, but only because of him. She wanted him to lust for her. She wanted to drive him crazy. Tonight she would do it again. And she'd want him again, but there could be no blowing off steam with Cooper.

When she caught herself trying to remember if the batteries in her vibrator were still charged, she swore. "Damn you, Cooper."

❧

Amanda, dressed in sweats with duffle bag in hand, stared at the clock by her front door, then checked her wristwatch. If Cooper was a second late, she was leaving for the club.

The second hand swept toward the hour. The detective's Cherokee appeared.

Once inside the Jeep, he was all business. "Tonight's crowd should be rowdier. Not as many suits. More hats," he said, pointing to his black Stetson. "More money in the till."

They hashed over the possibility of a Friday night robbery. Satisfied with their plan of action, Amanda relaxed as they pulled into the parking lot behind the Prickly Cactus. He hadn't called her Mandy once.

At the dressing room door, he leaned close. "If some guy grabs at you, don't kick him in the teeth, Lieutenant. That's my job," he said. Then he slapped her on the rear and strolled down the hallway toward the bar.

Right before her last set, Amanda remembered that slap. As she moved down the stage, she focused on the guys wearing hats at the edge of the stage, especially the young ones. She licked her lips and blew kisses while she stripped out of her vest and skirt.

Down to her demi-bra and G string, she jiggled her breasts then wiggled her hips in each of their faces. By teasing them, she'd get to Cooper. Like a wave, they jumped to their feet and hooted and hollered. Amanda danced to the end of the stage and rolled her hips and pelvis, performing the bump and grind. One young cowboy lunged forward, but before the guy joined her on stage, a large hand shot out, clamped him on the shoulder and forced him back.

Cooper stepped forward and planted himself at the edge of the stage. If Amanda thrust her pelvis forward, she could tap him on the nose. Instead she pushed his Stetson back on his forehead and pursed her lips in a kiss. Cooper grinned.

She danced in a tight circle, keeping within an arm's length of her protector. With her back to Cooper, she lowered herself slowly to her hands and knees, then pumped her hips in time with the music. The crowd roared. She peeked over her shoulder. The grin on Cooper's face had disappeared. His eyes narrowed. He looked furious.

Pushing herself to her feet, she performed her finale. As she made her way around the stage to collect her tips, the men closest to the stage shoved bills in her garter. One cowboy reached for her G string. She felt a crisp bill, followed by his calloused fingers slide across her backside and beneath the thong between her cheeks, then quickly retreat as Cooper forced his body between her admirer and the stage.

She felt Cooper's hand cup her bare buttocks. As his warm fingers splayed protectively over her rear, he directed the cowboys to the black garter on her thigh.

Cooper walked along the stage as she moved on to collect her tips.

No one else grabbed her G string. No one dared. She could still feel the imprint of his hand as she pushed the beaded curtains aside to leave the stage.

Just as he said he would, he'd protected his partner. It was his job, but it was also sexy, sweet and macho.

⚜

Amanda shouldered her duffle bag and joined Cooper at the back door of the Prickly Cactus. "No Harolds tonight," she quipped.

He gave her a sidelong glance as they walked. "After that last show, I think you made more than enough tips."

"You were right," she said as they approached his Jeep. "I doubled them."

"I noticed."

When Cooper unlocked the passenger door and opened it for her, she thought about turning around, grabbing him by the lapels of his leather jacket and kissing him senseless. Instead, she climbed into the Jeep and reached for her seatbelt.

He remained silent and well within the posted speed limits as he navigated the Jeep through the city streets, then onto the freeway. By the time they reached her street, Amanda had made her decision.

Despite the rules, she wanted Cooper. Wanted to know the splendor of his lovemaking. Wanted to feel him inside her.

"Would you like to come in?"

Cooper pulled up at the curb and switched off the engine. "I'd like nothing better, but I've got a lead on those retail heists. One of my informants says he knows where the stuff is warehoused. I'm going to check it out."

"I'll go with you."

"Thanks, boss, but you might spook my informant."

Amanda leaned over and stroked his lean jaw. "Just tell him I'm your *woman*."

He reached up and caught her hand in his. "I'm having a hard enough time concentrating on work as it is."

"You don't seem to have any problem at the club."

"I don't when Candy or Lucy is on stage. But you . . ."

In the near darkness, she couldn't see his expression. His voice was level, devoid of humor or sarcasm. "What about me?"

He slid his hand slowly up her arm, then placed a fingertip on her lower lip. "Don't tease me, Mandy. You have no idea—"

"I'm not teasing, Cooper."

"What are you saying?"

She turned her head and kissed his palm. "I want you, Wes."

"You would choose tonight."

"The night's not over."

He leaned back in the bucket seat. "You're determined to go with me, aren't you?"

"Uh-huh."

"Then put some clothes on. I can't think business when you're almost naked," he said as he opened his door.

"I'm decent," she protested before the door slammed shut.

He walked around to her door and pulled it open. "Any underwear, Mandy?"

"Well, no."

He took her hand. "Then think layers."

She heard the thunk of the car door as she stepped into his arms. "You have no trouble at the club."

"The hell I don't." His hands drifted down her back, beneath her sweatshirt, and under the waistband of her sweats. He cupped her buttocks. "If the robbers had come in while you were on your knees, I'd have given them the fucking money."

His erection, thick and promising, pressed into her belly. "How much time do we have?"

"Not enough to do you justice," he said, setting her body away and taking her hand. "Let's go inside before we start rolling around on the front lawn."

"Ever done it on a lawn?" she asked as they covered the short distance to her front door.

"Not since college." He took her key and unlocked her front door. "I want you naked, Mandy. And once I'm inside you, I'm gonna stay awhile."

"That a promise, cowboy?" she asked as they stepped inside.

He shut the door, yanked off his hat and pulled her into his arms. Their bodies met breast to thigh. "We'll see whose knees give out first."

Amanda wrapped her arms about his neck and kissed him hard. The phone rang. Reluctantly she broke the kiss. "It's my mother. She always calls when I'm out on late assignments."

He closed his eyes. When the phone rang again, his hands slid down her back to rest on her bottom. "I'll take the call in my bedroom while I dress. Don't disappear, Cooper," she said in her Lieutenant's voice as she stepped out of his light hold.

"I wouldn't think of it, boss," he said, slapping her on the backside as she turned away. "One of us might come to our senses."

Amanda grabbed the receiver from its cradle. "Hi, Mom. I got to make this quick, I'm working another robbery case," she said as she pulled off her athletic shoes without untying the laces.

"Did the package arrive?"

"It arrived a couple of days ago," Amanda said thinking of the unopened package she'd shoved under her bed. Her grandmother's recent death had been difficult. She couldn't bring herself to open the box.

"Her only regret was not seeing you wear it before she . . ."

"I'm sorry," Amanda said softly. "I wish I could have made her happy . . . I . . . I'm going out for a while. We're working a case."

"It's awfully late. Who's we?"

Knowing her mother worried, she tried to assure her by letting her know she wouldn't be on her own. "Detective Cooper. He works for me."

"How old is he?"

Amanda rolled her eyes. "Don't start matchmaking. Cooper's definitely not husband material."

Her remark did little to dampen her mother's curiosity. It irked Amanda that her mother thought being a bride more important than making Lieutenant. "Is he single?"

With one hand Amanda shucked her sweat pants. "About as single as they come."

"Let me speak to him."

"Not a chance. He's an employee, not a date," she said opening her dresser drawer to retrieve a pair of lacy panties and bra. "We're working an important case. Cooper doesn't have time to talk to you."

"Give me the phone, Mandy."

Amanda started at the voice behind her. She spun around. How long had he been there listening? Cooper stepped closer. She motioned him back into the living room. Grinning like a Cheshire cat, he dropped his gaze to her bare crotch and kept coming. She yanked down the oversized sweatshirt as his hand closed over the receiver. For a moment, they wrestled silently over the slender piece of sand-colored plastic, then he thrust his hand between her legs.

Caught off guard, she forgot the receiver and grabbed at his hand. Then his forefinger slid inside her.

"Mrs. Forbes, this is Detective Wes Cooper. How are you?"

His voice was far too calm for what he was doing with his hand. He turned his head so she couldn't reach the receiver.

"Are you crazy," Amanda cried, lunging forward. His finger plunged deeper. His palm fastened over her mound. Although both her hands gripped his wrist, she couldn't free herself without retreating away from him and the telephone. She hesitated, hoping he'd relax his guard. He moved his finger to-and-fro bringing back the heat which had been simmering since she'd stepped on stage to dance for him.

"Yes, I have to agree. She's very pretty." Cooper turned. His gaze moved over her, then dropped to where his hand cupped her possessively. "Yes, she does have beautiful red hair."

Wrenching her body free of his invasion, Amanda stepped back, then lunged forward. Cooper reached for her again. She jumped back. He winked, then licked his finger.

"Don't worry, Peggy," he said into the receiver. "I'll see that she's safe and sound in her bed as soon as possible."

At the use of her mother's Christian name, Amanda lunged forward. She had to disconnect the call. To her surprise, he thrust the receiver in her hand.

"Say goodnight, Mandy," he whispered.

Although her heart pounded and she was mad as hell at Cooper, she tried to sound calm, "I call you tomorrow, Mom."

He dropped to his knees. She danced away from him. The stretched phone cord pulled the base off the bed stand.

Cooper caught it. "Come over here, Mandy."

She glared at him and shook her head. "I've got to go," she said into the receiver.

"Is Detective Cooper as handsome as he sounds?"

"No, Mom," Amanda replied. "He just thinks he's irresistible."

When Cooper gave her a you-don't-mean-that look, Amanda said a quick goodnight to her mother and tossed the receiver at him. He dodged the missile and fastened his gaze on her exposed crotch. "Come here, Mandy. Let me show how much I like red hair."

"How dare you talk to my mother."

"She just wants you to be happy. I can make you happy."

"I don't think a quickie was what my mother had in mind. Watch out, Cooper. She's not trying to find me a lover."

"I want to kiss you."

"Forget it. Get out and let me get dressed or we'll be late."

"We've got time for a kiss." He took off his leather jacket and tossed it on the bed.

Be careful what you wish for, you just might get it. All of a sudden Amanda's anger dwindled. She had to laugh at the irony. Here was Wes Cooper in her bedroom on his knees wanting her, and she was ordering him out. How many times had she fantasized about this very situation? Far too many to count.

As if attuned to her moment of indecision, he cocked his head to one side and lifted his arms. She moved into them.

But Cooper didn't pull her down into his arms. He kissed her. Right between the legs. His tongue lapped at her hidden entrance, easing aside the delicate folds. She felt his big hands curl about her thighs. Hot and gripping, they held her while his tongue explored with slow, deliberate caresses.

Pushing his knees between her ankles, he urged her legs further apart to give him unrestricted access. Amanda complied. Her hands fell to his shoulders. She needed to touch him. She wanted him naked. She slid her hand to his neck, then under the collar of his western shirt. The top snap popped open. His muscles bunched beneath her fingers.

She gave no thought to forbidding his actions. Nothing existed except Wes and the exquisite pleasure he gave her.

He licked her soft flesh. With each lush stroke she felt herself opening to him. Each stroke pushing him deeper inside her. He delved, once, then once again. Her legs trembled. Her knees slumped, yet his hands held her steady.

His tongue withdrew. Using the tip, he slowly circled her heated entrance. She wanted him inside her. Willed him to please her. "Again," she whispered.

She waited for him to enter her. Instead his tongue skimmed over her bud, back and forth until her whole body burned with wanting him.

He drew back a fraction and blew gently. His warm breath flowed over her heated flesh. Lightly he sucked at the tender flesh of her inner thighs.

She moaned. Wrapping her fingers in his hair, Amanda turned his head, demanded his loving. Again he laved her swollen flesh until she quivered. Then he blew gently. His hot breath teasing her heated sex.

His tongue delved inside. Exploring her recesses, he mapped every soft fold until Amanda felt swollen, ready to burst. His tongue withdrew and rested against her entrance. Amanda felt a trickle, hot and molten, slide from her. A harsh groan tore from his throat, then his mouth covered her fleshy outer lips, caressing them, kissing them, making her wetter still.

When his tongue settled on her bud, Amanda cried out. A tidal wave of pleasure engulfed her. Wet and full, she rolled her hips, enhancing her pleasure and easing the great pressure building inside her.

His hands skimmed the back of her thighs and up to the cleft of her buttocks. His fingertip dipped inside her moist channel from behind.

She lifted one leg and settled her naked thigh on his shoulder. Using his body for support, Amanda pressed her swollen flesh to his mouth. Her hips moved, heightening her pleasure, bringing her to the edge. Gently he drew her bud between his lips and suckled. Her back arched. She thrust her pelvis forward, demanding more. Waves of pleasure, moving from the epicenter of his loving, flowed throughout her body.

The muscles in her legs trembled beneath his hands as her orgasm eased. As if knowing he'd pushed her to the limit of pleasure, Cooper laved the swollen tissue. Stroking her. Easing her tender flesh. Bringing her back to earth.

At that moment everything important centered between her legs. She pulled off her sweatshirt, tossed it aside and looked down at him.

His hot blue gaze concentrated for a heartbeat on one nipple, then the other. He licked his lips and grinned. Damn, but he was sexy when he grinned.

"They're beautiful, Mandy. But if we don't get moving, my snitch is gonna fly."

Chapter Three

Amanda stared at him in disbelief as he eased her bare leg off his shoulder and drew himself to his feet. Was he made of steel? Her knees still felt weak. Her body languid. The last thing she wanted to do was dress and meet a snitch in the warehouse district.

She glanced at the bed as he picked up his jacket. She wanted to toss aside the Southwest patterned comforter and make love until the crisp new sheets were hot and slick with their sweat.

His head cocked to one side. That ever present grin teased his lips. Lips that had given her so much pleasure. "You coming?" he asked.

Before she could mouth an answer, he strode out of her bedroom and her fantasy. Amanda frantically looked about for her clothes. Where did she leave her bra and underpants? If she didn't move quickly, he'd be gone.

She snatched her sweatpants from the floor, then grabbed her shoes. Her sweatshirt had disappeared. She rushed to her closet and grabbed a jacket, then raced out of her bedroom.

Cooper turned as she ran into the living room. His mouth dropped open as she shoved her arms into her sheepskin coat. "Get my duffle bag," she ordered, grabbing her key ring dangling from his right hand. "I'll need my gun and badge."

"You can't—"

"Let's go, Detective," she said, pushing past him. She opened the door and stepped onto the walkway. Although she wore socks, the flagstone felt like blocks of ice.

Without looking back, Amanda ran to his parked vehicle. The cold night air nipped at her legs and curled up her bare thighs. Cooper climbed in behind the wheel, tossed her duffle bag onto the back seat, then reached over and unlocked the passenger door.

She hopped in as he started the engine. When her bare butt made contact with the cold leather seat, she jumped.

The Jeep lunged forward. She heard him stifle a laugh as he flipped on the heater, then pushed the lever to high.

No wonder he was laughing, she thought as she maneuvered into her sweatpants. She'd run out of the house, naked except for a coat and socks, after letting him . . .

Twice he'd taken her to climax. Pleased her to distraction. At least this time he'd taken off his jacket.

At this rate it would take her a month to get him down to briefs. If they had a month.

She was playing with fire. Passion fire. Teasing a flame which could easily go out of control. Deep in her heart, Amanda knew she'd have to give him up. They both had worked too hard to throw it all away for a fast burning passion fire. . . .

Or was it a heartfire?

Could this be the real thing? Amanda glanced at Cooper. Lights from passing vehicles flashed across his lean features. "Warm?"

She pulled the deep pile coat across her naked breasts. "I'm fine," she managed. "Can we make it on time?"

"Yeah, if I concentrate on the road."

"Then drive, Detective," she said, trying to dispel the aura of sensuality between them. Like a thin fog it circled them, pulling them together. At the club it blew like a hot wind. In her bedroom it had changed once again. She'd been the explosive, waiting for his spark.

She wanted the passion. And him. But was she ready for love and commitment?

"We're almost there," he said, breaking into her thoughts. "I'll leave the car keys."

"I'm coming with you," she said, suddenly afraid for him.

"Then I might as well kiss this off," he said, pulling into a deserted alley. He switched off the headlights. Slowly he navigated the vehicle down the narrow strip of asphalt. Twenty feet shy of the street, he braked to a stop. Cooper turned off the ignition and handed her the keys. He reached for the door latch, then his right hand shot up to switch off the interior lamp.

Amanda grabbed his lapels and pulled him toward her.

He wrapped his hands around her wrists. "Don't. I have the scent of you in my nostrils and the taste of you on my lips. I can barely think for wanting you."

For a long moment Amanda stared at him. His face was nothing more than a shadow, but she could feel the warmth of his body, the rhythm of his breathing, the solid strength in his hands. Her heart pounded against her ribs. Partly in fear, wildly in love.

Reluctantly she released her grip. "Be careful, Wes."

"Give me forty-five minutes," he said, then pulled away. She heard the soft click of the door opening and shutting, then watched as he disappeared around the corner.

Amanda started at the tap on the driver's window. She'd been waiting, chewing her nails to the quick, expecting Wes to return from the direction he'd gone. Instead he'd approached the vehicle from behind, taking her off guard. She reached over and unlocked the door. He slipped inside and she dropped the keys into his outstretched hand.

"How did it go?" she asked as he drove slowly out of the alley and onto the deserted street. Although her voice sounded calm, she'd never been so frightened for anyone in her life. But then she'd never been in love with her partner.

Love. Waiting for him, wondering if he were safe, Amanda realized she'd never experienced such powerful emotions. Such need. Alone in the Jeep's dark interior, all she'd heard was her thundering heart. Now it thundered in relief. He was safe.

"The place is full of stolen merchandise. I'll need a search warrant."

"I'll take care of it first thing in the morning." *After we go back to my place and finish what you started.* She needed to hold him.

"Got to do it now. They're moving the stuff this weekend. I'll drop you off at home, then roust Tom out of bed."

"No way, Cooper. I'm going with you."

"I can handle this, boss," he said, glancing over at her. "You're not exactly dressed for work."

She stiffened and didn't say a word to keep from revealing her disappointment. He'd distanced himself from her. She could feel it.

He reached over and squeezed her hand. "Tom and I have worked this case for months. It's our collar, Lieutenant."

Relief washed over her. He wasn't pushing her away, but doing his job. Too many times she'd seen commanders step in and take credit for cases they'd assigned and forgotten. Until they were solved.

"If you need anything, call me." She watched the play of passing street lights flit across his face. "I'll back you a hundred percent." She was rewarded with that irresistible grin.

Ten minutes later, he parked in front of her house. She turned toward him and unbuttoned his jacket. "Turn off the lights, Wes."

At the flip of a switch, they were plunged into darkness. She leaned toward him. Her hand slid beneath his open jacket to wrap around his solid torso. She drew him close. "I want to know how I taste," she said right before her lips met his.

She kissed him hard. Thrusting her tongue into his mouth, showing him as powerfully as she could how much she wanted him, how much she loved him. His arm slid about her back, he held her tight to his chest for a short heartbeat, then relaxed. Reluctantly she ended the kiss.

"You taste lush and sweet and wonderful," he said as his hand dropped away. "And I gotta go."

At five o'clock, Wes's Jeep pulled up in front of her house. Amanda hadn't heard from him all day. She opened the door as he strolled down the walkway. He looked exhausted. "Did you get any sleep?" she asked.

He shook his head. "Grabbed an hour while waiting for the warrant. The place is staked out. We want to nail them inside. Tom is at the warehouse. Grimes is covering the Bosom Buddy."

She stepped back to let him inside. "But he was on leave till next week."

"Captain got an okay from his doctor. Besides Grimes is a regular at the Buddy. He'll fit right in."

She closed the door. "You didn't need me at all."

"I don't need a Lieutenant telling me how to do my job," he said as he pulled her into his arms. "But I need you, Mandy. If I didn't, I'd be at the stakeout with Tom."

He slanted his head and captured her lips. His hands snaked into her hair. His lips moved over hers as his tongue penetrated her mouth. She wrapped her arms around his lean torso and held him tight.

Her hands slid down to cup his firm buns. When she reached for him, he pulled his mouth from hers and sucked in a breath. "Take it easy, honey. I've had no sleep and I've been wearing this hard-on for most of the last three days. If you touch me, I'll burst. Then I'll never get back on my feet."

Amanda folded her arms across her chest. She'd spent the day worrying and wrestling with her feelings. Being in love was hell. Knowing Wes was facing a potentially dangerous situation frayed her usually calm nerves. This would never work. Her perspective as task force leader was shot. "Let me call someone in to cover the Cactus. Then you can rest."

He reached out and planted a large hand about her waist. His other hand cupped her chin. "If you think I'll let anyone watch you dance—"

"Fifty guys watch me dance."

His whole body tensed. The muscles in his arms bunched beneath his black shirt. His eyes burned into hers. "Fifty strangers watch Blaze. If I'm not there, *you* don't dance."

"Maybe I should remind you this is a job—"

His grip on her chin tightened slightly. "What's happening between us . . . this isn't casual . . . at least not for me. This has gone way beyond a job and you know it."

"And it has to end when this job is over," she said. Despite the heartpain, she'd made an executive decision for both of them. She wouldn't be responsible for damaging Cooper's career. Nor was she ready to resign. She loved him, but love could be so fickle. Too many of her friends were divorced for her to believe otherwise. She worked too hard to gamble on love.

His hand slid from her waist as his eyes closed tight. He moved his head slowly, side-to-side in denial. As he opened his eyes, he said, "End?"

She wanted Wes. Maybe it wasn't love at all and this passion would burn itself out, but odds were if they became lovers, they'd be discovered. Whenever she looked at Wes, Amanda felt her temperature rise. Someone was bound to notice. "We can't lose everything just because we've got the hots for each other."

He released her chin and ran his fingers along her jaw. "What is it you want from me, Mandy? Am I just a guy to put out the fire after you dance?"

"Of course not. You've built your life around your job," she said softly. "Both of us have. If the Captain finds out you'll be back in uniform and I . . . it's—"

"It's not worth a career." His hand dropped to his side. He stepped away from her and opened the front door. "Let's go to work, *boss*," he said as he marched out.

Amanda started out the door, then remembered her duffle bag. By the time she ran outside, he was sitting in the Jeep with the engine running. His lean facial features looked like stone. Cold and immobile.

All the way to the club he didn't say a word, which suited her just fine. Logic and training told her she was doing the right thing. But all the training in the world couldn't keep her heart from breaking.

Why did she have to fall for a fellow cop? Amanda thought of all the men she'd dated, but not one of them had touched her heart. She'd wanted the perfect combination of hero and hunk. She'd found it in Wes.

Strong, honest, and willing to put his life on the line if necessary, Wes had her complete respect. He made her proud to be his boss, but more than that, he always made her feel. He had the power to make her laugh, to make her forget her rank, and to break her heart.

What on earth had possessed her to use the term "hots"? She didn't have the "hots" for Wes Cooper. She loved him. Too much to get him busted down to a patrol car.

Or so she told herself. Deep in her heart, she knew she was taking the easy route. So many times, she'd challenged the odds and won. She'd received several commendations, some for valor. When she thought about testing the odds of love, Amanda didn't feel the least bit brave.

❧

Both Candy and Lucy, eager to enjoy Saturday night, had left the club before Amanda finished her last set. Back in her dressing room, she plucked the bills from her garter. The tips were meager compared to the night before, but Amanda hadn't lived up to her previous performance either. All night she'd felt the pain in her heart much more than the beat of the music. Although Wes was somewhere in the blackness beyond the lights, she hadn't felt his heated gaze. Not once had he approached the stage.

She pulled off her boots, then unclasped her sequin-covered bra. After dropping the bra into her duffle bag, she bent to remove her G string. As she stepped out of the garment, the dressing room door burst open. Wes filled the doorway. His big hands hung at his sides and his fingers moved as if his hands itched. The frown marring his handsome face softened into a grin as he stepped forward and shut the door with a decided bang.

He shucked off his jacket, letting it fall to the floor, then reached for his belt buckle. "Okay, Mandy, I'm your guy."

The look in his blue eyes alarmed her. She licked her lips, half in fear, half in excitement. He wanted her. Intended to take her. Right now. Right here. She stepped back. The G string slipped from her fingers. He kept right on coming. She knew she should protest, but her tongue refused to move. It might be the nineties, but something inside her coiled, heated and waited to be taken.

Her gaze dropped to his hands ripping at the buttons of his fly. She sucked in her breath when he freed his erection. Then his hands were in her hair, pulling her head back. His mouth covered hers as his hands slid down her bare back to grasp her buttocks.

In one fluid motion, he lifted her up and pushed her back against the dressing room wall, exactly as he had in her fantasies. Trapped between his hot body and the cold wall with her legs open, she anticipated his passionate invasion. Ached for it.

Holding her buttocks firmly with one hand, he reached for her breast. He cupped, then lifted and molded her flesh to his. Slowly he squeezed, a sweet compression of his palm and fingers. Beneath his powerful hand, her breast swelled and ached. Her nipple thrust against the textured skin of his palm.

His hand slid from her breast, down her torso, strong fingers teasing her excited flesh. Everywhere he touched became heated. He dipped his fingertips between her legs as if testing her readiness, then wet her aching nipple with her moisture.

When his mouth covered her breast, a cry caught in her throat. He suckled. With each deep tug, waves of desire rolled through Amanda. Hot, heavy waves building between her legs until the need for Wes was unbearable. She grasped his erection. Her hand pumped his rigid shaft.

Wet and primed, her muscles pulsed. When she guided him toward her heated center, he grabbed her hand. Amanda moved her head in protest. This time she wanted him inside her. Not his long experienced fingers, not his sensual tongue, but him. All of him.

"Make love to me, Wes. Now."

He lifted his head and looked her right in the eye. "You're much too bossy," he said as he reached into his back pocket and pulled out his cuffs and snapped one on her wrist.

Her lungs sucked in air. "I could charge you with sexual harassment," she said, her voice husky with desire.

"Then do it. But we both know who's been harassed. And honey it hasn't been you."

"Use these often?" Amanda asked, excited all the more by the cuffs.

Wes grinned. "Only with uncooperative Lieutenants," he said as he cuffed her to his wrist.

Amanda reached down and grasped his erection. His shaft flexed beneath her rapidly moving fingers. "This could cost you your detective's badge, Cooper. Put you back in a patrol car until retirement."

He locked the fingers of his cuffed hand with hers. "Put your arm around my neck."

She released him. He lifted her high until his belly pressed her center. As his lips closed over her nipple, she whispered. "You must look damn good in uniform."

She arched her back. Her taut breast ached. A delicious heat coiled between her legs.

All Wes had to do was touch her and she was powerless to resist him. How could she work with him, see him daily and not want him? He lifted his head, then slid their clenched, cuffed hands gently beneath her buttocks. Her weight securely anchored, he slipped his free hand between her legs. He dipped his finger in her drenched slit. After a few heartbeats, he withdrew his finger and ran the soft tip along her lower lip. It was slick with desire. Her desire.

She wanted to kiss him. Put her lips on him and taste him. She wanted to feel his full, thick erection in her mouth. She needed to feel his heated blood pumping beneath her lips.

As if understanding her thoughts, Wes's shaft moved against her bottom. Inside, her muscles flexed.

"You're wet, Mandy. Wet and hot. If you don't want me, tell me. If this isn't extraordinary, tell me. If the job's more important, tell me."

Amanda couldn't speak. The lie wouldn't come. To remain a couple one of them would have to sacrifice their choice assignments. If they were discovered, both of them could face serious consequences. In her wildest dreams she'd never believed she'd have to choose between a man and her career. Wrapping her legs tight around his torso, she pressed her wet center against his bare belly. She was going to have the man. She'd have to figure out the rest later.

When she licked her lower lip, he slanted his head and kissed her. He shifted her bottom and pushed her up higher against the wall. Fishing in his shirt pocket, he retrieved a small foil packet and forced it in her free hand. "I want to feel your hand on me. Then I want you."

The cool steel blue gaze she'd known had shifted. His eyes burned hot. Blue fire. Without breaking eye contact, she tore open the foil packet and positioned the condom between her lips.

His heated gaze shifted to her mouth and he stepped back. She dropped to her knees between his legs. Her fingers enclosed him, and his breathing increased. He raised one eyebrow as she positioned her lips on the tip of his penis, then slowly rolled the latex down his hard length, sheathing him as she took him deeper in her mouth. His eyelids partially closed, then opened. He whispered her name.

His strangled voice warned her he was on the edge. Slowly Amanda removed her lips from his pulsing erection. In one supple movement, he pulled her to her feet, lifted her against the wall, and entered her. A trickle of sweat trailed down his temple.

Once again he locked her fingers in his, binding her to him as surely as the cuffs bound their wrists.

Needing to feel more of his hot flesh, she grasped the top snap of his western shirt and in one quick yank, the snaps gave way popping like firecrackers.

Shockwaves rippled through her body as he filled her. Wide open and wet, she welcomed him. He buried his shaft deeper, plunging again and again into her swollen center. His balls slapped against her sensitive flesh. His broad chest, damp with sweat, imprisoned her against the wall, crushing her breasts. With each thrust of his lean hips, he drove himself into her.

Joining them.

Their bodies made those lush sucking sounds of skin against skin and his heated flesh drove her to cresting madness. Then he went rigid. His shoulders and chest heaved. Her breath caught. Her legs clamped his torso, binding him to her.

Chapter Four

Wes's body convulsed and released in heavy waves of pure ecstasy. Mandy held him tight, both inside and out. Her green eyes glowed. Her lips parted slightly. Her breathing, like his, puffed in uneven gasps. He'd pleased her. Satisfied her.

He slanted his head to cover her mouth. He wanted to kiss her while he was still deep inside her, surrounded by her splendid wetness.

He loved the lush feel of her. All of her. His tongue sucked at the hot recesses of her mouth. Her sex flexed and pulled at him.

She needed more.

Her breasts heaved and her nipples tantalized his skin, sparking his tired, sated body to life. He rocked his hips and deepened his kiss. Despite the ache in his legs, Wes willed himself to stay hard. She was still unbelievably wet. Soft and sweet, and demanding. His woman. His love.

He felt her body shudder, then clamp down on him. He pushed his way past her tight folds. Once. Twice. Buried himself. Her sex rippled along his length. Grasping. Releasing. Finally, she stilled.

Their lips parted as she relaxed. Inhaling deeply, he filled his lungs with air. Her scent lingered in his nostrils. She'd taken everything he had to offer. He closed his eyes and buried his face in her hair.

His legs jerked. His thighs vibrated as the exhaustion hit him. Yet he didn't want to let her go.

He hadn't wanted it this way. He'd wanted to love her in that soft bed of hers. He'd wanted to fall asleep with their still damp bodies entwined and the smell of her hair scenting the air he breathed.

Instead he'd shoved her up against a wall, handcuffed her and taken her.

Wes wasn't sure just when he'd fallen in love. But he had. Still embedded in her sweet warmth, he felt a moment of panic. After having her, he couldn't go back to his old life. He didn't want one-night stands or afternoon romps. Quickly done, easily forgotten.

But Mandy wanted nothing more than that. She wanted his heat. His sex. When the operation ended, she wanted the partnership dissolved.

What the hell was he supposed to do? Go to work each day and pretend she meant nothing? Or worse yet pretend she didn't exist? When had all the damn rules changed?

For a moment he longed for the old days when he'd been the one with the love-them-and-leave-them attitude.

Her lips touched his neck. Soft, gentle nipping kisses. Sweet, and tender. He loved for her to touch him. He lifted his hand and sank his fingers into her long, red hair. He placed his lips to her temple and felt the pulse of her heartbeat. He wanted to remember this moment: her soft breasts crushed to his chest, his hand in her hair, the descending rhythm of their heartbeats and the sweet aroma of their mating.

What would she do if he told her he loved her?

He wanted to say the words he felt in his heart, but given the present scenario she'd probably laugh. Besides Mandy didn't love him. She wanted him, she liked him, but she wasn't in love with him. He'd rather be shot than have her tell him to get lost.

He opened his eyes. She was so damn beautiful. He stroked her hair, then stepped back a fraction. Her legs uncoiled as he withdrew from her warmth. Despite the harsh glare of the dressing room lights, her skin held the pink flush of sensual heat. She had no idea what she did to him.

Maybe it was better that way.

"Wes—"

He wished she'd call him Cooper and maintain the cool distance of passing lovers. She had no right to say his name as if . . . He pushed aside the delicious, completely reckless thought.

He uncurled his fingers and released his tight grip on her hand. "The key's in my pants pocket."

She bent her knees and sank slowly until her weight was balanced on her toes. Her thighs were spread wide. Her gaze focused on his dwindling erection. Damn but this was embarrassing. Why the hell had he cuffed her? Why the hell did he feel so damn possessive?

She fished the key out of his pocket and stood. With quick efficiency she unlocked the cuffs, then dropped the key in his palm. For a long moment they stared at each other. Wes wanted to kiss her, tell her he'd transfer to another precinct, anything to keep her. As long as there were criminals, he'd find work, but he'd never find another Mandy. His hand closed over the cuffs.

What should have been a loving moment, felt awkward and embarrassing. He hadn't been embarrassed with a woman since high school. But then he'd never cuffed a woman before. And he'd cuffed the woman he loved. He pulled up his jeans and turned away.

"I've got a stakeout in progress," he said. Without looking at her, he grabbed his jacket and slammed out the door.

❧

Amanda paced. She'd been prowling her office like a caged cat all morning. And it had nothing to do with the stack of reports on her desk.

Wes Cooper was driving her mad.

All day yesterday she'd waited for the phone to ring. Ached to hear his voice. Twice she'd entered the garage and opened the door of her Firebird only to slam it closed. She wanted to go to him, to tear off her clothes and demand he make love to her.

But pride had overruled her foolish heart. After a few glasses of wine, driving was out of the question.

She rounded her desk again, aware of the black lace garter belt, smoke-colored nylons and the slight scrap of lace barely restraining her breasts, all hidden beneath a soft, clinging forest-green, knit sweater and matching straight skirt. And she knew exactly what had possessed her to dress so daringly.

The possibility of a tryst with Wes flooded her already alert senses. The mere thought of his hand slipping beneath her skirt and his long fingers inside her made her eyelids flutter and her sex wet. After what had happened Saturday night in the dancers' dressing room, the idea of an unoccupied elevator or a stolen moment in her office was far more exciting then stripping off her clothes on a lit stage.

If nothing else, Wes had taught her that fantasy could become real-ity. That wild, uninhibited sex with the right man was not only feasible, but more exciting than she'd imagined. And utterly satisfying.

Saturday she'd been sated, but Wes had only given her a taste. She wanted more. And she wanted it now.

Too bad it was noon and the place buzzed with human traffic. If only she could wish humanity away for a short hour.

Forcing herself back to her work, Amanda sank into her high-backed, executive chair. The action only heightened her awareness of her lack of underwear. She pushed up the long sleeves of her sweater and picked up a report. The recent crime statistics danced before her eyes. All she could see was Wes's lightly furred chest and the trail of dark hair leading down his lean torso.

She rubbed her wrist. Her breath caught at the memory of Wes filling her. . . .

A bold knock at her office door brought her back to the present and the stack of Monday morning reports. She smoothed back an errant strand of hair which had worked itself loose from her hair clasp. The image of Wes's hands in her hair . . .

Quickly Amanda pushed the thought aside and bade her intruder to enter.

When the object of her fantasies stepped into her office, file folder in hand, and quietly closed the door, Amanda sat back and crossed her legs. "I expected your report first thing this morning, Detective."

"I've been busy," he said, dropping the case file on her desk and easing his big frame into a chair.

His eyes had been on her since he'd opened the door. He stared at her now. As she rubbed her wrist, she regretted the rash decision to forego underwear. Wes had the power to make her forget everything except how wonderful it felt to be in his arms. Her pulse quickened. Fire caught in her middle and spread to her lips, her breasts and burned hot between her legs. If he touched her, she'd be lost.

This wildness had to stop. Where was the tight control she'd always kept over her emotions? Her feelings for Wes were so powerful, she felt breathless. Her mother had once told her she'd know true love because it would be like a bullet in the heart. Since her mom had never faced a real bullet, Amanda had scoffed.

Not anymore. Loving Wes scared the hell out of her. And it hurt.

"Keeping you satisfied is hard work."

Amanda felt the air in her lungs go still. She swallowed hard. Resisting the desire to touch him, she clasped her hands before her on the desktop. "I understand you had an interesting Sunday. Twelve arrests. Over a million dollars in merchandise recovered."

"I had a far more interesting Saturday night," he said, leaning forward. His forefinger slid along her wrist. The gesture prompted every synapse to fire. Her skin felt hot. She shifted her weight.

Wes grinned. "Miss me?"

"You could have called," she snapped, thinking of all the waiting she'd done. All the worrying.

"Any time you need me, boss." He smiled. A knowing smile that told her he knew she'd been wanting him.

Amanda hated his taunting tone, but it had been her own words, defensive words, which had set the rules. She couldn't blame Wes. She'd asked for sex, temporary loving without complications, and that's what he'd given her. What he planned to continue giving her.

All she had to do was ask and he'd deliver.

All he had to do was touch her and she'd surrender everything.

Everything including her heart. Wes owned her body and soul, except he didn't know it. Amanda couldn't let him know it. Not until she had a little time to get used to being in love and decided how to handle the situation. What if Wes didn't love her? What then? And if he did, was he ready to commit himself to the inevitable changes their relationship would demand? Was she?

He stared at her as if he expected her to speak.

The words of surrender had been on her lips Saturday night. When he separated his body from hers, she'd felt a hollow, empty place in her heart. A place only his love could fill.

If she said them now . . .

He started to rise. "You haven't told me about yesterday," she said.

"It's all there." He poked his index finger at the case file he'd deposited on her desk. "Besides you can hear the details when we meet with the Captain."

"He's called a meeting?"

Wes nodded and pushed himself to every glorious inch of his six foot two frame. Her gaze slid from his face, down his chest to rest on the button fly of his well-worn jeans. The soft material clung to his hips, outlined his . . . left nothing to her imagination. She wanted, needed to see him naked and hard.

He leaned over her desk. A sexy grin played at the corners of his mouth. His blue eyes sparkled. "Something I can help you with, Lieutenant?"

Amanda pushed her chair back and uncrossed her legs. He wanted her. She could see it in his eyes. Blue fire. What would he do if she told him she wasn't wearing underwear? That nothing but the stream of civil servants passing her door prevented his lifting her skirt and taking her.

An odd sense of power, erotic and potent, came over her. Wes wanted her as badly as she wanted him.

He felt the change in her the moment she uncrossed her long, glorious legs. The offer, subtle to any other observer, was blatant to Wes. The wave of desire that hit him was as shocking as the idea of taking her right here, right now in her office.

As she pushed herself out of her chair, he caught the gentle movement of her breasts. His hands itched to cover the twin mounds outlined beneath the clinging material of her sweater. He couldn't will away the erection stretching his jeans. He didn't want to. Just looking into her sultry green eyes as she moved toward him gave him pleasure. He liked the way she made him hard. He liked the way she made him feel. Hot, thick and full of lust. And something else. Something catching in his chest. Just as hot. Just as potent.

Something he'd never felt before.

He couldn't think. He reacted. He pulled her hard against him as he stepped back. Blocking the door with his weight, Wes covered her mouth with his. She tasted of cinnamon and sugar. He licked at her lips. He wanted to strip her naked and taste her from head to toe. Explore every hollow and curve.

He pulled up her sweater. A scrap of black lace barely covered her breasts. Her peaked nipples beckoned him. "Come home with me tonight, Mandy."

Pushing his tongue beneath the black lace, he captured her nipple and suckled. A muffled cry tore from her throat. She arched, pushing her breast against his mouth.

Needing no further encouragement, he caught the soft knit of her skirt and pulled it up over her hips. She was naked. She'd deliberately left herself bare for him. If she wanted it wild and dangerous, he was the man to give it to her.

He locked the office door and carried her to her desk. With a sweep of his arm, he cleared the surface. Files tumbled and pens flew as he lowered her onto a leather-trimmed ink blotter. He reached for his belt buckle, then paused. He wanted her. He wanted to feel her tight sex, but he couldn't make love to her without protection. Neither could he ignore her parted thighs. He brushed her red curls with his fingers, played between the folds of her delicate slit until his hand was wet with her need. Her hips bucked and pushed against his hand.

Her muscles clamped down on his fingers reminding him of how tight and wet she was.

"Please, Wes. Please."

Her hands clutched his shoulders. He heard the strain in her voice, knew she teetered on the precipice of orgasm. He withdrew his fingers and pulled her to the edge of the desk, lifting her buttocks so that she straddled his thigh. Friction mounted with each forward thrust and her breasts bounced provocatively. Wes felt her slick heat through the thick material of his jeans. When she found her release, her body arched and another stack of files balanced on the desk's edge slid to the floor.

She shuddered against him, grasping futilely at the fabric covering his aching shaft. "Don't make me come in my pants, Mandy. Not here," he whispered, wishing they were anywhere but in her office.

To his surprise, Amanda slid from the desk to her knees. She made quick work of his belt. Her fingers tore at the buttons of his jeans and eased his swollen erection free of his briefs. When she guided him into her mouth, he groaned. The erotic combination of her lips and tongue with the rhythmic use of her hand sent him over the edge. He closed his eyes as she drew him deeper into her sweet mouth.

He rocked lightly on his heels, savoring each delicious tug of her lips, every caress of her tongue and the erotic movements of her hands. Even as he came, he wanted, needed to be inside her tight, wet sheath. As his climax eased, the sounds of footsteps, voices and ringing telephones beyond the closed door reminded Wes of where they were.

Reluctantly Wes stepped back as Mandy glanced over her shoulder at the disarray of her desk, then back at his flagging erection. A horrified expression filled her eyes. He reached down and pulled her to her feet. Gently he pushed her skirt over her bare hips. "Have I told you how much I like red hair?"

She shook her head and tucked her reddened nipples beneath that scrap of black lace passing for a brassiere, then quickly yanked her sweater down.

He reached out. He wanted her to look at him. He wanted to kiss her, let her know everything would be all right. She didn't move. He lowered his arms and adjusted his clothes.

"I love red hair, Mandy," he said, trying to ease the situation as he buckled his belt. They'd lost control, both of them. Neither of them had given a damn where they were. Wes couldn't recall ever wanting any woman this badly. "Especially those soft, red curls between your legs."

"What are we doing, Wes?" She stepped away from him. "Have we both gone completely insane? Anyone could have walked in here . . . caught me on my knees. . . ."

Despite the glow of her flushed skin, her lush mouth was pulled into a decided frown and her green eyes. . . . She regretted what just happened. Had she regretted Saturday night?

"I locked the door," he said as she moved to the opposite side of her desk. He wanted to hold her, wrap his arms about her and never let her go. "Maybe we should try this at home, in bed for once."

She folded her arms before her and looked at the files scattered on the floor. "Maybe we shouldn't be doing this at all."

"And maybe the sun won't rise tomorrow," he shot back.

"What time are we supposed to meet the Captain?" she asked ignoring his remark.

He looked at his watch. "About five minutes ago," he responded. The last twenty minutes had passed in a heartbeat.

"Why didn't you say something?"

"I was busy." He looked down at the wet stain on his jeans and touched the spot with his fingertip.

"Don't ever come in here and lock the door again," she snapped. He looked at her and her cheeks blushed an adorable pink. Her shoulders squared. "Is that clear, Detective?"

"Very clear, Lieutenant." Turning on his heel, Wes yanked open the door and, leaving it wide open, headed straight for the Captain's office.

Five minutes later, Amanda sat, legs crossed, before Captain Miller's desk. His balding head was bent over the report of yesterday's warehouse raid. Detective Tom Jenkins sat in the chair next to her while Wes leaned against the wall across the room.

Although her gaze remained on the Captain, out of the corner of her eye, Amanda caught Wes's fingers brushing at the still damp stain on his jeans. Again, she felt her neck and face flush with embarrassment. She'd lost control, and Cooper loved reminding her of it.

"Can this be right?" the Captain asked as he poked a thick finger at a list of merchandise recovered. "Panties?"

Cooper grinned. "A truck load of goods intended for a chain of expensive lingerie shops had been highjacked, but we didn't expect to find it yesterday. This group specializes in electronics."

Inside, Amanda groaned. The last thing she wanted to discuss was lingerie.

The Captain shook his head. "But this amount? Can it be correct?"

"You wouldn't believe what a few inches of satin and lace can cost," Cooper said. Amanda could feel the grin in his voice. He was enjoying this. "Some women have stopped wearing them entirely."

When Tom Jenkins looked at Wes, then at her, Amanda shifted in her seat.

"You'd know," the Captain responded, then gave her a sheepish look. "Sorry, Lieutenant."

Amanda merely acknowledged his remark with a slight nod. She was the last person who should be offended by the sexist statement. After all she was one of Cooper's conquests. She glanced at him and immediately regretted it.

He was sucking on his fingertip.

The same fingertip he'd put inside her. She tried to control the hot blush creeping up her neck to her burning cheeks. She heard him chuckle.

Next time they were alone, she'd kill him.

"Good work," the Captain said looking first at Cooper then at Jenkins.

"It was Wes's snitch that provided the information," Jenkins added.

"But I couldn't have done it alone. And the Lieutenant . . . she backed me up. Gave me a free hand so to speak. I hope I lived up to her expectations."

All eyes were on her. Amanda forced a smile. She hadn't missed the duplicity of Cooper's declaration. She considered a set down, but his performance had been superb. Every single time.

"You haven't disappointed me yet, Detective."

On the way back to the squad room, Tom pulled Wes aside. His dark eyes looked worried.

"What the hell was all that?"

"What?" Wes asked, hoping Tom hadn't picked up on the emotional darts being tossed back and forth between he and Mandy.

"I know you, partner. Tell me you aren't doing the Lieutenant."

Wes decided not to lie to Tom. They'd been partners too many years. "So far we haven't made it to a bed, but I intend to remedy that real soon."

Tom grimaced. "Are you nuts? You can't screw the boss." Anger swept through Wes. Mandy wasn't a convenient screw. "It's not like that. I'm crazy about her."

"Damn right you're crazy. You'll end up working southside in a patrol car. I don't know about you, but I'm too damn old for that shit."

"I love her, Tom."

Tom looked at him and shook his head. "You're gonna ask for a transfer, aren't you?"

Wes nodded.

"We've got it good, partner. What happens when this blows over?"

"This isn't going to blow over. I intend to marry her."

"Marry? Now hold on, Wes. You're talking about house payments and dirty diapers. Spit-up on your jacket!"

"Yeah, I know." The idea of marriage and kids hadn't been a conscious thought until now, but he wanted them. Deep in his heart, he wanted them. As badly as he wanted her.

"No, you don't. I know. It ain't easy."

"And you wouldn't have it any other way." Wes knew Tom was devoted to his girls, and the only way he'd leave Carol was in a casket.

Tom shook his head in disbelief. "Most cops' marriages don't work. But two cops. It's ridiculous. She's a career woman, Wes. Amanda

Forbes has brass written all over her. Is she willing to give that up for babies?"

The thought that Mandy wouldn't want his babies tore at his guts. She could have her career. She'd probably make Captain, too. But he wanted a family.

"Have you told her you want kids?"

"I haven't asked her to marry me, yet."

Tom's mouth dropped opened.

"Don't worry, partner. When I get around to asking, she'll say yes."

Wes turned to walk away, then glanced over his shoulder at Tom. "Close your mouth, partner. You're catching flies."

Chapter Five

Amanda opened her front door to find Wes leaning casually against the frame, a fancy black Stetson in his right hand. "Why are you here, Cooper?"

He stepped inside, pushed the door closed and turned the lock. Looking her right in the eye, he said, "For you, Mandy."

Amanda strolled into her living room. Wes followed. She bit the inside of her cheek to keep from grinning, then she turned to face him. He'd be furious if he realized how predictable he was. She'd known he couldn't resist the challenge she'd made this afternoon in the Captain's office.

Wes's gaze settled on the lit fireplace, then moved lazily over the chilled champagne resting in a silver ice bucket, to the sheepskin rug she'd spread out on the floor, and finally upon the handful of foil packets she'd scattered on the hearth.

"Expecting someone?" His blue gaze fastened on her. Slowly he perused her oversized black sweater, her bare legs and feet, then back to her face. He rubbed a knuckle against his cheek and grinned. "Expecting me?"

She lifted her chin a fraction. "Maybe."

"You got anything on under that?" he drawled.

She kept her voice as cool and as lazy as his. "Maybe. Maybe not."

He glanced at the shiny foil packets decorating the hearth. "Planning on using those tonight?"

Noticing the erection beginning to strain his well-worn jeans, she gave him a sexy grin. "Maybe."

He moved toward her. His big hands flexed. "How do I get past maybe?"

"Strip," she said, sidling over to the sheepskin rug. His gaze locked onto her bare thighs as she sat down and curled her legs close to her body. "You've stripped for your women before, haven't you?"

He shook his head slowly. "Naw, I usually just let'em tear my clothes off."

Amanda separated her legs just enough to let him know she was bare beneath the sweater. She kept her voice low and seductive. "Shuck your clothes, cowboy."

"That an order?"

"Naw, that's a privilege."

He tossed his Stetson onto her couch, then hooked his thumbs in his leather belt. "No music?"

Amanda smiled as she reached for the remote control she'd left beside the champagne bucket. She punched a button and "Achy Breaky Heart" began to play. The skin around Wes's blue eyes crinkled as his face split into a wide grin. He hitched a hip on the padded arm of her couch and slowly pulled off a boot. He dropped it, then took off the other. He reached for a sock.

Amanda laughed as he twirled both his socks in time with the music then tossed them over his shoulder. When he rose to his feet and began to unbutton his shirt, her heart raced. He moved his hips from side-to-side, performing a sexy two-step. Turning around, he pulled the shirt off his shoulders, then let it slide slowly down his arms, leaving his back bare and beautiful for her perusal.

He spun around to face her and his blue eyes locked with hers as he reached for his belt buckle. For the first time Amanda understood how a man might feel while she danced. Her cowboy wasn't Nureyev, but he was seductive. She licked her lips at the expanse of his chest, the defined bulges of his arms, and the long, familiar fingers working the buttons of his jeans.

She shifted her legs, aware of the moisture pooling between her thighs as each button popped open, exposing his taut belly then a thatch of dark hair. Then it struck her, he wasn't wearing underwear.

He'd stolen her act.

Her lips parted as his jeans slid down his rock hard thighs and freed his fully aroused shaft. Deftly, he kicked the jeans aside.

Naked and beautiful, and obviously quite proud of himself, he closed the short distance between them and stood before her. "Enjoy the show?"

Incapable of answering in words, Amanda rose to her knees, removed her sweater and did what she'd planned as a prelude to a long night of lovemaking. She took him in her mouth.

When her lips touched the smooth skin of his erection, her eyes fluttered closed. His big hands molded to her scalp, holding her, urging her to take more of him. Encouraged, she explored his taut flesh; tasting his skin, feeling his need, and surveying the length of him. Smooth as velvet. Hard as steel.

He felt so good. She planned to take her time, all night if necessary. There was a lot of her cowboy to love. Using the tip of her tongue, she teased the underside of his shaft. Her action brought a strangled moan. His.

She wrapped her fingers around the base of his erection, massaging and stroking, increasing the tempo. She wanted to make him come, give him the earth shattering pleasure he'd given her. She needed to feel the power of her loving course through his body.

She'd always strived to be the best, to meet every challenge. Including giving Wes Cooper the loving of his life.

"I can't hold back," he said in a husky voice laden with passion.

She slid her hand between his legs and cupped his sac. He groaned, an unintelligible moan of pleasure. With slow, sensual strokes, she urged him on. Increasing her tempo until his salty fluid filled her mouth.

Amanda slid her lips from his erection, licked them, then looked up at him. Sweat stained his brow. His eyes glowed with a soft fire she'd never seen before.

"Do you have any idea what you do to me?" he asked as he dropped to his knees.

"Touché, Cooper."

An odd smile curled his lips as his fingertip touched her wet lower lip. She leaned forward and licked his lips. "Like how you taste?"

"As long as I'm on you," he said as he slanted his head to capture her mouth.

His kiss was lush and sexy. Their tongues mingled with his pleasure, and his hands cupped her buttocks pressing her sex tight to his. Big, hot and solid, he made her feel delicate, sensual and soft. He guided her down to the plush sheepskin rug. Instead of covering her body with his, he knelt beside her. For the longest time he just looked at her.

A raw gentleness had replaced the blue fire in his eyes. He touched her hair, then ran his fingertips along her jaw, across her lips. He touched the tip of her nose.

Wes could make the simplest gesture sexy. And loving. For the first time in her life she understood how it felt to love a man. No words were necessary. She felt it in her heart. Like wildfire it spread throughout her body, radiating through her skin in waves of heat.

His hand moved down her neck, drifted over her shoulder to her breast. He cupped her flesh, molding it to his palm. He massaged the mound until it swelled beneath his hand. She rubbed her thighs together, trying to ease the sweet pressure between her legs. She wanted to feel his hot mouth tugging at her breast. Needed him to ease the tender ache in her taut nipples.

Inching his way along in gentle, sensual caresses, he skimmed her curves. She pushed gently against his hand, urging him to quell the fire he'd started hours ago in her office.

As he splayed his hand across her belly, his eyes glowed with blue hot desire, raw and palpable.

Every inch of her skin felt hot, every part, lush. Turned on. His fingers curled and gripped her short curls. A possessive act, reminding her of the night he'd escorted her around the stage with his hand on her backside.

That night he'd let the audience know she belonged to him. Tonight he was making the same declaration.

"How can you want this to end?"

Amanda wanted to shout "never," but before she could answer, his fingers dipped inside her. When he leaned over and licked her nipple, then took it deep inside his hot mouth she realized he didn't want a verbal response. He was determined to prove she wasn't strong enough to deny the passion. That neither of them could endure another night without being together.

Desire flared as his fingers slowly stroked her. Using his tongue and lips, he explored each breast as if to reacquaint himself with her body. Then he suckled deeply, drawing a strangled moan from between her parted lips. "Wes, please, Wes. I'm burning for you."

Her ache intensified as he ceased his erotic massage and dipped his hands into the melting ice surrounding the champagne. His cold fingers grasped one hot nipple making it constrict into a hard kernel. As his other hand dipped into her hot center, he covered the contracted nipple with his mouth.

The contrast between hot and cold teased her senses. Again he dipped his fingers in the ice. This time he pinched her nipples until she couldn't wait for his hot mouth to ease her ache.

His ice cold fingers probed her sex, teasing her body in easy, yet provocative strokes. He'd heat her to boiling then cool her down and start all over again. Her sex was drenched, her nipples a bright red. Amanda arched her back and pelvis. She wanted him inside her, filling her. She reached over and plucked a foil packet from the hearth.

Gripping his hair, she eased his head back. "I want you. Now."

His fingers moved deeper. "Forever or just tonight?"

Amanda met his intense gaze. "Love me, Wes."

"I can't just walk away from you, from us."

She was too wet and excited to discuss the difficulties of being in love with him. "I burn for you."

Rolling to his knees, he pulled the packet from her fingers and kneeled between her thighs. Wet and aching for him, she watched as he sheathed his bold erection in the thin latex.

Taking her about the waist, he lifted her up like an offering. His hot breath caressed her breast, then his lips closed about her distended nipple. Every nerve ending quivered as he suckled. The breast he ignored tingled.

As if understanding her need, he released her swollen breast and captured the other. He drew deeply, sending rivers of desire to pool where his engorged shaft touched her sex.

He pulled back, his gaze lingering on her swollen and sensitive nipples. A hungry, sensual gaze, telling her how much he loved pleasing her. Slowly, he lowered his head, his tongue laving first one nipple, then the other. Her sex throbbed as he suckled hard on her breast. Wrapping her arms about his neck, she thrust forward, embedding him inside her.

Unrestricted, except by his hands guiding her buttocks, Amanda rode him with abandon. Setting the pace, she squeezed his flesh as she withdrew, then released as she pulled him deep inside.

She closed her eyes. She wanted to feel his love. His passion. His hard heat. Hot sweat formed between their thighs. The tempo increased. Her belly slapped into his. His fingers kneaded her hips. The musky scent of him filled her nostrils.

Poised at the brink of rapture, she opened her eyes. His intense gaze locked with hers and held as she came in slow, magnificent waves.

She collapsed against his sweat-dampened chest. Heat radiated from their flesh, filling the air with her perfume, his scent, their passion. Her knees gripped his hips. She wanted him inside her, forever.

She clung to him as he withdrew his swollen shaft. Although she'd climaxed, Amanda still pulsed with need. Guiding her gently to her knees, his hands grasped her waist as he knelt behind her. The velvety tip of his penis teased her heated opening, then slowly filled her.

Her breasts bounced in erotic rhythm with each penetrating stroke. His hand slid along her belly to her breast. He rolled her sensitive nipple between his thumb and forefinger until her sex throbbed in response.

His thrusts slowed. She felt an exquisite pleasure as his body vibrated. Amanda knew he was riding the edge. His hands caressed her thighs and hips in measured rhythm.

The sweat between their bodies sealed his thighs to the backs of hers as they moved in unison. His hand slid to her belly, and his finger teased her aching bud.

She lowered her head. Her back arched, driving him deeper. His breathing surged as fast and hard as his thrusts.

Amanda gasped, a strangled sound escaping from her throat, as the tempo of their lovemaking escalated into a wild, primitive coupling. His belly slapped her buttocks and his balls lapped against her clit until an unbearable heat built, then burst into orgasm. He thrust deep and held, then shuddered as her sex contracted about his fully embedded shaft. His breath exploded in hard labored gasps similar to her own. He gripped her wet curls until her contractions ceased, then slid his fingers between her swollen labia and rubbed her clit. She cried out as she came.

Moving his fingers in slow circles, he eased her back to earth.

Remaining inside her, he lowered her to the rug and buried his face in her hair. Lying on their sides, he tenderly stroked her belly, caressed her mound.

"I'll never get enough of you," he said, his voice still husky from their lovemaking.

The words of a lover or a man in love? "Never is a long time."

"Not long enough."

Her heart swelled with love. Amanda knew the love she had for Wes would last a lifetime.

Neither of them spoke for a long time. Content in the warmth of his embrace, Amanda listened to the measured rhythm of his heartbeat as he kissed her hair and neck.

"I'd like to stay the night," he said. "I want to sleep with you. Feel you next to me all night."

She reached down and touched him. "You won't get much sleep."

Laughter rumbled in his chest. "Didn't expect to."

Satisfied and deliciously sore, Amanda rolled onto her side and faced the dying fire. Wes curled his big body around hers. His arm wrapped possessively about her and his hand cupped her tender breast. His relaxed shaft rested against the cleft of her buttocks. Their loving had begun like the fire, hot and consuming. Now the two of them were like the glow in the embers. Still hot, but out of fuel. She closed her eyes.

On the verge of drifting off, she felt Wes kiss her shoulder. A soft, gentle touch that told her he cared.

"I love you, Amanda." He whispered so low she wasn't sure whether he'd said it or she had dreamed it.

It had to be a dream.

Amanda awoke as Wes brushed his lips over hers. She was in her bed, but she couldn't remember when they'd changed rooms. The bedroom was still dark, except for a pool of light spilling onto the carpet from her bathroom. He was leaning over her. "What time is it?"

"Around four," he said, moving away from the bed. "I just wanted to say goodbye."

"Four?" She rolled over and turned on the bedside lamp. He was dressed in a western-cut, black suit, white shirt and string tie. He looked more like an oil baron than a cop.

"I have to testify at the Delancy trial, remember? My plane leaves for Dallas in two hours."

"Thanks for telling me goodbye," she said, pleased that he hadn't slipped out of her house like a one-night stand. "You must be exhausted."

"I'll catch up tonight at the hotel." He picked up his fancy Stetson, placed it on his head, then ran his fingertips along the brim. "How do I look, boss?"

"If the jurors are women, they'll be eating out of your hand."

"I'll be back in time to pick you up for Thursday's shift at the Prickly Cactus. See you in my dreams," he said as he walked toward the bedroom door.

"I had a dream about you last night. I dreamed you told me you loved me."

He stopped mid-stride, then turned and faced her. His expression was thoughtful. "And if it wasn't a dream?"

"It changes everything."

He arched a brow. "You want me to say it was a dream?"

She shook her head. "This is serious."

"Yeah, I know."

"Then you better get going. If you miss that plane, your boss will have your cute ass in a sling."

Wes grinned and left the room. He called back to her. "Did I tell you today how much I love red hair?"

A moment later she heard the front door close.

On Thursday, Amanda left the office early and hurried home. She'd spent two days thinking about Wes. A few nights in his arms was one thing, but being crazy in love with him presented all kinds of problems. There was no middle ground.

They couldn't sneak around until the fire burned out, because Amanda knew the flame Wes had ignited was as close to eternal as it could get. Which meant their relationship had to be permanent, their commitment lasting or not at all.

Knife in hand, Amanda dropped to her knees and retrieved the package stored beneath her bed. With sentimental tears teasing the corners of her eyes, she carefully cut the tape sealing the box. Remembering her grandmother's stories, Amanda lifted the lid and pushed aside the thick pad of tissue.

She fingered the delicate lace, smoothed the transparent material, then lifted the seed pearl headdress. Her maternal great-great-grandmother had first worn this veil in the late 1800's and for the last hundred years, each mother had passed the veil to their daughter to wear on her wedding day.

Now it was her turn.

Before the mirror, Amanda adjusted the cap of pearls onto her head, then fluffed the long veil over her face and shoulders. The lace trim touched her thighs.

Did Wes love her enough?

Never one to back down from a situation, even if it meant she might lose, Amanda decided her course of action.

"I hope you've done some thinking, Cooper," she said aloud. "Cause if you haven't, you're in for one helluva surprise."

"What would you have done the other night, if I'd tossed you out of my house?" Amanda asked, glancing at Wes. His eyes were fixed on the road ahead. They hadn't said more than two words to each other since he'd arrived and hustled her into the vehicle. He glanced over and winked at her. "I'd have rented a room by the airport, and jacked off while I watched a couple of dirty movies."

Amanda grinned. "When's the last time you masturbated, Cooper?"

"Can't recall. But I'm sure I enjoyed myself."

"I'd like to talk to you after the shift at the club," she began. "That is if you don't have plans."

For a quick second, his gaze connected with hers. "I was hoping you would take me home."

"We've got to talk. I'd rather it be at the club. I've made arrangements with the owner for us to lock up the place."

"Why do I get the feeling I'm not going to like this? If it's over, just say it."

"And stop jumping to conclusions. I want you to be certain about your feelings."

"I know how I feel."

"Then we'll talk later." Her heart pounded. Wes had no idea what she had planned for him later. The truth of his feelings would be tested tonight.

A short time later, Wes escorted her to the dressing room door. He pulled her in his arms and kissed her hard. She loved his lush kisses. His tongue parried and warred with hers. His mouth was hot and demanding. His hands cupped her backside and pulled her against him. He was already hard.

"I'm starved for you." His lips brushed hers again and as he turned to leave, he said, "Stay off your knees, Mandy. That is until we get home."

Lucy, eyelash wand in hand, looked up as Amanda opened the dressing room door. "You been out front?" Lucy asked. Amanda shook her head and dropped her duffle bag. "Better take a look at the stage," Lucy warned.

Curious, Amanda left the dressing room and rushed to peek through the beaded curtain. Her jaw dropped. Up to the front, right in the middle of the stage stood a shiny brass pole. Amanda's eyes widened as Wes strolled to the edge of the stage and ran his fingers up and down the slick metal. The grin on his face was priceless.

Back in the dressing room, Amanda looked at Lucy. "What do I do with it?"

"Hold it, wrap yourself around it," Lucy said in a matter-of-fact voice. "Just pretend it's a big cock. They'll get the idea."

"Did you know about it?"

Lucy shook her head. She applied a generous amount of lipstick to her lower lip. "I requested it months ago. That thing will double our tips."

Amanda sat down and untied her athletic shoes. "Double," she said, wondering if that shiny brass pole would help her with Wes. She remembered the grin on his face as he ran his fingers along the metal.

"Men like to look at you in this business, but if you really want them to put down their money, each and every one of them has to feel what it would be like to make it with you. They become the pole, if you know what I mean. Then the money just flies out of their pockets."

"Maybe it's because they need the room in their pants."

Lucy laughed. "You're catching on, Blaze. If you can make yourself wet out there, guys will pay for it."

Amanda performed five times, each dance a prelude to her big finale with only Wes to watch her. She'd chosen an unconventional way of speaking her mind, but then their relationship hadn't been ordinary. When she'd told Lucy her plan, the dancer had readily agreed to help.

She'd just placed the veil on her head when the cellular phone in her duffle bag rang. As she listened, Amanda expelled a sigh of relief. The gods were smiling on her. Quickly she made a few arrangements, then fluffed the veil over her face.

Nervous as a cat, Amanda stood behind the beaded curtain. The main club was empty except for Wes, waiting for her at the bar. According to plan, Lucy started the music and hurried out the back door as Amanda stepped onto the stage.

Dressed all in white, Amanda began to dance. She'd chosen her costume of white high heels, white nylons, and matching lacy garter belt and skimpy bra, for Wes. The long wedding veil was for her and all of her female ancestors.

By the time she'd gyrated her way to the brass pole, Wes had planted himself center stage. Her back braced against the pole, Amanda lowered herself slowly. The gauzy veil obscured the view, but with her knees spread wide apart, it was obvious she wore nothing but her red hair. As she pushed herself to her feet, she pumped her hips up and down. Despite the filmy material, Amanda could tell she had Wes's full attention. Dancing around the pole, Amanda lifted the veil to reveal her bare backside. Standing before Wes, she grasped the pole and lowered her upper body until she heard his sharp intake of breath.

Looking through her parted legs, she winked at him. He dropped into the prized center chair for a better view. Ever so slowly, she pulled herself erect. Her hands grasped the pole, then pulled and pushed in prolonged, sensual motions, letting him know exactly how it would feel should she do the same to him. She circled the pole several times, thrusting herself up against its length. Moving directly behind the slender metal rod, she placed her high-heeled feet on either side. She flipped the veil back from her face and over her head. Flush against the brass, she dipped, rubbing herself up and down the shiny metal. Wes grinned and licked his lips.

Looking straight into his blue eyes, she touched her tongue to the slick brass and rose slowly. By the time she stood erect, he'd pulled off his hat and had planted himself at the end of the stage. His big hands flexed.

As the music ended, Amanda felt a sheen of perspiration, fueled by exertion and a liberal dose of pure passion, break out on her flesh. She sauntered to the edge of the stage. She wanted him to feel the heat exuding from her body, to inhale the scent of her desire.

"You proposing, Mandy?"

"I told you it was serious."

"Can't have my wife dancing around a pole," he said running his fingertips along her nylon clad legs.

"I only dance for you, cowboy."

"Let's keep it that way," he said as his fingers touched her bare thighs. "I'm sure we can rustle up a replacement for this job."

"Job's over. Jenkins and Bates made the collar at the Bosom Buddies."

She expected him to be disappointed about missing the action, but his attention was focused between her legs. "If you've got something to wear to cover these," he said, brushing the curls between her legs with the backs of his fingers, "I'm up for a quick trip to Nevada. We can get hitched, and make it back by morning shift."

"The Captain will have a fit."

"Yeah, but at least he'll understand why I requested a transfer."

For several heartbeats, Amanda couldn't speak. All she could think of was that Wes was not only ready to hop in the Jeep and make it official, he was willing to change his assignment for her. Her heart swelled.

"My best suit is already packed. That is, if you're sure how you feel."

"I'm sure. I've cleared our schedules until Sunday."

Wes gave her that sexy grin of his. "It might be fun to make it in a bed for once."

Her cowboy was old enough not to be caught up in the heat of the moment, but did he realize how marriage would change his life. She wanted forever, nothing less. "Sure you're ready for this? Ready for one woman? Ready for—"

"Are you, Lieutenant? I'll want babies," he said, sliding his big hand over her almost bare belly. His fingertips slipped beneath the lace trim of her garter belt. "A couple at least."

Amanda's heart began to pound. "As long as they're your babies."

"I plan to marry once, Mandy. Only once."

"Any other demands?"

"None of this feminist shit about keeping your own name. I like the sound of Captain Amanda Cooper." He gave her a concentrated stare. "But at home, I'm the boss."

"Anything else I should know?"

He dug into his jean pocket. "Just this."

Amanda felt her heart do a flip-flop at the sparkling diamond ring he held up to her. He lifted her hand and slid the engagement ring on her finger.

"I love you, Mandy." He held out his hands and she stepped into them. His lips grazed her belly. "Are you always going to be a step ahead of me?"

Feeling his hot breath caress her curls, she answered, "Always."

About the author:

B. J. McCall lives beneath the redwoods of Northern California with her husband, two dobermans and a loquacious parrot. While working as a 911 dispatcher/desk clerk for a small, coastal town, she met her husband of twenty years. That brief career, and the possibilities explored on the Police Chief's desk, provided the inspiration for her story.

Blood and Kisses

by Angela Knight

To my reader:
A good vampire is hard to find.

Sad, but true. It seems most vampire heroes (with a few wonderful exceptions) are either whiners or psychopaths. Which is really too bad, because I just love the idea of a romantic vampire. All that menacing sexuality, superhuman strength and animal hunger . . .

Besides, you know any guy who's been seducing women for three hundred years just *has* to be good in bed.

On those rare occasions when I do find the perfect vampire, he's always paired with a heroine who has the fixed bubbliness of a Laker Girl combined with the raw intelligence of a Boston Fern. By chapter three I'm chanting, "Bite her, Bite her, bite her . . ."

Why the hell would a three-hundred-year-old nobleman be attracted to a woman who wants to be reincarnated as a rainbow? Puh-leeeze.

So when Alexandria Kendall graciously allowed me to write another novella for *Secrets III*, I knew just what I wanted to write about—a civilized vampire hero and a heroine who is neither vampire nor particularly civilized. And while I was at it, I explored some of my favorite vamp fantasies.

I hope you enjoy the results. Thanks!

Chapter One

Her neck burned as though venom pumped through her blood. Beryl St. Cloud reached up and gingerly touched the wound, resisting the urge to scratch. It had finally stopped bleeding, but that bastard Tagliar would sink his fangs into her again if she wasn't damn lucky.

And for Beryl, luck meant finding Jim Decker. Now.

She ducked into the open maw of the nearest bar, then stopped to let her eyes adjust to the poor lighting. Like the rest of the Huff-Hamilton Interstellar Station, Hot Shots served a clientele of spacers, merchants and mercenaries, and she knew better than to rush in blind.

Even after Beryl's eyes adapted, the dive's interior was dark enough to make her back itch. The only illumination came from the fluorescent bar that shed gaudy pinwheels of light over tables and patrons. Not the best conditions to spot a man she'd never met, but she made a careful scan of the room anyway. She was damned if she'd get in a hurry and miss him.

There. A flash of red back in the corner. Beryl snapped her head around and recognized the crimson shimmer of a vampire's eyes staring back at her. He turned his head and the glow disappeared, winking out as the angle of reflection changed. A chill rippled across the back of Beryl's neck, but she started for his table anyway.

Her right hand automatically twitched toward the laser torch that hung on her belt, but she'd hardly win friends drawing down on a possible savior, so Beryl forced her fingers to curl into a fist just short of the torch's comforting pistol grip. She relaxed only slightly when she got close enough to recognize the vampire from Bill's description.

She'd found Jim Decker at last.

He'd attracted a crowd. Three men and a woman, all dressed in the matte black skinsuits favored by mercenaries. The woman stood between Decker's long muscled thighs, her breasts taunting inches from his face. He glanced up at her, then turned his head again to watch Beryl walking toward them.

"Come on, vamp, let's play," the woman jeered, obviously frustrated with her target's slipping attention. She shook her long blonde hair back and arched her spine to display her breasts. Her skinsuit was so tight the contours of her areolas were visible.

"Thanks, but I'll pass," the vampire said dryly. The intensity of his gaze made Beryl's steps falter.

"Oh c'mon, bloodsucker, I know you want a piece." Waving a viblade under Decker's aristocratic nose, the merc purred, "All you have to do is bleed a little for it."

The vibrating blade of that combat knife could cleave steel like paper, and one slash could sever a human arm. Beryl quickened her pace. Decker, however, didn't look particularly worried.

"How about it, perv? You want me bad enough to bleed?"

"Actually," the vampire said, dismissive, "I don't."

The blonde flushed. To either side, her two companions watched in grinning appraisal, their cold eyes fixed on the anger growing on her pretty face.

Beryl recognized this game. The female merc was green, a rookie trying to prove her steel to both her fellow warriors and herself. Unfortunately, she was also dumb as a deck plate, or she wouldn't have picked a vamp for a target. Decker could rip her throat out before she saw him move.

Yet the vampire just sat there, anger tightening the sensual contour of his lips, high, strong cheekbones throwing shadows on his angular face. His eyes were blue except when the light ignited them into a red glow. A flowing white shirt stretched over his broad shoulders, caressing ridges of muscle before tucking into black pants. "Go away, little girl," Decker said softly, his deep voice gently threatening. "You're beginning to irritate me."

"What's the matter, vamp?" the blonde merc taunted. "Don't you have the guts to try for me?"

"Maybe the perv's just not interested, Clarke," one of the men said lazily. His lip curled into a sneer. "Maybe he only does little boys."

Muscle bunched in Decker's cheek, and he turned his head slowly until his gaze locked on the male merc, burning as steady and hot and red as a laser sight. The man took an instinctive step back. Then, as if realizing he'd look bad in front of the others if he retreated farther, he stopped and put an unsteady hand on the butt of his torch.

"Or maybe," Beryl said, shouldering into the group, "the vamp knows Clarke doesn't have what it takes." Swinging a leg over one of Decker's hard thighs, she settled onto it, putting herself between him and the merc's weapon. "Maybe I'm the one he's waiting for."

Beryl ignored the startled look in the vampire's eyes and drew a forefinger hard down the cut running from her chin to her collar bone.

The pressure made it bleed again, a fat hot bead that looked black and wet in the dim light as it rolled down the length of her finger.

Until, her heart pounding a combat drumbeat in her ears, her mouth dry as sand, Beryl offered her blood to Decker.

The vampire caught his breath. His eyes flicked to meet hers. Focused, sharpened to arc light intensity. Beryl swallowed, aware of the powerful muscle of his thigh between her legs, remembering all too clearly the moment when Tagliar had grabbed her, the feel of his breath, the burn of his fangs.

God, what was she doing here? You could never count on anybody but yourself. You sure as hell couldn't count on one vamp to protect you from another.

His big hand came up and closed gently around her wrist. Beryl blinked at the masculine heat of his fingers, so different from the undead chill she'd expected.

He bent his head, his gaze still locked on her, and opened that lushly male mouth as he guided her forefinger between his lips. His tongue began a slow, velvet swirl around her fingertip. Paused. Swirled again. His eyes slid closed as he sucked gently.

Beryl's nipples hardened, ached in time with each slow pull as she stared at the dark, gleaming crown of his head. She'd expected to have to endure him.

"Jesus," said Clarke hoarsely, revulsion and fascination a sickly mix in her eyes, "that's disgusting. Let's get the fuck out of here before I heave my rations."

The mercs, laughing uneasily, beat a hasty retreat from the saloon, but Beryl was aware of nothing except the astonishing carnality of Decker's tongue. Inside her a small voice babbled, *But he's a vampire. . . .*

Finally he lifted his head and lowered her captive hand. "What's your name?"

"St. Cloud," she breathed. "I'm Beryl St. Cloud."

"Jim Decker." He studied her. "So who did you piss off?"

Beryl rocked back, disoriented by the cool tone contrasting so starkly with those molten demon eyes. "I beg your pardon?"

"Somebody must be seriously ticked if they sent Damian Tagliar after you."

Feeling her jaw drop, she made an effort to close her mouth. "How did you know?"

"I can smell him on you." Decker nodded shortly at the cut on her neck. "You fought him. Must have done a damn good job, too, because you're still alive. I'd love to know how you pulled that one off. Tagliar doesn't often miss."

Beryl swallowed, remembering the sick terror of returning to her station hotel room to find the assassin lying on her bed, an erection swelling his trousers. *"Let's get started,"* he'd said. *"I want to make you come at least twice before I kill you."*

"I shot him in the eyes with a laser torch at point blank range."

"And fried his optic nerves like eggs." He nodded, approving. "Blinded him. One of the very few ways to slow a vampire down for any length of time. You bought yourself at least four or five hours while he heals."

"Time which is rapidly running out because I spent most of it looking for you." She rose from his thigh, trying to regain a sense of control.

He sat back in his chair. "How much?"

"Time?"

"Money." Decker's face hardened. "How much money are you offering me to kill Tagliar for you?"

That knocked her off balance, thought Decker. Good. She'd been playing him from the moment she'd slung those incredible legs over his and offered him her blood like Eve giving Adam the apple. She must think she could give him one red taste and he'd be willing to kill for more, but he knew damn well he'd never *get* more. Not without forcing her.

For a moment Decker let himself imagine it. The arch of her slim body against his, deliciously feminine, flooding his head with the musky woman scent he'd already drawn into his lungs under the stench of Tagliar. The slow penetration of his teeth into her throat. Blood pouring over his tongue in hot, liquid copper intoxication as he spread those magnificent thighs and pushed inside until she was triply impaled on his fangs and cock.

"I wasn't planning to offer money," she said, her voice cool now, steady. "I'm afraid I'm maxed out."

He banished the erotic vision and cleared his throat. "St. Cloud, if you expect me to do Tagliar out of the goodness of my heart, expect again. I'm nobody's knight in shining armor."

St. Cloud frowned, her twenty-third century mind not catching the reference.

"I don't work for free," he clarified with a cool mockery he was far from feeling.

"I don't expect you to." Her fine jaw squared. "I plan to pay in blood."

Was she saying what he thought she was saying? No. Forget it. She was trying to play him again.

Decker stood, an attempt to establish his dominance he regretted the minute he was on his feet. She looked entirely too damn tempting. And close enough to grab.

St. Cloud was dressed casually, but somehow she looked sexier than the blonde had in skinsuit and pouting nipples. The baggy white top draped over her round breasts, its short sleeves revealing the graceful female muscle of her long arms, just as tough neonylon shorts hugged her hips and showcased lust-inspiring legs. Yet despite all that luxuriant femininity, something in the alert, easy way she held herself hinted of combat training, and a lot of it. Decker had known enough mercs to bet St. Cloud was a pro, and a damn good one at that.

She didn't have a bimbo's face, either. Her features were strong, intelligent, with softly rounded cheekbones and a stubborn jaw, a pair of dimples punctuating a lushly wide mouth that looked like an engraved invitation to sin. Her eyes were as dark as the richly curling hair that tumbled around her sculpted shoulders. There was no fear at all in that midnight stare. He'd never realized how erotic a steady, level look could be. As though all he had to do was reach out for her, and she wouldn't run.

"Let me get this straight," Decker said, torn between scaring her off and snatching her into his arms, "you're offering me blood for my protection against Tagliar?"

"Yes." She didn't even blink when she said it.

"Why?"

"I am . . . I *was* a mercenary, Mr. Decker. I know what it would cost to hire a vampire bodyguard, and I know I don't have that kind of money." She hesitated and squared her finely muscled shoulders. "In fact, there's only one thing I have you might be interested in."

Heat spun into his cock, tightened his balls. He fought to ignore it. "St. Cloud, I've got a hemosynther back on my ship. I've been living on synthetic blood for five decades, and I can go on living on it for five centuries. Why would I be willing to fight Damian Tagliar just to taste your pretty white throat?"

"That depends on how long it's been since you've had a woman."

"You'd whore for a vampire?"

"To keep from being raped and murdered by another vampire? You bet your ass."

"Am I supposed to be flattered?"

"No." She gave him a smile stripped of amusement. "But then, if you accept, I'll owe my life to the fact that vamps have a hard time getting laid."

Which was no more than the truth. When Decker came into the Life back in 1986, women were not a problem. He'd needed no more than a pint or so a night, and he'd enjoyed the challenge of seduction. He'd lived that way for two hundred and thirty years.

But fifty years ago scientists discovered that vampires really did exist, setting off an orgy of stakings and anti-vamp legislation. A blood test was developed to identify the virus that caused vampirism, and vamps were forced to obtain licenses or face execution. Strict laws dictated, among other things, that vampires were no longer allowed to conceal their condition. And because the social stigma attached to vampirism was so great, Decker now had a hell of a time even buying a woman a drink, much less getting her into bed.

But even if he'd had his pick, he'd still find Beryl St. Cloud a tempting proposition.

"What's to keep you from crying off after I've staked Tagliar?"

"You." Her brown eyes were unblinking. "We both know there's nothing to stop you from taking me. You certainly have the strength. And I'm willing to sign a contract giving you the right."

That seductive idea almost finished his resistance, but he fought it off. There was no way she was serious. "What makes you think I won't kill you as quickly as Tagliar?"

"Bill Anderson."

He frowned. "Bill?" He hadn't seen Anderson in . . . it must be fifteen years. Which was a shame, because Decker had never met a better man. There was absolutely no bigotry in Bill. He honestly didn't give a damn whether you drank hundred proof or hemoglobin, as long as you treated your mercs well and delivered a good paycheck. That clear-headed intelligence was one factor in the success of Occam's Raiders. It was also the reason Decker had left Anderson in charge of the mercenary company when he'd walked away. "What about him?"

"I succeeded Bill as commander of the Raiders after he retired."

Decker sat back. "You run the Company? Why didn't you say so?"

"Because I don't. Not anymore. I disbanded it."

The Raiders had been dissolved? He hadn't realized he was so out of touch. "Why?"

"That is a very long story. Which ends with a vampire after my ass," St. Cloud said, so shortly he knew there was a lot more to it. "When I found out Tagliar was hunting me, I called Bill. He told me my only hope was to go to you for help, so I hit the Spacer's Computer Net to pinpoint the location of your ship, and here I am." She shrugged.

"I trust he'll vouch for you."

St. Cloud reached into a pocket for a chipcard. "Give him a call." Decker took the card from her long fingers and stood to find a com unit. He located one in a corner even dimmer than the rest of the bar and slipped in the chipcard, which began beeping out the code for an interstellar call. The card spent fifteen minutes playing connect the dots with various computers before linking him with someone in the Anderson household.

Decker had become adept at recognizing the faces of acquaintances under the mask of age, so it took him only a moment to see his clever, wicked executive officer in the 90-year-old who finally came to the com.

"Decker! Good God, you really don't age, do you?" Bill's mouth stretched into a white smile under a shock of hair the same color. That grin was definitely familiar, but it brought home to Decker just how long it had been.

"Hi, Bill. Enjoying retirement?"

"Hell, no. I'm bored to tears." The old man paused and studied him, his blue eyes sharp and perceptive. "I take it you've met my kid."

That rocked Decker back on his heels. "St. Cloud is your daughter?"

"Nah." Anderson waved a hand that still looked the size of a deck hatch. "It just seems like it. I've known her since she was sixteen. You gonna help her, Deck?"

"Maybe. What's the story, Bill?"

"She really is a great kid, Deck. Have I mentioned her dad was a member of the Raiders?"

Decker shot him a warning look. "Bill, you're not going to bullshit me into forgetting the question."

The old man grunted in disgust. "Hell, that's no surprise. You're the hardest man to bullshit I ever met." Settling back in his chair, he thought for a moment before he began. "Okay, here's the situation. Beryl's been running the Raiders for ten years now, and she's done a good job. Lost a couple battles, but won a lot more. Good fighter, dead-on shot, even kicks ass hand-to-hand, which is not easy for a woman. She's got guts. Tactically she's a goddamn genius. But romantically her judgement sucks."

"Doesn't everybody's? I remember that little blonde you . . ."

Bill grinned. "Shut the hell up, would you? My wife's in the next room. Anyway, a couple years ago she fell in love with this pretty prick, his name was Daveed Zahn. I never could stand that sonuvabitch. Found out why when the Raiders were involved in this action on

Dyson's World last year, and they were ambushed. Zahn had sold them out to the enemy. A bunch of the Raiders got killed. . . ."

Decker straightened in his chair. "Who?"

"Nobody you know. All of 'em came into the Company after you left. Deck, it's been fifteen years. That's a whole career to a merc."

He sighed. "Good point. Go on."

"Anyway, one of the ones that got fried was Zahn, which was a good thing, or Beryl would have killed him herself. She and the rest of the company were captured, had to ransom themselves by handing over their troopship, which was in orbit at the time. Luckily the opposition was hard up for ships, or they'd have been dead."

"So where does Tagliar come in?"

"Well, back home some ugly accusations got made about whether Beryl was in on Zahn's plot. The survivors of the mercs who were killed threatened to sue, and damned if Beryl didn't sell out and pay off. She pretty well busted herself doing it, too."

Decker frowned. "I hate to say it, buddy, but that doesn't sound all that innocent to me."

The old man's jaw took on a stubborn jut he recognized from a dozen old arguments. "She didn't do it, Deck. I know that kid. She would no sooner have betrayed the Raiders than she'd have hacked off her own arm with a butter knife."

"Okay, okay. Go on."

Mollified, Bill said, "Anyway, the Mercs' Union held an inquest and determined there was no evidence she'd sold out, but apparently somebody wasn't satisfied with the results, because soon afterward she got a tip Tagliar had been hired to do her. She contacted me to ask how to kill a vamp, and I told her the only chance she had was you."

"You're probably right."

"Will you help her?"

"Yeah. Hell, I'd stake Tagliar for the pure joy of it."

Bill grinned. "I told her you would. Good thing too, since she doesn't have any money to pay you anyway."

Decker sat up. "You told her I'd do Tag for free?"

"Uh, yeah." The old man looked suddenly uncomfortable. "Hope you don't mind, Deck. You've always had a soft spot for women, and besides, Beryl's a good kid."

After that there wasn't much Decker could do but say his goodbyes and cut the connection. For a long moment he sat frowning in the darkened com booth, then reached into the top of his boot and pulled out the ironwood knife he carried in case he ran into a vamp who needed killing. He stared at the slick black wood, with its wicked point and serrated double edge.

If she knew he'd take Tagliar out for free, why did St. Cloud offer to become his mistress? Trying to set the hook, maybe? Or maybe, having talked to Bill, she'd assumed Decker would gallantly refuse her offer once he heard the story. Which he might have, if not for his lingering doubts about whether she really had been involved in Zahn's betrayal.

And if he found out she had . . . His hand tightened on the knife's carved wooden hilt. The Raiders were his people, though the ones he'd known were probably long retired. Still, he'd formed the Company, and he felt a responsibility to it. If Beryl St. Cloud had betrayed it, she would pay.

Slipping the blade back into his boot, Decker strode back to the table. She looked up at his approach, her eyes dark, wary.

"All right," he said shortly.

St. Cloud's expression didn't change. She certainly didn't look like a woman who'd just reeled in her sucker.

"But this is not a one night stand, St. Cloud," he told her. "The going rate to stake a vamp is twenty thousand, and nobody's ass is worth that much for one night. You're mine for the next year. Agreed?"

She didn't even blink. "Agreed."

He nodded shortly. "I'll draw up a contract. Where's your kit?"

"Back at my hotel." She shrugged those luscious shoulders. "But then, that's where I left Tagliar. He's probably gone by now, but . . ."

"Screw it. We'll have somebody deliver it when we settle your bill. Let's go." He turned away without waiting for her agreement.

"Wait." St. Cloud caught at his forearm. "Where, exactly, are we going?"

"My ship." Decker headed for the entrance without waiting to see if she'd follow. He knew she would.

After all, she had no place else to go.

Somehow, this wasn't going quite the way she'd thought. Beryl had expected finding Decker to be tricky, and she'd figured it wouldn't be easy getting him to protect her. Instead, he'd talked to Anderson and simply agreed without another word.

What had taken her off balance was his lack of . . . enthusiasm.

Oh, right, St. Cloud, she thought, disgusted. *He's supposed to be eager to risk his neck for a chance at yours.*

Still, this cold, matter-of-fact agreement left her puzzled. He seemed almost disinterested, though she could have sworn she'd seen erotic hunger in his eyes before he'd gone to talk to Bill.

Oh, God. Bill. Her stomach sank. Bill had told him about the Raiders.

Beryl reached out and grabbed Decker by one hard shoulder and tried to haul him around. It was like grabbing a cliff, but he stopped and faced her. In the bright light of the station corridor, his eyes were a vivid electric blue.

"If you think I betrayed the Company, why did you agree to protect me?"

"Because I'm not sure whether you did or not." He lifted a dark eyebrow. "Did you sell out your men, St. Cloud?"

"No!" Rage swelled in her like hot oil bubbling through water. She was damn sick of being accused of betraying the people she'd loved most.

"Then why'd you settle? Must have been a good bit of change to pay for something you didn't do."

Her rage cooled as the guilt under it rolled to the surface. She slumped, suddenly drained. "It was my responsibility to protect them, and I didn't."

"I doubt that was the first battle you lost."

"Fuck you, vampire."

Decker made a gesture as though warding off her weary anger. "I'm not accusing you of incompetence, St. Cloud, but you know as well as I do that every commander loses battles. I did. Bill did. And you did. So why'd that one hit you so hard?"

She discovered she could no longer meet his eyes. "Because I should have seen what Daveed was, and I didn't." Since the age of sixteen, she'd been a warrior, and a damn good one. It was all she was, all she was good at. And Daveed Zahn had stripped it all away. Now she'd fallen so far she was forced to whore for a vampire to save her life.

Hell, if they'd sent a proper assassin after her, one who would have ended her life with one clean shot . . . But they hadn't even allowed her the dignity of an honorable fight, an honorable death. And she had enough self-respect left not to settle for what they had in mind.

So she had no hope but Decker, the vampire who'd led the Raiders as they should be led. She knew his history, she'd heard the stories since she'd been sixteen. Few had died under his command, and the ones who hadn't had gotten rich from his victories.

Why had he been the only one she could turn to?

"Do you want me or not?" Beryl snapped.

For a long moment Decker looked at her as if weighing her, testing the pain he could read in her face. Suddenly the darkness lifted from his features and relief filled his eyes, followed by compassion. "You really weren't involved with Zahn's plot, were you? This hurts you too damn much."

But before she could answer, his gaze shifted into the distance, and his eyes narrowed, his lips peeling back to reveal his canine teeth lengthening into fangs. Crouching, he snatched something out of the top of his boot, then rose and grabbed her elbow. She looked down and saw he held a serrated black knife almost as long as her arm.

"What are you doing?" Beryl gave her arm a jerk, but it was like pulling against an industrial vise.

Decker started towing her up the corridor at a pace just short of a run. "Tagliar's coming."

"Damn," she murmured. "I'd hoped to have more time . . . Wait, how do you know that? For that matter, how'd he manage to find me so fast?"

He shrugged. "We can sense each other when conditions are right. As for tracking you, he's following your scent. He doesn't know we're together yet, but he will. If we're lucky, we may have just enough time to get this done."

"Get *what* done?"

Decker ignored the question as he drew her into the main atrium, a huge, vaulting chamber filled with trees and vegetation under the dome of a hologram night sky. An immense ringed planet hung overhead, casting a soft, butter yellow light that illuminated the park. The patter of falling water vied with birdsong in air fragrant with honeysuckle, but the vampire didn't even seem to notice as he plunged down a curving gravel path. She scrambled after him.

"Tagliar's got me at a disadvantage," he explained, his voice grim. "Synthblood is a lousy substitute for the real thing; it provides nourishment, but not the psychic charge that taking a human does. And it's that energy which strengthens us. Tagliar's an assassin, and he feeds well and often. Me, I've been drinking synthblood since the Vamp Legislation passed."

"So because you've been living like a monk while Tagliar's been gorging on other people's lives . . ."

". . . He's going to kick my ass. Unless I take you *now*."

Beryl's gut twisted at the thought, but she forced herself to consider it calmly. And she calmly thought it was a bad idea. "I can't give you that much blood, Decker."

"Of course not, but blood's only part of it. When a woman climaxes, she produces a hell of a lot of psychic energy. Tagliar likes to take that energy by force before he kills, but mutual passion gives a better charge than rape. That, and given that I'll have taken you more recently than he's fed, could balance the scales."

They'd stepped into a clearing. An elaborate fountain splashed water high into the air. Decker headed for one of the marble benches that surrounded it, Beryl resisting the urge to tug against his grip.

"I hope to hell you're not expecting me to generate burning passion on the spot." She dropped down on the bench next to him. "I hate to say it, but I'm just not in the mood."

He gave her a grin so heart-stoppingly charming she blinked in surprise. "You let me take care of that."

Easing closer, Decker reached for her.

Unwillingly, her mind spat an ugly memory of Tagliar: *"I want to make you come at least twice before I kill you."*

"Shhh," the vampire breathed, his fingers brushing her mouth in a feathering caress. "I won't hurt you."

But another thought occurred to her, and she frowned. "What about the vamp virus?"

"You can't catch it from saliva," he told her patiently. "You'd only become a vampire if you drank my blood while I drank enough of yours to weaken your immune system."

Her last reasonable objection banished, Beryl forced her muscles to relax. It was like going into battle, she told herself. Just plunge in and worry later. If there was a later.

A rueful chuckle rumbled warmly in her ear. His hands came up to cup her face, lifting her head so her eyes met his. "Work with me here, darlin'."

There was such kindness in those eyes, an understanding that seemed to speak directly to something in her she never acknowledged. *I know how lonely you've been. I know how you've feared and hid it, I know how you've wanted to reach out, but there was never anyone there. I know how you've suffered.*

Part of Beryl yearned to accept that silent offer of understanding, but the rest was pure soldier, and she had learned to distrust anything she wanted that much.

He's three hundred years old, she thought, as his strong fingers gently explored the rise of her cheekbone, the whorl of her ear. *And he's survived most of that time because he knows how to give women exactly what they want, and give it so well they're willing to sacrifice blood to get it.*

Yet those blue eyes looked into her, called to the vulnerable girl she kept locked within a hard shell of cynicism. And that girl wanted him.

He's a giggolo with fangs.

But the warm glide of his fingers didn't feel like pretense. He leaned closer, brushed his lips against her forehead. She forced herself to let go of her fear, to close her eyes.

And surrender to the vampire.

There was something so disarming about her, Decker thought, as she finally relaxed against him. She looked like sex and sin, she thought like a soldier, but underneath . . . Dreamily he played his hands over her, tracing the fine muscles of her shoulders and down to the thrust of her round, full breasts, letting the connection between them build.

What was it Anderson had said? She'd been with the Raiders since she was sixteen. What the hell had Bill been thinking of, to let a child fight with that gang of killers?

Despite the ghost of that girl he could sense inside her, she was far from childlike now. Pulling her closer, Decker felt her relax another increment as he slowly seduced her into forgetting Tagliar.

He cupped one pretty breast, filling his hand with silken warmth. The thin shirt she wore was no barrier at all, and her nipple budded tightly. He began to stroke her, taking the little peak between thumb and forefinger and squeezing until she gasped in his ear. His vampire hearing picked up her pulse as it took on the rapid thump of desire, and Decker smiled.

Craving more direct contact, he reached under her loose shirt and found the taut, female globe shuddering with her heartbeat. A shiver of his own rippled through him. God, it had been so long.

Decker slipped his fingers up to the eager point he'd been toying with and gently twisted, using all the skill he'd honed for three centuries. Beryl moaned, her breath hot on his skin as she arched her back. Silently begging for more.

She was no virgin, yet she'd never felt such arousal. Her nipples were hard and desperate, and Decker was giving them exactly what they needed, tugging, crimping them between his fingers, building her flicker of cautious desire into a blaze. Beryl twined her arms around his back and held on. She wanted his mouth, she wanted his fingers, she wanted. . . .

But he's a vampire, said the little voice. Beryl told it to shut up.

His breath gusted warm across her ear, then his tongue tip traced the sensitive whorl. Blindly she turned her head, met his mouth with her own. His lips were seductively smooth against hers as his slick, wicked tongue glided inside. His hand found the tender flesh between her legs through the fabric of her shorts. She moaned against his mouth.

Her questing tongue found the sharp length of a fang, jolting her for a moment. But then his right hand tugged gently at her nipple, and his left pressed urgently against her sex, right *there*, at the spot she most needed him, and Beryl shuddered. Long, clever fingers increased the pressure, and she arched into the muscular warmth of his body, moaning. He felt so good holding her. Not like a predatory vampire looking for blood and sex, but a tender, loving man.

And God, she'd had too few of those.

She felt the gust of his breath on her throat, the careful press of his teeth. His tongue bathed her skin. Something stung her neck, built quickly toward pain, but his hands were working her body with such skill she didn't care. The pain became a deep, drawing ache, but somehow instead of puncturing her pleasure it only spurred it. Beryl whimpered, shocking herself with the helpless passion in her own voice.

Then Decker began to feed.

The first tug of his mouth sent a wave of erotic delight through her so hot and dark she gasped in startled lust. He was holding her locked against him now, one arm around her back, a hand fisted in her hair. Ruthlessly Decker shoved the other down the waistband of her shorts and thrust two fingers into her slickness as his thumb sought her clit. Beryl arched her back and moaned, her voice high and trembling with passion. He growled back, still drawing deeply on her skin. His thumb circled her hard little bud. The dark, exotic pleasure was abruptly unbearable, burning through her in time to the suction of his mouth and the pumping of his hand. His fingers flexed within her, making her wish for his erection. She sought it out, finding his cock wonderfully hard and hot and long behind the frustrating barrier of his pants. Decker sucked harder on her throat and twisted his long fingers deep, and she hungered for that splendid, forbidden vampire cock plunging into her as he drank. It would feel so thick, so merciless . . .

The ecstasy burned hotter. And hotter. And exploded.

Beryl screamed.

And *felt* him in her mind, taking everything she had and giving it back, savagely bright and strong. Under his delicious spur, something in her burst again, wiping out everything else but that starburst of rapture. Which slowly, slowly faded like a spark dying in the night. Until at last he drew away.

"Don't stop," she moaned, pulling weakly at him.

"No, darlin'," he murmured. "You can't give me any more, or I'll hurt you."

"Oh." She wasn't sure she cared, but could only muster the strength to hang there in his arms, exhausted.

He began to tongue her slowly, painting wet, warm paths along her neck until Beryl stirred enough to ask, "What are you doing?"

He said something technical about vampire saliva and enzymes promoting healing. She barely listened, floating in lassitude as he licked the small wound he'd left, his tongue moving in long strokes over her throat like a cat bathing a kitten. Too sated for further conversation, Beryl simply lay back in his possessive arms, eyes drifting closed as he tongued her.

She was actually drifting off to sleep when a familiar voice snarled, "You been fucking my prey, Decker?"

Chapter Two

Decker lifted his head as a lightning strike of primitive rage forked through him. He'd found his woman at last, her blood was in his mouth, her hot cunt waited for his first thrust, and now that idiot Tagliar wanted to play games. "Go away, bloodsucker. I'm busy."

"I can see that," Tagliar said, eyeing them from the edge of the clearing. He was a big bastard, taller than Decker by a good three inches, with the muscle to back up that size packed on his long bones. He was handsome enough to have been a successful vampire back before the Legislation, but Decker suspected the chill arrogance in his hazel eyes repelled more women than his pretty face attracted. Tagliar had killed so many humans so easily he'd forgotten anyone could give him a fight.

Right now that cold gaze was crawling over the swelling lower curve of Beryl's breast, revealed by Decker's hand still thrust beneath her shirt. He let the hem drop.

"Well, well." Tagliar grinned at Beryl in nasty insinuation. "I never dreamed you'd climb onto another vampire's cock so soon after feeling my fangs. You must have liked it."

"And you know just how much, Tagliar. I could tell by the way you screamed when I pulled the trigger." Beryl really should have had fangs of her own to go in that smile. "How are your eyes, vampire?"

Tagliar lost his grin. "Better off than yours, once I dig them out of your head. Take a walk, Deck. The bitch and I have business."

Decker stood and moved to shield Beryl with his body. "You always were a little stupid, so I'll spell it out for you. She's mine. You don't get her."

Tagliar reached into his belt and pulled out an ironwood knife that looked more like a machete. "The knight in shining armor rides to the rescue. Come on, cock sucker, I want to dent your gleaming ass."

"God, Tag, where do you get your dialogue—the Asshole Channel?" To Beryl, who looked as if she was wondering what a "channel" was, Decker muttered, "You still have your torch?"

She nodded, drawing the weapon from its holster. He noticed from the readouts it held a full charge and wasn't surprised. Beryl was a professional to the soles of her battle boots.

"Remember, that's just a backup." Decker showed her the knife. "Nothing will really put a permanent hole in a vampire but this."

Beryl's eyes widened. "Is that *wood*?"

"Next best thing to a stake." He eyed Tagliar, who was pacing around the area as if choosing a good spot for a fight. "How else would two vampires fight?"

Having found a suitable spot for a brawl, Tagliar turned to watch them with reptilian attention.

"Let me help, Decker." Beryl's eyes were cold as she stared at their enemy.

"Sorry, that's my job. You're safer on the sidelines." She looked so offended he had to smile. "I hate to mention this, darlin', but you're only human."

"Don't rub it in."

From across the fountain, Tagliar called, "Any day now, Decker!"

Beryl shot the big vampire a look of pure loathing. "Gut him."

"I'll certainly try." It was time to start.

⁕

Before her eyes, the amusement drained away from Decker's handsome features until nothing was left but chill determination. Without another word, he walked away to meet his enemy. Beryl could only clench her fists and ignore her churning stomach. It went against the grain to watch someone else fight for her while she did nothing. She knew she was no match for a vampire's strength, but failing to try felt cowardly.

The duel started so fast she almost missed it. A flash of color, the muffled thud of big bodies slamming together like enraged bulls, and the two vampires were locked in a writhing clench on the ground.

Decker caught Tagliar's wrist, stopping the wooden blade an inch from his chest. His biceps howled as he fought the strength of his opponent's massive arm. Sweat rolled, stinging, into his eyes. Still the knife pushed closer. Tagliar met his gaze and grinned.

Decker released the vampire's knife wrist, simultaneously sweeping his free hand around in a chop that slammed into Tagliar's forearm and knocked the big blade aside. It thumped into the grassy turf that covered the deck, burying itself halfway to the hilt just as Decker slammed a fist into Tagliar's narrow nose. Blood splattered. He jerked his head back from the hot, red spray and kicked, launching Tagliar into the air with one thrust of his legs. Decker rolled to his feet as Tagliar, cursing, somersaulted to his own.

Decker circled to his right. Something wet and warm rolled toward his mouth, and he knew from the scent it was Tagliar's blood. He fought the temptation to lick it off, knowing one taste of his enemy's blood would plunge him into the territorial madness of vampire combat. He needed all his intelligence and skill if he was going to keep Tagliar from killing him and taking Beryl, and the blood rage could strip it all away.

Tagliar lunged again, setting off a flurry of strikes Beryl couldn't even follow. When the two separated, Decker had a foot-long slash across his torso.

A chill skated Beryl's spine. She'd been in everything from bar brawls to battles between interstellar armadas, but this fight was different. It wasn't just the combatants' vampire strength that seemed so alien, it was the vampire rage that contorted their features into something feral and inhuman.

Then Tagliar confirmed that impression. Looking directly into Decker's eyes, he licked the bloody point of his knife, his smile demonic, his tongue abnormally long, pointed like a snake's.

Decker stiffened, and his jaw thrust forward before he dipped his head and tongued the blood from his own blade. Yet instead of Tagliar's nonhuman relish, there was distaste in his eyes, a repugnance mixed with resignation.

What the hell is that all about? Beryl wondered, and waited for the fight to start again.

For several beats the only movement was Tagliar licking his knife as though savoring an ice cream cone. Both vampires seemed to be waiting for something. Finally Decker coiled into a crouch and Tagliar lifted his head from his blade. A low growl rumbled, she couldn't tell from whom.

They hit each other so hard she could hear the meaty thud from across the park. One knife spun away and the other fell into the grass, but the vampires didn't seem to notice as they ripped at anything they could reach with fangs and clawing hands. Blood sprayed the deck, animal growls sawed the air, and for the first time Beryl realized how far from human they really were.

Her stomach twisted as she remembered she'd just agreed to put herself at Decker's mercy. And she wondered if there was really all that much difference between him and Damian Tagliar. . . .

Rage heated Decker's consciousness into a roiling boil that made thought impossible. Just as he'd feared, the other's vampire blood had triggered a flood of hormones that plunged him into a killing rage, but he'd had no choice once Tagliar had licked that damn knife. The vamp rage doubled strength even as it made strategy more difficult, and he couldn't afford the disadvantage.

The reaction was even stronger because Beryl's blood also ran in his veins. Beryl, his prey, his woman, his mate. *His.* Tagliar dared think he could take her away.

And Decker was going to kill him for it.

Fangs bared, he launched himself at Tagliar, grabbing him by the throat as the force of his dive threw them both into the fountain. Decker howled at the shock of hitting cold water, but forgot his discomfort as Tagliar flailed and clawed at the hands still clamped around his neck. Snarling, Decker dug in, his nails gouging so deep blood curled into the water. The sight spurred his frenzy even higher.

Somewhere, far back inside the red riot Decker's mind had become, a last fragment of human intelligence rejoiced. His gamble had paid off. By taking Beryl as he had, he'd gained the strength to defeat Tagliar. All that remained was the kill.

Decker watched hazel eyes widen as Tagliar realized he was about to die. In a moment his neck would break, and though that wasn't enough to kill a vampire, it would paralyze him long enough for Decker to tear his head off his shoulders.

Snarling into Tagliar's face, Decker curled his fingers deeper, tighter.

"Not this time, bloodsucker!" Tagliar gasped, fumbling at his boot until his fist shot up holding a backup knife. He thrust it right toward Decker's eyes. Instinctively Decker jerked back, avoiding the blade but relaxing his hold.

Tagliar threw him off, rolled to his feet and lunged out of the fountain. Snarling, Decker shot to his feet.

But before he could leap after his enemy, a hot red point appeared on Tagliar's shoulder. The vampire stumbled, roaring in shock at the pain of the laser blast carving into his body. Unfortunately the wound wasn't enough to stop him. He recovered and kept going, running hard.

Decker instinctively turned to look for the ally with the torch. Behind him, Beryl was holstering her weapon. Their gazes locked, and she froze there just beyond the stone lip of the fountain, her eyes going wide.

Water beaded her mahogany curls, and the white top she wore was wet through from the splashing kicked up in the combat. Her nipples were clearly visible, dark and puckered under the fabric that clung to her breasts like a man's hand. The twin globes looked taut and full and tempting.

And she was his.

He'd fought for her and won. He would have killed for her. Instead he'd forced Tagliar to flee for his life.

Now he owned her.

The human intelligence that was slowly struggling back to life knew he should go after Tagliar. But his Beast was in control now, and his Beast wasn't interested in whatever threat Tagliar might be later. Its only focus was the woman who stared at him now, her expression stunned.

It took him a great effort, but at last he managed speech. "Come. Here."

Unconsciously, Beryl took a step back. Decker stood in the middle of the fountain, his shirt ripped off his back, thin runnels of blood rolling down his muscled torso from the countless cuts that marked him. His hair was slicked tight to his head, and water beaded on the taut planes of his face. And there was nothing at all human in his eyes.

"Come," he growled. "Here."

Beryl had made her living facing death, and fear was not a new feeling to her. Yet now she felt a fear both physical and sexual that was alien to her tough merc pragmatism, a fear not only of his strength and his vampire hunger, but a woman's fear of a fully aroused and dominant male who'd won a right to her.

"You'll kill me," Beryl said, and was instantly ashamed of the implied cowardice in the protest.

"Fought for you," Decker rumbled. "Mine."

Damn him. Beryl stared at him, taking in the muscled power of his body, the hard bulge of his arousal. He was right. He had fought for her, and he'd won. And if it had only been sex on his mind, she'd have gone to him at once, because even in her fear she felt the hot tug of his attraction. After all, she'd already given herself to him tonight.

But that had been the sane Decker, not this hungry vampire who'd clawed and bitten at Tagliar like a wolf. If she submitted to him now, there was no telling what he'd do to her.

And yet . . .

And yet Beryl St. Cloud had never backed down in her life. She'd made this man a vow, and she owed it to him to keep it. If she ran from him now, she might survive, but she'd be broken. Better to die than break.

He purred in pleasure as his woman came to meet him, her head up and her shoulders back, presenting her breasts to him like a gift. Decker reached for them, found he disliked the clammy feeling of her wet shirt, and impatiently ripped it open with a single pass of his hand. Freed, her breasts trembled, taut and pale and wet. A bead of water clung to the end of one nipple like milk. He wanted to suck it away.

But as he bent toward her, Decker looked up into her face. Beryl looked back, as expressionless as a warrior going into a battle that might kill her.

It was that impassivity which awoke the human in Decker from his bloody vampiric haze. And he realized that if he took her blood now, he wouldn't be able to stop. He'd kill her.

Decker looked down at her breast, at the hard, tight point waiting for him, and shuddered with a wave of lust. He couldn't let her go. He craved her wet heat clamping tight around his aching shaft, craved her long, slender female body, her warmth, her humanity. Her. He growled low in his throat at the tearing frustration.

Beryl looked up and met his gaze as he reached out a long hand and closed it around her forearm, his fingers almost burning her with their hectic heat. She sucked in a breath at the stark conflict in his eyes, the hunger struggling with conscience.

"This way," he rumbled.

Decker pulled her into the fountain's spray. Blindly she sloshed after him, wondering as falling drops hit her face what he had in mind. Then they were through the spray, moving toward the sculpture that stood in the center of the fountain. Constructed of countless sheets of metal polished to a mirror sheen, the structure reached almost to the vaulted ceiling ten meters overhead.

Decker pulled her to it. "Bend over."

She hesitated, frowning, until he caught the back of her head and gently forced it to lower. Automatically she grabbed one of the metal plates for balance, and saw Decker moving behind her in its polished surface. His big hands caught the waistband of her shorts and jerked them down her legs. The motion brought his face close to her back, and he froze there, his eyes widening, his nostrils flaring as though catching her scent. Then his eyes drifted closed, and he inhaled again as if deliberately savoring her. Decker's lips parted, revealing the white length of his fangs.

He jerked to his full height. Clenching his eyes shut, Decker threw his head back, visibly fighting for control even as his powerful hands caught her bare, slick hips to keep her from escaping.

Beryl stood motionless, sensing that if she moved she might shatter the delicate balance in the battle Decker obviously fought with himself.

His hands stroked over the curve of her bottom, up her back, brushing her ribs. Watching him in the sculpture's countless mirrors, she realized he was careful to keep his head up and back from her vulnerable body, as if struggling not to bite her.

He'd chosen this position to keep her safe.

Bill was right about Decker, Beryl thought, awed. Here he was, so far gone he could barely speak, yet still he fought to protect her from his own ravenous hunger. That said a lot about the strength of both his principles and his willpower.

For the first time since meeting Decker, Beryl relaxed, knowing that despite his feral, erotic appetite she was safe with him.

Then long masculine fingers slipped into the folds of her core, and all thought vanished from her head. As Beryl's eyes widened, Decker delicately began to strum her, testing her heat, her textures. At the same time, his other hand smoothed over the tight muscle of her thigh. She squirmed and swallowed a moan at the sudden, ferocious pleasure.

Behind her, Decker smiled a tight, lunatic smile. His Beast still clawed for control, but he'd had three hundred years to learn how to ignore his vampiric needs in the name of seduction. Instead he focused on the sight of her heart-shaped ass and the rosy, pouting petals of her sex. And those sweet, taut breasts that seemed to swell as he stared at them, silently pleading for his lips.

Beryl was everything he'd ever wanted, everything he'd ever dreamed about in all these lonely decades. A woman who wouldn't break, a woman who could keep up with his demands and give as good as she got.

Slowly, hungrily, he slipped a finger into her. She was still wet from her earlier climax, and he eased another finger in. Beryl caught her breath. And grew still wetter around him. Decker smiled and licked his fangs.

Beryl bit her dry lips, watching Decker in the mirrored surface of the sculpture. He stood behind her, his broad, powerful body dewed from the fountain spray, the thick tendons of his forearm working as he played with her. The feral expression that had chilled her earlier was fading, leaving only a ravenous sensuality and animal possessiveness. He reached for his fly, and despite herself, she shivered. Wanting to see him, she twisted her head to gaze at him over a shoulder as he freed himself. Long. His shaft was long and thick. Eager for her. Helplessly Beryl set her feet farther apart in welcome.

Decker's hands closed over her hips, drew her backward until the thick head brushed her bottom, found her wetness. And slid inward endlessly. Beryl ducked her head, biting down on her lower lip at the pleasure.

He growled in satisfaction and slowly began to stroke. She shut her eyes and tightened her grip on the plates in front of her. Cool water foamed around her ankles as Decker's hot cock tunneled and withdrew. She threw her head back, letting the spray from the fountain hit her face and dew on her skin. Each hard thrust pulled and twisted at her creamy flesh, his rigid length delving deep into her, feeding the emptiness of her own steadily sharpening hunger.

Opening her eyes, Beryl watched him take her in the mirrors, his handsome head thrown back so the cords of his neck stood in relief, the powerful muscles of his torso lacing as they worked to drive his length in and out of her.

His blue eyes opened and caught her watching him. Whatever he saw on her face spread a satisfied male smile across his own. Deliberately, possessively, Decker began to thrust harder and harder, driving the breath from her lungs and forcing her onto her toes. Pleasure raked her with needle claws each time his big shaft plunged in. She cried out, a wordless plea for mercy and for more, and he took her still faster, pumping ruthlessly.

Beryl felt her climax coming in driving waves as brutal as he was. Even as she opened her mouth to scream, Decker lifted her, pulling her away from the statue and into his arms. Her back hit his hard chest. He shifted his grip, caught her under her thighs and forced her right down on his straining cock. Strong vampire hands lifted her and dropped her and lifted again in time to the merciless pumping of his hips. She shrieked at the incredible sensation, her head falling back against his shoulder as he plunged even deeper than before, all the way inside. All the way to her heart.

She came then, her body twisting against his hands. He held her easily. Beryl was still quaking when he suddenly stiffened and drove himself to the hilt inside her, roaring out his pleasure as he came.

Long minutes passed as she hung in his arms, the spasms of after-shock gripping her sex. When it was over at last, she could only slump there, listening to the hot throb of his heart as his muscled chest worked behind her head.

"You okay?" His voice sounded hoarse, but otherwise back to normal.

"Yeah." Beryl grimaced at the rough croak her throat had produced.

"Can you stand?"

"I'm willing to try."

Gently he put her down. She gasped as her shaking thighs protested her weight and instinctively caught his wrist to brace herself. When she looked up, she was startled at the wary look in Decker's eyes, as if he expected her to lace into him for his feral sexuality.

Beryl said the first thing she thought of. "Well, that was fun. Where are my shorts?"

A grin of relief rather than humor spread over his handsome face. "Glad you enjoyed it. God knows I did." Spotting the bottoms, he stooped and fished them out for her, giving them a helpful wringing to get rid of the water before handing them back. Beryl struggled into them, swearing at the chilled, wet fabric.

"At least it's the middle of the graveyard shift, so there won't be many people around to wonder what the hell we've been up to," Decker told her, pouncing on the rags of her shirt floating past. "And my ship is docked on this deck, so we don't have far to go." He wrung the torn fabric and helped her slip into it before fastening his own pants. "Are you ready?"

"God, yes." She was shivering in her dripping clothing. "Please tell me you've got a ship suit or something I can put on until I can get my own stuff."

"I'm sure I've got something, though I won't promise it'll fit."

Beryl nodded, relaxing a little herself. Decker was definitely back to normal, an idea that filled her with a curious blend of relief and regret. As erotic as the encounter had been, she wasn't likely to forget the hungry Beast that lay beneath his civilized, intelligent facade.

"Wonder where that bastard Tagliar got to?" he murmured. His eyes caught the light and ignited with a spark of red.

And Beryl realized that Decker's Beast was never buried very deeply.

Chapter Three

The mercenary lifestyle isn't one that affords a lot of physical privacy, so being sopping wet and next to nude didn't bother Beryl all that much when she and Decker walked onto the station's hanger deck. She didn't even blink at the spacer who openly leered as she approached, but when the man went pale and backed up, she turned to see what had spooked him.

Behind her, Decker was baring his fangs.

Realizing she'd caught him threatening the spacer, Decker shut his mouth and looked sheepish. "Sorry." To change the subject, he said, "There's my ship."

Beryl turned, followed his pointing finger. And resisted the urge to gape. Compared to the troopships and fighters she'd crewed, the vessel was huge. Like most merchanters, it was laid out in the standard "Bucky Ball" shape, like two geodesic domes placed lip to lip, but she did spot one unusual feature. A series of bumps on the outer hull. Positron cannons. A lot of them.

"What did you do, raid an armory?" Beryl asked, doing a silent count and raising her brows at the total.

Decker grinned, as proudly wicked as a mischievous boy. "Hey, it's the merc motto, 'you can never have . . .' "

" '. . . too many guns.' " Beryl finished. "Yeah, I know." Watching a passenger airlock open and a ramp slide down from the ship's side, she asked, "By the way, why did you retire from the Raiders? You're immortal, so age obviously wasn't a factor."

"Actually, my immortality is the reason I retired," Decker started up the ramp, his long legs eating the distance into the primary hatch. "When you live damn near forever, you can only do something just so long before you get sick of it. And I got really sick of war."

"But why a merchanter? You don't seem the type to haul cargo."

"It wasn't what I had in mind," Decker admitted as they started down a long, narrow corridor. To either side of the bulkheads lay the cargo holds that took up the vast majority of the ship's considerable volume. If he'd followed the standard layout, both Decker's living quarters and the engines would lie at the vessel's core.

"I'd planned to go back to Earth," Decker continued. "Thing is, I'd been running the Raiders since the Vamp Legislation, and I didn't know how bad things had gotten. Once I'd been on the planet for a couple of months, I realized I didn't have the patience to deal with the laws that limit what vampires are allowed to do for a living, what relationships they can have. Not to mention all the intolerant sons of bitches who rapidly got on my nerves." He shrugged. "It finally dawned on me I could either lose my temper and kill a bigot, or head back to space. I've been here ever since. It's lonely, but nobody gives me any shit."

Beryl nodded. Mercs in general had a low tolerance for bureaucracy and rules, and she wasn't surprised Decker shared that attitude. "Still, those fifteen years must have felt like a prison sentence."

He shrugged his broad shoulders again. "Like anything else, it's what you make out of it. I've found ways to keep life interesting." Decker grinned suddenly. "You, for example. By the way, we'll need to stock up on food supplies for you. Give the ship's computer a list of what you need, and I'll order it."

She nodded as they reached the end of the corridor and stepped into the lift. "Quarters," Decker said, and the lift smoothly moved off at a steep diagonal.

He yawned, one hand lifting to cover his mouth not quite fast enough to hide his fangs. Beryl was reminded of a lazy tiger. " 'S'cuse me. You may want to order in dinner, since I don't have anything on hand. Just charge it to the ship."

"What registry?"

Decker grinned. *"Bram Stoker."* He eyed her, then sighed and rattled off the ship's ID code. Beryl had the feeling she'd missed a joke.

The lift doors opened on Decker's living quarters, and he led her on a tour. Spacers of every sort tended to have cluttered living areas, chock full of keepsakes and toys to break up the lonely monotony of space travel, but Beryl had never seen anything as opulent as Decker's shipboard home.

Some kind of early rock played in the background, a haunting blend of sax and drum and guitar. Thick carpet in vivid shades covered the deck, and plants and artwork were everywhere, filling niches in the walls or occupying graceful stands carved from genuine wood.

The bridge, where most solo spacers did their sleeping, was dominated by a circular bed inset in the floor in a shallow pit. The mattress was heaped with colorful silk pillows and covered with a vast silky black fur throw, and around the pit clustered enough plants to stock a jungle. Beyond lay the ship's command center with its arching control panels and viewing screens, all of them up-to-date tech.

Beryl cleared her throat and said, "This is . . . impressive."

Decker laughed. "You mean it's a bit much. True." The bridge door opened, and an ink black cat the size of a lynx glided in. He stooped to pick up the enormous feline, giving it an affectionate stroke. "Basically I've turned the *Stoker* into my own private pleasure palace, pets and all." He gave her a wicked grin. "All I needed was a harem."

"A sadly under-supplied harem," she observed dryly.

"I wouldn't say that." His long fingers scratched under the chin of the big cat, which rewarded him with a rumbling purr. "By the way, this is Lestat, so named because he likes to rub up against you and then take a chunk out of your nearest juicy body part."

Beryl eyed the cat cautiously. "I'll keep that in mind."

"That would definitely be a good idea." He strolled toward one of the bulkheads and tapped a spot. A section of the wall slid back to reveal a well-stocked closet. Putting down the cat, Decker reached into the closet and pulled out a one-piece jumpsuit he handed to her. "One of my ship suits. It should do until you can have your own gear delivered. It'll be a bit baggy, but it's dry and in one piece."

"Which is more than I can say for my current wardrobe." Eager to get out of her dripping clothes, she started stripping, then paused. "You don't mind?"

"Who, me?"

Decker watched with acute male interest as she undressed. Beryl felt a flicker of unease mixed with feminine awareness that was foreign to her normal merc practicality. Trying to ignore him, she tugged on the ship suit, which was just as baggy as he'd predicted. Luckily the sleeves and legs were short, so at least she didn't have to roll up the cuffs. She slanted another wary look in his direction.

The vampire broke the rising tension with another jaw-cracking yawn. "Sorry. Look, I'm going to have to hit the bunk. Between the fight and our other . . . activities, I'm done. Care to join me?"

"Not just yet. I'm not particularly sleepy at the moment."

"Well, feel free to curl up when you're ready. In the meantime, the com is over there; it's pretty standard, but you can ask the ship's comp if you need help with it . . ."

"I think I can figure it out."

Decker gave her another quicksilver grin. "Yes, I'm sure you can." He headed toward the sleep pit, stripping off his shirt and kicking free of his pants as he went. This time it was Beryl's turn to watch with appreciation.

Decker had a tough, strong body, broad and well-muscled, as beautifully cut as a Greek statue. He stepped down onto the mattress, giving her an appreciative view of his tight, firm butt and long legs before he more or less fell into the fur. Within seconds he was as bonelessly asleep as an exhausted child.

"I guess you're entitled," Beryl muttered, and went to familiarize herself with the ship's control console. It was pretty standard, except for the banks of automatics that controlled all those positron cannons. She'd seen merc cruisers less well-armed.

Content that she knew the layout of everything important, Beryl ordered the comp to download a list of menus from the station's delivery restaurants, made a selection and had the computer call it in. She made a second call to her hotel to arrange to pay her bill and have her bag sent over to the *Stoker*.

Then, stretching, she turned and froze in sheer erotic appreciation. Decker lay in the bed with his muscled arms flung wide, his thick cock hard with a nocturnal erection. His mouth was open in a slight smile that revealed the points of his fangs.

Beryl grinned. "Bet I know what you're dreaming about."

Her gaze slipped to his erection. She could almost feel its width plowing her again as Decker possessed her cunt and drank her blood. Beryl had never been . . . taken like that before. For her, sex had always been either a race for pleasure or a slow exchange of comfort. But Decker had swept her into a hurricane of sexual sensation and given her no choice but utter surrender.

Frowning, Beryl headed for the lift to wait for the deliverybot. She wasn't used to being so out of control. One of the things she'd learned early as a merc was that losing your grip could get you killed. A little fear was good, kept you on your toes, got you thinking, but terror was pure, caustic poison, freezing the muscles and the mind, setting you up for whoever wanted you. She suspected the wild lust she'd known with Decker was just as bad.

Besides, her judgement about men in general was badly flawed. God knew Daveed had royally worked her over, appealing to her need for companionship, for closeness, only to set her up for betrayal.

The thought triggered a familiar surge of rage that Beryl automatically fought down to manageable levels. Zahn was dead now, he'd been dead for months. There was no point in indulging in anger now. It was all gone out the airlock.

Just like the rest of her life.

As soon as the thought crossed her mind, she rejected it. Self-pity was one emotion she couldn't tolerate.

The plain fact was that her situation had changed. She was broke and dependent on a vampire for protection against another vampire. As part of the deal, she had to keep her own vamp sexually satisfied. There was no point in bitching, she just had to play the situation out as best she could and wait for the wheel to turn. It always did.

One way or another.

The lift doors opened. Beryl strode down the corridor, stepping out the main airlock to discover the deliverybot still hadn't arrived. Sighing, she folded her arms and leaned against the *Stoker*'s slick, cold hull to wait.

Patience, like controlling her anger, was something Beryl St. Cloud had learned very well.

Brooding, Beryl stared out across the huge deck as cargo bots scurried around loading and unloading the surrounding ships. Her best course was to keep her relationship with Decker on a business footing. She'd made a deal with him to provide sex and blood for his protection. She'd just make damn sure to keep her emotions out of it . . .

"Well, well, it's the deviant with the vampire boyfriend."

She snapped her head around and found the mercs from the bar standing at the base of the ramp. Two of them anyway, the woman and one of the men, both of them sneering.

Beryl grinned back in lunatic delight. She was suddenly in the mood for a good brawl. And it damn well had nothing to do with Decker. "Well, well, it's the greenie trying to prove her stones," she purred.

"I am not," Clarke hissed, "a greenie."

"Honey, you're so green your hair's grass."

Clarke flushed and pulled her viblade. "Let's see what color your blood is—if there's any left."

"Sorry, darlin', I'm saving it all for my one true love." Beryl fell into a crouch.

"Pervert." Bigotry and bloodlust in her eyes, Clarke charged up the ramp.

Now that the fight had started, Beryl's mind ticked off the tactical situation with the cool of a targeting computer. Clarke was armed, a considerable advantage, but she'd blunted it by pulling the knife too soon and attacking uphill. She'd have done better to hold the weapon back and wait for Beryl's attack.

Instead Clarke tried to impale her on the viblade like a cocktail olive.

Beryl pivoted out of the way, grabbed Clarke's knife hand and used the momentum of the blonde's charge to slam her into the airlock hatch. Pinning her there, Beryl slowly twisted Clarke's blade hand back while applying agonizing pressure to the merc's elbow with her free hand. The combination proved too much, and Clarke dropped the viblade with a curse.

"Computer, open hatch," Beryl called, and stepped back just as the airlock opened. The merc fell in with a yelp. "Close hatch and ignore commands from occupant." The computer obeyed, trapping Clarke between the inner and outer hatches as Beryl pivoted to face the remaining merc.

He still stood at the foot of the ramp as though he hadn't bothered to move, arms folded, an assessing expression in his eyes. "Who are you?"

"Beryl St. Cloud."

He nodded slowly. "Occam's Raiders. Thought I recognized you. Richard Keven of Andrikov's Commandos."

Beryl's brows flew up. "We tussled with you on Jovan a couple of years back. That was a hell of a fight. And how is the Black Russian?"

"Still cusses you when he's sober. When he's drunk, he says you're the best he ever faced." Keven paused. "And he's right. What the hell are you doing with a vampire?"

"It's a long story." A muffled thumping vibrated the hatch. "And I don't think Clarke has the patience to listen."

"Let her stew, the little idiot." He grimaced. "I can't believe she threw away her advantage like that."

"She just needs seasoning. And maybe a little less desire to prove the size of her stones."

"I'm just not sure she'll live long enough to get 'em."

"Hey, we did." As Keven chuckled, Beryl spotted a vehicle gliding toward them on a bed of antigravity. "Unless I'm mistaken, that's the deliverybot with dinner. Care to join me?" Another series of thuds. "I've even got enough for your friend."

"We've already eaten, thanks." He sighed. "I suppose you'd better turn the little greenie loose. I obviously need to give her more combat training before she gets somebody killed. Like me."

Beryl considered the idea, then nodded. "Open outer hatch, computer." She ducked as Clarke came out swinging.

"None of that, you little twit," roared Keven, striding up the ramp. "That's Admiral St. Cloud. She'll eat your ass like a cocktail cracker."

"Admiral St. . . . ?" Clarke must have heard of Beryl. She subsided immediately, then rallied enough for a sullen growl. "I want my viblade."

Beryl nodded sweetly and handed it to Keven. "And no, you can't have it back," he told her. "You'll cut your own arm off. Let's go, we've got some remedial hand to hand to go over."

Keven led Clarke off, chewing her out all the way.

Beryl was still grinning when she collected her meal from the deliverybot.

Carrying the hot pack of food, Beryl walked onto the bridge and flopped into the center seat. Decker still lay in glorious nudity in the bed pit, though she noticed his erection had subsided.

Too bad.

Forking moo goo gai pan into her mouth, she eyed him. He certainly made great scenery. She'd gotten out of the habit of noticing male bodies because ogling your subordinates was bad for morale, but in Decker's case it was safe to make an exception. Which was a good thing, Beryl admitted silently, since she'd been ogling him since she'd met him.

Munching, she meditated on the hard, rippling territory. He'd honed his body to perfection, though with his vampire strength, he could have gotten away with flab and still kicked any human's ass. But then Tagliar would probably have kicked his.

Beryl sucked her fork and wondered if Decker had to fight vampire duels on a regular basis. Of course, that build might also fall under the general category of maximizing your advantages, a solid policy for any smart commander. Or it might just be a way to attract girls.

Beryl grimaced and shoveled in another bite, chewing vengefully. Why the hell should it bother her that Decker had spent three hundred years seducing women? His past had nothing to do with her. She'd never cared about Daveed's sexual history.

Then again, maybe she should have.

Beryl jabbed a piece of chicken viciously. Something furry brushed her ankles, and she looked down to see Lestat looking at her in an obvious demand for food. "Sure, cat. Decker's pets have to stick together."

But as she plucked the bit of meat off her fork and gave it to the animal, she realized what she'd just said.

A pet? Her? *Screw that.*

Beryl St. Cloud was damn well nobody's pet. She'd won two wars, six space battles, seventeen ground engagements, and more bar brawls than she could shake a bottle of ale at. She had her own power, her own hunger, and it was time her vampire found out she also had teeth.

Beryl put the hot pack down on the deck with a thump, not even noticing when the cat buried its muzzle into it. Slapping the seal of the ship suit open, she shucked it off and tossed the bundle across the bridge without looking to see where it landed. She stalked down into the pit and crouched, naked, to stare at all that sprawled muscular male nudity, at the sharply cut features that looked almost innocent in sleep.

All hers.

She expected him to wake the moment she touched him, since every merc she'd ever known was a light sleeper. But Decker was also a vampire, and vampires slept like deck plates, as Beryl discovered while delicately stroking the powerful arch of his ribs. His skin felt wonderfully smooth and warm under her fingertips, but he didn't so much as twitch an eyebrow. She grinned, wickedly intrigued. *Let's see how long he can sleep through this.*

A lovely ruff of chest hair spread over his pecs and down over his belly tempting her fingers to comb through it, savor its silky texture. Beryl sighed, enjoying the sensuous contrast between the soft hair and the hard, warm flesh that lay beneath it. She couldn't remember the last time she'd touched a man just for the pure tactile pleasure of it. Exploring Decker made her realize she'd been cheating herself.

So Beryl set about savoring her vampire, discovering the way muscle wove around bone in each of his massive shoulders, the thick bundles of biceps and triceps, the hard beauty of forearms cabled with tendon. His long, agile fingers caught her attention, with their intriguing white ridges that must date back to his human life, back before medical science could instantly eliminate scars. Delighted, Beryl went on to the arch of his ribs, broad ripples curving toward the rock hard plates of the abdominals that lay over his belly like armor.

His cock was in full, glorious erection, its flushed head hovering over his navel.

Her gaze flew to his face, but his eyes were still closed, though she could glimpse the tips of his fangs in his slight smile.

Beryl's answering smile was predatory. She wanted him *now*, without even waiting for him to wake up. She wanted to take him as mercilessly as he'd taken her after his fight with Tagliar. Take him and own him.

She didn't pause to reconsider. She just swung one leg over his hips, grabbed his stiff length in one hand, and impaled herself in one delicious swoop. She'd grown so wet inside that his cock slid in like a knife into clotted cream. Biting her lip to stifle a moan, she looked down at him.

"Beryl!" Decker's blue eyes were wide and startled, his handsome features dazed. Beryl gave him a triumphant smirk and rose, then sank down on him again. He reached for her, but she grabbed his hands and pushed them back down to the fur spread.

"Forget it, vampire," she growled. "This time you're mine."

He blinked. She glared back. Both of them knew he could break her grip like an infant's. Instead Beryl felt his big body go slack under hers, surrendering. She hummed in satisfaction and pushed off for her next stroke.

Her deliciously wet heat stroked Decker's shaft, her full breasts bouncing as she ground down on him. For once he was utterly stunned. In three hundred years no woman who'd known he was a vampire had ever tried to seduce him.

Seduce hell, Decker thought, staring up into her fierce, beautiful dark eyes. *She's practically raping me.*

He licked his fangs and fought the desire to grab her, roll her under him, and plunge deep. Clamping his hands into the fur spread under him, Decker gritted his teeth and held on. He could sense how much she needed to be in control, and he was damn well going to give it to her.

But God, that long, lithe body, those gorgeous breasts . . . He eyed her bouncing nipples hungrily and promised himself a taste later.

Beryl leaned back to grab her ankles with both hands, seeking a deeper penetration as she rolled her hips hard. Her slick, hot walls slid up and down his long shaft, and the taut arch of her spine pointed her breasts at the ceiling, the erect stems of her nipples in tempting relief.

His Hunger boiled up, carnivorous and savage. He fought it back.

Sweat rolled down Beryl's ribs as she pumped up and down, her body arching until her hair brushed his ankles. His glistening shaft slid in and out between her thighs with a speed that made his head swim. The lush eroticism of that sight was almost more than he could stand, and he had to fight his body's leap toward pleasure. If he came too soon . . . But then she writhed over him with a low moan that quickly built to a sustained primal scream, her core clamping and releasing his shaft.

His control exploded. Decker's hands shot up, closed hard over her slim shoulders, pulled her down and under him in one powerful sweep without even breaking the connection between them. His Hunger roared through his defenses, stoked by the purely masculine lust she'd built so relentlessly.

Beryl's dark eyes flared wide for just a moment in surprise before his head swooped for the delicate white length of her throat. The smell of her skin filled his skull with female musk and the rich copper of her blood. Quivering with the force of his need, he sank his fangs into her until the burning red liquor flooded his mouth, and his cock, sunk deep in her wet depths, hardened even more.

Beryl gasped in shock at the warm velvet of his lips and the sharp edge of his fangs. For a moment there was pain, but the burn of pleasure followed, pumping with each pull of his mouth as he drank. Her fading orgasm hammered back into life. She shrieked.

LINK.

A psychic vampire bond snapped into place between them like a door banging open in Decker's mind. Suddenly he *was* Beryl, feeling himself, the width of his own cock, the edge of his own fangs. He could feel what she felt as she came, the pulsing beat deep in her sex, the fire in her nipples, the ache in her throat. The echo of her pleasure drove his own even higher, and he fed it back to her, showing her how her own wet silk walls clasped his cock as her smooth throat arched against his mouth.

She felt him. He was there with her, in her mind, raw and male, strong and dark, vampire lover taking everything she had and funneling it back to her in pounding, glorious waves. There was no separation between them, no way to tell who was Beryl and who was Decker. She, who'd always been alone, at last knew what it was like to touch another, feel another, be another.

And it was too much. *Get out of my mind!*

"Shit!" Decker shot away from her as though something had picked him up and blown him back.

Still pulsing hot from the pleasure, Beryl groggily lifted her head. He crouched at the other side of the sleeping pit, a wary expression on his angular, handsome face. One big hand rubbed his jaw as though he'd taken a punch. "You know, for somebody with no psi," he grumbled, "you have a hell of a psychic force field."

Beryl licked her lips, feeling dazed. "What are you talking about? What happened?"

"We linked. Mentally. Vamps do that, when the emotional connection is strong." He shrugged his wide shoulders. "Then you tossed me the hell out of your head."

"Oh." There didn't seem to be anything else to say. She sat up and curled her arms around herself, feeling suddenly cold.

Decker studied her intently, then gave her a small sympathetic smile. "Mind if I hold you? I promise not to do whatever it was that pissed you off." He paused. "Ever again."

She considered it. "Okay."

Moving back to her side, Decker pulled her gently into his arms. Beryl sighed, feeling his warmth and strength enfold her again. Gradually, she began to relax.

"You know," he said, after a long pause, "Linking really isn't so bad. I think if you gave it a chance, you'd like it."

"Oh, I liked it," Beryl said, remembering the pure, bright core that was Decker. It had felt so seductive, so delicious. So warm. "I think maybe that's the problem."

"What do you mean?"

His heart was thudding under her ear. She relaxed against his chest, feeling the hard muscle under her cheek. This she knew how to deal with, bodies, flesh. Sex. This was safe. Allowing him into her mind was not.

Beryl went lax against Decker as she sank quickly into sleep without answering his question. No surprise, really. She was exhausted.

He frowned, knowing he probably shouldn't have fed from her so soon after the last time. He'd better make sure she had a session in the ship's regeneration capsule to build up her blood again.

Thoughtfully, Decker combed his fingers through the tangled silk of her hair and listened to her heartbeat slowing into the languid rhythms of sleep. He'd never linked with a woman so completely after such a short time. Hell, he rarely managed to link with his partners at all, since the act required a special kind of kinship he'd encountered only a few times in his long life.

Yet Beryl had pushed him away. He couldn't help but wonder why.

The next day, Beryl, Decker and several cargo bots pitched in to load a shipment into the *Bram Stoker*'s holds.

"Hey, boss," the *Stoker*'s computer said, its feminine voice echoing in the huge space.

Decker put down a crate with a grunt. "What?"

"I just got a call from a Zalman Wirth. Asks if we can run some emergency medical supplies to Dyson's World. Want to talk to him?"

"Sure." Decker walked toward the intercom pickup, leaving Beryl standing frozen with a crate in her hands.

Dyson's World. The scene of her worst defeat, and the last planet she'd ever wanted to set foot on again.

But she wasn't calling the shots this time; Decker was. Besides, the load was medical supplies, and she damn well wasn't going to say a word about it.

Jaw set, Beryl put the crate away and picked up another from the pallet.

His conversation finished, Decker returned a few minutes later. Whatever he read on her face must have given her away. "What's wrong?" His eyes widened. "Shit. Dyson's World. Wasn't that where. . . ."

"Yeah. Don't worry about it." She hefted a box at random and stashed it. "War's over, I'm not a merc anymore. It's done."

Decker studied her with eyes that seemed to see right to her core. "Wirth said they've been hit by Red Plague, and the death toll is climbing fast. They have to have the meds to save the dying and inoculate the rest, or I'd call him back and tell him to kiss off."

Beryl looked up in surprise. "Why would you do something like that?"

"It bothers you."

"I'm a big girl now, Deck." She shrugged. "Besides, this is your business. You can't blow off a commission because your resident piece of ass has bad memories of a business partner."

"I don't see you as a piece of ass, Beryl."

To her surprise, she realized he was serious. "Why not?"

Decker turned and hefted a huge crate that should have taken three men to lift. "A lot of reasons. Including that link we had last night."

She forced herself not to stiffen as he went on, "I learned a hell of a lot about you in those few seconds. Some of it I already knew, like your courage, integrity and sense of honor. I'd found out about those when you came to me after the fight with Tagliar, though most women would have taken one look at me and run like hell." He set the box down, adjusted its position. "But during the link I also discovered that you're hurting over that bastard Zahn more than you let on." He looked up, locking her in an intent blue stare. "I can help you with that."

Beryl set her teeth. "Look, Decker, I appreciate your protection from Tagliar, but that's all I need from you. Any other problems I have I'm more than capable of solving myself." Pivoting, she grabbed a crate. "Where do you want this?"

Decker gave her a narrow glance, then gestured. She stalked off to put the box down where he'd instructed.

Brooding, Decker watched Beryl stack crates, and knew there was something growing between them he'd never felt before.

I'm just horny.

Unfortunately he'd known himself too long to pull off that particular lie. True, he was lonely, and he'd probably be attracted to any receptive female after his long celibacy. But Beryl was something more. Her toughness, decency and strength demanded his respect just as her body demanded his desire. What he felt might not be love, not yet, but it was recognition.

She was not only his mate, she was his match. And after three hundred years, Jim Decker knew just how rare it was to see your heart mirrored in another.

The trouble was, Beryl didn't recognize their rare spiritual connection, and she certainly didn't realize how precious it was. He was going to have his hands full getting her to see what was happening between them. And as stubborn as she was, she wouldn't make it easy.

But no matter how long it took, he damn well wasn't going to give up.

Chapter Four

Decker brought the ship out of SuperC, punched in the realspace coordinates for Dyson's World, and faced Beryl. She sprawled in the navigator's seat, Lestat draped across her lap as her long, clever fingers scratched behind his furry black ears. *Beryl and that cat have a lot in common*, he thought. *No matter how they purr when you stroke them, it doesn't mean love.*

He grimaced, suspecting he'd just crossed the line into being a prick. For God's sake, the woman had given him a month of hot blood and hotter sex. What more could a vampire want?

Everything, whispered a little voice he'd been trying to ignore without much success.

"I've got a feeling I should apologize about last night," he said, partly to silence that damn little voice.

Beryl slanted him an amused look. "And well you should. All those screaming orgasms gave me a sore throat." Letting her head fall against the back of her seat, she shut her eyes with a cream-licking smile. "Inconsiderate bastard."

He cleared his throat. "I meant the psilink. I know you don't like 'linking,' but honest to God, it's not intentional."

Beryl's gaze slid away from his. "I never said I didn't like it."

The question was out before he could censor it. "So why do you always toss me out on my ass?"

The cat leaped from Beryl's lap, leaving her fingers to beat a quick tatoo on her thigh. "Decker, it's not intentional."

"Yeah, there seems to be a lot of that going around," he muttered, and winced as he heard the edge in his own voice.

Beryl snapped him a look. "Are you trying to pick a fight, Deck?"

"No, but I'm losing interest in avoiding one."

"Well, don't." Evidently deciding to take the vampire by the fangs, she leaned forward and braced her elbows on her thighs, fixing him with an earnest stare. "Decker, I get the impression you're trying to make our deal into something it's not. And I'm telling you, you're going to screw it up."

That did it. "The only one screwing things up is you, because you refuse to admit this is becoming a lot more than a business deal."

"Look, I need your protection, and you need my blood. It's a very simple arrangement and it's mutually satisfying, but it ain't love. If you start calling it something else, it's going to blow up all over us." Her fingers were beating that tatoo on her thigh again.

"Daveed really worked you over, didn't he?"

"Jesus." The muscles in her jaw rippled. "He's got nothing to do with this, Decker."

"Oh, yes he does, and it's a good thing the son of a bitch is dead, or I'd kill him." Figuring he'd better get out before he said something he couldn't take back, Decker rose and stalked toward the lift.

"Where are you going?"

"To check those damn medical supplies we're supposed to be delivering."

"We start our approach to the docking station in fifteen minutes," Beryl reminded him. "You'll have to pilot us in."

Decker didn't look back. "You do it. You're the one who's always got to be in control."

Beryl growled a few choice mercenary phrases toward the hatch he'd closed behind him.

Men. They had to make everything so damn complicated.

She spun her chair to face the control panel. On the three view screens above it, Dyson's World hung in space, a perfect glowing sapphire of a planet. Her irritation gave way before a thrust of pain.

This was where it had started. Daveed's betrayal, the deaths of her people, and her destruction.

She'd fought with Daveed that day too, when her merc troopship first fell into orbit. *"You never let me get close,"* he'd said, his full mouth sulky under the long fringe of his bangs. *"The only thing you really want from me is cock, because the only thing you really care about is your goddamned Occam's Raiders."*

Beryl watched the lovely blue globe swell in the view screen. "Was that why you let them buy you and destroy us all, Daveed? Because I couldn't give you enough?"

But that was one question she'd never get an answer for. Daveed was dead, along with far too many of the Raiders who'd depended on her to lead them to safety. Leaving Beryl to grieve and wonder.

If she'd been willing to give Daveed more, would they all be alive?

Docking the *Stoker* was a bitch. The merchant was so damn big piloting it into even a space station's cavernous maw took a skilled ʋand on the stick. Beryl managed it, though not without a few choice words for Decker and his attitude.

No sooner had the ship settled on its struts than a call came in from the hospital representative who'd ordered the shipment, a surprisingly burly man who looked more like a star marine than a paper pusher. They exchanged pleasantries and arranged to meet at the *Stoker's* primary airlock.

Beryl shut down everything and went to the hold to give Decker a hand, but when she got there, he hefted the crate onto one broad shoulder and told her with chilling courtesy that he didn't need help.

Simmering, she trailed him to the main hatch. While they waited for the airlock to cycle, she eyed his rigid profile. "So Decker, how long are you going to freeze me out?"

He rewarded her impudence with a glacial stare. "Until I get hungry enough to want a fucking snack."

Beryl refused to let the sting show on her face, but he apparently sensed it anyway. "Hey, that's all we are to each other, right? I'm the bodyguard, you're the ass. Who could want anything more?"

"Don't be a prick."

"Oh, why not? I'm so good at it." He banged a big fist into the airlock control button.

Beryl's mouth was open to retort when the hatch opened.

Tagliar stood on the other side, big, blond and grinning, an ironwood knife in one fist. "Hiya, Deck." He lunged while Beryl was still blinking in shock.

"Decker!" She instinctively grabbed him to pull him back from Tagliar's attack, but she was too late. His big body lurched and stiffened, and the crate hit the ground with a crash. Decker toppled, sheer dead weight pulling him out of her arms.

"Deck . . ." Beryl whispered in horror.

Hard vampire hands yanked her forward to hit Tagliar's massive body with a jaw-snapping jar. "Ah," he purred, "alone at last."

Her grief turned to instant rage. "You cowardly son of. . . ."

Tagliar's mouth mashed off the end of the insult with a vicious faux kiss. Gagging, Beryl managed to jerk back just enough to lift one leg and fumble at the top of her boot. The bastard had hurt Decker. He was damn well going to pay.

Tagliar pulled back at last, his grin was white and reptilian on his handsome face. "Nice. Very nice. I'm going to enjoy this." His big hand came up, stroked the side of her face. "I just love the taste of a woman's blood when I rape her. It's got that certain zing. . . ."

At that moment, Beryl's fingers found the wooden hilt protruding from her boot top. She snatched the knife free. "Which is why I started carrying ironwood, you son of a bitch."

And she drove the blade into the vampire's side, the whole of her body behind the thrust.

Tagliar grunted and staggered. Grimly triumphant, she waited for him to fall.

Instead the vampire caught himself, his lips pulling back from his fangs in a snarl. "You'll pay for that, bitch." Tagliar's head started to lower toward hers.

"When hell freezes over," Decker said, rising behind him like Banquo's ghost. His blood-slicked hand caught Beryl's around the knife hilt.

Tagliar tried to turn, but the blade dug deeper with Decker's strength behind it. He froze. "Goddamn it, haven't you died *yet*?"

"Nothing counts but the heart, Tag," Decker said. "And you missed. I won't." He drove the knife upward, dragging Beryl's hand along for the ride as he cleaved right through Tagliar's ribs.

The assassin roared and slapped Beryl away like a poker chip. She flew through the air and slammed into the interior airlock doors so high she slid down a meter and a half before she hit the floor.

Everything blacked out.

When she faded back to full awareness, Tagliar lay sprawled on the deck. Decker was bent double, his hands braced on his knees, his handsome face gray, bright crimson slicking him from midchest to knee. Beryl realized not all the blood was Tagliar's when his eyes rolled back and he collapsed across his enemy.

Tagliar might have missed the heart, but he sure as hell hit something.

"Shit." Beryl rolled to her feet and lunged for Decker, ignoring the resultant detonation of pain in her concussed skull. Grabbing a double fistful of Decker's bloody shirt, she ripped it away. No stranger to injuries after fifteen years as a merc, she still blanched at what she saw. Blood was gushing from the wound as though Tag had nicked the aorta.

Cursing, she balled up the shirt and mashed the wadded material against the wound, hoping pressure would slow the bleeding. "Computer," Beryl yelled toward the hull pickup, "call the station's mediunit. We've got a critical here. And send down the portable so we can stabilize him."

Which was when a female voice demanded, "What does it take to kill you, bitch—a starkiller nuke?"

Startled, Beryl jerked her head around to see six armored soldiers with laser rifles trained on her from the airlock hatch. In the lead stood a tall woman dressed in a dark blue uniform of the Dyson Space Service. Judging from the elaborate braid on her padded shoulders, she must be the station commander.

She was also one of the most beautiful women Beryl had ever seen. Her features were strong and lovely, and her skin was the color of clover honey, the golden tone a stark contrast to her vivid turquoise eyes and curling red hair.

Beryl's stomach lurched in recognition followed by sick fear. "Nice seeing you again, Lacey," she said, fighting to hide her reaction. "Call a mediunit, would you? This man is dying."

Lacey curled a well-shaped lip. "Don't be an idiot. He's a vampire. He's already healing." Compassion had never been Arith Lacey's forte.

"God, Lace, even a vampire couldn't survive a chest wound like . . ." Beryl lifted the sopping rag of his shirt. The bleeding had already stopped.

Lacey strolled over on her long, booted legs, turquoise eyes assessing the damage. "That sonofabitch Tagliar *did* miss, didn't he?"

Beryl went numb. "You hired him."

"You bet your ass." Her lush mouth curled into a smile that suggested torture chambers and long screams. "You know, St. Cloud, when Decker wakes up, he'll have to replace all that blood. Which means he'll be one hungry vamp. And I know just who to feed to him. . . ."

Beryl braced her legs and concentrated on staying upright between the two troopers who held each arm. She didn't think they'd broken her ribs, but she wasn't willing to swear to it.

On the other hand, she was dead sure she could feel a painful smorgasbord of bruises blooming all over her body. Lacey and her armored buddies liked to play rough.

After they'd all gotten bored with beating her, the guards had marched Beryl off to the chilly confines of the space station's brig. Then, as if that wasn't severe enough, they headed right through to solitary confinement, an area even less inviting than the rest of the jail. Racks of horizontal tubes were sunk into the bulkheads, each holding a mattress barely wide enough to accommodate a man's shoulders. If you didn't have claustrophobia when they put you in, you would by the time they pulled you out. It reminded Beryl of a morgue, which, under the circumstances, wasn't exactly comforting.

"What I want to know," she said to Lacey around a cut and stinging lip, "is how the hell you got in Occam's Raiders to begin with."

The redhead was watching a trooper load Decker into one of the tube bunks. He was still out cold. "Our boy here has a weakness for a pretty face." Lacey laughed. Beryl had never liked Lacey's laugh, and now she realized why; the woman sounded like she spent her off hours burning puppies with a laser torch. "Do you know, he once reprimanded me for being too bloodthirsty? Imagine, a vampire calling *me* bloodthirsty."

"Did it ever occur to you that should tell you something?"

Beryl tried to duck the backhand she got for that comment, but the troopers held her still.

"You've got a very annoying holier-than-thou streak, St. Cloud," Lacey said. "You really ought to muzzle it. Particularly considering I haven't forgotten the way you drummed me out of the company."

Beryl snorted. "You were lucky I didn't torch your ass. And don't think I wasn't tempted. The Raiders don't beat prisoners, but you just couldn't keep your hands off that kid. He was, what? Fourteen?"

"Fifteen." Lacey leaned too close, vivid eyes narrowing. "And by the time I get done with you, you're going to know just how he felt."

"Yeah, well." Beryl spat blood onto the deck, aiming for a polished boot. "And next time I'm going to torch you until you burst into flame."

Lacey came around the tube after her. The gut punch buckled her knees, but Beryl stiffened them. "Now that we've established we both hate each other's guts," she wheezed, when the redhead had stepped back and the urge to vomit had faded, "why are you still holding a grudge? God knows you must have been sacked before, what with your charming personality."

"This isn't about your firing me, you idiot." Lacey's pretty turquoise eyes narrowed to evil slits. "This is about you *failing* me."

"The only one I failed is that kid by not shooting you."

"Don't play stupid, St. Cloud, you know what you did. The one thing, the only thing, I've ever counted on you for, *and you fucked it up.*" There was a chilling glitter in Lacy's fixed stare that was a long way from sane.

"I have no idea what you're talking about."

"You know exactly what I'm talking about." She reached out a long arm and snagged Beryl by the collar, jerking her onto her toes. "You let Daveed Zahn die, you stupid little cunt."

Beryl, astonished, hung in the big woman's fist. "Daveed died in an ambush."

"I know that. Who the hell do you think set it up?"

Her heels thumped into the deck as Lacey dropped her and turned to pace too quickly. Beryl blinked, wondering if the ringing in her ears was interfering with her hearing. "You arranged the ambush?"

"Of course. And it worked like a charm, didn't it? You and your Raiders waltzed right in."

Beryl suddenly remembered laughing dark eyes and a strong arm curling around Lacey's waist. "Jamin died in that attack, Lacey. He was your lover for six years. Doesn't that mean anything to you?"

Lacey looked startled, as if she could see no reason why it should. "But Daveed was the one I really wanted," she said, in a chillingly reasonable voice. "You know that. He told you so, and then you kicked me out of the Raiders."

"You were having an affair with Daveed?" Beryl was more stunned than she'd been when she'd discovered he'd sold out the Raiders. She could imagine her gentle lover doing something stupid out of hurt and anger, but he'd never sleep with this borderline psychotic.

"Drop the astonished act, St. Cloud. I know damn well he went running to you, because you sacked me a week later."

"I sacked you because I caught you beating that kid."

"Bullshit. We both know the little bastard deserved it. Not that it matters, I wasn't out of work long. They were throwing this lovely little war right here." She folded her arms and rocked back on her heels, smug. "High Command recognized my talent."

Everything began making an ugly kind of sense. "And then the Loyalists hired us."

"It was perfect," Lacey agreed, her face lighting up. "Because I knew the Raiders so well, High Command sent me into Loyalist territory to spy on you. And that's where I found Daveed in a dancebar."

She just might throw up on Lacey's polished black boots. "Oh, God."

"He was drunk, and he wanted to talk. In retrospect, I really don't think he was tracking well enough to wonder what I was doing there. He must have assumed I was working for the Loyalists."

"He told you our plans." And suddenly Beryl could see his face, in the moment before the guerillas had closed in, in the moments before he'd died. Stark white, shocked. *"My God, I've killed us. This is all because of me . . ."* Once the battle was over, Beryl had remembered what he'd said and thought he'd sold them out. So had the other Raiders who'd overheard. It was a logical assumption, because Daveed had been the only one other than Beryl herself who had known the route she'd planned.

"You'd just had a fight, which evidently wasn't all that unusual to hear him tell it," Lacey continued, her eyes bright with malice. "So I pumped him for your plans, patted his hand, fucked him witless and sent him home. I was worried about him the whole time we planned the attack, but I knew you'd take care of him. You're so very good, you know."

Beryl swallowed bile. Daveed had been stupid, yes, he'd deserved to get his ass kicked for criminal carelessness. But his betrayal hadn't been the intentional treason she'd suspected. "And he died."

"You let him die, you bitch." Lacey's long legs covered the room in two strides. Beryl tried to duck, but the troopers held her still for the punch. "I trusted you to keep him alive, and you failed me!"

"You set up the ambush, Lacey," Beryl said over the hard ringing in her head.

"I worked for the Rebels, bitch. That's what I was supposed to do. And you were supposed to keep Daveed safe."

At the corners of her vision, Beryl saw the two troopers exchange a quick glance over her head. *Yeah, boys, your boss is a nutbar.* "So you hired Tagliar."

"Of course. It was the perfect death for you, or would have been if your pet stud here hadn't killed him." She smiled slowly. "But I think this is even more perfect."

With a flourish, she gave the pallet a shove. It rolled neatly back into the insolation tube, carrying Decker's unconscious body. "Put her in with him," Lacey ordered the guards.

Beryl tried to fight, but one too many head blows blunted her struggles, and soon she was stuffed in on top of Decker. A single lightbar let her see the vampire's gray face as she sprawled across his chill chest, and her mouth went dry with worry. He'd lost far too much blood.

Something hit the back wall next to her head and fell to the mattress. As the hatch thumped shut, she saw it was the ironwood knife they'd used to kill Tagliar.

"This is the lovely part," Lacey's voice said over the tube intercom. "When our friend comes to, he'll need all that blood he lost to Tagliar.

He's going to be very, very hungry. And you'll be the only lunch in town."

"So what's with the knife?"

"You care about him, you fickle bitch, I saw it in your eyes when Tag stabbed him. So you can live, if you can kill him. Or more likely, he'll kill you." Lacey snickered. "Perfect."

Beryl's stomach rolled. "What if he kills me, Lacey? What will you do to him?"

"Oh, turn him loose, probably. I've got nothing against him. He was a marvelous commander, y'know. For a bloodsucker."

Then the tube fell silent.

Until Decker murmured, his voice sounding as cracked as his chapped lips, "Jesus God, I wonder what she'd do if she had it in for me."

"You're awake?"

He paused to swallow. "Barely."

"You okay?"

"Hell, no." As she stared down at his face, she saw the fine muscle shift in his jaw. "Get off me, darlin'."

Realizing she must be hurting him, she tried to lever herself away, only to come up against the padded ceiling. Attempting to shift to one side, she found there was no room there either. "Damn. There isn't anywhere to go. My head's bumping the ceiling and your shoulders scrape the walls."

He opened too-bright eyes just enough to look at her. "Where'd they put us, a coffin?"

"No, an isolation tube." She stared around at the thick white padding. "They use it for punishment or something."

"Barbarians. We didn't even do shit like this in the Twentieth Century." His face was gray, and dark shadows ringed his eyes.

"You need blood, Deck."

"You're telling me." Decker's eyes drifted closed.

"I can probably spare a liter. . . ."

His eyes snapped wide. "Don't say that."

She frowned at him, wondering about the veiled panic she could read so easily. "Look, if you take a little from me, you'll have the strength to break the lock on this damn tube. Then you can find a nice juicy guard while I go looking for Lacey and kick her psychotic ass out the nearest airlock."

His face went even more gray. "Good plan. Unfortunately it's got a fatal flaw."

"Yeah?"

"If I took you, I wouldn't be able to stop."

Beryl snorted. "Oh, bullshit. When you first fought Tag, you were so worked up you couldn't even string a sentence together, but you didn't hurt me then."

Decker looked away. "I hadn't lost this much blood. Beryl, if I were human, I'd be dead."

She could believe it. There was a blue tinge to his lips, and the skin was cracked.

He closed his eyes again. "You have to use the knife."

"You mean jimmy the lock? I don't think so. The blade would probably break."

"I'm not talking about the lock, Beryl."

His meaning suddenly penetrated, chilling her until she froze. "You want me to use it? On you?"

"On me."

"Forget it."

"Beryl . . ."

"I'm not going to stake you, Decker. It's not even an option."

"Then sooner or later I'll kill you."

"Deck, you stopped scaring me the day I met you, so don't even try it."

Decker's head snapped up off the mattress, his lips peeling back from fangs at full extension, his eyes glittering red in the dim light. *"If I didn't love you, you'd already be dead."*

Startled, Beryl jerked back so hard she bumped her head on the roof of the tube. Decker let his head fall again and squeezed his eyes shut as he spoke. "I'm in control now, just barely. I don't know how long I can hold out. You have to stake me before I lose my grip completely."

Beryl's ruthlessly tactical merc mind analyzed the situation, calculated possible solutions and concluded he was right. Everything in her rebelled anyway. She didn't even stop to wonder why. "Forget it. Killing you is not an option. Period."

His blue eyes opened, locked with hers. "Beryl, I'm begging you. Don't do this to me. I can't stand the thought of coming to and finding you dead on top of me."

"There are other alternatives."

"Name one."

"Make me a vampire." The words were out of her mouth so suddenly she blinked in shock.

Beryl St. Cloud, willingly become a vampire? Surrender her human nature to an alien one created by a disease? Give up eating and sunlight to drink blood and become an object of bigotry?

Or remain a human, kill Jim Decker, and grieve for him for the rest of her life?

Put like that, it was no choice at all. She'd rather drink blood for the next three hundred years.

Decker was shaking his head. "I already considered that, but it won't work."

"Why not?"

"To pull it off, you and I would have to link completely. That's what vamp psi is for, so the vampire can guide his mate through the transition. Without linking, you'd die from the blood loss you have to suffer to be successfully infected by the virus."

"So we link."

"You've never let me form the link, Beryl. You've always evicted me from your mind. If you did that when you were teetering on death's door, the transition would fail and you'd die. And I wouldn't be able to save you."

Beryl rested her chin on his chest and slipped her arms around him, instinctively offering comfort in the face of his anguish. "I don't think we've got a hell of a lot of choice, Decker. You don't want to kill me, and I'm sure not going to kill you. Changing me's the only alternative."

"But it's not an alterative, because it still comes down to me draining you, and I'm not going to take that risk."

So frustrated she wanted to scream, she stared into his eyes. And knew he would never give in.

Decker lay under the solid warm torment that was her body. The air was so full of her scent that the roots of his fangs ached, and the fact that she was bleeding from a dozen small cuts made the problem even worse. He knew the least touch, the least movement, would be enough to tip him over into blood madness.

Ironically his very weakness had saved her so far. Had he been even a little more healthy, he could never have controlled the Hunger, but he was so weak, the raw inertia of his body helped him control his vampire instincts.

But if Beryl kept pushing him. . . .

Decker knew what ecstacy awaited him under the smooth surface of her throat, the warmth, the heat, the pure female essence that would give him back his life. But he could also imagine all too well recovering from that sensual delirium to find her lying limp and cold across him. Beryl, all her wit, all her intelligence, all her courage gone, destroyed by his mindless need to live.

Killing her would destroy him far more effectively than an ironwood knife driven into his heart.

He loved her. He could see it so clearly now, in the moment he was so close to losing her. Nothing else mattered, not even the knowledge that he didn't mean anything to her. She was just too scarred by Daveed Zahn to let another man in that close.

But scarred or not, loving him or not, she was going to get through this alive. Even if he had to die himself.

So Decker slid his hand up and found the ironwood knife where Lacey had tossed it. "You're going to have to use this, Beryl. You and I both know that."

She looked at him. "Yeah. I guess you're right."

And she took the knife out of his hand.

For just a moment something in Decker gave a kick of shocked protest that Beryl would give in so readily. But he dug his hands into the padding of the tube and braced himself.

Which is why he didn't react fast enough when she sliced a thin, shallow cut across her own throat. It wasn't deep enough to be fatal, but blood welled and ran in a narrow scarlet ribbon down her white skin. She met his eyes calmly. "Live or die, Decker, we do it together."

Her blood scent hit him in a hammer stroke, and the Hunger surged in Decker like a demon rising out of hell. And he knew he was lost.

"Damn you, Beryl." He snatched the blade away and nicked his own wrist with a pass of the knife. Pushing the wound to her mouth, he fastened his lips against the cut in her neck and began to drink.

At the first taste, the Hunger stripped his sanity away.

Decker's blood seared through her mouth and down her throat like some sweet, impossibly potent liquor. At the same time his mouth worked against her skin, the sensation making her nipples pull into heated, longing points. One strong hand came up, closed hard over her rump and began to knead with demanding strength.

Gasping at the overwhelming combination of his blood and his mouth and his hands, Beryl tried to pull away. Yet the taste of him was so seductive, she had to drink again.

So she drank, dimly aware that Decker was taking from her more greedily then he ever had before as his fingers stroked and probed. Her sense of time stretched out as starbursts detonated behind her closed eyelids. Her lips were growing numb.

Drunk, Beryl thought. *I'm getting drunk . . .*

Whirls of color spun out behind her lids, comets, stars accelerating away into the dark, shifting toward the red. She was beginning to feel cold, so cold, warmth running out of her until the only source of heat was Decker's lips against her throat. They'd felt so chill at first, but now she could see them glowing against the curtain of her closed lids like crimson stars.

Desperately, instinctively ravenous, Beryl drank Decker's blood as he drained her. And never quite realized when she died.

Chapter Five

Decker listened to her pulse going thready and fought his instinctive panic. He ached to link with her, knowing if he waited too long she'd vanish so deeply into death he'd never win her back. But he also knew if he tried to form the link when she was still capable of shielding herself, she'd eject him from her mind. And then she'd die anyway.

So he counted her stuttering heartbeats and waited for his moment. And prayed to the God of his childhood that he wouldn't misjudge it. *Now.*

LINK.

The connection snapped into place, he felt it lock in, but still he didn't sense her. Worried, he opened his eyes to find himself standing on a bare, sandy plane, as completely flat as if it had been smoothed by a giant's hand. Above him an aurora painted dancing red and orange light over the night sky. There was absolutely nothing else around.

Decker frowned. This place was a dream they were having, he and Beryl between them, a symbol of their shared mental reality. Which was why her absence worried him. Had he let her fade too long, go too far into death?

Then he saw the statue.

It stood there on the horizon, a biped figure silhouetted against the glowing darkness. He concentrated. . . .

And was right in front of the statue between one blink and the next. In this place, logic took a holiday, and reality was whatever he made it. Or more accurately, reality was whatever it *was*, deep under the surface of the real world.

Which was why Decker wasn't surprised to find that the statue was actually a suit of medieval armor, pitted and locked in rust. And when he saw the breastplate was molded to accommodate the lush curves of a woman's torso, he knew something else.

Beryl was in there.

Decker leaned down to peer into the helmet's eye slits, but there was nothing inside but utter blackness. His heart jumped in his chest as he realized he had to get her out of that cocoon of rust *now,* because if he didn't connect with her soon and guide her through the vampire transition, she would die.

Taking a deep breath to calm himself, Decker dug his fingers into the rotting steel of the gauntlet covering her right arm. The plate crumbled in his ruthless grip until he could touch Beryl's skin.

Cold. God, she was cold as a corpse.

But as he touched her, light flared from his fingers and lit the gray flesh with a faint, soft glow.

Tossing the mangled chunk of metal away, Decker grabbed another piece. As he peeled it back, he glimpsed the barest flash of a vision: a very young child, a woman, and a man. The adults were dressed in the mesh merc skinsuits popular twenty-five years before. The child was crying, but her mother crouched and held her close. *"We love you, baby. We'll make sure you're always safe."*

Decker knew the vision was a fragment of Beryl's memory, but he had no time to puzzle over it. He grabbed the next section of armor and peeled the rusted plate away.

There was the male merc's face now, ravaged with grief. *"She never saw it coming, Beryl. She didn't feel any pain."*

Decker shuddered at the agonizing grief that flashed through him with that memory, but he didn't stop. Grab and pull.

The merc sat at a dingy table, his thick shoulders hunched. Beryl, twelve now, caught him by one beefy arm. *"You've got to get work, Dad. We need money."*

Another section of armor fell apart between Decker's impatient fingers. Now he recognized a younger Bill Anderson, shaking his head at the fifteen-year old Beryl. *"He's always been a good man."*

"Maybe. Fact is, he hasn't given a rat's ass since mother died," Beryl growled. *"I should have let him eat his torch five years ago."*

Crunch.

Beryl's face, screaming. *"Daddy!"*

Decker reached up and jerked the helmet off to look into her dark, grieving eyes. "It wasn't your fault, Beryl."

"Bullshit," she said, her gray lips barely moving. "I was so busy trying to prove to Bill what a badass I was, I didn't see the sniper. So Dad deliberately stepped into the shot that should have burned right through my skull. He loved me, and I killed him."

"No," Decker said softly, "you loved him, and he used you as an excuse to die."

He reached out, touched her face, and the connection snapped to full strength.

Decker was Beryl was Decker was Beryl, fusing into a mental mobius strip of awareness until it was impossible to tell where one left off and the other began. He could feel her strength, her intelligence, the wary love for him that had grown so stealthily even she hadn't known it. Just as she could feel his own solid love, sense how precious she was to him, precious as only something could be after three centuries of searching for it.

And each feeling the other, they flowed together.

Beryl's chestplate cracked like an eggshell giving way. Armor fell around her in flakes of rust as she straightened, shaking out her wings, extending them wide until they stretched twelve feet across.

Blinking her glowing red eyes, Beryl stared over her shoulder at the huge delicate membranes, taking in their iridescent rainbow sheen. Her soft lips parted, revealing fangs. "What the hell are those things?" she gasped.

"Bat wings." A weary grin spread across Decker's face. "Don't worry, they're not real, just a symbol that you sucessfully made the transition. You're a vampire, Beryl. You're going to live."

Beryl awoke sprawled across Decker's warm, hard chest. A wave of chill skated on icy feet over her skin, and she shuddered, remembering with brutal clarity the moment when her father had taken the torch blast for her. "I'd forgotten. How the hell could I have forgotten that much guilt?"

"I don't think you did," Decker said, lifting a hand to stroke her hair, his voice rumbling through his chest. "I think that's why you'd never let me into your mind. Why even Daveed, the poor son of a bitch, could never really touch you."

"Where are we?" Beryl tried to lift her head, but her skull felt like solid lead. She let it fall with a whimper.

"In the tube." He stretched under her, his powerful body rippling. "We never left."

"God," she moaned, cracked lips burning, "I'm so weak . . ." Something that felt like pebbles shifted in her mouth. Unable to move, Beryl pushed out her tongue and watched in dull horror as two teeth rolled out onto the bunk's gray padding. Exploring with her tongue, she felt a pair of sharp points where those canines used to be. Fangs.

It was true. She was a vampire. Panic and nausea twisted her stomach. "Oh, God, Decker," Beryl groaned, and swallowed bile. "I feel like hell."

"It'll get better once you feed."

Feed. Jesus, she was a *vampire* now. She was going to have to bite someone, drink blood . . .

Merc that she was, Beryl cut the thought off. You did what you had to do to survive. She'd chosen this, and now she damn well wasn't going to whine about it.

"Get ready, kid. It's time to go." Decker slipped a muscled arm around her waist and braced the other hand against the tube ceiling. He gathered under her, then slammed his booted foot against the tube hatch in a hard, solid kick. The latch broke with a scream of metal, and the door slammed open so hard it crashed into the outside wall. A shove of Decker's hand sent the bunk rolling out of the tube. He flipped off of it the instant it rolled to a stop, the arm around her waist keeping her tight against him as he moved. She squeezed her eyes shut and fought the roll of her stomach.

"What the hell . . . ?" a male voice shouted.

Decker was gone. Deprived of his support, Beryl fell against the bunk and concentrated on breathing, dimly aware of the sound of a struggle that ended almost before it began.

"Beryl, darlin'. . . ." Decker's voice sounded velvety and coaxing over a muffled squealing.

Beryl didn't see how she could stay on her feet, much less walk. "Jesus, Decker, I don't think I can. . . ."

Then she smelled it.

It was wonderful, seductive, musk and copper, raw sex and heat. The very scent strengthened her. Beryl's eyes snapped open. She rolled erect and almost fell, slapping a hand to the bunk to steady herself.

Decker was holding a guard, one hand buried in the man's collar, the other clamped over his captive's mouth to hold his neck in a tempting arch.

The guard. He was the source of that wonderful smell.

Beryl ran into Decker's muscled shoulder as he snatched the man away from her instinctive lunge. "Control, sweetheart. You don't want to kill him."

Good God. She wanted to drink his blood.

Even as her old human nature recoiled in horror, Beryl, driven by her new Hunger, babbled an incoherent promise. Decker let her ease close enough to look into the guard's face. His eyes were round and white with terror.

That fear dug through her vampire instincts to touch off compassion. "I won't hurt you," Beryl said, and hoped she could keep her promise as she bent for his neck. The guard yelped behind Decker's hand, his voice muffled. She ignored him and put her mouth against his throat. The vein was there, running hot and strong under the skin. Beryl hesitated. What if she accidently killed this man? "Decker . . ."

"Your body knows what to do, darlin'," he said, his voice soothing. "Just go with it."

She bit down carefully. Hot liquid spun into her mouth. It didn't taste anything like blood. It was crimson and burning and sweet, though not as lush to her senses as Decker's blood. Pleasure flooded her, and Beryl hummed against the guard's warm throat. He stiffened, his strong male body forming an involuntary arch, and she crooned reassurance to him while she drank.

As his blood rolled down her throat, lust curled in her belly until she found herself slowly dragging her nipples across his chest. He moaned, the sound husky with arousal as he lost his fear.

Until, too soon, Decker said in her ear, "That's enough, darlin'. You're giving the poor bastard a hardon, and you're making me jealous."

Beryl lifted her head and licked the blood from her fangs. "More. Please, Decker . . ."

"There's a whole hemosynther on the *Stoker*. You can have as much as you want when we get back. Come on, be a good girl . . ."

Reluctantly, she let go. The guard promptly collapsed.

Beryl frowned, looking down at the limp body sprawled on the deck. A few hours ago she'd have shot him if she'd had a torch, but what she'd just done seemed different. She was aware of him as a man now, not just an enemy. And she didn't want to be responsible for his death. "Did I hurt him?"

Decker smiled drily. "No, you just showed him a really good time. As soon as the meditechs give him a pint or three, he'll be pistol whipping the prisoners again." He took her arm, his grip firm but gentle as he began to lead her toward the nearest door. "Let's go, sweetheart. We have to get to the ship . . ."

"I feel . . . better." She felt better than better. She felt high, soaring. Invulnerable. Immortal.

Decker was studying her anxiously. Beryl wondered why she'd never noticed the love in those blue eyes before. "Yeah, well, be careful. It's a great buzz, but it's deceptive. You haven't really had enough blood to sustain you, and I'm afraid you're going to collapse before we get you home."

The brig hatch opened and bloodscent flooded Beryl's senses. "Ever heard of security cameras?" Lacey purred.

Beryl spun, falling into an instinctive combat crouch. The redhead stood with a laser torch pointed at Decker's broad chest, a gang of nervous troopers at her back.

Lacey sneered at him, ignoring Beryl for the moment. "Watch it, vampire. No matter how fast you are, you're not faster than light."

Beryl saw her chance and didn't stop to think about it. She leapt.

The explosion of powerful vampire muscle took even Beryl by surprise as it drove her into Lacey and halfway through the gang of guards. They all went down in a tangle, but Beryl twisted around until she ended up on top of Lacey with the bitch's torch hand clamped in one fist and her fingers wrapped around the redhead's throat. "I don't have to be faster than light, Lace," she gritted. "I just have to be faster than you."

Lacey stared at Beryl in terror, taking in the fangs, the glint of red in her eyes. "You let him *infect* you?"

"You sound surprised. Didn't you watch the whole show on your precious security cameras?" She caught a movement out of the corner of her eye and added, "By the way, my compliments on your guards. They're like potato chips, I just can't keep my fangs out of them . . ."

The soldier lying under them stopped trying to work her weapon free, her eyes going wide.

"I hate to interrupt the fun, darlin'," Decker whispered. It took her a moment to realize he was speaking directly into her mind through the link that had formed between them during her transition. *"But we really need to get out of here before one of these people grows a spine."*

"Good point," she thought back. *"Want to take the bitch hostage?"*

"Sounds like a plan to me."

Decker took three running steps forward and cleared the pileup on the floor in one bounce. Before anybody could react, he strode back and hauled Beryl upright, though she still held Lacey locked in her ruthless grip. While he was at it, Decker snatched a couple of torches away from their erstwhile owners.

"All right, people, this is how it goes down," he said, covering the stunned group. "Commander Lacey here is going to provide us with an escort away from your dubious hospitality. If anybody screws with us, I'm going to feed her to my hungry partner. Does everybody read clear on that?"

"No!" Lacey growled, jerking against Beryl's hold as her eyes went wild, "Don't let them take me! That's an order!"

"Shut up, Lacey." Beryl's lip curled as she inhaled the redhead's scent. Unlike the guard's, there was something about it that made the hair stand on the back of her neck, something bitter and acrid. Even the bloodscent that underlay the bitterness smelled like food, not sex.

"She's female, Beryl," Decker pointed out, his mental voice amused.

"*As for the nasty underlay, that's just pure viciousness.*" Beryl got the sense of a frown. "*She didn't smell like that when I knew her.*"

They headed for the brig exit, Lacey's bootheels scrapping on the deck as Beryl hauled her along. Decker brought up the rear, pointing his torches back toward the guards who followed at a respectful distance. They were obviously torn between making the ordered rescue attempt and a reluctance to take on two pissed-off vampires.

"They don't look too eager to risk their necks for you, Lace," Beryl observed, aiming a malicious grin at her enemy. "I wonder why?"

"Fucking cowards," Lacey snarled at her troopers.

"They're not cowards, Lace, it's just that you're such a charming bitch they can't stand the thought of dying for you. Don't try it, pal," Decker added to one of the guards who was attempting to work his way in closer.

Looking sullen, the man fell back.

The remainder of the trip to the hanger deck where the ship was docked was nerve-wracking. Lacey struggled the whole way, apparently deciding she didn't want to wait for rescue. Beryl controlled the bigger woman easily at first, but soon she began to tire.

Decker was right, the guard's blood hadn't been enough. Her newly changed body had to have more. Beryl fought to keep her grip hard and her step confident, knowing that if Lacey sensed weakness, all hell would break loose.

Somehow the two vampires remained in control all the way back to the hanger, though Decker was forced to fire a few warning shots as they got close to the ship. Beryl barely flinched at the high-pitched whine of his shots, concentrating on putting one foot in front of the other and keeping one hand clamped around Lacey's wrist.

"All right, boys and girls, here's the way it goes," Decker called to the guards, who'd hastily taken cover. "We take off, and your commander goes with us. We drop her off at Freeboot Station, where you pick her up. If nobody gives us any crap, and if she's a good girl, you'll get her back with no tooth marks. Otherwise, all bets are off."

As he covered the guards, Beryl hauled Lacey past him toward the *Stoker*'s airlock. If she could just make it inside, she could collapse in peace. "Open hatch," she husked. The ship's computer, recognizing her voice, obeyed.

Suddenly Lacey yanked hard, and Beryl stumbled as her numb, chilled fingers lost their grip. Stooping, the redhead pulled out a length of sharpened wood from her boot top and pivoted to drive the weapon right for Beryl's chest.

It figures the bitch would have a stake, Beryl thought, and met her rush with a single, sharp punch that slammed right into Lacey's face with a wet crack. Blood sprayed up her arm.

Blinking in surprise, Beryl realized she'd just killed Arith Lacey.

"Jesus, Beryl!" Decker dove for her and scooped her up before Lacey's body even hit the ground. Gathering Beryl against his chest, he swept her inside the airlock amid the high whine of powering torches. "Close hatch, computer! Activate antigravs and ready weapons. And get the mediunit up to . . ."

Beryl watched his mouth keep moving, but a loud, mechanical buzz drowned out whatever he might be saying. Darkness flooded in.

Decker carried Beryl onto the bridge, where the cargobots had already set up the mediunit. Laying her down on the unit's bed, he left her to its automated care. Though every instinct demanded that he see to her himself, Decker knew that if he didn't get them away from the station, she'd die anyway.

Without bothering to wait for clearance, he lifted off and piloted the *Bram Stoker* toward the hanger's primary airlock hatch, which obediently opened for the huge craft. Decker knew the station defense force didn't dare risk a fight inside the landing deck because the *Stoker* could crack the space base open with just a few shots. Which is why they didn't have anti-ship weapons mounted in the deck either, since their own fire could be just as deadly to them.

For a moment Decker considered opening fire anyway, then instantly dismissed the idea. There were too many civilians aboard, and he liked to keep the body count down when he could.

Decker tensed in his command chair as he waited for the huge airlock to cycle. The minute the *Stoker* was out in space at a safe distance, the station would try its damndest to blow them to hell. The key to survival was to fly an evasive course at maximum speed, avoiding enemy fire until they were far enough out to pop to Super-C, where no weapon could touch them.

The massive doors began, slowly, to open. He threw a quick look over his shoulder where the mediunit was giving Beryl a transfusion and allowed himself to commit her lovely profile to memory.

Then he turned back to his monitors, saw the doors were opened just enough, and punched the *Stoker* to full throttle.

And prayed.

Chapter Six

Beryl crouched on top of a massive crate and waited for her opponent, scanning her surroundings with a predator's patience. She could read every label on every crate, though it was so dark in the hold she shouldn't have been able to see a damn thing. Since she was a vampire, it might as well be day.

More than two weeks had passed since the *Bram Stoker* had blasted its way out of Dyson's space. Thankfully Decker had avoided any major loss of life, and the planet's officials decided to let the whole thing drop. Particularly once he'd threatened to sue for false imprisonment over Lacey's actions.

Still, the *Stoker* wouldn't be accepting any more shipments to Dyson's for at least a couple of decades.

Meanwhile Beryl had finally completed the transition, becoming, Decker put it, an honest-to-Anne-Rice vampire. Whoever the hell Anne Rice was.

She was surprised at how easy she'd found the adjustment. It was probably because she was a spacer, and vampires did better in space, where there was easy access to hemosynthers, no dangerously unfiltered sunlight, and no bigots. Oh, she'd have to deal with those things eventually, but there was something about sharing the Life with Decker that made the negatives of vampirism seem like a small price to pay.

Still, Beryl needed to learn how to control her vampirism, from the great strength it had given her to the fantastically acute senses.

Which was what she was doing down in the cargo hold, waiting for Decker to subject her to another one of his "training exercises." She knew from painful experience that she'd suffer cuts, lacerations and general blood loss in the process, but she didn't much care. She and Decker always ended up naked at the end of the session, which made for a hell of an incentive.

But first she had to find him.

Beryl could tell he was nearby, because she could smell that deliciously tempting Decker scent that never failed to make her nipples harden. Still, though she scanned her surroundings like a hungry cat, she couldn't quite pinpoint where he was.

Beryl curled her lip in frustration. She might be a vampire now, but he still held the advantage of experience, size and strength. And he used it ruthlessly.

But this time she'd take him.

If she could find him.

There was a higher crate twenty feet away that looked promising. Ignoring the small voice that insisted that she couldn't possibly make it, Beryl gathered herself and sprang. For a single, gorgeous instant she was flying. Then she hit, bending her knees to absorb the jolting shock of landing.

Warily, Beryl straightened and was relieved to discover she hadn't broken every bone in her legs this time. Earlier this week she'd misjudged a jump, and though she'd healed with amazing speed, she was in no hurry to repeat the experience.

With a sigh of satisfaction, Beryl folded herself into a crouch and scanned her surroundings again.

There. Something moved off to the left, half-hidden behind a short crate.

She could clear the distance in one bounce, but Beryl's mercenary's instincts told her she should approach more cautiously. Yet the Hunger was thrumming high and eager, and she wanted Decker *now*. Her grin revealing lengthening fangs, Beryl jumped, her body stretching into the air like a pouncing tiger.

Until she saw the glint of metal at the height of her arc and realized she'd made a serious mistake.

A cargobot. He'd suckered her with a cargobot.

Beryl twisted in midair just enough to avoid crashing into the low-slung, tentacled robot as it trundled along. She hit rolling, instinctively trying to put herself as far from Decker's target area as she could.

Taunting male laughter told her she'd failed as strong hands grabbed her. "You've got to learn to manage the Hunger better than that, darlin'."

Beryl only snarled and fought to flip clear, knowing that if Decker got a good grip, she'd never get free.

Decker fought to hold her, laughing and wincing as a small, hard fist connected with his chin. She knew good and damn well she couldn't possibly win, but she was too stubborn to quit. It was one of the things Decker loved about her, but it was a pain in the ass at times like this.

Decker ducked a second punch and grabbed her fist before she could cock it again. She slammed a knee into his gut, and he whoofed out a breath, managing narrowly to hang on to the hand he'd captured. Jerking back, he flipped her onto her stomach and dragged her arm up between her shoulder blades. A half nelson was painful even to a vampire, but Beryl went right on struggling.

"I don't suppose," he asked, midway between gasping and chuckling, "you'd consider a graceful surrender so I can nibble your throat and screw you senseless?"

"I have a better idea," she panted back. "*You* give up so I can nibble your throat and screw *you* senseless."

"Oh, no, that wasn't the agreement." He whipped the length of thin magnetic cable out of his pocket and lashed it around her captive wrist. "The winner bangs the loser, remember?"

"Hey! What do you think you're doing?" She fought to escape as he went after her free hand.

"I just want to devote all my attention to nibbling, kissing and playing with your lush and—cut that out—lovely body." He finally managed to snag her flailing fist and lash it to the one he'd already captured. "Without having to worry about you trying to get away, knee me somewhere painful, or sink your needle fangs into my anatomy."

"I just don't want you to get bored, Deck." She gave him a feral grin. "Don't you get tired of winning all the time?"

"Nope." He pounced on her ankles with a second length of cable. He had to duck several kicks before he could get them tied. Satisfied he had her neatly lashed, he rocked back on his heels and flipped her over onto her back.

Then Decker reached for the neck of her coveralls.

"Don't you dare . . ."

Rrrriiiiiiippp!

"You dared," she observed drily, watching him strip her with a couple of ruthless swipes.

"I dared," he agreed. "What are you going to do about it?"

Beryl smirked. "Plot my revenge."

"The mind boggles." Actually, she did look rather intimidating. Though her bare, white breasts arched upward temptingly and her lush little cunt smelled of desire between her long legs, her eyes glowed red in the darkness and her fangs peeked from her parted lips.

Decker displayed his own long teeth. He loved a challenge.

Bouncing to his feet, he bent, scooped her into his arms, and deposited her, naked and squirming, head down over his shoulder.

"Oh, look," she purred from somewhere below the small of his back, "Decker haunch."

"Bite me and I'll paddle your little ass," he growled, and started toward the bridge. He had a sudden urge to take her in a bed this time.

"First bondage, now spanking," Beryl mused. "Decker, you're getting kinky. I think I like it."

"Slut."

"Guilty. But you can't say immortality will be boring with me along."

"Truer words were never spoken." He carried her into the lift, where he spent the ride trying to avoid her playfully snapping teeth.

It scared him, being this happy. It had been too damn long.

At last he strode onto the bridge with her and dumped her into the sleeping pit, then pounced with a growl of delighted lust.

It was past time to play.

Decker's hot mouth closed over her nipple with astonishing delicacy after the roughness of their game. Beryl watched him, the fan of his lashes against his hard cheeks, the way he drank her scent with flaring nostrils as his tongue flicked out to tease her hard pink point. His scent flooded her senses, male and vampire and blood and sex, a heady blend potent as straight whiskey, hot and sharp. She writhed, instinctively pulling at the cable that bound her, wanting to touch, wanting to hold him and taste him and pull him deep.

He growled at her as she moved, the sound blending hunger and humor.

One big hand came up to pluck the nipple deliciously, warm fingers indenting the soft, white skin of her breast.

"Let me go, Deck," Beryl pleaded, her voice husky. "Let me touch you."

"No way, kid. I won, and I'm keeping you just the way I like you. Naked and helpless." His teeth nipped her as his clever hands worked her body, spanning her waist and gliding over her tight, quivering belly.

"Bastard," she moaned, wet heat flooding between her thighs.

"You bet." He reared away from her suddenly, his eyes striking red sparks, and grabbed his shirt in both hands. Old-fashioned buttons popped and bounced across the room as he ripped it open, the motion arching his spine. She watched hungrily, taking in the broad, lovely torso with its fluid roping of muscle. Catching his eyes, Beryl licked her fangs and grinned.

Decker grinned back, springing to his feet to peel off his boots and strip the tight black trousers down his muscled thighs. His erection sprang free, thick as her wrist and hard enough to jut upward at an angle, his testicles nestling full and taut to its underside. She growled in appreciation.

Decker stood over her, his cock and his fangs aching in full erection, both eager to be buried in her. And Beryl looked up at him, fearless and feral in her bonds, her nipples long rose stems. She treated him to a deliberate wriggle that made her lovely breasts bounce and the muscles work in her lush thighs. A blood vessel pulsed in his temple.

She was his. His woman, his mate, his match, his equal. Even his willing prisoner when it suited her. Here, after three hundred years of searching, was a woman he didn't have to protect from himself. Because Beryl didn't need protecting. She could take his strength and give it back to him.

And for the first time in far too long, he deliberately set his Hunger free.

Beryl saw his powerful body coil, the flame leap high in his eyes as his fine features drew taut. "Mine," Decker growled, as he had that first night he'd taken her.

And it was back, visible there in his eyes for the first time since she'd met him his Hunger, his Beast, the part of him he worked so hard to control. Had she still been human, it would have terrified her, the naked animal lust in his eyes, the power that radiated from him as he bent toward her.

Instead she freed her own Beast to match his.

Decker didn't like her ankles tied together, so he broke the grip of the magnetic cable and lashed each of them to the opposite wrist. She submitted with a deep, throaty purr that built to a rumbling growl as he shifted to bury his face between her thighs.

Her scent flooded his brain, salt and musk and vampire and female, so eager for him, predator to his predator, pussy to his cock. He growled deep in his throat and feasted on her slick red flesh, opening her with his fingers and licking in long strokes. He sucked and tongued and bit until her wetness covered his face, intoxicating and goading him. Instinctively, helplessly, Decker worked his hips, grinding his cock into the bedding.

To give himself a moment to regain control, Decker lifted his head and watched as Beryl tossed her head in her dark hair, gasping and pulling against her bonds, as lost to the Hunger as he. Growling triumphantly, he buried his face between her legs again, both hands simultaneously reaching up to seize her lush breasts.

Beryl whimpered, mindless in the face of Decker's ruthless skill and the Hunger he'd unleashed. He was everywhere, big body and slick hard muscle and talented hands and wicked mouth. Everywhere but where she wanted him: inside. *Now*.

Then he reared over her, and Beryl's mind lit with a ferocious, animal joy as Decker came down on top of her, spearing her on an endless rush of broad, rigid cock. Then his face was against her throat, and she felt the hot/cold prick of his fangs. Instinctively she bent her head to seek out a thick vein throbbing in the muscle of his shoulder. And bit deep, savoring the burning brandy flood of his blood over her tongue.

Decker promptly let go and pulled away. "Bad girl," he rumbled. "I won, so I get to bite *you*. Those are the rules."

Before Beryl could frame a protest, he flipped her onto her belly and propped her shoulders on the rim of the sleeping pit. Then he speared her again. Beryl gasped at the molten sensation of his length sliding deep. Without so much as a pause, he pumped his powerful hips, sliding in and out even as his strong fingers tightened on her waist, dragging her closer so he could reach up even further. Beryl shuddered helplessly, hissing at the raw, brutal pleasure.

And then his mouth was on her neck again, his fangs slowly penetrating her throat, driving a spike of pleasure right into her skull. She screamed at the deep pulsations of orgasm as his pumping hips rammed his cock in and out.

But Decker didn't slow down. Instead he suddenly pulled his fangs away so he could mercilessly pound her rump. The sensation of his massive erection pistoning inside her was maddening, and Beryl gasped incoherent pleas. He ignored them, wrapping a fist in her hair to hold her writhing body still while he fucked her even harder.

Another orgasm shuddered through her, ripping her voice into a spiraling howl of pleasure. Decker stiffened against her, then suddenly dove for her throat. His fangs entered her again even as her climax hit its brutal peak.

Link!

She felt him, *was* him, felt her own hot, slick walls gripping his cock, felt the smooth muscle of her ass pressing into his groin. Felt her blood rolling sweet and burning down his throat until it was impossible to tell where Decker left off and where she began. They were one.

And she felt his love, shining even through the animal heat of his Hunger, bright and pure, just as she could see her love through his eyes.

As the urgency of the Hunger burned away, extinguished by the power of their pleasure, the love remained, until they were left sated and tangled together on the huge mattress, surrounded by its warm glow.

"Decker?"

"Mmmm."

"If you don't untie me right now, I'm gonna be stuck in this position for the rest of my life."

Without opening his eyes, Decker grinned. "What a lovely thought."

"Decker, I know where you sleep."

"Oh, all right." He dragged himself upright and untied her, then gathered her limp body against his.

"When I get my strength back in a day or two," Beryl said, her voice pleasantly blurred by exhaustion, "I'm going to demand a rematch."

"I'm counting on it." Contented, Decker smiled and curled around her. "You know," he added into her hair, "for a pair of vampires, it really can be happily ever after."

"God, Decker," she murmured, "you can be so corny sometimes."

He bit her.

About the author:

Angela Knight lives in the wilds of upstate South Carolina with her son and her handsome cop husband (who really ought to have fangs to go with the look he gets in his eyes on certain dark nights).

She loves handcuffs and politically incorrect romances, and likes to mix the two whenever possible—and she's secretly relieved whenever anybody else admits to doing the same.

The Barbarian

by Ann Jacobs

To my reader:

"The Barbarian" brings home lusty appetites honed in harems of the East. When he discovers to his pleasure that the bride the king has provided him along with rich estates in England appreciates and shares his enthusiasm for varied bed sports, he is a happy man. Little does he know that from healthy lust will grow a love of a lifetime.

I hope you enjoy the fantasy as well as the gritty reality of this tale of sex and love set in the harsh and unforgiving medieval times. Erotic though this story may be, it is romance as well—the story of one man and one woman, searching for happily ever after.

Chapter One

Giles deVere's promised bride was apparently intent on denying him entry to Harrow Castle. This day, not even the cool rain could cool his impatience to end a useless siege and take this castle he had earned with his sword and lance.

As he sweated within the confines of his chain mail he came to a decision. His coffers brimmed with gold captured from the infidel. He would spend some to repair the damages he was about to inflict upon his own property. "Rolfe, ready the catapults, and set men-at-arms to preparing a ram. We take Harrow on the morrow," he told his brother, who sat his destrier but a few yards away.

"This is your castle now, Giles. Would you cause it such grievous damage?"

"I would have Harrow Castle and my reluctant bride in my power without further delay. Those within the walls who defy me will learn how I earned the name Barbarian."

At first the name, earned by merciless killing of infidels on battlefields in the Holy Lands, had disturbed Giles. Later, after many victories, he came to relish his image as a fierce warrior obsessed with victory no matter what the costs. Such, he told himself, was the lot of a third son—and now, through his bloody service to King Henry, he had gained the prize of land and title his birth had denied him.

His prize had belonged to a robber baron he had chased down and delivered to his fate at Henry's court. The old earl and his followers had purportedly wreaked havoc on the midlands since the time of Stephen with their raping, killing, and debauched acts. No doubt they had earned the punishment Henry had meted out.

All Henry had required in return for granting him Harrow, and all its lesser fiefs, was that Giles wed with the old earl's only remaining child, a lady of the somewhat advanced age of sixteen, for whom her father had neglected to choose a husband. Smiling, Giles fantasized that bedding the Lady Brianna would bring him pleasures equal to those he remembered from his stint as master of the harem in a villa captured from an infidel prince.

Together he and the eunuch Arnaud, who would be his wife's protector, would tutor her in the sensual arts. Giles would conquer the lady Brianna with his body as surely as he would quell her master-at-arms's foolish resistance tomorrow with his weapons of war. Be she fair or ugly, the lady would soon be his love slave.

❧✦❧

"The Barbarian shall never possess Harrow Castle. Never possess me!" Even as she said it Brianna of Harrow feared she spoke a lie. The castle might have survived a siege. It was falling quickly, however, to the Barbarian's mighty army. The gate was giving way to a battering ram even now while boulders hurled from catapults rent the curtain wall. The battle-hardened retainers of Giles deVere outnumbered her protectors by close to a hundred men.

If only, Brianna thought angrily, her true brother had not perished in battle! She would not be standing here with her illegitimate half-brother Eudo, the odious monk her sire had retrieved from his cloister in the hope of having him named heir to Harrow. The very one who had read her the king's letter which ordered her to wed the brutal warlord who had quelled her father's army and delivered him to Henry to be tortured and executed just two months past.

She wanted not to become the instrument of the Barbarian's vengeance, no more than she wished to give herself to the man Eudo described as monstrous in appearance as well as actions. "I would escape him, my brother," she said, meeting the monk's beady gaze as he approached.

"If you would flee, the time must be now," Eudo observed, pausing at her side, his coarse brown robe flapping in the breeze.

"I like not the idea of a religious life." Brianna's body had heated at the sight of maids and men-at-arms coupling in the great hall, at the sounds of soft moans and whimpers they made. She had dreamed of finding the rapture her maids whispered about, of possibly even sharing affection with a handsome lord who would sire her children—the heady joy her lady mother had found in the arms of a virile young lover ere she died.

"Like you better the notion of coupling with deVere? From all accounts, he is more demon than the devil himself. If you make haste, you may escape his ravishment."

Eudo was right. Celibacy held more appeal than coupling with a monster whose very name made strong men speak in hushed tones. Turning from the shattered window, Brianna took boys' clothing from a trunk. "Fetch me a pot of the oil and tar the defenders use to try to quell his invasion," she told Eudo. "And hurry. They batter now at the hall entry."

Her nose wrinkling with distaste at the stench of the peasant garments, Brianna removed her gown. She had donned the filthy rags and was tying baggy chausses when Eudo returned.

"What do you with this?" he asked, setting down the pot of hot tar and kitchen grease.

She sat before the polished metal, staring at her reflection as she grasped the long braid of her hair. "Give me your dagger. I shall be shorn soon enough when I reach the protection of the convent. For now I would improve my disguise."

Hacking mercilessly, she had soon reduced what had been waist-length hair to a series of uneven clumps that stood out like a haystack from her head. "Rub the tar into it. 'Twill change the color." Since childhood, all had commented on the beauty of her pale, silky hair. None would recognize her now, with hair as short as any boy serf's and as black as tar. Even Brianna would not have recognized the pathetic reflection that stared back at her.

Sounds of clanking metal and anguished cries of the wounded and dying came ever closer. At a great crashing noise, Brianna whirled to find the solar door blocked by a huge warrior, bloody sword in one mail-covered fist. Trembling, she assumed the diffident posture of a peasant caught above stairs in the master's solar.

Lifting off his helm as if to improve his vision, he glanced about the solar before settling his gaze upon Eudo. "You, man of God. Get you with my men outside. Your tonsure will protect you from harm." He watched Eudo slink through the door before turning his attention to Brianna. "You are no serf boy, *madam*. You would have done well to take the time to bind those thrusting breasts."

Heat came to Brianna's oil-caked cheeks. Conqueror he might be, but this warrior seduced her senses with his hot, dark gaze. Pity she could not wed with him instead of the Barbarian he must call lord. Her nipples swelled against the rough cloth of her disguise, as she boldly imagined the hard muscle and tough sinew this beautiful man must be hiding beneath the accouterments of war.

"Your name, madam," he demanded, his voice deep and compelling, his Norman French too perfect for him to be any but a nobleman.

"Brianna of Harrow, my lord. I would that you help me escape your master. I would take refuge in a convent before I'd wed with him." This warrior's stance, his demeanor, and his hot, needy gaze made Brianna fantasize that he would give her a taste of the sexual pleasure the convent would deny her for eternity. "I would make it worth your while, sir knight."

The warrior frowned. "What you offer is for your lord husband alone, my lady. And he is as dear to me as mine own self."

Fie! The fates had no mercy, that such a knight would be so loyal to the monster she would now be forced to wed! "You will hand me over to the Barbarian?"

He nodded, his lips parting to reveal a row of straight, healthy-looking teeth. Brianna fancied that the hot look in the warrior's eyes was lust, though she knew not how she could inspire lust, filthy as a swineherd and as ragged as the poorest of villeins. Would that he had come upon her ere she had hacked off her hair!

"I cannot allow you . . ."

"You have no choice."

Before she could catch her breath to cajole him further, the mail-clad knight was upon her, lifting her over his shoulder and striding purposefully downstairs into the great hall.

"Set me down, you great oaf!" Brianna shuddered at the sight of carnage left in her hall by the Barbarian's army. Olaf. Geoff. That old man-at-arms who used to pat her on the head as she walked by him at his post. Dead. Their lives forfeited as they tried to protect her from this man's master. "What have you done with my brother? Does he lie somewhere, as dead as these men who only did my bidding?" she asked as she searched the hall for Eudo.

"The monk I sent from the solar? I expect he rests now in Harrow's dungeon, milady, along with all we found still living when we took the castle. Fear not. My men would not harm a man of the cloth, not unless he took up a sword against them."

Brianna considered that unlikely. Ungodly Eudo might be, but his sins ran more toward dipping his wick into the honey pots of castle wenches than to defending them with sword or lance. Not even holy orders could cool men's lust, but at least Eudo hadn't looked upon her that way since she had reminded him rather forcefully that she was his sister, and a lady whose virginity must be saved for her husband.

Her husband. Not the white knight of her dreams, a gentle warrior who would woo her with tender care and make her burn for the touch of his hands. Not the dream lover for whom she would be more than the vessel for him to spill his seed. Not the beautiful but fearsome warrior who held her now and made her burn. No, from the tales she had heard, she feared that the man King Henry had ordered her to marry would make her vicious, scheming father appear a mere carica-ture of wickedness.

She imagined her fate as bride of the Barbarian Giles deVere, shuddering at the thought that he must wield the sword between his legs more brutally than most.

"I beg you, let me escape!" Desperate, she beat his back with her fists, causing him to swing her off his shoulder and against his mail-clad chest.

He smiled in the way Brianna fancied a stalking predator might, his dark gaze riddling her as if with fire. For a moment she thought he might set her free, if only to watch her scurry like a trapped rat for freedom that was not in the cards. Then she knew. *His reference to his men. The aura of leadership about him. This man, as gorgeous as he was to look upon, had to be none other than Giles deVere, the king's Barbarian and her betrothed husband.*

Brianna's heart clenched with fear—or was it with a primal need for the heat this man stirred within her breast? "What say you, sir?" she murmured, her gaze steady as she looked into his laughing eyes.

"I think not, wench. I rather fancy the taming of you, once we wed and I have you to myself. I am Giles deVere, Earl of Harrow. Your husband ere the sun sets this day."

Chapter Two

"By God, Giles, Henry did you no great favor!" Rolfe looked as if they were facing the might of the king's army, not one small, filthy damsel who strained against Giles's restraining arms.

Giles laughed, earning himself another furious pounding from his virago's tiny fists. "She will tame soon enough, brother, once I've taken her to my bed."

"Barbarian! Think you to ravage me as your battering ram sundered the gates of my castle? Never, as long as I draw breath." She pounded Giles's chest until he tightened his grip on her wrists and held her at arms' length.

"Protest will get you naught, Lady Brianna. Rolfe, summon the priest." Weary from fighting to gain what was already his, and angered by having had to search for his bride once he had breached the castle defenses, Giles yearned for peace—and the gentle touch of a woman.

Somehow he doubted he would find either this night with Lady Brianna, although he had no doubt he would find fire. If she brought a tenth of the passion to their marriage bed that she had demonstrated in her attempt to escape him, they would both flame and burn. None too gently he handed his reluctant bride over to two of his knights, instructing them to bring her to the chapel when the time came to say their vows.

Giles would follow his sovereign's orders with dispatch. The hurried ceremony would hardly befit the joining of an earl of the realm with a niece of the dowager queen. But he would not wait. The deed must be done and sealed, ere he venture out to take possession of Harrow's lesser holdings.

An hour later Giles stood before the chapel still in armor, the stench of battle filling his nostrils. Although he thought himself immured against the softer emotions, he shuddered when his young brother booted aside a body as he strode across the bailey.

Two men at arms struggled to drag his bride through the bloody maze. Like him, she came to be wed in the garments she had been wearing when he found her: filthy chausses and a torn tunic that would befit a serf boy. Her hair, hacked off unevenly and smeared with mud and tar she must have taken from one of the vats her men poured on his as they scaled the castle walls, made Giles shudder with revulsion until he envisioned how he would use this sign of her rebellion to conquer and tame her.

Briefly he pictured Brianna in the silk and velvet garments that filled several of his trunks. She would be a beauty, with those indigo eyes staring at him from a perfect oval face scrubbed clean of filth. Those long legs indecently displayed in boys' clothing would clasp him to her when he spilled his seed, and her full, ripe breasts would make delightful pillows for his weary head. Blood rushed to his groin as she approached.

"I will not wed with you," she hissed as Giles's men shoved her to his side.

Giles grasped her hand. "Neither of us has a choice, my lady."

"I will refuse the vows."

Nodding toward his men, Giles grabbed Brianna's chin and forced her to meet his gaze. "You will wed with me or you and the rest of your people will die. Think you I might hesitate? Look about you. Your foolish attempt to hold this castle has cost many lives. Will you make the toll go higher?"

"Nay. I will say the marriage vows. Be wary, Barbarian, for I make another vow this moment. Someday, somehow, I will make you pay for all you take from me this day."

"Defy me and you will be the one who pays, *wife*."

Giles had no taste for raping a reluctant virago, but he didn't think rape would be necessary. Brianna hated him with a passion—but he would soon turn that blood lust to passion for every sexual pleasure he would introduce. Looking to the back of the chapel, he nodded to Arnaud. Then he clasped Brianna's hand and turned back to the priest.

"Strip her, bathe her, and tie her to my bed."

With that terse order Giles shoved Brianna into the arms of a giant, scowling minion who had ordered her cringing chambermaid Elise to leave, the moment he strode into her father's solar. Never brave, the maid had wasted no time scurrying away as if since Brianna had wed, hers was no longer the voice the servant must obey.

Furious, she struggled with her new captor as she imagined her bar-

barous husband hurrying belowstairs to supervise disposing of the bloody remains of her people who had died trying to defend her home. How, she wondered, could God have bestowed such physical beauty on the beast she had been forced to marry? Why had the brief touch of his lips on hers made her body ache for more? And why had he left her in the care of this fearsome giant?

She glared at the giant as others from the Barbarian's army emptied buckets of steaming water into a tub they had placed before the fire. "Out!" she commanded after the men at arms completed their chore. "Think you I will bathe whilst you gape?"

"What charms you may possess hold no interest for me, my lady. Disrobe and bathe as your lord husband Giles directed." Only the giant's lips moved. The rest of him remained as still as a tree in a peaceful forest.

"Nay. I am no camp follower to flaunt myself before a man. Remove yourself!"

"I remain."

Brianna stomped a foot, wishing the Barbarian's head were beneath it. "Then I shall leave." Before she had taken two steps toward the door the giant had her in his grasp, his hands like a vise around her waist. "Unhand me!" she screamed, kicking out blindly in the hope of inflicting some pain on this implacable brute.

She might as well have saved her energy. Before she realized what was happening he had her naked and immersed to the neck in the steaming tub. His arms resting on his massive chest, the giant stared down at her. Humiliated, for no man but her husband should see her thus, she tried to cover her breasts with her hands.

"Bathe, or I will bathe you," he ordered, and from his implacable expression Brianna surmised that he meant what he said. Squelching her embarrassment and uncovering her breasts, she took up a bar of soap and tried in vain to scour the filth from her hair.

Finally giving up, she scrubbed her body free from dirt and grime as the giant watched, his bland expression unchanging. Did seeing her naked not make him burn with lust? Brianna stole a surreptitious glance at the giant's crotch. Nothing. No jutting bulge beneath his chausses, the sure sign of a man's readiness to mate.

Was there something wrong with her that she did not inspire this man's lust? Brianna gazed over at the bed where tonight the Barbarian would consummate their farce of a marriage. Perhaps like his servant, her husband would not desire her. Why did that thought not make her smile?

❧

Chilly winds passed into the great hall, through gaping holes made by boulders hurled from his own siege engines. Giles shivered as he sat in a tub set before the hearth, soaking away the evidence of battle from his aching body. His cock twitched, reminding him his bride awaited her deflowering in what was now his private chamber.

Rolfe, he noted when he glanced about the hall, had found a cooperative wench to ease his lust. Giles grinned. His brother, despite the time he had spent subduing Turkish harem girls, had much to learn of the subtleties of sex, lessons Giles himself had applied himself to with enthusiasm in the harem of an infidel prince whose castle he conquered while on Crusade.

His harem here would house just one reluctant bride. Giles hardened as he contemplated the tricks he would teach her. The sensual toys. Arnaud. As he had conquered her land, so he would conquer her, enslave her until she would beg to do his bidding.

Giles wondered what the lady Brianna might know of the sensual arts. Nothing, he decided as he watched the castle wenches servicing his men in the plain sight of all in the hall. While he imagined his bride, having lived in this place all her life, knew what coupling entailed, he was certain he would be the first to teach her the art of making love.

Ducking his head under the water, Giles rid himself of the last of the soap and grime. He rose and stepped from the tub, moving to the fire as he rubbed a rough linen towel over his body. After years of fighting he welcomed the luxurious earldom Henry had given him along with the intriguing vixen he could hardly wait to tame.

❧

"You are clean. Get out ere the water cools." The giant grasped Brianna under the arms and heaved her out of the tub. "Dry yourself. My lord dislikes wet bed linens."

Shivering, Brianna stepped closer to the fire and rubbed the linen briskly over her body and hair. She risked another glance down her captor's still-placid body, but that did little to allay the terror she felt at being here with him, alone. Naked.

"Lie down," he ordered, taking the damp cloths from her hands and nudging her toward what had once been her sire's huge bed.

The bed linens smelled fresh, sweeter than any she had known existed. And softer. Weary of fighting a fate she knew was as inevitable as the Barbarian's victory over her sire's depleted army she protested not when the giant rolled her onto her back. The touch of meaty but strangely soft hands against the still-damp skin on her belly startled her from her lassitude.

"Do not touch me!" Perhaps she had been wrong. Maybe this strange giant of a man lusted for her after all. She must not let him take what Henry and the Church had decreed belonged to the Barbarian.

"Be silent."

"I shall scream for my lord husband. He will kill you." *More likely he will slay me, as will be his right if I come to his bed not a virgin.*

"I but follow my lord's orders." The giant shrugged, then drew out four silken cords from his tunic and secured them to Brianna's wrists and ankles. Her struggles were for naught except to make her pant, more from fear than from exertion. "Lift your hips," he told her, his tone matter of fact as he gazed at her naked body.

His tone suggested she would be wise to comply. Big, imposing and not hard upon the eyes, yet somehow different from the men she had known, the giant intrigued Brianna as much as he intimidated her.

Although it wasn't easy to do, the way he had bound her limbs to the four stout posts at the corners of the bed. Brianna arched her back and lifted her hips. A soft cloth, even softer than the bed linens, brushed her buttocks as the giant slid it beneath her body.

Helpless. In all her sixteen summers she had never felt so impotent. She watched her captor rummage through a carved chest he had placed close to the bed. Half expecting him to bring out some instrument of torture, Brianna gasped when he produced a pot, curiously shaped, of colors that reminded Brianna of her mother's precious stained glass window, the one the Barbarian's missiles had shattered during the first hour of his attack.

Opened, the pot produced an aroma that stung Brianna's nostrils. Unfamiliar, exotic, pungent, yet not altogether unpleasant, she thought as she watched the giant dip a finger into the pot and bring forth a slick, pink paste. When he smeared the paste over her mons and between her legs she gasped, shocked that he would touch her there. Whatever this substance was caused her to squirm from its heat.

"What do you do?"

The giant grunted a reply she couldn't understand, but the warmth and tingling, and an unfamiliar ache deep inside her body, terrified her more than her huge, implacable captor. Was he about to rape her? Gathering her courage Brianna raised her head and blatantly stared at the still-unthreatening juncture of his thighs.

"I told you, my lady, your woman's body interests me not." Brianna thought he sounded somehow sad, yet she very nearly believed his words.

She looked for the first time at the giant's round, placid face. Light gray, ringed in blue, his eyes bespoke a softness she'd not expected. His cheeks were smooth, as if he grew no beard, but from the stubble on his scalp she guessed he had recently shorn the hair from his head. "Tell me what you do," she implored.

"I ready you for my lord Giles." With hands gentle despite their size he rubbed the paste into her skin, then wiped it away with a soft cloth.

Chilled air swirled against her body. Brianna hadn't thought it possible to feel more naked than she had, spread open and helpless, tethered hand and foot to the bed posts. But she did. Unbelievably she wanted to move—to feel something—to feel a caress between her legs where the giant had just removed that strange warm substance. What was happening to her?

He rummaged through the chest again, bringing out a filigreed silver vial. Uncapping it he held it over her tingling mound. Brianna practically screamed with frustration at the sensation of slick, slithering warmth sliding slowly, tantalizingly downward until it anointed her most secret places with a sensation the likes of which she had never imagined.

"Please," she implored. She wanted more, but of what she did not know.

When he spread the oil, massaging it into her denuded skin with practiced skill, every nerve in her body screamed in need. Then he stopped and set the containers on top of another chest, and she burned.

What was he doing? She watched him bring items from the first chest and arrange them one by one atop the chest that now held the pot and vial. First, a string of large, translucent pearls. Two silvery spheres engraved with exotic symbols, and a hood made of sheer black silk. A glittering blue-green feather and another, stiffer one she thought might have come from a peregrine falcon. An oval-shaped blood-red cylinder of glass, rounded on one end and stoppered with an ornately carved ivory handle on the other. Finally he brought forth a small dagger with a golden hilt and a thin blade honed to a razor edge.

"What . . ."

"Be silent." With large, smooth-muscled arms the giant pulled one last item from the chest, an exquisite bed cover of sable furs, and tossed it over her tethered body. "Lord Giles comes," he said as he stepped back, apparently inspecting his handiwork.

Moving to the bed again, this strange man took up the black cloth he had laid out on the chest and wrapped it about her hair. Suddenly she pictured herself as she must look with her chopped-off hair, still clumped up with the tar she hadn't been able to wash completely away.

"Thank you," she said, and she watched the giant nod as he stepped away again.

Chapter Three

Her husband took her breath away. The Barbarian in armor had intimidated Brianna more than she would ever admit. Still damp from his bath, his glistening blue-black hair cut short in the Norman fashion and his lean cheeks scraped free of the stubble she had noticed earlier, Giles appeared even more deadly than he had when he burst in upon her as she prepared to flee. His masculine beauty both terrified and entranced her.

She trembled as she recalled the sudden heat that had flowed through her body when he brushed his lips across hers to seal their marriage vows. It was as though, now, every cell of her scrubbed and denuded skin came alive in the presence of his potent male sexuality. When she strained against her bonds, each motion caused the fur coverlet to caress her as if it were some living thing.

This butcher who had slaughtered so many of her people, and most likely conspired to cause her sire's execution at the king's hand, had the look of a dark angel. An angel sent to release the tension that now sizzled throughout her body. This could not be the demon who had stolen all she held dear. If he was, she didn't care. Her bound fingers itched to feel him and her treacherous body urged her to surrender to her conqueror.

"My lady," he murmured, his devastating smile seducing her as he sat on the edge of the bed. The bed robe he wore, deep blue velvet that matched his sparkling eyes, gaped to reveal a light dusting of dark hair against his heavily muscled chest. Brianna squirmed at the growing heat deep within her belly, and the tickling sensation of the fur as it settled between her legs.

She wanted to feel his chest hair tickling her naked breasts. God help her, she needed this man to take her. Anything to soothe the restless, tingling need his simple presence evoked in her.

She watched him turn to the giant, who stood before the fireplace, arms crossed, as if observing a scene in which he played no part. "Is all in readiness?" Giles asked, his voice low and husky as he returned his gaze to Brianna's naked breasts.

"Yes, my lord. Your bride awaits your pleasure."

Giles smiled, showing those gleaming white teeth Brianna had noticed earlier. She felt rather than saw him reach out and touch the silk that covered her mangled hair. "You may seek your bed, Arnaud," he said, and only then did the servant move, inclining his head toward his master before striding from the solar.

Brianna gasped as Giles shrugged out of his robe, lifted the sable throw that covered her, and tossed both to the floor. She didn't need to look to his manhood to sense that he wanted her. The predatory gleam in his eyes, and the way his tongue darted out to wet his lips as his gaze raked her heated body, made his intention clear.

Still she had to look. She strained to raise her head, but from her vantage point she could see only his flat, ridged belly and the ruby tip of his penis that obscured his navel. Her mouth watered as she braced herself for his possession.

She expected him to fall upon her like the beast he was, but he did not. Instead he picked up a feather from the array of objects the giant had set out earlier and sat cross-legged in the space between her legs. Leaning over her he used the tip of the feather to trace a line from her lips to her quivering center, sending chills all the way to her toes.

His muscles rippled with every motion, calling her attention to the breadth of his shoulders and depth of his massive chest. Only a few scars marred golden skin Brianna longed to touch. She needed to see him fully, feast her eyes on the masculine perfection of his sculpted body. "Please," she whimpered as she strained against her bonds.

"Christ's bones, but you're lovely," he muttered, re-tracing the feather's path with a callused finger. "Soft. As pale and precious as these." He lifted the strand of pearls and trailed them over the same path the feather had taken, then let them swing slowly between her wide-spread thighs. Each jewel, cool and smooth, sent a shock wave deep inside her belly as it gently bounced against her naked, open core. His avid gaze set her on fire. "Dare I release your bonds?"

Moisture gushed from her body and trickled slowly downward as he watched, touching her only with his gaze and the pearls, which she felt swinging faster, bombarding her with sensation.

"I would touch you, husband." She had an overwhelming need to touch this stranger she had just wed, entice him to end this torture and fill the emptiness that burned deep within her. Writhing, she tried to pull free of her bonds.

"Be still, Brianna." Harsh words, yet softly spoken in a deep melodious tone very different from the way she had heard him speak to his followers, and her, ere he had shed the accouterments of battle.

"Free me, my lord." By now Brianna was unsure if she wanted freedom or continued enslavement. His heat scorched her when he raised up on his knees and covered the bonds on her wrists with long callused fingers. Hovering hardly a hair's breadth above her naked body, he pulled away when she strained desperately upward to brush against his massive chest.

"Nay. This night I would have you know you are mine, to do with as I will. I would have you know you cannot escape me." His breath blew warm and sweet against her cheek as he toyed with the knot at one wrist, giving Brianna the feeling that he regretted his decision to have her bound.

His heart beat a steady cadence she could feel, so close was he—yet still apart. "Had you not sworn vengeance on me, Brianna, I would loosen this tiny hand that you might feel the luscious softness of yourself, and the strength of my sword that will pierce you and make you a woman."

"Please. Upon my honor I would do you no harm this night." Her fingers itched to touch him, to explore sun-kissed skin that looked like satin pulled taut over muscles of iron. Had she lost her mind? She must have, to want this man after all he had done to her and her people. But she ached for him. Desperately and mindlessly, in spite of all that had gone before.

'Twas as though this mating had been predestined. As if God had fashioned this man only for her, and sent him here to unleash the fierce animal need in her to become one with him and only him. She had to touch him. "Please."

He smiled and shook his head. Trailing the pearls over her mons and up her body he let them settle in the hollow between her breasts. They seared her tender skin, but his moist, sweet breath burned nearly as hot before he covered her mouth and plunged his tongue deep inside.

Against her belly she felt the sword he would wield to pierce her maidenhead. Fearsome though it was, huge and rigid yet pulsing with life, it made her tremble more with mindless passion than with terror. Her body already wept with need for her lord—her enemy—to take her, to fill the pulsating void that before this night she had never realized was there.

The closely shaved stubble of his beard rasped her skin as he moved down her body, pausing to nip and tongue her nipples before burying his face against her hot, tingling mons. His tongue laved every newly sensitized inch of her there before he moved lower still and lapped at the throbbing knot of nerves he had awakened with the touch of the feather.

When he raised his head, she saw the heat of his passion in eyes so dark they seemed almost black in the dim glow from the candles. "Behold me," he said, rising on his knees and sliding forward until the glistening rosy tip of his throbbing cock nearly touched her lips. "Taste the sword that will pierce you, Brianna. Do not hurt me, or I will take your maidenhead without a lover's care."

Why would she hurt him? Every fiber of her being wanted his full possession. She ached to learn him by feel and touch as well as with her eyes. With both battle-hardened hands he cradled her head, lifting her until she could lick away the salty pearl of moisture she watched emerge from the slit from whence would flow his seed.

Long and thick and gently curving upward toward his flat, muscled belly, his sex enthralled her. Unable to free her hands she sampled him again with her tongue, not knowing why except that she would do anything to fill the emptiness inside her.

Savoring the musky scent and slightly salty taste of him, she clasped her lips around the ruby knob of his penis and sucked him in, swallowing and caressing him with her tongue until she could feel the coarse bush from which his manhood sprung tickling her lips.

'Tis strange, she thought, *that feeling him throb in my mouth makes the emptiness in my belly more intense.* Still she continued until he shuddered and jerked away.

"No more, my lady, lest you unman me," he said, his voice hoarse as he slid back down her body and positioned himself between her widespread legs. "I will go easily. I do not wish to cause you unnecessary pain."

More than anything she had ever wanted, Brianna wanted him to make them one. He felt so smooth, so hot and hard as he rubbed himself along her wet, slick slit. She couldn't move, couldn't wrap her arms and legs about his hard male body and draw him home. But she could watch.

She raised her head. His huge hot cock slid slowly into her body, and she relaxed her inner muscles to ease his way. He stretched her almost unbearably, yet she welcomed his fullness, and the sharp pain and tearing sensation that made her cry out when he breached the last defense of her maidenhead. Thrusting gently, he sank fully into her until she could not see where she ended and he began.

"Tis done. You are mine." The soft, wet kisses he placed on her lips gave sweet punctuation to his harshly spoken words. As if he found her gift precious, he withdrew ever so slowly and slid back home, over and over, faster with each careful stroke, until she felt the pain recede and sensed her body accepting that this man—her enemy and yet her husband—had made her part and parcel of himself. Sensation robbed her of reason and she gave herself over to it.

Brianna had never felt so full. It was as if she were perfectly attuned to the sight and smell and taste of Giles. The way the muscles in his arms bulged as he braced himself above her, almost in concert with the throbbing of his cock within her woman's place and the soft rasp of his chest hair against her puckered, aching nipples, drove her wild.

A hot, urgent feeling began deep in her belly and radiated outward. Her inner muscles clamped down on him when he withdrew, only to relax when he plunged harder and deeper with each measured thrust of his hard, lean hips.

Straining at her bonds she cried out, needing to draw him closer, clasp her limbs about his warrior's body and swallow him up. The heat bubbled through her veins, and she screamed at the kaleidoscope of sensations. His mouth came down on hers, muting the sound. His tongue plunged deep, in time with the cadence of his thrusts. Suddenly a dam burst inside her, sending shards of pleasure-pain to every cell in her body and consuming her as his hot seed shot deep into her womb.

When he rolled to his side, she missed his strength and heat.

⚜

"You are mine." Raising himself off the mattress and staring down at her sweat-glistened skin, Giles bent to sip at a rosy nipple. "Methinks Henry did me no great disservice when he gave you to me," he murmured as he rolled to his side. "You may speak."

Sated, Giles was of a mind to loosen her bonds. He fancied having her learn his body with her hands and mouth, the way he had just learned hers. That must come later, he told himself, thinking of the lesson he had yet to teach his bride.

"If I am yours, why did you bid your manservant to touch me?"

Giles met Brianna's solemn gaze. That had not been the response he expected. "Arnaud?"

She nodded, staring down toward her denuded mons as if to remind him what he had allowed Arnaud to do. "He touched me there."

"He didn't violate you, though." Giles pulled his trophy, the soft white linen stained with her virgin's blood, from beneath her hips and held it up for her to see. "He could not, even should that have been his intent. Arnaud is not a man."

"Not a man?"

"He is a eunuch."

Her eyes widened. "I do not understand."

"Look on me, Brianna." Rising, he knelt beside her shoulder, his sex plainly within her line of vision. "What do you see?"

"Your manhood. 'Tis not so big now." Still her tongue darted out and moistened lips that had recently clenched his cock so sweetly. He felt himself becoming hard again under her questioning gaze.

"That's because you just wrung the life from it, sweeting. Watch. It recovers even as we speak. I am a man. A whole man. When I look upon a woman I swell and harden."

"And a eunuch does not?"

"No. Eunuchs have no seed sac." Lifting his half-hard penis he bared his scrotum to her gaze.

"How sad. I knew not that some men lacked . . ."

"They are not born that way. Rather, eunuchs are made. The seed sac is taken, in much the same manner that stallions are gelded. Sometimes the rod is removed as well, as it was in Arnaud's case."

"But why? To create keepers for reluctant brides? You are even more of a beast than I first imagined." Brianna turned her head away, as if repulsed by the sight of him.

"I am not the one who took Arnaud's manhood." Giles gently stroked her cheek. "He fell victim to a Saracen's blade two years past. Rolfe and I came upon him in the desert, near death, and nursed him back to health."

"He was your servant?"

"Nay. He was lord of a great estate in the south of France. Not wishing to return no longer a man, he bade us inform his family of his death and asked me to take him as my servant . . . one of the gifts I would make to my bride."

"Gift?"

"A protector and defender, Brianna. One in whom I—and you—may place complete faith and trust. One who can pleasure you without risk when I am gone to battle."

"You would allow this?"

"From the infidel I learned the benefit of ensuring a woman's sexual satisfaction. Arnaud can ease your lust, yet hone it to a fever pitch for me. I need never fear needing the horns of a cuckold as long as he draws life, for he will guard your life and virtue with his own."

"Why would he do this, Giles? Does it not make him regret his state?"

"His state, pitiable though it is, gave him immense value in the East by making him acceptable to guard and protect the highest born women of the harem. By giving him that value here, in a Christian land where otherwise he would be useless, I give him purpose for having survived and returned."

Brianna met Giles's gaze before looking again at his pulsing rod. Her small pink tongue darted out and licked her upper lip. "If he is as you say, how can he . . . ? Is this the purpose . . ." She glanced at the articles Arnaud had arranged on the chest by the bed.

Her avid gaze suggested hunger as well as sexual curiosity. Brianna, he thought with satisfaction, would take eagerly to all the sensual arts. Her plump rose nipples beaded up as if begging for the touch of his tongue, and he bent to oblige them before reaching for the pair of silver spheres. Gently he rolled them against her cheek so she could feel the movement of the drops of mercury inside and hear the tinkling of the balls as they bounced together in his hand.

"Arnaud can use them to bring you release. They can also enhance the pleasures we share together. That is why he assembled them here this night. Feel the spheres. They can intensify your wanting," he told her, shifting his hand to her satiny mound and lower. With his fingers he spread her outer lips and inserted the balls, one at the time, deep into her vagina. "Milk them, as you milked me so sweetly," he ordered, pausing to cajole her nipples into rock-hard little peaks with his thumbs and forefingers.

"They feel cold. Not warm and alive. I would know more of my bride-gift. How he came to be unmanned."

"He killed a Saracen whose brothers set upon him and staked him out naked in the desert sun. As Arnaud tells it they slit open his seed sac, took his testicles, and forced them down his throat."

Brianna squirmed, apparently unnerved by Giles's graphic description. "But I thought . . . you said they took his rod as well," she murmured, beads of sweat forming on her brow.

Apparently her slight movement had set the mercury in motion. Wondering how long it would take for the spheres to drive her into a sexual frenzy Giles continued his story. "They did not. A Saracen physician we captured finished what the infidel warriors had begun. By the time my men and I came upon Arnaud his wound had festered into a mass of dried blood and pus. The physician cut away the rotted flesh that had been his seed sac and rod, and fashioned an opening for him to pass water through, that he might live. Thus Arnaud became a complete eunuch, the kind the infidel princes pay dearly for to guard their harems."

When she began to writhe in earnest Giles reached inside her and retrieved the silver spheres. Never had he seen a woman respond so quickly and completely to the slightest stimulation. That this wanton was his wife made him want to thank Henry again for his unexpected gift.

"After he realized he would not die, Arnaud pledged his life to me, and asked to serve me as the harem eunuchs serve the infidel. While he recuperated Arnaud befriended the physician's wives and concubines, and learned the sensual arts they practice. Soon afterward I conquered an infidel prince's palace, and placed Arnaud in charge of what had become my harem. There I learned of sexual pleasure I had never dreamed existed, erotic delights far more devastating than I had ever known. Skills Arnaud will help me teach to you."

❧

Hot and needing her husband's mighty sword to ease her, Brianna raised her head again. "Release my bonds," she whispered, not certain she wished him to comply. There was something exciting, forbidden, about being bound and helpless to the desires of this mighty conqueror.

"Soon."

With trepidation she watched as he lazily looked over the remaining items on the chest. "What is that?" she asked when she saw him grasp the strange red glass cylinder.

His other hand settled on the hood that covered her ruined hair. "A dildo. Puny as it is, it should soothe you while I rid you of this." With that terse reply Giles took the cylinder and inserted it where he had removed the spheres. Turning back to the chest he picked up the dagger. Brianna gasped, terrified that now her bridegroom intended to kill her.

"Fear not, sweeting. You pleasure me too much for me to wish you dead. Since you chose to hack away your hair in your effort to escape me, I intend to finish the job. I am going to cut away the unsightly mess you left behind." Lifting her head he loosened and removed the wimple.

"You are going to shave my head, as if I had taken holy orders?"

"Yes. The feel of your bare scalp in my hands will pleasure me more than running my fingers through this tar-caked stubble." He loosened but did not release the cords that bound her hands, and she felt his warm breath on her cheek as he raised her to a sitting position, placing pillows at her back. With one hand he pulled the short fringe at her brow taut. She shuddered when he made the first pass of cold steel across her scalp.

"Why did you not order Arnaud to do this?" In one way Brianna thought she would have preferred the eunuch's impersonal touch to Giles's sensual application of the blade to her skull.

"Because I wished to claim your body before taking your hair." The rasp of the dagger and the weightless feeling as locks of her hair fell away gave her a perception of freedom despite her bonds.

Her internal muscles constricted about the cool, smooth dildo, and she felt a scalding drop of moisture drip down the slit between her legs. The fact that Giles wanted to perform this act himself made Brianna feel in it a purely sexual excitement that overshadowed the shame of being punished, she supposed for the sin of having tried to defy her lord and master's will.

How can the touch of cold Toledo steel make me feel so hot? she wondered as she focused her gaze on her husband's dark, impassioned face. The small jagged scar that marred one otherwise perfect cheek stood out in the dim light, a white and stark reminder that Giles was the Barbarian—warrior without equal, thief of all she held dear.

He rose above her, moving the slow, sensual drag of the dagger across her scalp. His warm, firm cock nestled in the hollow between her breasts, gently abrading her skin with the bush of coal black pubic hair that surrounded it.

She had to touch him. When he shifted positions again she tried to take him into her mouth.

"Cease!"

His terse order lacked conviction. She rested her chin on her chest and tickled the tip of his penis with her tongue. He shifted forward and she took him deep into her throat. When he let out a tortured-sounding moan, she curved her lips around him.

Her head felt naked, yet he kept stroking it with callused fingers, as though searching for tufts of hair his knife had missed. Within her mouth he pulsed with life, and when he pulled away he shuddered.

Suddenly she felt bereft. The dildo didn't fill her the way he did—the way she needed him to fill her now!

"You've too pretty a head to hurt," he said, and the familiar pungent smell of the paste Arnaud had used to denude her body made her realize what he intended.

"No!" *Do not destroy the illusion that you have left me with a short, pale pelt to hide beneath the wimple I must wear to cover my shame.*

"Yes." He set the jar beside her head, where she could see its mottled colors out of the corner of her eye, and straddled her belly. Reaching behind him he removed the dildo.

"Open to me."

He slid down her body until his cock nestled between her wide-spread legs, then thrust upward to impale her.

He filled her completely, and she willed him to move. He did not, except to lean forward. With one hand he steadied her head, while he reached with the other hand into the jar and withdrew a handful of the pink paste.

"I do this to rid you of the stench of oil and tar. I would not have reminders of battle in my bed. Weep not. You cannot feel me pulse within you and yet not know I desire you shorn as much as I could want you if you had kept your flowing locks. Besides, the hair here will grow back. Until it does, you will like feeling my hands and tongue caress the naked skin no one has ever touched before."

At the same time he smoothed a layer of the paste over her scalp, he began slowly to slide in and out of her. Soon she was climaxing again, the way she had before when he had primed her with ever faster and harder rhythmic thrusts of his mighty sword.

The sensations kept building within her, making her oblivious to all but his thrusting cock, his hard male body, and his warm hands massaging her naked scalp. When he anointed her there with fragrant oil, her skin prickled, sending sensual messages pounding through her body.

She thought she could take no more, but when he lowered his head and plunged his tongue into her mouth as he increased the rhythm of his hips, she convulsed around him again just before he bathed her with his seed. The stark pleasure was too much, and she lost consciousness.

When morning came Giles took the black silk from the chest and positioned it over Brianna's naked scalp. His rod grew hard and ready as he watched her, totally naked but for the headcovering someone had decreed that married women must wear. His hands trembled with the need to caress her as he tied thin laces that secured the sheer silk covering and made it conform to the contour of her perfectly oval skull.

As he tugged on his chausses and pulled a short black tunic over his head, his gaze kept wandering back to his bride. Brianna had proven herself a sexual wanton, for which Giles uttered a silent prayer of thanksgiving. He looked at her and marveled at her stubborn spirit that must have prevented her from begging him to free her. Finally he had loosened her bonds, unwilling to wait longer to feel her tiny hands upon his manhood, her legs entwined with his as they slept. Unchecked, Giles surmised, Brianna's strength would be his undoing unless he proved himself to be her master in every way. Tossing the fur coverlet over her, Giles turned to the smaller of the two carved chests and drew out a small velvet bag.

Chapter Four

"Arnaud!"

The solar door opened and the eunuch appeared. "My lord?"

"The deed is done," Giles muttered, as he tucked the square of bloodied linen which proclaimed he had consummated the marriage into the waistband of his chausses. "I go below stairs to break my fast. Summon my lady's attendants and set them to fashioning braids from the locks she hacked off yesterday. I fancy such a favor to hang from my lance. When the lady Brianna awakens, summon me. I would present her with these gifts ere I ride out." After handing over the bag he had brought from the chest, he strode from the room, intent upon discharging duties less pleasant but no less necessary than the taming of his reluctant bride.

"You!" While she slept, Brianna thought furiously, her husband had left her with the strange giant he had assured her was not a man at all. Her muscles ached from her deflowering and the delicious ravishments that had followed.

"Lord Giles bade me watch you sleep and summon him ere you awakened. Wish you to break your fast?" Arnaud shifted in his chair, making Brianna wonder if he still felt pain from the ordeal that had taken his manhood.

"I wish to go below. The servants will expect their instructions."

"As my lady wishes." The giant rose and called out to someone beyond the closed door.

Suddenly she remembered Giles had shaved her head. Her scalp didn't feel especially cold, though, the way her hands and feet did where the sable failed to cover her. Curious, she raised a hand to her head.

Her fingers skimmed over thin silk when she touched her forehead . . . her scalp . . . even her cheeks and chin. A wimple. Not the starched, white linen one Elsa had set out the night before, but one so sheer and clinging, so revealing that her husband's blatant mark of possession would be evident to all. The very covering the giant had placed on her yestereve.

Brianna hated the way she ached even now to feel Giles's hard, warrior's body join again with hers. Hated her own weakness for taking such pleasure in the way his hands and mouth caressed her as they stole her independence—her very self. Loathed that she had lusted for him even as she felt him run his blade against her scalp, knowing he was shaving off her hair.

Her cheeks heated with embarrassment as she recalled how she had taken his huge cock in her mouth and suckled him even as he completed this subjugation of her person.

She smiled. While Giles had marked her his in a way she could not conceal, he had revealed his weakness for female flesh. Her flesh. She would bring him down with his own sensual arsenal. She would order her giant, unmanned wedding present to teach her how.

"Arnaud, will you teach me how to pleasure my lord Giles?"

"As my lady commands."

"I would learn at once. You will begin my lessons as I put on my clothes." Brianna rose, no longer shy at having Arnaud look upon her naked form, but anxious to don the clothing Elise had set out for her ere she scurried away the night before. "What did you do with the clothing my maid laid out yestereve?" she asked when she noted the bare top of the chest where she had last seen the garments.

"I put those rags away. Lord Giles has provided you garments fit for a great lord's bride." She watched Arnaud remove garments from her husband's larger chest and lay them on the bed. "My lord assumed you would be mourning your lord father when he had these garments made for your bride-gifts. There are others in the chest, ones you may wish to wear when the mourning time is done."

A black silk shift, so sheer she could see through it and so slippery it nearly slid through her fingers, would surely caress the sensitized skin on her body just as the wimple, fashioned of the same transparent stuff, was already fondling her scalp. Brianna felt her nipples tighten and her belly cramp when she set the shift down and looked at the outer garments.

The Barbarian had apparently spared no expense. The heavy black silk bliaut and sleeveless hooded cotte of loosely woven black wool shot through with silver threads must have cost him much gold. She was about to pick up the girdle of silver links, obsidian, and garnets when the giant eunuch stilled her hand.

"Come. My lord Giles will be here presently. He wishes to present you with your bride-gifts ere you don your clothing." When Brianna turned about she saw that Arnaud had moved a chair near the solar's large glass window and that he was placing some coals from the fireplace into a small metal brazier. "Stand here," he ordered when she approached, confused.

"What do you do?"

"I fire the needle to pierce your skin for the jewels he will give you."

Brianna reached to brush back her hair but encountered only the feel of silk against her fingers. "No one will be able to see them," she murmured regretfully as she tried in vain to uncover her earlobes.

"Lord Giles will see. Stop. You will tear the silk. I will show you how to unlace that later. Stand here in the light. I will ready you for the insertion of your other adornments."

"What?" From a small cloth bag, the likes of which Brianna had never seen, Arnaud poured a handful of sparkling mounted stones onto the table.

"You please me, Brianna. I would adorn you with rubies, set in pure gold from the land of the infidel. Stand still, that Arnaud may numb your skin for the piercing." Giles appeared beside her, his entry as silent as a stalking cat's. When he spoke his hot gaze raked over her naked, burning skin.

The ointment the eunuch was smearing onto her belly and around her upthrust nipples burned, then left the skin it touched feeling as if it were not there. "What do you do?" she asked, alarmed at the lack of sensation when Giles pulled a nipple taut between his callused fingers.

"Insert the wire, Arnaud," he said, and when the hot, sharp prick of the needle passed through her flesh she knew. As Brianna looked down to see rounded, heavy gold wire protruding from behind either side of the nipple Giles still held taut, he grasped her other nipple and tugged it just before another hot, tingling sensation passed through her body. Before she could do more than register that the eunuch had pierced her body twice with red-hot gold, he did it again, this time into her navel.

"Do not move," he ordered, raising up from his task and reaching onto the table. "The jewel, my lord."

Giles let loose her nipples to quiver against the cooling gold, and he went to his knees before her. Whatever he placed into her navel felt cold and hard, so foreign that she barely noticed the pain when Arnaud passed the thick gold wire through the other side of her navel.

Giles put his lips where the needle had pierced her skin. Touched, Brianna reached down to tangle her fingers in his glistening short black curls.

"Behold, Lady Brianna," he said after a moment, positioning the mirror Arnaud had handed him so she could see the huge, glittering ruby that winked from within her navel. "This is for my pleasure.

These," he said, reaching up to touch her nipples with a gentleness that surprised her, "will be for yours."

"I wish to see them." When he moved the glass higher she saw how four small rubies formed caps for the gold wires Arnaud had threaded behind each nipple and through narrow gold circlets. Her flesh stung, yet the little peaks quivered proudly, forming a rose-red puckered center for each of the jeweled rings.

"Oh," she murmured, imagining the delicious feeling of slippery silk—or the velvety moisture of the Barbarian's tongue—abrading the upthrust, sensitive tips. That thought made her instantly hot and wet.

"Care you to look upon your face now?"

Arnaud had removed the wimple, and Brianna's earlobes throbbed when he pierced them and inserted earrings that felt nearly as heavy as her knee-length hair had been before she cut it. Suddenly Brianna feared to look, aware that the girl she had been yesterday was no more.

"I would feel them first." Tentatively she raised her hands to touch the hard, cold jewels in her earlobes. Then, bolder, she skimmed her fingers over her scalp as if learning by touch alone the satiny texture and shape of a self no longer defined by the pale, wavy hair that now rested . . . where? "Arnaud, where is my hair?"

"My lord Giles ordered your ladies to weave the long strands you hacked away into braids."

Giles met her questioning gaze. "I fancy hanging one from my lance at the tourney three weeks hence. Want you to see yourself now?" he asked again.

She inhaled deeply. "Yes." Slowly she raised the mirror and met her own wide-eyed gaze.

A bald woman with sparkling rubies in the lobes of delicate shell-like ears stared back at her. Her eyes looked huge. She did not look repulsive, as she had feared, but she wasn't Brianna, either.

Myself? Nay! I fear I have become some otherworldly sexual creature of my lord's creation.

She raised a hand and touched the satiny-smooth surface of her scalp, amazed at how soft it felt. The Barbarian had done this with his own hands, and he had made what should have been a humiliating ordeal into a sensual, almost sexual experience.

She needed him to fill the suddenly throbbing core of her with his thick, pulsating manhood. Squirming now with lust she did not understand and could not control, Brianna set down the mirror and reached out to him.

This creature is me. A sensual, sexual fantasy made real by this man. Giles. My enemy . . . my lord.

Brianna craved Giles's touch. "Lie with me," she begged as she imagined his dark, battle-hardened hands binding her head to his velvet-smooth, iron-hard cock, his fingers digging into her scalp to hold her steady for the voracious invasion of his tongue.

She yearned for him to cradle and massage her scalp while his talented tongue tortured nipples raised and puckered by his sensual gifts of gold and rubies. When she remembered how he had licked and suckled her as they lay sated after a mighty climax the night before, she burned.

"You need time to recover from your deflowering, Brianna," Giles told her as he cupped her mound in one callused hand. "Arnaud will see to your needs and teach you how best to satisfy mine. I go now to secure the lesser properties of Harrow. My brother Rolfe will see to repairing the castle defenses here. Arnaud, while I am gone, do as your lady bids."

With that Giles dropped a casual kiss on the top of Brianna's head and strode from the chamber.

"If you require relief, lady, I am here to oblige you." Arnaud moved to the chest by the bed and picked up the dildo.

"Nay." She needed not to be reminded how Giles had soothed her lust with that poor excuse for his mighty sword while he ravished her yestereve.

The giant eunuch shrugged. "Perhaps the spheres?"

Brianna hesitated. She hurt with wanting, so much she hardly noticed the soreness from the piercings or the dull aches from newly-used muscles in her belly and thighs. When she had lain motionless last night, the gentle motion of the silver balls in her vagina had soothed the urgent need until Giles had replaced them with his mighty rod and given her relief.

"Perhaps," she said, conceding that her lust overwhelmed her modesty. "I will lie down that you may insert them."

"That is not necessary. Bend forward."

Desperate for relief, Brianna obeyed. The cold metal of first one sphere and then the other slid past the cheeks of her bottom, over smooth skin slick with her own juices and into the aching, empty spot that had lain dormant until the Barbarian awakened it.

"It is done."

Brianna straightened, her legs trembling slightly as the motion caused the spheres to shift within her body. "I would dress and go below stairs now," she told Arnaud.

"As you wish, my lady."

Silently he slid the silk shift over her head, letting it settle on her shoulders. The scooped-out neckline caught on her protruding nipples, making her wriggle in response to needle-like sensation that caused her inner muscles to clench and set the spheres in motion within her body.

She closed her eyes, then forced them open. Glancing down she saw the ruby-studded rings that defined her nipples—reddened, puckered nipples that jutted proudly against the transparent material. Automatically she reached to touch them, wincing slightly at the pleasure-pain the slight pressure caused. Brianna felt her inner muscles begin to twitch again, and the spheres rocked harder against the sensitive lining of her vagina.

She could hardly stand still while Arnaud tightened the laces of the heavy silk bliaut. The feel of smooth silk pulled taut against the skin of her jeweled belly nearly drove her over the edge toward insanity.

Realizing that the bliaut left her breasts bare save for the gossamer fabric of her shift, she gently rubbed her nipples again, then pinched and rolled them between her fingers. They tingled and stung, and swelled proudly against the ruby-studded rings.

Brianna was beyond caring what, if anything, her eunuch protector might think. Instead of gaining release, though, she only intensified the fire inside her.

"Sit, my lady." She did, and the spheres rocked together. Her gaze went to the juncture of Arnaud's legs. Nothing. Not even the slightest evidence of a sleeping sword. Giles apparently had spoken the truth when he said the giant possessed neither cock nor balls.

"Summon Lord Giles!"

"He has ridden out, my lady."

"I die. Do something!" Brianna's insides were on fire, and the eunuch's gentle touch as he smoothed the black silk over her skull and around her neck was stoking the flame. She barely felt him tighten the material under her chin or secure it with lacing that began at the crown of her head and continued down her neck. Desperate now she rotated her hips as she reached between her legs to seek the knot of nerves Giles had awakened yestereve.

"Help me." Layers of fabric kept her from her goal.

"Move to the edge of the chair." Arnaud sank to his knees and raised her skirts. Spreading her legs wide she watched as he bent his head and took her in his mouth. Impassively he suckled her until she shuddered. Then he pulled out the silver balls and, with a warm damp cloth, he wiped between her legs.

"That gave you no pleasure, did it?" she asked, relieved in body but inexplicably still yearning for what the eunuch could not give.

"Nay. I but do my duty to my lord Giles. He saved my miserable life, encouraged me to learn the ways of the Turkish harems. When he expressed the wish to bring some of the infidel customs home, I offered myself to him. The Saracen devil who stole my lust along with my manhood made me good for naught but to serve a master in some man's harem. I preferred to do it for Lord Giles than live out the balance of my existence there in the land of the infidel."

"Tell me of these harems."

Arnaud's laugh seemed devoid of mirth. "Every Saracen's home boasts a harem. And every harem has its eunuchs, most of whom were sold into slavery and gelded as small boys. Eunuchs like me, the Saracen physician who healed me said, are rare and costly because most who are made as I am die from the operation that removes the rod as well as the seed sac. All but the wealthiest of the infidels must satisfy themselves with guards who have merely been castrated in much the same way that your hostler might geld a stallion."

"You truly have no . . ."

"Naught but a tube of blown glass through which to pass my water. Were I in a sultan's harem I would wear this as an ornament in my turban." He reached inside his tunic and pulled out a clear, hollow tube that flared at one end. "Would you that I prove I pose no threat to you or my lord Giles?" Arnaud's hand went to the tie on his chausses.

Brianna shook her head. "Nay. Pray tell me if it pains you, though, for I know something of the healing arts. I would try to ease your suffering."

"What is not there cannot cause pain once the wound heals, Lady Brianna. Come, I will accompany you as you see to my lord's household." Arnaud picked up the intricate girdle from the bed and fastened it about Brianna's still-trembling hips.

Reaching beneath the weblike veil Arnaud had secured to her head with a beaten silver circlet, Brianna touched the sheer black wimple beneath it. All would be able to see that beneath the sheer fabric her head was shaven smoother than a nun's.

She would not cower in her solar, or hide beneath her long-dead mother's starched linen wimples. Suddenly, as she saw Giles's men supervising repairs within the hall, Brianna wanted them to know she had bowed her head in obeisance to the power of their lord, Giles deVere, now Earl of Harrow. From his jovial young brother Rolfe to the crustiest man-at-arms, her lord husband's men treated her with respect. None, however, would tell her more of her fallen warriors than that those who lived languished in the castle's dungeons, their fates to be decided at Lord Giles's convenience.

Brianna had to see for herself. With her giant protector at her side she hurried to the dungeon, trying hard to ignore the dank, musty smell as they descended narrow stone steps. Her sire had not allowed her here, where it was whispered that he subjected his prisoners to the vilest forms of torture. "Hold the light, Arnaud," she said, expecting at any moment to hear the screams of those who had survived the Barbarian's attack the day before.

She heard no screams. Were they all dead? Her sire, she had heard, had tortured his prisoners for weeks ere finally sending them to their deaths in the outer bailey. Could her husband, so fierce yet so gentle as he initiated her to the pleasures of the flesh the night before, have put her men through such an ordeal that they had succumbed in less than a day?

"This way, my lady." The torch in Arnaud's hand lit the way into a large room ringed with iron-barred cells. "On your feet, Norwen, and bid your new countess welcome," he ordered the young man-at-arms who stood guard within the chamber.

"My lady," he murmured as Brianna looked past him to the score of her father's men who lounged within their cells. "Wish you to speak with one of the prisoners?"

"Nay." 'Twas enough that she saw Eudo, glaring at her as he gnawed on a joint of roasted meat. Apparently he and the others, a motley crew of men-at-arms Brianna knew not by their names, waited here under guard for her husband to decide their fate.

"What will be done to them?" she asked, not at all certain she truly wished to know.

Arnaud shrugged. "When Lord Giles returns, he will offer them the opportunity to serve him as they served your sire, if they are willing to swear fealty to him. Except for the monk. He will be escorted to his cloister, with an account of the evil he has perpetrated here, unless Lord Giles chooses to deal with his punishment himself, monk or no."

Was the Barbarian so confident that he would allow those who fought against him in his midst? Brianna did not understand. Her sire had dispatched his enemies with ruthless abandon, sparing no mercy to those defeated in battle. "What evil?" she asked, glancing at Eudo again as the eunuch's prediction of his fate registered in her mind.

"Your armorer accuses him of having raped his eight-year-old daughter, causing her to bleed to death, milady. There are witnesses."

"No! I did not know." Brianna shuddered with distaste.

"Lord Giles tolerates no rape, and no violation of children. Your brother, if you have forgotten, violated another vow, the promise of chastity he made to the Church. I doubt that his abbot will take this kindly."

"What will happen to Eudo?"

"You love your brother well?"

"Nay. He is an odious man. And not my true brother, but my sire's get on a peasant wench. Upon my true brother's death my sire brought him back from his cloister in the hope of making Eudo his heir."

Arnaud glanced at the tonsured creature chewing on his meat. "He should have known that could never be. A bastard and a man consecrated to the church. Perhaps the one, but not the both."

"My sire was a determined man."

Curious, Brianna met the eunuch's gaze. "What will his punishment be if he is sent back to the abbey?"

"Castration. Possibly torture and death. I know not the customs here in England, but in France no abbot would allow a brother who committed such a sin to live. Yon churchman might be wise to beg Lord Giles to mete out his punishment."

"Perhaps you are right."

Arnaud nodded. "Lord Giles will not go easy on any man, let alone a supposed man of God, who has raped and caused the death of an innocent child."

"I may not hold him dear, but Eudo is the last of my blood relatives, Arnaud. Surely my husband would not have him put to death?"

"Nay. 'Tis a sin to kill a priest or monk. Cease your fretting. The worst that will happen to him at Harrow is to lose his manhood, and in a much more humane manner than if his gelding takes place by one not versed in the Infidel's methods. Rolfe, Giles's young brother, may indeed have already ordered the monk be made a eunuch." Arnaud gestured toward the fire at the center of the dungeon, where a burly man-at-arms was heating a small, open iron ring in a pincer-like device.

"Nay!" Brianna could not imagine the agony that white-hot ring could inflict upon a man's private parts.

" 'Tis kinder than hacking them away with a knife, Lady Brianna. He will feel pain when the ring is clamped tightly about his seed sac, then naught but numbness, or so those who have been gelded in that manner say. In a few days his balls will rot and fall off."

"Oh." This travesty might well have been ordered by her husband's young brother, but Brianna had no illusions that Giles would not have done the same, or worse. "My lord husband is indeed the monster he was painted to me before we met," she muttered, angry with herself because she lusted for him even now.

"Do not tell me you do not relish his attentions. According to the houris in the harem, Lord Giles is a most skillful lover. Come, I will instruct you in how to please him if you have satisfied yourself that your people fare none too badly here."

When she sought her room that night and for the seven more lonely nights that followed, Brianna immersed herself in the pleasures of her eunuch's impersonal but thorough ministrations.

Each night Arnaud bathed and oiled her, using his hands and mouth to relieve her when her lust became too much to bear. As he did, he instructed her in the ancient arts the houris mastered to please their infidel masters. Brianna ached to put her new knowledge to the test with her own absent lord.

On the eighth night as Arnaud applied the pink paste liberally from her neck down to her toes, she ran her hands over her thighs and upward. Idly she twisted the gold balls on each end of the wire that held the ruby snugly within her navel. The piercings pained her no more, but rather reminded her of how Giles had placed his marks of possession on her body. God, but she yearned for his return.

"Lord Rolfe has had a message. Lord Giles returns on the morrow," Arnaud said, shifting his gaze from his task to look her in the eye.

"Think you I can entice him?"

"My lady, you could make a eunuch's useless cock stand up and swell for want of you."

She smiled. "I could? Surely not. Do not tell me I excite you, Arnaud." Twirling the wires behind each nipple Brianna tugged lightly, still amazed that the delicious tingling shot from her breasts straight to her womb.

"Nay. But had I my rod, I would be forced to bind it tightly between my legs while in your presence, lest your lord note its enthusiasm and decide I needed it no more. Never fear, Lady Brianna, you will enslave Lord Giles." After wiping the paste away he rubbed heated, fragrant oil into her satiny skin. After he had completed her toilette, Arnaud offered her relief. Brianna declined, secure in the knowledge that by this time on the morrow, she would be learning the Barbarian's hard, fit body as intimately as he had learned hers. She promised herself that she would be well upon the way toward enslaving him, the way he already had subjugated her to his iron will.

Chapter Five

God's teeth! Giles thought, his gaze raking the prize that might well be worth more than the pile of stone and wood she had defended. *Brianna.* Garbed head to toe in his colors of black and silver, the small replica of his shield set proudly over her silken mons, his bride brought a smile to his lips and an instant hardening to his groin.

"My lady," he murmured as he dismounted and brushed his lips across her cheek. "I trust you are recovered."

Ruby lips curving upward into a smile, eyes sparkling, Brianna sank into a curtsy. The rubies twinkling in her ears beneath sheer silk made him want to see other jewels meant for his eyes only. "I am well, my lord," she murmured softly as she knelt, her perfectly oval head modestly covered yet not concealed, bowed before him as if in an act of obeisance. Or was it an act of seduction?

Blood pooled between his legs. "Rise, my lady," he growled, using one hand to pull her to her feet. Now was not the time, and here was not the place for his cock to swell in anticipation of her sweet mouth's beckoning warmth. "My other possessions came into my hands without a fight. Come, I would that you show me my castle." *And ease my aching within your tight, wet woman's place if God grants us a moment's privacy among the casks of wheat and wine.*

"I will show you the storerooms." Her smile made his cock twitch with anticipation as they descended narrow stairs to the castle storerooms.

Tightening his grip on her hand, Giles pulled Brianna to him and pinned her between his body and the stone corridor wall. He felt her heartbeat quicken when their bodies made contact through layers of clothing that somehow heightened passions they were intended to cool.

"I would have you now."

"Shall we seek our chamber?"

"Nay." Jerking at the string of his chausses, he loosened them and let them fall about his knees. "Lift your skirts and lean across yon wine cask."

When she complied he rubbed himself along her hot, wet slit. Finding his way easily, he thrust home hard and deep until his sac rested firmly against the knot of nerves he had learned was key to a woman's pleasure. His hands found puckered nipples upthrust proudly against the pressure of the jewels.

Wanting to hear his new bride scream with pleasure he set to fucking her in earnest, pulling her nipples rhythmically with each inward thrust that brought him ever closer to release.

Her inner muscles contracted fiercely around his cock, milking him dry. With a feral growl he gave up his seed. It took him a moment to recover and draw up his chausses.

That fast, hard coupling had hardly taken the edge off his lust. Giles barely managed to beat down the need to claim his bride again until after the evening meal. In the lord's chamber now, his own clothing discarded, his blood burned hotter as he watched Brianna disrobe.

Naked now, she stood before him, her gaze raking his already fierce arousal. "I would place my mark upon you as you did me. Behold the man in this picture," she told him, and his gaze followed hers to the opened page of a pillow book he had brought back from the East. "I would watch Arnaud make you thus."

He bent and ran his tongue over the incredibly satiny skin of her scalp, pausing to trace the rubies that adorned earlobes as soft as velvet.

So she wanted Arnaud to shave his cock and balls. The idea of anyone wielding a blade so near his genitals alarmed him, yet the idea of her running her tongue over newly bared skin had him instantly rock hard and ready.

"As you wish, Lady Brianna." Bellowing for Arnaud to enter, he positioned her on her knees above him, her silken sex within easy reach of his tongue. "I would take my pleasure whilst you take yours, however."

On the bed, his legs as wide-spread as hers had been on their wedding night, Giles lapped Brianna's honey as Arnaud wielded his dagger. Slowly, stopping ever so often to scrape the hair from the blade, the eunuch began at the crack of his arse, scraping the blade against his skin and testing each inch by rubbing a finger over it. Giles struggled to hold his seed, nearly failing when the dagger reached his nearly-bursting seed sac.

He suckled her harder, swirling his tongue around her sex as Arnaud grasped his cock and scraped away the thick bush at its base. He barely felt the eunuch's touch when he spread the paste between his legs. The chilly air swirled about him as warm, musky oil scented the chamber.

"So satin smooth. I like you thus," Brianna said, her breath beating a soft cadence against the sensitized skin of his crotch as she leaned forward and touched him. Then she took his rigid cock in her mouth and drew it deep into her throat while she rolled his balls between her tiny palms.

Christ's bones, if he wasn't going to come again. "Enough!" Pulling her off him he flipped her onto her back, coming over her and driving home in one hard thrust. The sensation of silk against silk, her satiny slit wet and hot against his own denuded skin, sent fresh desire to every nerve in his body.

Each thrust and parry, every movement felt magnified a thousand times. When it was over Giles realized he had submitted to Brianna's lust as certainly as she had fallen prey to his.

Twice in the night he awoke to the feel of her hands and mouth on him, and twice he rose to the occasion, pouring himself into her as he cradled her silken scalp between his own roughened hands.

⚜

Brianna slept until midday, waking to find Giles gone but Arnaud on hand to help her dress. Embarrassed when she recalled all she had done with Giles the night before, she managed to contain her sexual excitement as the giant tended her piercings and creamed away her body hair. As gently as if she were a child he dressed her, this time in a white gown and sheer white wimple beneath the same black bliaut, cotte and veil she had worn the day before.

"You may seek your own pleasures, Arnaud," she murmured when he finished lacing the wimple and adjusting the circlet that held her veil in place. "I would see to the needs of my people."

The giant shook his head. "My lord wishes me to accompany you, my lady," he told her. "He would that you attend his court this day."

"Court?" Giles wished *her* to witness his passing sentence upon her people?

"He tries and punishes those who defy his rule. He would have you at his side."

Brianna saw no way to defy the Barbarian, not as long as his giant eunuch was there to enforce his orders. After the pleasure he had given her last night she wasn't sure she even wanted to defy her lusty husband. "Very well. I would break my fast, ere I join my lord Giles."

"Damn! I've not the stomach for much more of this," Rolfe muttered, shifting in his chair next to Giles as they listened to the tearful accusation by the chief armorer that one of Giles's bowmen had raped the man's twelve-year-old daughter.

Giles tried to ignore the swelling in his groin that had begun the moment he saw Brianna enter the hall. "What say you to this?" he asked his man.

"She enticed me, milord."

"Then you may have the privilege of bedding the wench nightly. You will wed with her as soon as can be arranged." Giles cast his gaze upon the miller and his comely young daughter. "See that the banns are called," he told them before waving his hand in dismissal.

Rising, Giles strode to Brianna's side and stroked her cheek. "Come with me," he ordered, his rough warrior's fingers tracing rosy lips as soft as satin.

"Giles! There are yet men in the dungeons to be tried," Rolfe called out.

The prisoners could wait. Giles would not. "Let them languish a bit longer, brother. You may hear and decide the minor cases yet before the court. We shall return." Lifting his wife into his arms he strode up the winding staircase, intent upon easing the lust that grew every time he dipped into her honeyed heat.

Each time it was the same, yet different. Today she disrobed him with the skill of a infidel courtesan, her tiny hands making feathery patterns on his cock and balls. She used her tongue to dip into his navel, her hot breath to tickle the skin of his belly.

His fingers trembled as he unlaced her wimple. Naked now, she knelt before him, suckling his seed sac as her hands grasped his cock. Giles shuddered. Her greedy attentions were certain to drive him mad.

"Cease, my lady. I would spill my seed where it may take root."

Her pink tongue darting out to moisten her lips, Brianna looked up and met his gaze. "I would that you take my other maidenhead," she said. "Arnaud tells me that can give you greater pleasure than . . ."

"He is wrong." Giles had never particularly relished the act she offered. Still, his blood pumped faster when he imagined that tight, rose hole clutching at his sex. After all, this was his wife, not some nameless wench left over from a dead infidel's harem. "If this is what you want, I shall be happy to oblige you."

"It is." Rising, she positioned herself upon the bed on hands and knees, as though she expected him to mount her and take his pleasure. Amused at his wife's innocent eagerness, Giles turned to the chests by the bed and drew out a vial of oil.

"Arnaud must not have prepared you for this, my lady," he murmured as he oiled a finger and very gently worked it around her puckered rear entry. "I would not hurt you. And I would have you do what I do to you, to me, as well." When Brianna turned to meet his gaze he offered her the vial of oil, anticipating her gentle touch on a part of him none had ever breached.

She dipped her index finger into the vial as he turned on the bed. Her first touch felt as gentle as a soft breeze, as tantalizing as a melody coaxed from a lute. When she invaded him he tensed at the unfamiliar yet not unpleasant sensation. "Oil the dildo and place it where your finger is," he told her, needing to know whether what she asked of him would cause her pain.

Slowly, as if she too feared hurting him, she inserted the dildo. Discomfort gave way to a full, stretched sensation as she seated it fully, its handle resting within the cradle of his buttocks. He moved carefully, surprised to find his sex tightening further from this new, forbidden invasion.

Brianna sweetly caressed his throbbing cock before turning back to him. "It is my turn to learn new pleasures, my lord," she murmured, presenting him another dildo as she twisted around to give him access to her lush, rounded buttocks.

Gingerly he entered her again with one finger, then two. When her moans told him she was ready for more he inserted the dildo, inch by painstaking inch, until its rounded head rested flush against her puckered, pink ass. Positioning himself behind her, he buried his cock within her hot, wet woman's place and began to move.

Almost immediately lust overcame Brianna. Sensation upon sensation, silk against satin, white hot and so intense each movement stole her breath away, washed over her as Giles pumped rhythmically into her from behind. His battle-roughened hands chafed her breasts, the fingers plucking at her nipples and tugging gently at the jeweled rings . . . his hot, hard rod piercing her over and over . . . the ivory jostled into a matching rhythm as his balls pounded into its protruding head.

Her climax came quickly, too quickly, and only when she had rested did she realize Giles had withdrawn both dildos. His cock, still rockhard and pulsing moments after she had felt his seed flood her womb, prodded against the opening to her rear passage.

"Brianna?" She loved the husky timbre of his voice. Answering his unspoken question by moving to take the tip of him within her, she braced herself for this second deflowering Arnaud had described.

Later, as she lay in his arms, Brianna considered this man who was her husband, the man all called Barbarian. He was a paradox—a man who killed in battle without remorse, but who forced marriage on his own man for having deflowered a servant girl, and tempered his passion with gentle care that he not hurt her as they slaked their mutual lust.

She certainly hadn't conquered the Barbarian. She wasn't certain that she had even begun to tame him, but she felt sure she had pleasured him at least as much as he had pleasured her.

On the morrow she would sit at her lord husband's side as he finished meting out judgment on those of her people who still remained in her father's dungeons. Rubbing a hand experimentally over her hair that now felt like the down on a newborn babe's head, Brianna lay her head on Giles's shoulder and went to sleep.

Court began after the mass and a morning meal. After listening to Giles's merciful decisions regarding her people who had defied him, Brianna felt almost happy that King Henry had sent this man to rule in her debauched father's place. Lulled into a sense of contentment, she leaned back in her chair and imagined running her hands and tongue over every inch of her husband's lean, muscular body. Especially the silken skin of his magnificent sex.

When she glanced up and saw her half-brother Eudo being dragged into the hall by two burly men-at-arms, she shuddered at the memory of that molten ring and its grisly purpose. She loved Eudo not, yet he was the last of her flesh and blood. Would Giles punish him further, or return him to his cloister relieved only of his manhood?

"What is your complaint, my man?" she heard Giles ask a freedman she recognized as the castle's armorer.

Her gaze shifted from the armorer to Eudo as the man brought forth a tale that made Brianna's blood run cold. Despite the grisly evidence, she wished she could doubt that her brother, a monk who had long since taken final vows, could have brutally raped the armorer's eight-year-old daughter and left her to bleed to death upon the cold stone floor. "No!" she cried. "This cannot be."

"Hush, my lady. Let the witnesses speak." As if he cared that the accusation caused her anguish, Giles patted her knee beneath the table.

The witnesses' accounts convinced Brianna of her brother's guilt. The sly, unrepentant look on Eudo's face confirmed it. Brianna found herself gawking at his neat, recently-trimmed tonsure and wondering if it would save him from her husband's justice.

"What think you?" Giles asked, his voice low enough that only she and his brother Rolfe could hear.

"There is no doubt of his guilt. I ordered him gelded with the iron ring a sennight past. Were he not supposedly a man of God, I would have seen him suffer a painful death instead," Rolfe replied, his expression fierce.

"You cannot kill one who belongs to the church." Brianna could not bear for Giles to have a monk's death on his soul.

Giles appeared to be pondering his decision. Finally he spoke. "Brother Eudo. You richly deserve to die. I shall leave your fate to your abbot, however. I return you to the cloister under escort, with a letter describing the crime for which you have already lost your balls."

Eudo clasped his crotch through the coarse brown cloth of his monk's robe, his face paling further and his gaze meeting Brianna's. "Have you not done enough?" he croaked, and Brianna touched Giles's hand to gain his attention.

"Cease, my lady. Were this loathsome creature not of the church, I would personally see him not only castrated but disemboweled, drawn, and quartered." Turning toward the people of Harrow who attended the court, he spoke again, his voice deep and clear. "Those who take unwilling wenches in my demesne will be dealt with harshly. The sentence will be carried out immediately." Giles rose and pulled Brianna from her chair. "Come, I would write to the abbot of Brother Eudo's sin."

"What will happen to him?"

Giles shrugged. "If his abbot is a godly man, he will see to the evil monk's demise." His hand at Brianna's waist, he steadied her as they climbed the stairs to the solar.

"Mercifully?" Shuddering at the memory of her father's enemies screaming in agony as the horses rent them limb from limb, Brianna wished a less grisly death for her half-brother.

"I know not. Certainly you would not have the man live after what he did to that child?" Settling into a chair and selecting a piece of parchment, Giles began to pen a letter. "What is the monk to you?"

"He is my father's bastard. When my brother was born, Father dowered him into the cloister, where he remained until my true brother perished in battle. Then Father brought him home, in the hope that the king would allow Eudo to stand as his heir."

Giles met Brianna's gaze, his expression thoughtful. "And you hold this man dear?"

"Nay. He is of my flesh and blood, however. I would wish him a quick and easy death."

Setting the quill aside, Giles took Brianna's hand and pulled her onto his lap. "I would not displease you, my lady. Want you that I . . ."

"No! I could not rest should you have a churchman's blood on your hands, no matter how richly he may deserve it. I beg you, my lord, to return Eudo to the monastery, but to beg the abbot for his mercy." Unable to resist, Brianna caressed the raspy stubble of her husband's beard.

His manhood thickened, prodding at her thigh. "For you, there is little I would not do. Would you have me ask the abbot to let him live?"

"Nay. For what he did to that poor child Eudo deserves to die. Because he is of my blood, I would save him the suffering of torture."

"Then I shall request it. Better yet, I shall send Rolfe with his escort, to voice my wishes directly. One can never be certain someone at the abbey has the knowledge of written words." Calling out for his brother, Giles crumpled the parchment and tossed it into the fire. "Would you wish your brother farewell?"

"Nay." Reaching down to caress his swollen cock, Brianna wanted it inside her. More than lust, although he certainly inspired that, this man filled a space in her heart that had lain fallow since her lady mother's death. "I would love you," she whispered. "Speak to your brother. I will await you in our chamber."

Giles was so hard, he hurt, and he relayed his message for the abbot to Rolfe with haste. Handing over a pouch of coin to be donated to the abbey in return for the favor he would ask, he bid his brother farewell, cautioning him to complete his journey quickly, that he not miss the tourney scheduled to honor Giles as the new earl of Harrow.

Brianna trusted him to honor his word, he realized as he strode to the bedchamber they shared. He liked that. In bed she was everything a man could want. That had been his hope ere they wed, but now he yearned that they might become friends as well as lovers. Impatient, he stripped off his tunic before he opened the chamber door.

For a moment he wanted to commit murder, until he reminded himself that the man sitting on the edge of his bed rubbing oil into his wife's luscious body was not a man, but Arnaud, and that he had charged the eunuch with Brianna's care.

※

"Join me, my lord husband." Naked, her body tingling from the fragrant oil Arnaud was rubbing into her skin, Brianna watched as Giles quickly divested himself of his clothes. Like a pagan god, he stood before her, magnificently naked and aroused, scowling at the eunuch as he smoothed the oil gently over her breasts.

"Arnaud. You may leave!" Giles's voice was tight, as if it were all he could do to restrain himself from grabbing the eunuch and tossing him from the chamber. "Now!"

"As you will." A bland expression on his face, Arnaud ceased his ministrations and hurried away.

Giles sat where the eunuch had been, and traced a feathery pattern with his fingers over Brianna's breasts. "Like you the eunuch's touch?"

He is jealous. "Well enough. I find it soothing," she replied, her heart beating faster at the thought that Giles might be coming to care for her.

"Does my touch soothe you, too?"

Brianna smiled. "Nay. You enflame me. Come, ease the ache that begins each time I look upon your warrior's body."

"You no longer think me a barbarian?"

Shifting so she could feast her eyes upon his pulsating erection, he bent his head and took her nipple in his mouth. With his tongue he rotated the jeweled ring, sending a burst of heat through her. Instinctively she reached out to cradle his satin-smooth scrotum, rolling his testicles gently between her fingers.

"I think you a good man, my lord. Much more merciful than my late sire. I would offer you my thanks for treating my brother more gently than he deserved." Her breasts tingled as he suckled first one and then the other, the slight tug of the rings enhancing the delicious sensation. "I would taste you," she murmured, her tongue tingling at the prospect of laving his clean-shaven manhood.

"Love me because you desire it, not as thanks."

"I do love you." The man called Barbarian because of his legendary fierceness in battle had taken Brianna's heart, as surely as he made her body go up in flames.

"Then say my name. I yearn to hear it from your tender lips." Straddling her, yet holding himself just outside her reach, he seared her with a heated gaze.

"Giles."

He moved closer, close enough for her to breathe in the musky, clean scent of his arousal yet not near enough that she could feast upon his flesh. "You please me, Brianna," he murmured, "more than I ever dreamed a woman could. I know not of courtly love, yet you have found a place within my heart." Suddenly he rolled onto his back, legs and arms spread wide. "Do as you will with me, sweeting."

He tasted of salt and sweat and sex. His skin had the feel of velvet to her questing tongue, and his heart beat ever faster as Brianna caressed him with her hands and mouth. Pointing her tongue she lapped up the bead of moisture from the very tip of his engorged cock.

She wanted his mouth on her. She wanted his cock inside her, stretching and filling her. She wanted to feel his seed bathe her womb, that she might give him the heir all men wanted more than any other gift. Rising, she straddled him, positioning herself before taking him slowly within her body.

His callused hands chafed at her tender breasts as he rose to her, driving deeper with each upward stroke of his powerful body. The tension rose, breaking into a glorious climax. When her senses returned she felt him still hot and hard within her body.

"Giles?"

"Hold on." Deftly he rolled over, taking most of his weight on his massive shoulders. Slowly, he began to move above her, stoking her flame again until this time her climax came on the heels of his own.

"I pray to bear you a son come next spring," Brianna murmured as she lay quietly in the glow of a late afternoon sun that sent shadows over their entwined bodies.

Giles pulled her a little closer and rubbed one hand lazily down her back. "I would be as happy with a daughter, sweeting. Although the thought of losing you to childbirth is more than I can bear," he added after hesitating for a minute, and Brianna thought those words sounded as if they were being torn from his very soul.

He had said not the words she longed to hear, but Brianna sensed she had gained his love. "God willing, I shall bear you healthy babes for years to come, my love. I would not leave you, not for all the rewards of heaven."

Epilogue

Giles proved his strength in the tourney the following month, winning the fealty of those who remained of the old earl's followers. His talisman, he said, was the braid of Brianna's pale golden hair that she hung from the tip of his lance ere the ceremonies began. That night she told him she was carrying his child.

On the first day of the following spring, Giles paced with his brother and the eunuch Arnaud while Brianna brought forth their firstborn son. Mother and babe thrived, as their doting father would tell all who chanced to visit Harrow Castle. Peace abounded in the land in the coming years as the earl and his countess loved and made love. Giles deVere, the Barbarian of minstrels' lore, confined his warfare to the tiltyard, and the wielding of his legendary sword to the chamber he shared with Brianna, his wife and his only love.

Secrets

Volume 4

An Act of Love

by Jeanie Cesarini

To my reader:

It wasn't until I read Secrets Volume 3 in print that I thought of continuing the story that began in "A Spy Who Loved Me." Paige and Christopher had triumphed over evil and found their happily ever after. Lewis Goddard would meet justice. I turned the last page with a satisfied sigh—until Shelby piped up, "You're going to leave me a fifteen year old on the lam forever? No way! I want a happily ever after, too!"

Shelby was right. After all she'd been through, it wasn't fair to leave her a fictional loose end. She deserved a chance to overcome her past and find the man of her dreams. Guided by her hopes and fears, I honored her request, and now, dearest reader, just turn the page to find out how . . .

Take 23

Fractured light slashed across his face. His eyes were shadowed, dangerous. Feral. Shelby Moran issued a moan of half-hearted protest when he pushed the blouse over her shoulders, stripping away her last defense.

Cool air glazed her naked skin, but only for an instant before his strong arms enveloped her, every hard muscle of his body crushing her against the splintered warehouse wall.

"There isn't time," she pleaded, knowing as surely as he must how easily they could be discovered, *killed*. "We'll be caught. . . ."

Shelby tried to talk some sense into him, into herself. He needed to be strong, to push her away, because God knew she couldn't tell him no.

He ignored her. His mouth came down on hers, biting, full of darkness and urgency, his kiss stripping away her last vestiges of resistance.

To hell with common sense. To hell with tomorrow. All that mattered now was the air sizzling between them, the way she ached to feel his hands on her bare skin.

"I'm taking you, baby. Here. Now." His voice was gravelly, rough with unrestrained desire.

Stroking the column of her throat with a calloused hand, he drew the kiss from her mouth as surely as he drew the strength from her legs. "You're worth dying for."

She believed that he meant it. Need skittered across her nerve endings, and she fitted her thigh between his, seared by the proof of his desire, branded by his heat. He would take her violently right on the bare stone floor. No tenderness, no romance, just urgent sexuality.

She would not resist. She wanted him.

And he knew how much. Oh, yes, he knew. He would use desire as a weapon just as he used touch to banish her will.

His hands slid down her neck, over her shoulders. He cupped her breasts greedily, rolling her nipples with rough fingers. She moaned aloud. Her heart throbbed in her chest, almost too hard.

Running unsteady hands over him, she buried her fingers in the crisp curls on his chest. He didn't seem to notice how she trembled. His hard thigh slid between her legs, his hand explored her breast, his tongue made love to her mouth. Just as he would make love to her.

She *should* be tingling by now, riding a wave of desire that blocked out everything but their passion. She *would* feel it if only she could focus, if her heart would stop pounding and let her concentrate.

His mouth seared a path along her jaw, his teeth tugging on her earlobe. A cold sweat broke out on her forehead. A fine sheen of ice that warned of trouble.

Shelby breathed in deeply, a sound much like a sigh. She didn't resist when he dug his fingers into her skin and dragged her to the floor.

Concentrate.

Every inch of his hot skin scorched her as they stretched out on the hard floor, legs twined together, arms grasping.

The pounding in her chest eased slightly, and she closed her eyes to everything except the moment.

Feel. Respond.

He rolled her beneath him. Her legs parted, and he wedged himself between her thighs. A shiver slithered through her, icy sweat flowing freely when she felt his masculine length nestling against her. Goose-bumps raised along her arms.

Concentrate.

Stroking the firm roundness of his buttocks, she focused on the play of his muscles as he moved on her, trapped her beneath his grinding hips. His mouth crushed hers. Her chest tightened. She struggled to dislodge the breath that clogged in her throat.

Dragging her hands down his back, she raked her nails until he growled. In a few minutes they would be finished. . . .

Her long hair caught beneath his elbow as they turned together. Her neck snapped backward, not painfully, but so unexpectedly that her pulse erupted in her veins, all her efforts at concentration smothered beneath a blast of emotion.

Fear.

Her lungs burned. She struggled for air. Her heart hammered so hard against her ribs she thought it might burst. Unable to stop herself, Shelby shoved wildly to dismantle one hundred and eighty-five pounds of muscular male from her body.

"Cut!" the director yelled.

The command barely sliced through her panic. She'd blown it.

Bright lights flooded the set, exposing her shame beneath the harsh glare of reality. She could feel their gazes on her—production workers, cameramen, stage hands. When her co-star sat up and stared at her, Shelby covered her bare breasts with shaking hands.

She felt ridiculous, *ashamed*, but those emotions came only in the wake of a frighteningly real struggle to draw one more breath, to stave off a choking black void that swirled at the edges of her vision.

"Cut! Cut! Cut!" The director's voice sliced through her spinning thoughts. He threw a towel at her co-star. "Everyone get back. Give her air. She's fainting."

Shelby wanted to tell him she would be okay, but her throat was so tight, she could only draw in a trickle of air.

Suddenly Wes D'Angelo was pulling her to her feet, wrapping a robe around her shoulders. "You haven't eaten today, have you?" His voice was abnormally loud, but sounded so far away through the clouds in her head. "Hypoglycemia, don't you know. Everyone, take a break." He half-dragged, half-carried her from the set.

The shadowed coolness backstage did nothing to calm her racing pulse, nothing to ease the choking sensation that robbed her of breath.

"God damn it, Shelby. You promised," Wes yelled. "You promised you'd go see your therapist."

She wanted to tell him that she *had*. She'd been seeing Doctor Pich for weeks now, but her throat constricted precluding any attempt at speech. Dark spots whirled before her eyes. Her legs felt like lead.

Wes kicked open the door to her dressing room. "Here, sit down." He pushed her into a chair and shoved her head between her legs.

Mortified that this had happened again, that he should see her this way, Shelby felt tears press against her eyelids. She wanted to shrivel up and evaporate.

"Come on, babe. Breathe deep." He stroked her hair. "Come on. Breathe with me. In, out."

Shelby tried. Her ears rang. Her hands shook. She fought unconsciousness with huge gulps that let in only fragile ribbons of air.

She felt stupid, stupid, stupid.

But finally, after an eternity of false starts and unproductive gasps, the sound of Wes's voice calmed her, and she drew her first real breath.

"There you go, babe. You've got it."

Tears streamed down her cheeks. She could hear the ragged edge to his voice, his impatience. "I-I'm sorry."

"Half the women on the planet would give up their Xanax to get naked with Mr. Hollywood out there, and you have an anxiety attack."

She wanted to curl up and die.

He took pity on her. "They're getting worse, aren't they?"

Nodding, she wiped the tears from her cheeks. This was a nightmare. "I—I'm seeing a therapist."

Wes ran manicured fingers through his stylish long, gray hair and emitted a harsh laugh. "I hate to point this out, but it doesn't seem to be working."

"I'm trying, Wes." She sat up straight. "Really."

He started to pace. "What the hell are we going to do? We still have sex scenes to shoot. *If* we can get the first one on film."

Readying for battle, Shelby thrust her arms through the sleeves of the robe and belted it around her. She recognized his tone of voice. Sarcasm usually preceded intimidation.

"Can you shoot the stunts? Give me a week or so to work with Doctor Pich. I'll be ready by then. Promise."

"Been there, done that, got the T-shirt, babe." He frowned. "It's not only your box office sales riding on this film, but my future."

A flash of anger warmed her. It wasn't her fault that his career was at the breaking point. "Don't you think you're over-reacting? I'm one person. I can't . . ."

"This movie has to be a success, which means you have to film the sex scenes." He knelt before her and stared into her face, his own clear gaze icy.

"Get a double."

He blinked. "Forget it."

"Why not?"

"Fans are paying to see *you* on screen."

"Fans pay to see Charlie Brent," she pointed out. "But he got a double so he didn't have to show his ass in *Robin Hood*."

"When you earn out what Brent does, you'll have *carte blanche*, too." He swept his hair back with an impatient swipe. "I'm calling an acting coach."

"You want me to *act* my way through an anxiety attack?"

"You're an actor, aren't you?"

The man was an idiot. A brilliant director, but an idiot just the same. "I won't."

"You will."

Gripping the arms of the chair, Shelby leaned toward him until their noses almost touched. She wasn't backing down. "I'll report you to the union."

"I'll sue you for breach and smear your little problem all over the papers."

"Damn it, Wes!" Anger evaporated, and in its place came the sinking feeling of despair. She wanted to tell him to take a hike and storm out of the room.

But her legs still felt weak. Shelby didn't trust herself to stand. She *was* backing down. "Who?"

Wes stood and smiled at her. "Someone who could coach a monologue from a brick."

A Cameo Appearance

Jason Gage spun away from the computer monitor and snatched the telephone from the cradle. "Gage, here."

"Do I address you as doctor or professor?" The male voice came from another lifetime, no, another *world*, and Jason stared at the receiver, shocked into silence. Wes D'Angelo?

"Are you there, old man?" Wes asked. "I'm ignorant on the nuances of academic address."

Jason's fingers itched to slam down the receiver. Caller ID would definitely be included on his next budget proposal. "How about I solve your problem and hang up?"

"Leaving Hollywood hasn't improved your temper, I see." Wes's deep chuckle only piqued Jason's already strained temper.

"What is it?" Wes asked. "Doctor or professor?"

"Doctor."

"Of what?"

"Psychology," he growled, not in the mood to play twenty questions with someone from a past he had put behind him long ago. "What do you want?"

"I have a problem, Doctor Gage. I need your help."

A dull ache began at the base of Jason's neck, and he rolled his shoulders to ease the tension, wishing he had attended the dean's faculty meeting instead of begging off to work on his lecture. Wes D'Angelo and his problems had always given him a headache. It looked as if five years away from Tinsel Town hadn't changed that.

"Forget it, Wes. I'm on the lecture circuit right now. I'm only in town for a week, and I don't have time for anything except preparing my next presentation."

"You're breaking my heart." A disbelieving snort echoed through the receiver. "You haven't even heard my proposition."

"No."

"No?"

"Whatever it is, the answer is no." Couldn't get much clearer than that. Whatever Wes was, he wasn't deaf.

"We used to be friends."

Jason leaned back in his chair, gaze focused on the computer screen, every blink of the cursor reminding him how much time he was wasting on this telephone call. "We were never friends. You were one of my father's cronies who just happened to insinuate yourself into my career."

"All right. I'll settle for a friend of the family." Wes laughed. "It's been a long time, though. We haven't spoken since you coached Charlie Brent for me and launched him into super stardom. He's getting 17.5 *million* a picture now. We were a helluva team."

Jason couldn't deny that. Whether he acted or coached, his collaborations with Wes always yielded spectacular results. "Does this trip down memory lane have a point?"

"Just trying to jog your memory, so you'll be feeling magnanimous when I ask you my favor."

"I've already said no."

"This is a new favor," Wes explained. "I just want you to listen. Give me five minutes for old time's sake."

Had he really forgotten how persistent Wes could be? He hadn't forgotten. He had simply blocked it out. Wes had gotten him into more scrapes than he cared to recall, had opposed his retirement with more underhanded tricks than Jason could count on both hands. Wes had only been interested in using his fame to stay on top. That had hurt.

But on the other hand, Wes had stuck by him after the accident which had claimed both his parents' lives. Wes had been there when everybody else had turned away. That counted for something.

"Start talking."

"Good. I'd hoped you'd come to your senses." Wes laughed, but Jason didn't miss the relief in his voice. "You've heard of Shelby Moran?"

Who hadn't? The raven-haired beauty had burst upon Hollywood like a storm. Even he was impressed. More than once he had found himself calling in favors at the local video store to get her latest releases. "You've been doing a great deal of work with her lately."

"I'm flattered you've been paying attention." Wes's voice dropped a notch. "Have you seen her in anything? She's good. *Really* good. She could be great."

Jason agreed. Back when he had been coaching, he would have given his right arm for a student with Shelby Moran's potential. But now, at forty-one, he'd been out of that business for five years and had no intention of backtracking.

This conversation was going nowhere. "I'm not interested in coaching *anyone*. No matter how good she is."

"I just need you to teach her some techniques to help her through this problem she's having."

An image of the willowy, green-eyed actress flashed through his mind, but Jason's image didn't involve problems. Shelby Moran looked perfect as far as he could tell.

He shouldn't ask, should just hang up the phone right now and change his number, but the lure of those bedroom eyes was just too much. It had been too damn long since he'd had a date. "What kind of problem?"

"She freaks out during sex scenes."

Surprised, Jason sat up in his chair. "Any history of sexual abuse?"

"Hell, I never thought to ask." Wes emitted an unsteady laugh. "I'm not a psychologist. All I know is that if I don't get her through filming, I won't have an eligible release for the awards."

"Couldn't have that, could we?" Jason glanced out the window, squelching a rush of familiar emotion and letting the serenity of the landscaped university center him.

He knew what it felt like to be used as a vehicle to further someone else's ambitions. Looked like Shelby Moran was filling the bill now.

"Will you help me, Jason?"

He didn't hesitate. No matter how fast his pulse raced when he thought of being face-to-face with Shelby Moran, she'd have to learn for herself what the price of stardom was. "Sorry, Wes. Not my line anymore."

"She just needs a little coaching so she can deliver a decent performance without hyperventilating."

The accomplished young woman he had seen on screen contrasted sharply with the image Wes depicted. "If Shelby Moran has emotional issues, coaching won't help. Get her into therapy."

"She can deal with her problems on her own time," Wes erupted. "Right now I've got a film to direct."

"Compassionate as ever, aren't you?" Jason couldn't keep the bitterness from his voice as he took a deep breath to dispel his distaste.

This situation was not something he wanted to get involved in. Even if the thought of coaching Shelby Moran through sex scenes made his heart beat faster. "Let her go, Wes. Let her get the help she needs."

"You don't understand . . ."

"I understand completely. Shelby Moran is the most promising actress to come around in a while, and you're riding on her coattails because your last three films bombed."

"Ouch." Wes laughed, but the edge to his voice didn't fade. "You know how this business is."

"That's why I'm out." Jason rocked back in his chair. He stared out at the campus grounds, lush with the green of summer. The serenity of the scene reflected his peace of mind. No matter what the pros and cons of his new life, he was much better off out of Hollywood. "I won't change my mind. Good luck."

A heavy silence greeted him before Wes said, "I'm sorry, old man, but I must ask you to reconsider."

His flat tone made Jason's hackles rise. He braced himself against the ax he sensed about to fall.

"I haven't read anything about you in the rag sheets in what . . . three, maybe four weeks?"

Jason didn't answer. He propped his feet up on the window ledge and waited for Wes to play his hand.

"You must be enjoying all that privacy. I mean, I know how much you resented the paparazzi dogging you all the time. Even now they don't really leave you alone, do they?"

"So?"

"You're a mystery. Hollywood gifted you with stardom and you tossed it back in their faces. They're fascinated. Helluva career move."

"Your point?"

Wes laughed. "Remember that seedy little blue flick you made back in '74? The one that earned the X-rating and cost your father a fortune to keep from being released?"

Jason remembered very well. It had been one of his first attempts to break free of a career that had consumed his entire life. "What about it?"

"I have a copy sitting in my film vault."

Jason clutched the receiver and struggled to keep the revulsion from his voice. "I don't care if you release that. I was a kid for Christ's sake."

"*You* might not care, but the *paparazzi* will," Wes drawled. "Ready to step back into the spotlight?"

He wasn't, and the bastard damn well knew it. Jason exhaled a harsh breath. "Don't pull this crap on me."

"I asked nicely. You said no."

Was he bluffing? Jason didn't trust Wes as far as he could throw him. It had taken five long years to achieve the degree of privacy he enjoyed now. Five years to be able to walk out his front door without facing the flash of cameras, to drive to the university, or the airport, or the damned grocery store without outrunning the paparazzi.

He had been Chase and Elena's son, Hollywood's golden child whose entire life had been public domain. After his parents had died, the world had grieved with him, then watched him grow into adult-hood, delighted, angered and, above all, entertained, by his antics.

Until Jason turned his back on them.

Now he was an enigma. His only defense was the utterly *ordinary*, utterly *uninteresting* life he led.

Was he willing to step back into the spotlight now when, for the first time in his life, he could finally open his eyes without being blinded by the glare?

Jason gripped the receiver so tightly that his hand trembled. "Give me her address."

Star-Struck

Shelby crossed the foyer and cast a quick glance at the grandfather clock. Eight on the dot. The acting coach Wes had hired was right on time.

Lucky her.

Stopping just short of the door, she stood with her hand poised over the knob and calmed the flutters in her stomach. The moment of truth had arrived in the form of a stranger, and she was totally unprepared. No matter how hard she tried to gear herself up, the idea of tackling this problem still made her queasy. Maybe she should just give up acting?

But she couldn't give up life. With a little luck, if she could learn how to film a sex scene, she might be able to perform one in real life, too.

Taking a deep breath, Shelby cleared her thoughts and placed herself in the mindset of cordial hostess. *Open the door. Greet the guest.* She could do this.

The doorbell chimed again.

Rolling her shoulders to dispel the last of her tension, she settled a smile on her face and turned the knob.

"Hello." Shelby peered out at the powerhouse of a man who stood on her doorstep, faded jeans slung low on trim hips and expensive athletic shoes bracing long legs firmly apart. Her heart dropped to her feet.

Jason Gage?

No way. The lengthening twilight cast him in silver and shadow, and she quickly took in his casual, but masculine stance, his well-toned body. He radiated intensity, the robust energy of a man in his prime, a self-possession nobody half his age ever quite managed to pull off.

Experience. That's what it was. This was a man who had lived. She could see it in the chiseled planes of his face—a handsome face, an interestingly rough and experienced face. A face she had studied in stark clarity on film. A face she had seen grainy and shadowed on tabloids in the supermarket.

Jason Gage. In the flesh.

"Miss Moran?"

She had heard his voice a thousand times. Deep and strong, like a velvet murmur, his voice conjured up images of dark bedrooms and slick bodies.

Leaning back against the balustrade, he looked terribly roguish, just as he had when he had played Frankie Worth in *The Last Rebel*. He folded his arms across his chest and scowled before Shelby realized she had missed her cue. Jason Gage apparently was not amused by the way she kept gawking at him.

"Are you going to invite me in?"

Heat singed her cheeks with the force of Pepe's Beyond The Border Salsa. "Of course. Please." Feeling really stupid, she stumbled back against the door and allowed him to enter.

Striding past her in a burst of masculine grace that trampled what was left of her composure, Shelby suddenly found herself staring at his impossibly wide shoulders. The torchiere lamps illuminated his hair, thick wavy hair that was neither brown nor auburn, but some wonderful russet color in between.

Swinging back around, he sized her up with brilliant black eyes. "Are you coming?"

Shelby nodded. There was no recovering from this one. She'd flopped. Big time. "I'm so sorry. It's just—well, I wasn't expecting *you.*"

"Obviously." His full mouth tightened in a frown.

Get a grip, Shelby. Forcing herself into motion, she pulled the door closed and sailed past him, taking the opportunity to steady her nerves.

Leading him into the living room—a room large enough to allow her some breathing space—she moved as far away as politely possible. "May I take your—" She glanced around for whatever he had brought with him. Coat? Briefcase? Garment bag? "Keys. May I take your keys?"

"No." He hooked them onto his belt loop. Assessing the room in one even glance, he did not look pleased by what he saw.

She had decorated the room herself, just as she had the rest of the house. Stripped and refinished the woodwork by hand, fitted the cornices above the windows, selected everything from the draperies and floral arrangements to the mirror above the fireplace and the cloisonné vase that sat on the oriental-inspired "biblot" table beside the door. The result was a Victorian drawing room washed in shades of pink and burgundy that sent a tingle through her every time she glanced around.

Granted, Jason looked like a stallion in a field of dandelions against the backdrop of curio shelves and ornately-worked étagères. So was it her taste in furnishings that offended him, or did she herself displease him?

"Are you ready to work, Miss Moran?"

"I *was*. Until I saw you." She brushed an errant strand of hair from her face, then forced her arms to her sides. She didn't know what to do with her hands. "I *really* wasn't expecting you."

"Can you handle it?" he asked on the edge of an impatient breath.

"I don't know."

He seemed almost relieved, and she would have bet her bottom dollar that he would rather be anywhere in the world but here.

"How on earth did Wes talk you into this?" she asked bluntly.

"Blackmail." The reply was just as succinct.

That certainly wasn't what she had expected.

"The weasel!" Plopping back into a chair, she eyed him curiously. "Must really have the goods on you."

Those sable eyes bored into her. "No comment."

Yep, she'd bet that Jason Gage would rather be roasting in hell right now.

She tried to act composed, *recovered*, but the breath caught in her when he sat across from her, so close she couldn't help but notice the way his long body folded in a neat display of muscle, how he looked oh-so-masculine on her delicate Queen Anne settee.

"Wes told me a little about what's going on, Miss Moran. You sure you're up to this?"

"Absolutely."

Not!

"Then we need to cover a few ground rules." He compressed his mouth into a thin line. "If you want me to work with you, you'll have to agree to protect my privacy. I am not out of retirement and don't want to deal with the backlash of anyone thinking I am. This was one of my conditions to Wes."

"That's quite acceptable, Mr. Gage. I'm not exactly eager for media coverage either."

He blinked, and what she thought might be the start of a smile tugged at his lips. He managed to control it. "I don't imagine you are."

Slipping off her sandals, Shelby tucked her feet underneath her. She needed every relaxation technique she could think of right now, starting with casual posture. "I have a few questions of my own. The first of which is what you think you can actually do for me."

"You sound skeptical." He raised an eyebrow in that wonderfully quizzical expression she remembered so well from *The Longest Day Of The Century*.

He had played a quirky scientist in that one. A comedy that still made her laugh even though she must have seen it thirty times.

"Oh, I'm definitely skeptical. This was Wes's idea."

"But you agreed."

"No, Mr. Gage. *I* threatened to report him to the union." Shelby flashed her brightest smile. "*He* threatened to leak my problem to the press."

Jason let out a snort that might have been a laugh. "He is a weasel, isn't he?"

"Absolutely. But I've decided to make the best of a bad situation. Have you?"

He studied her for a long moment, and when he finally nodded, Shelby sucked in a breath that reminded her she'd almost forgotten to breathe.

"We'll call a truce." He leaned back on the settee and rested an elbow on the cushioned arm. "You had a few questions. What would you like to know?"

In the blink of an eye, all aggression left his expression, and she suddenly faced a man who reminded her of . . . her therapist.

Shelby laughed. "I was so surprised to see you, I'd forgotten."

"What?"

"You're a psychologist now. I read it in the papers."

He nodded.

"Are you here to coach me or psychoanalyze me?" She wasn't sure she was comfortable with either.

"I'm just here to help." He steepled his fingers before him and offered his first real smile.

Ohmigosh! Her heart skipped a beat, and she struggled to draw a decent breath through a chest that suddenly felt way too tight.

No wonder Jason Gage had been a star. He oozed presence like nobody she'd ever seen before. One smile, and she not only knew she was in the same room with him, but on the same planet.

She was *never* going to be able to work with him.

"I plan to take you back to your acting basics, Miss Moran. Relaxation. Concentration. Then we can move into sense and affective memory."

She didn't know whether to laugh or cry. "I've used every trick in my repertoire. Know any magic?"

"We don't need magic." His deep velvet voice made her chest squeeze even tighter. "You're obviously hung up somewhere. We just need to figure out where and find you some other stimuli to draw from when you perform."

Shelby let out a sigh. "You're talking coaching, not psychology. Right?"

"You'd be surprised at how closely the two are related. But I have no intention of prying. You fill in the blanks whenever you feel it's necessary. Fair enough?"

She nodded, not trusting herself to answer while experiencing such a strange mixture of relief, apprehension and foolishness. Relief that she wouldn't have to take a trip down memory lane. Apprehension because she didn't think she could avoid it. Foolishness because she needed Jason's help but couldn't seem to think straight when she looked at him.

"You're still worried."

He *knew*. As if he could see straight through to her soul, Jason Gage knew she had a horrible secret. But she had already spent years in and out of therapy working through all the emotional baggage from a dark past. She refused to believe that anything constructive could come from rehashing old memories.

Jason must have sensed her turmoil because he reached out and took her hand. "You can trust me, Miss Moran."

Tension melted. His grip was strong, warm, *giving*. Shelby knew in that instant no matter what the paparazzi wrote about the infamous Jason Gage—no matter how surly, ungrateful or selfish they portrayed him—they didn't have a clue about the man himself. This was a man who had been coerced to come here, yet he was willing to help. If he said she could trust him, she could.

And the protective way he held her hand said everything.

Shelby decided right then and there that she was going for the pot of gold at the end of the rainbow.

Her fingers tightened around his. "Can you teach me how to perform a sex scene?"

"Yes."

She lifted her gaze to find him watching her. With concern. And determination.

She believed that he would never hurt her.

Shelby swallowed hard. "Do you think you could teach me how to perform *sex*, too?"

Wouldn't Miss this Show . . .

"Your trouble isn't just with performing a sex *scene*, but with having sex?" Jason kept his voice level and his gaze steady, but it was a damn good thing he was sitting. Otherwise he might have hit the floor.

Shelby tried to pull her hand away. He held on.

"Yes." She breathed the word in a sigh, and something fluttered in his chest at the vulnerability he saw in her eyes.

God, she had beautiful eyes. Greener than the lawns at the university during summer session, her eyes attracted him just like that inviting place did.

"For how long?" He forced the words out, struggling for professional distance when all he wanted to do was stroke away the frown that creased her brow.

"I didn't have any problem filming sex scenes until about a year ago." She shrugged, a gesture that admitted defeat more eloquently than words. "Sex has always been a disaster."

"Always?"

She cast him a crooked grin. "Always."

Blood thudded through his veins. Shelby Moran wasn't at all what he had expected. Not by a long shot.

"Why has sex been a problem?"

Jason felt her agitation even before she jerked her hand away. Shooting to her feet in a fluid motion that drew his gaze along the slender lines of her body, she ran a hand through hair the color of soot and paced before the fireplace. "I don't know why."

"I said I wouldn't pry, but it would help me immensely to know if you have a history of sexual abuse."

"I don't," she answered defensively before turning to face him. "Something happened once. A long time ago. But it's all over now. I worked through it."

"This *something* doesn't have anything to do with your inability to perform a sex scene or have sex, does it?"

"No," she answered decidedly, then shrugged in obvious exasperation. "Oh, I don't know."

At first he thought she was trying to convince him, but he quickly realized she must be trying to convince herself.

Time for a new approach. "You asked me earlier if I thought coaching would help, and I'm going to ask you the same thing now. Do you think coaching will help?"

"Yes."

Apparently she was willing to settle for a sex life based on acting. That said a lot about what she was willing to sacrifice.

This was a problem Jason hadn't anticipated, and they already had a significant one. His professional detachment had vanished the minute she had opened the door. One look at her, and his blood had started pumping double-time.

Shelby Moran was definitely not what he had prepared himself for. She was tall, a bit too thin, a bit too lanky. He knew her runway model body filmed well, yet he couldn't help but wonder if those slender shoulders could bear the emotional burden she carried.

What had happened to her? So many tragedies could befall a beautiful young girl that inwardly he cringed at the possibilities. She must have been really young, because he knew she was only twenty-six now.

She seemed determined, though. He could see purpose in the stubborn tilt of her chin and the firm set to her lush pink mouth.

But Shelby was an actress, and a good one. While Jason didn't think her vulnerability was an act, in his experience, a vulnerable starlet was a contradiction in terms.

"This is more involved than I was led to believe. What do I get out of the deal?" he asked, needing to verify the impression he had formed about Shelby Moran.

Her back stiffened, and her straight black hair glimmered like glass as it swung with the movement. "The satisfaction of knowing you helped someone in need?" He wished she would turn around so he could see her face.

Jason came to his feet. Crossing the room, he stood behind her. Although she was tall, the top of her head only reached his chin. She jumped when he placed his hand on her shoulder.

"I'm no altruist."

"You'll get to have sex with me." Her words stabbed at his conscience.

"That's not much of an enticement. You've already said you're a disaster in bed."

She spun around, and his next challenge lodged in his throat when he gazed down at her exquisite face. Jason knew what it felt like to want. Shelby wanted to work through her problem more than she wanted anything else. He *felt* her longing like an electrical surge through his body. The strength of the connection he shared with her stunned him.

"I guess you'll just get to keep your secrets, then." Her green eyes sparkled, and he suspected she was fighting back tears. He felt chagrined.

"Wes won't let you off the hook, Mr. Gage. He's got a vested interest in me."

Jason didn't point out that he'd get to keep his secrets simply by coaching her through sex scenes. He would help Shelby, and maybe while he was helping her, he could alleviate some of the restlessness he had been experiencing since the start of his current lecture circuit.

Unable to resist, he ran his thumb along the full curve of her bottom lip. Her skin was soft to his touch. Warm satin.

"If I'm going to be your sex coach, perhaps you should call me Jason."

Her liquid gaze met his, and her lip trembled. "You'll do it?"

"I'd be honored." He meant it.

"All right, *Jason.*" Her mouth curved upward into a smile. "What about the logistics?"

"We'll work here. I've got my bags in the car."

That seemed to fluster her. "Wow. Great." She ran a jittery hand through her hair and backed away. "I'll go make up the guest bedroom while you get your stuff. Okay?"

He let his hand drop to his side, amused that his skin still tingled from where he touched her. It looked as though Shelby wasn't the only one star-struck.

"I'll go get my things."

Her relief was almost palpable. Spinning on her heel, she disappeared. Jason recognized retreat when he saw it, and for the first time in a very long time, he felt like smiling.

The Divine Comedy

Ohmigosh! Shelby swung into the guest bedroom, the only bedroom besides her own in the oceanside cottage. She pulled the door closed, sorry that she hadn't plunked down more money for a larger place.

But why had she needed more space? Up until twenty minutes ago, the only people who ever visited her had been Paige and Christopher Sharp, her "family-by-love" as she thought of them. After everything they had been through together during the years, she and the Sharps were so close they could have easily sacrificed the second bedroom and held a slumber party in hers.

For the first time ever, her comfortable little home seemed entirely too small. She couldn't get far enough away from the man in her living room to make even a stutter in her racing pulse.

"Calm down, Shelby," she told herself. "*Getting away* isn't the idea here. You wanted someone good. Jason Gage is the best." She stared into the mirror, aghast when she took in her rumpled hair and pale cheeks.

She should have at least put on some makeup. Biting her lips for color, she smoothed the front of her white cotton romper, then dragged her fingers through her hair. Yanking open the door to the cherry armoire she had refinished herself, she selected a set of sheets.

"Shelby?"

She could hear him calling her through the closed door. This house definitely wasn't big enough. "In here," she yelled.

The door opened, and he suddenly filled the room with his sheer masculine presence. As he hoisted the garment bag over the door and placed his briefcase on the desk, she watched the taut muscles play in his shoulders.

This was like living a scene from *Heaven's Traveler*, her very favorite Jason Gage film of all time. He had played the role of Max Brandauer, a grudging angel of sorts, who had appeared to help the cast resolve their troubles—sometimes to very unexpected results.

Her pulse rushed like a tide as she stared at him across the bed. He was tall and beautifully proportioned. The most gorgeous angel she had ever seen with his melting black eyes and rich russet hair.

He was her very own Max Brandauer. An angel who would help her through this mess.

The idea delighted Shelby, but she couldn't help wondering what the twist would be—Max the angel *always* managed to turn the expected into the unexpected.

She shook the fanciful thought from her head along with the flat sheet. "I'm in the middle of a film. Haven't been home much," she said by way of explanation for the unmade bed.

He grabbed an edge of the sheet as it floated down. "No maid?"

"Place really isn't big enough to warrant one. It's only me here."

He cornered and tucked the sheet into place with the practiced moves of a veteran. Shelby was considerably less adept, though not from lack of practice.

She couldn't keep her eyes off him. The tanned cords of his neck contrasted sharply with his white collar. The rugged angle of his jaw stood out beneath a five-o'clock shadow that burnished auburn on his chin. Everything about him fascinated her and filled her with silent expectation.

The sensation was completely unexpected. *Unfamiliar.* Shelby had summoned emotions, coaxed them, stifled them, built upon them— whatever the role she was playing at the time called for. But she had never actually *felt* this way before.

She fluffed a pillow. Jason caught her hand and stopped her short. His fingers twined through hers. His touch seared straight through her body.

"I'm making you really nervous, aren't I?"

Suddenly she was aware of the bed as if it were another living presence in the room. "Yes."

"Do you think you'll be able to work though it?" He cast her a wry grin that stole her breath. "You're beginning to make me nervous, too."

It took a second for his admission to register, but when it did, Shelby groaned.

How on earth am I going to work with him?

But she reminded herself that he was here to help. No need for pretense or artifice. She had already admitted her deepest, darkest secret.

Well, almost.

Laughter bubbled inside. "I really am sorry. I've met my share of fans who lose it when they ask for my autograph. Suddenly I can relate." She tightened her fingers around his. "Maybe the next time I meet one, I'll take his hand, look into his eyes and smile. Let him know it's okay."

Their gazes locked. His sable eyes glowed with laser intensity.

"It is okay, Jason, isn't it?"

"I don't bite."

"I'll be glad about that, I'm sure."

His expression warped into charming, and he turned into Max the angel before her very eyes. "I wouldn't count on it. I see the potential for brilliant results here."

"Really?"

He lifted her hand and brushed his lips gently across her palm. "We have chemistry, Miss Moran, or haven't you noticed?"

"Oh, I've noticed."

A tingle sailed up her arm. Whether it was his touch or his words that made her feel so . . . *alive*, Shelby didn't know, but that she was able to feel anything at all thrilled her. "Max Brandauer."

"What?"

"*Heaven's Traveler*. My favorite movie of all time," she admitted, not caring if she made a total jerk of herself by acting like a groupie. "I can't help but think of you as Max, coming to help me."

He laughed, his warm breath gusting across her palm and making her shiver. "Are you always so creative in your choice of stimuli?"

"Whatever helps me deliver the most believable performance."

"If Max does it for you, then Max I shall be." He let her hand slide away, and she felt the loss of his touch more intensely than she could explain. "Are you ready to start?"

"Yes."

Grabbing the antique chair from the desk, he placed it in the center of the room.

"I have a studio."

He slanted an amused glance at the bed. "This bedroom seems to be as good a place as any."

He had a point. But when he motioned her to the chair, Shelby had to force herself to sit, all at once apprehensive and excited.

"It's late. Why don't we start with some relaxation techniques? I want to see what kind of control you've got." He knelt beside her, so close that his voice pulsed against her ear. "You're very tense. We'll work through it and tackle more in the morning."

"Okay."

"Go limp."

Shelby closed her eyes and sank into the chair, arms resting on the armrests, head draped over the crest.

While she would have liked to relax at will and impress him with her usually exceptional control, she swallowed her pride and worked each muscle group, knowing that unless she became totally responsive this exercise would never work.

Silence seeped through her body, chased away the nervous tension. She retreated into herself, focusing on the breakers that combed the shoreline with rhythmic harmony just yards beyond her balcony. The steady tick-tock of the grandfather clock in the foyer.

And Jason. She could hear his deep even breathing, feel heat radiating from his body.

Suddenly his strong, warm fingers touched the sensitive skin beneath her bare knee. He lifted her leg and flexed it, and though other coaches had touched her exactly the same way a hundred times before, Shelby experienced a crazy little shimmer that kindled her skin like a sunbeam.

She willed herself to relax, but her mind feasted on this new sensation. She could smell him, unadorned by cologne, yet alluring and male, with his own unique scent. Hear the hushed quickening of his breath as he circled the chair and knelt before her, feel the raspy tread of his palms skimming her hips, nudging her diaphragm.

Only the strictest of control kept her from shivering while he worked his hands up from her waist and along her bare arms.

"Got some work to do here." His fingers glided along the bridge of her nose and over her eyelids. As if it were his pleasure and not his job, he explored her every curve, charted the lines of her muscles, committed his new knowledge to memory. "Open your eyes."

He stood oh-so-close, his face only inches from hers. Their gazes locked. She saw the flare of desire in his eyes, noticed a vein throbbing in his brow, even though his expression otherwise revealed no more than a professional interest.

He traced the curve of her brow with his thumbs, then outlined the hollow beneath her eyes.

"Let the tension drain away." His breath fanned her face like a gentle burst. Intimate.

Shelby let her eyes drift closed and focused on the stillness she had created within.

"Now relax here." His thumb circled her mouth.

She yawned wide, knowing she looked ridiculous, not caring. The last of her tension fled, and she sagged against the chair utterly limp, savoring the emptiness of controlled relaxation.

"Great. You've got it." He stroked her neck, a feather-light touch that tested her control. "Let's work on sense memory. Pick an object. Something simple."

Drawing her mind into the exercise, Shelby summoned an image of the only object she could concentrate on at the moment.

"What are you focusing on?"

"You."

"Why me?" She heard surprise in his voice.

"Trying to focus on a chair or a lamp would be impossible with you in the room."

He chuckled, a husky desirable sound that made her tingle. "All right. Add me to your memory bank."

Sweeping his hand across her eyes, just enough to stir the air and remind her to keep her eyes closed, he said, "What do you see?"

She conjured his image easily. "I see you the way you looked when I first opened my door. Everything about you waiting, impatient. You looked just like Frankie Worth in *The Last Rebel*." She could feel the smile in his laughter and narrowed her focus from the whole man to more specific details. "You're jingling keys in your right hand. Your keychain has the emblem of a Jaguar and the letters XJR-S. Your shoulders are straight. Your legs braced. You wear expensive athletic shoes, and the sole of the left one is worn down from the way you carry your weight."

Jason whistled. "What highly developed observation skills you have, my dear."

"I'm just getting started." Shelby laughed, liking that she had impressed him.

She guided her mind's eye upward along his legs. "Your jeans are just starting to show wear. The cuffs beginning to get thready. Judging by the way you move in them, I'd say they're comfortable."

"They fit well."

Amen. They hugged his thighs just enough to hint at the muscles beneath. And he had a great butt. Not flat. Not rounded. Curved just enough to make her want to touch.

Oh my!

Surprised at where her mind had wandered, Shelby forced herself to focus.

"Your tan magnifies the color of your eyes. Black. Like sable. Burning eyes. You have a strong face, an interesting face with just a hint of arrogance, as if you've seen a lot in your life and are determined to stay above it." Pausing, Shelby sharpened the image in her mind. "Straight nose. Blade-like nostrils that flare just a bit when you inhale. Full, erotic mouth. A mouth that makes me think of . . . kissing."

"Go with it, Shelby." Was that a catch she heard in his voice?

"You lick your lower lip when you're thinking. Your tongue darts out. It looks soft, textured, sort of like rough velvet."

"What does my tongue make you think of?" His voice simmered with some barely-checked emotion, and the sound slid right through her.

"*Taste*," she answered honestly. "Makes me wonder what you taste like."

The Anticipated Tragedy

Jason sucked in his breath, a reaction that could have been shock at her boldness, or something more, but a reaction that made Shelby realize how much she wanted to know.

Instead of summoning the emotion from the inner well she kept carefully filled at all times, this desire glowed from within. He was having the most amazing effect on her.

"Let's move on to your other senses," he said in a gravelly whisper. "What do you hear?"

"Your voice. Throaty and deep, yet controlled. I like the richness of it. You're breathing is shallow, not deep and even the way it was a few minutes ago. I'm making you . . . uncomfortable?"

He laughed, so near that strands of her hair trembled against her cheek. "Not uncomfortable, Shelby. Aroused. You're having an incredible effect on me." With a light stroke of a fingertip, he tucked the hair behind her ear.

She opened her eyes and met his gaze, surprised that his feelings mirrored her own. "I know."

"That surprises you?"

"You look so . . . hungry."

His gaze burned into her. "I am."

"You don't look very happy about it." She lifted her hand to his cheek, needing to touch him, needing to know that what she felt was real.

"You've shot my professional distance straight to hell."

"I'm glad."

"You feel it, too." It was a statement, not a question.

"I've never felt like this before," she admitted, trying to translate the elusive feeling into words. "I create sensations that I believe are appropriate, but I don't feel, Jason. I act."

The fire in his eyes blazed, and to her amazement, his reaction stoked that ribbon of flame inside her.

"I want to make you feel." His declaration was so simple, yet so potent. When he lifted his hand to her face and traced his fingers along her jaw, she shivered. "Concentrate on the way I make you feel. Describe it to me."

Her eyes drifted close, and she focused on his fingertips, the feathery light brush against her skin.

"The air between your fingers and my face feels heated, electric."

He molded her jaw with the strong warmth of his palm. "Now?"

"Aware. The strength of your touch. Of you."

His hand trembled as he traced the shell of her ear.

"Little tingles are spiraling down my neck. Almost like tickles."

She sensed his nearness, but when his breath puffed hot against her ear, she jumped, the tiny flame inside her flickering wildly. Her mouth opened, but the only sound to escape was a surprised gasp.

Jason chuckled.

"Build on that feeling." He traced the curve of her shoulders, then his hands trailed down her bare arms in a slow silken progression that made her tingle in the wake of his touch.

"Are you committing this sensation to memory?"

Her senses were so heightened that even his voice rippled through her. She whispered a hushed "Yes" before feeling him withdraw.

Suddenly he was in front of her, slipping the sandal from her left foot and tracing the arch, the rise of her ankle, the sweep of her calf.

She hadn't realized her legs were so sensitive, that a simple caress of his hand could be intimate. Even though their only physical connection was his thumb circling the underside of her knee, Shelby felt him everywhere.

His deep, even breathing resonated like music in her ears. His maleness seemed to glow from him, until she was sure she would melt beneath its brilliance.

His mouth.

He pressed a warm kiss to the tender curve below her knee, and pleasure radiated outward. Real pleasure. That's what this was. Somehow she knew. Not from any prior experience, but because this was what she always dreamed it would feel like.

"Jason." She breathed his name on the edge of a sigh. "I feel so . . . alive. I'm glowing inside."

"Let it build." His breath gusted against skin moist from his kiss, and a delicious shudder billowed through her body.

His touch was so gentle, so *right*. She didn't resist when he coaxed her knees apart. His fingers tempted, teased, but she sensed his hesitation, knew he waited for some sign to continue.

Shelby opened her eyes. Seeing him wedged between her thighs was a purely sensual experience. She had known this existed, just hadn't experienced it for herself.

Until Jason.

He met her gaze boldly. She recognized the emotion that sharpened his features, hooded his eyes. Her heart fluttered with the knowledge that she was affecting him, too.

"Don't stop," she said simply.

"Tell me how you feel." The command was a caress.

"I feel . . . connected to you. Filled by you."

He slid the hem of her romper up her leg, and his gaze held hers as he ran his tongue along the inside of her thigh. "Does my touch overwhelm you?"

She shifted uncomfortably in the chair as unfamiliar sensations pooled between her legs. "No. Yes."

A smile lifted the corners of his mouth.

Drawing up on his knees, he leaned so close that her breath ruffled his hair and made it tickle her nose. She felt a rush of such tenderness that she couldn't resist pressing a kiss to the top of his head.

Emotion played across his face, so fleeting that she couldn't pinpoint his mood. Had she offended him? Her breath caught. Her whole being filled with waiting, until his nostrils flared, and she recognized what she saw in his face.

Need.

Jason struggled, his battle to calm the desire that lurked in his expression plain for Shelby to see.

Raising her hand, she stroked the tense curve of his jaw. Burnished stubble rasped her fingertips, an odd, yet visceral, sensation, and she watched while he tamed his hunger.

Jason had to be the consummate actor. His chest rose and fell sharply, but within seconds, he had leveled his breathing.

And Shelby recognized what else she had seen in his face.

Loneliness.

She knew that feeling intimately.

"You're doing the most incredible things to me." He fixed her with a crooked smile that made her pulse jump.

"Ditto."

He stood and held out his hand. "Come, *student*. It's time to continue our studies supine."

She took his hand. Her mouth went dust dry as they stood so close he filled her vision. When his fingers dropped to undo the buttons of her romper, she looked up to study his face. A face that held such a fascinating blend of strength and hunger and isolation.

The buttons popped open, one by one, and the romper parted. He focused on his task as if she was the most important thing in his world. She liked the feeling. She liked Jason.

"Nervous?" His fingers brushed her stomach and her muscles contracted.

"No."

It was the scariest thing she had ever admitted, but this felt right. Jason felt right.

Now if only she could trust herself.

Here was this wonderful man, her very own Max the angel, and she could screw up at any time.

Shelby drew a deep breath. Doubt would get her nowhere. Clearing her mind of negativity, she focused on the stimuli Jason presented her—the tingle that shimmered through her when his hand brushed her hip, the strange sensations that stole the strength from her legs.

He pushed the romper from her shoulders, and it slid down her body in a whisper, leaving her standing in only her bra and French-cut panties. His burning gaze raked her boldly. The vein in his temple throbbed. The muscles in his throat worked as he swallowed hard.

Shelby had never felt so beautiful in her life.

There was wonder in his expression as he traced the arch of her shoulders with warm palms, barely touching her, yet scorching her skin with his heat. His hands trembled as he skimmed her arms, her breasts, her waist, her hips. And even as she marveled at the wild ache that pulsed low in her belly, she let the sensation wash through her, not needing to draw upon the wealth of emotions she kept stored in her actor's memory. Not needing to act.

She *felt*.

For the first time in memory, she felt.

Jason guided her onto the bed with a tender touch, his smile encouraging her to lie down, to trust him.

She did.

"Concentrate on what you're feeling, Shelby. Just tell me to stop if you're uncomfortable."

She smiled at him, gifted by the eager light that flared in those beautiful black eyes. Closing her own, Shelby cleared her mind, sharpened her focus to the way her insides trembled.

The bed dipped when Jason sat beside her. "How do you feel?"

"Excited."

"Good."

He slid the pillow from beneath her head so she lay flat, and she heard it fall to the floor with a thump. With light strokes, he brushed the hair from her face and smoothed it around her.

She must look decadent, like an innocent maiden on the sacrificial altar. She had played a similar role once, but then she had evoked angst and fear. Now all she felt was anticipation. Hope.

She sensed Jason's gaze. When his fingertip trailed from her chin down the arch of her neck, a stream of tiny embers ignited inside her. A hot ache grew in her throat, made it impossible to swallow, to speak, to do anything but let him guide her along this path of arousal.

He outlined the straps of her bra with his finger, his touch gentle, teasing, as he dipped beneath the lace to trace the curve of her breast.

As he followed the contours of her stomach, her abdomen, the womanly pillow of her sex, she quivered.

"Oh!" Had she really uttered that heartfelt sigh?

When his mouth grazed her ear and his hot breath gusted across her skin, Shelby knew without a doubt that she had. Sparks lit inside her like fireworks, tiny flames sparkling to life as he circled his tongue in that sensitive place behind her ear, then sprinkled gentle kisses along her neck.

Her eyes shot open when he stretched out beside her. He gathered her into his arms. Shelby could only gasp as her body fit against his in all the right places.

His wide shoulders created a haven, the perfect place to lay her head. His pulse beat steadily beneath her cheek, and she marveled as her own pulse quickened.

His earthy male essence filled her senses, heightening her awareness. The strong arms that held her close protected her, cherished her, as she and Jason lay together in a haze of sensation. Slipping her arms around his waist, she marveled at the trim hardness that hinted he enjoyed physical activity, another clue to the only man who had made her *feel*.

Shelby *felt* his clothing rasp her bare skin. She *felt* his muscled thighs buttress hers, pulling her close until she could feel the hardness of his desire against her.

He explored the contours of her back, trailing his hands upward along her spine, his touch gentle, knowledgeable.

Jason knew how to stoke the fire inside her, and when he unfastened the hooks of her bra, she experienced no uncertainty, no panic. Only the swell of her breasts as they grew heavy with expectation.

He cupped her bare breast with a strong hand, his thumb circling her nipple, until the ache inside became a pull of desire between her legs.

She arched against him.

"Do you like this?" The hunger in his whisky voice was no act. He wanted her, and his hard body radiated his need, a palpable force.

"And this?" Knowing fingers tugged at her nipple until it hardened into a tight pearl.

Tendrils of sensation rippled through her. Exquisite.

"Tell me what you feel."

"I feel . . . I *want*."

More.

She wasn't sure what more was, but she quickly figured out what would further their quest for fulfillment.

"I want to feel *you*." She slipped her hands into the waistband of his jeans and tugged at his shirt.

Needing no further urging, Jason kicked off his shoes while Shelby slid the shirt up, revealing a wealth of bronzed skin, the smattering of burnished curls.

He ripped the shirt over his head and tossed it aside. The breath hitched in her throat at the sight of his wide chest, all strength and sinew. All man. All desire.

Eagerly, she lifted her arms to him.

Jason sank into her embrace. She could feel the urgency he held in check as her breasts crushed the hot wall of his chest, rasping the crisp curls until her skin tingled with the need to feel him touch her.

Somehow he must have sensed her need. Cupping her breasts, he dipped his head, and his hot mouth fastened onto a nipple. Shelby moaned. Nothing in her experience had ever prepared her for the intensity of this sensation. She had heard, had dreamed, but, God, she had never *known*.

He created magic. In her body. In her mind.

The fire blazed.

He laved her nipples with a swirling tongue. She moaned. She wanted.

He knew.

His hands drifted down. He rolled the panties over her hips, and with his foot slid them between her legs until they joined the rest of the clothes on the floor.

With a flash of white teeth, he tugged on her nipple, and the exquisite sensation that followed robbed her of speech. She could only stare at him in wonder, not knowing anything except that she didn't want him to stop.

Jason apparently had no intention of stopping.

Placing a hand over her abdomen, he began a leisurely descent toward her most intimate place. He parted the tuft of hair between her legs, rounded the soft swell of her sex with deliberate slowness and dipped his fingers between her thighs. He fondled that tiny pearl of her womanhood until the fire inside her blazed into hot sensation.

Her thighs parted, and she pressed upward into his touch.

A ragged groan escaped him, and he captured her mouth with his, sharing his arousal with the hot sweep of his tongue.

Her mouth burned, her senses spun, and she met his kiss with a demand of her own.

Don't stop.

He didn't.

He stroked the tiny pearl of her desire, his fingertips testing the moist heat between her legs until she gasped at the wildness of the sensation, cried out her urgency against his lips.

He slid his finger inside.

The fire between her legs became a pulsing beat that thrummed through her entire body. Her sex throbbed around his finger as he massaged her with sizzling strokes, forced the flames higher with every sensual thrust.

Suddenly Shelby understood. An explosion waited just beyond the fire inside. Just a few more strokes. She could *feel* it.

The flames blazed hotter. Heat scorched every inch of her, singed the edges of her hope to experience this ultimate joining.

She writhed against him, drew upon his lips, urged him to take her beyond the flame.

Jason did.

He stormed her with touch until she could see the fire just ahead in the distance, feel the heat burn. Need flared so bright she thought she might explode.

Her senses reeled.

The flame was so close she could almost touch it.

Almost.

Then the breath clogged in her chest. Her heart pounded too hard. And Shelby tumbled into the black tunnel of fear.

The Ironic Farce

He had lost her.

Even though he'd been anticipating it, Jason almost missed the signs that it had happened. Her ragged breathing. Her trembling muscles. Her clammy skin. For an instant he had thought she was climaxing, but the deathlike paleness of her face quickly snuffed out that hope.

Her emerald eyes stared at him—unfocused, glazed with her own private terror. She pushed at him with shaking hands, tried to sit up. As he spun onto his knees, lifting her, trying to coax her back with soft words, he could feel her panic.

"It's all right, Shelby. Breathe with me."

Her lips parted. She tried. God, how she tried, but he could tell from her strangled gasps that she wasn't succeeding.

Her chest rose and fell rapidly. Tears suddenly trembled in her eyes, spiking black lashes into star-points before they spilled over pale cheeks.

His heart throbbed so hard in his chest it hurt, because of her fear. His helplessness.

Locking one arm around her, he stroked damp hairs from her cheek. "Breathe with me, honey." Puffing his cheeks in example, he wiped his expression clean, refusing to let her see his concern, realizing that in all his years of acting he had never had to struggle harder.

White lines ringed her mouth. Each gasp failed.

"Come on." He could hear the edge of alarm in his voice and struggled to hide it. "Exhale with me. One. Two. Three. One. Two. Three. Now take a deep breath."

A wheeze.

"There you go. Let's try again."

Holding her tight, as if he could chase away her fear by strength alone, Jason counted and breathed, again and again, until her trembling lessened and her eyes began to focus.

He smiled at her, relieved when she drew her first real breath. "It's all right, honey. You're going to be all right." He wiped the tears from her cheeks.

Shelby met his gaze with eyes that sparkled like jewels. Her expression crumbled. A sob, aching and terrible to hear, tore from her lips. He eased her back onto the bed while deep racking sobs shook her slender body and clawed at his heart.

When Jason cradled her against him, cheek to cheek, he realized her face was not the only one wet with tears.

This was his fault. He was supposed to be coaching her, not making love to her. But she had been so responsive. And so completely thrilled.

He had wanted to bring her to climax. She'd been so close. He still ached with need, but that no longer mattered. The sound of her pain chased away everything else from his mind.

With her face buried in the crook of his neck, Shelby cried her heart out. Lifting the corner of the comforter, Jason pulled it over her, feeling an unfamiliar need to protect, to offer a safe shelter against the storm that raged within her.

She clung to him, her trembling lessening by slow degrees, and he felt relief, far more than he ever believed possible. The way tears moistened her hair into a dark frame around her face touched him, and the way she bit her lower lip to stop its quivering tugged at his heart.

Helping Shelby face her demons suddenly seemed more important than anything he had ever done in his life.

It was an awesome feeling.

"I'm sorry," she whispered, her voice muffled against his skin.

He almost smiled. Raising himself onto an elbow, he peered down into her face. "Why's that?"

"I freaked you out."

His cheeks still felt sticky from tears, so to deny her claim would have been ridiculous. "I knew this might happen when I signed on. That's why I'm here, remember?"

She gave him a tight smile and sniffled loudly.

"Give me some of the credit, honey." With a finger on her chin, he lifted her face. "I wasn't doing my job. I was making love to you."

"You gave me what I wanted. You were so gentle." Hurt and longing flashed naked in her gaze. "And I was *feeling*, Jason. Really feeling."

Her shoulders slumped. She looked so defeated that he could only watch her grimly as he thought desperately for some way to make her smile.

"Come on. It's not so bad. We've only just started." He tweaked her nose the way an adult might do to a child, and when her tear-spangled eyes widened, he felt like a fool.

He rolled to the side of the bed. "I'll get you a tissue. Want something to drink?"

Sitting up in a graceful motion, she gathered the comforter around her. "I'm some kind of hostess. I dragged you into bed before I even offered you a drink."

Now he had made her feel self-conscious, too. What the hell was wrong with him?

"I won't hold it against you." Jason beat a hasty retreat.

After retrieving a box of tissues from the bathroom and giving it to Shelby, he made his way to the kitchen. A water cooler held a place of honor in the corner, hinting at Shelby's predilection for healthy drinking, but Jason headed toward a wine rack he spotted on the wall opposite the refrigerator.

He could use a glass.

Selecting a decent merlot, he searched through the cabinets for glasses, hoping Shelby hadn't been saving this bottle for anything special.

The uniform neatness of her kitchen hinted that no special event was forthcoming. Life on location left little time for anything else, and Shelby's immaculate home indicated that she didn't make time for much besides work. The delicate furnishings and design revealed no trace of a male in her life. He found himself pleased to an absurd degree.

This coaching session was turning out to be full of surprises. His reaction to Shelby was the most incredible of them. His taste in women had never run in any specific direction, but Shelby was about ten years too young for him and definitely in the wrong business.

Jason made his way back toward the guest bedroom, reflecting on all the twists his emotions were taking. He found Shelby wrapped in the comforter, perched on the window seat with moonlight silvering her hair. The sight of her brought a lump to his throat. She was so beautiful. She struck some primitive inner chord in him. He belonged here. No matter what bizarre events had brought them together, Jason was meant to be in this room with her.

He had never been more sure of anything in his life.

"I brought wine." Silently crossing the room, he sat beside her.

She accepted a glass and sipped without looking up.

"Do you still think you can help me?" Her question ended with a plaintive sigh.

"I can help you act," he replied honestly. "But I don't know enough about what's bothering you to do much beyond that."

Her gaze locked onto his, and he could almost feel her determination flare between them. "I'll settle."

"But will you be content?"

That elicited a smile. She shook her head. "Probably not now that I know what I'm missing. Beggars can't be choosers."

He wanted to tell her she wasn't a beggar, shouldn't have to settle, but he held back his opinion. Only Shelby knew how much effort she was willing to put into her recovery. Jason couldn't force her, no matter how much he wanted to.

Perhaps his coaching could facilitate changes in other areas, though. He had a theory. "I think the key is affective memory. If you want to act through your anxiety attacks, you're going to have to draw stimuli that gets you out of the trauma mode and into a sensual one."

"What happens if I haven't had any sexual experiences that are . . . well, *pleasant*?"

He anticipated her question, if not her blush. "We create them."

She sipped her wine thoughtfully, then held the glass out in a silent salute. "That works for me." Her fine black brows drew tight in a frown, but she held his gaze steadily. "You're sure you don't mind? This could get messy."

He admired the courage it took for her to admit that. "I don't mind."

"Why?"

It was a simple question, but Jason didn't have a simple answer. "You touch me."

"Pity?"

"No."

"What then?"

"I don't know," he replied truthfully, not at all sure that revealing his emotions was prudent. But his professional distance had bailed on him already, and he just didn't feel like acting right now.

"I think I know what you mean." The smile that softened her exquisite features encouraged him.

Taking a sip of wine, she set her glass on a low table beside the window. Her slender fingers grazed his when she plucked the glass from his hand and placed it next to her own. "You're a nice man, Jason."

He couldn't suppress a snort of laughter. "I've been called a lot of things. Nice generally isn't one of them."

"I can't imagine how anyone could miss it," she said, shifting in her seat. The sight of her long shapely legs stretching out from beneath the comforter drew his full attention. "Unless no one knows the real Jason Gage. Do you keep him hidden away and play a role for the world?"

Her question struck so close to home, he could only stare at her in wonder.

Yes.

The answer filled his mind, and even though he could not actually admit it, Shelby must have seen it clearly on his face.

She swept a light touch across his cheek. "Then I am flattered you let me glimpse the real Jason Gage. It's easy to think of you as Max Brandauer, but I think the man far surpasses the angel." She rose in a fluid motion that nearly took his breath away.

"You're also a very attractive man, and I suddenly find myself wanting you very much. Unless you have something else planned for the night." Her voice lowered to a throaty growl. "I'd like to rehearse again now."

Jason blinked. It took him a moment to realize she had slipped into character. Right before his eyes. Effortlessly.

Letting the comforter fall to the floor in a whisper of satin, Shelby stood before him naked, the willowy curves of her body gilded in the golden spray from the lamp.

"Will you make love to me, Jason?"

The First of Many Retakes

Every drop of blood in Jason's veins plummeted to his cock.

Apparently his voice had gone along for the ride, because he couldn't seem to form a coherent reply. His mouth opened, he felt the muscles in his throat work, but only a ragged gasp came out.

He had the vague thought that an accomplished actor should do better, but quickly cut himself a break. He was a man, after all—a man sitting a mere foot away from a naked Shelby Moran. If that in itself wasn't enough to leave him speechless, all the feelings she was stirring inside him were.

"Here, let me." She slipped to her knees, and her breasts jingled suggestively with the motion. When she gazed up at him, summer eyes hooded with desire, Jason realized her face was level with his crotch.

Oh, God.

Pale fingers flashed in the lamp light as she unbuttoned his fly and slid the jeans down his legs. Her every movement was slow motion, designed to entice, and though he knew this was the Shelby he had seen many times on the screen, in character, *believable*, he was helpless to resist her.

With her direction, he stepped out of his pants and stood before her in his briefs and socks. She leaned back on her haunches and inspected him boldly.

"Oh my." She maneuvered the briefs over his thickening erection. "You are gorgeous all over."

His cock accepted the compliment graciously by rising to full attention.

Shelby chuckled, a full-throated sound that ruffled through him like a shiver. Her breath gusted across his skin, hot and sweet, and he braced his legs apart to control the effects of her assault on his senses.

The fresh, faintly floral scent of her hair wafted through his awareness. Sooty strands of her hair fluttered over her ruby nipples in an enticing game of Peek-A-Boo. The seductive strokes of her hands scorched his flesh as she explored his thighs. Her fingers dipped and teased the sensitive skin between his legs, making his cock jump toward her hand like a heat-seeking missile.

Shelby slid her fingers in a sinuous glide around his hips, cupping his buttocks with both hands and urging him toward her. He could sense the hint of her breath on his skin, imagine the moisture of those lush lips.

A sound of satisfaction emerged from someplace deep within, some hidden place that echoed through his body only when his beast awoke. A sound that burst forth as a groan.

She responded to his need. Her body arched sinuously toward him, and her dark head dipped low. The breath solidified in his throat when her tongue glided along the length of his shaft in a slow wet spiral.

His hips thrust forward of their own accord. He balled his fists and fought the urge to pull her toward him, to demand an act that should only be a gift.

With smooth fingers she caressed his buttocks, urging him closer as she drew him into her mouth, sucked on him with long blissful pulls. A shudder ripped through him. His legs shook. He wondered how long he could stand.

Forever.

His body surged. The pleasure, so pure and explosive. It had been so long. Too long. The hot velvet walls of her mouth drew his arousal to life, worked his body into a sweet frenzy. His world spun out of control, and he speared his fingers into her hair to guide her rhythm, unable to stop himself, craving what she so lavishly offered.

Black silk swayed down the trim lines of her back as she worked his cock with generous strokes. She cupped his balls with a gentle hand. But it was the sight of her slender waist flaring into the gentle curve of her hips that undid him.

Without fully willing himself to, Jason pulled her into his arms and staggered back toward the bed like a drunk. She landed full length on top of him, her graceful body draped over his in all her naked glory. Every feminine inch branded him, fused reason and pleasure together in violent turmoil.

He could only groan when her mouth captured his in a kiss. Her tongue darted into his mouth, demanding, sending currents of erotic need coursing through him. He joined the game, and suddenly his world narrowed into tongues that dueled in hot abandon, seeking, searching, warm breaths coming together as one.

Her hair cloaked them in shadow. Like a sooty waterfall it brushed his shoulders, snagged the rough skin along his jaw, threaded into their mouths. Cool silk when everything else between them raged out of control.

Her fingers seared trails of fire along his neck, shoulders. Her breasts crushed against his chest, pebble tips grazed his skin, shattered him with sensation.

He could feel her heart throb in time with his. Bodies in sync. The sensation was unfamiliar, yet it filled him with longing to become a part of her. He *needed* to plunge deep inside her, to ride together on this tide of desire.

With shaking hands, he traced the furrow of her spine. Blindly he met her kisses. His body blazed with unfulfilled desire, but though she lifted him on the crest of a breaker, a tiny voice in his head reminded him that her lovemaking was all a performance.

She was acting.

He wanted to be more than her co-star. He wanted to be her lover.

He shouldn't push her.

But couldn't stop himself.

Wedging his erection between her thighs, he teased her soft opening, finding her dry as a scattering of fallen leaves.

A sober reminder that he was here to help.

He had to slow down. Had to make her feel . . . *something.*

His erection was a white-hot ache between his legs. Every inch of his body pounded, strained for release.

Arching his hips, he pressed into her softness, trying to ease the ache, control it. No one had ever actually died from unfulfilled desire. At least no one had ever documented it.

Slipping his hands between them to fondle her breasts, he brushed her nipples in slow circles while he tasted her mouth with his tongue and drank of her sweetness. Shelby gasped, her breath catching in her throat like a sob. She trembled in his arms.

He recognized her struggle for concentration and cheered her on with a reassuring touch.

"Remember how good it felt when I kissed you here." He demonstrated with a light brush of his lips across her ear.

"And here." He pressed feathery kisses down the graceful column of her neck.

She didn't pull away, and encouraged, he caressed the curve of her waist with a light stroke.

She shivered.

Poised on the brink. He could see it in her heavy-lidded gaze when he lifted his mouth to hers. He traced her lower lip with his tongue, sensuously, and when a sigh slipped between her parted lips, a sound of pure pleasure, Jason knew she was winning the battle to combine her feelings with her ability to act.

Unable to resist, he fondled the curve of her buttock, pressing into her softness, the satin warmth of her thighs molding his erection, a bittersweet agony.

Her teeth caught his bottom lip in a light nip. Jason tilted his head back and stared into her face.

Her eyes sparkled.

"You're a nice man, Jason Gage." Her breathy voice quickened the need inside him. "A nice man with a problem."

She caught the length of his erection in slim fingers and gave a knowing tug.

He groaned.

"Need a hand?"

Another slow pull with those long fingers saw him bucking unceremoniously.

Shelby laughed, the twinkle in her eyes telling him she was back in character. The swelling ache in his crotch threatened to engulf him. Jason struggled for control.

But when she bent over him, rosy lips parting to take him inside, she proved his control was all an illusion. With erotic strokes of her swirling tongue, Shelby lifted his desire to the edge, until his body only knew sensation. His concern that her lovemaking was a performance disappeared like smoke into the night.

She bobbed over his cock, her tongue laving the bursting head in slow, wet strokes that coaxed waves of sensation outward from her touch. Fighting the urge to spear his fingers into her hair and guide her strokes, he sank his fingers into the sheets, buffeted by sensation. Struggling for control.

But thought vanished completely when Shelby rose above him like a goddess of Venus, ivory shoulders thrust back, ruby-tipped breasts temptingly displayed under the fall of smoky hair.

His heart stuttered in his chest.

Stroking his wet cock against the folds of her sex, she took him in inch by glorious inch.

He had died and gone to heaven.

With her eyelids partially closed and a secret smile curving her erotic mouth, she welcomed him into her body until he hilted. Heat bound them together as surely as if they were one.

The shapely beauty of her body and the sleek caress of her skin taunted him. She dipped low, breasts rasping his chest, mouth caressing his cheek, then arched back as she rode him.

His legs shook, and with a strangled groan, Jason clasped her buttocks, lifted her off him, then plunged back inside as he crested, and wave after wave of ecstasy crashed through him.

But sanity returned with Shelby's triumphant smile. She sparkled, fresh as the grass after a summer rain, lifting his spirits even though he felt like a cad.

She had performed. He had come.

She was thrilled.

"I did it, Jason." She smiled ecstatically at him as though he had actually done something. "I really did it."

He sucked in another deep breath. Closing his eyes, he was dismayed, but not surprised, to find the sight of her beaming face burned into his eyelids. No help there.

He opened his eyes again. "Honey, you've got some work to do on your climax."

"Ha!" She laughed and eyed him imperiously down her slender nose. "I was great."

His legs still vibrated with the intensity of his orgasm. "No doubt there."

He still tingled from the effects of her greatness warring with the heaviness of satiation that weighted his body. Christ, he was too old for this. He wanted to roll over and die.

But Shelby did the rolling. Right off of him, eliciting his groan when the cool air hit his skin. Retrieving the comforter from the floor, she covered them and molded herself into the contours of his body as if she belonged there.

Her cheek rested in the curve between his shoulder and neck, her long legs threaded through his, and he couldn't have resisted stroking her smooth skin even if he had the energy to try.

"Are you okay?"

"Takes us old guys longer to recover."

Her disbelieving laughter rippled through the air. She ran slim fingers through the mat of fur on his chest. "Not my angel. He's beyond such a mortal concept."

"Trust me." At the moment, Jason felt the fifteen years between them like a century.

Shelby only smiled and snuggled closer. He sensed her elation, her joy, and wouldn't dream of spoiling her victory. He held her, resting his cheek on the warm silk of her hair.

She had accomplished something wonderful tonight. She had worked through an anxiety attack and seemed to have created a pleasant sensual experience for her memory scrapbook.

Jason supposed he should feel some sense of satisfaction that he had done his job. He didn't.

His ego was bruised. He knew she couldn't overcome her trauma in

one session, but . . . Jason inhaled sharply as the truth struck him—
his *head* knew.

Apparently rational thought had nothing to do with Shelby.

He traced the curve of her shoulder in wonder, and when she sighed
softly, he realized she had fallen asleep.

A smile tugged at his lips. She felt so right wrapped in his arms. She
belonged with him.

And then he understood.

Rational thought had no place around Shelby because his heart was
calling the shots.

How in hell had this happened?

Special Effects

"Someone named Paige called while you were in the shower," Jason told her when she appeared on the balcony. "I let the recorder pick it up."

Nodding, Shelby half-sat on the balcony railing, close enough to Jason for polite conversation, but far enough not to get sucked in by his magnetic presence.

Her jitters were back in force this morning. Just the sight of him— tall, masculine, gorgeous—and the memory of his hands on her body stole the words right out of her mouth.

"I hope it wasn't a call you were waiting for."

"A friend," she explained. "I'll call her back later."

Much later. Like after the sun went down, so Paige wouldn't realize she hadn't been on the set all day and get on the next flight out of Washington. As welcome as her presence would be, Shelby had Jason and his request for privacy to consider at the moment.

She sipped her coffee and tried to alleviate a pang of guilt for blowing off her dearest friend in the world.

Paige and her husband Christopher knew about the return of her anxiety attacks, and they had been calling every few days just to say hello. They were worried about her. Shelby didn't know what she had done in a past life to deserve Paige and Christopher Sharp, but it certainly hadn't been anything she had done in this one. They were gifts from heaven personified.

"Is she a close friend?" Jason asked, peering at her through gold-rimmed eyeglasses.

"Like a sister."

"Wes didn't mention anything about your family, and I don't recall ever reading that you had any."

"I don't." Shelby smiled warmly, charmed that he was interested in her. How gentlemanly. How *Max the angel.* "My parents died when I was young. I lived in foster homes until I went to live with Paige in college."

Instead of offering the well-intentioned, yet unnecessary, sympathetic remarks she had come to expect whenever mentioning her upbringing in the foster care system, Jason asked, "Did you meet her in school?"

Shelby shook her head. "Through a volunteer program when I was about eight. She's been 'family-by-love' ever since."

"Are you a loner, Shelby?"

"Seems that way, doesn't it? Maybe that's why I'm such a control nut." She chuckled softly, then something he'd said earlier came to mind. "So you think my problem is a control thing?"

"Control is definitely a part of you," he said with a knowing smile. "You seemed much more comfortable in control last night."

Damn. Heat seared a path straight to her cheeks. Shelby averted her gaze to the silvery shoals barely visible beneath the breakers as the tide shifted.

The sight helped calm her, helped her focus. Dawn broke in ribbons of blush and gray just beyond the horizon, awesome and uplifting.

Humbling.

She was lucky to be alive. Ten years ago she had traveled a different path, a path that had almost killed her. But with lots of luck and wonderful people like Paige and Christopher, she had turned her life around and made something of herself.

She could get over this problem.

With Jason's help.

"Have I said thanks for last night?"

He glanced up from the laptop computer open on the table and laughed. "Honey, I should be the one saying thanks. My knees are still weak."

Heat bloomed in her cheeks again. She liked the way he called her honey. "I was good, wasn't I?"

"I'm going to kiss Wes the next time I see him."

He was teasing, she knew, but she was flattered all the same. Jason appeared different this morning. And it wasn't just the wire-framed glasses that made him seem like the height of academic masculinity. Like the time he played August St. Germain in *Conversations With Godfrey.* She had loved him in that film, with his sexy European accent.

"Hmm."

Her gaze trailed over him appreciatively. This morning he seemed content, drinking his coffee and working on his laptop. His laughter came easily. He looked at her with an almost tender expression. Perhaps sex did that to him.

Sipping her cooling coffee, Shelby remembered what sex did to her.

Her previous experiences had been such busts that she rarely made the effort anymore.

Awkward.

That one word summed up her entire sex life in a nutshell. Usually so worried about doing it right, she could never relax, let alone feel.

But she had felt last night with Jason. Exquisite new sensations that she had no names for, but somehow knew only he could make her feel. And when she remembered all the delicious tinglings and flutterings that had made her sigh aloud, Shelby knew she would not be content until she experienced them again.

What was happening here?

She had expected to *act* with her coach, not *feel*. But Jason had done the impossible, and now her emotions were getting all tangled up. Her heart went all soft and mushy whenever she looked at him.

She was playing with fire.

That's what was happening. Jason Gage had no use for Hollywood— a well-documented fact. She lived and breathed Tinsel Town. This situation was a disaster in the making.

She eyed him curiously, but he seemed oblivious to her scrutiny as he scowled at the computer monitor, then bashed out a rush of words on the keyboard.

A frown drew his brows together and compressed his lips into a straight line. She had explored the heat of his mouth with her kiss, had tasted the strong angle of his jaw with her touch. Her fingers tingled when she remembered caressing the muscular hollows of his chest, and how his broad shoulders blocked everything from her vision except for him.

He wore a robe now, loosely belted at the waist, and a tempting length of hard thigh was exposed, reminding her of how his hairy legs had twined between hers. How the pulsing shaft of his erection had felt inside her.

Hot. Thick. Swollen.

The sensitive place between her thighs prickled with memory.

Setting her coffee cup on the table, Shelby recognized this as the same feeling she had experienced last night when Jason had touched her. A budding ache that spread outward like the petals of a flower.

Shifting her bottom on the railing, she found that pressure only increased the sensation. Swirling tendrils of warmth spiraled into her belly and down her thighs. She held back a gasp of surprise at the tiny pinpoint of desire that just begged to be touched.

Casting a surreptitious glance at Jason, she found him engrossed in his work. She considered retiring to her room to investigate her newfound sensuality, but was afraid of losing the fragile sensation.

Propping a knee on the railing, Shelby stood in a relaxed stance that left her legs parted just enough to explore. She pretended to adjust her robe and slipped a hand inside. Her fingers felt cool as they skimmed her abdomen, her touch curiously decadent as she sought that secret place.

She zeroed in on the tiny bud with a light touch, and her sex seemed to gather in a pleasurable squeeze. Increasing the pressure slightly, she rolled her fingertip around the hard pearl until a shimmer of pure sensation rippled through her.

Oh.

Another stroke of her finger. Another wave of pleasure. Her breasts swelled. Her nipples grew hard until they peaked through her robe like pebbles.

This was what she had been missing, what she hadn't allowed herself to feel.

Until Jason.

Every sense heightened until she could smell the breath of the ocean on a breeze and sense the summer heat that lingered just beyond dawn. The way the chenille robe lay against her bare skin like a tickle.

The sensation blossomed. She shifted on the railing, pleasure building inside her, as delicate as spun sand, yet as steady as the tide. Her whole body felt languid, dreamy, carried away on a wave of warm sensation.

When the robe slipped from her shoulder, exposing her breast to the ocean breeze, she couldn't bear the thought of moving a muscle to cover herself.

Until she heard Jason suck in his breath.

Shelby glanced up to find him watching her. The raw hunger on his face sent a ripple of excitement through her.

"I'm onto something here." She barely recognized the sultry voice as her own.

"I'll say." He grinned the most crooked, crazy grin, and her gaze traveled down to his lap, where his erection jutted from between the parted folds of his robe.

Instead of feeling awkward or ashamed, his reaction only enhanced her arousal. Emboldened, Shelby indulged the sensation.

One tug on the belt, and her robe fell open.

Jason's eyes widened.

She smiled at him, encouraged, then dipped her finger into the soft folds of her womanhood.

Wet.

Like the petals of a flower after a spring rain. Pleasure unfurled, blooming inside her, urging her to nurture the feeling. Instinctively she rocked her hips, seeking, amazed by her response. So simple, yet so irresistible.

She fondled herself with long strokes, inspired by the way his gaze slid over her, slowly and seductively, by the yearning in his hooded eyes, by the erotic fullness of his mouth.

A sensual current passed between them. Her breath quivered on the edge of expectation. Her gaze slid down to his thick shaft, swollen, *ready*, gleaming with the tight sheen of arousal as it surged in response to her attention.

Jason slipped his hand around it, fingered the wide head in a slow teasing glide in time with the rhythm of her own heated caresses. She felt the sexual connection between them like a magnet, and the breath caught in her throat at the intimacy. The pleasure inside her mounted.

She sighed.

He stood and silently closed the distance between them.

Her heart smiled at the hunger in his gaze. Carried her even higher on the crest of elation.

Lifting a lock of her hair from her breast, he wound it around his finger, the wonder in his expression dazzling, the simplicity of touch not enough.

She arched toward him, needing, uncertain.

Jason knew.

He caught her nipple between a thumb and forefinger and squeezed. Need spiraled through her body and pooled between her legs, a long melting pull that made her heart beat faster and her insides tremble.

He slid his hand down the length of her arm until his palm covered hers and gently pressed against her sex. She writhed against the pressure as the glow inside swelled and mounted.

A low murmur of erotic wonder slipped from her lips. Her breath came in a long surrendering moan as the ultimate pleasure burst upon her, sprinkling through her like a sweet summer shower. Barely able to stand, Shelby clung to him.

Holding her within the circle of his arms, Jason rained soft kisses along her brow, rocking her tenderly against him until her heartbeat slowed to normal and she could breathe in more than a ragged gasp.

His throaty whisper echoed in her ear. "My, my, you have made progress."

"What about you?" His hot erection branded her.

With a finger hooked beneath her chin, he lifted her face toward his. "Watching you find satisfaction means a great deal to me."

His sweet words humbled her. Searching his face, Shelby saw the truth in his tender gaze, the contentment of his expression. Laying her cheek on his shoulder, she blinked back a teary smile.

This was more than she had ever dreamed possible. Held against the broad chest of a wonderful, caring man, her body drowsy while the ocean breezes bathed them in a balmy warmth. He was Max the angel, and this could have been a scene from a movie.

Except she wasn't acting.

She had experienced real pleasure, and her heart brimmed with Jason's touch.

Not the actor who had drifted into her life like an angel, but the man.

Her hand slipped between them to fondle him. "Let me watch you."

It was neither a question, nor a demand, but Jason lifted his head in obvious surprise, a quirky half-smile curving his lips.

She thought for an instant he might refuse, but suddenly his strong hand surrounded hers, and with quick, sharp strokes, he guided her in the method of his fulfillment.

His hot sex jumped in her hand, and she could feel the blood surging, feel the power of his arousal. Excitement rushed through her. The feeling amazed her.

Jason amazed her.

His glasses rested crookedly over eyes half-closed with desire. The chiseled planes of his face relaxed, and his mouth melted to kissable softness. She couldn't resist raising on tiptoe to press a kiss on those lips.

His arm banded her close, and he returned her kiss with abandon.

Her heart turned over.

And as their mouths met and their bold strokes lifted him toward fulfillment, Shelby understood the gift Jason had bestowed upon her. He was vulnerable in his passion, yet he was willing to share that vulnerability with her.

Suddenly she knew that Jason was right. All along her problem had been a control thing—she had never allowed herself to be out of control. He had seen so quickly what had taken her ten years to understand.

But that wasn't so surprising. Jason Gage was an incredible man.

And never more so than at the moment of climax. He bucked sharply, once, twice, and then, as a growl tore from his throat, he spurted his passion over her stomach.

With a delighted laugh, Shelby leaned into him, sealing their naked bodies together with his love juices, just as she hoped to make her newfound ability to *feel* a constant part of her life.

Fade-In

Shelby learned something else about Jason Gage that the tabloids had never reported. He was a wonderful cook. As they sat in her bed, naked, feeding each other like lovers, she decided she liked a man who was full of surprises.

"Open up." He speared a bite-size portion of crepe with his fork and held it to her lips.

"I shouldn't." She shook her head. "Wes will kill me if I gain an ounce."

Jason set the fork on the plate, and in one very graceful, very unexpected motion, pushed her onto her back. He raised himself on his elbows and gazed down at her, his powerful lower body pressing her into the mattress. "Do you always worry about what your director wants?"

Shelby sighed. "Wes is a tyrant. You know that."

"*I'm* a tyrant, and you have to keep up your strength because I plan to work you hard today."

"Is that so?" she challenged, laughing at the way his brows knitted together in a threatening frown.

He swooped down to catch her mouth in a kiss. A sweet kiss that tasted of coffee and syrup and horny male.

His kiss challenged her. Rewarded her. Only Jason had ever kissed her this way, a long easy joining of souls that felt so right. Charmed, Shelby melted into his embrace.

He took her face and held it gently as he explored her mouth with a dreamy intimacy. Her immediate, automatic response surprised her— she wanted to touch him.

And when Jason broke the kiss and gazed at her with a tender promise in his gaze, Shelby knew he had found the key to unlock her heart.

The realization filled her with sudden fear.

Rolling to her side, she retrieved her coffee cup from the night table, averting her gaze under the pretense of thirst.

"Better get in my quota of caffeine if you're expecting much from me today." She sounded nervous to her own ears and wondered if he noticed.

He did.

Lying beside her, he caressed the tense muscles in her shoulders with comforting gentleness, not asking, not speaking. Just being.

It was so simple. She had been shielding her emotions behind an impenetrable wall, never leaving herself unprotected for an instant.

That's why acting suited her so well. She had all the control. But *feeling* wasn't about summoning up emotions from her memory bank, it was about trusting her heart. Whether the result was pleasure or pain.

She had been afraid.

Even though ten years had passed, she was still afraid.

"It's about being vulnerable, isn't it?"

His brows shot upward. "A revelation. When did this take place?"

"When you were at the brink of orgasm."

He grimaced. "Guess I'll have to work on my performance. I wasn't trying to provoke deep thought."

"I don't want you to act. Your responses were what made the moment so powerful."

"Did they now?" His words hung in the air between them.

Something in his oddly wry expression made her wonder if . . . .

"Does my acting during sex bother you?"

His slight nod and ironic chuckle made her admonish gently, "It really shouldn't, you know."

His gaze never wavered. "I know."

Propping herself up on an elbow to face him, Shelby took his hand, determined to make him understand. "You're a wonderful coach, Jason. Please don't take my troubles personally."

"I don't." He lifted their joined hands to his heart, and her spirits soared. "This isn't about coaching. I can coach you just fine when I'm not thinking about making love to you. Tell me you don't think about it, too."

"I do."

"I'm glad." The smile that brightened his face stole her breath.

Or was it panic?

"You really shouldn't be." She squeezed his hands wistfully, then pulled away.

"Why's that?" He rolled into a sitting position in one graceful burst of muscle and sinew that she couldn't help but admire, then leaned back against the headboard and folded his arms across his chest, waiting.

"I make notoriously poor choices in men. You're no exception. You're here to coach me. Then you'll have to go."

"What if I don't want to?"

"Then we've got a problem."

"Which is?"

She exhaled in growing exasperation. "The most obvious is that all the years you've spent getting out of Hollywood, I've spent getting in."

"Quite true." He chuckled, although she didn't see anything to laugh about.

"You don't see that as a problem?"

"Not really." He fixed his gaze on her legs and caressed the length of her thigh with his toe. "We're back to control again, Shelby. If I'd wanted an *easy* scenario, I wouldn't have chosen you, but I must confess it was the last thing on my mind when I knocked on your door."

Chosen?

"I'll bet it was," she muttered, desperately trying to ignore an admission she just wasn't ready to deal with. "You really didn't look happy to be here."

"And you're skirting the issue." He faced her, affection glowing in his eyes. "I don't expect it to be easy, but I'm willing to make a few sacrifices to be with you."

"Sacrifices?"

He shrugged. "Maybe sacrifice isn't the right word. Letting go of some previously held misconceptions might be better."

Shelby shook her head to indicate that she didn't understand. But she desperately needed to. Her heart was fluttering wildly out of control and her mouth felt as dry as dust.

"I haven't been happy, Shelby. Not for a long time. I thought it was my lifestyle—acting, coaching, the lack of privacy in Hollywood—but the truth is, I'm just lonely." He slipped his foot between her knees and nudged her legs apart with a seductive grin. "I just didn't realize how lonely until I met you."

She had guessed, had seen glimpses in his handsome face. Amazed as she was that someone of Jason Gage's status could be lonely, his admission also broke her heart. She knew the feeling intimately. But instead of running from acting, she had buried herself in it.

That was the *real* problem. Not the logistics of where they lived and worked, but the reason she felt all alone.

Her deep dark secret.

Somehow it always came back to that.

"You don't know anything about me, Jason. Not really."

"I know how I feel. Nothing else really matters."

Other things did matter, and the thought alone sent a shudder through her.

"Everything I feel for you is so new," she blurted. "I don't know if I can have a relationship, Jason. I don't know if I can *love*."

His smile was so tender that her heart turned over. "I'm willing to take the chance."

He took her hand and pulled her into his arms. "I'm not asking for anything, Shelby. Just a chance to explore these feelings with you. Given the dynamics of the way we met, I thought it best to be up front with you about how I feel."

An unfamiliar contentment warred with some very familiar doubts. Shelby ran her fingers through his hair, savoring the rich texture. She enjoyed so many things about him. The raspy feel of her bare breasts against his chest. The muscular heaviness of his legs draped across hers. But most of all she treasured the tenderness that softened his expression when he looked at her, as if he cherished her beyond anything else in the world and wasn't afraid to show it.

Could she ever share her past with him?

She had no ready answer. But risk was the key here, and Shelby decided she would risk anything to feel the way Jason made her feel. Tilting her mouth toward his, she gazed deep into his eyes and traced the curve of his neck with gentle fingers. "I'm game, Jason. Let's explore."

Fade-Out

Shelby had been game, all right. All afternoon Jason had coached while Shelby performed. He tested and she improvised. He loved her and she felt. They had explored their passion until they literally dropped from exhaustion.

And now after waking content in her arms, Jason knew what he felt for Shelby was real.

Love?

Did he know how to love? Shelby had voiced exactly the same concern earlier, but the truth was, he hadn't had much experience with that emotion in his own life. His parents had loved him, but their love had been all tied up with ambition and control. He had been the son to follow in their images, the shining example of what brilliant performers and wonderful parents they were.

Jason had no complaints, though. Chase and Elena had loved him to a fault, and they had always welcomed him back from his rebellious forays with forgiving arms. He was fairly certain that Shelby had never known that sort of unconditional love.

Lifting a strand of hair that had fallen into her face while she slept, Jason considered Shelby's emotional scars.

What sort of tragedy could have made such a vibrant young woman so terrified of intimacy?

Rape? Molestation?

Grief, like the sharp edge of a blade, stabbed his heart when he thought about the possibilities.

He sheltered her within the tight circle of his arms, feeling the steady beat of her heart. She nestled against him as though she belonged there.

She did.

Jason had never known such an inspired need to protect, to nurture. To love.

Like Shelby, he had shielded himself from this emotion, scorned the very idea. Why?

Her gentle breathing rippled through the stillness. He held her close, mulling the question. An ocean breeze sailed through the balcony doors, and goose-bumps sprinkled the slender length of her arms. Jason tugged at the sheet until her gorgeous body became a tempting vision of shapely curves swathed in pale yellow satin.

He exhaled a long sigh of satisfaction. Peaceful. That's how he felt. For the first time ever, that familiar restlessness didn't gnaw at him. He felt mercifully content.

For the life of him, Jason couldn't figure out why. He had experienced a lifetime of admiration from his fans, his parents' fans, but it had never been enough.

Why?

When the answer struck, so simple and clear, he almost laughed aloud.

He hadn't met Shelby.

The people in his life had needed Jason Gage the actor—needed his fame, his connections, his talent. Shelby needed none of those things. She needed *him*.

All along his quest for fulfillment had been a quest for love. Now he had found it. In a beautiful slip of a woman who doubted she even knew how to accept or return it.

Jason pressed a soft kiss to her silk-straight hair and felt a little thrill when she stirred in response.

He loved her. He wanted to wake up to the sound of her voice, the naturally bright way she spoke that matched the energetic way she moved. He wanted to experience her humor, test her anger, explore her intellect.

Share the secrets that haunted her.

The shrill bell of the telephone rang out, and he snatched the receiver from the night table before it screeched a second time and disturbed her.

"Hello," he rasped, trying to keep his voice down.

"Good afternoon," came the pleasant response. "This is Doctor Pich's office calling to confirm Shelby's appointment in the morning."

He recognized the name of a respected psychoanalyst who had offices in LA. Shelby was in good hands.

"I'll give her the message." Jason hung up the phone.

Glancing at the bedside clock, he slipped from the tangle of Shelby's arms and grabbed his robe from the floor. Unless he missed his guess, she would awaken soon, hungry. He was starving.

With a parting glance at the beautiful woman who had captured his heart, Jason made his way to the kitchen.

The phone rang again.

"Hello." Wedging the portable between his ear and shoulder, he returned to his task at the sink, drying leaves of romaine for a salad.

"Do I have the right number?" a feminine voice asked in apparent surprise.

"Depends on whom you're calling." He glanced down at the Caller ID where the area code read: 202. Washington DC.

"Shelby."

"You've got the right number, but Shelby can't come to the phone right now. I'll take a message."

Jason met complete silence on the other end.

"Who am I speaking with?" the voice demanded suddenly, and he couldn't help but notice the no-nonsense strength in an otherwise silky voice.

"A friend," he said, unwilling to give his name.

"Well, *friend*," she said, and Jason knew he hadn't made a friend with his evasion. "You tell Shelby that Paige called."

Oh, hell! "I'll tell her."

He returned the portable to the base with a groan. Paige from DC. Damn. Shelby was right—he didn't know enough about her.

But as he peered absently at the telephone, he noticed something interesting. She liked cutting edge. Caller ID. Portables and cell phones with all the buttons and bows. An elaborate answering machine. A state-of-the-art security system.

Another piece fitted into the puzzle about the woman he loved, and when she woke up, he'd tell her about Paige's call.

But when Shelby's anguished moan had sent him running toward her bedroom, questions were the farthest thing from Jason's mind.

He found her tangled in a sheet, drenched in sweat. A chill glazed the full length of his spine when he saw her deathly pale face, the tears that squeezed through tightly-closed eyelids. She was still asleep.

Two long strides saw him beside her. "It's okay, Shelby. Wake up." Jason knelt on the edge of the bed. "Wake up," he commanded, shaking her shoulder to rouse her.

Her eyes flew open, unfocused. Frightened.

He lay a reassuring hand over her heart to find it beating frantically beneath his palm.

A nightmare. Fear etched tight lines around her mouth. His own heart breaking, he gathered her into his arms, and she clung to him, her slender body trembling.

He lay back on the bed, stroking wet hair from her face as she came back from the horror trip she'd been on.

Anxiety attacks and nightmares.

He was tempted to call Doctor Pich. But just as quickly, he dismissed the idea. He wanted answers, but he wanted them from Shelby. Until she was ready to trust him. . . .

"I'm not really an emotional wreck, Jason." Her voice was ragged from slumber and tears. She looked up at him with a soul-melting gaze. "Except for a few quirks, I'm perfectly normal."

He squeezed her tight. "I know, honey."

"I feel like such a jerk."

"Helluva nightmare, hmm?"

"A doozy." A shadow clouded her brilliant gaze.

"Want to talk about it?"

He could feel her conflict in the way she tensed, and he wondered what bothered her more: reliving her nightmare or sharing it with him.

"Will it help?"

"Usually does."

She sighed, and her frown deepened. With his thumb he caressed the tiny crease between her brows, pleased that she hadn't refused outright, hopeful that she might open up.

"They frighten me," she said, trailing a finger along the nape of his neck. "I hadn't had a nightmare in years, and then all of a sudden— boom!—I'm having one every few weeks." She sighed again, sounded tired.

"What do you think triggered them?"

Nervously, she moistened dry lips, and her mouth dipped into an even deeper frown. He sensed her uncertainty, sensed her retreat. She shrugged.

Disappointment rushed through him. She wasn't ready to trust him yet.

"Doctor Pich's office called to confirm your appointment in the morning," he said, hoping to engage her in the conversation a little longer.

"I was going to blow it off. I know your schedule's tight."

"Do you think that's a good idea?"

Shelby tossed her hair over her shoulder and sent it tumbling down her back like a sooty waterfall. "Probably not," she admitted with a roll of her eyes. "But I don't want to waste any of our time together. Wes expects me back on the set Monday."

"I'll wait." Jason reached out and grabbed her hand. "Wes can, too."

She brushed her lips across his knuckles, sending his nerve endings skittering in rapid response, but she still looked troubled. "I won't take too long. Promise."

"I'll wait." Not only would he be here after her therapist's appointment, he'd be here until she was ready to trust him. However long it took, and it definitely looked like it might take a while, since she seemed so committed to steering the conversation elsewhere.

"Hungry?" She rolled to the edge of the bed and slid fluidly to her feet.

The sight of her silhouetted in the natural light of the open French doors was like a blast of fresh air.

"Read my mind," he said, not sure which was stronger: the hunger in his stomach or the hunger in his crotch. Propping a pillow behind his head so he could watch Shelby as she brushed her hair, he pondered the question.

Her hair tumbled in a glossy fall down her back, outlining the neat lines of her ribs and ending just short of where her waist curved inward.

Her long shapely legs and the graceful way she moved hinted at a natural athletic ability, and he wondered if she would bike along the coast with him or prefer to take long walks along the beach. Maybe he would luck out and she'd enjoy both.

God, he wanted her.

Setting the brush on the dresser, Shelby caught his gaze in the mirror. "I'm starved."

That answered the question of which hunger he'd satisfy first. "I'm working on dinner."

"You're a talented man, Jason Gage." She smiled and slipped into a light robe.

He hoped talent would be enough to win her, because she was so obviously comfortable being alone.

And then it hit him.

That aura of . . . something about her. It had been nagging at him since they met, but he hadn't known Shelby well enough to pinpoint what it was until now.

Guilt.

She wore it like a shroud. Whatever had happened all those years ago still haunted her in more ways than she seemed to realize. Despite all her years of therapy and hard work. Despite her protests of having resolved all her issues, Shelby had missed one very important thing.

She had never forgiven herself.

It was Jason's best guess, and it fit. Her avoidance of intimacy. Her willingness to settle for acting instead of feeling.

What the hell had happened to her?

The question gnawed his soul, urged him to his feet. Taking her in his arms, he buried his face in her hair and inhaled deeply of her moist feminine scent, staving off his own rising panic. Shelby could never love him unless she learned to love herself.

These Names Weren't on the Playbill

"Ding! Ding-a-ling!"

The doorbell chimed. Jason cursed aloud at the interruption, at the computer monitor, and at his own inability to concentrate on this lecture when his thoughts kept steering back to Shelby—just like an old trail horse kept heading back to the stable.

How was she making out at her therapy session?

He attacked the keyboard with renewed vigor.

"Ding! Ding-a-ling!"

The damned bell kept ringing. Jason resolutely ignored it, determined Hell would freeze over before he answered the door. Finally there was silence again, and he breathed a sigh of relief.

Until he heard the unmistakable sound of footsteps tapping on the wood plank floor in the foyer.

"Shelby, are you home? Your system isn't on." A feminine voice called out, and if Jason wasn't mistaken, this was a voice he recognized. "I saw a car in the garage and used my key."

With a groan, he shoved the chair back and stood.

Moving quickly through the house, he turned the corner and came face-to-face with a stunning woman who stood just inside the open doorway as if hesitant to enter. He ground to a dead halt, unable to stop staring.

Dressed in a stylish silk jumpsuit, a sapphire shade remarkably similar to her eyes, she was tall and slender and strikingly beautiful. A halo of wild red curls framed a delicate oval face, and Jason suddenly felt very undressed as her deprecating gaze swept over him in return, taking in every inch of his bare chest and feet.

"You must be the *friend*," she said dryly. Raising a finely-arched copper brow, she stared him down in a silent command to explain.

"Paige from DC?"

He didn't need her short nod to tell him he was right. He recognized both her voice and her tone, and he also sensed that Paige from DC was a woman used to getting whatever answers she wanted.

"I thought you had retired from show business, Mr. Gage."

She had recognized him, and to Jason's surprise he felt only a mild sense of amusement. Whether anyone discovered he was here no longer mattered. The idea of the media chewing over his love for Shelby didn't really bother him. Not as long as he had Shelby. "I have."

"Since Shelby hasn't mentioned word one about you, perhaps you can fill me in on the details. *Friend* doesn't really tell me much." She jingled her keys impatiently, gaze dropping deliberately to his chest. "Are you here in a professional or personal capacity?"

"Both."

"I've read about your new profession, Mr. Gage. Should I be concerned about her health?"

There was no mistaking the worry she tried to hide behind carefully controlled features. Paige from DC cared for Shelby very much.

Jason felt the first connection click into place between them. His defenses dwindled. "Call me Jason, please. I'm here in both capacities, and, no, you don't need to be concerned about Shelby."

"Where is she?"

"She had an appointment this morning. I expect her back shortly." He motioned toward the living room. "You're welcome to wait."

Paige didn't move from the doorway, though, and when a tall man suddenly appeared beside her, Jason understood why.

"Christopher, this is Jason Gage. The *friend*." She met the man's gaze with a wry grin. "My husband, Christopher Sharp."

Jason made the first move, crossing the foyer and extending his hand. The Sharps were important to Shelby, and he suspected he had some making up to do to remedy his first impression.

A *lot* of remedying if Christopher Sharp's scowl was any indication.

He was a huge man with a firm grip and an all-business stare. There was something naggingly familiar about him, too, but Jason couldn't place it.

What he could place, however, was that Paige and Christopher Sharp were a power couple. Definitely physical people, they seemed to flow together as if they had been cast from the same mold. Where one ended, the other began.

"Please come in and make yourselves comfortable," he said.

The Sharps followed him into the living room. Paige took a seat on the settee, while her husband loosened the tie around his throat with studied movements. Getting down to business.

"Shelby hasn't mentioned you as a friend," Christopher said, resting a large hand on his wife's shoulder.

She leaned into his touch so naturally that Jason felt a twinge of envy for the kind of closeness these two apparently shared.

He wanted a place in Shelby's world, and to earn one, he would have to make friends with the Sharps. The fact that Christopher believed he knew all Shelby's friends was revealing.

"I love her," he said simply. Might as well play his hand. He'd shoot straight with them and see what happened.

Paige quirked a copper brow. Christopher glowered. Their combined scrutiny was so intense that he could only surmise they found him seriously lacking as a partner.

"Does she share your sentiment?" Paige asked, elegantly and to the point.

Clasping his hands over his knees, Jason leaned forward and faced her with a smile, deciding in that instant he liked Paige Sharp very much. "Poised on the brink, I believe. I'm hopeful."

"Don't get too hopeful, Gage," Christopher challenged. "I'm not convinced you have anything to offer her."

Paige patted her husband's hand as he glared down from his lofty height. Some silent communication passed between them, before he said, "Shelby doesn't need a rogue."

"I agree." Even though Christopher was justified in his opinion, although news of his decadent youth had been greatly exaggerated by the media, Jason would not back down. "She's held herself back from love for a long time, and to be frank with you, I'm glad. It's given me the opportunity to meet her."

"When exactly did you meet her, Jason?" Paige asked.

"Two days ago."

Christopher snorted. "In which time I suppose you've formed 'an eternal bond with the woman of your dreams.' "

"Touché." Jason leaned back and folded his arms across his chest, unable to suppress a smile at Christopher's performance of a line from one of his early movies. "But, yes, it's something like that."

"She's not the woman to scratch your itch."

"No, she's not," he agreed, and the silence swelled between them.

"What Christopher is trying to say," Paige began delicately, "is that Shelby is a woman who has . . . a woman who needs . . ."

"What I assume you're trying to say is that she still has some issues to work out." Watching the two of them try to make their point without revealing anything was becoming almost painful.

"She's told you?"

He didn't miss the catch in Paige's voice, and Jason didn't hesitate. "She hasn't confided in me—yet. I hope in time she will."

"What difference would it make?" Christopher braced his hands on either side of his wife and stared Jason down.

He was being interrogated. No getting around it. All that was missing was a light and an observation window.

"I think trusting someone might help."

"Is that a professional opinion?" Paige asked.

"Not really. It's hard to assess her situation when I don't know what's troubling her. It's almost irrelevant, though, since I don't have any professional distance." He shrugged, smiling when he met Paige's sympathetic gaze. "Shelby deserves to know love. I intend to be the man she discovers it with. My gut tells me she blames herself for something that happened to her a long time ago, and I'm able to distance myself enough to know she can't love me until she lets that go."

Christopher thumped his hands down on the back of the settee in apparent frustration. "You talk good, Gage. But knowing what an actor you are, how are we supposed to believe you?"

Jason met the man's dark gaze steadily. "I'm not interested in whether you believe me. I'm interested in Shelby."

The front door opened, and he heard Shelby call out, "I'm home. Jason, do you have company?"

"You do." He stood as she appeared in the doorway, her eyes widening in amusement as they flicked over his bare chest. She glanced at her visitors.

A smile of genuine delight wreathed her features, and she literally did a little hop-skip as she sailed into the room, arms spread. "Paige! Christopher! What are you doing here?"

"Business." Christopher caught her in an enthusiastic bear hug and lifted her off her feet. "Paige tried calling you."

"I know. I'm sorry I haven't returned your calls. I've been—busy." She cast a sheepish glance at Jason before Paige wrapped her in an embrace that brought on a round of teary laughter.

Jason retreated to the doorway, intent upon leaving them to their greetings and taking the opportunity to get dressed. Christopher observed him warily while shrugging out of his Italian suit jacket. When he draped it over the back of the settee, Jason noticed a semi-automatic pistol in the shoulder holster strapped around his back.

And he remembered where he had seen Christopher Sharp before.

The Denouement

As her "family by love" sat down to a brunch that she and Jason had prepared, Shelby had never felt so content. Paige and Christopher behaved like protective parents, grilling Jason all during the preparation of the meal and looking as if they planned to continue between bites. She found their concern endearing.

Given their combined years in law enforcement, and elevated positions with the FBI, Shelby understood they were only interested in her welfare. They always had been.

In addition to a thousand kindnesses, Paige and Christopher had offered her the gifts of friendship and love.

And loyalty.

She owed them her life.

Except Christopher swore he owed her because if it hadn't been for Shelby, he never would have won Paige's heart.

The three of them were a family.

And as Shelby listened to them cross-examine Jason, she wondered if the time had come to add someone else into the equation.

Paige and Christopher were professional interrogators, but Jason was holding his own. He had a dry sense of humor that smoothly deflected Christopher's attempts to intimidate him. Paige was tough but kind, and Shelby guessed that Jason had already won her over.

He was charming and pleasant and confident, as though he had every right in the world to be sitting in her kitchen. He did. Because she wanted him there. Her heart fluttered every time their gazes met across the table.

Jason belonged with them. She could envision them together on the holidays like a real family. The only problem now was turning the image in her head into a reality.

She could never have *any* kind of relationship unless she opened her heart and shared her past—and let the pieces fall where they may. Her conversation this morning with Doctor Pich had left her thinking that perhaps putting the past behind her wasn't all she had to do—that she still had to make peace with the young girl who had gotten into so much trouble ten years ago.

"Simple, but not easy," Doctor Pich had told her, and Shelby agreed. Dredging up her past would be a risk. But, Shelby decided while gazing across the table at Jason who was laughing at some lame joke Paige had just told, Jason Gage was worth it.

"You *are* a marvelous actor." Paige caught Shelby's gaze and winked. "I *almost* believed you liked my joke."

"She can't tell a joke to save her soul," Shelby explained, delighted Jason had made the effort to be nice. "Yet for some bizarre reason that Christopher and I still haven't figured out, she humbles herself by trying."

"It's an exercise in humility," Paige quipped.

Jason stared at her over the champagne flute. Shelby rolled her eyes while Christopher massaged his temples as though pained.

Paige pursed her lips in a disgruntled moue. "Ignore them, Jason. I don't have a shred of humility in me. I have to work at it."

"I'll deliver a more convincing performance next time."

"Oh, you were wonderful," Paige assured him. "But I wouldn't believe God, Himself. I really can't tell a joke."

"No one's perfect, my dear." Christopher cast her a loving glance that made Shelby believe in soulmates. Then he patted Shelby's hand and said, "There'd be no living with her if she didn't have at least one imperfection."

"Humph." Paige tossed her napkin onto her plate in a fit of mock pique.

"Be careful," Shelby warned Christopher. "She'll get you as soon as you walk out the door."

"Not to worry. We'll be in meetings for the rest of the day. She has no choice but to be on her best behavior."

Paige nudged Shelby with an elbow and sighed. "He'll want me to be respectful, too, I bet."

Christopher nodded. "I'm the boss."

"Are you sure you can't stay?" Shelby took Paige's hand, felt her slim fingers squeeze tight.

"I'm sorry. I don't see how we can leave the hotel. We've just got so many meetings." She cast an accusing glance at Christopher. "He's going to work us to death. But we'll squeeze out for dinner once or twice. He promised."

"Just call. I'll make myself available."

Paige patted her hand, then faced Jason. "Perhaps you'll join us."

"I will."

Shelby's heart soared. He expected to be here a few more days. Hopping to her feet before anyone caught her blush, she began clearing the table. Before she even got the dishes in the sink, Jason appeared by her side and whispered, "Go say your good-byes. I'll get this stuff in the dishwasher."

She smiled. He smiled back.

"Sorry we have to run and leave you with the mess." Paige intruded upon their moment with a knowing grin.

"No problem," Shelby said. "Come on. I'll walk you out."

Sandwiched between the two people dearest to her in all the world, she led them to the door, sorry, as always, to see them go. "Make sure you leave time for dinner. We can come to the hotel if it's more convenient. I'll be back on the set Monday, and it will be at least another eight weeks before I can get to DC."

"Promise." Paige's eyes misted, and Christopher, always sensitive to their need for long farewells, took his cue.

Enveloping Shelby in those strong, loving arms, he rocked her against his chest. "You call if you need anything."

Shelby couldn't miss the concern in his voice. He was worried about her. Smoothing her fingers over his graying blonde hair, she stood on tiptoes and kissed his cheek. "I promise."

He gave her a squeeze, then let her go. "I'll get the car."

Paige faced Shelby with misty eyes. It had always been like this between them. Tears prickled the backs of her lids. She took Paige's hands. "Promise me you'll take care. No dangerous undercover assignments, okay?"

Paige laughed through her tears. "Ever since Christopher was promoted, he refuses to let me do anything that's fun. I've spent more time at Quantico this past year than I have in my entire career."

"Good. I worry about you."

"Ditto." Paige wrapped her arms around Shelby.

Paige radiated the same sense of security and contentment Shelby had always felt with her. "You're too good to me."

"Never!" Paige replied vehemently and gave her a tight squeeze. "Do you love him?"

Shelby nodded, unable to form the words past the swell of emotion in her throat.

"Then trust him, sweetie. I've never seen you sparkle the way you do when you look at Jason. He's a good man, and he loves you."

"You're so sure, are you?"

Paige rolled her eyes. "It's all over him. Besides, he told me."

"He did?" Her heart filled with hope.

"He did, and I believe him." She wiped the tears from Shelby's cheeks. "Just be happy, and call me if you want to talk."

"I will."

The sound of a car horn beeped, and Christopher pulled a rented Lexus up to the portico. The driver's door swung open and he appeared. "Come on, ladies, before we end up swimming out of here."

Shelby laughed and shooed Paige off. "Go on. I'll see you before you leave L.A."

She gave Shelby a parting kiss and headed down the stairs to where Christopher was holding the door for her.

He beeped one last time before driving through the front gate, and Shelby waved, distracted from her bittersweet thoughts by Paige's parting advice.

Trust him.

Her whole world had changed overnight. Literally. She was falling in love with Jason Gage. She finally had a chance for happiness.

But would Jason still love her when he knew what she had done?

"Hey. You okay?"

She hadn't heard his approach and spun around at the sound of his voice. His smile flowed through her like sunshine, chasing the doubt from her mind. His arm came around her, and she rested her head against his chest.

"I'm always sad when they leave."

"It's wonderful to have people you love so much."

There it was, that loneliness again. She snuggled against him. "They're my family."

They could be yours, too.

"What did you think of them?"

"Paige is lovely. The verdict is still out on Christopher. He thinks I'm too old for you."

Surprised, she glanced up into his face. Apparently he was serious. "Whatever makes you think that?"

"It's a guy thing. He looks at you like his beautiful young daughter, then he looks at me like some nasty old pervert."

Shelby blinked back her tears with a laugh. "Christopher is just protective. Besides, *I* don't think you're too old."

"Good thing. I had no idea you hung with such powerful people."

"I knew them when they were nobodies," she said in mock disdain. "Paige, at least. Christopher was already important when I met him."

"Tell me about them."

The afternoon sun bathed them in its warmth, and Shelby felt the glow melt the chill around her heart.

She told Jason how she had met Paige through a volunteer program.

Paige's father had recently died, so she had no family living. She sort of adopted Shelby, and they had become friends. Sisters.

"When did Christopher come into the picture?"

"Oooh! A love story." She sighed, long and dramatic, eliciting Jason's laughter. "Christopher had been Paige's instructor at Quantico. He swears he fell in love with her there, but Paige wouldn't give him the time of day. He chased her around for eight years . . . until this one assignment." Shelby swallowed back the lump in her throat. "He trapped her on an island where she couldn't get away, and then he stole her heart."

She shivered, and Jason's arms tightened around her. As much as she adored Paige and Christopher's love story, she hated the reason they had been on that assignment.

It had been because of *her*.

They had never shared the gory details. They hadn't needed to. Shelby already knew what kind of crimes took place on that island.

"That is quite a love story. So why don't you look caught up in the romance?"

Shelby rested her chin on his shoulder and stared out at the English rose bushes she had planted last spring.

They had grown untended in recent weeks, lovely in their wildness, and she marveled at their freedom to bloom, to grow unfettered by anything other than the need to reach the sun. She wanted to experience that freedom, too.

Taking a deep breath, she forced the words out. "I hated that Paige even went to that island. She was undercover for two years. It was terrible. A really ugly case."

Jason's finger locked beneath her chin, and he lifted her face toward his. The sun cast his features in sharp relief, the hint of burnished stubble outlining the clench of his jaw. His sable gaze seared into hers. "I read about the case, Shelby. I recognized Christopher from photographs of the trial."

Shelby's heart missed a beat.

Jason knew.

Her mind raced. She didn't know what to say. Retreat? Confess? The blood seemed to drain to her toes, and she felt light-headed, dizzy.

The moment of truth had finally arrived.

Break a Leg

Jason thought she would bolt, but Shelby pressed her eyes tightly shut and said, "Christopher should never have been so visible. Paige, either. *They* absorbed all the media attention to . . . to protect . . ."

He had never loved her more than in that instant. Somewhere within herself, she had found the strength to share her past. "Who, Shelby?"

"*Me.*"

Tears slipped between her closed eyelids. Jason leaned back against the balustrade, taking her with him, cradling her against his chest. "Want to talk about it?"

Shelby wiped tears on his shirt. "Paige and Christopher were protecting me," she finally said.

"From what?"

"The sordid facts." She blinked her eyes open, her expression one of profound sadness. "I was the witness."

As soon as he had placed Christopher, Jason had guessed she was involved, but as he recalled the details of that shocking trial, he called upon all his years of acting experience to keep his expression blank. "I see."

The silence lengthened, but he held Shelby's gaze steadily, even as a range of emotions flashed across her face. "That's it? No shock? No high-tailing it out of here?"

"You want a performance?" He couldn't help but smile, feeling some of his own tension fade. "I'm not surprised, Shelby. I told you I recognized Christopher. Knowing what I know about you, it wasn't hard to draw my own conclusions."

"You already know?"

"Well, I don't really *know* anything except what you told me, but I *guessed* enough not to be surprised." He dropped his arms so they rested lightly around her waist, and they stood, facing each other in the warm afternoon sun. "Honey, we all have shadows. I have more than I care to admit. Point is, I put them behind me and moved on."

"I thought I had."

He knew she had conquered her demon now. His throat constricted when he asked, "And then the nightmares started?"

She nodded.

"What triggered them?"

"Lewis Goddard was murdered in prison."

Jason exhaled heavily and rested his chin on the top of her head, feeling the weight of her statement like an anchor. He had read all about Lewis Goddard, the leader of a crime ring that produced custom porn films. He had been convicted of murdering his actors and sentenced to life in prison.

"I thought I had put the past behind me, Jason." The pain in her voice burdened the anchor a little more. "Life wasn't perfect, but it was good enough to content me. I had my family, my work, and if I was a little lonely sometimes well, it just seemed an awfully small price to pay."

"Why should you pay at all?" It was such a simple question, yet she seemed surprised.

"I've made choices. I have to live with them."

"You're being hard, honey."

Her beautiful green eyes grew flinty. "I made some hard choices."

Guilt.

Therein lay her true problem, and he was determined to help her see it. "How did you get mixed up with a crime lord like Lewis Goddard?"

"One of his talent scouts."

"Where did he find you?"

"My high school drama club. It was the only reason I was still in school. I loved to act." She laughed, a short unforgiving sound that quickly became a sob. "Paige used to bribe me. If I passed all my other classes, she footed the bill for acting lessons."

"Sounds like she had you figured out."

"She did. Until I met Goddard's scout and saw a shortcut."

Tilting her head back, she stared at him, and he saw regret. "It was a whole new world, Jason. An exciting one. Goddard's clubs. Premieres. Expensive hotels. Foster homes and high school just couldn't compete."

"You must have been so young."

"Barely fifteen."

His struggle with control slipped a notch, his hand trembling as he brushed an errant strand of hair from her cheek. He didn't trust himself to speak.

"Goddard was casting a film," she explained. "I auditioned and won the lead. I knew the whole situation was wrong. He might have been professional. He had the production company, the people, the credentials—but he wouldn't discuss the script with me."

"You never told Paige?"

She shook her head. "I already knew what she'd say. Everything I didn't want to hear."

Of course not. Most fifteen-year-olds weren't big on hearing the world wasn't everything they thought it should be. Perhaps Shelby didn't realize that. Massaging her shoulders, Jason kneaded away the tension knotted there, and she let her eyes drift close with a sigh.

"Lewis Goddard owned an island where we were scheduled to film, and it wasn't until I was there that I finally understood what he wanted me to do."

"Pornography?" The question tore from his throat in a growl, despite his best efforts to keep his emotions below the surface.

She seemed to have expected his reaction and pressed shaking fingers gently against his lips. Her eyes misted. "He had this really elaborate set-up for rehearsing. A 'method' he called it. A technique he used with all his actors to get them comfortable with each other." Her voice cracked. "He wanted me to practice the sex scenes with my co-star."

Jason held her close, offered his strength, even when her words seared through him like acid.

"He scared me, Jason. His people scared me. They had guns, but they were as terrified of him as I was. There was no way off the island. My co-star . . . Bobby," her voice broke, and he sensed she was remembering. "He tried to protect me, didn't want me to feel ashamed by what we were doing. He was a year older than I was, and he tried to act tough. He was just as scared. We figured if we just did what Lewis Goddard wanted, we could go home."

Jason stroked her hair, her shoulders, her back, as she choked out every word with the horror of a fifteen year old. "But we didn't go home. Even though we did everything he said. Even when we found out that the entire wing where we rehearsed was wired and he was watching—"

His body jerked in stunned surprise. He hadn't known. Certain details must not have been released to the media. He tried, God, how he tried, but no amount of acting skill could help Jason hide his reaction. He vibrated with a helpless fury unlike anything he had experienced before.

His fists clenched when he thought of Shelby, so young and scared, all alone except for her brave boy hero who was no match against a monster like Goddard.

Shelby clung to him, trembling hands stroking, offering comfort, as if he was the one about to break. He grabbed her hands, knowing what he had to do. Goddard was already dead. Paige and Christopher had helped Shelby find justice. He would help her find peace.

"There's more, isn't there, honey?" He could see it in her face. He had to make her understand that these were Goddard's crimes, not *hers*.

"It was a snuff film." The words spilled from her lips as if her torment ate at her from the inside, and he braced himself against the truth she needed to share, the truth that jeopardized his control.

"We had shut almost the whole movie. We thought we were almost finished, but then . . . during the last sex scene . . . someone *murdered* Bobby. Staged it so . . . so it looked as if *I* had killed him. I was there, on top of him, and suddenly there was all this blood and he was gagging . . ." Shelby began to shake.

"Jesus!" Jason exploded and scooped her into his arms. Carrying her into the house, he sat on the settee with her curled in his lap like a child, rocking her, while her sobs tore at him.

"Come on, honey. Breathe. It's okay." His own throat was raw, choked with tears as he fought back the image of a terrified Shelby, in trouble and alone.

And when she lifted her gaze to his, Jason thought his heart would break.

"Don't," she whispered, kissing the tears from his cheeks.

Cupping her face between his hands, he closed his eyes, unable to face her anguish. "I feel your pain."

"You shouldn't."

"I do." He pressed a tremulous kiss to her lips. "I love you."

Her tears flowed, and she tried to pull away.

He held her. "Don't turn away from me, Shelby. Share yourself. I want to understand."

And she told him. Huddled in a wretched ball on his lap, she told him how she had hidden in an elevator shaft for two days, stolen a personal watercraft and escaped to the mainland in the dead of night.

She told him how she had hitchhiked to Paige, cross-country from California to Virginia, with nothing more than the clothes on her back and the terror that Lewis Goddard would be after her.

He had been.

Paige had set Shelby up in the Witness Protection Program until she built a case strong enough to convict Goddard. Jason thanked God for Paige, who had cared for a young girl all alone in the world.

He held Shelby, their mingled tears streaming over his lips, a vision of her in the middle of a pitch black ocean, so desperately frightened, seared into his brain. Resting his brow against hers, he couldn't resist

the urge to touch her, to kiss her and feel her warmth pulsing beneath
his lips. She was so alive. Even in her grief, she made him feel alive.
And she had trusted him enough to share her past.

"Bobby's death still haunts you."

A shadow of despair clouded her features. "I met his mother at the
trial, Jason. She . . . she *thanked* me."

The contempt in her voice fitted another piece of the puzzle in
place. "Why does that surprise you? Your testimony convicted her
son's killer."

"You make it sound so . . . *noble*." She spit the word from between
clenched teeth. "There was nothing noble about it. I did the only thing
I could, and I was just fortunate enough to have Paige and Christopher
on my side."

"You're being too hard on yourself." Yet he understood, with all his
heart and soul, he understood. She had found the courage to seek
justice, no matter what the cost, but she still didn't think it was enough.
"The right thing wasn't the easy thing. You gave up your life to see
justice done. Lewis Goddard went to prison. *Died* in prison. Haven't
you suffered enough?"

He saw the answer gather in her eyes like a summer storm.

No.

"Bobby died. He was so sweet, Jason. He tried so hard to be brave
so that I wouldn't be scared." Tears spilled down her cheeks, her voice
ragged, grief-stricken. "He didn't deserve to die."

He kissed the tears away, tried to reassure her, to absorb some of
her anguish. She sobbed harder.

"I dragged Paige and Christopher into this . . . this mess. They
went to that island. They lived with those . . . criminals. All because
of me. Whatever I've suffered just doesn't quite compare."

He had to make her understand. His heart depended on it. "Forgive
yourself, Shelby, because until you do, you can't love me." Jason ran
his hands along her neck, her jaw, her cheeks. "The way I love you."

Relief broke from his lips in a sigh when she answered his plea with
one of her own. "Help me, Jason. Show me how."

It's a Wrap

Shelby slanted her mouth over his. She wanted him more than she had ever wanted anything before, needed him to help her feel something beyond this despair. He hadn't turned away. He knew everything, understood her demons, and he still loved her.

Jason.

She ran her fingers through his hair, kissing the tears from his lips, laughing, crying, drowning in a swirl of emotion that she *felt* inside.

A low growl tore from his throat, and he plunged his tongue into her mouth. He knew what she needed. He took what he wanted.

His kiss awakened her senses. Need roiled inside like a maelstrom. Desire forged a fevered ache low in her belly. Running her hands along his neck, she outlined the corded muscles with eager fingers.

Jason dragged her off the settee, protecting her within the circle of his arms as they rolled to the floor. She gasped as their hips locked, and his erection pressed into her softness like a command.

Running her hands along his waist, hips, buttocks, she rocked against that maleness, showing him boldly what she needed. No longer afraid. "I want you."

She had trusted him with her past. Now she would trust him with her heart. "Love me, Jason."

His look of bold desire made her heart swell and her body ache. He braced himself above her, and Shelby gasped at the savage beauty of him, at the fury of a passion that etched stark lines on his beloved face, at the glaze of need that burned in the depths of his sable gaze.

Tugging the shirt from the waistband of her jeans with jerky motions, he tore it open with rough hands, buttons popping in all directions as the fabric parted. He dragged her bra from her body with the shreds of her shirt and stripped the jeans down her legs in impatient strokes. She lay naked before him. His gaze scorched her, and she saw the fire in his eyes, recognized the need that drew his muscles tight. His chest heaved with ragged breaths. She felt his hunger. She felt his love.

All along he had coached her, caressed her, coddled her, always putting her pleasure first.

Not anymore.

His urgency fed her own, whipped through her until she understood in the vaguely-functioning portion of her brain just how masterful his control had been.

"I love you, Shelby." His voice was rough gravel, awakening such primitive excitement inside her, Shelby thought she might explode. She held her arms to him. Eager. Ready.

Suddenly his hands were all over her, searing across her thighs, molding the feminine mound between her legs, sweeping upward along her ribs, plucking at her nipples, until she cried out in abandon.

She arched against him as a current surged across her breasts, tightening the tips into eager crests. Sliding her hand between them, she stroked his male hardness through his jeans, wanting him to lose control and tumble with her into this whirl of erotic sensation.

He grabbed her with a wild strength, rolling her beneath him suddenly, stealing her breath with his kiss. Blood surged from her fingertips to her toes. Desire pounded like thunder between her legs. She would die unless he satisfied this ache inside, this urgency he had created.

He knew. Spearing his hand into her hair, his lips came down hard, and she met each thrust of his tongue, wanting to give him everything. Her body, her past, her heart.

Her trust.

A gift as precious as any she could give. But did she know how to be vulnerable?

The tenderness in his face as he gazed upon her, the love in his eyes, filled her with such hope that she felt the answer straight to her soul. *Yes.*

She had known it since the moment they met. He would never hurt her. With a half-sob, half-gasp, she held onto him as he lifted her to her knees, bodies pressed together, hearts racing. He broke their kiss only to yank the shirt over his head, and together they fumbled with the button at his waist, hands tangled as they slid the jeans down his hips. His sex sprang free. Hot. Hard. Shelby resisted the urge to touch him while he kicked off his clothes.

Powerful muscles played beneath the dark sweep of his skin. Burnished curls nestled in the ridges of his chest, veeing downward along the muscled lines of his stomach, circling the base of that splendid erection.

He was magnificent.

And he was *hers*.

Jason sat back on his haunches, taking her with him, and with a grateful sigh, Shelby let him pull her into his arms, awed by the feel of him against her. Her nails raked the muscles along his back in excitement as he thrust into her in one bold stroke, need unleashed, desire raging like a storm around them.

"Trust me, Shelby."

"I do."

He filled her. A moan slipped from her lips, a low, throaty sound that surrounded them. Her body trembled.

His hands locked onto her hips, lifting her off his thick shaft, then driving her back down. Sweat slicked their skin together. Passion built like a tempest, and Jason knew, oh, yes, he knew exactly what to do to push her into the midst of the storm.

He drew her into his rhythm, pounded into her with exquisite fury. She soared. Grinding out a sound of the purest male triumph, he watched her, knowing, as her ecstasy mounted. Exploded. She cried out, her sex clenching his in violent bursts, as the most incredible sensation of rapture whipped through her.

Driving into her one last time, he poured out his own pleasure while she clung to him, gasping, laughing aloud for the sheer joy of it.

She had never imagined climax could be so sweet. Even the delightful sensations she had coaxed from her own body did not compare with this heart-melting bliss, the languid glow that pulsed through her with the rhythm of her racing heartbeat.

Draping his arms around her hips, Jason leaned back against the settee and closed his eyes. "God, I'm too old for this."

She could feel his heart throb in time with hers when she rested her cheek on his shoulder. She had never known such contentment. Such peace.

"Marry me, Jason," she whispered into his ear. "Be my husband and make lots of babies with me."

He cracked an eyelid. "I'm *really* too old for this."

Shelby arched backward to gaze into his face. "I love you. I'm prepared to give up acting. You have another life now, and I want to be a part of it."

He rolled her off and under him with an agility that belied his earlier claim. "Never. You have a gift and I'll push you to use it until we're old and gray and performing for dinner theaters."

"*We're?*" she asked, not sure she heard him right. "You're retired."

"I think I could be persuaded into accepting a role or two. I'm having a helluva hard time envisioning you performing sex scenes with other actors." He nipped at her shoulder with a growl. "You'll be my leading lady, won't you?"

She gazed into his burning black eyes, suddenly unsure. "I thought you only wanted privacy?"

"I want a lot more now. I want love. I want you." He stretched out, wedging a leg between hers until her sex nestled warmly against his thigh. "I think we can come up with a compromise that lets us both do what we love. If you'll relocate north with me, I think after the initial shock, the media won't hound us too much. Some press will be good for your career."

The breath caught in her throat. "Are you saying yes, Jason?"

"Yes, Shelby. I'll marry you." His eyes sparkled.

"Are you sure?"

"I thought my life was making me lonely, and Hollywood was my life. I left. I was still lonely. Until now."

His tender expression warmed her straight to her soul, and her heart sang with the knowledge that she was living, not acting. She *felt* this swell of joy inside. "The babies, too?"

"At least six." He smiled a roguish smile. "I have to show Christopher I'm not too old to do you justice."

Laughter bubbled from her lips, and Shelby closed her eyes, savoring this moment of shared love. She had wasted so much time punishing herself over mistakes made long ago. Mistakes she had paid dearly for, had done everything possible to correct.

She *would* learn to forgive herself. With Jason's help.

"What about my past? There's always the possibility that it leaks out. Will I embarrass you?"

"Bad press, honey?" He quirked the bronzed slash of his brow. "I'm immune." Ruffling her hair back from her face with a tender touch, he said, "Besides, I've got a blue movie in my own credits. I'm sure Wes will be happy to tell you all about it."

Shelby wondered if that movie was what Wes had used to blackmail Jason into coaching her. She rested her head against his arm, basking in the warm glow of his love, not really interested. Right now all she could think about was how dashing he would look in a tux.

Even more handsome than Max Brandauer had looked when he gave away the bride in *Heaven's Traveler.*

And as Shelby envisioned Jason playing the role of groom before an altar, another thought occurred to her. "Should we invite Wes to the wedding, do you think?"

"Invite, hell." Jason laughed and pulled her into his arms. "We'll blackmail him into paying for it."

It was a grand plan.

About the author:

Jeanie Cesarini is a multi-published author who lives with her very own romance hero and their two beautiful daughters in the South. A transplanted Yankee, she particularly enjoys stretching out beneath moss-draped oaks and indulging in her favorite pastime: reading thrilling crime novels then soothing her jitters with a wonderful romance. "The Spy Who Loved Me" and "An Act Of Love" allowed her to triumph over evil, to create love from the harsh reality of crime and create a happily ever after from a past mistake. She loves believing that, at least in fiction, good always triumphs over evil and hopes Secrets' readers enjoy believing, too.

Enslaved

❧❦❧

by Desirée Lindsey

To my reader:

Everyone loves a good, angst-filled love story and adore a tender, provocative hero. Here's to vulnerable alpha heroes—to a sensate adventure with Nicholas and Crystal, their undying love, fierce passion, and all things as brilliant as his gift to her . . .

I give you award-winning seduction—may your hearts be *Enslaved*.

Diamond Necklace Contest

For more information, send a self-addressed stamped envelope to:

Diamond Necklace Contest
c/o Desirée Lindsey
P.O. Box 9806
Denver, CO 80209

Chapter One

Lady Crystal Halverton stood gazing out the massive wall of windows with her back to the man she knew so well—the man her husband hadn't spoken to in weeks. Not since they'd parted ways out-of-sorts with each other.

Nicholas Summer had come like she knew he would.

And she desperately needed his cooperation.

With her fingers, Crystal cleared a spot where her breath fogged the glass pane. The rains had stopped their battering ram of sound on the roof. Despite the warmth from the blazing hearth at her back, the sky above the rear courtyard looked utterly despondent and sent an involuntary shiver through her. The winds felt colder this year, she thought, as she watched the approach of winter whip leaves across the rolling lawn of Halverton Hall's vast gardens.

Where once the house had been filled with laughter and happiness, it felt empty now—more like a prison of failures each day her husband stayed away. The gloomy and dreary weather matched her ever increasing despair and she wondered how Nicholas would feel when he learned the reason behind her hastily penned summons.

"I was so afraid you'd left London," she told him. "Thank you for coming, Nick."

"The dispatch sounded urgent," the deep voice answered behind her from the gold-braided settee. "Are you all right?"

"Freddy really does feel badly," she said feebly, avoiding the concern lacing his question, "about the disagreement over the hounds. I know he'll come around soon . . . it's just his pride is so delicate."

"So you called me here today to smooth things over?"

That would be a whole lot easier than what she intended. "I needed to speak with you in private . . . about another matter."

Interrupting them, the liveried footman in green and gold entered the drawing room with a tray of petit fours and a fine, black Darjeeling tea reserved for those occasions when Lord Summer came to call.

Crystal nodded at the table, her guest was familiar enough to the family to dispense with formality. "Please, Nick, help yourself." Her heart started an erratic dance the minute the door closed behind her footman.

"It's obvious you didn't call me here to discuss how Fred thinks his hounds are superior to the ones I acquired in France." His gaze was on her profile, his voice low, intimate. "You look pale. Have you eaten today?"

"No," she told him softly, "and please don't press me, not today."

"All right. I'll talk about the weather until you're sufficiently bored."

She shook her head. "I suppose you indulge your paramours in the same way. I should be jealous if I were not your friend."

"Neglect shows on you, puss."

His endearment touched her. Made her heart clench. "I'm not sure I like being read so well."

"Don't be angry, darling. Remember we practically grew up together. Knowing what you're feeling isn't difficult."

She sighed. "You've always been better at reading people than most men. I shouldn't wonder it comes in handy with overwrought women."

"With you I take special pains. It gives me great pleasure to find I've not lost my touch." The deep timbre of his voice was teasing and caressing in turns.

No, she thought, *you haven't lost your touch.*

From the drawing room window the courtyard looked deserted and gray. Dark snow clouds edged the wintery sky. A handful of birds clung to branches, their little bodies fluffed against the cold. She felt a pang of pity for the poor creatures, who not unlike man, sought warmth and protection where they could from the harshness of life.

"I'm a friend, Crystal. You know I won't spread your secrets around for gossip. Tell me what's wrong and I'll try to help."

She rested her forehead against the window, felt the cool glass panes startling cold against her skin. *That's why I chose you.*

"I won't be leaving for Edinburgh until tonight." His cup clanked onto the table. "Come, let me take you out for a walk, and you can tell me how married life is beginning to bore you."

It was a joke with them, of course, her marriage to Freddy Halverton anything but boring. "I already went for a walk before you arrived." She knew he was only trying to pull her out of her melancholy shell.

"Then a carriage ride? I'll bundle you up and we'll race around the estate—see how many tongues we can set to wagging. We used to do that well, you and I."

His devil-may-care tone reminded her of the days when she would have thrown convention to the wind. Could she really have been so careless all those years ago? So young?

Contemplating the changes in her life, she turned from the window. Her gaze rested on her childhood friend with a fond appreciation of his disarming good looks. At thirty, the wealthy man of a thriving merchant-line, Nicholas Summer was the model of virility. A paragon of masculine grace that took her breath away. His hair was thick as sable, still a rich, dark brown. To her, Nicholas looked every bit the young blood she'd loved as a girl—back when he and Freddy Halverton had taken London by storm. Time had changed many things, but not Nicholas.

Nick was five years her senior and still possessed an air of danger, dark passions, and irresistible charm. In the circles she belonged to, his name purred from the lips of breathless wives. And here, in her drawing room, the incorrigible Lord Summer was lounged in a sanguine sprawl on her settee. Typical, she mused, how he tied his white cravat as if to proclaim a rakish disregard for convention, while Freddy on the other hand took great pains to affect perfection.

She closed her heart to that painful thought.

"I'm losing him, Nick," she whispered weakly, her stomach knotting in anguish as if voicing the words made final the acceptance of losing her husband's love.

The silent sympathy in Nick's vivid green gaze told her he had not missed the nuances, the long weeks Freddy spent away, presumably hunting at their cottage near Dover.

"For what it's worth, he's alone, Crystal. I know he doesn't keep another woman."

"Oh, and I guess that should make me feel better. They're all in your bed—is that what you're telling me?"

"I'm sorry, puss."

His sympathy was almost more than she could bear—her empty bed becoming a stark contrast to his. "I don't think there's ever been any question about *your* ability to sire, has there? Aren't you glad now you're not saddled with a wife who has trouble breeding?"

"I would still love you, puss," he said with mild seriousness.

She slanted him a disgruntled look. "But you wouldn't have made me happy, isn't that what you said?"

"Fred was the better man."

"Really? I wonder on whose authority you arrived at that falsehood."

"Fred hasn't stopped loving you, Crystal."

"Not yet." There was no animosity in her voice, only a strained tiredness. "But neither have I been able to give him an heir."

"Don't blame yourself. Have you thought it might be Fred with the problem and not you?"

For a man who'd probably sired half of England, Nick's announcement seemed a mockery of her pathetic handicap. She had pondered over everything until her brain ached. Pointing fingers, she had decided, did nothing to lessen the burden—the stark longing in her husband's eyes. Nor did it lessen the yearning in her own heart, when their friends had hoards of children they only casually acknowledged.

The *problem* was, regardless of who was at fault, the result of their inability to have children had slowly erected a wedge between them. Which was why she had desperately agreed to go along with Freddy's outrageous request.

"I will do anything to keep my marriage from falling apart, Nick, anything."

Then because she'd held it bottled up all week, the misery and sorrow gave way to hot tears. One by one they trickled down her cheeks.

Nick came out of his chair and closed the short distance between them. He drew her tight in genuine concern. "Don't cry, darling."

He held her closer, murmuring soft praises against her hair that made her throat burn with self-pity. In her weakened state, Crystal gladly accepted his charity. She leaned on his strength, reveled in his warmth, when she had for many weeks been bereft of warmth, of hope. She let Nick be her rock, let him comfort her. She was too weary to worry about convention, about ruining his fine linen shirt with tears. Grateful for what scraps of attention he gave her, she pressed her lips to his chest. In Nick's embrace she could forget the world, her troubles—the affection they shared for one another brought her no shame.

She drew in a ragged breath, felt his hand soothing the tightness from her neck. His fingers were strong, caressing. After going so long without a simple touch, being held by him felt close to heaven. Just like old times. At first she had worried about feeling nervous—but now it was as if all the years since their last kiss had been washed away. He smelled of rainsoaked forests and leather. Under her cheek, his chest was solid. He was the same way she remembered him at seventeen, yet different in remarkable ways. Muscles honed by action rippled beneath his shirt. He towered above her. Tall, powerful, infallible.

She sniffled against him, felt his arms tighten, his compassion reach out to her. "I don't know if I could bear your rejection, too," she whispered, clinging to him in a manner she knew was desperate.

"Shh, darling, I'd never do that to you."

"You don't know yet why I asked you here." She knew him. He'd probably never speak to her again, never hold her like he held her now as though he cherished her. Like Freddy used to cherish her. But then she'd already spent the night crying over Freddy. Worrying about the future. Its complications. Now was not the time to have qualms about her promise.

"Tell me what I can do for you," Nicholas prompted reverently, "and I'll do it."

So trusting, so irresistible, and so gallant. "I want you," she murmured softly, "to give me a child."

The slight stiffening of Nick's body told her she'd been right. He was shocked.

His chin was resting on her head, the noticeable change in his breathing curiously touching.

"Are you serious?" Though he sounded calm, his heart was racing against her cheek.

She nodded against his chest and sniffled. "Very serious."

At least he hadn't said no.

"In fact, Freddy is staying away," she explained in a breathless rush, "until I send him word you're going home. The staff is leaving tonight. It will be only you and I alone in the house."

"Fred gave his consent?"

Another shock, she knew. One he hadn't expected.

"His blessing really. Freddy said if anyone could get me with child it would be you. He wanted me to approach you." Remembering her husband's anguished expression and not understanding it had upset her horribly. The despair in his voice had scared her. He hadn't explained why he was suddenly adamant about having an heir, just that it was imperative she talk to Nicholas. When she had balked, Freddy had begged her in a strangely hoarse voice that had cut straight to her heart. She'd set her fears aside, assured him she still loved him, and agreed to do as he requested. "Nick, I know what you must be thinking. God help me, but I want to please Freddy so badly I agreed."

His hand smoothed her hair. "Good Lord, Crystal. How could a man live with himself after sending his wife to seduce his best friend?"

Overwhelmed by the same uncertainties, wanting only to be done with fulfilling her husband's wish, she bit her lip to staunch the flow of misgivings.

"Really, it isn't all as insane as it sounds," she defended softly, "I think Freddy's plan makes perfect sense." She had to believe that—she must. "We've tried everything—the countless potions, the doctors who had no answers. You're our last hope."

"Are you sure?" he asked gravely.

Heartened by what sounded like his acceptance, she looked up at him, praying he wouldn't disappoint her. "I've thought about this long and hard. Quite honestly, I don't want to talk about it all night. I don't want to hear all the reasons why we shouldn't. I want you to carry me upstairs and make love to me."

"Just like that?"

Certainly she sounded like a stranger even to herself. A woman driven by fear of failure to the point of desperation. But it didn't matter. Everything important to her was slowly deteriorating before her very eyes. She'd failed Freddy in the most elemental way as a wife, but she would not fail him in this.

"Perhaps not *just* like that." Blushing, she admitted, "It may take a couple of days."

"And if it takes longer?"

Her heart twisted with sorrow. "I have no choice. You should have seen him, Nick, the way he kept looking at me as though he was leaving and never coming back. I can't fail. He won't come home until I'm with child," she told him plaintively. "In which case I'm prepared for it to take as long as a month." She'd gone over the details in her mind into the wee hours of the morning. "I'll need you to cancel all your engagements. That way you can stay in bed with me until I'm certain—"

"Slow down." His arms dropped to his sides. "I didn't agree to anything."

Desperation clutched at her belly. "I know what I'm asking sounds absurd, but please don't say no. Can't you just imagine I'm one of your many paramours? I'll even keep the room dark—"

"I can't."

The statement rang out with deafening clarity. No margin for maybe. Just resounding denial.

Reeling with dread, Crystal pulled away from him. Her throat filled with a suffocating desolation. She kept her face averted, tried to draw on the strength of her resolve while the ruined remains of her future flashed before her eyes.

"You mean you won't," she clarified softly.

She watched his expression in the window's reflection where they stood in uncomfortable silence. She could feel his pity reach out to her, sense his struggle—while beyond the perfectly manicured lawn, the grounds of Halverton Hall looked as bleak as her childless marriage.

Swallowing hard at the tight knot, she turned abruptly away and blindly made her way to the table. She forced herself to drink her tea slowly as panic rose up her throat to suffocate her. Her husband's parting words rang in her ears, impaling her heart. "I'm not getting any younger, Crystal. I need an heir—a son to entail Halverton Hall to."

When she had told Freddy he was scaring her with his morbid talk, his lips had thinned into a stubborn line. "You care for Nick, don't you?"

All she'd been capable of was nodding.

"Then I must have your word that you will talk to Nick tomorrow before he leaves for Edinburgh."

The way he'd pressed her for a promise frightened her. She'd sensed something had claimed the husband she loved, something had happened that she couldn't fight, something horribly wrong that he wouldn't talk about. "All right, I'll speak to Nicholas," she had said at last, giving in. "I promise you."

"Thank God. I'm counting on you, Crystal."

Freddy had finished packing and left her standing in the middle of his bedchamber. No goodbye kiss this time. No sweet parting hug. Crystal had run to the window, sobbing silently as she watched him ride away. The way he'd withdrawn from her frightened and confused her. It was as if he'd, for some reason, locked her out of his heart.

Determined not to let this one small failure panic her, Crystal turned to Nicholas. "If you won't help me, I will just have to find someone who will," she told him convincingly, her head held high, her voice shaking with emotion.

Across the twenty feet that separated them, Nicholas stood rigid, a muscle clenching in his jaw.

"Don't you think this has gone far enough?"

"Not near as far as I intend to go."

Nicholas drew a deep breath to battle his fury, not caring to rationalize why her blithe statement twisted his insides.

"Then an advertisement in *The Whoremonger's Guide* should do the job," he remarked dryly, "or if you really can't wait, you could stand on Half Moon Street near the Strand and peddle your wares." He let his gaze rake her slender curves in a bold assessment while the image of her giving herself to a stranger ignited all the demons he'd thought conquered. "With a body like yours, you should do well," he went on heedless of her crushed expression. "Put some red on your lips, wear a halo, and your clients will be calling you an angel. After a month you might even start looking forward to their generosity, you won't need the pin money Fred gives you. Hell, in time, your husband may even find your broadened knowledge in bed enjoyable."

"Stop it," she cried, covering her ears. "Don't you say another word! And don't you dare take airs with me, Nicholas. If you really cared, then I wouldn't have to resort to whoring."

"Good God, listen to yourself. You're not making sense." Nor could he leave her like this, feeling alone and rejected. "Why would making love with me be different than with another?"

Afraid she'd break down in front of him, Crystal clutched her teacup. Already her fingers were trembling so badly she feared she'd look down to find the skirt of her simple blue frock speckled with tea stains. Dear God, to voice her innermost feelings now would be the absolute humiliation.

The obvious reasons came easier. "The difference is simple. With you, I wouldn't have to suffer the shame afterwards. No one would have to know how desperate my husband is besides you and me."

"Then again," she said softly over the cup's rim, "I was so hopeful you would not mind so much. That you might even look forward to bedding me." She sounded like a petulant child, and hated it, but he'd wounded her gravely. "Obviously things have changed between us without my being aware. Freddy was right when he said you would be difficult."

In the numbing silence that followed, the air filled with a breathless kind of expectation.

His gaze burned with green fire. "My God, Crystal, surely you know how hard it is for any man to deny you?"

"I don't know what I believe anymore." Her voice vibrated with sadness.

"You don't have to do this. You could approach the orphanage—I could help you with the arrangements if Fred won't."

She smiled weakly. "Then everyone would know something was wrong with us."

"Don't you mean Fred's pride wouldn't survive their pity?"

"The orphanage is out of the question." Her tone was implacable.

"Damn Fred. You shouldn't have to do this alone."

"If things go as planned, I won't *be* alone."

"Any man will do, is that it?"

Her bottom lip quivered. "We wanted you."

"Well I'm not for hire."

She took a deep breath as the last of her hopes dwindled. "We would have made a beautiful child," she said thickly, her throat convulsing. "If you had only consented."

He didn't move, didn't breathe.

For a briefest moment, something in those emerald eyes touched her with warmth. She thought he might change his mind. Then the moment turned, again.

Frustration pulled his mouth into a grim line. "What you really want is some fool. Preferably two. One to service you through the day, while the night shift sleeps. Preferably someone with blue blood. Perhaps you'd like me to help you search?"

His cool tone made her feel sordid and cheap. "Don't do me any favors. I shall flounder along quite well on my own."

He laughed harshly. "Floundering hardly begins to describe your inexperience with men. Do you even know what a courtesan wears to seduce her clients?"

"I'm not an ignorant school girl," she reminded him tartly. "And what I don't know, I'll learn. I have *friends* who'll help me. Women with experience who have always been eager to share their secrets." Her husband's anguished expression—her promise to him—stiffened her resolve. She slid her gaze to the clock over the mantle. Already having decided on a reckless new course, she approximated how long it might take to pen a missive to Sarah Brown—how long before the dispatch made its way to the Theatre Royal on Catherine Street. "My only regret is that I have wasted my time. Had I known you would be so difficult," she went on, "I'd have paid closer attention to them."

He smiled tightly. "I should have married you, puss. I'd have given you a house full of children and put you out of your misery."

"Don't be ridiculous. I was seventeen and naive. I would have made you miserable." Hoping she sounded calmer, she moved to stand beside him at the window. "You shouldn't worry that I hold it against you. Freddy was, after all, a very dear and persuasive young man."

"Like a bulldog with a one track mind," Nicholas said sardonically.

"I like bulldogs, they're a dependable breed."

"And I'm not, I suppose."

"Poor, Nick. You're the wolf all dogs dream about."

His gaze bore into her. "Wolves understand boundaries, Crystal. If you were *my* wife, I'd never allow another man to touch you."

The implied message warmed the barren regions of her soul. "Fidelity? Coming from you?" She searched his face, saw he was serious. "Somehow I find that hard to believe."

"There was a time your husband felt the same way. Have things changed so much in eight years?"

She looked away from him, gazing out the window in a dreamlike way a wistful child might. "Freddy wants an heir very badly. Have you never wanted something so much it hurts?"

When after a moment he said nothing, she looked up to find those intense eyes of his watching her. For one incredibly brief moment, some fierce and almost tangible emotion flickered within their emerald depths. Then, elusive as a whisper, that emotion burned away.

"You really don't have to answer." She had always thought it a terrible waste for a man as extraordinary as Nicholas Summer to have found no one to love, no one equal to his passion.

Sighing, she turned from the window and gracefully made her way to her writing table. "Please feel free to stay and finish your tea." Pushing aside a delicate china saucer, she picked up the heavy, lead inkwell before heading for the door. "I'm sorry to have troubled you—we needn't speak of this matter again."

"Crystal—"

"Thank you for coming. I hope your trip to Edinburgh is safe. Give my regards to your mother."

Chapter Two

A week passed before Crystal received word from her husband. He had changed his mind—his letter said he would be coming home the end of next week. His message implied he'd forgotten to settle an important matter with their solicitor. What she read between those lines was he wanted to know if she'd been successful with Nicholas.

That nervous gnawing in her stomach churned into nausea. She couldn't face her husband's disappointment, his anguish.

Crystal rubbed her eyes and pushed herself up in bed. She'd already wasted a week being desperately lonely and feeling inadequate. And her husband's dispatch had sent her into a bout of melancholy that had her servants tiptoeing down the hall past her bedchamber. Even her maid was afraid to disturb to her, her groom hesitant to bring her news.

This morning, she noticed bleakly, her able-looking butler waited like always. Thin as a reed and solemn-faced, he stood a discreet distance just outside her door, his eyes downcast. "It's all right, Graves, I know my husband isn't coming home." Her voice sounded raspy, tired. Her hair was a tangled mess, her nightrail wrinkled like her composure. She no longer cared what they thought.

"I beg your pardon, my lady," Graves muttered, wringing his hands together. "It's not Lord Halverton I came to see you about. It's your gentleman friend, my lady. Lord Summer seems awful worried about you. He's come to take you for a ride, he wants us to have you ready right away. Said he won't take no for an answer."

"Was he furious when you handed him his unopened letters?" She'd heard the commotion Nicholas made in her foyer.

"Yes, I was," came the deep voice from the doorway. Startling them, Nicholas stepped around Graves and approached the bed. Crystal's heart skipped erratically. Devastatingly handsome, Nick gave her no time to compose herself. She glimpsed the tight buff breeches hugging his long muscled legs. How the royal blue riding jacket cut in the height of fashion gave an added touch of arrogance to his impossibly wide shoulders.

The calmness in his voice was deceptive. Nicholas' fierce scowl had Crystal squirming.

"Sorry, my lady, I could not stop him," Graves apologized with redfaced embarrassment. "Lord Summer insisted on seeing you."

Coming out of shock by degrees, Crystal clamored to still her thundering heart. "It's all right, Graves. I will deal with Lord Summer myself." She sent Nick a fierce scowl of her own.

Graves hurriedly shut the door leaving Crystal alone with her testy visitor.

Before she could move, Nick bent down and gathered her into his arms. Still reeling from one surprise, she hardly had time to recover her wits before he was wrapping the counterpane around her transparent nightdress, pulling her onto his lap. They sat in silence. For all his glowering, he held her like a fragile china doll, his embrace curiously compassionate.

"I ordered you a bath," Nick told her softly, his hands unsteady. Coming in to find her looking pale and broken had instantly lanced his heart wide open. "Your maid told me you haven't been out of the house in days. After you have bathed we're going for a ride."

"A ride?" she parroted in a rush of trepidation.

"What did you think? That you could keep me away by simply barring your door to me?"

Her mind, now fully recovered from the shock, started working frantically for answers. "You ordered me a bath?" she asked nervously, aware he was watching her with a diabolical glint in his eyes. "Surely you don't intend—"

"To watch?" He could hardly stay angry with her looking so pitiful. "I thought that was what you wanted."

She averted her eyes. "I've changed my mind about your staying." He'd just barged in without a welcome and ordered her a bath. As if he hadn't wounded her pride not two days past. "You must leave immediately." Her hands lay fisted in her nightdress. "Now, before the servants start talking."

"A smart staff knows they will be dismissed without references should they talk."

Her gaze met his. "You brute, if you are bullying them—"

He put his finger to her lips to shush her. "They don't like what's happening any more than I do."

Because he was touching her, she tried not to respond, but the imploring tenderness in his voice breached her barriers. Something was passing between them . . . something fragile and warm. Comforting. Vital.

Knowing he shouldn't, but damned if he could stop it, Nicholas' finger searched the smooth texture of her lips. Her defenses were crumbling, the stiffness of her spine melting away under his touch. With a soft little moan that stroked his senses, she opened her lips to him, parting sweetly, giving him license to ravish.

"After your bath, I'm taking you away for a while." He abruptly shifted her from his lap just as the bath water arrived.

Because she knew he would, in fact, assist her if she didn't do as he wished, Crystal quickly disrobed behind a screen upon which graceful white swans were painstakingly painted. Some minutes later when she emerged from her bath all squeaky clean and smelling of gardenias, she found Nicholas holding a towel for her, his gaze averted.

"This is all very mysterious." Standing on tiptoe, she frowned at him over the top of the modest shield and snatched the towel. "Where is it we're going? Or is that a secret?"

"You will see." He chose a slate-colored riding habit with black braiding which he laid out on the bed with a fashionable little head-dress and limerick gloves. Lastly, he retrieved from the bottom of her wardrobe the leather boots of the same morose shade.

In the courtyard, Crystal's pretty bay mare tossed her head while dancing a tight circle around Nicholas' huge black stallion. The horses sensed the excitement, flicking their tails and snorting their disdain for being patient. Nicholas leaned from his saddle, made a last minute check of the mare's girth and then they whirled around and were off down the drive at a fast trot that whisked Crystal's demure little hat from her head. She left it where it fell, knowing she could retrieve it later and far too giddy with excitement to care. Riding in the morning was something she'd missed dearly. Up until a month ago Freddy had always ridden with her. Now, when he was home, he preferred staying behind, content to read his newspapers and debate the importance of rotating crops with his land manager.

Just to be out of the house was exhilarating. Nick knew her weakness for horses and wild gallops and as angry as she'd been at him, she couldn't stay mad. Not on a glorious morning like this. Color bloomed in her cheeks. The mists were just clearing, the air crisp. Her hair, soon free of its pins and tousled by the horses' fast pace through the countryside, clung in damp tendrils to her neck. Going for a ride with Nicholas was exactly what she needed, she realized, her spirits rising in spite of her misgivings about her husband's return. And when those thoughts would have darkened her day, she quietly pushed them away.

The horses raced around a bend in the road and came upon that all-too-familiar secluded glen where naive love had nearly been Crystal's undoing a decade ago.

Nicholas reined alongside her, his smile ready, his keen gaze on her face. "You remember where we are?" he asked, nudging his high-strung stallion next to the prancing mare. "You remember what we did here?"

She shot him a blushing grin and suddenly looked shy. Like all those years ago, he thought her as captivating as the first rays of sunshine peering over the horizon. He'd watched her transform from a vibrant young tease into the woman the ton claimed breathtaking. Their claims merely brushed the surface. To him, Crystal was as passionate and infuriating as any woman he'd ever taken to his bed.

Stimulated by that image, the burning flame in his gut twisted lower through his groin.

They dismounted in silence, his hands at her waist to assist her to the ground. Standing close to her, layers of consciousness registered upon his senses. She smelled exotic. Ravishable. Redolent of everything sweet. A sweet temptation belonging to another man. Best he remember that, should he start to lose his mind.

When Nick would have dropped his hands and turned away, she caught him around the waist and snuggled her head against his chest like a trusting child. Nick's heart thumped hard against his ribs. Lower, there was another part of him swiftly turning just as hard. "Come," he told her when he couldn't trust himself a moment longer, "I want to show you something."

Leaving the horses tied to a tree, he walked ahead of her through the knee-deep grass.

In the middle of a vast lush valley stood a lonely sentinel of young love, a huge overhanging oak dominating the view. Its massive branches were draped like heavy arms over a verdant glen, just as it had when Crystal and Nicholas discovered it over a decade earlier.

"Oh, Nick!" Crystal broke into a run, lifting her skirt over the tall grass, her hair flowing out behind her in brilliant golden waves. He stood for a moment and watched her, his chest constricting with emotion.

Crystal reached out her hand and captured his as he stopped near her under the cover of branches. With her other hand, she traced the deep grooves in the tree bark, the symbol of all her young dreams and fantasies. The jagged lines felt rough and smooth—much the same as the tempestuous fondling between inexperienced lovers. Surrounded by a perfect heart carved deep enough to last all eternity, her fingers lingered on their initials.

Crystal turned to him, her eyes misting with emotion. "I remember the day you carved this. You were wild and full of yourself and you told me you were eloping with me, that I didn't have any choice but to succumb to slavery. We were both laughing, because you kneeled in the grass like a beseeching knight pretending to kiss my hem and got grass stains on your breeches." She paused when the memory of what followed made her breath hitch. "That was the same day Freddy proposed to me . . . and the same day you later sailed for Italy." Still a painful memory after all these years, she lifted her hand to run her fingers over his name. "So why did you bring me here? Why now?"

He drew her into his arms. Gently at first, until she pressed closer. Then he held her as if the world would fall out beneath him. He held her without reserve, like he had all those years ago when he touched her in ways only a husband touched his bride. When he'd been out of his mind to have her and yet told her he wouldn't marry her. When she offered him what no gentleman of honor took. And he had regretted it every day since . . . denying himself that brief glimpse of heaven.

"I brought you here"—he swallowed—"to show you that things haven't changed. That it won't work." His lips brushed her hair. "You accused me of not caring. You're dead wrong, puss. It's because I care, I can't have you. Because if I bed you, I'll only end up hurting you."

Her pitiful little sounds of anguish made him feel like a insensitive bastard. He feared she'd break down. And perverse as it was, he almost hoped she would . . . so he could go on believing she was suffering as much as he had suffered these last eight years. Seeing her humbled should have made him feel better, but the exact opposite was happening, her utter unhappiness was shattering his soul.

"I don't know what to do any more, Nick. Nothing makes sense. I'm so afraid, so alone," she whispered at last. "If you would just hold me like you used to." So soft was her voice, he had to strain to hear her. "If you won't seduce me, then leave me a memory to hold onto. Please, Nick, just touch me."

What she asked of him made his heart hammer madly in his chest. "If I touch you that way, it won't be enough. We'll want more. You know how it was between us."

"I promise not to ask for more . . . please, Nick, I'm so empty, I feel so cold. I don't want to be alone—"

"Shh, puss." He kissed her hair and knew exactly how vulnerable she felt. "Come with me."

He led her away from their hiding until they found themselves in a lushly secluded area just large enough to turn around—where the shadows embraced them in a circle of intimacy. This time Crystal was no innocent, she was as knowledgeable about seduction as he was. Nick leaned his back against the rough tree trunk, feet braced on either side of hers, his head telling him to go slow, his heart ignoring rationale. For a brief moment of insanity, he damned to hell the consequences and crushing the skirt of her demure riding habit drew her tightly into his groin.

His head swam, his blood pumped furiously through his body. Her hands slid down his back, then lower to frantically draw him closer. The sounds of the meadow faded into a blood rushing beat pulsing loudly in his head. Wanting nothing more than to fill her ache, waiting for what seemed half his life to bring her to climax, he hadn't realized how that blazing need had taken its toll. He captured her wrists to slow her exploration, slow the tempo of their impassioned madness to a more bearable level of burning desire. What control he'd managed to hold onto was fading.

Her writhing body pressed hotly against his became a searing torture. So perilously close to release, the powerful urge to drive into her was so hot, so potent, his sex stiffened in painful need. Nick's last shred of thought, as he lowered his mouth to conquer, was he wanted her more than life, wanted to penetrate her every way imaginable. Penetrate her heart.

Crystal opened her lips to his mastery, felt him invading, tasting, demanding, making her swoon with cresting waves. Then their kiss went beyond carnal exploration and flared into a voracious flame of mating that burned brighter and hotter than either of them anticipated. Unconsciously, his hand slipped between her thighs in an attempt to seek the lush wetness his body craved. She quivered uncontrollably as he explored the folds of her skirt, the fabric a frustrating barrier hindering deeper penetration. His hands clenched in her skirt, his agony peaking, desire flaring, every nerve in his body preparing for the blazing moment when he touched bare skin.

Crystal cried out, sagging against Nick, panting for air, her weight supported solely by his thrusts . . . each exquisite penetration of material and mastery filling her womb with searing sweet friction.

Little moans of hot need brazed his skin where her breath burned, as she pulled the buttons free on his shirt to press her lips to his chest. A deep groan rumbled in his throat as her assault moved lower.

Her hands cupped his groin, groping impatiently, shamelessly asking for more when the high shrill pitch of a horse's scream dragged them abruptly back to reality.

Heart pumping in his ears, his body corded and tight, Nick held his breath and listened.

Crystal stirred from her rapturous delirium, her breathing strained. "Hounds! Do you hear them?"

"Christ!" Nicholas drew a rasp of air, took one last look at her dishevelled state, her luminous eyes, the flushed glow of passion brightening her cheeks, and decided there was no time to waste righting her tousled coiffure. Being interrupted by a pack of hounds in hot pursuit, and discovered by the riders not far behind the chase, would be damaging enough to a woman of social rank, but should that woman be another man's wife, the deed would be unforgivable. Crystal's reputation would suffer. And before Nick would see her destroyed, he'd vow to celibacy.

They emerged from the cover of the trees at a run.

Despite her skirt tangling her legs, Crystal tried to stay up with Nicholas as he pulled her along behind at a breathless pace. The horses danced in frenzied circles a few yards ahead. By the time Nicholas and Crystal reached the giant oak where the horses were straining their tethered bonds, the hounds burst from the brush. Out in the lead, a flash of red fur zigzagged across the open field less than fifty yards away.

The beautiful fox ran for its life.

"Poor thing," Crystal cried, doubling over with an effort to drag air into her lungs. They were both out of breath, their sides heaving, when Nicholas lifted her off the ground and onto her agitated mount.

"Ride for town," Nick shouted over the baying of ravenous dogs. "I'll circle around the forest and meet up with you later." When she hesitated, looking down on him with a crestfallen expression clearly laced with regret, he met her gaze for one dangerous moment longer, then smacked her horse on the rump.

"Why can't I stay with you—" Her words were lost in brisk departure, her horse already bolting off. Crystal's full concentration turned immediately to the task of keeping her seat.

Glancing briefly over her shoulder as her mount sprinted ahead of the snarling pack, Crystal's last glimpse of Nick was him racing in the opposite direction. Her heart pounding, her lips tingling and her body still trembling from her devastating encounter with blatant sensuality, Crystal rode hard and swift for home.

All the way back to London, the emptiness in her belly grew. It festered into a craven longing that she knew no relief from without Nicholas. When he'd looked at her with lust-darkened eyes just before they parted, she'd seen it in his gaze, realized in that fleeting moment before their intimacy had been shattered that Nicholas had been just as powerless as she to hide it. Damn the hounds! Damn their ill-timing!

Chapter Three

Like an anxious child awaiting the first glimpse of a fairy, Crystal sat perched restlessly near the window that evening, her gaze searching the shadowy landscape for a flash of black—for that instant man and beast would come into view. What could be wrong? Why hadn't he come?

She waited there the next day as well, determined more than ever to assure herself that Nick was coming.

It wasn't until the third day when her spirits started to flag, when her nerves were strung out, that her tryst with Nick in the forest started to feel more like a dream than a reality. She wouldn't yet accept that he was purposely staying away. She tried to tell herself his absence was only temporary, that he'd been just as carried away as she had, but the truth was, the more she grieved over what could have happened, the more foolish she felt. Nicholas had, after all, been quite clearly resisting. In fact, he had expressly told her he wouldn't bed her.

When, on the morning of the fourth day, Nick rode up to Halverton Hall, Crystal wasn't receiving him. That she decided quite out of self-preservation. She'd put that whole heart-wrenching scene in the forest behind her, she wanted nothing to do with that memory or those feelings.

Nick came back that noon only to be turned away again. He persisted a second time that evening and was told the same story. Lady Halverton wasn't accepting callers.

"He has threatened to climb the trellis outside your window, my lady." Graves gave reports on Nick's visits. "I think we should take it down right away."

"I'm sorry, Graves. Do you mind?"

"Not at all, my lady."

Crystal had kept her door locked every time she heard Nick arrive, she wasn't taking any chances of being caught off guard again. He'd not sweep into her bedroom and set her heart soaring with any more well-intended gestures that would end in disaster for her.

He'd sent her notes that she left untouched, sent her flowers she gave to the housekeeper. She could hardly keep up with the onslaught.

Yet in all fairness, if she were honest with herself, Crystal found Nick's persistence comforting. Even if it intensified those vulnerable feelings she was trying to ignore.

She swallowed against a lump of pain. In time, Nick would go away, stop trying to wear her resistance down. Leave her to her self-destruction.

Graves entered her room with another armful of wild white orchids. Nicholas knew they were her favorite.

"Lord Summer is not to be trusted anymore, Graves." She stared unflinching, the shadows of evening falling across her bed where she sat dragging her fingers through her snarled hair. "Tell the footman to shoot him on sight."

To his credit, the man's face gave only a hint of a smile. "If that's your wish, my lady, I'll see to it your orders are carried out."

"Have there been any dispatches for me besides his?" she asked dispassionately.

Graves' brows drew together in thought. "A letter arrived earlier this evening from Lady Sutherland, her footman delivered her apologies. Seems she has been visiting her sister in the country and didn't get your missive until morning last." He pulled two envelopes from his pocket and slid them onto the table just inside her door. "The other, I can't say who it's from, my lady. I was otherwise engaged with Lord Summer when the woman arrived. She didn't give her name to the footman."

Heartened by the news, her first time in what seemed days, Crystal glanced at the scant moonlight filtering between the drapes. "What time is it, Graves?"

"Just past ten, my lady."

Not too late. "I think I'll manage dinner now."

"Yes, madam," he replied with a beaming smile, "I'll bring a tray directly."

After he shut the door behind him, she slid from bed. A ray of hope bloomed in her dismal world as she reached for the letters.

An hour before midnight, Nicholas rode up to the Halverton's doorstep and handed the reins to a sleepy lackey. The response he received, however, from Crystal's young footman was not the one he expected.

"Sorry, sir, I have orders to shoot you on sight."

The dim light afforded by the street lantern gave the lad's boyish features a yellow tinge. Nicholas' brows slanted at opposing angles, his gaze fastened on the pistol pointed at his chest. "Orders from Lady Halverton?" he ground out.

"Yes, sir."

Patience gone, Nick contemplated the younger man's unrelenting stance, wondered if the insolent pup would like having the gun's steel barrel wrapped around his neck. Though it might make him feel better, he knew injuring Crystal's young footman would only make matters worse between them. "Is the Lady at home?" he said with forced civility.

"I can't say, sir."

Which meant in layman's terms, she had already slipped out. After a week of lying in bed, eating hardly enough to sustain a pulse, speaking to no one according to her maid, she had miraculously recovered. To elude him it seemed.

He should have found that knowledge encouraging, but dread of another sort wormed into his conscience. He'd grievously hurt her, now she was making his life hell. Hell he could manage, it was Crystal's sudden return of spirit that worried him.

Damn her, she'd not changed her mind.

Knowing he'd get nowhere with the footman, Nicholas visited Lady Halverton's stable. It was there he gleaned from a worried and reluctant groom that the Lady had taken a carriage to the Sutherland's soiree, that she hadn't said when she expected to return.

Nicholas didn't find Crystal at Sutherland's either. In fact, the Duchess hadn't seen her good friend for over three weeks and had only just sent a dispatch to Halverton Hall that morning inviting Lady Halverton to her social.

It was long after midnight by the time Nick approached the outer edges of civilized Town. London's East district was a mass of dark shapes, the streets a twisted maze of faceless shadows watching for prey—unsuspecting women like Crystal. A sense of urgency pushed at his weary brain. Nicholas turned his horse down a narrow alley, breathing in the stench of rot and filth. He followed behind a figure in a threadbare coat who was leaning heavily on the arm of some unfortunate woman in equally frayed clothes. Her lusterless eyes held a wariness, lines of fatigue and hard years were twisted upon her bony features. He dug into his pocket as he passed. "Bless you, your lordship, bless you," the woman rasped, her fingers clasping his like frozen branches to the gold piece.

He trudged on, towering brick walls flanking his sides. Flakes of snow started to fall, coming down in blurry chunks. February's chill settled in his bones like an icy hand gripping his heart. He'd already stormed the brothels along Covent Garden. The only establishment Nicholas hadn't searched loomed ahead, a fuzzy outline barely recognizable beyond the heavy fall of snow. Fear of finding Crystal there knotted his gut. He prayed he wasn't too late.

A thick layer of cigar smoke hovered over the opulent parlor where Madame Lucina entertained her guests. It stung Crystal's eyes, burned her nose. All around her, clients lay sprawled over plush-cushioned divans and their red satin counterparts. Chairs were arranged around the parlor filled with couples engaged in various forms of foreplay, some already advanced to positions that made Crystal's cheeks flame. She'd heard of wild orgies, she'd tried once to imagine them in her mind. But never in her wildest dreams had she expected this.

"You like watching, Countess?"

The foreign, wine-slurred voice in her ear sounded so far away. Her mind felt foggy, her mouth so dry. The hot breath on her neck sent a shiver of trepidation down Crystal's spine, the cold hand sliding up her arm startling her out of her daze.

Countess? Was that the alias she'd chosen? "Please, sir"—she looked around for her fur wrap—"I've made a mistake. I need to leave." The strap of her green gown slipped off one shoulder.

Smiling, her escort drew her closer. "Relax, Countess, you paid handsomely for my services. You want a child, I can give you what you want." His soft hypnotic voice drummed against her groggy mind. With his arm curled around her bare shoulder, he coaxed her up a flight of winding stairs to the private rooms preferred by the more prudent clientele. "Let me help you, *cara*, let me give you a baby."

"Yes, a baby," she whispered. Her tongue felt thick, sluggish. She was leaning heavily against him as he led her down a carpeted corridor. He opened one of the doors. She stumbled against him as he drew her into a dimly lit room with gaudy, red satin walls. "It's so hot," she stammered. "I can't think."

On the sideboard sat a decanter exactly like the one her escort had poured from downstairs. He carefully held onto her with one arm while filling a glass with ruby nectar. He offered her a taste. "Drink, Countess, the wine will help."

"Yes . . . the wine." Sipping the sweet potion, she stared straight ahead, the garish trappings wavering in and out of her vision. "You must tell me what I should do," she said stonily.

"Don't worry, *cara*." He reached up, traced his finger over her brow with slow mesmerizing care. "I will go slow."

Some minutes later, she roused from a groggy daze and found herself resting atop her handsome escort on a gold satin settee. He was smiling at her, the smile of an angel. A dark, mysterious, angel. Her thoughts returned, as if in some other dream, to the way he'd walked, the way he'd pulled her along by the hand up the stairs. "I chose you . . . did I tell you . . . because your smile"—she tried to focus—"reminded me of someone."

The raised voices of lurid laughter sounding from the other side of the door faded in and out of her consciousness.

"Then close your eyes, *cara*, let me kiss you like he kisses you." His lips grazed her bare shoulder. "Remember his hands . . . how they felt . . . let me touch you where he touched you."

Crystal was losing herself, helpless to do anything but follow him. The effect of his entreaty made her breathless, the vision he painted for her stroked a chord of longing in her that left her defenseless. He was caressing her shoulder, his skillful fingers tingling over her heated skin. Her head rolled back on the cushion, her eyes too heavy to open.

"Drink, *cara*, the wine is for you." He poured her more. "It works quickly, I promise." He curled his fingers around hers, lifted her hand with her glass to her lips. Crystal felt the liquid slide down her throat, felt the answering wetness hot between her thighs. Burning, she thought numbly. Between her legs she felt on fire.

"That's it, Countess, relax. I'll help that burning, I'll make it go away."

"Yes," she murmured, her body shaking with splintery spirals of need. She felt something cool—air—on her legs, his hand—she thought—pulling her skirt aside. Her throat made whimpering sounds. Then the growing heat between her thighs spread up, devouring her, arching her back—it pulsed in her womb, opening her to his coaxing. Muffled laughter came from somewhere, a woman moaning. But nothing mattered, not the dark stranger, nor the piquant odor of sin. "Help me, please . . ."

A draft chilled her bare legs, followed by the sound of decisive footsteps. "Move your hand any higher and I'll kill you."

In a cold, black rage, Nicholas stood over them, bearing down on Crystal and her lover like a fierce dark knight, snow still clinging to his cloak. The man on the divan stiffened. His hand had halted bare inches away from entering her, his head snapped around, eyes slitted, assessing his challenger. "She's not going to appreciate your interference."

Crystal moaned, tried to open her eyes.

Nicholas leaned over, gripped the man's throat. "What have you given her?" he growled inches from the foreigner's handsome face.

"Let him go," a woman behind Nicholas demanded, her voice one of authority, her heavy bosom heaving from the pace with which she'd hurried after the angry man thundering into her parlor. Lucina made an impressive figure in shear black silk, her lush breasts bared, hands on her hips. "The Lady consented to using an aphrodisiac." She paused for a deep breath. "I didn't know how familiar she was with them so I used a mild one. She should be fine by morning."

Crystal reached up, clutching for the angry visage of her savior when the fingery sensations gripping her body peaked. "Nicholas . . . help me." She cried out his name, panting, writhing.

Nicholas's gaze darted from Lucina to Crystal.

"Listen, I don't want any trouble with you, Lord Summer," the robust madame offered quickly. "If you want her, take her. We'll settle finances later."

Nicholas slowly loosened his grip on the foreigner's neck. The younger man made a hasty retreat, brushing past the curious onlookers filling the doorway who'd gathered for a glimpse of what promised to be a roiling battle.

"Back to your business, everyone," Lucina called out, clapping her hands. "There's champagne for all downstairs."

In the time it took the sheepish-looking footman to call for Crystal's carriage, Nicholas had gathered her in his arms. He took care with the folds of her cape, making sure they were wrapped tightly around her writhing body. Then he bent and brushed his lips along her temple. Whispered something in her ear that seemed to soothe her.

The concern evident in Lord Summer's ministrations for the beautiful Countess was readily noted by Lucina. In all the years she'd known the infamous seducer, not once had his actions shown such devotion to a woman. It was a brief thing, a moment of unguarded affection she might expect of a lover. This woman obviously meant something to him.

Chapter Four

In the carriage, Nicholas held Crystal in his arms. Her hair had come loose, waves of pale honey lay like a blanket of silk falling about her waist. Her breathing erratic, in her disheveled state, her beauty was devastating, the green shimmer of fabric against flawless skin drawing his gaze. But then she would have been captivating in a wool sack. A particular memory of a grey riding habit had haunted him mercilessly.

This time her fashionable gown, what there was of it, hung off one shoulder in a way meant to entice.

He was furious with her—with himself.

He felt his control slipping, he watched her agony peak. His need, despite his best efforts, swelled with every excruciating twist of her bottom against his lap.

Nicholas gritted his teeth. If she were his wife, he'd have pulled aside her skirt miles back, buried himself in her silken heat. But she wasn't his wife, he thought furiously. She wasn't even able to speak to him.

"Give me your hand, puss," he coaxed, her whimpering driving his body to madness. "Let me show you how to ride this out."

Her fingers clasping his hand were ice cold. He rubbed them between his own, then slowly drew them to the heart of her wanting. He pushed them under her skirt, between her thighs. She was hot, and wet, and the instant he touched her pouty cleft his shaft turned brick hard. The air left his lungs in a rush. Fighting back blinding carnal urges, he guided her fingers, pushing them slowly into her pulsing flesh . . . and heard the first piercing cry of her orgasm start low in her throat. His body responded, desire burned deep in his groin. Her weight setting atop him made his torture acute, the filmy layer of gown separating them unable to hide his raring arousal. For the second time in a mere week, he lived hell on earth, rational mind useless against a straining libido.

The aphrodisiac promised a slow initiation. Crystal's lingering ascent to impassioned madness, his abstinence a gradual death taking all night. The cantharides familiar to him sometimes lasted through morning.

She was panting, wanting more, her body arching against her hand. He turned his gaze beyond the window, tried to block out her begging. She would bring herself to climax without him.

By the time they reached Halverton Hall her exhaustion was acute. He knew she was at the limit of her strength, resting heavily against him now, waiting for the next soul-robbing orgasm. And he might have felt sorry for her, had she not scared ten years off his life.

"If you want my help, puss, you have to call off your watchdogs."

"Anything," she breathed tightly.

The carriage stopped with a jolt. "I'm going to get you into bed as quick as I can."

Carrying her past the gaping footman whose pistol was now tucked away, Nicholas met Graves at the door. "Lady Halverton would like the servants to leave as quickly as possible. My town house is empty, go there. Tell Burnes I'm staying here."

"But"

"Please, Graves, just do it," Crystal bit out.

At the top of the stairs, Nicholas kicked her bedchamber door open, waited until he laid her down on her bed. "Dammit, Crystal," he said, pulling her stockings down. "You little fool. What possessed you to go to Lucina's? What did you think you were going to find?"

"He wanted to help me," she rasped as shame washed over her. She lay helpless, utterly weary. Then her body bucked against his arm, cresting need splitting her in two. Broken gasps punctuated her whimpering. Her throat felt raw, her head throbbing. "He wanted to give me a baby. And you ruined it."

The words were barely a whisper, but he heard them. Grabbing the hem of her gown, he yanked the transparent green tulle over her head. "Turn over." He didn't wait for her to comply, he pushed her over onto her stomach. His hands worked quickly, peeling off her chemise. "That boy you wanted likes to work over his clients with broom handles." His hands were harsh, his actions driven by anger. "I was there when his last victim nearly hemorrhaged to death. She was twice your age and old enough to know what to expect."

He rolled her onto her back. "If I have to, I'll put a leash on you until Fred returns. You won't go anywhere without my permission." He tugged the coverlet over her legs.

She laid on her back, clenching her eyes shut, batting his hands away. "I don't need a keeper—get out." She would have railed at him, but her body convulsed, she started to climb again.

Gently, Nick guided her hand where she ached. "I'm staying the night. I'll be here if you need me." And shamelessly, her hand moved of its own accord.

Nick straightened, and watched, his breathing unsteady.

Candlelight from across the room, flickered over her face, the pain mingled with pleasure there, over the perfection of her slender curves, over rouged nipples distended and thrusting with each arch of her back. Light blended with shadows, contouring her full breasts, the valley leading down her abdomen. She was a temptress, pale as white silk. She drew her legs up, let her knees fall apart, her eyes begging him.

Mentally flogging himself for weakening, he swiftly approached the limits of his threshold. Christ, he even had her husband's consent. His release an arm's length away. He could smell her need. He'd seduced women with no remorse, less scruple.

"It's all right if you don't want to be my lover," she whispered fitfully, her eyes already drooping shut. "I'll settle for friendship."

"What happened the other day was a mistake." He heard himself say the unforgivable, felt the falsehood stick in his throat. "Go to sleep, puss."

Then dying inside, Nicholas turned abruptly and walked over to the window. He drew the drapes aside, stood looking out into a dreary sky.

His hands burned hot on her flesh, caressing her lovingly, sliding down her stomach. Her nerves came alive, tingling under the brush of Nick's lips against the soft curls of her woman's place, dragging strangled whimpers from her throat. He was all she imagined he would be, fierce, gentle, capable of rending her every screaming nerve with provocative sensation. She was drowning in a searing pool of bliss so deep and keen she cried aloud, its licking heat devouring her until she could fight it no more. Teasing her, tasting her and tormenting her, Nick carried her higher. Higher until her world quivered, until she thought she would die. His every move designed to make her shatter rushed upon her body in unmerciful waves of utter sweetness so poignant she wanted nothing but to surrender, giving in to the wild rapture of fire consuming her body and soul.

"Nick, now," she keened passionately, his weight pinning her to the bed, his body readied for entry. His eyes blazed down at her with a tenderness borne of devotion before he commanded her to behold the evidence of his madness. Gleaming in the candlelight, taut, straining, his beautiful arousal—all flared glory and dominate power—flexed under her very rapt gaze. All that glory was for her, pulsing with need, with a life giving potion her body ached to receive. He drew her nipple between his teeth, and they came together in a wild rapturous melding of flesh and bone and hot-blooded passion. She cried his name, beseeching, thrushing, wanting him

deeper, seeking complete domination, and he gave her more than she ever dreamed possible, lifting her with each powerful thrust until at last she shattered in half upon a cliff of sweet hot rapture.

Slowly the sensation brought Crystal awake, her body still hot and splintering, her mind instantly rejecting the brutal truth that her impassioned encounter was nothing more than a dream.

The heart-wrenching sickness that came with reality, following those first intense moments of loss, made her want to scream out in denial. Close on the heels of frustration came the events of last night to fill her heart with shame. Staring at a fragment of daylight streaking the ceiling, her mind still drowsy, she made the mistake of trying to move. Her involuntary cry brought Nick's head around. Her body felt terrifyingly heavy, her legs and arms weak.

"Feel better?"

Soreness forgotten, Crystal pulled the coverlet up under her chin. She couldn't meet his gaze. "I have a feeling I behaved very badly last night."

He smiled reassuringly. "You had an excuse." Hands at the middle of his back, he stretched.

From her view in the bed, Nicholas looked tired, his face drawn into a mask of polite regard, revealing none of the condemnation she'd expected. He said not one harsh word to make her feel foolish. "I'm sorry. I can't seem to get anything right. I failed miserably last night, didn't I?"

"No, you didn't fail. If I hadn't interfered you would have had what you wanted."

The weariness in his voice shamed her, brought a hot flush creeping into her face. He'd cared enough to come looking for her, and she would hug that solace to her heart in the empty days ahead. "Please don't tell Freddy, I don't know if I can face his disappointment."

Nicholas was looking out the window, the pale dawn light reflected in his eyes. He didn't speak. The tension in his body, the way he avoided looking at her, spoke of the tortures he'd lived last night. He'd wanted her, she'd seen it in his bold gaze when he'd peeled her clothes away, when he'd stared down at her before stalking away. No matter how hard he tried to hide it, the tiger lurking beneath the surface, eyes shining with heated lust craved her. His need to mate was riding him hard. Her scent had him prowling, primed.

Her cheeks flamed hotter, her brazen thoughts running wild. The image of him coming to her, kneeling between her legs, sent a shiver of latent thrills down her limbs. She was still tingling from her dream. If he touched her, she would melt. Only she knew he wasn't going to give in to the hunger.

Crystal sighed. She must be overwrought, she decided. In reality, she was merely missing her husband. Nicholas was an infatuation, the things she'd imagined him doing to her, her way of preparing for the ultimate seduction. Preparing her body to accept his child.

"You told me last night the woman nearly died. You know her, don't you?"

He stood there stonily quiet, as if not sure he wanted to answer.

"I know her, yes." His sigh seemed dragged from the depths of his soul. "She came to me because she thought I could help her get over her fear." He raked his hand through his hair. "I started out slow. I would spend the first hour doing menial things that required minimal contact. We spent many hours just playing faro. The progress has been slow, and she still flinches from my touch."

Sadness filled her heart. "He must have beat her very badly."

Nick looked over his shoulder at her, saw she didn't understand. "I didn't say he beat her, Crystal."

"I don't understand. I thought you said he used a broom handle on her?"

"Not in the way you are thinking." He waited for the impact to set in.

Slowly she shook her head, her eyes round, confused.

Taking pity on her, he told her gently, "What you did for yourself last night, he used a broom handle to intensify."

Her face turned pale as dawning horror filled her eyes, her shocked expression giving way to nausea.

"If he had hurt you, Crystal, I would have killed him."

She pressed her hand to her mouth afraid the churning in her stomach would come up. "I didn't know," she managed, gulping air. "I'm sorry."

"I can't go through another night like last night." His voice was raw, stark with emotion.

"Oh, Nick, I'm so sorry. So ashamed."

"But you haven't changed your mind?"

She dropped her gaze to her lap, slowly shook her head.

Chapter Five

During the next few days, her houseguest took great care to see to it that her spirits improved. Nicholas lavished her with tenderness. When she cried, he rocked her in his arms. When she refused food, he would ply her lips open and feed her with his fingers. She blushed with tingling awareness whenever he touched her. Last night, when he'd brushed her hair by the fire, she'd thought he might give in. She'd caught him looking at her—she'd seen that raw hunger in his eyes. Something had changed between them. How, she wasn't certain, but she felt it. Nick's devotion brought back memories, reminded her of how wonderful it used to be between her and Freddy. It brought pain, too. Reminded her of her inadequacies. Her failures.

When she was with Nick, she felt . . . well she felt whole.

While she loved her husband dearly, she imagined a very different relationship with Nicholas. A wild, impetuous one, like the one in her dream. Imagined herself giving him her body, his eagerness to show her all the things she'd heard about his wild excesses. Show her the passion absent from her life. She'd started imagining shameful visions where she ran naked through the halls, a lust-crazed Nicholas stalking her, growling her name in frustration. He was always fierce, lavishing her with caresses . . . with his mouth. Other times they had played like lovers, throwing pillows, laughing at each other, crazily and breathlessly in lust. In her daydreams his hands encoded unruly havoc on her senses. He'd whispered outrageous things in her ear, looked at her with stormy green eyes, plunged into her in fits of passion until she wailed his name to the rafters. But those visions ended up being wistful wanderings of the mind. Frustrating dreams.

Feeling more a failure than ever, Crystal hugged her arms around herself, barely aware of where her feet carried her through the house. Her emptiness was torture. It brought a lump of self-pity to her throat. God, she missed Freddy. Damn him, why couldn't he just love her again? Like he used to?

One thing was certain, she couldn't go on like this.

Despite Nicholas' efforts to turn her interests away from her problem, the heart of her sorrow was ever cropping up in her mind. She was tired of walking on eggshells, skirting the issues. Nick's patience seemed endless, while her frustrations mounted. The closer the day came for Freddy to return, the more agitated and snappish she grew.

Upstairs in her room, she'd read the note from her friend, Sarah Brown, inviting her to the Theatre Royal for tea. The note was an urgent reply to Crystal's plea.

She heard a noise coming from the kitchen and found Nicholas rummaging through the pantry, flour smeared on his face. Pans clanged noisily together, the homey smell of dough made her stomach grumble. He didn't notice her right away, intent as he was on finding whatever he sought.

It was during their conversation at breakfast he'd promised her fresh-baked bread, said she'd needed someone to look after her. That was when she'd told him what she needed was his precious manhood inside her. They'd argued then, and because she'd had a particularly restless night and hadn't slept, she'd been unusually sensitive. Shaming herself, she'd broken down and cried like a baby, and he had stalked from the room.

She noticed Nicholas had shaved and changed since breakfast. He'd shed formal dress for casual and the effect left her breathless. This afternoon, a sable lock of hair hung over one eye, his pale linen shirt was open at the neck, his sleeves rolled up. A picture of a perfectly domesticated rogue. Her gaze drank in his masculine perfection—his breeches hugging the tight lines of his buttocks, encasing his powerful thighs. The perfect man for the father of her child, she thought pragmatically. Only he didn't want her.

Nicholas found what he was looking for—was turning toward the table when he caught sight of her. His expression turned wary, as if weighing her mood.

"Hungry?" he asked, his gaze burning into her.

Crystal shrugged, tried not to notice how utterly appealing he looked all powdered with flour, his broad shoulders filling her kitchen. "I don't know why you insist on doing everything for me. I'm not an invalid—nor do I want to be pampered. Tomorrow I'm sending word that the servants are to return."

He scowled, let his gaze drag over her from head to foot. "You're dressed? Did you change your mind about going for a walk?"

Crystal felt his displeasure, heard that unrelenting tone in his voice. Her heart plummeted. She had hoped he would notice the extra effort she'd taken with her hair, the way she let it fall in unruly wisps about her face. Hoped he'd find her new jonquil day dress scandalous, notice how it molded her curves like a lover's caress. Her ploy only seemed to anger him.

"Aren't you tired of playing my keeper?" she shot back.

"Don't you like my cooking?" Brows drawn sharply, he concentrated on his task.

His cooking was divine, the way he fed her shamelessly erotic. "No," she lied, blushing. "You're only being nice because you feel obligated to protect me until my husband comes home."

His gaze pinned her, heat flaring into his eyes. For a moment he looked as if he might beat her. Vent all the frustrations she'd heaped on him. They both knew the part about obligation was only partly true. He was doing it because he cared about her, because he couldn't abandon her even pushed to the limit of his control.

"I'm sorry, I shouldn't have said that."

He angrily wiped his brow with a sleeve, left a flour smudge along his hairline before jabbing the dough with his fist. Every line in his body was taut, sprung to breaking point. Her shame deepened. "Please, Nick," she whispered, "forgive me." It was a plea from her heart—she felt it breaking. If he left and never came back she'd fall apart and never recover.

"Christ, this is killing me, Crystal." His voice shook with emotion, his gazed fixed on the table. "I can't leave you here alone. I can't seduce you and I can't go home. We're both going to go insane before Fred returns."

She wasn't sure which upset her more, the way he made her feel foolish and vulnerable or his attempt to make amends for having refused to seduce her. The part she couldn't bear any longer was his pity.

"That's why I'm going out. You'll have the house all to yourself."

His head came up, his expression grave. "You haven't had lunch."

Unable to endure another intimate meal with him, she turned and walked to the door. "I'm sorry I have no appetite for food." She paused to look over her shoulder at him. "I think I'll skip lunch—I'm rather anxious to escape my dungeon."

Then, before he could protest, she slipped out and ran down the hall. In the foyer she stopped only long enough to grab her cloak before hurrying out the door.

Crystal heard her name being shouted as a cold gust hit her in the face. She gasped, her breath coming in foggy puffs before her eyes. Shuddering from the dip in temperature, she stood on the step and quickly swung her cloak about her shoulders. Already a light blanket of snow covered the street, flakes melted on her cheeks. The icy chill bit her toes. Clutching her cloak tightly, she took a fortifying breath and fled down the street as if the hounds of death were stalking her heels.

Nicholas squinted into the cold gust whipping his hair. Turning his head one way then the other, he searched the streets for Crystal's dark shape. She couldn't be far ahead.

Without the protection of a coat, the icy chill quickly seeped through the thin linen of his shirt. Flakes of snow drifted into his face, clung to his lashes. He pushed on, heedless of his own discomfort. He had to find her.

Prodded by desperation, he almost turned the wrong way when a flash of color on the opposite side of the street caught his eye. No mistaking the yellow hem showing beneath her cloak.

He recognized the back entrance to the Theatre Royal.

A clandestine meeting, no doubt, with someone she couldn't invite to the house. Perhaps someone to fill her requisite needs. It would explain her rash behavior, her need to flee his protection.

Glowering, he started across the street.

Chapter Six

Crystal's mad flight came to an abrupt halt on the steps of the Theatre Royal where she'd intended to approach Sarah Brown with her dilemma. To her utter humiliation, Nicholas had caught up with her and despite all her squirming and kicking, he none too gently escorted her home.

They stood in the foyer out of the cold, both of them breathing heavily from the fast pace forced by his angry stride. "How dare you drag me through town!" she railed, trembling with fury, her humiliation making her cheeks hot.

"If you had come quietly," he lashed out in anger, his grip punishing her wrist, "I wouldn't have had to resort to force."

Wishing she was big enough to do him damage, she shoved her elbow into his rib, but he swiftly blocked her pitiful attempt.

Eyes shining murder, she glared up at him. "You have no right to tell me when and where I can go!" she panted angrily. "And if you don't like it, you are perfectly free to leave." Trying to ward off an intense feeling of loss should he go, she waited for him to stalk away.

To her surprise, he pulled her roughly against him. The intensity of his gold-sparked gaze filled with fierce possession sent thrills racing down her spine. "I've had enough. I can no longer stand by and permit another man to touch you. Nor will I let you bear a stranger's child. You leave me no choice."

His sudden words and their meaning stunned Crystal speechless, took all the fight out of her. The tension between them grew palpable. Dare she hope? She narrowed her gaze on him and in a small voice asked, "What are you saying?"

"I can't let you bed another man." His breath fanned her face, his thumb circled the tender skin of her wrist. She was painfully aware of his closeness, the flare of heat under his touch that burned up her arm and blossomed into her heart. She sensed his struggle with an inner demon—his defenses being hacked away. Then his grip loosened and he reached up to unclasp her cloak. It floated to the floor in a pool of velvet. His eyes simmered with emotion, his voice calm. "If you send me away I can't get you with child."

This time there was no mistaking his intent. Wings fluttered uncontrollably in her stomach. "You mean it?" she asked breathlessly, her heart soaring.

One minute they were squared off in opposing corners, the next, his arm went around her waist.

He buried his hands in the heavy spill of her hair, his fingers flexing helplessly. "My God, Crystal," he rasped against her temple, "you make me mad."

The heat in his voice ignited her blood. Instantly her arms encircled his lean hips. She smiled with rapturous delight and pressed her breasts against him, nuzzling her face into the curve between his arm and shoulder. His heart thundered against her ear. He smelled heady and wickedly male. "Oh, Nick, you don't know how divine you feel. I have dreamed of you like this—you pulling me into your arms—taking me right here on the floor." The image pulsed through her brain.

On a groan he bent his head and nipped her earlobe, drew it into his mouth. She sucked in her breath as he impatiently ran his palm down her buttocks and pressed her snug against his virile length. Her heart accelerated. He fisted a handful of her skirt—pulled it up and clasped her waist. When he pressed against her, thrust his thigh between her legs, liquid heat melted through her limbs, sensation dancing over her body. His hands grew impatient, he wanted her as fiercely as she wanted him. She wanted to weep with gratitude . . . with tears of joy. Her throat clogged with emotion, anticipation making her tremble as she lifted her leg to accommodate him. Looking up at him with a wild hunger that threatened to eat her alive, she arched her back in wanton submission—to give him reign over her body.

Supporting her head with his palm, Nicholas's mouth came down on hers, his vivid hunger stark in his eyes, his tongue thrusting into her sweetness. He devoured her like a man starved for love.

Her body responded on its own. Suddenly she was straddling his leg, the friction of material and muscle devastating between her legs, her heat soaking his breeches.

"Are you sure," he groaned tightly against her mouth, "you still want me?" He sounded in pain, his hoarse whisper tingling over her flesh. God love him, he was letting her know she could stop.

She closed her eyes, knew it was too late, knew she'd crossed over that fine line where nothing mattered besides Nicholas and his devastating mastery. His kisses, his caresses, his glorious shaft thrusting against her womb. "I've wanted you in my dreams. I've wanted you, it seems, for weeks." Her long bout of solitude, now ended, called forth vague visions of Freddy. They momentarily poked at her conscience before she pushed his stark face from her thoughts. She needed desperately to be touched. Loved. "I'll want you day and night . . . every hour we have together I'll cherish." She shivered in his embrace, her intense yearning singing through her veins.

"Dear God, I want you, Nick" Her voice shook with emotion, with deep longing, with desperation. "At last we can pretend we are lovers . . . that you're going to give me a beautiful child."

Nicholas felt her fear, her pain and knew he'd never be able to just walk away when the time came. He'd wanted her years ago when he'd not thought himself worthy. Lusted after her even now with a fierceness that scared him. Miraculously, she was his to plunder, his to cherish because her husband wanted an heir. Fool that Fred was, the man had no idea how rare a gift he'd given Nicholas, the precious woman in his arms was his . . . even if for a few weeks. Weeks that would end too soon, he feared. Dear God, he was doomed. He would regret making love to her, already hated the bleakness of his life without her once Fred came back. Growling an oath, Nicholas swiftly curled his arm under her leg to hold her against him as he moved with her to the hall table. With a sweep of his hand, he brushed the table's contents aside, gently edged her onto the top.

Under her bare bottom the hard polished surface felt cool and contrasted with the warmth emanating from his rigid shaft straining against her need. Heat swirled her woman's core. Her breathing grew ragged. When she thought she'd scream if he didn't take her, his hand moved between them. In an instant she gasped, his skin was hot, his palm massaging her mons. The shock vibrated to her soul. He touched her with a reverence she craved—with the skill that made her life seem so bereft. Before she could wonder at his tender regard, his finger spread her open, penetrated her velvety folds, made her cry out. She sagged against him. Writhing. Her keening cries echoing off the walls.

He waited with diabolical care while she came down from her climax, then skillfully plunged his hand deeper. Until she was careening. Panting his name.

Dragging in sharp breaths, she arched into him, heard his strangled groan rumble against her ear. Frantic for him, her nails tore at his shirt. While he stroked her, she anxiously fumbled at his waist, yanking buttons, rending fabric. She let out an exasperated sigh, her movements too slow for the escalating sensations flooding her body. He helped her then, his movements swift, practiced. When his heated shaft brushed her cleft, she whimpered. The feeling was giddy, the searing need in Nicholas' eyes wonderfully erotic. Wild abandon sang through her body and she opened her legs while he slid his arms under her knees—drew her to the table's edge.

Then with a wicked gleam in his eyes, he smiled down at her with wolfish possession and thrust into her. The exquisite pressure—his largeness stretching her, plunging into her body—raised her bottom off the table. Took her to the edge of ecstacy. Then he was drawing out, ramming in . . . and her world shattered.

As her climax clenched around him, Nicholas knew a moment of blinding passion, felt himself slipping into a vortex of intense sensation. He'd never felt so close to losing himself, so close to losing control. The shock bludgeoning his soul vibrated like lashes of a whip through his body. With Crystal he'd expected to be swept away—never so blatantly close to utter destruction.

His body sheened with sweat—her legs clamped around his waist in exquisite orgasm—Nicholas used his weight, pulled her luscious bottom tight and again drove himself into her. Her piercing cry mingled with his strangled groan as his body convulsed, his release exploding down his nerves, his seed pumping into her sweet body.

It was several long minutes later before he felt strong enough to move. His body still shaking from a tempest of passion, Nicholas held Crystal gently against his chest, his chin resting on her head. He breathed deeply, tried to steady his legs. Their impassioned union left him light-headed. He was still trying to recover when he felt her withdraw. Instantaneous regret assailed him. A sharp pain of dread twisted his heart. Now having gotten what she wanted, Crystal would realize her mistake. Being a loyal wife, she'd feel ashamed for coercing him, devastated by her abandon. As damning as that knowledge was, he spent a wholly irrational moment wanting to murder Fred for his selfishness. Then came the calm voice of reason tempering rash thoughts. While they'd both put him in this accursed situation, it was as much his fault as theirs. There was no excuse for his lack of resistance. For lusting after another man's wife.

No less inexcusable, he reflected harshly, was the fact that Fred wasn't around to ease Crystal's pain and soften her burden. "If I haven't just given you a child, Crystal . . . then the timing could be wrong," he told her gently, his voice gravelly and strained. "Would you like me to leave?"

She slid her arms around his waist and held tight, shook her head. "Just hold me, please," she uttered with a raspy voice. "I'm so frightened of being alone."

His own fear kept him silent.

"I didn't expect . . . I mean . . . I didn't know I'd feel so wonderful with you," she told him in a small voice.

Wonderful, he reflected, hardly began to describe the plush softness of her slick heat clamped around his sex.

"This wasn't supposed to happen." She trembled against him. "Lord, what have I done?"

As he expected, her recriminations and guilt weighed heavy on her conscience. She fell silent, dropped her head. Her neck was bared to him, her creamy skin flushed with passion against the daffodil gold of her gown. A gown he suspected she'd donned to torture him.

He brushed a kiss along her temple, willed his body not to move. Though she was no virgin to seduction, her inexperience beyond her husband marked her an innocent pawn. He still pulsed inside her, already wanted to whisk her upstairs for a long, intense initiation where they'd stay until they collapsed. With great effort, he fought down the urge. Christ, she was baring her soul to him and all he wanted to do was ravish her again. "Stop beating yourself up. I had a hand in this, I should have had better sense."

She stirred against him, the tiny pulse along her neck still beating erratically. "What we just shared was so beautiful," she said in awe, "it changes everything between us. Oh, Nick, you tried to warn me and I wouldn't listen. Now I'm going to lose you, too. . . ." Her voice broke.

"Shh, darling." He kept her impaled—afraid she might misunderstand if he withdrew. Slowly, he reached up with his hands and cradled her face between his palms, brushed her cheeks with his thumb. "I'm not leaving you, Crystal. I've already changed all my plans, I'm at your disposal for as long as you need me."

His tenderness made her want to wail to the heavens for the unfairness. She'd thought all her problems solved. She wondered now, with a dreadful ache, if she'd ever be able to return to her old life. To her husband. Then a sudden thought panicked her. "My God, what day is it?" She twisted in his arms, her face turning pale.

Nicholas felt a keen loss as she pulled away, her warm sheath withdrawing, their bodies no longer connected. In an instant he'd lost her and their fragile intimacy. "It's all right, puss." He willed his hands to be still while her absence caused havoc on his senses. "It's only Tuesday. The servants won't come back until I send for them."

She looked white as a sheet. "It's not the servants, it's Freddy! Oh God, Nick, he's due home today." She anxiously bit her lip. "I've got to warn him—get a dispatch to him. He can't come back now. Not until I'm sure."

Her words struck him in the gut, his reaction to the news sparking irrational jealousy. Damn Fred to hell, his week wasn't up. He didn't care to analyze why, he just needed more time with her. "If Fred were coming home"—he glanced at the window, saw it was growing dark—"wouldn't he have been here by now?"

She shook her skirt out and moved to the window, conscious that behind her he was fastening his breeches. "You're right, of course." She nervously peered both directions down the street. "I'm probably worrying over nothing." She lapsed into silence, her gaze searching the avenue below.

Her inattention gave him time to recover. For a moment he stood watching her, drinking in her slender beauty, the curve of her breasts— the curves engraved on his mind, those now hidden under the folds of her skirt. For some reason, her preoccupation at the window irritated him. Her agitation over Fred clearly put him in his place. What had he expected? She loved her husband, for Christsakes.

"I'll be in the kitchen—I'll see if I can't find us something to eat." There would be wine and cheese left over from the night before.

Distracted, she nodded. "We could picnic in my bedchamber and you could brush my hair 'til it shines."

He stiffened. "You want me to seduce you in your husband's bed?" His voice was hard, cold as steel.

She turned from the window to stare at him. It was the first time he'd given her any hint of his feelings, the first sign Nicholas showed that he resented her husband's presence. It was a profoundly disturbing thought.

"Freddy sleeps in the master chamber." A sadness weighted her words, there was no longer a need to hide her shame from Nicholas. "I sleep alone in my bed."

He paused by the door. "Then we'll dine in your chamber."

Chapter Seven

At the top of the stairs, the bedchamber door stood open to Nicholas. He noted the room was comfortably heated, in the hearth a fire blazed. Crystal sat at her writing desk, immersed in thought, her head bent over a parchment. The rich gold hue of her waist-long tresses picked up the glow of the firelight, shimmered with warm russets cast by the flames. The plush, white robe exposed an expanse of shapely calf, her delicate profile giving a glimpse of the seductive curve of her lips, the elegant tilt of her nose. If Crystal were his wife she'd be enslaved in his bed. She damn sure wouldn't be neglected.

His bare feet made no noise as he crossed the floor. She'd used an oak log, instead of coal, for the fire. The blaze heated his skin, the log crackled and hissed, sent sparks fluttering up the chimney. A woodsy smell filled the chamber. She had taken the heavy brocade counterpane from the bed and spread it on the floor in front of the fire.

Wordlessly, Nicholas kneeled and arranged their feast on the royal blue fabric fashioned as a table. In the larder he'd found wine, a brick of cheese and a tray of finger cakes.

Next to twin wine glasses, he set a bottle of port. Then he withdrew a small velvet pouch from the pocket of his silk robe and dropped it near the glasses.

Facing her, Nicholas stretched out on his side, hand propped under his head where he waited for her to finish the missive.

Crystal had heard Nick preparing their meal. She was keenly aware of his gaze fastened on her with those intense green eyes. He knew her well. Intimately now. As a lover did. In the foyer he'd given her a most cherished gift, lavished her with sensual warmth. In return she'd unwittingly hurt him by mentioning Freddy. She would have to guard her tongue until they came to an understanding about her husband.

Pondering her blessings, Crystal smiled to herself. In a week's time, if her monthly didn't come, she'd know she was carrying his child. The thought that she might already be pregnant was a heady one. It made her feel wondrously decadent, and horribly wanton. Nicholas, her gallant knight, had given her all that in a single afternoon.

What he had in store for them tonight, God only knew. But the prospect had her heart throbbing. Warm excitement skittered down her spine, spread between her legs in wet gushes of heat. Her body, now attuned to him, craved more. The yearning between her thighs dampened her robe, her body seeking its mate, reaching toward a fire that threatened to consume her.

Afraid she'd fling herself into his arms and beg to be ravished, she kept her face averted. Over the last hour she'd fought down the overwhelming urge to flee the room, run for her sanity. Throw herself at Freddy's mercy. Her fear, she tried to tell herself, was silly.

Her heart, though, nagged her.

When she'd exhausted all her reasons for delaying the inevitable, she rose to her feet. Nicholas' musky smell still clung to her skin, tremors still raced over her flesh where his hands had caressed her body a mere hour earlier. Swallowing hard, she forced her feet to move. When she came to the edge of the counterpane, she halted and let her gaze wander over him. Like her, he had changed clothes. His chest, she noticed, was bare under his robe, his skin gleaming like bronze in the fire's glow. He looked every bit the prodigal libertine. His robe of crimson silk heightened his aura of seduction, drew her gaze to the blatantly raised bulge straining against its silk sheath in randy display. Because she was watching, he moved his powerful body to give her a better view until his splendid erection lay bared for her pleasure. Her reaction to him was instant, sensation shot to her core. Liquid heat slid down her thigh, and her cheeks burned with shame while she stared in amazement. How she'd managed to accommodate his size, she didn't know. He looked enormous—his beautifully swollen head curved into a flat stomach lined with hard muscle. She noticed with awe the maze of veins running along his engorged length.

Blushing, her gaze flew to his face and riveted there. His eyes burned hungrily, his nostrils flared.

The letter she held in her trembling fingers floated to the floor near the counterpane.

Nicholas extended his hand to her. "Are you hungry?" he asked softly, subdued amusement dancing in his eyes.

She laid her fingers in his . . . felt the warmth of his skin, his vital strength. She melted to her knees beside his head. "Nick . . . I . . ." She wet her lips with her tongue. "We must talk first."

He swiftly curled into a sitting position and crossed his legs. "We'll talk later. Come . . . sit in my lap." He guided her bottom until her back leaned into his chest. Her hair spilled like waves of blonde silk over his arms—over his hands where they rested on her stomach. "I have something for you." He scooped up the pouch and dropped it in the folds of her robe between her legs. "Open it."

"You didn't—"

"Just open it," he persisted.

She bit her lip anxiously, her curiosity mounting. She shouldn't accept a gift from him. Yet fascinated by his persistence, she stared a moment at the black velvet pouch. It was heavy—she guessed the weight of a gold guinea. The soft velvet against her fingers felt warm as she slowly pulled at the drawstrings. Then her fingers dug into the bag . . . hit something that felt like a glass sphere. He'd given her a glass egg?

Puzzled, she held the glittering object up to the fire and inspected it closely. Firelight danced over the sphere. Prisms of color ricocheted off the many faceted edges. A beautiful crystal of some kind, she mused. Then her wedding ring caught her eye, sparkling with glittering fragments of light, its colors joining the rainbows on the walls. Her heart caught in her throat as dawning realization took her breath away. Diamonds this size didn't exist, or if they did they were worth a king's ransom. "My God, this can't be . . . tell me you didn't just give me a diamond."

He smiled warmly. "The mines I purchased in Africa have produced some amazing results. This one arrived a fortnight ago."

"Good heavens, I can't accept this." She turned to give it back when his hand closed over hers. Stanching her protest, he nuzzled his mouth along her neck, his tongue flicking over her sensitive skin, the smooth curve of her ear. Sensations ripped through her pulsing center, her vision blurred. "I want you to wear it, puss," he said softly near her ear.

She shuddered against him. Her nipples tightened against her robe, the swollen weight of her breasts tingling. It took all her will to whisper, "Wear it how? There's no clasp and no hooks."

"If you'll pour the wine, I'll show you," he lazily drawled.

The pulsing between her legs was spreading a carnal heat upward. She couldn't think, much less grasp the importance of his generous gift. Already aching for him, Crystal obediently did as Nicholas asked, while he shifted against her back and shrugged out of his robe.

When she'd accomplished the task, he carefully dropped the diamond into the wine of one glass. It clanked like a rock to the bottom. He slid his arms under hers and pulled her tight against him. Trembling violently, she became painfully aware of his splendid arousal pressing against her back. Her pulse raced out of control. His naked heat burned through her robe.

He fed her then with erotic languor, with his fingers, then gave her wine to wet her parched throat. Beside her, the glass with the diamond sat untouched, its presence a reminder of something mysterious to come. Nicholas was lavishing her, she knew, tantalizing her with his special sorcery. Soon the warmth of the fire, combined with her alarming consumption of wine, blended all the harsh edges of the room into a glowing flush on her cheeks.

When her robe slipped down her arms, a heady frisson of anticipation thrummed through her ravenous body. Nicholas rained kisses along her neck, murmured, "I've wanted to hold you like this . . . for a very long time." His voice was a rumble of heat against her neck. "Your husband will have his heir . . . though what I do now is not for him . . . it is for you." Slowly his hand reached for the untouched wine glass. "For all the long nights you slept alone in your bed. For all the nights I could have held you in my arms." With slow mesmerizing care, his other hand drew aside her robe, burned a path down her belly. She writhed against him, her near climax arching her back along his arousal. Driven to craving madness, she shamelessly drew her knees apart for him. The fire's heat warmed her bottom, her pouty cleft beautifully displayed with glossy wetness.

He nudged the wine glass against the luscious juncture. "Open your eyes, darling, watch me touch you." He dipped his fingers into the wine, let them trail wetness over her stomach—lower over the soft mound of darker blonde curls. He hooked his middle finger over the rim of the glass, tipped it into her vagina.

Her fingers dug into his thighs as sweet wetness trickled between her legs. "Easy, darling . . . now feel the pressure." With infinite care, he pressed the cool diamond against her pouty folds, held it snug, heard her sharp cry of pleasure. "How much do you want, Crystal?" he asked, pushing the slender end half-way into her.

She wanted more with a mindless desire, an insatiable craving. "Desperately," she whimpered, her throaty moan heady with need. She tried arching against his hand, tried to drive the jewel deeper. He moved his hand away, left the diamond lodged, watched her hips seek his assistance. "Hold still for me, darling. Watch my hand . . ." A paroxysm of shudders converged on her as he slid his flat palm down her stomach, cupped his fingers over the diamond and eased it into her. Her wetness poured into his hand, her panting cries brought him close to losing control. "You want it deeper?"

"Please, Nick . . ." she gasped, opening to him, rocking into his hand. "I ache . . ."

On the verge of wasting himself against her writhing hot bottom, he leaned her forward, shifted to his knees. Her bottom angled against him. He pulled her robe over her hips. The luscious sight of her sweet cleft engorged with a diamond made his pulse thunder. And because he could wait no longer, he nudged his head against the jewel, penetrated her, drove the egg into her pulsing wetness. A trickle of sweat snaked down his neck. Crystal's head was thrown back, hair wildly tossed around her slender beauty. His hands gripped her hips, he pushed in—felt her tight spasm, her keening cry—then pulled out with agonizing friction. He watched a climax shudder through her, saw the flame-light dance over her blissful features. And then the tempo changed as he slipped into her with his fingers—deftly withdrew the diamond and adjusted his grip on her with a restless, hot blooded urgency.

This time when he drove into her, he reached the depths of blinding need. He pulled back then pushed deeper, craving her—gorging on rapturous sensations, wanting to put his mark on her, each plunging stroke merciless, fierce, unchecked. Their bodies grew hot and sweat-sheened. And she cried for him, helplessly enslaved, wanting to be covered and penetrated, wanting him to fill her with his seed.

His knees forced hers further apart as he thrust into her, his hands clamped hard on her waist so she couldn't move, couldn't evade him, so he could conquer her, make her crave what he had for so long wanted to give her.

There was no rational thought, no remorse, only need and sensation and ravenous mastery. She invited him into her body, clenching around him as he penetrated her to the hilt and ground against her womb.

When he felt her coming, his own orgasm begin to crest, he tightened his grip.

She gasped.

Thrust deep against her womb, he wondered in a flash of insanity if she'd love his child, if he'd be permitted to visit, if it would be a girl or boy. Then his breath caught as she careened over the edge . . . and his back arched, his eyes shut, and he released sweet life into her body.

The log in the fire had long since smoldered to ashes when Nicholas was jolted awake by a noise. His gaze darted around the room, his brain trying frantically to locate something familiar, some clue to where he was. In the next instant he became aware of Crystal's nude form lying snug against him, her breathing steady, her head resting on his arm. Still groggy from sleep, he wondered if he was dreaming. He closed his eyes, remained motionless, and listened. There. Hollow sounding footsteps. Coming from the stairway outside the bedchamber.

A voice in the hall shouted for Crystal.

Heart thumping in his ears, Nicholas came instantly alert, his reflexes automatic as he clutched the counterpane and hastily covered Crystal as a shadow filled the doorway.

Crystal stirred against him. "What is it?—"

Nicholas had no time for a response.

Chapter Eight

"Crystal, where the blazes are you?" The voice coming from the shadow carried a distinct slur, the candlelight held aloft swaying in his grasp. When the intruder's eyes adjusted to the dark to find Crystal wasn't alone, he cursed.

In a heartbeat, her husband's gaze turned from shock into cold appraisal, his lips pressed together in a hurt expression.

Heart pounding, Crystal clasped the blanket to her bosom and tried to sit. "I'm sorry, Freddy, I wanted to warn you"—she pointed a trembling finger to the letter still lying where she'd dropped it—"I even remembered to use the special code we agreed upon." Shame strained her voice, and she desperately searched her mind for something to say to soothe his pride.

Nicholas got to his feet and hovered protectively over her, his face implacably calm. "I'll leave."

"No," she cried, then quickly realized the error of her outburst. "I mean . . ."—she fought for a calming breath—"I think as long as we're all together maybe we should talk."

Nicholas' face grew uncompromising, while her husband's grew fiercely forbidding. Why did she feel so wretched? As if she'd willingly cuckold her husband?

Nicholas bent to scoop up his robe and whispered close to her, "He's been drinking—now is not the time to discuss colors for the nursery. I'll leave." He swiftly tied his robe around his waist and walked toward his anguished friend.

Eyes curiously bright, Halverton barred his path. "Did you enjoy my wife?"

Nicholas' shoulder brushed against Freddy's in the narrow doorway. "Christ, Fred, isn't this what you wanted? Get a hold of yourself."

Halverton reached out and grabbed his arm. "Don't forget Crystal is my wife—"

"Freddy, don't." Crystal stumbled to her feet. She'd once thought her husband's disappointment unbearable, but his jealously was a thousand times worse. "Please. Nick's your friend."

The coverlet trailed across the floor behind her as she hurried to her husband's side. "Please, let's not argue tonight," she pleaded, looking up at Freddy's crestfallen face. The smell of sour ale almost overwhelmed her. The thought of him riding in his condition, the possibility of something happening to him, deeply frightened her. "You must be exhausted." She tugged on his arm. "Let Nick leave if he wants to." She slid a glance at Nicholas and hoped he understood she wasn't trying to evict him.

Fred looked down at her, his gaze momentarily softening. "I shouldn't have just walked in like this," he admitted at last in a strained voice. His pain was almost palpable. "I just didn't expect you to succeed, that's all." His eyes held a fatalistic glimmer. "I'm proud of you, Crystal, you've done exactly what I wished."

Giving her hand a squeeze, he turned to Nicholas. "What do you think, old friend? Another time, we could have made a stunning *menage a trois*?"

Blanching, Crystal's heart faltered. "Freddy, please you've been drinking—"

"Yes, I've been drinking." He laughed dryly, looked pointedly at the empty wine bottles strewn over the floor behind her. "But then so have you."

Crystal shuddered as the coolness of his tone sank into her heart. Nicholas kept dangerously silent.

Her gaze traveled to the hearth and guilt pierced her wavering courage. The evidence of their mating lay in disarray over the floor. Wine glasses. Trays of leftover food. Her robe. Amidst the clutter sparkled a fire evoked by the candlelight. Dear God—her diamond. An exquisite reminder of intoxication of another kind. She prayed Freddy wouldn't notice it.

That thought froze, when to her horror he staggered toward the clutter.

Crystal held her breath as he bent on unsteady legs and retrieved her missive from the floor. Her heart pounded in her throat as she looked at Nicholas. In that endlessly tense moment, their gazes meshed. No words needed. This was where their glorious union ended, their last night together. There would be no one there in the morning to feed her with gentle persuasion, no one there to soften her loneliness once Freddy returned to the country.

Her husband took the missive with him as he walked to the connecting door between their bedchambers. He was abandoning her again, she thought, disspiritedly.

"I'm meeting with a solicitor in the morning," he told them, "I'll be leaving early." The door opened with a whisper. "If you have a boy I'd like to name him after my father." Then he paused in the open doorway to look over his shoulder. "Stay as long as you like, Nick. She'll need you."

Crystal stared unblinking as the emotionless announcement of her husband's blow crushed her last hope. After she'd carried out his wishes, after she'd prayed he'd be happy, for reasons beyond her comprehension, he still chose to abandon her and all their hopes of happiness. She'd been so gullible, tried so hard to please him. While the only thing that mattered to him seemed his heir.

Feeling utterly bereft and alone, an old despair surged into her heart. For the innocent babe she could be carrying. For the love she tried to hold onto. And for Nicholas, who must be as confused as she was.

"I'm leaving for France at the end of the week," Nick said gently, "I'll call on you before I sail to see how you're feeling."

Nick's words jarred her out of her melancholy. She turned to stare at him in numb misery. God, no. "You're leaving?" she whispered, sounding pathetically close to tears. Her throat worked convulsively for air as she fought against the insane desire to cling to him—beg him to stay.

His hungry gaze devoured her for a breathless moment—then he told her very quietly, "The diamond is yours, Crystal. When you're alone you can wear it for me . . . and remember tonight."

The intimacy of his words hung between them like a caress. His regrets strained his features. Both of them felt the pain. The pull of something deeper. Something forbidden. Then because there was nothing either of them dare do about it, he turned and walked away.

By the following afternoon, Crystal's house was returned to its usual grim order. Freddy had left early as he'd promised and she'd awakened with a deplorable headache. Her lady's maid resumed her post, carried out all the mundane tasks that Nicholas had done for her with lavish seduction. She tried telling herself she was merely overwrought, it was her husband's love she longed for, that he would return, explain his rash behavior and once again restore to her her faith. Then she would remember last night and Nicholas invaded her thoughts. The way he'd looked at her in that unguarded moment before he left haunted her. After the precious time she'd spent with him, her emptiness seemed all the more keen. The diamond in her pocket was all she had left of him. A diamond and, she prayed, a child.

That week passed with agonizing swiftness. Nicholas stood at the bow of his yacht—early morning dawn peeking over the horizon on the

Thames—and stared at the bustling dock as he pulled away from shore. He thought over the past night's agony. He'd walked the street outside Crystal's house last evening, and later watched the glow of the hearth illuminating the window from his obscure post in a closed carriage. He'd kept a vigil there for hours—until the light faded and her room grew dark. He'd spent the night trying to relegate her to the place she belonged—out of his thoughts—but had failed.

He regretted, now, telling her he would call on her. She was the wife of his friend. A temptation. The precious taste of her was imprinted on his jaded soul, her passion flaring like flames searing an image on his memory. To have gone to her under the pretense of inquiring about her health would have been his utter destruction. It would have been dangerous to see her again. Torture to abstain from dragging her into the nearest corner and impaling her until he rid himself of the insane desire to keep her.

No. It would be better for them both this way. She'd receive his letter, find it sufficiently circumspect and be saved the burden of embarrassing goodbyes.

Paris offered an escape, her beauty unlike any Nicholas could remember in London. Trees sprouting new blossoms scented the air with their flowery fragrance, while the feminine crowd in their spring-colored walking gowns made a rainbow of swishing color along the sidewalks. Emerged from their cocoons after the harshness of winter, they chatted animatedly about the Paris *Season*, and which guests to add to their parties.

He approached a milliner's shop on the Rue Saint-Honore, his focus fixed on the opposite side of the street.

One woman in particular stood out from the rest, her wide smile curved up with feline pleasure as she caught sight of him coming in her direction.

Evette Collier was looking exceedingly beautiful, her pale violet gown molding voluptuous curves of a woman practiced in luring men into bed. A riot of dark curls cascaded down her back, her jaunty little hat with its enormous plume gave her a decided edge of sophistication. Her face was shaded by a matching violet parasol trimmed in the same lace that flattered her heavy bosom. Since she rarely emerged from her boudoir before noon, it was his fortune to have found her out and about.

They met under the canopy of a small pastry shop.

"Dear God, Nicholas, I thought I must be fantasizing about you again." She gracefully extended her hand, eating him up with her hungry brown eyes. "You look so edible . . . *mon Deiu*, I've been missing you," she purred with sultry sweetness.

Because she expected it, he took her slender fingers in his and brought them to his lips—let his fingers tighten perceptibly in a blatant caress of possession. He remembered their last encounter well—the cream eclair adorning his arousal—her tongue licking sweet confection from his shaft while she searched his face like a greedy child looking for praise.

She would do, he decided somewhat cynically. "If you're not busy, I would like to take you sailing on the Seine."

Her almond-shaped eyes sparkled with promises. "For you, I just canceled all my engagements. Perhaps you won't mind if I bring along lunch." She held up her recent purchase. "I've been famished for eclairs."

His smile lacked the characteristic enthusiasm. A year ago he'd have looked forward to rendering his body for her pleasure. Evette was amiable and extremely well versed in his tastes. She was everything another man might desire in a wife, while to him she represented everything that contrasted with the one woman he couldn't have. In that regard she was perfect.

An hour later as their carriage rolled to a stop at her doorstep, Nicholas helped her alight and escorted her into the house. When he'd not accommodated her in bed aboard his yacht she had been disappointed, but patient. She'd even been tolerant when he'd declined lunch.

It wasn't until they entered her drawing room where she firmly shut the door behind her and turned to face him that her composure shattered.

"All right. I've been throwing myself at you all afternoon and nothing seems to move you. What have I done to displease you?" she asked in pouty tones, her bosom heaving with each breath.

Nicholas settled into a chair as he tugged his cravat loose and tossed it over the back of the elegant blue settee. "Don't worry, sweetheart, it's not what you've done—it's what I'm about to do."

At the seriousness of his tone, she came to stand over him, looking down at him with avid regard. "And just what is it"—she dropped to her knees between his legs—"you're about to do?"

Time to sever ties with his heart. "I came to propose marriage." There he'd done the unspeakable—put an end to his torture.

Evette's gurgle of happiness made him feel like a cad. She climbed into his lap and kissed him hard on the mouth. "My God, Nicholas, of all your conquests, why me?"

His brows drew together. "Why not?"

She drew back to look at him and smiled. "You're not exactly thrilled about this, for one."

He shifted her off his lap and rose to his feet.

She was looking up at him with calm reproach. "You already have a string of devoted bed partners, for two. And three, you could have any woman you wanted eating out of your hand."

Crystal's lips sucking sweetmeats from his fingers flashed into his thoughts. The searing sensation was like fire hitting his groin. God help him, he knew of no other way to cut her from his life.

"If you want a declaration of love, I can't give it."

The dark beauty tilted her head and studied him. "You'll find I can be very practical when I need to be. And a practical woman would be a fool to decline your offer." She smiled complacently. "Under the circumstance, I guess I'll have to content myself with your wealth. When will our wedding take place?"

He recklessly tossed aside the voice of caution. Already set on a course of self-destruction, at this point he didn't much care whether he lived or died.

Eager to be done with it, he said, "Just as soon as we dispatch a message to London and the banns can be posted." The same recklessness that drove him from London, drove him to carelessness. "In the meantime, you're free to make any purchases you need at my expense. I'll go tomorrow and make arrangements with the bank to extend you funds." He watched her eyes go soft with some emotion and experienced an uneasy feeling in the pit of his stomach, but he heedlessly pushed on. "After lunch we'll visit a jeweler to select suitable rings."

Chapter Nine

Crystal clutched the badly crumpled note in her fist as she curled into a tight ball of misery in her empty bed and gave into despair.

Forgive me for leaving without saying good-bye..
Your devoted servant, Nicholas.

No regrets. No tender teasing. Just cool, emotionless words. And she'd read those words at least a hundred times since the message arrived yesterday morning. She'd cried after the footman left. Silently wept in misery when she'd drug herself up the steps and locked herself in her room.

He'd left her. He had told her he was going to France—still she thought he might stay. The cruel pain of reality hurt.

She'd never expected to miss him so much. What a fool she'd been to think she could make love to him, have his child, and resume her life as if they'd never shared soul-binding intimacy.

The maid banging on the door roused but a flicker of notice. "Go away," Crystal croaked, her throat hoarse, her head throbbing. Alone in her cold bed, she lay robbed of her will to fight. She had no strength left.

"Please, milady, open the door," the woman cried in earnest. " 'Tis four days since you ate last."

A scuffle of feet and voices penetrated her dim consciousness— sounded like Graves and her young footman—their voices muffled with concern.

God, why can't they just let me die?

The thunder against the door this time resounded around the room, hinges creaked under the assault. Weakly, Crystal pulled the pillow over her head to shut out the noise and the raspy sound of her breathing as she gasped for life. . . .

Minutes later, the door crashed in with a shuddering, wood-splitting boom.

Butler, maid, and footman poured through the opening, rushing toward the bed with fear on their faces.

Graves reached her first. "Draw back the drapes"—he shot over his shoulder to the footman—"open the window, quickly." He swiftly drug the pillow away from his mistress' face, dreading he might not be in time to save her.

Lady Halverton looked asleep. Deathly pale. He quickly leaned over her, put his cheek near her mouth. Faint breathing whispered over his face. Relief brought dampness to his eyes.

Wasting no time, Graves knelt and pulled his poor sweet mistress against his chest. She sagged over his arm like a limp rag doll.

Beside him, the lady's maid shrieked at the sight. "Is she dead?"

Graves shot her a quelling look that would have sent a lesser woman fleeing for cover. "Get yourself downstairs and fetch us a doctor."

For the next three days the doctor came and administered laudanum, bled Lady Halverton, and left. Graves had issued orders that all visitors were to be turned away with an understanding that his employer wasn't feeling well. It was the staff's duty to protect their grieving mistress.

On the fourth day, when their mistress didn't awaken, a sealed message was sent to Lord Summer's residence. It was Lord Summer she called for in her delirium. Graves hoped Lady Halverton's close friend might wish to be there to help her in some way.

Several days went by while Graves waited for a reply. Implicit directions issued by Lord Halverton before he left clearly indicated he didn't want to be disturbed, that if his wife needed anything the staff was to contact Lord Summer.

In Paris, Nicholas threw himself with a reckless kind of numbness into the farce of his engagement, while the exhausting hours of civility he'd been forced to maintain for the sake of his fiancée took their toll. He lived his own private hell, going through the motions of pretense. Most days he kept his misery tightly contained. But today his torment felt more acute, the knife blade pressed against his heart plunging deeper with each passing hour. All the eclairs in France—all Evette's seductive wiles—couldn't keep thoughts of Crystal from haunting his memory.

God . . . Crystal. She was scarred upon his soul. He craved her with a fierceness that knotted his gut. Like a man craves death when he finds his life at an end. Every time he plunged into Evette's willing body he saw Crystal's wanton beauty. Crystal opening to him . . .

writing against him . . . beckoning him to his doom with sultry blue eyes.

Today, he and his intended were traveling back to London. Back to face the music—where the pain of being near Crystal would drive him mad.

"You look like a man who's lost his only friend," Evette said reflectively as she joined him in the drawing room.

Not just a friend, he thought grimly, someone infinitely precious.

"I have no friends," he said moodily, staring out the window. "You must be thinking of someone else."

Patient as always, she gave him a sympathetic smile as she reached up and brushed a lock of hair from his forehead. "Shall we go then?"

Smiling tightly, Nicholas followed Evette out of the room. In the foyer they paused at the mirror for her to adjust her hat. He then waited while she slipped her fingers into the soft, kid gloves that she'd purchased with his money. Lastly, came the meaningless emerald engagement ring.

She smiled happily up at him and slid it onto her third finger.

Though innocent, the proprietary gesture seemed a particular favorite of hers . . . one that annoyed the hell out of him.

Two weeks after her ordeal, as early morning light filtered over the floor, Crystal was roused from her deathbed out of a dreamless slumber. A sickly feeling made her mouth water. A horrible rumble tightened her stomach. Her hand flew to her mouth in a panic as bile surged up her throat.

Stumbling from bed, she collapsed on the floor and grasped the chamber pot to her chest when her insides erupted.

She heaved and coughed. Then retched again.

Retched until her sides ached.

Several minutes passed before she felt the cold floorboards beneath her. Now wide awake and trembling, she weakly laid her head back against the bed for support and wondered if she was dying. Her mouth tasted vile. Sweat soaked her nightrail. Vague memories of Graves' face close to hers—his muffled voice speaking to her—stirred her recall. The doctor's face, she remembered, had been there, too.

Beyond that she couldn't remember.

My God. How long had she been in bed?

She'd no sooner set the chamber pot aside, when the door burst open, followed by the doctor. His face registered shock when he spotted her sitting on the floor.

"I'm pregnant," she whispered weakly, remembering now the joy of discovering she'd missed her monthly courses just minutes before her utter desolation surrounding Nicholas' ill-timed note.

The doctor knelt beside her and helped her back into bed. He regarded her with open concern and smiled kindly. "Yes, you are with child, Mrs. Halverton. Don't worry, in time the sickness will go away." He indicated a bowl of broth. "Though I didn't mind feeding you, it's good to see you up and about. How are you feeling?"

Her ears were still ringing. "Death would be preferable."

"Yes, well, you must eat if your baby is going to be healthy."

The memories of the last few weeks came back to her then with horrifying vengeance. Freddy's cold words. His anguish. "Does my husband know?" she asked anxiously. "Has he come home?"

The doctor reached for the bowl of soup, his face blank, his eyes avoiding hers. "Eat first, then we will talk."

Crystal did as he asked. And Doc Phillips entertained her with stories of a patient who'd delivered a fine baby boy. How the mother had lost several babies. How she'd lost all hope. He told her how happy the parents were now, how brave they were to keep trying.

Although Crystal's first two spoonfuls of beef broth had rumbled her stomach, by sheer determination for the baby's sake, she kept them down this time. Her baby would be all right. He must be all right.

Feeling decidedly stronger after a couple of mouthfuls, she finished her broth and set the bowl aside. The doctor's solemn calm worried her—something about the way he avoided her gaze sent a tingle of premonition down her spine. "What aren't you telling me?"

Surprising her, he reached for her hand, took it between his cool palms. His skin felt leathery soft against hers—the wrinkled-lines around his kind, brown eyes bore into her with pity.

Her heart fluttered erratically. "What's wrong?" she whispered, her throat closing tight with fear. Dear God, not the baby. "Is it the baby?"

"My dear woman, your baby will be just fine." He patted her hand, squeezed it tightly. "It's you I'm worried about, you've lost weight, you're still very weak . . ." His voice faded as he traced his finger over the blue veins of one delicate white hand.

"Dear God, what is it? Just tell me!"

Heaving a deep sigh, he said, "Lady Halverton, it pains me to see you like this. Your distress is a grave concern. I want you to know that this has not been an easy decision for me, that your health is a priority. But"—he regarded her closely—"I knew you would want to know that there has been . . . well . . . a death in the family."

She paled. "A death?"

"Yes, your husband asked that I not say anything about his illness, he didn't want you worrying. He died peacefully—"

To Crystal's panicked brain the words hammered like blows of death along her shattered nerves—and she heard nothing beyond the word "died." Tears flooded her eyes, rolled down her cheeks in warm streams. Not Freddy, she cried. Not now.

With a sickening clarity that clogged her throat, she realized now part of why he had withdrawn from her, why he seemed so insistent she approach Nicholas. He wanted an heir because he was dying. He wanted Nicholas to be the father.

Nicholas to be the father . . .

Blood pumped the litany though her veins, throbbed like drum beats against her temples—made her head spin.

Plunged into grief, she shivered uncontrollably while her future swam before her eyes with painful clarity. Dear God, Freddy wasn't coming back—the anguish she hadn't understood when he looked at her was because he loved and wanted her taken care of. While she'd been feeling sorry for herself, scared and lonely, he had spent his last days alone.

Oh, Freddy, I'm so sorry, I didn't understand.

She could imagine it so well, how Freddy had planned ahead, planned on Nicholas being there for her. But Nicholas had left. She was completely alone—her life suddenly turned inside out. She was a widow carrying a love child created out of passion with a man whom she'd coerced into seducing her.

The bleakness and pain of her loss rippled through her body.

She gasped for air, fought off encroaching darkness. The doctor's voice faded in and out, muffled by the surging black numbness dragging at her subconscious.

With a vague awareness, she felt Doc Phillips lifting her shoulders—then something foul smelling—a liquid tasting like laudanum was being poured between her lips.

A few ragged breaths later she felt no more pain.

"Has Lord Summer returned from France?" Crystal asked in a small voice the next morning as her lady's maid entered with a breakfast tray. "He should be notified"—she took a deep breath—"of my husband's . . ." She swallowed hard, and fought a new rush of tears.

The woman nodded sympathetically. "Yes, my lady, Lord Summer has just returned from Paris. A note was delivered to him this very morning." She plopped the heavy tray on the bedside table. "Incidently, Lord Summer has announced his engagement to a Miss Collier.

The banns have been posted, and the wedding is scheduled for the end of this week. 'Course, knowing how fond you are of him, Mr. Graves took the liberty of sending your congratulations."

Crystal felt the blood draining from her face.

From the doorway, Graves cleared his throat. "That will be all, Miss Jones."

Mumbling an apology, the lady's maid scurried out of the room.

Still reeling, Crystal stared round-eyed at Graves, her chin trembling. "Exactly when were you planning to tell me? After the wedding?"

Looking justifiably contrite, he dropped his gaze to the floor. "Forgive me, my lady. After all that's happened, the doctor said it was best we didn't add to your distress."

Utterly devastated by the news, she turned from him and rolled onto her side. Her heart pounding in her throat swiftly brought back the sick churning in her stomach. To describe her intense feeling of loneliness as distress was achingly inadequate. Her husband was gone. Their last moments together were etched on her mind with images of his fatalistic sorrow. In a few days time, she would be laying him to rest along with her future happiness. Her emotions this morning felt shredded beyond repair.

Now, the shock of Nicholas marrying tore her heart wide open in a wholly irrational way. The pain of it mixed with a searing, illogical jealousy. Envy toward this other woman clutched her chest, while she struggled with the burden of her guilt.

Dear God forgive her, her husband's body wasn't even two days cold. While she knew now what Freddy intended—that she turn to Nicholas—it still felt like she was betraying him. And Freddy, he must have known all along she was in love with Nicholas. Hopelessly, recklessly, and shamefully in love.

She wrapped her arm protectively over her abdomen, the precious life growing there. The love she felt for Nicholas burned like blazing coals.

Her heart twisted with pain. With her newfound love came the gut-wrenching realization that while she loved Nicholas with every fiber of her traitorous heart, he had been looking for a wife.

Nicholas had helped her out of kindness—given her the child she wanted—nothing more.

She heard the shuffle of footsteps as Graves left the room. She wouldn't cry, she told herself sternly. She had the new life within her to get her through the days ahead, she would survive this, dammit. But being in a breeding way had a way of making even her sternest intentions buckle.

Turning her face to her pillow, she gave into overwhelming grief, silently sobbing for Freddy . . . and only after her tears exhausted themselves, did she curl into a tight ball, whimpering Nick's name.

Chapter Ten

In Summer's London town house, Evette dropped her bundle of hat boxes and extravagant purchases in the hall before entering the drawing room where her soon-to-be husband sat brooding over a glass of brandy.

She kissed his cheek affectionately and plopped down beside him. "Oh, my toes are aching with a vengeance." She kicked off her shoes and propped her feet up on the nearest cushioned footstool. "I must have visited every shop in the city."

He stared into the empty hearth without comment, the dispatch from Halverton Hall balled tightly in his fist.

"Tell me, darling, who is this Halverton woman I'm hearing about?"

Nicholas' attention swung to his fiancée as he tried to remember what it was he had decided to tell her when the time came. His thinking moved slowly, thanks to the effects of good brandy. "Why do you ask?" he queried darkly, his head throbbing with a passion.

"No reason, I suppose. It's just she has recently lost her husband—"

"So I've just learned." His vision blurring, he set his glass aside.

Taking pity on him, Evette closed her eyes, rested her head against the cushioned settee. "I'm sorry, darling, about your friend. I found out about it from Her Grace, the Duchess of Sutherland. She just happened by the same shop I was in and I overheard her talking about the poor widow and how the doctor found her near death in grief."

Nicholas abruptly rose to his feet, his heart hammering.

When he didn't speak, she opened her eyes to find him restlessly prowling the floor like a caged cat. So, he was in love with the woman—the rumors she'd heard were true. "I heard that you know Lady Halverton quite intimately."

His gaze turned on her with a fierceness that burned with animal wildness. "Why don't you just ask me if I fucked her?"

She grimaced. "It's all right, darling, I understand now where your preoccupation comes from." As composed as she looked her voice held a distinct quiver. "Don't worry, I told you before I'm a practical woman. And a practical woman doesn't expect fidelity. I just wish you weren't in love with her."

Evette's blithe statement left Nicholas momentarily stunned. Was it love? This feeling tearing him apart? Christ, only a complete fool would fall in love with a married woman. A widow, he amended, haphazardly.

"I knew you really didn't want to marry me, not when you were obviously pining over another woman. The hell of it is, I am going to regret losing you. No man has ever given me pleasure the way you have."

That tremor of emotion she'd tried hiding from him, had he recognized it for what it was months ago, apparently ran deeper than he thought.

Because she was being brave, because he suspected he'd just broken her heart, he offered her what he offered no other mistress. "Whatever you want, Evette, it's yours. I'll see that you receive it."

Sighing, she pulled the engagement ring from her finger, and resolutely handed it to him. "Since I shall have to live without you, I should like a place of my own. I've always thought how nice it would be to live in some exotic heathen desert—maybe have my own ship, so I could sail about like you have, maybe retire and live in a harem of some handsome young sheik. Perhaps I shall even marry one of those rugged buccaneers from America, who knows? Surely with enough gold I could choose the life I wanted, and not be left destitute by every man who falls in love."

Closing her eyes on a deep sigh, she wiggled her toes. "Now please be a dear, won't you, and send Bessy down to rub my feet. I really am having a wretched day."

Nick gave her a parting kiss for old time's sake, and hoped he didn't appear as eager to bolt from the room as he felt. "By the way, this town house is yours. Tomorrow I'll have the yacht transferred into your name." Feeling expressly generous in his present state of inexplicable joy, he stopped at the door and added, "You'll find an account in your name as well with enough to buy your own harem of young men, should you decide on that. We've shared good times, Evette, and I wish you sincere happiness. God knows, you have just given me mine."

Evette waved him off, bravely staunching the flow of tears until after he left the room.

Nicholas walked until he was reasonably certain no one would notice, then he ran, his long strides taking him the rest of the way to Crystal's front doorstep.

When he knocked, he never expected her to answer the door.

It seemed they were both incapable of speech while for a fleeting moment time stood still.

The misery he saw in her face deepened the dark circles beneath her eyes. She'd lost weight, her face pale, thin. Her ethereal beauty, so fragile, so easily destroyed, twisted his gut into a knot of guilt.

"You're back?" she whispered raggedly, her eyes suddenly bright with tears.

He should offer his condolences, but he didn't. "France held no interest for me. All I thought about was you."

Her bottom lip quivered. "Is that why you're engaged now?"

The misery in her voice clamped around his heart with a force that left him reeling. "I'm not leaving here until we talk. If you want me to beg you, I will."

She pulled him into the foyer then, shut and locked the door. When she raised her eyes to his, all the suffering she'd endured glimmered in their depths. "I wanted to die when you left. If you think I'm going to give you up, I won't."

He slowly reached for her hand, drew it to his lips. "Let me hold you," he whispered roughly, pressing his mouth to the soft flesh of her palm. "God, let me love you, puss."

And because Crystal loved him to distraction, she couldn't deny him. Suddenly, the other woman didn't matter. Uttering a soft moan, she went into his arms. She shuddered in his embrace. Ravenous with need, he nuzzled her neck, his breathing searing her flesh as he devoured her with his hot mouth, nipping and suckling her ear. His hand cupped her bottom impatiently.

Heat emanated from his body, sank into her bones, and Crystal weakly clung to his solid length in desperation. The pain, when he left this time, would be worse than cutting out her heart, but she wanted him. Fiercely. Completely. Filling her with his engorged desire, with the liquid fire burning between her legs. For a time he was hers, for now that had to be enough.

With his other hand, Nicholas clasped her hard against his chest, the supple feel of her pressed along his length, the faint smell of gardenias unique to the woman he'd never thought to see again becoming an ache in his heart that wouldn't go away. He wanted to carry her upstairs, lay her down before a blazing fire and ravish her until he collapsed. Yet he held back, trying to tell himself she was recently widowed and understandably grieving.

He tried telling himself he could live without her should she no longer need him. But deep in his heart he knew he couldn't let her go. Crystal was his, she should have been his eight years ago.

She was pressing her breasts against his chest, her hand greedily massaging his erection through his breeches. Alas, in the space of a heartbeat, nothing in the past mattered. He wouldn't worry about the future, somehow the future would take care of itself. But Crystal . . . Christ, he needed her in irrational ways.

As her hand slipped down the front of his breeches, his spine stiffened. When she clasped her warm fingers around his shaft, he thought his heart would stop. Bludgeoned by the hot-spurred urge to rut against her hand, he came near to ravishing her right there on the floor like a randy youth. But he wanted her begging . . . wanted to hear her crying out his name like she had in his dreams.

His fingers locked around her wrist. "You'll waste me," he rasped hoarsely, "if you touch me like that. Give me your hand."

He heard her muffled protest against his chest as she tried to twist her hand free of his grip. "It's your choice, puss," he whispered softly, "either we wait until Graves finds us like this or you wrap your legs around me right now and let me carry you to bed."

He waited for what seemed an eternity, then his willful little puss lifted her leg to his waist. As soon as her wetness seeped through the fabric stretched taut over his erection, he knew there was no evading what was destined to be his utter surrender. Hell and heaven vied for dominance over his soul, and with a mindless urgency he lifted his hips into her . . . seeking that which was his. Just as restless, Crystal's hands drew him in tightly, her cleft grinding against him. Aware that she hovered near climax, he glanced at the hall table, remembered the afternoon when they had the house to themselves.

"No, puss, this time I want you in bed." He took her hand then, lifted it to his lips, drew her finger into his mouth. Crystal sagged against him, whimpering, writhing. His tongue flicked over her finger, tasted her, wet her and an answering throb pulsed through her veins. "I can't wait," she moaned, her nails digging into his back.

The smell of her heat clenched his groin. Mutual lust burned between them. Victim of the same pained pleasure she felt, he slid her finger from his mouth . . . then remembering a dark night in a certain carriage, he slowly drew a ragged breath and guided her hand between her legs. She was drenched, her labia pulsing for him . . . his already straining erection lengthened a painful minuscule more. He swallowed his groan. Like an impassioned fool on the brink of spilling his seed, he gritted his teeth, pushed his fingers and hers between her swollen folds, deeper into her silken passage. "Stay with me, puss," he breathed tightly. Gently holding her hand in place, he felt her shuddering near orgasm. "Hold on, darling. I'm going to carry you now very carefully up the stairs. Don't move your hand . . . wait for me . . . and I'll show you how much we've missed you." *I'll love you like you wanted me to years ago.*

Fingers laced, he cupped her bottom and lifted her, let her weight settle against his hips where he held her hand trapped between them. "Hurry, Nick," she whimpered, resting heavily against him. "Please hurry."

Taking great care, he managed the stairs, having to stop but once when Crystal's body tensed against a climax at the top of the landing.

In her bedchamber, he lowered her onto the counterpane and followed her down. His brain quickly registered the fire someone had started in the hearth, the medicinal smell clinging to the room, at the edge of his vision an empty bowl setting on the side table. Stark reminders of Crystal's fragile health, of the missive from Graves awaiting him upon his return from France.

Fool that he was, he might have lost her and never been given the chance to tell her what it was that took him so long to come to terms with.

Pinned beneath him, she writhed. And he lowered his head, ran his tongue over her parted lips, tasted the sweetness of her breath. Her nails clawed at his back. Impatient. Frantic. "Please," she gasped, ripping his shirt from his breeches. "I need you inside me."

Sweat trickled down his back. His heartbeat thrummed through his veins. Braced above her on one arm, he grabbed her shoulder, half lifted her from the bed, bent his head to suckle her bottom lip, his mouth harsh, his fingers biting into her flesh. Working quickly with his other hand to pull the barrier of her skirt out of the way, he crushed her hard against his chest, forced her mouth open with his, plunged his tongue deep into her throat, the need to possess eating at his brain. He couldn't stand the thought of her lying like this with another man. She belonged to him . . . somehow he would have her.

Or at least that was how he imagined it, his cool reasoning responded, as he roughly raised her hips to admit his pounding thrust.

He took her with a fierceness of wild abandon, he kept her wanting him all night, wooing her, tasting her, spilling his seed into her luscious body, neither of them wanting to break the intensity of their rapture, neither of them talking of tomorrow. They made love with tender caresses, with exquisite slowness, and long into the morning when dawn spread over the floor, when at last he poured his soul into her with the gentleness of a man sealing his vow upon her heart.

Nick stood naked at the window, peering through the drapes at the tangle of late afternoon traffic, of carriages blocking the street below.

Crystal lay sprawled over the counterpane, wondrously displayed for him in her big bed, her pale beauty bared to his scrutiny, tendrils of tangled gold encircling her shoulders. He ached for her with raw need, wanted her with a recklessness that would very likely kill him. Was it love? Or madness?

Evette had called it love.

He'd been a fool to think Evette could make him forget his little puss. Crystal's every graceful gesture was engraved on his memory. The way she smiled at him with that engulfing heat in her eyes when he touched her, the way she glared like a mutinous child when he insisted she eat. Sated now, her eyes closed in slumber, her lips curled in repleted aftermath, he imagined what it might be like to have her like this in his bed, in his life. More than anything he wanted to be the one at her side when she woke in the morning, the one to bring her to shuddering climax in the middle of the night.

Already he wanted her again. The heat from their mating filled his nostrils, the faint essence of her scent lingered on his dampened skin. His hungry gaze devoured. Her alabaster beauty stood out in stark contrast to the passion flushed pearls of her nipples. Lower, wavy blonde curls nestled between her legs—its silken wetness a greedy sheath for his rampant sex.

He pulled his gaze away from her, looked out the window. The thought of taking another mistress made him see how ludicrous were his plans of putting Crystal out of his mind.

"You're not going back to her, are you?" a small voice rose in the solitude.

Nicholas started, swung his gaze toward the bed again. Sitting cross-legged in the middle of the mattress, her hair spilling over her naked-ness in golden dishabille, sat his precious reason for living. So pale. So fragile, he thought. Utterly vulnerable in her sultry pose. Utterly desir-able. The anguish in her eyes gave his heart a painful tug. "I thought Evette would help me forget you. The marriage I sought was to drive a wedge between us."

Her gaze went to his erection, and the way her eyes devoured him made it difficult to concentrate. He knew what she was thinking. "When I laid with her, it was you I saw, Crystal. When I fucked her, it was your body I wanted. Christ . . . you have tortured me."

Her gaze rose to his, shimmering with hope.

He heaved a deep, soulful sigh. "In response to your question, the answer is no."

"Oh, Nick," she cried happily, launching herself off the bed at him.

With a wolfish grin on his lips, he easily caught her in his arms while the impact knocked the air from his lungs.

She was mewling with delight, raining joyful kisses to the hollow of his throat, his chin, her smile more radiant than any sunrise he'd ever seen.

"Crystal, I'm not going to lie to you," he murmured against her hair, "and tell you there aren't going to be consequences to my rash actions—"

"I know." She pressed her cheek to his heart and the vital warmth there. "The banns have been posted," she murmured, "the entire city of London knows. What will we do?"

"That depends on you."

"On me?"

With slow deliberation, he drew her chin up with gentle fingers until he was looking into her soul. She held his fate in the palm of her hands. "Tell me what you want me to do." He was letting her decide. He was walking the edge of a blade.

She blushed under his heated scrutiny, the trust there. "I want your love," she said simply, as if her entire existence weren't held in the balance by his response.

"Is that all you want, puss?" His voice was silky deep, his words bringing flags of crimson to her already flushed face. Biting her bottom lip, she dropped her gaze.

Finding her maidenly embarrassment charming, he didn't wait for an answer, but lifted her into his arms and carried her back to the bed. He perched on the edge with her in his lap, held her nakedness nestled against his broad chest. "Maybe you still need reassurance." His fingers were kneading the tension from her spine.

Crystal's body shook with the intensity of her joy, overwhelming happiness making her vision go blurry. Within Nick's embrace, she felt warm and safe . . . protected. What he gave her was so incredibly wonderful, his tenderness a balm to her deprived soul. She tingled where their bodies touched.

Groaning, he bent his head and captured her mouth, drove his tongue between her teeth and plunged into her sweetness.

The fire blazing through his body evoked a yearning in Crystal that shuddered like lightning upon her soul. She clung to Nick in glorious abandon, felt his heated desire nudging against her bare bottom. His sensuality left her giddy, breathless. "I prayed you would come back to me," she rasped.

"Did you?" His hand on her back grew unsteady. "Perhaps you were feeling just a trifle guilty?"

She drew back to look at him, her lashes spiked with joyous tears. "How do you mean?"

"How long were you going to keep me in the dark before you told me you were carrying my child?"

Her cheeks flamed anew under his heated gaze. "That was my secret," she told him. "Besides, I didn't think you would appreciate the burden when you were to be married. Who told you? Was it Graves?"

"Graves had nothing to do with it." He moved his hand up, cupped the heavy weight of her breast, grazed the swell of alabaster beauty with his finger "Rather a simple observation on my part. You see, I notice every little change in your body."

While wanting desperately to hold onto him, to have him say the words she needed to hear, she still couldn't ignore the fact that he'd gone to Paris to look for a wife. "If this woman loves you like I do, she won't let you go."

His smile flashed white against dark features. "So you admit you love me?"

She twisted her hands together. "I have for some time—I just didn't know how much until you announced your engagement." She swallowed against the lump of pain at the thought. "Oh, God, Nick, I'd rather die than watch the two of you together—"

"Shh," he soothed, running his fingers through her hair, knowing he would move heaven and earth to keep Crystal now that his child grew deep within her womb. Now that their love was out in the open. "Don't worry, puss, the engagement to Evette is off. You're the one I'm in love with." He crushed her tight. "No other woman has ever driven me to madness the way you have." His body was trembling with the fierce need to penetrate her, his voice husky, possessive. "Is that what you wanted to hear?"

Glancing away, she nodded against his chest.

He tenderly ran his finger along her jaw, brought her chin around so he could peer into her liquid blue eyes. "Marry me, Crystal—put me out of my misery."

Her lips parted on a gasp. Thinking she was dreaming, Crystal warily scanned his face for what she sought as dizzy elation left her fighting for breath. There was no denying the devotion in his eyes was a sweet murmur of the love she needed. That love made her go weepy, her acceptance shining in her eyes.

He brushed a tear away. "I really should let you sleep—"

She shook her head. "I'll sleep later." With trembling fingers, she boldly reached for what she wanted more than sleep. More than nourishment.

His smile strained, his shaft responding to her feather-like strokes, he shifted with her in the bed and covered her with his body. "Are you certain you want more?"

"Mmmm." Eyes shimmering, she snuggled her breasts against his softly-pelted chest, reveling in the roughness of hair braising her skin. The hard length pulsing in her palm. "Remember, you promised me a house full of children"—she quivered where his fingers invaded—"and I shall explode if you lick me there again."

"Then open to me, puss," he murmured against her neck, "I want to feel you wet and climaxing around me." Nuzzling her breast with his lips, he captured a lush coral nipple between his teeth and drew on the tight nub with gentle tugs. His one hand penetrating, invading, his tongue lathing one tender peak, then the other, he took her over crest after blissful crest. Until she arched in hot abandon, parting her pale thighs to accept him, her fitful pleas whispering against his ear.

Still, he held back until she was drenched and thrashing beneath him—then guiding himself into her love-swollen sheath, he tipped her bottom up to take all his engorged desire . . . and heart pumping, plunged into her with all the driving fire of possession. She was all the woman he needed . . . the mother of his child . . . the only woman he had ever loved. And he thoroughly branded her his with each ravishing thrust . . .

About the author:

When Desirée Lindsey isn't writing romantic passages, she's taking care of the farm, the menagerie of animals her husband added to her chore list, and reading what she loves best—historical romance. To her, elegant gowns, horse-drawn carriages and gallant knights are the embodiment of everything romantic and dashing. She gave up the city life and her RN degree to pursue writing romance while enduring freezing temperatures, tornados and coyotes on the eastern plains of Colorado where she, her husband of many years, and their two children reside. She secretly admits to thriving on the outrageous and sultry, and loves weaving her stories with sinful splendor. In her opinion, there is nothing more captivating than a hero whose speech is wickedly masculine, his voice a velvet rumble . . .

My fondest regards to those who stood by me during the making of this sensual journey; my heartfelt thanks to my own alpha hero, Jeff—you're the magic in my life; to my son, Jeffrey, and daughter, Demi—Mom adores you both. To my mother, sisters and brothers for your never-ending faith and love. To my cherished friend Laura Altom and our writing journey together. Warmest of thanks to cohorts Amy Sandrin, Lynda Cooper, Maggi Landry, Terri Clark, Joyce Farrell, Audra Harders, Chelley Kitzmiller and the dozens who have believed in *Enslaved*. To my gracious editor and mentor, who patiently stood by me and nurtured with praise. You women are the stuff our heroines are made of.

Lastly, but certainly not least, my very humble gratitude to the Divine presence in my life whose love for us all makes faith possible, dreams come true and miracles happen.

Out of which *Enslaved* was born. Enjoy!

The Bodyguard

by Betsy Morgan and Susan Paul

To our reader:
Alana Manley's drug of choice is men. Kaki York's last assignment was Desert Storm. What happens when this female bodyguard is hired to protect the Oscar-winning actress from a stalker, and herself? Put on your jammies, crawl in bed, and read on . . .

Chapter One

P.S. I think you should know, Alana Manley's drug of choice is men . . . Ka-say-yo! Lee!

Eyes wide, Kaki York read the last line of the fax for the third time. Her eyebrows knit together. She sat in nothing but an old oversized T-shirt with her shapely legs curled beneath her on the couch in her rented beach house in Savannah, Georgia.

For God's sake, what kind of statement was that? It sounded as if Master Lee was trying to tell her this woman was a nymphomaniac. Surely not. The Seoul-born martial art expert was no doubt just having his usual problems with English.

The summer moon hung low in the sky casting a million sparkles on the water, and the evening air smelled sea-fresh coming through the open window. A scent of magnolia blossoms came to her from beyond a weathered white-picket fence. Down the road, lighted shop windows offered an endless variety of treasures that would have fascinated her at another time. But what had arrived earlier today—the request—was all that concerned her now. It was also the reason for her earlier video store run.

So much for a quiet three-month vacation, Kaki thought, as she pointed the remote control at the VCR and pushed play.

The previews of upcoming attractions ran. She took a handful of hot buttered popcorn from the bowl and popped several pieces into her mouth. Only the faintest trace of a smile hovered on her lips as she savored the salty delight.

She watched with interest as Alana Manley's latest box office hit began on the television screen. Still, she could not imagine why Master Lee wanted her to be this woman's bodyguard. If someone was stalking Ms. Manley, it seemed to her that a team of security professionals was in order—not just one black belt.

Taking a deep breath, she stretched. Her thoughts on the matter were unimportant. The man who had taken her in when she was orphaned at seven years old, loved her as his own daughter and taught her everything he knew about Korean Karate, had asked her to come to New York. And she would. It was as simple as that.

Kaki knew of Alana Manley, of course. Who didn't? She had flirted with the camera for most of her twenty-nine years. When the actress received an unprecedented thirteen million dollars for the meaty role in her latest feature film, it had made headlines across the globe. But Kaki had never seen one of her movies. Until now.

There was a quick flash of Alana's face; the rich auburn hair, the sensual long lashed, chocolate colored eyes, the natural pout of her full red lips as she sat in a straight-backed chair and adjusted herself to a more comfortable position. Kaki shook her head. Alana Manley really was lovely. If only she had looks like—

The camera closed in on the stunning star, who sat with her legs spread wide apart. Kaki could clearly see that she wore no underwear. When Alana rested her fingers on her naked sex, Kaki choked on her popcorn, spewing more than a few pieces across the room. Grabbing the bottle of pop she took a long swig, hoping to quell the spasm in her esophagus. It didn't work. She choked again. Then coughed, which sent a stream of the carbonated liquid up the back of her nose.

Jesus, Kaki thought, shooting to her feet. Had she survived the officer's candidate school at the Great Lakes Naval Academy and Desert Storm only to die, drowning in a river of Coke?

With a groan, she snatched a tissue from the box on the coffee table and flipped off the tape. After blowing her nose several times, washing her face, and taking a few moments to regain her composure, she took a seat again. Head in her hands, Kaki thought few things ever surprised her. She had seen a great deal in her thirty years, but this was definitely something that had taken her by surprise.

The next afternoon, in her luxurious penthouse in New York's elite Central Park West where she spent most of each summer, Alana Manley, not surprisingly, was perfectly groomed. She knew what a man wanted and just how to give it to him.

Unlike most women who had used sex to gain opportunities and open doors that would have otherwise been closed to a struggling actress, she was not ashamed of the fact. Why should she be? She had not only enjoyed the ride, but was now one of the highest paid leading ladies in the motion picture industry. And though her morals were in constant question, her talent as an actress never had been.

As her gaze drifted to the golden statue on top of the white and gold marble mantel, Alana realized accepting the Oscar for Best Actress had been the most orgasmic experience of her life. With a smile, her thoughts spiraled to the evening ahead. There was always hope.

One of the biggest secrets to her success with men was focus—

undiluted, undivided attention to the man she was in bed with. She concentrated totally and completely on him. She made him feel he was the only man in the world, that he was the sexiest, most desirable, most wonderful lover she could possibly have.

"Nothing is a bigger turn-on," Alana said turning to Jenna Tucker, her assistant, "than knowing you are the object of someone's desire and that you are the sole center of attention. Surely the best way to make love to a man is to let him know that you are truly carried away by desire."

Alana was in a hurry, but she took a few extra minutes to explain the reasons why she was such a success, on screen and off. "Now, scoot . . . or I will be late," she said, tapping the crystal of her gold Cartier watch with a perfect, red varnished fingernail that would match her evening heels. "And I am never late."

Jenna nodded knowingly. "Would you like me to run the errands for you, Ms. Manley? When Mr. Lee phoned this morning he said that under no circumstances should you go out until your new bodyguard arrives."

Alana waved a hand dismissively. "Mr. Lee was a dear friend of my father's when he was alive, and because of that he worries far too much about me. If every well-known person went into seclusion because of a few crank phone calls, there would hardly be anyone on the streets of New York. Besides, this will not take very long, and you know I really like to do these things myself."

"I know," Jenna said. "But I still do not think this date tonight is a good idea, Ms. Manley. You don't even know this man. Maybe you should cancel—"

"Not on your life!" Alana cut in with a musical laugh.

Jenna's reply was an expansive sigh.

Alana shook her head and gave her assistant a sweet smile over one shoulder. "For heaven's sake, stop worrying. James has been my driver for years. He is perfectly capable of handling any situation that might arise, he's an ex-marine. He is also very devoted."

"He is in love with you," Jenna corrected with a raise of her eyebrows.

"Nonsense," Alana said shrugging into her jacket. "He is just lonely, that's all, and enjoys the attention I give him."

Jenna started toward the door. "If you say so, Ms. Manley," she said. But mumbled under her breath, "There is a big difference between being lonely, and being lonely for much too long."

Two minutes later, Alana Manley secured the last huge ruby and diamond earring to her dainty lobe, put on her Foster Grants, and hurried out of her suite.

As she went into the warm July day, she thought it really was a shame that she never stepped more than halfway out onto her balcony overlooking the park, but she was afraid of heights. She had chosen this suite because it was the best. Had she been able to find a penthouse on the first floor, she would have gladly leased it.

James had the limo waiting. "You look stunning, Ms. Manley," he said as he opened the door and waited for her to get in.

"Thank you, James," she said genuinely pleased by the compliment, but not surprised.

Once he had pulled the black limo away from the curb, Alana instructed him to head uptown to a special French bakery. She smoothed a nonexistent wrinkle in her classic DKNY suit and thought about the man she was to meet at the Opera later this evening.

In the handwritten missive delivered yesterday, by a very good looking and impeccably dressed young man who had awaited her reply, Hunter Morgan had simply requested the presence of her company the following evening. And should she accept, he would like her to wear a red velvet gown and wait for him in the small main vestibule of the Metropolitan. They were seeing Verdi's Aida.

Hunter Morgan.

They had never met. Ironic, Alana thought, that he had picked her favorite color as the means by which to recognize her in a veritable sea of fashion.

Alana might not know Hunter Morgan personally, but she knew him by reputation and that was enough for her. In the ruthless world of acquisitions and mergers, he was notorious. A financial genius. A legend. Insatiable womanizer. He was heterosexual, totally. Alana also knew that the Metropolitan Opera House, which opened in 1883, was paid for, in part, by his great-great grandfather who was one of New York's most famous, and infamous, nouveau riche. Today, Hunter was considered one of the most eligible bachelors in the world, if not the most eligible. He lived moment to moment, "The public be damned."

Only one fact emerged consistently from the tabloids.

No one woman had ever captured his heart. Or, his attention for long.

Alana smiled. We'll see who's the hunter and who's the game. I may not be as civilized as you think.

She was, she suddenly realized, looking forward to the possibilities, and only woke from her daze when James brought the limo to a halt. She stepped out and entered the shop. The fragrance of freshly baked brioches was so overpowering that she could not restrain from buying her favorite white-raisin beignet and eating one on the spot. Then, she asked the clerk for two babas su rhums, the ultimate pastry, before directing James to the next destination.

The limo approached the block-long restaurant from the Broadway side, where the cafe was, then turned left at Twenty-sixth Street, pulling up to the main entrance. She stepped through the door and once inside, was immediately greeted by the owner, Charlie Magaddino.

"Ms. Manley," Charlie said as she approached. He took her hands and smiled handsomely. "Always a pleasure, especially when you are alone."

Alana returned his smile. "Kind, as ever," she said. "You are very sweet."

Charlie gazed at her appreciatively. "Your paté de foie gras will be ready in just a moment. If you will excuse me, I will get the bottle of Chambertin you wanted."

Jenna Tucker greeted Alana at the door and took her packages. "I will take care of the food and put the wine to chill. Is there anything else you would like me to do?"

"Yes," Alana said. "Please arrange the jasmine scented candles around the bedroom and turn down the sheets. Oh . . . and do not forget to slip that little something under the pillow."

"No ma'am."

⚜

From a seat by the window on wings of steel, John Pierpont "Hunter" Morgan glanced at the lights over the city as his pilot circled, waiting for clearance to land at LaGuardia.

A half-smile formed around the corners of his mouth as he picked up the remote control and fast-forwarded the videotape until he reached his favorite part. To him, Alana Manley was "sex on a stick," and he would pass the time enjoying the spectacle.

Silently, sipping Dom Perignon, Hunter wondered what she would think if she knew that he had had a video camera installed behind the mirror in her bedroom. That her every movement for the past two months had been secretly recorded. He almost laughed aloud as he recalled how easy it had been to buy the cooperation of the hotel's head of security.

Sometimes the couplings he watched were rough, almost brutal, the men seeming to thrust into her before she was ready, as careless of her pleasure as they would be a whore. But, he thought with satisfaction, those men never returned to her bed.

This one, however, whom Alana called Damian, a tall, muscular man with American Indian features and long dark hair, bound in a meticulous ponytail, had been in her bed several times this month alone. There had been some straight sex, of course, but there had been some interesting variations, too. All of which Hunter was eager to try himself.

The swarthy skinned man was now shirtless and shoeless. Hunter could see his manhood, still restrained by his tight fitting and faded jeans, was hard with erotic desire. When Damian held out his arms to Alana, Hunter could see her nipples were already pointing through the thin silk of her chemise. He immediately felt the corresponding hardness in his member and unzipped the fly of his tuxedo pants to release it.

Smiling to himself, Hunter took one more sip of champagne from the Waterford Crystal flute and watched them undressing each other, deep in the throes of lust. Within seconds they were both naked, and Alana was in her lover's arms.

Her body engrossed Hunter, the lovely skin and the graceful legs, the beautiful face with its full chestnut waves flowing around her shoulders like Renaissance paintings of angels.

When Hunter watched Damian go down on his knees before the dainty auburn V of tight curls that concealed Alana's pink lips that he had no doubt were moist and swollen with readiness, he wrapped his hand around the hard length of his distended cock and stroked until the size surged almost painfully. His eyes shone as he watched Damian lift his head to Alana's breast and let his tongue curl around one nipple and heard her gasp.

Damian then drew his head back at once and Alana groaned with the loss. Her body squirming and crying with the injustice of it all. Damian's white grin was wide and wicked. "I did not hurt you, did I?"

"No," Alana whispered in frustration, breathlessly. "You did not hurt me."

She uttered a sigh as Damian lifted her to the bed and knelt over her. Alana opened her legs wide, but remained passively on her back and quiescent, as he licked her nipple, running his tongue over the hard point until she grasped her breast in her hand and held it to his mouth like an offering and begged for his teeth.

Hunter continued to watch as Damian slowly nipped at Alana's flesh, teeth just grazing the sensitive skin of her areola, but deliberately avoided the jutting peaks of her nipples that were hardened in obvious anticipation of his mouth; her body, arching, and stiffening with its fever. While his tongue tormented her, his skilled fingers worked on her other breast, gently rolling the hard swollen flesh, until she reached between their bodies and found his thick hard sex with her hand.

Damian immediately stiffened and moaned. Reaching down farther, Alana touched his taut sac, softly caressed it with her fingers, his breathing harsh and ragged, and Hunter's body stiffened with hunger. He tugged hard on his sex.

Damn her, he thought furiously, watching Alana lay down on her belly, drawing Damian on top of her. She had everything he wanted, beauty, variety and intensity . . . and her appetite was insatiable. Tonight he would have her, make her plead with him, more than she had ever pleaded with any man for what she craved.

What Hunter saw was stimulating beyond control, and his right hand worked instinctively on his own erection, bringing himself closer and closer to the brink. His breathing turned ragged as he watched Damian draw up and look at Alana's small tight buttocks under him, caress her, then slide his hand under her smooth belly, between her legs, and place that thick hard erection deep into her.

Hunter immediately became engulfed by his own need of Alana's slick opening, her rough little mouth and the warmth inside her. As he watched Damian ride her with one vicious thrust after another, and heard Alana moan against the silk sheets of the bed, Hunter's right hand tightened on his cock, worked the member, abusing his shaft as if he meant to break it off. When he saw Damian jerk in the throws of climax and Alana shudder beneath him, Hunter stiffened and gasped.

The opera house was jammed with congenial noise when Hunter Morgan arrived. A good many people were there whom he recognized immediately, and so was Alana Manley. Her eyes enormous, dark and clear, as she sipped her wine, waiting.

Hunter could see the woman he would be fucking tonight, and for as long as he wanted, was perfectly at ease. He walked forward through the crowd, getting the usual stares from several available women who were none too happy to see him heading for the Hollywood star.

Alana turned at the soft touch on her shoulder and found Hunter Morgan's eyes burning as blue as the heart of a red-hot flame. With a slight movement, and no effort, he pulled her close, against the hard length of him.

Alana's eyes widened and her breath caught in her throat. "Hunter?"

"And so . . . our evening at last begins," he whispered as he kissed her cheek almost nonchalantly, and his fingertips descended to her breasts.

"B-but . . ." Alana protested.

A quick hard kiss instantly silenced her. Then he took her by the elbow and led her up the tight angular main staircase at a good pace.

With her heart pounding she hastened to keep up with him. Hunter Morgan certainly was an appealing figure in his evening clothes, and the thought crossed her mind that they made an attractive pair. But there had been something in the depths of his eyes that she found disturbing. Her feelings for this mysterious and forceful man were definitely mixed. How could she be excited, yet frightened at the same time?

They were among the last people to enter the auditorium and they hurried to their seats in Hunter's private box on the second tier. Alana remained silent, not knowing what to say. He came close then, and kissed her. She did not embrace him as she wanted, but she did slip her tongue between his lips, and for a few seconds their kiss deepened. Then he drew away.

"You're dazzling in red," Hunter said.

"Red is my signature color," she replied with a sensual smile.

Just as they settled in, the houselights faded, and he pulled out a set of foldable glasses and handed them to Alana. She immediately checked out the other boxes around and across from them for familiar faces.

She was looking forward to hearing the beautiful and powerful Leontyne Price sing; her performances were always such a rare treat. But unfortunately she knew that Mayor Rudolph Giuliani's bratty kid—who had been on David Letterman more times than she—would be giving Ms. Price a run for her money tonight. He was already screaming and rolling wildly all over his father's lap.

With a sigh, Alana shifted her gaze to the boxes across from them. She saw Donald and the strumpet from Dalton, Georgia in deep conversation. Then she caught a quick glimpse of a cherry-faced man with red hair sitting in the shadows and realized it was the rather robust Senator Pat Moynahan, whom she liked very much. Just as Luciano Pavarotti, the great tenor, became visible in the wings, the house went black.

When Hunter moved his chair closer to her, Alana received a shock. But, a pleasant shock. When he reached out and cupped the back of her neck in his hand, drawing her face close to his, she was lost. In an instant the atmosphere in the private enclosure was transformed.

Hunter brushed his lips over hers in a slow sensuous way. She wanted to taste him and responded immediately by opening her lips. He kissed her slowly and surely. His warmth flowed through her body; he did not let his lips rest for long. She wanted more. So much more. She shivered and tiny tendrils of excitement snaked their way through her lower stomach. When he moved to the cleavage between her breasts, her nipples hardened and ached. She breathed hard and fast.

Abruptly, he stopped.

"Well," she said, and forced her breathing to slow.

"Do not talk," he said as he pulled the velvet of her gown up over her left knee, over her thigh, and placed his hand beneath it. Reaching between her legs, he brushed his fingers over her garters before sliding them into the crotch of her silk panties. Her clitoris hardened and throbbed sharply.

After a minute Alana obeyed, feeling hopelessly vulnerable as Hunter arranged her gown with his free hand so that to a casual on-looker nothing would seem the least bit out of the ordinary. Then, she finally felt the pads of his surprisingly cool fingers touching her soft lips and a thrill ran through her as she inhaled sharply.

With a crooked grin, Hunter said quietly, "Next time we are to-gether I would prefer that you do not wear panties."

She nodded, but stayed still, holding her breath. Hunter turned and said something cordial to the elderly woman in the box to his left. At the same time he slid a single finger between her wet lips and caressed the swollen bud within at the same time.

Beyond caring, lost in her own lascivious dream world, Alana's sex throbbed and her thighs tightened. When Hunter continued to brush his fingers quickly and cleverly over her opening, slick with desire, it was so tantalizing she almost moaned aloud. The movements of his fingers began to drive her crazy and Alana could do nothing but bite her lower lip to keep from crying out.

She finally gave in and leaned back, closing her eyes. "Just relax," she heard him say.

How could she? Hunter's fingers were flying across her inflamed sex. First rubbing furiously, then flicking and pinching. From a great dis-tance Alana could hear the insistent music of the orchestra as it ac-companied a moving soprano and tenor duet, but was fully aware of Hunter's blue gaze intently staring at her. In a slow movement that was almost imperious, she raised her hips against him in an effort to in-crease the pressure against his hand, but he moved his hand gently away.

Instantly, her gaze met his.

"Not yet," Hunter murmured softly.

"B-But I—" whispered Alana, beseeching him with her eyes.

"I will bring you to climax, but when I decide. And that will not be until much later this evening," he said very softly, but clearly, then lowered his mouth onto Alana's open one.

At Alana Manley's penthouse suite, her chauffeur was not happy. He had wanted to wait for Alana at the opera but she had sent him on his way.

Exactly two seconds after the bell chimed James snatched open the front door. The woman standing in the hall promptly stated her reason for being there and his jaw dropped open. After a moment he placed both hands on either side of the doorjamb and leaned forward as if wanting a closer look.

"You are Ms. Manley's what?"

Kaki looked him in the eye. "Her bodyguard," she said for the second time.

James stared incredulously. "This is a joke, right?"

"No," she said clearly. "This is not a joke. I was hired by Mr. Lee to serve as Ms. Manley's bodyguard. I assumed my arrival was expected."

"Your arrival?" James laughed. "Hardly!"

Forcibly, she kept her temper under control. "My name is Kaki York."

He laughed again. "Khaki? As in the pants?"

"Sort of," she said, irritated. "The spelling is different. And before you ask no, I'm not joking about that either."

James continued to stare as the strawberry blond beauty with the dancing green eyes. She stood in front of him with all the pomp of a seasoned Marine.

The big man shook his head. "Mr. Lee must have lost his mind."

Kaki's face flushed hotly. "I believe you will find Mr. Lee to be in full possession of all his faculties."

James immediately straightened to his full height, which was impressive. "That is a matter of opinion."

She clasped her hands in front of her and took a deep breath. "May I come in?"

He boldly swept her sleek figure with the keen gaze of a connoisseur. "Only if you are here to apply for a job as a secretary."

Kaki smiled indulgently at him, as if she were preparing to speak to a slow child. "I hold a black belt in Taekwondo. Korean Karate," she said easily. "And I served five years as a captain in the United States Navy."

The ex-marine placed his hands on his hips. His glance was piercing. "I am sure that qualifies you to be a very well rounded person, Ms. York. But I do not believe Ms. Manley needs someone who can tie knots and just happens to look good in bell-bottoms. She needs a professional bodyguard."

Kaki stood stiffly; her every muscle tensed. Already exhausted from lack of sleep, the last thing she needed was this big jerk giving her a hard time.

"If necessary, I am prepared to demonstrate my expertise," she said with pleasure.

"Oh, this I have to see," James said with a chuckle. He stepped aside and gestured for her to enter. "Please."

Once inside, Kaki turned to face him. "Now?"

James grinned smugly. "Of course."

In a split second he was on the floor with his face pressed firmly against the cool marble, and his left arm jacked up behind his back in an inescapable hold. Kaki's knee rested firmly against his spine, just between the shoulder blades, and she was pressing a Heckler and Köch 9mm calmly to his right temple.

Having no other choice, James spoke through his teeth to the floor. "I hope that damn thing is not loaded."

Kaki could not help it. She smiled. "I am afraid it is, but I assure you that I have the safety firmly in place."

James made a low sound in his throat. "Thank God for small favors," he mumbled. Then erupted, "Now let me up!"

Kaki's response was immediate. She released her hold on him and with a catlike swiftness. Calmly, she sheathed the 9mm in the holster at her back.

He stood abruptly and faced her. They stared steadily into each other's eye, until James turned his attention to Mr. Lee who was just coming through the front door.

Tommy Lee had witnessed the whole humiliating display. "I see you two have met," he said casually. His gaze shifted to Kaki and he bowed gallantly.

She smiled, widely. "Master Lee . . . Yo-bo-say-yo," she said, respectfully returning his bow before moving forward to give him a big hug.

"Oh joy, you are friends," James said as he righted his clothes. "And she speaks Korean, too." He pinned Lee with an unpleasant look.

"You cannot be serious about hiring a woman to guard Ms. Manley," he snapped, looking more than a little insulted.

Lee remained an undaunted figure in his black silk suit. "She handled you quite well."

"I am not the stalker," James grumbled.

Lee's hooded eyes smiled. "True. If you had been, this unpleasant business would be concluded."

James stiffened.

Lee ignored his reaction and returned his attention to Kaki. He gazed proudly at the slender figure in a navy blazer and jeans. "Kaki was one of my best students. She is a third degree black belt and an ex-Navy Seal. She also spent time stationed in Kuwait during Desert Storm, and served as one of General Norman Swartzkopf's personal bodyguards—"

"I'll just bet," James interrupted, smiling at Kaki wickedly. "A man in Swartzkopf's position no doubt has his perks. And she is definitely a pleasure to look at."

Kaki swallowed her need to tell this man to jump up her ass. "Master Lee, since Ms. Manley does not appear to be in at the moment, I will go and check into my room now."

Tommy Lee sighed. "I am sorry to say that against my advice, Ms. Manley has gone out for the evening, but I would like you to stay for a moment. There are some things the three of us need to go over." He paused to run splayed fingers through his ink-black hair. "You and James will be working closely together. It is important that you establish a good working relationship."

Kaki nodded and the two shook hands guardedly.

Lee focused on James. "I realize that you have been in Ms. Manley's employ a long time and that you care about her a great deal, but who I hire as her personal bodyguard is really none of your business. You are her chauffeur."

The chauffeur? Kaki almost laughed, but suppressed it when she saw James narrow his eyes at her. She would need his cooperation to protect Ms. Manley and she did not need to alienate him any further.

Lee continued, "After threatening phone calls, and the dead cat you found in the limo last week, Ms. Manley needs a personal bodyguard. A good one. Kaki is one of the best in the business. She is also one of the few who have the unique qualifications needed for this assignment."

"Does Ms. Manley know her new bodyguard is female?" James asked.

"She does. And she is quite pleased with my decision," Lee said.

James paced back and forth. Lee stood stolidly. "The dead cat signals the stalker has psychotic aberrations."

James stopped then, leaned against the wall and crossed his arms. "And I suppose she is an expert in that area, too?"

Kaki stood still, her temper simmering. How many times had she gone through this scenario? She was beyond tired of it, but this time refusing to take the position was not an option. She owed Master Lee much. She loved him like a father. No, this obstinate man could give her considerable problems, but she would not refuse to guard Ms. Manley because of him.

She couldn't.

Kaki tensed as she remembered the day she and her sister, Nikki, became orphaned.

"I am here to take you to the county home," the woman from social services had said matter-of-factly, just after the funeral of their parents.

Kaki felt tears rising as she thought about how the cruel fates had left two little girls alone in the world. Her sister and she had been inconsolable, and uncontrollable. No one could handle them. They were shuffled from one foster home to the other, until finally, a judge had ordered them taken to Master Lee. To be taught discipline.

She smiled thinly. They had learned discipline and respect, yes. More importantly, this gentle warrior had taught two little girls to believe in love again. Now grown, both experts in the martial arts, they were secure in the knowledge that as long as Tommy Lee lived, they would never again be alone in the world. She had traded in her ribbons and bows for a karate uniform and learned how to persevere and excel, and even become one of the best of the best. All because of Master Lee. She would not disappoint him now.

"James," Lee said interrupting Kaki's thoughts. "Kaki has experience dealing with this type stalker. What better cover for a bodyguard than posing as Ms. Manley's assistant? A male could hardly do that and go unnoticed."

James reluctantly agreed with a raise of an eyebrow. "Jenna is her assistant."

Tommy Lee did not miss a beat. "And she will continue to be. To any outsiders, Kaki will appear as nothing more than a newly hired employee. In my opinion, if the stalker believes Ms. Manley is unguarded, he . . . or she, for that matter, is more likely to make careless mistakes that could lead to a quick apprehension."

James seemed to hesitate, but nodded.

Kaki closed her eyes briefly, relieved.

Chapter Two

At the Metropolitan, Act III was underway but Alana Manley sat nearly oblivious to the ominous opening. Seconds later as everyone leaned forward to see the stage she only felt the thrill of anticipation. Still aroused by Hunter's bold onslaught, she wiggled in her chair and unconsciously adjusted herself into the best position for stimulating the sensitive area of her ripe flesh.

"You are enjoying yourself I see," Hunter said with the raise of a dark eyebrow, his amusement of her present situation evident by his derisive expression.

He casually leaned back in his chair with a look on his face in which Alana was positive she saw a tinge of devilment. She said nothing in reply and quickly shifted her gaze back to the stage. Much to her surprise he made no further comments, and she was able to put the world aside and enjoy Price and Pavarotti's final duet.

When the lights went up for the last time everyone stood and bellowed bravos, getting a small wave from the performers in return.

At precisely fifteen minutes before midnight Alana and Hunter entered the lobby of her apartment building on Central Park West.

The elevator attendant, with his immaculate white gloves, pressed a button and within seconds they exited on the top floor. Without a word Alana removed a single key on a silken cord from her evening bag. In the dim light, she turned the key in the latch and the scent of jasmine assailed her senses as she preceded Hunter into her penthouse suite.

With a firm grasp on her hand, he stopped her. "I think I have found Paradise."

Alana tilted her head and looked directly at his handsome face, the slightest shadow of facial hair on his jaw. She kept still as her lips curved into a smile. "I have arranged a surprise for you . . . come inside."

Hunter's hand slid up the pale silkiness of her bare shoulder, drifted lightly over her throat, and gently cupped her face. "I would be delighted," he said, then lifted his gaze to the specially set table in the middle of the living room.

Easing her hand free of his hold, Alana lifted her chin so that her gaze softly commanded his. "The food comes much later."

His mouth brushed hers with a light caress, twice. His sweet breath was warm on her face. A moment later they made their way across the marble-tiled foyer. The slow, driving beat of Ravel's Bolero enveloped them as their eyes adjusted to the light. Shimmering candles lit the entire suite and Alana was pleased with the effect.

Following the path that the music set Alana led Hunter into her bedroom. Silently they moved past the turned down bed that was sprinkled with rose petals and into the large bathroom, where long-stemmed white roses in a crystal vase shone through the flickering light.

Alana turned to face him. "Wait here for just a moment and do not undress; I want to do that for you."

"You've planned ahead." Looking intrigued, Hunter smiled and leaned casually against the counter to wait.

"Being prepared saves time," she said in a caressing tone and left him to enter a small dressing room with mirrored walls, though she made certain to leave the door open so that he could have a good view of the show. And he would watch with pleasure, she thought, if the expression on his face was any indication.

She undressed, slipping out of her formal gown without haste. Nude, except for her garter belt and stockings, she slipped her pedicured feet into a pair of high-heeled slippers and wrapped a red silk kimono around her. Without speaking, she went into his arms.

"You are so beautiful," he breathed, rubbing his cheek against hers. He kissed her deeply and pulled the pins, one by one, from her hair until it fell like a fragrant curtain over her shoulders.

"So are you," Alana said, slowly kneeling at his feet and then sliding her hands up Hunter's tuxedo trousers until her fingers closed on the zipper. "Relax," she whispered, opening his fly, smiling up at him as she eased the black material over his lean hips and peeled away his pants. The swish of fabric sliding down his legs was distinct, as was the slap of his trousers hitting the tile of the bathroom wall when he kicked them away.

The white silk of his briefs revealed his erection and Alana smiled to herself.

His gaze from under the fringe of dark lashes was unmoving. Gently grasping his erection through the silky fabric, he ran a practiced hand down its length, and she sucked in a breath as its sized surged on demand. "Then do so, darling," Hunter said in invitation. "I want you to undress me and pleasure me while I watch. I enjoy that," he whispered, then released his gentle grip on his sex and waited.

Alana stared at him, her eyes glazed with sharp desire. "Oh, I will," she assured him. And she was starving for him. The pulsing in her vagina was already spreading a carnal heat upward; her nipples hardened against the cool silk of her wrap, the swollen weight of her breasts tingling.

She began by opening her robe, just a little, to expose the deep cleavage of her full breasts, and then she raised her head and kissed the sensitive flesh of his inner thigh. He unbuttoned his jacket. She held his gaze intently, focused on the deep cleft in his strong chin, the full pout of his lips, his sky-blue eyes, the shiny blackness of his hair— the tanned, sculpted muscles of his torso. Shrugging out of his satin-lapeled jacket, he tossed it aside.

When he pulled his tie loose at the collar and reached for the pearl buttons on his white silk shirt, Alana touched his hand. "I want to do the rest." Her voice was velvet soft.

Hunter exhaled softly and nodded. Again, he rested his hands on either side of himself and gripped the edge of cool marble.

"Good," she murmured with a faint smile, opening the front of her robe fully and releasing her breasts. The cool scented air in the room immediately caused the darker area around her nipples to tighten and wrinkle.

"I like what I see," he said softly.

Alana smiled and lifted her hands to cup her breasts and hold them up, as if offering them to him; the tips of her fingers traced and toyed with her nipples until they were stiff jutting peaks.

Hunter's breathing became labored. He raised a hand to run his palm across the rosy hardness with a feather-light touch. He inhaled deeply. Alana moaned. And seeing the storm that raged in his eyes, she knew then that they would ride the heat of passion like a comet burning both ends of the night. She could hardly wait to feel the hunger of his strong arms, the magnificent hardness of him plundering her intimate feminine flesh. She yearned for him, heated, damp and swollen, was ready for him. But she refused to give into the baser need to expose her soft opening and beg him to take her—no. Hunter Morgan would be the one to beg.

Now Alana moved with conscious effort, slowly running a single finger just inside, and along, the elastic waistband of his briefs. The thick muscles of his hard well-defined thighs tensed, the lean hips too.

She gazed blatantly at his splendid erection, long and thick as it strained against his briefs. Touched it, felt its heat radiating through the soft material.

Hunter sucked in a breath; his head fell back. Her long, cool fingers freed the velvety hardness from its constraints and gently cupped the hanging sac behind, teasingly played with him as she might roll Chinese balls in her hand to relieve the tensions of the day. His body radiated with unreleased passion and it pleased her. She wanted to torture him. Exquisite torture. She knew she had succeeded when he groaned breathlessly, his sex jerked with the intensity of its throbbing blood flow, and he spread his legs wide. The soft tender parts of her swelled unbearably and the inner walls contracted.

With eager anticipation she caressed the taut-capped vermilion head; the supple softness of his firm shaft. Taking the warm hardness in her hand, she wrapped her fingers around its thick width and squeezed—just a little. She raised his strong member then, and pressed her face to the hard, smooth flatness of his lower abdomen, nuzzled the thicket of soft curling dark hair that spread from the root all around his thighs and up in a decreasingly thin line to the navel.

God, he was magnificent, she thought, and devoured his naked charms with her gaze, inhaled his sweet manly scent, laved greedily the sweet bag of nature's sweets beneath with her warm wet tongue. He moaned and closed his eyes. The long muscles of his thighs trembled with anticipation. He shoved his fingers deeply into the soft chestnut waves of her hair.

Alana continued to torment him, her hands making endless movements to caress and stimulate his genitals. When his hanging sac became taut between his thighs, drawn up in pleasing wrinkles, her lips nipped, kissed, and traced it as her fingers ran lightly up the sensitive branched vein and down the full length of him until his hips were inching up toward the warmth of her mouth.

He reached down and took a breast in each hand, rolled the nipples simultaneously between thumb and forefingers, and an answering pull tugged deep within her stomach. Her sex instantly filled with a rush of hot moisture; she inhaled deeply of the scent of their mingled arousal heavy in the air. Knowing she did not want to go further now, she forced herself to move away and took a deep cleansing breath.

"Are you not as hot for me as I am for you?" he demanded as he dragged her up from her knees and into his strong embrace.

She sucked in a quick breath at the jarring sensations he evoked within her being. "Oh, yes," she said instantly. "But first . . . I want to bathe you."

He ran his warm palm up her neck and cupped the back of her head. "Do you?"

Straightening, she stood before him, and raised her emerald gaze to meet his so far above. "Very much so," she said, and without protest Hunter allowed her to remove the rest of his clothing, kissing every inch of him as she did.

"I've never had a lover bathe me," Hunter said. "You intrigue me, Alana Manley, in many ways." Bending his head low, his lips touched hers lightly before gently sliding his tongue over them, which sent a shocking bolt of lightning deep down inside her. So hot was the strike that Alana moved away from him. Abruptly his hand tightened on her back and pulled her close again with an authority that left her with no doubt who was in command, and it remained firmly pressed against the base of her spine.

"Do with me as you will, darling," Hunter said, reaching out to slide the pad of one finger across the tops of her breasts. "But please, take your time."

Then, in the flickering candlelight, Alana saw his tattoo. She blinked. It was fascinating—a small Bengal tiger expertly depicted in full color and waiting to pounce on his left shoulder. Oddly, she had never made love to a man with a tattoo before and it was wildly arousing. She traced its outline with a sculpted nail, kissed it wetly and ran her tongue across the length of it.

He placed a finger beneath her delicate chin and lifted her face to his. "I am, after all, the hunter," he said cutting into her thoughts.

Alana's wide eyes gazed up at him. "I guess so." The words rode on a breathless whisper.

She left him then to run his bath, adding rose petals and a foamy azure liquid from an antique frosted glass decanter. She picked up the champagne bottle from the iced bucket nearby, leaned over and poured him an icy glass of wine. "You will enjoy this much more after a few glasses of champagne." Handing it to him, she patted the water.

With the raise of a dark eyebrow, he stepped into the scented bath and relaxed in the tub. "Won't you join me?" he gently queried.

"No . . . not this time. I have some other things I need to do."

"Ah, more surprises," he said, smiling at her across the candlelit space. "Then I won't keep you." he finished in a low whisper.

Turning, she headed for the door, and then, looking back over her shoulder, quietly said, "Don't start anything without me."

He laughed. "I wouldn't think of it. Besides, it might be frustrating for you to watch."

Alana agreed.

She returned a few minutes later carrying a small sterling silver serving tray filled with white mushroom caps that were stuffed with glistening caviar. And as Hunter lay back and soaked in the soothing warmth, she finger-fed him the appetizer.

Later, after she had soaped his body and shampooed his hair, she wrapped his naked body in the cleanest, softest white terry-cloth robe. Reaching up on tiptoe, she kissed him. His searing blue gaze scanned her face and his arms pulled her tightly against him.

"Not yet," she said and wiggled out of his embrace.

Hunter's dark brows rose slightly. She poured him another glass of champagne. Slipping her hand in his free one, she led him into the living area where they would eat a late supper and gestured toward the finely set table. "There is room at my table. Why don't you pull up a chair?"

His eyes lit up and his expression was one of pleasure. His brushed her cheek with his fingers. "I would be delighted." Taking a seat, he set the crystal glass aside. "My appetite is both voracious and wholesome."

She laughed musically. "I would not want it any other way."

As Alana bent to light the single candle in the delicate holder there was no mistaking the look in his eyes. Then with a wink she disappeared into the kitchen.

Expelling a pleasant sigh, she thought that all men, if they were truthful with themselves, wanted a woman to be a lady in the living room and a whore in the bedroom. And she intended this night to be a perfect blend of ecstasy and lust.

Five minutes later, she returned with the petits de foie gras and Chambertin from Charlie Maggadino's restaurant. Placing them before Hunter, she took her seat and gazed out at the summer night, with its magic moon, through the sliding glass doors that led to the balcony.

She was about to shift her gaze back to him when she caught a definite glimpse of a shadow cutting the bright moonbeam's path in two. Someone was out on the patio. She froze, then the wind howled. She shook her head. How silly she thought—her suite was the penthouse, her balcony over a hundred feet straight up—it had only been the clouds riding on the wind. Suddenly thunder rumbled in the distance and she stared at Hunter. "It looks as if a summer storm is coming."

"I believe it is already here," he said, "and I intend to try in every way to make it roll out of control." His wicked grin caused them both to smile.

For the next hour, they ate and laughed and kissed across the table. When they were finished, Alana slowly and deliberately glided over to the CD player on the other side of the room and changed the disk. To the seductive tune of Kenny G's saxophone, she padded her way across the wool carpet and back to Hunter. She slipped out of her kimono, and let it fall. Leaving it in a lovely heap on the floor, she drew him by the hand and into the bedroom.

Motioning for him to join her in bed, Alana slid her hand under the pillow and pulled out two silk scarves. Hunter did not hesitate. He removed his robe and tossed it on a gilded chair. Lying next to her now, he clasped his hands behind his head and settled his back comfortably against the satin covered feather pillows.

Reaching over to finger the long lengths of red silk she held loosely in her grasp, he asked, "Are those for me or you, my darling?"

She looked back at him, her emerald glance direct in his heated gaze, and saw a blaze of desire as blue as the center of a hot flame smoldering in his eyes.

"Which would you prefer?"

He hesitated for a moment, as if undecided. "I think, sweet Alana," he said, turning on his side to face her and sliding his foot between her legs, "this time I will let you decide and set the pace . . ."

She arched a finely shaped auburn brow and scooted forward, which enabled her to apply more pressure to the top of his foot and her swollen clitoris at the same time. "I told you that red was my signature color," she purred as she trailed the silk scarves along the inside of his muscular thighs and over his enormous erection.

Hunter shifted his gaze to her pale pink garters. "Every shade, I see."

His insistent arousal was hard and huge like his body. She kept her gaze riveted to the ostentatious display as she placed her hands on his shoulders and urged him to lie on his back again. Then she straddled him. Supporting herself on her knees, she placed a scarf in each hand and knelt above his rigid length. Heat radiated between their bodies. His strong hands spanned her waist; he lifted her, guided his erection toward her drenched vulva. When she locked her elbows and held her bottom fast in its raised position, stopping him short of penetration, his fingers dug into her buttocks. "Now what are you up to?"

"Wait and see," she whispered. She bent down to nip his lower lip with her teeth. "I want to play a little game," she said. "You are up for it, aren't you?"

Hunter's stiff instrument remained pointed to the opening of her slick sex as surely as a divining rod to water. He first gave his searing member an intent perusal, then directed his attention to the succulent double pout between her legs and jammed his fingers inside her, hooked them on her pelvic bone and pulled her up so she was almost raised off her knees. "What do you think?"

She glanced downward and grinned. "Is this going to be my choice, or not?"

He pulled his fingers out so abruptly she almost lost her balance and impaled herself on his erection. "I'm willing . . . this time, but there is something you need to know." His eyes were an icy-blue, hovering for a moment as he raised his drenched fingers and touched them to her lips. "If I'm not pleased—fully—I will punish you. And enjoy every minute."

Alana opened her mouth, snatched his fingers between her teeth and sucked her essence from them. When she released them, she smiled fully, then ran the tip of her tongue across her white even teeth. "Agreed," she said without a single reservation. "I choose that I am now the hunter . . . and you are the game. You must do as I say and obey my every command, but I promise I will not hurt you," she said with a mischievous grin on her full red lips.

Hunter threw back his head and laughed.

But he stopped when she took his wrist and quickly and efficiently tied one of the scarves around it, then brought it up to thread the red silk through the brass headboard before securing his other wrist to it. Once she had him tied securely to the headboard and was certain that he was propped up nicely against the pillows, she unstraddled him and left the bed.

"Where are you going?" he demanded.

Alana stood next to the bed gazing down at his full, straining arousal and then shifted to his face. "Wouldn't you like me to entertain you?"

"In this bed," he said without amusement.

Alana shook her head and smiled back over her shoulder as she walked away. "Not yet."

First she picked up her vanity stool and positioned it at the end of the big bed and in front of a full-length wall mirror. She placed one foot on it allowing Hunter a clear view of both her backside and her front in the flickering candlelight as she removed the high-heeled slipper, unhooked her stocking from the pink lace garter, and slowly rolled it down one shapely leg. Then she took the transparent ribbon of silk and tossed it at his feet.

Hunter tensed on the bed. His sex was so firm, sculpted like his body, and she felt like jumping on top of him and riding him, but it was too soon. He had not begged her yet. But he will, she thought with pleasure.

"Enough of this game, Alana, come here," he said in a not-to-be-denied tone.

"Not yet," she said again softly and placed her other foot on the stool and went on to repeat the same motions as before, removing her other stocking. Unhooking her garter belt she sighed and allowed it to slip slowly from her waist to the floor.

Hunter groaned and instinctively tried to sit up, but was held fast to the headboard by the thin silk bindings. He jerked the bindings again in frustration but did not say a thing.

Alana gave him a seductive smile and placed her palms on the seat cushion, thrusting her bottom high in the air. Her full breasts dangled beneath her. His gaze immediately focused on the arousingly inviting reflection in the mirror of her firm buttocks and the plump moist slit down the center.

Leaving one hand on the stool for support, she slowly slid the other up the inside of one thigh before threading it between her legs, allowing it to rest only after she had slipped her middle finger deep inside her. She groaned and her head lulled a little to the side, her nipples hardened visibly.

She looked at Hunter through huge eyes glazed with desire. For a moment the throbbing heartbeat of Hunter's stiff member entranced Alana.

"You agreed this night was my choice." She paused for a short time to move her finger slowly in and then out of herself; she arched her back at the pleasure it brought. "I only wish to give you pleasure. Surely you agree that the greater the desire, the greater the pleasure."

Hunter's muscular hips involuntarily jerked, seeming to search for what she was intentionally denying him as he watched her fingers in the mirror, glistening wetly, again slip out of the heated entrance to his paradise and begin to pluck and play with the swollen bud of her pleasure.

Alana did not stop pleasuring herself when she asked, in a breathless whisper, "Do you truly want me to stop? Would you go back on your word now?"

"I never go back on my word," he ground out through clenched teeth.

She smiled in a wickedly seductive way. "I thought not. If I come to you . . . will you let me do as I like with you—however I like—and without protest?"

He said no more, only nodded.

Alana had known he would, and she could see from the state of his arousal he wasn't at all opposed to the idea.

She moved then to the end of the bed and climbed his hard body like a tree. This time she not only heard, but also felt his deep muffled cry of frustration.

In the rented suite just across the hall that evening, Kaki York could not watch the monitor one more second. She flipped it off, and the other four too. Raking a hand through her hair, she seriously wondered if she could handle this assignment after all. Twenty-four-hour surveillance had suddenly taken on a whole new meaning.

At first she had been thrilled to find Master Lee had installed a high-tech security system that enabled them to monitor Alana Manley's movements by way of hidden cameras strategically placed throughout her penthouse. She had agreed that they would have a much better chance of catching this psychopath if she was not seen as being joined to Ms. Manley by the hip day and night, dogging her every move. But now, she would have preferred to be sleeping on the hall floor outside her front door to watching her sexual escapades . . . more to the point, that man's . . . on a full color screen.

So, she thought, this was what Tommy Lee had meant when he had said that Alana Manley's drug of choice was men. Dear God, she hoped this would not go on every night—she would never survive.

Kaki was so lost in thought that she never noticed Jenna Tucker ease in the room, only to walk away in disgust—or heard James Kulick come into the room to relieve her.

At the sound of James' voice, she nearly jumped out of her skin. He looked so different from the way he had looked in his chauffeur's uniform. Propped against the door jam with his arms crossed over the wide expanse of his chest, he was dressed in faded jeans, a black denim shirt and cowboy boots. He looked rumpled and windblown, but handsome.

"Some bodyguard," he said with dripping sarcasm. "The monitors are off and you did not even hear me come in."

Kaki bristled. "Maybe you enjoy voyeurism, but I do not," she said with enough force to cause James to arch a dark eyebrow. "Nevertheless, I will try to do better in the future." She nervously wiped her palms on the seat of her jeans. "I am a bit overtired at the moment. Are you here to take over the watch?"

He nodded. "That's what I'm being paid for."

Kaki stood with a brief sigh and a yawn. She picked up her nine-millimeter off the desktop and returned it to her shoulder holster. "Wake me at six. We need to check Ms. Manley's suite for security leaks before meeting with Tommy Lee to discuss what else needs to be done," she said and brushed quickly past him, heading straight for a cold shower and bed. Over her shoulder, she said, "Enjoy." Her voice held the smallest hint of huskiness.

James yelled after her, "Pleasant dreams." His deep voice held a derisive tone.

She absolutely refused to respond.

"Are you still hot for me?" Alana asked as she pressed her pelvis hard against Hunter's already painfully distended erection.

His eyes were heated, restless. "Yes."

She slid her hand between them and pressed her fingers to her pulsing labia. Shifting beneath her, he groaned as the back of her hand touched the heavy weight of his testicles. She moved from her position and slid her legs between his outspread legs, kneeling above him. "Do you want me to touch you?"

"Only immediately," he said with a grin.

His perfectly formed penis stood rigidly upright. She touched him delicately, tentatively, as if he were a rare jewel that held the secrets to her unquenchable thirst for the rare hard stone before her. She ran the tip of her finger up and down the bulging veins, the moist, glistening slit at the tip, the swollen hard taut globes drawn up tightly against the root.

Lifting his hips, he made a sound in his throat, a low growl, as she lifted the shaft to better stoke the velvety skin. With him bound and unable to respond in kind, it gave her a sense of power to see him strain for her touch. She watched his erection swell even more, the dark pink peak stretch its skin to what looked like the breaking point, his pulse quickened and forced out the transparent droplets of arousal.

He sucked in a harsh breath when her tongue flicked over the tip, then curled into her mouth as she tasted his salty essence with leisurely decadence. Her mouth hovered the merest breath away from the little ridge of skin where the shiny red head was joined to the shaft. "Are you in a hurry to be inside me?" she whispered, then enveloped his penis with her mouth and held it, not moving, but hugging it like a snug vagina.

He could barely think. It took him a moment to catch his breath, to speak. "I don't want to wait much longer."

Thumb and forefinger encircled his sex, and she moved her hand up and down the shaft in the same rhythm as she sucked the tip of his sensitive head. With the other hand she used mild finger movements over his testicles. When she stopped, he groaned in frustration.

She rose up then and kneaded his strong chest muscles with her hands, her fingers rolled and tugged the small hard nipples—her lips kissed and sucked. "Do you want to be inside my mouth . . . or plumb the depths of my inner passage?"

He opened his mouth to speak, but she quickly pressed the pad of her index finger to his lips, stopping him. "You may choose either place, but I won't let you come in my mouth."

"Do me," he said huskily.

"But what do you want me to do?" she asked.

"Anything you want. Everything you want."

"What if I want you to do me first?"

"Come here then," he said to her.

Instantly she moved over his chest until positioned just a few inches above his face, with her knees planted on either side of his head. Almost ready to burst, she moved herself down so that she was directly over his mouth, so close that she could feel the warmth of his labored breath on her clitoris.

She moaned and gazed down at his handsome face; she used her fingers to open herself wide for him. "Open your mouth and lick me . . . suck me."

"With pleasure" he said, and then his tongue, long and pointed, snaked out and lashed the sensitive area of skin that marked the pathway to her pleasure. She reveled in the rough wetness of his tongue skimming across her clitoris repeatedly, his teeth nipping, she rotated her hips and groaned loudly. The faster he licked, the harder her fingers dug into his hard muscled shoulders. When he took her fully into his mouth and sucked the hardened and protruding nub as if milking her passions—from far inside her a guttural cry escaped, a desperate whimper of passion and she was off his face and scrambling down his body to reach his thick, throbbing member.

Quickly straddling his hips, she roughly shoved his stiff sex inside her, slid down the full length of him, stopping only when her groin met his. He cried out in savage grunts from the searing pleasure.

She drew air into her labored lungs, sweat beaded on her forehead, between her breasts. Wanting him beyond the power to comprehend, she began to ride his hardness and his erection quickened with the first pumps of pre-orgasm.

"No! Slow down," he growled, his body barely in check. He held his breath, closed his eyes, and focused his mind on everything but the carnal urgency that had taken control.

She stopped her movement. "I want to come now," she said on a suffocated breath and leaned forward to brush sensitive nipples across his wet lips. He responded by sucking first one then the other greedily.

Licked and bit them until she could stand it no longer and pulled her breasts away. "I want you now, right now," she said and threw her head back. As she did so she gripped him, feeling his ribs under her palms, and rotated her pelvis shamelessly against his groin, controlling his penis to such a degree that she flipped the head against her cervix, amplifying the pleasurable sensations to the extreme.

His gaze pinned hers. "Now then, hurry," he growled raggedly, already beginning to ejaculate. "Damn you!"

She gripped his rigid sex with her interior muscles and began sliding back and forth toward his shoulders, faster and faster, with an almost rough, brutal vengeance until she climaxed, her scream echoing in the sumptuous candlelit room. He cried out from the pleasurable pain and eagerly thrust his pelvis to meet her desperate movements until his back arched, his eyes shut and he gushed into her.

Alana's body was aglow with sensual heat when she released Hunter's wrists from their silk bindings and fell into his strong embrace.

Lying in a cocoon of pillow and satin sheets, he shook his head and smiled. He tightened his arms around her. He said, "Next time, darling, you will suffer the torments of the damned before I allow you release."

She snuggled more deeply into the crook of his arm. "I look forward to it."

Chapter Three

Four hours, and a cold shower later, James Kulick was still as eager and edgy as a tomcat on the prowl. And, if that was not enough to put him in a foul mood, his hand still hurt like hell from when he had punched the wall.

He pressed his fingers to tired eyes. Alana's way of life with her constant parade of lovers had always irritated him, but until now, he had never had to see it so . . . up close and personal. He could, of course, just tell her how he felt. And he'd be wasting his breath. He wondered how much more it would take to make her stop. Now eyeing the fresh set of scraped and bruised knuckles, he swore. Alana Manley was going to drive him over the proverbial edge.

Kulick shook his head. He was relieved Alana's assistant had arrived at work on time this morning, and that keeping an eye on Alana was now her responsibility for a while. He was a bundle of raw nerves; he needed a break. After glancing at his wristwatch, he turned and stepped out of the bathroom.

Drying his wet head with a towel, he went into the living room. Past the kitchen, and down the hall he found Kaki's bedroom. He knew she had picked this one before he saw the suitcase on the floor. He'd smelled her, as a predator does his prey.

Maybe it wouldn't be so bad working with her after all.

The door was not shut, so he pushed it all the way open and plowed in to wake her—at least that had been his intention. Instead, he froze just on the other side of the doorjamb.

As stunned as if he had been hit with a two-fisted punch, he scanned the enticing buffet of femininity laid out before him on top of crisp white sheets. There was hardly any resemblance to the woman he had seen just a few hours ago. This woman was one of slender, voluptuous grace; he was awed by the unexpected and sumptuous display.

A spiking surge of lust ripped through his senses. A droplet of sweat slid down his temple and his still semi-aroused member shot as hard as a woodpecker's lips. He touched the throbbing ache at his groin. He wanted her. All of her.

Just as instantly, he realized what he had been thinking was crazy.

He told himself that he would have been able to set his thoughts aside if . . . if Kaki York had not been lying on her stomach with only a short slip of a gown to hide her curves, which also happened to leave her long slender legs completely bare. His mouth tightened.

James stood for a long time and watched her sleeping in the mellow light of early morning, struck suddenly by the reality of her beauty, noting her soft, metered breathing; that her right cheek rested on the white cased pillow her arms were tucked beneath. She was an arresting sight with her red-gold waves starkly flowing in casual disarray on her pale shoulders and her shapely little rearend in clear view.

Weary and frustrated, he groaned inwardly and then shook it off, forcibly took back control of his wandering mind. He smiled a little— just a quirk at the corner of his mouth. His careful steps muffled by heavy carpet, he approached the bed and stopped at the edge.

Taking one end of the damp towel in each hand, he spun it tight, and took aim. When he let it fly, snapping the terrycloth in a "crack the whip" fashion at just the right moment, the homemade weapon hit right on target.

"Bull's-eye."

Kaki shrieked in pain from the solid whack to her bottom and sprang to her feet with amazing speed for a person who had been deeply asleep just seconds ago. But having already witnessed just how fast she could react, James was not too surprised. Still, he was shocked that she had cocked her automatic weapon and aimed at his head in the same amount of time.

She must have been sleeping with the damn thing. Okay, so he was impressed—a little.

Under the circumstances he dropped the offending weapon at once and raised both hands high in the air in mock surrender.

"All right, I'm sorry. Now you can put the gun down." He stared directly down the cold steel barrel of her nine-millimeter.

Kaki murmured something he could not quite make out before she eased the hammer back in place, flipped on the safety, and lowered the weapon. Not unaware, but certainly unconcerned that James was a man of considerable size, she advanced on him with determination. When she reached the object of her wrath, she stood on tiptoe so that she could look him directly in the eye.

Then she jabbed a finger in the middle of his wide chest.

"Ow!" He feigned injury.

She poked him in the chest again—harder—and he gave her an I-can't-believe-you-did-that-look.

"Let me tell you one damn thing, you giant flaming jackass . . . If you so much as even think of doing that to me ever again, I swear to God that I will shoot you dead without a second thought."

James almost laughed but thought better of it, then his gaze shifted from her face and slowly drifted to her heaving milky-white cleavage. When he saw a red flush spread up her slender neck and flame on her high-boned cheeks, he lifted a brow. "You, blushing?"

She said nothing. Slowly she breathed deeply, as if trying to gain some semblance of composure, but her gaze remained steady. He liked that—a whole lot. Because, for some reason, he was positive only a privileged few had ever seen Kaki York flustered.

He raised a hand and fingered his chin thoughtfully for a moment. "Well, I have to say that you don't exactly look like a natural born killer, sweetheart."

Despite her state of undress, her gaze stayed cool and level. "Neither did Lizzy Borden," she said. "So don't push your luck, big guy."

He laughed this time and shot her a look that said he was not all that intimidated by her threat. Folding his arms, he ran an appreciative gaze over her compact figure that was barely hidden by the thin layer of silk.

She sighed. Men were so predictable.

Kaki held up her hand like a stop sign. As an ex-naval officer with five years' experience as a member of an otherwise all-male special forces' unit, she had learned to recognize the signs, confront the problem before it got out of control, so all involved could return to the business at hand.

"Wait, don't tell me," she said with an absent wave of her hand. "The wet hair—the towel. I've got it. You've just had a cold shower and it didn't work. You're still hot and bothered from viewing Ms. Manley's Sexual Olympics. And—" she crossed her arms and tapped a finger on her lips "you want to go to bed with me."

James stepped forward and slipped his arms around her. "That about sums it up."

She had to tilt her head back to meet his dark gaze. "You don't even like me and yet you want to screw me."

He shrugged and flicked a finger down her hair. "One has nothing to do with the other. I want you, Kaki, and I want you bad. Now, why don't you admit that you want me, too."

Her eyes narrowed as she stared at him. "With you?" Kaki snorted. "In your dreams, Kulick."

She broke free, turned, and shoved splayed fingers through her tumbledown hair. Irritation scored deep between her finely shaped brows as she placed her weapon on the nightstand.

With resolve, she went over to the chair, yanked on her robe, nearly cutting off her breathing in belting the sash too tight, and watched James advance. She glared at him. An attractive man in a rugged sort of way, she thought objectively. Nicely built, and definitely not unappealing, even if he was a bit rough around the edges. A pity he was such a horse's ass.

"Sorry, James. I am not interested. Besides, we have work to do. I'm taking a shower. When I'm finished we can go over every inch of Ms. Manley's apartment for security leaks. I'm sure there are only about a million and one." Kaki's voice was flat as she turned and headed toward the bathroom.

But he was not giving up that easily. He was hard with lust.

He followed her across the room and took her in his arms again. "Alana won't be out of bed until way past noon. Believe me, I know. And Jenna's with her now. We have plenty of time to finish what we started."

"We haven't started anything, James." She slapped his hands and shoved his arms away. "I have no intention of having anything to do with you sexually. All I have to do is work with you."

She only sighed when he placed a hand on her shoulder, preventing her from putting any distance between them.

"Come on, Kaki, you didn't wear a nightie like that to bed for no reason. You knew I would be turned on after watching that little scene in Alana's bedroom. And seeing you like this makes me hotter," he lowered his head and murmured against her ear.

His warm breath sent a shiver down her spine, and she could feel him stiff and rigid against her bottom, which caused a passionate fluttering deep in her stomach. Appalled at her reaction to the feel of his body against hers, her mood took a decided turn for the worse. Now, she was no longer mildly irritated—she was pissed.

Keeping her back to him, she said, "I did not wear this gown in the hopes that a longshoreman wanna-be would feel me up while I was asleep."

Anger glinted in her voice, and . . . something else that she did not care to identify. But the quick elbow to his ribs had him coughing up a breath and allowed her to break free. She tossed her hair back and walked over to the nightstand to retrieve her weapon. Without hesitation she turned to face him, took steady aim, and calmly pulled back the hammer.

She took a step closer. "Keep it up, and the question of whether or not I will continue to work with you and not mention this unfortunate incident to Master Lee will be the least of your worries. I will shoot your dick off."

"For God's sake, Kaki, calm down."

"Funny, that's exactly what I was going to suggest to you."

James set his massive shoulders. "Fine."

Saying nothing, Kaki watched him lean against the chest of drawers and cross his arms over the wide expanse of his chest. She hadn't expected him to give up that easily, but she was so relieved that she didn't think to question his motives. Lowering the revolver she sat heavily on the edge of the bed.

James Kulick. A dangerous man for her to be alone with, she thought. She hadn't simply felt anger when he had snapped her rearend with a wet towel and then taken her in his arms. She hadn't felt anything she could remotely describe as simple. And then, when he had pressed the hard length of his erection to her, what she'd experienced was nothing short of a primal soul-searing arousal.

What in the world was the matter with her? This kind of thing did not happen to her. Gut-deep, red-hot arousal for a man she hardly knew and was positive she didn't like? This was insane, she told herself. The entire situation was insane—that was the problem—and her involvement with these people had only just begun.

Suddenly, she had the distinct feeling that if she didn't get the hell-out-of-Dodge, and fast, she'd be sucked into this . . . this . . . decadent world of sexual debauchery in which Alana Manley obviously reigned as queen—with all the mesmerizing force that Alice was drawn through the looking glass by the White Rabbit.

With a groan she fell back on the mattress and covered her eyes with a forearm. When she removed it two seconds later to see if James had left the room, he was just pushing off the dresser. And his state of arousal was undeniably evident. She would have had to be blind not to see his erection, hard and straining against his denim jeans.

She could have gotten up, used her gun—used any one of the defensive, or offensive moves that were as much second nature to her as breathing. Even if she was feeling a small surge of curiosity, even of lust, she could ignore it. She'd done it before. But as she watched him approach her with fascination, she didn't want to fight the clouding of her senses. But why?

Kaki had no idea.

"Why don't we start over?" James drawled.

Blood pounded hotly in her temples. She didn't answer, but she didn't say no either. That surprised them both.

If she had, he might have stopped. Maybe. Maybe . . . she didn't want him to.

His gaze drifted from her face to her breasts. One glance like that from him, and her insides began to melt. She could feel the sudden rise of her chest as she began breathing just a bit more quickly. Damn him! she thought. Why didn't he just go away? Her nipples hardened against her negligée. His gaze on her like a caress while the cool silk clung to her body. Her face hardened.

Wearing this gown had been a mistake. A big mistake. Huge.

She immediately jackknifed into a sitting position and he came to stand in front of her. Though her gaze was focused on something other than his face, she could feel him gazing down at her. Assessingly. Lasciviously. She tilted her head back to look into his eyes. He was just kneeling.

"Enjoy the view?" she taunted him, desperately trying not to let him see how his nearness affected her.

There was a tawny glint in his deep brown eyes and dimples appeared in his tanned cheeks. "Love the view," he said in a new and almost silky voice. Then took the gun out of her hand and set it aside.

She did not protest; she was more concerned with the feel of blood rushing to her face. Why was her body doing this to her?

James gave her no time to think. He reached out and cupped the back of Kaki's neck in his hand, drawing her face close to his. She gasped at the surge of heat that rushed through her traitorous body, touching parts of her she had forgotten existed.

He pulled her to him, brushed his lips over hers in a slow, sensuous way, and what was left of her control vanished. She responded almost immediately by lifting her cheek to his. He kissed her again, slowly and surely. When he eased her back on the bed and stretched his long length out beside her, Kaki began breathing hard and fast.

A tremulous silence hung between them. James was pressing against her. He caught her confused, frightened glance and held it.

"J-James, no . . . stop let me up—"

"Don't talk."

She tried to get up. Ignoring her wishes, he caught her shoulders, pushed her down on the bed and slipped the thin straps of silk from her shoulders, exposing her, and kissing the soft pink skin of her breast. She half-closed her eyes and her head lulled to one side. He touched a nipple and it came erect and hard; he pinched it, rolled it between his fingers. Her lips parted and a sigh escaped, her breath came unevenly, her body trembled with lust under his touch. He cupped her other breast in his hand and squeezed. Her stomach jolted.

It was as if her body had an existence—needs all its own and she had no control over how she responded. Reason no longer existed. She could only focus on wanting him, needing him, feeling the long hard length of him inside her.

"I want you," he said plainly, as if there was ever a doubt in her mind.

"I-I shouldn't. We—"

"But you do—and we will," he said.

He bent his head and kissed her breasts, kneaded her nipples, took them into his mouth. He sucked gently at first, and then with forceful pleasure until they swelled into distended rigid jewels . . . until, she could stand it no longer and arched her back like a cat in heat.

"Don't you?" he asked as his mouth trailed over her breasts, then her stomach. He slipped his hand between her thighs and lightly skimmed her moist opening with his knuckles.

Kaki cried out, her back arched. Her legs fell open, but when she lifted her hips in an unconscious attempt to increase the pleasurable pressure with his hand, he removed it. She groaned and her hips jerked at the loss.

"Don't you?" he asked again, with more force this time. She squeezed his arm.

"Say it," he demanded.

When she still didn't respond quickly enough, he snaked a hand slowly up the sensitive skin of her inner thigh until he reached the apex of her need. She bit her lip in anticipation of the pleasure of his touch, breathing in the scent of her own arousal. It didn't come. His fingers barely brushed the soft, damp curls around and above her intimate flesh.

Her green eyes opened wide and she forced herself not to squirm. "Why are you doing this?"

"If you want me, say so," he demanded in a husky tone.

"I want you. I can't bear it any longer."

He probed at her entry, cupped her, making tiny caressing circles with the callused pad of a finger over her erect clitoris. A mist of perspiration broke out on her brow. He took his hand away. A tremor rocked her slender frame. Her lips parted in a gasp. She peered at him intently, her emerald eyes ablaze with unfulfilled passion.

"Where do you want me?" He grazed a hard jutting nipple with his teeth. She moaned; he bit down and sucked. Fire surged through her.

"Inside me," she gasped.

Only then did he release the hard pink tip abruptly and lick it, once. "No, not yet," he said.

Her clitoris throbbed in protest, her vagina contracted. Then, she felt his hands moving down to her waist, her hips, removing her gown altogether. In seconds, she lay completely naked on the bed, the air cool around her. She smelled the sandalwood from his heated body and her nudity was suddenly exciting to her under his gaze. He rose to his knees and placed a pillow under the small of her back so that her breast and belly and thighs formed a smooth slanting line.

"Stay," he murmured in a deep low voice. She did, and an undisguised desire met his eyes.

He stood up, turned his shirt over his head with one hand and tossed it on the floor. His sable gaze caressed hers, promising to fulfill her every dream as he removed his socks and boots, ripped open his jeans, stripped them and his briefs down to his feet. She rose up, braced herself on her elbows, and through the haze of her growing excitement she gazed at his dark handsomeness, his brooding, moody eyes, that held her captive.

Straightening before her, James was uncaring of his nudity and her gaze was inexorably drawn to his rampant erection. His engorged penis stood proud and taut, the ridged head broad and swollen, reaching almost waist high. She had never wanted anything so badly in her life. Her vagina shot heat upward and a rush of liquid heat skimmed downward through her inner walls that opened. She swallowed, opened her mouth to speak, shut it again.

"Do you want me?"

She didn't answer, but he waited, stroking the softness of her inner thighs.

Moments later she breathed, "Yes." She had to have him now. Passion and a hot-blooded need overrode her doubts, nothing mattered but putting out the fire he had ignited in her very soul.

Gently grasping his erection, he ran a practiced hand down its length. "You are sure you want me," he said placing his legs on the inside of hers. She thought she would die. When he gently pushed her thighs farther apart, she lifted her hips, tentatively seeking relief from the burning desire.

He didn't come to her; he arched a dark eyebrow in question.

"Yes, I want you," she whispered, then his fingers touched her heated entrance and dipped softly into her lush wetness, aching and swollen for him. She gasped, shivered, her skin rising up in goosebumps.

His lips curled into a seductive smile. "You are so hot," he said softly, stroking gently, sliding his expert fingers inside her.

She gasped, her head fell back. In a second he was on top of her, his impossible hardness resting smooth and hot against the wet mouth of her sex, with a hand braced on either side of her head. Her fingers wound their way into his thick hair. She moaned, her hips rose. His mouth came down on hers roughly, his tongue powerful in its onslaught. She devoured the taste of him.

"I can't wait," he said in a husky rasp as he reached down and eased her apart with expert fingers. Her breath caught in her throat. "Are you ready for me?"

"Umm," she breathed, her lips quivering softly.

He gave her a crooked, rueful smile. Spreading her legs wide with his knees, he fitted the tip of his penis to her. With control he slipped in and out, moved the swollen head of his erection over her hard slippery crest, teasing her repeatedly until she too whimpered and moaned, rotating her hips, lifting them, trying to draw him deep inside her.

Her body was so near orgasm it was rigid under his, and he could no longer control himself. He thrust solidly into her, as deeply as he could possibly go. She cried out at the tight heat that flared all the way to the pit of her stomach; her arms twined around his strong solid neck desperately and pulled him tightly to her. He penetrated her in an increasingly deepening rhythm until she became feverish beneath him, thrusting her hips up to meet each new, driving invasion of her body. Clinging to him, she cried out his name and he moaned. Her fingers tangled in his hair, he drove in deeper and deeper still, sending her spiraling along the waves of passion.

Whimpering breathlessly she clung to him; she was hot around him and he was shuddering on the brink. Her panting cries of release sent him over the edge. His back arched and the powerful rhythm of his lower body plunged into her, out of control, until he felt hot desire pumped uncontrollably down the length of his engorged shaft. His hands harshly gripped her hips like a man possessed and he lifted her, pulled her hard into his last violent penetrating thrust. Holding her with firm hands, his chest heaved and his body shook as he ground himself against her until the madness finally ceased.

Sapped of every last ounce of strength, he collapsed on her, gulping in air as she did the same beneath him.

As soon as Kaki drifted back from the idyllic depths of pleasure, the enormity of her acquiescence hit her. What had she done? She was a trained professional in the middle of an assignment and she had totally forgotten about the client she was supposed to be guarding . . . And just to indulge herself in a wild bout of mindless, lustful sex! Good God, she had lost her mind.

When she stirred beneath him, James lifted his head and trailed a finger down her throat. "You're stunning. Absolutely stunning. Do you know that?"

She grabbed his hand to keep from losing her mind again. "Get off me!" Her voice was harsh with self-disgust.

James' eyes glinted when they met hers. "What?"

She gave him a razor-sharp glance. "Get off me!"

When he didn't move, she grabbed his thumb and bent it back until he did.

"Dammit all to hell, Kaki!" he said, shooting to his feet and checking to make certain his thumb wasn't broken.

When James whirled, the raw fury in his face was staggering, but she didn't see it. She was halfway to the bathroom. "Come back here!"

She didn't.

He swore and went after her. But just as he caught up with her, she slammed the door in his face and locked it. "The next time I see you, Kulick, it had better be in Alana Manley's suite!"

"Fine!" he shot back at the pain-in-the-butt behind the closed door.

"You'll want it again, Kaki York," James muttered to himself as he snatched up his clothes and moved quickly out of the room. "Sex with me is like country music—you try not to listen, but you just can't help yourself."

Chapter Four

Kaki had to admit that she did not feel any better after her quick shower. This was clearly the beginning of a very bad day. She glanced at her watch. It read 8:30. Thirty-minutes until she was to meet Tommy Lee in Alana Manley's suite. With a sigh she finished dressing in a loosely fitting banana-yellow silk shirt and her favorite pair of Guess jeans. After tying her hair back into a ponytail, she pulled on her high-top sneakers.

She was deep in thought when several hard knocks on the door broke the silence. With a loud groan she went to answer it. Expecting to see James Kulick, she snatched the door open with considerable force. The young man she faced instead, started.

"Sorry," Kaki said and gave him an apologetic smile. "I thought you were someone else."

He shoved a manila envelope at her. "Ah . . . sorry to disturb you, Ms. York, b-but this is for you."

Before Kaki could thank the messenger, he was gone. With a shrug, she closed the door and made her way across the room to sit at the table. Examining the outside of the large envelope she saw it was from Tommy Lee, which she thought odd considering she would see him in just a few minutes. She shoved aside the light breakfast she had ordered from room service and opened the envelope. Dumping the contents out on the table, she read the note first.

Dear Kaki,

I am sorry, but I have been called out of town on urgent business. Ms. Manley is expecting you, so do not worry. You can handle this assignment without me.

James is a stubborn man, but he can be a great help to you. He is not just a chauffeur; he is also a very good bodyguard when he has to be. Not as good as you, of course. But then I didn't train him. Do not underestimate his abilities, Kaki. He spent ten years in the Marines as an explosive expert and he handles a gun with expertise. Let James cover your back; he is a good man. I have already spoken with him and he has agreed to help.

Enclosed are the threatening letters Alana has received. I had them

dusted for prints, of course. Nothing. Go over them and see what you can come up with. I will be in touch.
Lee
P.S. Keep a close eye on Alana. She is not taking these threats nearly as seriously as she should.

"Damn." Kaki's voice was flat as she stared out the window.

Tommy Lee knew she preferred to work alone. Why, she wondered, did he insist she needed James' help? Well, there was no way to ask Lee. So she might as well just accept that she had a partner.

Kaki leaned back in the chair with an expansive sigh.

Now she had to spend a whole lot of time with James Kulick. And she would have to share information with him. And she had the distinct feeling she would have to fight him off every five minutes.

She shook her head. Smart move—having sex with him, she told herself. And she knew it was not just anger she felt because of that. There was a lot more emotion mixed up with the anger.

But she was not going to think about him now. No, she would think about him later.

Alana Manley would have slept until noon, if the ringing telephone had not jarred her to consciousness. Still, she lay in bed for a moment, unwilling to surrender the comforting darkness, fighting the fact that she had to answer the phone.

She groaned in protest. Mornings were always a bad time for her because she rarely went to bed until several hours past midnight. But this morning, she had had even less sleep than usual. Because it had been close to dawn before Hunter Morgan left her bed—almost five o'clock.

The ringing persisted. Alana reluctantly pushed her sleep-mask up onto her forehead with one hand, while she groped blindly to pick up the telephone's receiver with the other. Only because she had to. If she didn't, it would just keep on ringing.

"Hello."

Heavy breathing.

Anger shot her upright. "Who is this?"

"Whenever I see you touching someone else, my headaches begin. I don't like headaches," said the rather cryptic and oddly asexual voice on the other end of the line.

Alana's stomach lurched and she shot to a sitting position. "Who is this?"

Icy laughter. Click.

The caller I.D. displayed "unknown." A chill ran down her spine. She braced herself.

Obscene caller.

Yes, the statement was one that could have frightened anyone and her name had not been used. It was just some pervert dialing random numbers.

Suddenly she wished Hunter Morgan had not gone to Los Angeles for a business meeting this afternoon. Quickly she slammed the receiver back into its cradle and unconsciously wiped the palm of her hand on the bed sheets as if she had touched something dirty. She drew a deep, steadying breath to chase away her nervousness. After all, this wasn't the first obscene call she'd ever received. There was no reason to be afraid.

It was only when she stood that her legs buckled and she had to sit on the bed to recover.

❦

Kaki knocked on Alana Manley's door at precisely 9:00 a.m., and if it had not been for her nervousness about meeting the movie star for the first time, and seeing James Kulick again, she would have paid closer attention to the telephone repairman who stood waiting, a little too patiently, for the elevator.

Jenna Tucker opened the door and let Kaki in with apparent reluctance. Then when she'd introduced herself, Jenna said, "I know who you are."

Kaki ignored her and instinctively looked at the doorjamb, studying the lock's strike plate. As she examined the brass plate in the door, she found that the jamb was set improperly. With a sigh, she thought one swift kick or shoulder roll to the door and she could break right through. The penthouse suite might be the priciest, but she could already tell that the security here was cheap.

"Something I can help you find?" Jenna asked, eyeing her with a frown.

Kaki's face was blank. "No, thanks. But would you please tell Ms. Manley that I would like to see her?"

The younger woman looked at her as if she had lost her mind. "At this hour?"

"Yes," Kaki said without hesitation.

Jenna shook her head. "If you'll wait here, Ms. York, I will see if Ms. Manley is awake."

"Thank you."

Taking a seat on the nearest chair, she wondered where James was—she'd thought he would be here when she arrived. She was glad he wasn't. She was unsettled enough without having to deal with him, too.

Five minutes later, Alana Manley walked into the room and Kaki stood.

Alana wore a deep red silk kimono. The rich, vibrant chestnut waves that fell in disarray about her cameo face and continued well past her shoulders, shimmered under the morning sunlight that shone through the floor-to-ceiling windows. Obviously she had just gotten out of bed. And Kaki thought she had never seen a lovelier woman. Much more attractive than she appeared on screen. Even her toes, the nails expertly manicured and painted a British red, were pretty as they peeked out from under the floor-length swish of material as she walked. Deep sable eyes dominated her thin, fine-boned face.

Kaki shook her head. Nobody had pretty toes.

Yes, Alana Manley did. No wonder, she thought, that the men came looking for her.

Then Alana smiled, and Kaki saw warmth and friendliness, and she gave a small sigh of relief.

"Thank you for coming," she said softly. "I'm Alana Manley."

"Kaki York."

Alana nodded. "I'm glad you agreed to take the position as my personal bodyguard."

Kaki looked at her in surprise. "May I ask why?"

Alana laughed as she crossed the room and took a seat on the sofa. She motioned for Kaki to do the same. "Because I have seen you in action and I was impressed. That's why."

Stunned disbelief spread over her face as she sat next to Alana. "Me? When?"

Alana didn't answer at first because Jenna came into the room and poured coffee for them both.

"Thank you," Kaki said, taking the dainty china cup.

Jenna inclined her head and left.

Alana cradled her own cup in her hands. "Mr. Lee is very proud of you. Did you know that?"

Kaki nodded, the telltale flush of embarrassment heating her cheeks. "Sometimes more than he should be."

"I have seen what you can do, remember?"

Kaki nodded again. "But where? I can't imagine."

Alana took a sip of her coffee, then lifted her gaze to meet Kaki's. "My father and Mr. Lee served together during the Korean War.

Though my father was a Marine, and Lee, a Special Forces instructor in the South Korean Army, they were assigned to a joint unit and became close friends. When my father died, Mr. Lee kept in touch. He somehow felt it was his duty." She paused then to place her cup on the coffee table in front of them. After tucking her legs beneath her and adjusting the red kimono, she clasped her long-fingered hands in her lap. "Anyway . . . when I started receiving these crank phone calls I contacted him and asked his advice. He knew I'd already hired James and that he was my bodyguard/driver so to speak; that he was very capable. Still, Mr. Lee did not feel James alone was sufficient protection for me under the circumstances and strongly suggested that I hire you. He also sent me your resume, along with a tape of your win at the 1995 National Taekwondo Championships. And, as I said before, I was impressed. With everything." She smiled then. "Someday, Kaki, you must tell me about being the only female member of the Navy Seals. It must have been delicious having those hard-bodied and dangerous men all to yourself."

Kaki discreetly rolled her eyes. After what she had seen last night, she was sure Alana Manley would have thought so. She cleared her throat and took another sip of coffee. "I have to admit, Ms. Manley, I never thought of my expertise in quite that light before."

"That's too bad," Alana said in a tsk-tsk fashion. "Obviously you need someone who can teach you to appreciate the joys in life. And I am just the one to do it, too." She smiled devilishly. "And please, call me Alana. For heaven's sake, we are going to spend nearly every waking moment together until this . . . this person is caught. We certainly can't stand on formalities the entire time."

"Yes, ma'am. I mean, no, ma'am," she said, flustered.

Alana shook her head emphatically and took Kaki's hand in hers. "No, ma'ams—no, Ms. Manleys—just Alana, okay?"

Kaki smiled. "Then Alana it is."

"Good!" She stood then. "If you'll excuse me now I will go and get cleaned up."

Just as she turned to leave, Kaki said, "Ms. . . . ah, Alana." she corrected quickly. "If you don't mind, I need to check the apartment for security leaks."

Alana smiled over her shoulder. "Do whatever you like, my dear. As of right now, you are in charge."

With that, she exited the room as gracefully as she had entered.

Kaki immediately got to work. She checked the locks, then the windows and door alarm. Within thirty minutes she knew that she would have to build an entire new security system.

Three hours later, James Kulick sat slumped on the couch in Alana's penthouse suite drinking a cup of coffee. He watched with aggravation as Alana and Kaki talked out on the balcony behind closed French doors.

"What the devil do you think they are talking about?" he asked Jenna as she made her way past him with a light lunch of salad, cheese and wine in her hands.

"How should I know?" she shot back over her shoulder.

James grumbled in response, snatched up the remote and flipped on the local television station.

"And now the national news," the commentator announced just before a picture flashed on the screen, and he almost dropped his coffee cup on the floor.

Without shifting his gaze from the television screen, he shot off the couch and went to the French doors. He rapped hard on a glass pane with his knuckles. "Kaki, Alana, get in here!"

The door opened and the two women came inside. "What the devil is wrong with you?" Alana demanded.

James still did not shift his gaze and pointed to the TV.

Alana immediately sat in the nearest chair before she fell down. "Oh my God!" Alana exclaimed, clamping a hand over her mouth.

"What is it? What's the matter?" Kaki asked, placing a hand on her shoulder.

When Alana did not answer, Kaki's confused gaze shifted to James. He shook his head.

Alana listened intently, not saying a word, her tawny-colored eyes widening with horror as the details unfolded. A successful male model had been found dead in his New York City apartment early that morning. Murdered. Shot in the head. Execution style. With a dead cat left lying on his chest.

A twenty-six-year-old man who had appeared on the covers of hundreds of romance novels. A man simply known as Damian. And now he was dead.

Chapter Five

The phone rang and James answered it. When the short conversation was over, he turned and faced the women. "Lt. Ballard is waiting for me downstairs in the lobby. I'm going to meet him. Alana, you and Kaki, don't unlock this door. Not for anyone. I'll let myself back in."

Alana and Kaki agreed as James pulled the door to, locking it securely behind him.

When James reached the lobby, he quickly assessed the man standing before him. The lieutenant was a powerful man with a sun-darkened complexion and the hulking presence of someone not to be argued with. He appeared to be in his middle to late thirties, with striking blue eyes and a handsome face with sharp features and a full day's stubble adding to his roughish air. His blonde hair was buzzed short in a no-nonsense style. The man looked as if he would be at home on a Harley, riding at the speed of light, with a Lucky Strike dangling from between his even white teeth.

"What can I do for you?" The lieutenant sat down and tipped back in a chair, nonchalantly surveying the room.

James was not to be fooled. He knew the lieutenant well. "As I said on the phone, I'd like to look at the file on this Damian fellow." Lt. Ballard didn't respond right away, but reached for a crumbled pack of cigarettes resting in his shirt pocket. He took one in his teeth and lit it with a scarred Zippo lighter that had seen its better days. Finally, he said, "What does Damian have to do with this case of yours?"

Now James became irritated. "Do you know that Ms. Manley was one of Damian's lovers, that she has received several threatening letters over the last few months and phone calls, and found a dead cat in her limo."

"A dead cat?" the lieutenant said with a straight face.

James couldn't decide if Lt. Ballard was toying with him or not. His brother had a way of annoying him with practically no effort at all.

"Yes, a dead cat," James shot back. "You have to take this seriously J.T. Someone is terrorizing Alana Manley and we need to know what

kind of danger she could be in so that we know how to go about
protecting her."

"Who is with her now?" J.T. asked.

"Kaki, her bodyguard."

J.T. swallowed. "Kaki?"

"Did I stutter? Kaki is a woman who has a blackbelt and comes
highly recommended. Alana is safe for now, but if you don't get off
your butt and hand over the Damian files, that might not be for long."

After deliberating a moment, Lt. Ballard pulled a cell phone from
his back pocket. When he spoke, James realized he had called the
station.

"Could you please bring me the files on the murder investigation of
that model, Damian? I'll be waiting at Alana Manley's penthouse in
the lobby."

When J.T. ended the conversation, James focused on his brother.
"Brother or not, I'd better not hear any of this leaked to the press or
I'll have your butt for obstruction of justice, you hear me?"

"I think you have it backward, J.T. We're not trying to interfere with
your investigation, but bring justice to whoever committed this murder,
while protecting other potential victims. That's all."

"Okay, fine."

At that moment, a uniformed police officer entered the hotel lobby
and hurried over to the two men, handing some folders to the lieutenant.

"Thank you." J.T. dismissed the young officer with a nod.

As the man left, J.T. handed the folders to James with a final ad-
monishment, "Be careful."

James nodded. "I will."

Within twenty minutes James and Kaki settled down in the rented
suite they used for twenty-four hour surveillance of Alana with the files
Lt. Ballard had provided. For the next hour they reviewed them, along
with penciled summations of telephone calls, the autopsy report, and
photos taken at the crime scene.

They went over the files first. Ballard hadn't been kidding when he'd
said Damian was a lady-killer. From the notes it was apparent that his
affairs had been extensive. One particularly lengthy memo about an
interview conducted with a near swooning and current lover named
Bitsy Maxwell, caught Kaki's attention. Though married, Bitsy claimed
to have been involved with Damian for the past two years. She also was
convinced that he had recently become romantically involved with a

"certain unnamed Hollywood Hussy," and only because she wouldn't leave her husband for him, but there was nothing much beyond that. James was the one to shove reports about a second and third homicide under her nose.

"What the hell?" Kaki asked, scanning the papers.

"The Telex is from the Fort Lauderdale Police Department," he said. "It's about a homicide that took place exactly seven days before Damian Scott's. This guy was also killed at about the same hour of the night." He paused to point to the other. "From the Chicago Police Department about a homicide on the south-side that took place over a month ago—"

"All three have the same MO," Kaki said. "Shot in the head at point-blank range with a 120 grain nine-millimeter bullet, but I still don't understand where the dead cat that Alana found in the limo fits in with all this."

James clasped his fingers behind his head. "Probably just someone trying to throw the investigation off track."

"We'll soon find out. For now, I'm off to bed," Kaki said, trying to yawn and stretch at the same time.

With that, she headed for the door. James stood and followed her. They both stopped in the hall and said goodnight before going into their rooms.

♣

Muffled sounds coming from Alana's suite awakened Kaki. Jumping from the bed, she snatched her jeans from the floor and pulled them on under her T-shirt. Taking her 9mm from the nightstand, she checked the load, tucked the revolver in the back of her jeans and headed for the door.

When Kaki burst into Alana's suite, she started screaming uncontrollably. Just then something was slipped around her neck.

Instantly, she knew it was a piece of rope that was gripped in the man's hands and he was tightening it around her neck.

Her throat burned. Her lungs ached. Darkness stole over her.

Chapter Six

The stranglehold jerked even more firmly around Kaki's throat. Reaching for the gun in the back of her waistband she fought the darkness. She lost her grip and the 9mm fell and hit the floor. Along with it, a good amount of hope. Dammit!

She struggled to get her fingers under the rope, but it was already cutting deeply into her flesh. The assailant twisted it harder.

Kaki knew that she only had seconds to get away before she lapsed into unconsciousness. She lifted her knee and kicked backward with all her strength, but she missed. Her assailant having evaded the blow twisted the rope still tighter.

She tried to cry out, but no sound escaped her throat. Hell, she couldn't even draw a breath. Her face burned like fire, and her eyes felt as if they were popping out of her head.

Desperate, Kaki jammed her elbow into her attacker's stomach. The move caught her attacker offguard and he stumbled for a second, which caused him to loosen his grip on the rope.

That was all Kaki needed. Spinning, she brought up her right knee hard and caught the man between the legs. With a scream, the attacker staggered forward and lunged for the door. Kaki fell to the floor just as the elevator across the hall lurched into motion again. Frantically, she groped for her gun. She had a much better chance if she got to her gun. But she was weak from the attack, and too slow. When the elevator halted and the doors flew open, the attacker shot out into the hallway.

With a sudden burst of strength, Kaki sprang to her feet, and tackled the man. The man threw her off and she staggered backward, her head throbbing from the impact. She looked up in time to see the man pull a gun from inside his jacket. She leapt forward and hit his wrist with a knife-hand strike. The gun popped out of the man's hand before he could fire a shot, and spiraled across the floor. Either she was seeing things or his entire hairline shifted several inches to the right.

At the noise, James ran into the hallway and toward her. Kaki shook her head to clear it. He stopped dead in his tracks as he spotted her gasping for breath.

"You, okay?" He narrowed his eyes, lifted her chin with his forefinger and assessed the damage to her neck.

She nodded the affirmative.

"Hurry, he's getting away," she managed to shout painfully, louder this time.

Kaki rested for a millisecond, drawing a deep breath as she bent with hands on her knees.

"Let's go get the sonofabitch." She gingerly tested the ligature marks with her hand.

James grabbed her elbow and steered her down the hall towards the front door. They exploded onto the sidewalk at full speed. They would have to double-time it to catch up.

They had traveled several yards when James stumbled. He swooped down and lifted something off the pavement and shoved it into Kaki's hand.

She glanced at the object, it was light in color and hairy, and she flipped it over. A wig!

The hunted assailant came into view through the bobbing shoulders of the cops up ahead. A long ponytail danced across his back, bouncing up and down with each step.

James and Kaki gained quickly on him. They rushed past like a hurricane, the perpetrator only a few feet away.

"Stop," James screamed as he reached out desperately and nabbed the flying hem of the baggy jacket between thumb and forefinger. He quickly worked a handful of fabric into his palm, jerking back hard as he dug in his heels, coming to a sudden stop.

The suspect lost his footing and hit the pavement hard. He jumped up immediately and turned on them in a fury.

"Jenna," Kaki whispered, eyes wide in stunned disbelief.

James took Jenna out with one punch.

Epilogue

Kaki leaned back in the rattan chaise and slipped on her shades. James sat, legs outstretched, ankles crossed, in the chair next to her, zinc oxide white on his nose. She suspected that behind his dark sunglasses he was intently surveying the scene. One that included dozens of topless women.

St. Tropez, not a bad place to resume her vacation. Alana had insisted on sending them on the trip after they apprehended Jenna, possibly saving the actress' life.

She shook her head. "James, I still can't believe Jenna was the one. I would have never guessed in a million years that she was a lesbian. Much less an obsessive psychopath."

He stretched and yawned, "Kaki, we have been over this at least a thousand times. Her apartment was practically wallpapered with Alana's image. The diaries spelled it all out. She had been in love with Alana since the first time she laid eyes on her. Over time she just got sicker and sicker, acting on more and more of her twisted fantasies."

"My money would have been on Hunter Morgan," Kaki observed. "That is one twisted bastard."

"Yes, twisted," James turned to face her, "but not twisted, obsessed, psychotic bastard."

Kaki picked up the Pina Colada from the table adjacent to her chair and took a long drink, "I hope Alana won't be too upset with us for declining her offer to stay on as her permanent security team."

He shook his head. "I'm sure Hunter Morgan will protect her quite well until she hires another bodyguard. Besides, I'm looking forward to exploring Savannah. The South and Southern Belles have always fascinated me." He shot Kaki a wicked grin. "I am just dying to eat a Georgia Peach."

Kaki tried to smother a chuckle and failed. "What if I told you that I know where you could find one right here in San Tropez?"

James lifted an eyebrow. "I'd say show me."

"Just walk this way . . ."

About the authors:

Although Betsy Morgan and Susan Paul both live in South Georgia, less than ninety-miles apart, they met for the first time at the Romantic Times Convention in Fort Worth, Texas. Kathryn Falk, Lady Barrow, introduced Susan, a multi-published author, and Besty, an aspiring one. She suggested that they keep in touch. As they did just that, Susan and Betsy decided it would be fun to collaborate on a story.

The Bodyguard, Susan's second story for **Secrets** (*"Savage Garden"* appears in **Secrets Vol. 2**), and Betsy's first, is the result. Was it fate that the infamous Lady Barrow intervened? Who knows?

Susan and Betsy certainly think so!

The Love Slave

by Emma Holly

To our reader:

To me, good erotica is like a glass of wine with dinner, slightly decadent, darkly exciting and—who knows—if it gets my pulse pounding, it might lower my cholesterol! A good romance, however, is dinner. I've gotta have it, no ifs, ands, or buts.

When I saw my first *Secrets* collection, my writer's imagination was sparked. Romance and erotica entwined in a single story? What a yummy idea. I knew I had to try my hand at it. I hope you enjoy my attempt in *The Love Slave*, and I hope you come back for more!

In the days before Empire, the country of Srucia was a collection of loosely affiliated city-states. Chief among these was Ammam. Nations far and wide sent tribute to the Lady of Ammam, whose formidable army had held the scourge of Southland at bay for four generations. Despite local rivalries and the ever present threat of invasion, this was a time of peace. The old ways flourished, especially the tradition of the love guard.

Chapter One

Princess Lily tied the scarlet ribbon beneath her breasts. She was seventeen today. Though her gown blazed the white of maidens, the ribbon declared to all her approaching womanhood. Today she would select her love guard, the trio of slaves who would protect her person and teach her the mastery of men. Thus prepared, in one short year she would choose her official consort.

Not a moment too soon, according to her mother. To Lily's dismay, Lady Fortis liked to call her the Royal Doormat. In front of people.

It was fortunate she could not see her daughter dressing herself. Lily had let her maids leave early for the fair. Her toilette was simple and they were good maids; they never slacked or grumbled and Lyn did have an eye for one of the jugglers. But perhaps this was exactly the sort of thing a doormat would do. She *was* running late, though even her mother could not have predicted that her hem would rip and have to be mended.

Lily bit her lip. Who was she trying to fool? She even looked soft. She hadn't her mother's height, or her spectacular bosom. She supposed she was pretty. Her hair was chestnut brown and hung past the curve of her bottom. Her eyes shone as green as the Indje in flood, and last week the miller's son had assured her that the roses on the chapel were not softer than her lips.

Her mother thought she was sleeping with the miller's son, cutting her teeth on him, as she put it. She would be angry to discover she was not. Lily was saving herself. Nurse had raised her charge on stories of her own homeland, where the king ruled above the queen and women preserved their virginity for their husbands, or at least for their One True Love.

This sounded romantic to Lily, even heroic, considering how strongly the pleasures of the flesh could call to a healthy girl. Fortunately, only a year remained until she married. Unlike her mother, she intended to wed a man she could love, a man too gentle to require mastering. He would also be a powerful prince, of course, one whose alliance would benefit Ammam's people.

Bolstered by her daydream, she leaned out the window of her tower. In honor of her birthday, white and gold pennants had been strung between the six corners of the castle. Though times were peaceful, soldiers patrolled the rose-granite ramparts. *Strength is peace,* Lady Fortis said, and she made sure her men stayed keen. Their armor was polished, their shields bright. Fully a third wore Ka'arkish chainmail, which was neither iron nor steel, but some substance known only to the dour Northern metalsmiths. The mail, which was twice as strong and much lighter than plated steel, was invariably a trophy of war. The Ka'arkastanians would part with but limited quantities and were unmoved by threats or charm, both of which her mother had employed.

As if aware of her attention, one soldier waved from the nearest tower. Lily couldn't remember ever seeing a soldier wave at her mother. Lady Fortis paid them well, deeded land to her officers and sent a sack of gold to any soldier who married a local girl, but she did not encourage familiarity. Lily wished she could fault her mother's iron manner, but the evidence was against her. Ammam's knights fought more fiercely than any except the Yskutians, and everyone knew they were a race of sorcerers who could not fairly be compared.

With a small and all too familiar sigh, she craned her head in the other direction.

She found distraction in plenty there. Stands had been erected in the courtyard so that the townsfolk and nobles could watch their princess select her love guard. The candidates hailed from every corner of the continent. It was considered an honor to serve the Lady of Ammam, the greatest Lady yet, many said. Though Lady Fortis had fought no major battles, she had wrought more changes through treaties and building projects than the last three ladies combined.

Lily despaired of matching her. Who feared Ammam's princess? Who respected her, for that matter? Soldiers waved at her. Maids felt free to run off and play, and never mind she'd told them they could. She shouldn't have told them. On this of all days, she should have been strict!

Oh, cease your puling, she thought, with a disgusted shake of her head. No one makes you a doormat but you. If you dislike it so much, do something about it.

"I will," she said to the empty chamber. "I will learn to rule and my people will respect me. What's more, I will begin today." The words were almost firm by the time she reached the end of her declaration. Still, she jumped when she heard a rattle at the door.

"There you are," said Nurse, huffing and puffing from her climb up the tower stairs.

Lily beamed. Nurse was a small, round woman. Lily adored her more than anyone in the world except for her mother's lover, the wise and quiet Vizier. The one time she'd defied her mother was for Nurse's sake. Lady Fortis had wished to dismiss her, saying that the woman was encouraging her romantical ways. Lily had to admit she had a point.

Now Nurse looked about the chamber, no doubt searching for a maid to scold. "What have you been doing, child? The scryer has been waiting on you this last hour."

"Oh!" Lily covered her mouth with both hands.

"Oh, indeed," said Nurse, though not unkindly. "Must you be late for everything?"

It seemed worse than pointless to explain about the fair and the juggler and the unexpectedly torn hem. She hung her head. "I'm sorry. I'll try to do better."

"Pshaw," said Nurse. "You know better than to apologize to the likes of me."

Lily released a silent sigh. It seemed changing would be harder than saying the words.

The scryer waited in the shadows on the courtyard's east side. She wore a long grey gown with a cowl. The Jewel of the Third Eye, a coin-sized opal from deep in the southern desert, glimmered above the bridge of her nose. Lily stiffened. The scryer intimidated her as much as Lady Fortis, despite being young and kind. She had been trained by the Yskutians and shared their otherworldly air. Lily feared she would peer into her soul and read her un-princesslike thoughts.

Now the scryer placed long, slim hands on her shoulders. "Just follow my lead, Princess. I'll tell you what I wish you to do. There's no need to be nervous."

Lily tried to heed her but she'd never seen such a crowd at the castle. Thousands thronged the walled courtyard, all waiting for a glimpse of their heir. In a way, this would be her first act of rulership. If she chose unwisely . . .

"Hush," said the scryer. "Follow your heart. Then all will be well. Although—" She paused. Was it Lily's imagination or did the woman's eyes twinkle? "I would not advise choosing a slave who will not rise to your hand."

Lily nodded. She did not, however, have the faintest idea what the scryer meant.

Lady Fortis opened the festivities by thanking her neighbors for sending the flower of their manhood into Ammam's service. One by one, the representatives of each country filed up the steps and set an offering at her feet. The offering was not grudged. Many love guards went on to hold high posts after their year of service. Vizier himself had been her mother's slave and none save the Lady wielded more power. His native country was guaranteed fair hearing on any issue.

Lily listened to the speeches with half an ear. I will choose the biggest, meanest slaves I can find, she vowed, and I will master them. They will tremble at my air of command. Her face twisted with a grimace. More likely they'd die laughing. Perhaps she'd be better off with a few medium-sized, moderately mean slaves. Surely mastering those would be challenge enough. Squirming in her demi-throne, she gazed around the courtyard in search of likely candidates.

Six gilded cages had been erected on the lawn, each holding a score of slaves. Clearly the cages were more symbol than reality. Any of the young men could have squeezed between the bars, had they chosen to do so. Lily eyed them. They were not the peasants she'd expected. Though clad in kalisaris, the plain white skirts of quarry workers, the sheen of their skin and hair proclaimed them the sons of good homes. It was impossible to tell which ones might be mean, or even moderately mean. To a man, they stood calmly.

She wondered if she could have borne the prospect of slavery so well.

Finally, the flowery speeches ended. The scryer glided up the dais, bowed to her mother and handed Lily a small golden key.

"Come, Princess," she said in a melodious, carrying tone. "Come choose your guard."

Lily followed her graceful figure across the springy coastal grass. She hoped she didn't look as awkward as she felt. This was what came of being late! If she'd met the scryer ahead of time, she'd have been instructed on what was to come.

When they reached the first cage, the scryer directed her to unlock the door, then called a candidate to the entrance. He looked as nervous as Lily felt. She ventured a reassuring smile.

"Hast thou lain with a woman?" asked the scryer.

Lily's eyes widened at the question, but the candidate did not flinch.

"I have not," he said in a voice that barely shook.

"Lift your skirt," ordered the scryer.

The candidate did so. Lily tried not to choke. He was naked beneath the clean white linen. His sex dangled, thick and pink, between strong, hairy thighs.

"Cup him from beneath," said the scryer.

A subtle nudge broke Lily's paralysis. Her mother would be horrified to discover she had never handled a man's naked organ. Hesitantly, she curled her fingers beneath the swaying shaft. It was smooth, like silk.

"The sac as well," corrected the scryer.

As gently as she could, she gathered the joggling bundle and lifted it toward the scryer's view. A sound broke in the candidate's throat. Within her hand his cool, soft flesh began to swell. The candidate flushed, but it seemed he could not curb his body's reaction. When his organ had risen beyond the horizontal, the scryer positioned her hand above it and gazed into the man's eyes. After a moment's silence, she said, "This candidate speaks true. He is worthy of service."

Then she called the next young man to the door. Goodness, Lily thought, anticipation and alarm shivering in unison down her spine. Surely they couldn't mean for her to touch them all?

But they did. She had not imagined such a variety of organs existed. Some were long, some short, some wide, some thin. Some sported fetching cowls which slipped back as their owners' shafts lengthened in her palm. Others were as bare of adornment as a monk's shaven pate. She saw penises as pink as the inside of a shell and as red as a maple in autumn. She saw penises that jerked like hunting dogs and others that rose as gently as a curtain blown by a breeze.

Her skin grew warm and cold by turns. They were lovely, all of them, and so magically responsive. A heavy pulse settled between her legs. Oh, that this entertainment ever had to end!

Only two of the candidates were pronounced "impure" by the scryer, and only one failed to rise in her hand. With so few eliminated, she did not know how she would choose. She could not tell one man from another, having spent precious little time gazing in their faces.

Then, at the fourth cage, one of the candidates set himself apart. He was a comely youth, lean and strong and as fair as any girl. His light brown hair hung to his shoulders in waves. When he stepped to the door, he clutched a handful of daisies over his heart.

"Princess," he said in the deep tones of a man grown.

Lily fought a smile. What a naughty puppy. With a low bow, he held out the humble bouquet, which he'd obviously plucked from the lawn surrounding his cage. She glanced at the scryer, who nodded that she might accept the gift. She, too, seemed to be fighting amusement.

"Hast thou lain —" she began her ritual interrogative.

One of the candidates erupted from the back of the cage.

"Cheeky bastard!" he shouted, and took a flying leap at the first candidate's back.

Lily shrieked and dropped the flowers as the men tumbled onto the lawn and began to scuffle. Stop it, she thought, unconsciously wringing her hands. Oh, please stop it. Then she saw the blood. With that, her fear left her. She grabbed Daisy-boy by the scruff of the neck.

"That's enough," she said in a tone of such ringing authority she barely recognized it.

Daisy-boy was not as impressed as he should have been. Still full of fight, he swung his fist towards her face. The spectators moaned. At the very last second, he checked the blow. Immediately, he fell to his knees. "My lady." He pressed fervent kisses to the hem of her gown. "Queen of my heart. Princess of princesses. Please forgive me. I was overcome by passion."

"Bastard," muttered his attacker, who sat on the grass nursing a bloody nose.

Lily looked at him. His hair was as red as his temper, but his looks rivaled his foe's. Where Daisy-boy's face was clever, however, this man's was painfully honest.

"These two," she said, the words leaving her mouth almost before they'd reached her brain. "I choose these two."

"Very good," said the scryer. "With luck they will fight as valiantly for you as they do against each other."

"They had better," she declared, and impressed herself by administering a playful cuff to Daisy-boy's ear. The crowd roared with laughter. Their approval rushed to her head like wine, but she couldn't afford to lose her wits now. One slave remained to choose.

She found him in the last cage. Even supposing the last two failed to impress her mother, this one surely would. He stood apart, his arms crossed over a powerful chest. He was taller than the others and broader, not a youth verging on manhood but a man in truth. A smoky cross of hair marked his torso. He had the warm, bronzed skin of Ka'arkastan and the slanted eyes of Yskut. A half-breed. Brute strength paired with age-old sophistication.

She shivered, half in fear and half in interest. Did she truly dare choose this slave?

His eyes, as black as his shaggy hair, narrowed when the scryer beckoned him forward. Such a terrible stare, so full of anger. I couldn't, she thought. But then something strange happened. His dark eyes bored into hers, and a hot stab of feeling pierced her heart. *You,* said a voice in her mind, all joy and trembling. *It's you.* His glare intensified. She didn't care. She felt as if she had stumbled across a friend she'd been missing for years and had never hoped to see again. It was almost like one of Nurse's stories where the lover comes back from the dead.

Nonsense, she thought. This glowering fellow was no object of romance. Her nerves must have unbalanced her mind.

"Hast thou lain with a woman?" the scryer asked in her lovely, gentle voice.

Hope tightened the back of Lily's neck. Or was it dread? He couldn't be a virgin, not this towering man with the shadow of a beard and the hot, knowing eyes.

But "Yes," he growled in a voice like rusty iron. He did not sound happy about it.

"Lift your skirt," said the scryer.

Lily bit her lip. Slowly, sullenly, he lifted his brief white wrap. His sex was as big as the rest of him. The shaft hung heavy and thick over the curve of his scrotum. He had one of those cowls that had fascinated her on the other men. She longed to see it slide back over his arousal. No longer shy, she reached out to cup him.

Nothing happened. He did not warm, or twitch, or swell. The only sign that he knew she touched him was the ticking of a tiny muscle in his jaw. She suspected he was doing it on purpose. Perhaps he knew some arcane Yskutian trick for controlling his body. Enough, she thought. She might not be masterful, but she had learned a thing or two about the male anatomy today. In this, at least, she would rule. She moved her hand up his heavy shaft. She felt a quickened pulse, a flicker of movement beneath the smooth outer skin. She stroked him again.

"Do not do this," he said through gritted teeth. Beads of sweat glistened on his forehead. "This is not my will."

She hesitated. What did he mean? Had he been kidnapped into servitude? If that were true, he should have shouted it to the skies. He would have been released at once. Perhaps he was reluctant to serve, but that would make mastering him all the sweeter. Do it, she ordered herself. Don't be a coward.

She stepped closer and let him feel her quickened breath, and let her hardened nipples brush his chest. Yes, that was the secret; the evidence of her arousal woke his own. His manhood stirred in her hand. Encouraged, she petted the beast until it rose, until it throbbed to each gentle stroke as to the lash of a whip. Now that he'd come to heel, his sex was harder than any she'd held before. As red as her own red lips, it curved upward like the strut of a longbow. A tear of moisture appeared on its naked tip. Lily swept it away with her thumb, then gasped at the melting-smooth skin his cowl had revealed. His thighs trembled with strain.

"You had better stop, Princess," he growled. "Unless you want everyone in those stands to see your slave spill his seed."

He said the word as if she truly were a slavemaster, as if she were going to chain him to an oar and work him into an early grave. But his scorn did not matter. What mattered was that he had said it. *Your slave. Yours.* The victory was heady.

"I choose him," she said, releasing the man so abruptly he staggered back a step.

"Very well," said the scryer. "The choosing is complete."

The candidate's huff of disgust could be clearly heard by all.

Chapter Two

He was every bit as surly as she'd expected, though not as disobedient. He stood quietly behind her chair with the other slaves during the banquet, an interminable affair of speeches and course after course of heavy food. Torches lined the hall, flickering over tapestry and stone. Lily had a table to herself. She wished she dared offer the men some of the food she wasn't eating and the wine she wasn't drinking, but her mother watched her like a hawk. Probably Lily ought to be doing something she wasn't, something masterful, but she honestly couldn't think what.

Of her three slaves, only Daisy-boy was cheerful enough to speak. Ian was his name. He and the redhead had reached a truce. She didn't pretend to understand it, but she'd seen men behave this way before, as if the spilling of blood cemented friendship. The redhead, called Col, was trying to pretend his broken nose didn't pain him. The court physician had taped it but Col refused the crushed ice Lily had obtained for him. Beneath the tape, his nose was swelling like a plum. Finally, the sight grew too much for her.

"Slave," she said. "I—I order you to apply this ice."

Col's spine snapped straight in surprise. "As you please, Mistress."

There, she thought, handing him the bowl. That wasn't hard. She'd ordered him to do something he didn't want to do and he'd done it. Her glow of triumph so warmed her she was able to ignore her mother's baleful glare, and the fact that the brooding Ka'arkish hulk was staring stonily into the distance and had missed this demonstration of her power.

Ian said his name was Grae. He was two months younger than her pretty boys, just shy of nineteen. Lily didn't believe it, but Grae confirmed Ian's claim with a curt nod.

"But you look so much older," she said.

She could only imagine what he read into that. His chest rose and fell and his gaze heated. He was staring at her breasts. Lily clutched the jeweled stem of her wine cup, abruptly aware that her nipples were tingling. The effect unnerved her, but she forced herself not to flinch. When Grae looked away, his face was hard.

"I worked with my father," he said.

She eyed his muscular arms. "Was he a blacksmith?" The beast pretended not to hear.

She knew she should force him to answer but her father appeared then, a silent shadow at the end of the hall. He rarely attended public functions, preferring to remain closeted with his books. Lily should have been flattered, but her throat tightened with dread. He glided down the central aisle, oblivious to the whispers. He was tall and straight and wore garments as black as his beard. Eyes turned towards him as he approached the high table. As always, his spirit seemed deeply withdrawn. Only his eyes, the same olive green as Lily's, glittered with secret life.

He climbed the dais where Lady Fortis, his wife, sat shoulder to shoulder with her beloved Vizier. He bent and kissed her cheek, then continued his measured journey to Lily's side. He put his hand on her shoulder. His fingers were heavy and cold. She looked up at him, into the grave, handsome face that seemed to know neither bitterness nor joy.

"Felicitations on your birthday," he said in his husky, seldom used voice.

He left as silently as he had come.

Ian murmured something humorous, but Lily didn't hear it, didn't hear anything until they returned to her tower and Nurse revealed that all her maids had been dismissed.

"These laddies will do for you now," she said with a laughing glance at the slaves. "Dressing and bathing and building up the fire. Two will share your bed each night and one will guard the door."

"Share my bed?" Lily repeated, unable to hide her shock.

"Aye, Princess," Nurse confirmed. "But there'll be no funny business unless you wish it. Their virginity is yours. They cannot give it to you nor any other without your permission."

Grae had been examining each of her six arrow slits. At Nurse's words he snorted, probably his version of a laugh.

"You," Lily said, as imperiously as she could. He turned to face her, arms behind his back, stance wide, like a soldier awaiting orders. Sensing mockery in the pose, she decided then and there that he would not sleep in her bed this night. "You will stand guard."

He smiled, not a nice smile, though his teeth were white and straight. "As you wish, Princess. But it might be more efficient to break the night into watches. Even I need to sleep."

"Watch your tone," Col warned, his fists clenching at his hips. "She is our mistress now."

Lily expected another fight, but Grae inclined his head and took a symbolic step back.

"Forgive me," he said, but it seemed to Lily he apologized to Col rather than to her.

Lily bathed herself behind the painted screen. She knew she would have to overcome her shyness at some point, but tonight she was reluctant to allow the men such intimate access to her person. To make up for the lapse, she ordered Col of the broken nose to brush her hair dry before the fire. That was pleasant, though Grae kept up a constant mutter about the poor security arrangements in the tower.

"You have my permission to see to it," she finally said. "Just leave off your nattering."

He opened his mouth to protest her choice of words, then shut it and strode off to stand watch in the entryway.

"I need a weapon," he barked a minute later. "My belongings are still shipboard."

With Ian's help, Lily tugged open the heavy door to the arms closet. She grabbed the first sword and dagger that met her eye. They were also the finest: Ka'arkish steel with elaborate Laravian hilts. Grae tested the hair-splitting edge on his thumb and grunted.

"These were expensive," he said. It sounded like a complaint.

"So were you," she responded, which silenced him nicely. Her mother would be proud. Lily felt as if she were growing more authoritative by the minute.

When he turned away, however, the sight of his back made her breath catch. He'd been whipped. The firelight turned the faint net of scars to silver threads, too many to count. The marks were old; he must have received them as a youth. But who would whip a child until no unmarred skin remained? Her eyes burned, pity and fury mixing in her breast. Her hand crept out.

The heat shadow must have warned him. He went rigid before her fingers met skin. He said nothing but she knew. He did not want her to see this. He did not want her pity.

The dilemma baffled her. Was showing pity weak, or was obeying his unspoken demand? At a loss, she withdrew just as Ian called her.

"Come, Princess," he said.

Ian, apparently, required little direction. He had pulled back the green brocade hangings of her bed. He had turned down the pink silk sheets and set a carafe of cool water on the side table. Less confident than his partner, Col stood on the opposite side blinking nervously.

Oh, well, she thought. Might as well get it over with. Holding her nightgown out of the way, she climbed the two mahogany steps that abutted the footboard. The frame had been carved to resemble a grape arbor, complete with vines and fruit and delicate birds. All her life this bed had been her sanctuary, witness to her dreams and tears, the imaginary boat for a thousand imaginary journeys. How changed it seemed tonight, how fraught with foreign dangers.

Ian steadied her as she crawled to the pillows. She lay down on her back. Col pulled the covers up to her chest. Then they both climbed in on either side of her. Under the sheets.

Lily ordered herself not to protest. The night was cool and they wore naught but their linen skirts. She simply wished the bed were wider. Two pairs of hairy legs warmed her through her gown. Two broad shoulders. Two sets of inhaling and exhaling lungs. With a grimace, she closed her eyes and pretended to sleep.

For many minutes all was silent. Then, as if a hidden signal had been passed, two long bodies turned to hers and two long arms draped themselves across her belly. Col nuzzled the curve of her neck like a babe, his poor nose hotter than the rest of his face.

Her sex pulsed at the seeking gesture. Were they asleep? Did they think she was?

Col snuggled closer, his leg shifting restlessly against her side. The sheets rustled. Something warm prodded her hip. After the day she'd spent, she could not fail to recognize the throbbing shape. He was aroused. His leg moved again, crossing hers, and the shape flattened against her side. He rolled his hips forward once, twice, then moaned low in his throat.

"You, too?" Ian whispered.

"God, yes," Col said. "I don't think I can bear it. She's so soft and she smells so nice. And I'm so hard it feels like it's about to fall off."

Ian adjusted his head on the pillow. "You know what the slave trainers said. Your pleasure is hers to dictate. You can't even take yourself in hand except she give you leave."

Col moaned and squirmed again. "I don't need to take myself in hand. If I lie here and smell her for a few more minutes, it'll spill all by itself." Lily felt his toes curl where they were wedged between her feet. "Do you know how long it's been since I came? Six weeks counting the ship's journey. People our age weren't meant to be celibate this long."

Ian laughed but he, too, sounded pained. He reached across her to pat Col's arm.

"It was worth it, Col. We were chosen, both of us. Our families will be proud."

"Our families don't have red hot pokers stabbing them between the legs."

Lily couldn't help it. She snuffled out a laugh.

"Princess!" Ian exclaimed.

"It's all right." She flattened her hand across her chest to calm the laugh. "I was awake."

Col groaned, mortified. She turned and hugged him, which made him groan the louder.

She smoothed her hand down his hard, perspiring chest. "Let me give you ease."

He practically tore the kalisari out of her way.

"Ah," he sighed as she explored his stiffened length. "Ah, yes, Mistress. Softly, softly. Your little fingers are so—"

Her fingers wandered over his swollen sac, stifling whatever he'd meant to say. Lily cocked her head. "You feel different from before. Plumper."

"His balls have drawn up," Ian said, pressing tightly to her back. He'd pulled up his skirt. His hardness was a pulsing rod that pressed and released against the cotton-clad crease of her buttocks. His voice grew huskier. "It means he's about to spill."

Heat swept Lily's body. She wanted to feel him spill. She wanted to make him do it.

She tightened her hand around the thickened shaft. She pulled upwards, then pushed back towards Col's belly. Twice she did this, slowly, reveling in his growing heat, in the tightness of his sexual skin, in his harsh, panting breaths.

"Oh, no," Col moaned. He cursed then and shuddered. A hot burst of moisture jetted against her gown. He shook and grunted with each climactic spasm. He had not quite finished when Ian clutched her hips, cried out and dampened her gown as well.

"Ah," both men sighed, and sagged bonelessly against her.

Happy to have pleased them, she stroked Col's thick red locks.

"Princess," Ian muttered.

Col began to snore.

Her mouth fell open in disbelief. She understood they were tired, but what about her? No doubt her mother would have cuffed the bounders awake. Of course, her mother wouldn't have offered to please them in the first place. Once again, she had done everything wrong. She sighed and squirmed onto her back. One night's frustration wouldn't kill her.

But Grae had his own opinion on the matter.

"Out!" he ordered, grabbing each man by the foot and yanking him down the mattress.

"Wha—" Col said, fighting for balance.

Taking advantage of his confusion, Grae grabbed his arm and pulled him fully out. "Neither of you knows how to treat a lady. Therefore, you will take the first watch."

"It's not their fault," Lily protested. "I didn't ask—"

"You shouldn't have to ask," he roared.

She couldn't suppress a squeak at the volume of his voice. Ian squeezed her shoulder. "He's right, Princess. Col and I behaved abominably and we will do as he says."

But *I'm* supposed to be training you, she wanted to say.

Before she could, Col and Ian disappeared to take up their post in the entryway. Grae remained. He glared at her from the foot of the bed as if she were responsible for putting him in this position. But if he regretted his decision to interfere, that was his concern. She would not sit here trembling like a rabbit at his disapproval.

"Well," she said in as steady a voice as she could muster. "Why don't you show me how a lady should be treated?"

Grae's face tightened, but she knew he wouldn't back down. With a long warrior's breath he grabbed the flint from her bedside table. Though moonlight poured through the room's narrow windows, he lit the brass lanterns that hung from the posts of her bed. When each was burning merrily, he climbed inside and pulled the hangings shut. Immediately she felt as if she were breathing steam instead of air. He was so big, so unyielding and intense. Anticipation shivered through her limbs. What would he do to her?

"Your gown is wet," he said. "Give it to me."

She could not think of a good reason to disobey. Her hands shook as she wriggled the cambric up her legs and pulled it over her head. She held it out to him, crumpled in her hand. He did not take it: he was too caught up in staring at her naked breasts and belly. The silk sheet still covered her lap but he stared at that, too, as if his eyes could burn through the slippery cloth.

To her relief, he was not unmoved by what he saw. His quarry man's skirt stood out as if he'd lodged a club beneath it. Now she must take control, she thought, before she lost the chance.

"Grae," she said. He flinched at the sound of his name. "Grae, take off your skirt."

"Later," he growled.

"Now," she insisted.

Their eyes clashed. His hands moved. In a swift, angry motion, he discarded the kalisari. His sex was beautiful, red and strong. A single blue vein twisted from the deep slash of his navel, through his gleaming black thatch and down his shaft to the big, heart-shaped glans. Fluid glistened on the ruddy tip. She licked her lips.

"Don't," he said, though she hadn't moved. "Don't make me forget what I'm here to do."

"What are you here to do?"

"This," he said, and swooped down on her.

He kissed her temple, her cheek, the tip of her nose, the line of her jaw. The blows were soft and warm, hungry, but fleeting. With a low growl, he nipped the skin of her neck between his teeth, and then finally, finally settled his body and took her mouth. Their tongues met at once, wet and sweet and wonderfully curious. It was a deep kiss, but soft. She'd never been kissed like this before. She felt as if he were opening her entire being through the sinuous seduction of her mouth.

She moaned with pleasure, and tried to kick free of the sheets. As impatient as she, he lifted and stripped them down. Again he stared. She was naked, bare to his gaze. Gently, ever so gently, he ruffled the mink-brown curls between her thighs. The tender gesture brought the sting of tears to her eyes. As it had in the courtyard, a shadow of recognition fluttered across her awareness. Her soul seemed to know this man. She tugged at his arms, wanting him against her.

To her dismay, he sat back on his heels. "I can't," he said, his black eyes shuttered. "Not my skin to yours. I couldn't bear it."

"You can't," she repeated.

"Unless you're offering to let me take you. Completely." His expression gave nothing away. Not slyness. Not longing. Lily wished her own face were as blank but she knew he could see every flicker of hurt, of anger and frustration. She pressed the back of her wrist over her mouth to keep her groan inside.

"Hush," he said, and then his hands were on her: long, delicious strokes that swept her from breast to thigh. "Hush. I'll take care of you."

She wanted to resist but she melted at his touch. He bent closer. His lips captured her nipple, tugging and licking. He kissed a wet trail to her second breast, then down the inside of one arm and onto her belly. He licked her navel and her anger dissolved in a giggle. She felt his answering smile against her skin and thought he might be human after all. Gently, he grasped her thighs in his big, hard hands. She tensed at the pressure.

"Don't worry," he said. "I've done this before. Just not the rest."

"The rest?" she said, though she knew. She knew.

"I've never been inside a woman. Not my cock inside her cunt."

The words sent a shudder through her sex. Moisture overflowed her, warm and creamy.

"Oh, that rest," she said, pretending he hadn't devastated her with those hard, male words.

He smiled and looked up from her belly. His eyes seemed to slant even more in the lamplight. His brows were wings of coal, sardonic, mysterious. "Yes, that rest. How do you think I earned those pretty stripes you were admiring?"

The answer was no clearer than before, but the sudden descent of his mouth erased the question from her mind. In seconds, he'd wrung an anguished cry from her throat. Never had she felt anything so lovely as his tongue moving on her sex.

"Tell me." He paused and applied a different motion. "Did you like that better? Or this?"

She could not answer. Everything he did sent thrills through her secret flesh. He slid two fingers into the first inch of her sheath. She moaned so loudly she heard Col mutter in alarm from across the room.

Grae chuckled. "Like something inside your pretty snatch, do you?"

"Yes," she said. "Yes. Just don't stop. Please don't stop."

She shouldn't have said "please" but it was too late to take it back. Still chuckling, Grae took her in his mouth again. A heavenly tension coiled inside her.

"Oh," she cried. "Oh, yes."

He pushed her legs wider and worked his shoulders under them. His breath warmed her. His tongue lashed her. His fingers beat a soft tattoo just inside her gate. Her sheath tugged at the intrusion. Her hands tangled in his rough, night-black hair. She was so close.

"Mmn," he hummed into the tiny kernel of her pleasure.

She broke with a low, quavering cry, shattering into a thousand shards of wet sensation, sweet as chocolate, sharp as wine. Like chocolate they melted. Like wine they sang. Her body arched and went limp. Tenderly he kissed her. One last kiss beyond any need for kissing. A chink in his brutal Ka'arkish armor.

An answering tenderness welled up inside her, too powerful to resist. "Grae," she whispered. She sat up to knead the stiff muscles of his neck.

For a moment, he relaxed into the caress, but only a moment. Her face burned with embarrassment as he eased her back and straightened the covers. He blew out the lanterns. But he could not leave. He had ordered the others away and now he must stay. In silence, he stretched out beside her, on top of the covers, with his back to her breast. She heard his heel strike the footboard. The bed was not quite long enough for him. The rhythm of his breathing filled the curtained space. It told her he did not sleep. It told her his need for release had not abated.

She touched his naked hip. He stiffened.

"Hush," she said, and kissed his shoulder. She rubbed a circle around his hip. Her hand crept over his side and into the velvety hollow of his groin. He quivered like a shying horse. His skin felt different from hers, more substantial, but smooth. She reached the edge of his pubic thatch. The heat of his arousal pulsed over her fingers. She combed through the crisp, curly hair.

A callused hand slammed over her wrist. "No," he said.

"But I want to help you. You need it."

"I need it too much, Princess. If you touch me now, I won't stop until we fuck. So unless you want to give up that precious virginity of yours . . ."

"You wouldn't dare."

"I wouldn't have to dare. I'd make you beg."

She wanted to deny it but she couldn't get the words out. She wriggled her hand free of his grip. "Perhaps," she said in a tone too shaky to impress, "I would make *you* beg."

His laugh was humorless. "When hell freezes over. I may be a slave but I have my pride."

"But how can my pleasuring you injure it?"

He thumped the pillow and resettled himself. "I have my reasons."

"I order you to tell me what they are," she said and this time the words didn't shake at all.

"Order me to mop the floor, Princess. My soul is my own."

"Perhaps I should call the others. They were grateful for my favors."

If she hoped to make him jealous, she failed. "The others don't have what you want."

"You don't know what I want."

"Don't I?" He turned and licked slowly up the side of her face. "You want a strong man you can break, Princess. A man whose spine will make a nice, satisfying crack."

"That is not what I want!" Actually, this was precisely why she had chosen him but he had no right to think so. Certainly not to say so. "Oh, turn around and go to sleep," she snapped.

"As you wish," he said, but so mockingly the victory was hollow.

Chapter Three

He refused to let her pleasure him.

Lily did not understand. Her pretty boys reveled in pleasure. Every night they taught her marvelous things. How to make a man shiver from a single touch. How each man liked to be stroked differently, yet in some ways were the same. She learned to listen for the hitch in the breath, for the moan or whimper that signaled their deepest pleasures. She also learned what pleasured her. The men had taken Grae's scolding to heart. She no longer had to ask, though sometimes she did. *Kiss me here,* she would say and they would quiver with excitement as each competed to fulfill her request. The more daring her demand the better they liked it.

Grae was different. If she made demands of him, he gave her what she asked twice over. He was not satisfied unless he left her weak with pleasure. But he never let her turn the tables.

"I do not understand him," she confessed to Ian one night as they lay in a sweaty tangle, half way to dreamland. "Where is the harm in taking release from my hand? Why does he insist that he will only come inside me?"

Ian stroked her hair. "When a man makes love to a woman they are lost in the madness together. But when a woman makes a man come, by himself, he is utterly in her power, and at his moment of greatest vulnerability. I believe Grae is too proud to put himself in this position."

"If that is true, why are you not too proud?"

"I," said Ian, "am not an idiot."

His explanation obsessed her even as Grae's resistance did. But to force him was not the victory she craved. She must do what he threatened to do to her. She must make him beg.

She ordered him to clothe her each morning, from shift to gown to slipper. He would rise from the task so desirous his hands would shake. Then she would clothe him. The kalisaris she reserved for her private enjoyment, jealous of the pleasure her slave's bare bodies might give the ladies of the court. For public wear, she ordered fine uniforms from the seamstresses, baby-soft velvet and silk, a caress for them to carry through the day. The cloth was gold and white; her colors for her men.

She loved sliding the hose up Grae's long legs. The muscles of his calves cried to be held in the curve of her palm. The tender skin behind his knee was ticklish, and his thighs were admirably hard. The current fashion in tunics was short, mid-thigh, with a long leather belt to cinch them at the waist. Grae's waist was narrow. She would wrap the leather thrice, then smooth the ends over his bulging groin. He winced every time she did it.

Sometimes she would slip her hand beneath the hem and give his sex a squeeze.

"It would take but a moment," she would say. "A few quick strokes? Perhaps a kiss?"

The answer was always the same. "Only if you are offering yourself to me."

That she would not do. Her virginity belonged to another, to her One True Love.

When Ian and Col shared her bed, she made certain the curtains were open, made certain Grae could hear everything they did.

Alas, when they left to take their watch, he would come to her bed and make a mockery of all she'd learned. The pleasure he showed her obeyed no rules. He was a fire licking over her skin, a storm at sea that made one long to drown. She could not control her response to him and still he refused to relinquish control over himself. A kiss was all the caress he would allow her.

So she kissed him. She kissed him awake in the morning while his sex lifted the sheets in hard, surging throbs. She kissed him in the vestibule at chapel. She kissed him until their lips burned from the friction, until their eyes glazed with hunger and their lungs heaved like bellows.

"Don't," he would say and she would stop. Until the next time.

"Why?" she finally asked. "Are you afraid I'll treat it as a weakness to take advantage of?"

"I know you will," he said.

His words hurt, though she could not deny them. He was only here so that she could master him. But was that so awful? Col and Ian did not suffer under her yoke. Grae would be happy, too. Her determination to prove it grew. Each kiss might be the kiss that broke him, each night *the* night. She began to long for bedtime. Col and Ian did, too. They smiled at the ringing of each evening bell, full of shared anticipation. Only Grae grew surly as the night drew on.

Fortunately, her days were full or the wait would have been intolerable. Her hours with the tutor were increased and twice a week she sat in Audience, once with her mother and once by herself. She preferred judging simple matters on her own, experiencing none of the doubts she felt in Lady Fortis's presence. Common sense unraveled most of the knots her people brought to her. When it didn't, she would set either Ian or Grae to investigate. Ian had a nose for gossip and Grae could stare the truth out of all but the most hardened criminals.

Col was simply a dear. He rubbed her neck if she sat too long at her studies. He organized her appointments and ensured she got everywhere on time. Most importantly, he saw that anyone who came to her was treated well from the moment they arrived to the moment they left. As a result, she had the most even-tempered petitioners of anyone on her mother's staff.

"I do hope you're not planning to go home when your year is up," she said to Col one day. "I don't know how I'd manage without you."

He blushed to the roots of his blazing hair. "It is my honor to serve you."

Touched, Lily took his hand and pressed a kiss to its palm. The flame of adoration that lit his sky-blue eyes embarrassed her.

It disgusted Lady Fortis. She sent Lily a small leather crop with a note.

Infatuation fades, it said. *Respect does not.* Lily immediately threw both on the fire. To consider whipping a slave for such a reason! Far better to remain a doormat.

In any case, she doubted Col was truly besotted. She had noticed he jumped to do Ian and Grae's bidding as eagerly as her own. She suspected he needed someone to devote himself to. Unlike Ian, who made friends at every turn and Grae, who appeared to need none, Col seemed lonely. No doubt he would have given his heart to any woman who was kind to him.

Would that Grae were as easy to win!

One night she ordered him to bathe her. There was a chamber beneath the Great Hall, where a hot spring had been diverted through the castle. It was a large, echoing room, tiled in flowery blue and gold designs. It smelled of copper and eucalyptus, an earthy scent. She set Col and Ian to guard the door and handed Grae a pot of lavender soap.

"Strip," she ordered as she floated in the shallow end of the steaming bath.

He pulled off his clothes, his eyes never leaving her body. He was hard already. With a caution she suspected had nothing to do with the heat of the water, he descended the steps.

"You must stand," he said hoarsely, "if you wish me to bathe you." She stood. The water fell to her knees. For a moment, he closed his eyes.

"You've seen me naked many times," she whispered. "Does it still move you?"

"You know it does, Princess. You have only to look at me and my body readies."

She took the pot of soap from him and set it on the marble ledge. She clasped his slender waist and looked into his hot, black eyes. His nostrils flared. His tongue touched his narrow upper lip. He wanted her kiss, she knew, wanted the one pleasure he allowed her to give.

She rose on her toes. She twined her arms behind his corded neck.

"God in heaven," he swore, and swallowed her whole.

She had never known him to be so desperate. He would not end the kiss. He would not let her go. Tighter and tighter he held her, owning her mouth with the avid penetration of his tongue. Twice he lost his breath and broke for air. Twice he clutched her more greedily than before.

Lily stroked the furrow of his spine. His scars tickled her palms and a cry of pity escaped her control. A growl rumbled in his chest. He gripped her bottom and hitched her closer, off her feet, into the angry throb of his groin. She couldn't bear it. She had to touch the part of him he'd denied her. She squirmed her hand between their bodies. She grasped the angled root.

"Don't," he said and shoved her away so hard she almost lost her footing.

"Damn you," she said, her hand on the floor of the bath to steady her. "You are my slave!"

He had just enough shame to look down at the steaming water. "Why must you torture me? I obey you in all things but this. Can you not leave me one scrap of pride?"

"How can this hurt your pride? It is your duty to obey me, as much as it is your duty to mop the floor or stoke the fire."

"I did not choose to be a slave," was all he said.

Lily slapped the surface of the water. "Tell me who forced you then. I'll have them arrested. I'll set you free if that is what you truly desire." There. She had thrown the gauntlet between them. His lips narrowed to a hard white slash. He was shaking with anger.

"If you are protecting someone—"

"No," he said firmly. "No one."

"Then you must fulfill your contract. All of it."

For an instant his eyes held a plea for mercy but they hardened so quickly she thought she must have imagined it. "I cannot," he said. "Do you wish me to turn you over to the guards? Do you wish me to send you home?"

His expression blackened. "Do what you think best."

She did not understand him. He behaved as if he did not want to be sent home. Surely his freedom was worth the disgrace. As for turning him over to the guards, he must know she would never do so. She covered her face. Some slave mistress. No wonder her mother doubted her ability to rule. But there were at least two men who were willing, even eager, to let her rule them.

She straightened with decision. "Col! Ian!"

Grae gaped at her. Clearly, he hadn't expected this.

"Yes, Mistress?" Ian said, his smile all sidelong charm.

"This slave feels unable to carry out his duties. You and Col may assume them."

"Our pleasure," said Ian, and promptly began to strip.

Grae watched with narrowed eyes as they soaped her body, lingering over her breasts, her bottom, the plump cushion of pleasure between her legs. Col washed her hair, kneading her scalp in slow, tingling circles. Her sighs of pleasure were not feigned.

When they had rinsed her, she walked into deeper water and directed Ian to hop onto the marble ledge. She put her hands on his knees and eased them apart. Her head was level with his groin. The heat of the water had softened him but now, as her breath washed his sex and her hands rubbed his muscled thighs, he rose to full glory.

"Now," she said. "We will show this man how a slave accepts a gift from his mistress."

Ian looked at her, his eyes wide. He had told her of this act, but she had not done it yet. "Are you sure, Mistress?"

Lily smiled and took the very tip of him in her mouth. From the corner of her eye, she saw Grae scowl. You could have had this, she told him silently as she worked the hot, rounded flesh. These groans could have been yours, these shudders of pleasure.

"Mistress," Ian cried, a tight-throated plea for release.

She gathered his sac in one hand and rolled it. She clasped his root in the other and squeezed it. As she drew on him with her cheeks, her tongue laved the magic spot beneath the head. He had shown her this the night before, a sweet gathering of nerves that could wring an explosion from the stubbornest organ. And Ian's was not stubborn at all. His knees tightened around her ribs. His hips contracted, pushing his sex further into her mouth. He spread his fingers wide against her cheek; to feel her suckle him, to feel himself burst.

"Mmn," she hummed, just as Grae had the first time he made her come. She heard him curse and then Ian jerked in climax.

"Ah," Ian said. "Yes-s."

Afterwards, he and Col did not wait for her to ask. They carried her from the pool and lay her on a heap of thick, gold toweling. Amazingly, Ian had not flagged.

"Let me," he said, his shaft rising strong and pink. He pressed it lengthwise between the lips of her mound. "Let me love you, Princess."

He was not a slave then. He was a man asking a man's right from his lover. Lily stroked his long, wavy hair and looked into his portrait-perfect face. He was a good man, fickle perhaps, but kind. He would not hurt her. For a second she thought: It would serve Grae right. But this was not a gift to be given in spite. This was a gift for her One True Love, whoever that might be. She had waited this long. She could wait a little longer.

"No." She cupped Ian's face. "I am not prepared to take that step."

"As you wish," he said, and he and Col brought her to her peak by other means.

Lily watched Grae brush her blue velvet gown by the chamber window. She did not need to oversee the work, but she had no duties for the hour and she had noticed on occasion that his company had the power to calm the turmoil within her, even if he was the one who had caused it. She was certain she was not falling in love; that would have been ridiculous. Assuredly, she only craved his company because he was a wonderfully quiet man.

His hands were sure at the task. She could tell he had consulted her favorite maid, for he was almost as clever now as Lyn. It struck her again that he refused to do anything poorly.

Except obey her. He did not do that very well.

"You should give them leave to take one of the maids," he said as he dabbed a mysterious concoction on a spot of grease.

"Give who leave?" she asked, entranced by the movement of the tendons in his wrist.

"Col and Ian. They were required to be virgins for the choosing ceremony, but it isn't natural for boys their age to remain celibate."

"Boys their age!" She stepped between him and the window, forcing him to look at her. His face was infuriatingly calm. "They're older than you. And they've expressed no interest in 'taking the maids' as you put it."

"Well, they wouldn't express it to you, would they?"

"You think I'm vain, don't you?" She hovered humiliatingly close to tears. "You think I can't imagine them looking at another woman. But for your information, I'm not such an idiot as that. I may be passably pretty for a princess, but I know I'm not the most beautiful woman in the world or the cleverest or, to hear you tell it, the nicest."

"If you're feeling possessive, you could take their virginity yourself."

Ooh, why did he do that? Why did he say the one thing that would hurt her most when it would have been so easy to make her happy? He could not have made it clearer that he cared naught for her virginity himself. She was not used to being disliked, and yet she was not entirely sure he did dislike her. Sometimes, when he touched her in the dark, he seemed almost to cherish her, which made such comments cut all the deeper. Furious with herself, and with him, she swiped her arm across her eyes. She looked out the window. A group of squires were running a mock joust in the courtyard. They didn't have horses so they rumbled along on wheeled trolleys, trying to unseat each other.

It was far easier to picture Grae out there, rather than in here cleaning her gowns.

"I do not think you vain," he said. "And you are more than passably pretty."

She blinked and turned to him. She couldn't believe it. He'd actually given her a compliment. Two, in fact. Of course, being Grae, he spoiled it in the next breath.

"You need to remember that Col and Ian are men, not toys."

"And you need to remember they're slaves." Oh, she hated the way that sounded, even as she said it.

He shook her dress and held it up to the light, his lips pursed, his thick, black lashes shielding his eyes. "You are their mistress," he said, agreeably enough.

But she knew he didn't mean: You are their mistress. Their pleasure is yours to dictate. He meant: You are their mistress. Their happiness is your responsibility. She flushed. Fairness demanded she think on what he'd said, though heaven forbid her mother should ever hear of it.

The three of them lay sprawled across the rumpled shelter of her bed. For once, she had closed the heavy curtains. The lanterns were lit. They cast a golden glow across the green brocade. Ian's silky head lay in her lap and Col was rubbing her feet. Their kindness tore at her conscience. Tradition dictated that she disregard the feelings of a slave.

Pride dictated that she do nothing which could be viewed as currying Grae's favor.

What does your heart say, she asked herself, and perdition take the rest.

She cleared her throat. Both men looked up at her and smiled. "I was wondering: would you like to take one of the maids? Assuming you know one who'd be agreeable."

The men exchanged a glance, their brows sporting identical furrows. Ian was the first to speak. "You want to watch us swive, er, make love to one of the maids?"

"Watch you?" Her hand flew to her breast. "Heavens, no! I simply thought it would make you happy to, you know, do as other men."

"Ah," Ian said. "You mean give up the dreaded burden of our virginity." He tapped her heated cheek. "No, Princess, we prefer to wait until you're ready to accept that gift yourself."

Col nodded energetically. "Yes, Princess. We'd rather give that to you."

"But what if it's a long time? What if it's never?"

Ian captured her hand and kissed her fingertips. "Nonetheless. We prefer to wait."

"Besides," Col's face reddened, "it's not as if we aren't enjoying ourselves."

Lily relaxed onto a mound of pillows. "You're right, Col. There's a lot to be said for fun."

To herself, she added: 'Tis a pity it's not enough.

Chapter Four

Lily's mother summoned her to her private office, a small chamber in the heart of the keep. So ornate was the carving on its marble arches and so bright the glow of its stained glass windows that it resembled the inside of a jewel box. Lady Fortis sat writing at her desk, her straight, wheat-colored hair trained back by a golden fillet. Though her pose was informal, she wore her robes of state. The purple velvet was so heavily embroidered with gold it crackled with her movements.

Lily stood on the thick Laravian carpet and waited for her to look up. She clasped her hands behind her back, squeezing them rhythmically to ease her nervous tension.

Finally, her mother set the quill aside and closed her ledger. Her eyes were the color of a winter sky, a pale, clear blue. Her face did not show her age. It was a pretty face. Only the stern set of her mouth hinted at the determination for which she was famed and the dissatisfaction of which she was capable. Her gaze took inventory, skimming over Lily's emerald green gown. Her lips thinned a fraction more.

"You have not taken your slaves. Nor have you disciplined them."

There was only one way she could know this. With difficulty, Lily swallowed her fury at being spied upon. "They are very well-behaved," she pointed out as calmly as she could.

"Yes, I'm sure the experience is valuable, so long as every man you meet is as eager to please as they!" Her mother leaned forward. "You must make them yours completely. You must impress upon them the awareness that you are the source of every pleasure and every pain. That is the way of mastery. Every woman who rules must taste this draught, must know she has this power."

"I—I prefer to master them my way."

"Pray tell, what is your way, Lily? To stuff them with comfits until they beg for mercy?" Her mother's fingertips pressed the surface of her desk as if to force her will through the polished wood. "You are meant to cut your teeth on them, Little Cub. Then when you take a husband, no matter how powerful he may be, you will rule him."

"As you rule Father?" Lily said, the question coming from some hidden depth.

Enraged, her mother slammed both hands on top of her ledger. "I will not have patriarchal ways return to Ammam. You will learn to rule if I have to beat it into you."

Perhaps hysteria put the words in her mouth. Perhaps her slaves truly had increased her confidence. "Ah," she said. "I'm sure being beaten will go far towards teaching me how to rule."

Her mother's lovely face darkened with fury. No sarcasm was allowed but her own. Lily braced for an explosion but a low laugh cut her short. Vizier had entered from the adjoining room. He was neither tall, nor handsome. He bore just enough weight to qualify as corpulent, and his greying hair had been creeping back for years. His nose was large, his teeth crooked. He did, however, have the cleverest eyes and the warmest smile she had ever seen. Now he turned both on Lady Fortis.

"Come, love," he said in his merry way. "Don't be angry when your cub shows her claws."

"Beast!" she spat and flung an ivory bauble at his head.

Experience had quickened his reflexes. The bauble missed him by a foot, hit the chamber door and rolled back across the carpet. It came to rest at Lily's feet. When she picked it up, it snapped in two.

A superstitious shiver crossed her nape. The trinket was a hollowed-out map of the world, a gift from the Yskutian ambassador. Unlike other countries, Yskut did not offer tribute to Ammam, not even in the name of diplomacy. Their reasons for gift-giving ran deeper. They responded neither to wants nor demands but only needs, and those needs were defined according to Yskut's own inscrutable standards.

If the ambassador, for whatever reason, thought her mother needed this trinket, Lily was loath to see it broken. She stared at the two halves lying like eggshells in her palms. Delicate ribs of longitude and latitude connected the continents, on which tiny rivers and mountains had been etched. The piece was a marvel of the miniaturist's art.

"I'll take this to Father," she said. "I've heard he is clever with—"

"You will not." Her mother was breathless, half-standing with anger. "You will not go near that bloodless little man. Throw the thing away. It doesn't matter."

Lily slipped the pieces into her pocket and fought the urge to nod. A nod would have been a lie. She had no intention of throwing the globe away. Instead she waited for her dismissal.

"Yes, yes." Lady Fortis waved her towards the door. "I know you cannot bear my company another moment. But remember what I told you, Lily. I want results."

She'd reached the threshold before resentment overcame caution and made her turn. She ignored the incipient chatter of her teeth.

"You will see no results unless you remove your spies, Mother. I will not master these men for the entertainment of servants."

Her mother's eyes narrowed, but Lily stood her ground.

"I will not wait much longer," her mother warned.

Lily sensed this was as close to a concession as she would get.

Vizier caught up to her halfway down the Corridor of Ancestors. He had a quick walk for a stocky man, full of energy.

"Lily, wait," he said. He swung his arm around her shoulders and steered her into a statuary alcove. That she did not resist was a measure of her affection for him. He began precisely as she expected. "Do not be angry with her, Princess. She cannot help what she is."

"How convenient for her."

Vizier hid his smile by rubbing a finger across his upper lip. Then he smoothed her long dark hair behind her shoulder. "Do you know, Lily, it irks your mother no end that your servants are always better-mannered than hers, always more skilled at their tasks. Do you suppose that, on some level, she's aware that she frightens her servants out of countenance and resents your ability to make yours love you?"

Lily scraped her slipper against the base of her grandfather Harry's bust. "She gives me no credit for anything." She sounded, to her dismay, like a petulant child. She cleared her throat and spoke more firmly. "I will master them."

Vizier patted her back. "It seems to me they are mastered already. They leap to do your bidding before you even know what it is. What you choose to do in the privacy of your chamber is your business. Your mother merely wishes to believe that her way is the only way."

Lily nodded, but his words did not lighten her gloom. He lifted her chin on the edge of his hand. "What is it, Little Cub? What troubles you?"

"Grae won't obey me."

Vizier's brows were tufts of grey above his clever eyes. They creased together in confusion. "Grae? Ah, the Ka'arkish lad." Deciding this discussion required more ease, he made himself comfortable on the alcove's small bench, then patted the space beside him. Lily sat and leaned into his big warm chest, just as she had when a child. How often she had prayed he were her parent, her only parent. Now he kissed the top of her head. "Men are led by different things, Princess. Some by fear, some by greed, and some by love. But some will only follow the dictates of their own will. To know which are which is not a bad lesson for a ruler to learn."

"But Mother—"

He smiled and shook his head. "You are one of very few people who has the capacity to set your mother on her heels. She respects you more than you know. More than she knows, in fact."

Lily shook her head. Vizier was, as always, trying to be kind, to mend the ever-growing rift between princess and queen. But Lady Fortis did not respect her. And unless Lily found some way to rule her unruly slave, she very likely never would.

Lily had noticed that, while Grae might think like a soldier, he certainly didn't sleep like one. Nothing short of shouting in his ear would wake him. To her amazement, he'd grown increasingly affectionate in his slumbers. This night, he squirmed over to her side of the bed, took her in his arms and slung his leg over her hip. Her heart squeezed in her chest, even though she knew better than to trust the actions of a sleeping man. How would it be, she wondered, if he turned to her this way when he was awake, not for the sake of giving her pleasure, but for his own comfort, out of his own wish to be loved?

She bit her lip. It was a foolish question. Why should he crave her love? More to the point, why should she crave his? No, she did not. She could not. She craved the pleasure he gave her, as did he; even now his arousal, which had softened in sleep, rose against her hip.

He muttered and pressed closer.

Idiot man, she thought. She raked her fingers through his thick, black hair, then gently stroked her nails down his naked back. His buttocks were so narrow for a man his size, narrow and round and covered in a fine, silky down. They seemed to invite fondling, nay, demanded it. Lily ran her fingers over their contours and they clenched.

She thought back on caresses Col and Ian had enjoyed. Would Grae share their pleasure? She ran her thumb between the two globes. His breath sighed from him. Encouraged, she reached further, further until her fingers nudged the heavy swell of his sac. He uttered a sound of discomfort. She withdrew at once but he shifted closer and higher. His turgid shaft pulsed against the meeting of her thighs, even harder than before. He liked what she'd done. Heat swept her body like the blast from an open bread oven. If she lifted her leg an inch, his sex would snap upward between her thighs. She could rub her hungry bead of pleasure against the shaft. She could pretend they were making love without risking her innocence.

"Grae," she whispered, scratching back up the furrow of his spine.

He moaned and his eyes rolled behind their lids, but he did not wake.

Gathering her courage, she pushed up against the leg that weighted hers. The head of his sex sprang free. She wriggled down until she caught him in a slippery pubic kiss. Gingerly, not wishing to crush him, she lowered her thigh. At once his body tightened around hers. His arms clutched her back and his leg caught hers in a vise-like pressure. Apparently, she need not have worried about hurting him, for he seemed to crave more force and more. He rubbed his cheek against hers like an anxious cat, his beard rough on her tender skin.

She squirmed against his body as best she could. His sex was held almost too tightly to move, but its velvety skin shifted over the rigid interior, as did the skin of her thighs. He moaned, a sound of such longing it brought an answering rush of moisture from her sex. She rolled her hips again and felt teeth grip the muscle between her neck and shoulder.

"Hey," she whispered. The teeth withdrew and were replaced by a tongue. It lapped her, soothed her, a primitive, animal caress.

Satisfied he would not hurt her, she resumed her slow, rocking thrust. After a moment, he joined her, sighing at each motion, and growing warmer and warmer until a fine sheen of perspiration covered his bronzed Ka'arkish skin. Her hands roved, delighted by this unexpected freedom. She measured the breadth of his shoulders. She counted his ribs. She stroked her way down his bent leg to the sole of his foot. His toes curled when she stroked his instep and a new, more emphatic jerk entered the movement of his hips.

He would do this if we were making love, she thought, *if he were near the end.* The realization inspired a secret thrill. Her own arousal spiraled closer to its edge, but suddenly she didn't care. She wanted his orgasm, his seed bursting hot and strong between her legs.

What matter that she would steal it from him unawares? Whether he admitted it or not, he needed this release. The desperate pounding of his sex told her so, the hitch of his breath, the brazier heat of his skin. He was a healthy young man. If Col had been crazed after six weeks, how much moreso Grae after ten?

She'd be doing him a favor.

Her mind made up, she returned her hands to his bottom, encouraging each thrust to come a little harder, a little faster. His moans turned to pants. His fingers clutched her so hard her muscles tingled. And then he went wild. His speed doubled. His sex seemed to grow still longer between her thighs. His teeth scored her shoulder again. He stiffened and held tight—

"God!" His eyes flew open and he shoved her from him.

A burst of seed hit her belly. He cursed and fumbled between his legs. With the fingers of one hand he pinched the tip of his erection so hard its skin whitened. His other hand did something she couldn't see behind his sac. Whatever it was, it halted his release mid-spurt.

"You," he said. He backed out of the bed, panting and glaring as the hangings tented out behind him. "Have you no honor?"

Despite its recent mistreatment, his cock still pointed heavenward, looking, if possible, even bigger and redder than before. The sight brought a smile to Lily's face, then a giggle.

"Oh." She covered her mouth. "I'm sorry, but it—it just looks so angry."

Grae turned a black look at his sex, then sighed. "Princess. Don't you understand the meaning of the word 'no'?"

"If you hadn't woken you'd be feeling grateful right now."

He sighed again and crawled back into the bed. "That's besides the point. Now, if you don't mind, I'd like to get some sleep."

"At least tell me why," she demanded. "Surely I deserve that much."

He flopped onto his back and crossed his arms. "I'm here for the sake of my family's honor, but I judge slavery no honor myself."

"So you suffer my brutish rule for their sake."

"I never said you were brutish."

Her laugh was thin and bitter. "At least you give me that."

"Princess." He touched her arm in the dark. His breath hitched. For a moment she thought he would pull her against him, but his hand slipped away. "Can you not be satisfied with mastering Col and Ian?"

"No, I cannot," she said, "for, as my mother was kind enough to point out, they require no mastering at all. It is precisely you I must break, because you resist."

"Then we must remain at odds."

He sounded weary, sad even. Was he sorry? Did he wish they could be friends? Oh, damn her stupid heart for caring. She gritted her teeth. "Do not force me to harsher measures."

"You must do as you think best," he said.

Ha. She knew his ways now. He meant to shame her conscience by this and yet, if she did resort to force, he would dismiss her as a brute, perhaps the same sort of brute who had flayed him as a boy. That her pride would not allow. Or her stupid heart.

But how to tread the line between force and persuasion? She despaired of finding a way.

Chapter Five

The answer came to her in the night. Her conscience was not strictly comfortable with the solution, but neither was it uncomfortable. The plan would work, she believed, and more than anything she was weary of the stalemate between her and Grae, weary of her mother's censure and wearier still of her own self-doubt. She told herself she was not too soft to rule. She could make a difficult decision when required.

She thrust back the bed hangings, tired from her sleepless night but filled with resolve. The sun flooded the chamber in long, slanting rays. Grae mumbled something and burrowed into his pillow. If no one disturbed him, he would likely sleep for hours.

Ian smiled as she stepped naked from the bed. "Princess, your beauty outshines the sun."

"Aye," Col agreed. He caught sight of Grae and his mouth twisted in disdain. "Shall I wake the sluggard, Mistress?"

"Nay," she said. "We have business to discuss to which he is not privy."

Ian held a robe for her. "This sounds interesting."

"I hope you continue to find it so once I tell you what I plan. I am depending on your aid."

Col went down on one knee with her slippers. "You may rely on us. Always."

But always was not necessary. Only the length of one night.

She began her day with breakfast, then a bath, then fell asleep as Col and Ian massaged her with scented oil. She woke to find they had wrapped her in a blanket and carried her to a sunny corner of the rose garden. Her head lay in Ian's lap. Col sat nearby, polishing the blade of a dagger she had given him the week before. It was a traditional Ammish weapon, small but dangerous, a weapon a woman could wield. Col treated it like the Crown Jewels.

"Oh, no," she said, rising to her elbow. "My duties—"

Ian pushed her down. "Col has taken the liberty of rescheduling your appointments. You have a bit of a headache, don't you know, and dearly need your rest."

"For tonight," Col said meaningfully.

"You know," said Ian, "I am almost reluctant to help you. That Ka'arkish lunk does not deserve the delightful gift you have planned for him."

Lily snorted through her nose. "I doubt he will view it as a gift."

"The man is an idiot."

Col nodded so hard at his friend's statement that a dragonfly sheered off in fright. On the matter of Grae's idiocy, at least, they could all agree.

The weaving room lay beneath Lily's bedchamber. Like her room, it was girded by six narrow windows, three overlooking the courtyard and three with a view of the land between castle and harbor. A large metal rack was bolted onto one wall. The weavers wound yarn into skeins on its hooks. These hooks were sturdy but not sharp, the space between them large enough for one grown man. One stubborn man, she thought with a nervous smile.

While Grae consulted the metalsmith on the feasibility of installing a porticullus-style door at the base of her tower, she and Col and Ian shoved the looms against the walls and poured fresh oil into the lamps. The men built a fire in the hearth and carried a round table to the center of the room. The utensils with which she set it were pure, polished silver, the cloth a fine white linen. A six-branched candelabra awaited the approach of dusk.

Then they began their search. After much scrutiny, they found one spyhole in the door and another in a chink between two floor stones. She stoppered both with a sense of virtuous rebellion. Her mother had not actually promised to stop spying, and Lily did not wish to lead her into temptation. This was to be a private evening.

Her nerves were aflutter, but she was pleased to see that Grae had bathed before returning and, without being reminded, had changed into his kalisari. Still wet, his black hair was combed behind his ears and caught in a short queue. He looked clean and strong and male.

He was also on his best behavior, neither surly nor silent. His manners were not as fine as her other slaves' but they would suit. She had chosen a simple meal so as not to make him self-conscious, and had succeeded. He ate with gusto. They spoke animatedly on the upcoming harvest, on the prospects for trade between Ammam and the nomads of the Southern desert. Ian displayed the knowledge of a diplomat, Grae the common sense of, well, Grae. By the time she served the fruit course, he was lounging back in his chair and cradling his wine cup to his chest. He seemed to know he had impressed her, and to be enjoying it.

He waved away her offer of candied ginger. "This night is too sweet to spoil with sugar."

He smiled into his cup as he said it, but she knew he meant the words as thanks to her. She almost regretted what she was about to do on this, the friendliest evening they had ever spent.

"Are you comfortable?" she asked, her heart pounding like a jackrabbit's.

"Very." He stretched his legs under the table. His eyes were heavy. The wine was not drugged but deceptively strong. She and the other men had imbibed little.

Wishing to lull him further, she stroked the hard tendons of his forearm. "You do not wish to use the garderobe?"

His brow puckered at the personal nature of the question. "No-o."

"Then I suppose we are ready."

Col and Ian had risen. They grabbed Grae's chair, tilted it back and dragged it on two legs to the yarn winding rack.

"Hey!" he protested, still more confused than angry. By the time he thought to struggle, his arms were stretched above his head and his wrists bound firmly to the hooks. He tried to kick Ian and Col away but was no match for their united efforts. They forced his legs apart and tied those to the rack as well. "What are you doing?" He twisted in his bonds. "Let me go!"

Lily ignored him. Shivers of excitement coursed through her limbs. He was hers now. She could do as she wished and he could not stop her. She turned to Ian. "His kalisari must be removed."

Ian laid one finger along his lean, handsome cheek. "If you don't mind, Princess, I think Col would like to do the honors."

Col bared his teeth and flashed his fine Ammish dagger. He seemed almost as excited as Lily. Her eyes slid down his well-knit body. He was aroused. His white skirt stood out with the thrust of his erection. Awareness shifted inside her. Suddenly she recalled how Col would sometimes touch Ian as he pleasured her. She had thought he was being helpful, but perhaps . . .

Ian read the suspicion in her eyes. "Yes. We are both flexible that way."

Both! She should have been horrified, but the thought that they would enjoy Grae's subjugation as much as she did aroused her. A quick pulse throbbed between her legs, as if a warm fist were closing round her sex. Unable to speak, she nodded for Col to continue.

Though it would have been easier to unwrap the thing, Col slid the dagger up from the hem of the kalisari, slicing the white linen by inches. The top of Grae's thigh appeared, then his hipbone, and then the short length of cloth fell free.

His sex hung between his legs, soft as yet, but not entirely still. It had lengthened already, and darkened, and was beginning to harden. Before Lily could ask, Ian dragged a thick Laravian prayer rug in front of the rack. Sighing with anticipation, she knelt before her slave.

"Don't," Grae said before she'd even touched him.

"There is no more don't," she said. "There is only my will and your pleasure."

His eyes were screwed shut, his body braced for some terrible blow. She leaned forward and blew lightly on the skin of his sex, just that, no more. He rose. Higher. Thicker. Redder. His knees trembled. She had the power now. A rush of dark pleasure suffused her veins. She understood then what her mother felt when servants cowered before her.

Ian handed her the ostrich plume. She began at Grae's feet. She teased them with the feather, then her lips, and finally her tongue. She rose to his calves. She kissed the ticklish spot behind his knees, then proceeded up his thighs. She ran the feather over his sac and up the ridge that girded the underside of his shaft. The rosy head, now bare of all covering, merited one brief swipe of her tongue.

He cursed when she moved away.

"You are not ready yet," she said.

His eyes shot sparks of pure obsidian fury. But he could not say he was ready. That would have meant agreeing to all she did.

She kissed his nipples, searching each from within its whorl of hair. They were tiny but hard and he heaved outwards as she suckled. She kissed her way up his neck, over his Adam's apple to the cleft in his chin. She licked the hollow beneath his lower lip, but she did not kiss his mouth. That he had allowed, so that she would not do.

She descended again, following the line of his breastbone. His ribs expanded and sank. His belly quivered. His sex was so erect she had to pull it from his body.

"Don't," he said one last time, the word a groan more of longing than dread.

She smiled and wet her lips and drew his manhood into her mouth. This time, his groan had no words to it. Like his body, it betrayed him. He thrust forward, straining off the rack, nearly overwhelming her with his length.

"Careful," Ian warned him.

"Tell her to be careful," Grae gasped. "I never asked for this, never—Oh, Lord."

She wrapped her hand around his base and suckled him, slow, deep tugs that drew the skin of his cowl first over and then down. She swirled her tongue around the heart-shaped tip, loving the smoothness of the skin beneath, the power of the flesh it concealed, the vitality.

Grae's moans changed in tenor, growing alarmed.

"Tell them to leave," he begged even as his hips canted towards the descent of her mouth. "I'm tied now. You have me at your mercy. Please. Just tell them to leave."

She let him slip from her lips. She looked at the plea in his eyes, then at Ian.

Ian nodded and smiled. "It is a fair request, Princess. And we have tied him securely."

With their departure, a silence filled the room. The lamps hissed in their oily globes. The rack creaked under Grae's weight. Their breath whispered in synchrony. Still kneeling, she loosened the ribbon that snugged her gown beneath her breasts. His lips parted, eyes locked to the motion of her fingers. She pushed the gown and shift down to her knees, then stood long enough to kick it free. She was glad for the fire they'd lit earlier, though by now it was embers. Her nipples were as sharp from the cold as they were from anticipation.

He wet his mouth as he stared. She knew he wanted to kiss her breasts.

"I make you a promise," she said. Her lips trembled, for this was the moment on which her victory hung. "I will not force you to come unless you beg. I will bring you to the edge and release you . . . and then I will begin again."

"Lord above," he said, the words hoarse. "You have brought me to the edge already."

Her laugh warmed her throat like wine.

"Princess," he said, smiling in spite of himself at the sound of her joy.

She took him again and there were no more words, only the sweet rise and fall, the smooth hot flesh, the catch in his breathing, the sound like a whimper caught in his throat. He pushed at her, his body begging though he would not. She took him deeper, sucked him harder. Her tongue was a weapon of pleasure. She caught his sac and cradled it in her palm. It felt so heavy, so full. She squeezed it lightly and lashed the pleasure spot beneath the head of his sex.

He cried out as if in pain. His sex swelled in her mouth. His hips jarred forward. One more pull would slay him. She paused, savoring the frantic palpitation on her tongue.

"Please," he said. "I beg you, finish it."

Elation filled her. She closed her eyes and drew on him one last time. Then he came, long months of denial pouring out in a quivering, moaning flood. The taste of him was hot and rich, sweet and strange. He shook, crying out with each pulsing burst. She soothed him with her mouth, with her hands, sucking him gently now and stroking the hard, tremulous flesh of his hips.

At last he sagged, hanging from the rack as if she had drained the last of his strength. Exhaustion overtook her as well, more from the release of tension than from the arduousness of her efforts. She rested her cheek against his belly.

She had done it. She had made him beg.

Then the rack gave a groan as loud as any he had uttered *in extremis*. The hook that had held his left wrist fell to the stone, ringing as it struck. She gasped, speechless with horror. A second hook dropped a moment later, and then it was far too late to call for help. He bore her to the floor with his weight. Covering her mouth with one hand, he stretched her wrists over her head with the other. She heard another clank and knew his feet were free as well.

She screamed her outrage into his palm. He could not do this. He could not steal her victory. But he could.

"Now, Princess," he said, dark and gloating. "We'll see if you know how to beg."

He rubbed his body over hers, chest to chest, legs to legs, and everywhere he rubbed sensation flowed like honey through her limbs. She struggled to squirm away before he discovered how her body betrayed her. It was too late. He already knew. He bent his head and suckled her breasts, drawing her nipples into long aching buds. Removing his hand from her mouth, he swept it between their bodies and curled his fingers over her nether lips.

"Yes, Princess," he said, drawing their tips through her wetness. "Show me how much you want me."

One knee wedged between her thighs, then two. He widened them. He shifted higher. She hadn't imagined he could recover so soon but he was rigid with arousal. His sex slipped against hers, vibrating with lust. He anointed himself in her moisture. He pulled and pushed between her folds, catching her tenderest spots on the smooth, swollen ridge of the head.

"Don't worry," he whispered, hot fire against her ear. "I won't take you unless you beg."

She moaned, resisting and weakening by turns. He moved again, realigning himself. The tip of him pressed her gate, entered. Oh, it was sleek and hot. Her body wept for more. He must have been able to feel her tears. They were pouring from her like cream from a jar.

"No," she moaned, but her body pushed up at him, craving all of him, the full, hard length.

"*No* will not get you what you want," he said. He slipped his thumb over the pearl of her pleasure. He pressed it back against the bone, initiating a heart-stopping rhythm that he echoed with his cock. The blunt head pushed against the barrier of her virginity. Her body clenched, willing him to take her with all its strength.

Grae gasped and bit the tender lobe of her ear, but he did not break his word. "A simple 'please' will do," he said, his voice rasping like an iron file.

The sound of it destroyed her. She could not hold firm. She wanted him inside her. Wanted to swallow him utterly. "Please," she said, tears spilling from her eyes. "Please."

"Thank you, Lord," he breathed, and swiftly increased the pressure. He steadied her hips. "Now, Princess. Hold tight."

Her maidenhead gave way with a brief pinching sensation, such a little feeling for such an irrevocable change. He slipped inward. Halfway, no more. His eyes slid shut. He shuddered. And she remembered this was his first time, too.

"Princess." He kissed her temple. "Lift your knees, Princess."

But she was stunned. He was inside her, heat and fullness stretching her secret flesh. Her gift was gone. Her victory was gone. She wanted to cry but her tears had dried. What a miracle this was! She could feel the blood throbbing in his shaft, jittering against the pulse of her sheath.

"Princess." This time he squeezed her captive wrists. "Lift your knees."

She could not resist the urging of her flesh. She lifted her knees and he pressed farther in. Her wonder intensified. So intimate, this locking together of body parts. With a sigh, half resignation, half relief, she crossed her ankles in the small of his back.

He groaned and shoved one more time until he hilted. A long shiver rolled down his powerful body. "Ah, Princess." He turned his face back and forth across the spill of her hair. "I hope you're with me. I'm afraid this isn't going to last very long."

He lifted his head. They stared at each other. Anxiety pinched the corners of his eyes, but she could hardly breathe for the chill-like waves of pleasure sweeping her body. Delicious, intoxicating. All she could think was that she wanted more. She licked her lips. A smile played

over his mouth. He ran his hand down her side and cupped her buttocks. "Are you with me?"

She couldn't bring herself to say the words but she dug her heels into
his back and levered herself towards him. He pulled back against her
strength, then let it ease him in.

"Mm," he said, a sound of profound enjoyment, and let her do it
again.

She would not let him go. She could not. He stretched her hands
high above her head and all she had to hold him were her thighs and
calves. She would not be helpless, though. She made the most of the
power she had. He had to fight her for every withdrawal. He began to
laugh between his moans.

She was sure her One True Love would not have laughed and yet she
could not bring herself to mind. He was making her feel the magic: the
soft tingling rise, the ache, the helpless tightening deep inside. Now,
her body demanded, but she clenched her teeth against the plea.

"Now," he growled, thrusting faster and changing angles so that he
caught her just so, where the ache was deepest. His hand tightened on
her wrists. Her heart leapt with an excitement she could not deny. This
badly he wanted her. This much. Shoving deep, he ground himself
against her.

She cried out. Her back arched. She felt his mouth on her breast,
clinging, tugging, and the climax slammed through her. Her sense of
her body narrowed to three points: nipples, sex, wrists, all flaming like
comets in a velvet darkness. He pinned her, held her by those three
glittering points. She would have flown to pieces without him.

Then he flew to pieces himself. His long groan of ecstasy should
have been music to her wounded soul. The grateful kiss he pressed to
the curve of her breast should have soothed her like a lullaby. But
when she came to herself, she remembered. He wasn't her One True
Love. He was just a stubborn slave who'd proven once again she was a
fool to believe she could master him.

He withdrew carefully, giving her body a chance to relax. He released her wrists and cradled her close. He stroked her back. He urged
her head to rest against his shoulder. They might have been long-lost
lovers.

But they weren't. When the memory of passion faded, he would
return to disliking her as much as ever. And she— She feared she had
never disliked him as much as she wished.

"Sorry," he muttered into the tumbled silk of her hair. "Can't keep
my eyes open a minute longer."

She waited until he slept, then wriggled free and stood. He curled tighter on the small prayer rug. He looked cold. Vulnerable. Young. She doubled the linen tablecloth and tucked it around him. Then she pulled on her gown.

The aches and pains of her body were nothing to the ache in her heart.

Chapter Six

The tears came as soon as she stepped into the torchlit stairwell. She could not return to her room. Col and Ian would be there, doing whatever it was they did that she had not suspected them of doing. Despite her curiosity, she did not wish to take them unawares. They would stop at once, in any case. They would ask her what had happened and she would have to share the humiliation she did not want to face, much less recount. She looked down the stairs instead, at the barred wooden door Grae was hoping to fortify against intruders. It led to a passage inside the curtain wall and from thence to the main keep.

She did not know the hour, but Vizier might yet be in his office. She could take her troubles to him.

She shook her head even as the idea formed. Grae had dosed her with her own medicine. While Vizier might not scold, she could not bear to find judgment in his eyes. Sniffing hard, she swiped her sleeve across her eyes. She didn't need disapproval. She could supply that herself. She needed pity. She needed mothering. She needed—

She needed Nurse. Nurse would understand her loss. Nurse would take her side no matter what. Oh, if only she hadn't been sent back to town with the maids. Three slaves, no matter how willing, could never take her place.

But maybe there was a way. She crept to the bottom of the stairs and pressed her ear to the wooden door. All was quiet. There was a gatehouse in this section of the wall which, in this time of peace, was sometimes left unguarded. From there, town was a brisk walk away. Nurse was staying with her daughter. Lily had visited their home more than once. She knew she'd have no trouble finding it. Her heart began to race. The prospect of doing something forbidden, and perhaps a bit dangerous, pushed aside her disappointment and her shame.

The town was fortified, not as formidably as the castle, but it did have its own crenellated wall. She was obliged to slip in by the bachelor's gate, the door young men used to meet their sweethearts on the sly.

At this hour, only torches and the occasional candle in a window lit the winding streets. The shops had closed and she had wit enough to avoid the taverns. She'd grabbed a cloak from the empty guardroom. Though her velvet gown showed beneath its hem, the few people she passed paid her no mind. A wonderful sense of freedom filled her. Her strides lengthened on the cobbles. Tonight she was not a princess, not an heir, just a woman on a journey to meet a friend.

She passed a shuttered bakery and smiled as a skinny cat darted from an alley.

Without warning, hands yanked her off her feet and dragged her backwards into the shadows. They covered her mouth, preventing her from crying out. For a second she thought Grae had followed her, but the hands were too rough and the body smelled too foul.

"Well, well, well," said a grating voice. "What have we here come slumming in its fancy slippers?"

The hands spun her around and thrust back the hood of her borrowed cloak. Three men faced her, two young and one old, all wearing the brown and gold of the Tanner's Guild. One of the young ones held her by the shoulders. He was tall and wiry and had a skinny hooked nose.

The old man whistled. "Don't that beat all. It's her Ladyship's brat."

"I've come to visit friends," she said with as much dignity as she could muster.

"I'll bet you have," cackled the one who held her. "Come for a taste of town rough, eh? Three slavey boys ain't enough for you castle ladies. But you can forget about getting your slap and tickle here, Princess. We've higher matters on our minds."

"Like a charter," piped the other young one.

"Aye." Hooknose's grin bared crooked yellow teeth. "And now we've got the leverage we need to ransom ourselves a bit of self-rule."

Her body tensed against a shiver of fear. "My mother won't give in to blackmail. This is not the way to get what you want."

"Oh, ain't it?" said Hooknose. He continued to cackle as he dragged her into the dark.

They stashed her in a root cellar with her hands tied behind her back, her ankles hobbled, and a cracked piece of leather gagging her mouth. She could hear them moving about on the floor above, arguing over the proper composition of the ransom note. From the sounds of their contention, she might molder here for weeks.

I should have screamed when I had the chance, she thought. But she had no experience with screaming. For that matter, she had no experience with being in danger.

Her captors, such as they were, left her in the cellar all night. Sometime before dawn she wrestled her gown above her waist so she could relieve herself in the corner. The last time the town had petitioned for the right to govern themselves, Lady Fortis had fobbed them off with a sewer system. And here her daughter was, making the place smell like a midden again.

She dreaded her mother's reaction to this fiasco more than she dreaded anything those would-be councilmen might do.

Overcome with frustration, she banged her head against the wall. Though she'd managed to free her ankles, her wrist bindings held fast, despite rubbing them against a stone until her arms felt ready to fall off. The tiny paper-covered windows were too high to reach. Nor could she raise much of an alarm with a soggy swatch of leather in her mouth. Not even her captors could hear her muffled shouts, or so she assumed, since they did nothing to silence them.

Damn, she thought, damn, damn, damn.

The clatter of hooves on the cobbles outside brought her head up. More conspirators, she thought, but then she heard shouting and the clash of metal. Was she being rescued? Was it her mother's men? Oh, God. If it was, she almost wished she could stay a little longer.

It wasn't her mother's men, though. It was Col and Ian. They burst into the shadowy cellar with an impressive splintering of wood.

"Mistress!" said Col.

"Princess!" said Ian.

Lily struggled to stand. Her pride might hang in shreds, but she'd meet them on her feet.

Ian clucked over her scratches like a mother hen. He worked the gag off, then sliced through the ties that bound her wrists. She immediately flung her arms around his neck. To hell with pride. She was so happy to see him she could have cried. She did, in fact, just a little.

"There, there." He patted her back. "It's all right now. There were only five of the rascals and the fifth was so scared of me and Col, he ran off with his tail between his legs."

Pushing back from Ian, she peered around him at Col. He looked as if he'd been through the mill. His clothes were bloody and tattered. The state of his face suggested his nose had been broken again. Ian, however, barely bore a scratch. He wore a hooded hauberk even finer in make than Ka'arkish war mail. Black as pitch and shiny, the rings were so closely linked she could not see between them. They flowed over his form more like cloth than metal.

Curious, she stroked the slippery sleeve. "Where on earth did you get this?"

"Er," Ian shuffled his feet. "It's Grae's. Corking good stuff. Fellow broke his knife on it. Grae gave it to me when he saw he wouldn't make it."

Lily put her hand to her throat, suddenly icy cold. " 'Wouldn't make it?' "

"Oh, no, Princess." Ian squeezed her trembling shoulders. "No, Princess, he's fine. He's just, well, I don't believe he's ever sat a horse before and he couldn't get the beast to cross the last stream. Col was hot on your track. He's keen on hunting, you know. And Grae insisted we go ahead without him. When he found you missing, he said he had a feeling something was wrong. He didn't want us to wait."

"And he was right," Col said, sliding his precious dagger back into its scabbard. He shook his head morosely. "He's going to be angry that he missed this."

They all stiffened at the sound of hoofbeats, quite a lot of them, coming their way.

"Damnation," said Ian. "That last fellow must have gone for reinforcements."

Footsteps thundered into the house, shouts rising as fallen companions were discovered.

"Quick." Lily thrust a shovel into Ian's hand. "Bar the cellar door."

"We'll be trapped," Col protested, even as Ian jammed it through the handle.

"No, I'm small. You can shove me out the window and I'll run for help. The town is loyal—most of it." Lily hated the thought of leaving Col and Ian to their fates even for the few minutes it took to summon help. They might have taken down four men, but it sounded as if they faced a good deal more than that now. Already the reinforcements were pounding at the cellar door, slamming it with their shoulders. Tears coursed down her face as she ran to the tiny window. "Hurry, Col, give me a leg up."

Col hefted her towards the sill. The door creaked and began to splinter. Ian faced it, sword at the ready, preparing to defend her escape. Lily punched the oil-covered paper off the window.

"God keep you," she gasped.

But her shoulders wouldn't fit through the narrow opening. She moaned in despair, then sucked a deep breath. At least she could call for help.

"Wait!" said Ian, his voice sharp. Lily realized their enemies had stopped ramming the door, even though the uproar had increased. Ian trotted up the stairs and pressed his ear to the wood. "I hear fighting. My God, Grae's out there. He must have run here on foot."

Lily dropped to the floor and flew to him, closely followed by Col. Ian yanked the shovel from the door handle. "I can't leave him alone out there. You stay here and guard her, Col."

"Like hell," Lily and Col said as one. The odds were bad enough.

Ian conceded with a brusque nod. He thrust the shovel at Lily. "You take this, Princess. If anyone comes through this door, you clobber him first and ask questions later."

She waited in terror, jumping at every crash, straining for the voices of her friends. Grae's rose loud and sure, directing Col and Ian, heartening them, warning them of danger. Once, she heard him grunt in pain and clutched the shovel so hard one of her nails broke. He's out there with no armor, she thought, against God knows how many men. She tugged the doorhandle, meaning to help, but he must have been close because she heard him curse.

"Stay there, damn you," he ordered, almost slamming it on her fingers. "We're coming."

Finally, after what seemed like an eternity, silence fell in the smoky little house. Weak-kneed and trembling, she poked her head around the cellar door. Bodies lay everywhere, bleeding, unconscious, more than a dozen by her count. Horrified, her gaze roved the scene of carnage until, like a homing pigeon, they found Grae. He leaned over his knees, panting, liberally splashed with blood but apparently hale. His expression was weary and drained.

"They're not all dead," he said, reading her unspoken dread. "Most just knocked out."

Ignoring her churning stomach, she examined the bodies, turning each onto his back so she could memorize the features. She might sympathize with their cause, but her mother would want to know who had been involved in the conspiracy. It was especially important not to accuse anyone unjustly, for the queen's response was sure to be fierce.

With the end of the fighting, townspeople began to arrive. Lily assigned a hostler and his staff to secure the house, and then she and her rescuers began the slow walk home. Ian led her along on his horse until they reached the spot where Grae had tied his own recalcitrant steed.

"Let her down," he said. "I'll see she gets home."

Ian looked at Grae's horse, stolidly munching grass beneath a shady oak. Clearly he doubted the wisdom of handing her over to an inexperienced rider.

"You take my horse and ride ahead," Grae said, the tightness in his jaw all that betrayed his embarrassment. "Tell the queen what happened and that her daughter is well."

"What about you?" Ian asked.

"The princess and I are going to walk. We have important matters to discuss."

Lily looked at Grae. He was pale and angry. She didn't want to face him alone but she knew she must. Men were dead today who would have been alive if she had not run from her troubles. She swore it would not happen again.

"It's all right," she said to Ian. "I'm sure the danger is past now."

Col gave Grae a hard look, but he didn't protest, either. "Don't be long," was all he said.

As soon as they'd turned the horses towards home, Grae took her arm, his fingers like steel on her elbow. He led her into a copse of trees that marked the edge of the royal game preserve, walking faster and faster until she was panting to keep pace.

"Please, Grae," she said, stumbling over a root. "I can't keep up."

Abruptly, he yanked her towards a fallen log and sat. Without a word of warning, he turned her over his lap and began to spank her. Hard, stinging smacks rained over her bottom from the small of her back to the top of her thighs. Lily cried out but she could not wrench free. He seemed determined to leave no inch of flesh unpunished.

"What," he said, with a particularly hard whack, "did you think you were doing?"

"Ow." She clapped a hand to her injured fanny. He immediately pulled up her gown so he could spank her bare skin. That stung even more. "Ow! Grae, stop. I was visiting my nurse."

"In the middle of the night! By yourself?" He let fall another volley of blows. "You are the heir. How dare you endanger yourself that way?"

Oh, her bottom was on fire. She'd never been spanked, never. How did children bear this? Each blow seemed to sizzle on her skin. And how humiliating it was! No doubt that was his purpose, for he showed no mercy. She wriggled to escape, but he held her too tightly, and spanked her all the harder for trying.

"I was upset," she pleaded. "Grae, you took my maidenhead. I was saving myself."

"Lord Almighty." His hand stopped and came to rest on her burning buttock. The blood pulsed in her skin. Her bottom felt huge. Like the center of the world. He was breathing hard. His little finger curved down between her cheeks. Its tip nearly touched her sex. Her sudden surge of arousal confused her. How could she be feeling *that* now? "You ran away because I took your virginity? When you'd forced your will on me exactly the same way?"

"I didn't run away," she grumbled, squirming under his hand. He didn't let go. In fact, though his hand didn't move, it seemed to caress her. "I went to see Nurse. She's very sympathetic. Haven't you ever wanted sympathy even when you knew you were wrong?"

He chuckled and now his hand did caress her, no mistaking it. His big rough palm moved in a winding figure eight over her cheeks. It hurt terribly, and yet it felt wonderful, too. Her sex liquefied and trembled, desperate to be filled. Then she registered the state of his lap.

"You're hard," she gasped.

"Aye," he said. "As a rock. You've got the prettiest bottom I've ever seen and right now it's glowing like a rose. You can't imagine what I felt when I thought I'd never hold it again."

"That's what you were worried about? My silly bottom? By God, you could at least pretend you feared for my life. You're a beast, Grae, an utter beast."

"I'd like to take you like a beast." The gutteral declaration sent a fresh thrill to her sex. "I want to rut inside you until we both explode. My cock is aching for it, Princess. I need you."

The way her heart jumped, he might have said "I love you."

She let him turn her so that her head faced his feet and her legs formed a "V" around his waist. Her head was lower than her hips. She felt dizzy, off-balance. She gripped his ankles to steady herself as he worked his hose over his hips. His shaft fell free, settling against the crack of her bottom, its heat burning hers. She thought he would take her but he stroked her first, dipping his fingers into her welling sex and then playing them over her curves. The moisture was warm, then cool. Slippery. He smoothed it into her crease, tickling the bud of her anus, then back over the marks of his spanking. He pinched them lightly.

"Does it hurt?" he whispered, his voice tense with arousal. They were sharing a secret, something forbidden.

She shook her head. "It's hot, though. Sensitive."

"Ah," he said. He rolled his hips as if her words had destroyed his patience. Good, she thought, for she had none herself. He took his sex in hand. He pressed the head inside her sheath, then dragged her body up his legs until she held him completely within her. "Touch yourself, Princess. You can reach better than I."

She hesitated, but he coaxed her, praised her. When she did as he asked, his breath caught in his throat and his cock jerked inside her like a spawning fish. All he could see was the motion of her arm, but that was enough to excite him.

"Yes," he breathed. "Yes, that's beautiful."

His hands moved over her bottom. He spread her cheeks like a man preparing to split an orange. His thumb probed the little bud. His thumb was slippery. And it was sliding inside her.

"Oh," she said, as a strange excitement shimmered up her spine.

He began to move in tiny surging rocks, first his thumb, then his cock. Pleasure rocketed through her, multiplied, fractured, like prisms splitting each feeling into its rainbow parts. She came in a burst of color and light. He laughed, thrusting faster, stroking deeper.

"Again," he whispered, bending forward to kiss her spine, to lick it like the animal he'd claimed he wanted to be. Her gown was caught beneath her arms. His calves tensed under her hands. "For me, Princess, come for me."

"Together," she gasped.

"Quick then. If I let go, I won't last a minute. I've been starving for you too long."

"How long?" she asked.

He groaned, took a firmer grip on her hips. "Forever. Since I met you. Since you touched me that first day. Oh, I can't—"

And then she couldn't speak, either. They pounded at each other as well as they could. The position was awkward but they needed hard blows, deep blows. His thumb tensed inside her. He pushed further, stroking her with its pad. It was so unexpectedly delicious, that double penetration, that sense of being overfilled. She clutched at him, pulling for her second crest. He shuddered under the grip of her sheath. She was so wet. She could hear how wet she was. And he, he swelled. He strained. He grunted and bumped the neck of her womb, a subtle, delirious pressure. So deep. The heat rose in her belly, the blissful ache of need. He cursed and said, *please, please, please.* And he broke. Oh, it was lovely. Forceful. Noisy. He spewed inside her with a long, low moan and, like one wave pushing another to shore, his climax crashed into hers, a foaming, sparkling convulsion that receded slowly, sweetly, on a weary chorus of sighs.

Afterwards, he spread her stolen cloak and eased her to the ground. He had spanked her. She could imagine her mother's horror but, thinking back, she did not feel diminished. He had meant to punish her, but had ended up giving her pleasure, a pleasure in which he had been as rapt as she. The weakness, if weakness it had been, was shared. In its way, it had changed them as much as the morning's brush with danger. He seemed open to her now, as if he'd let down his guard. She teased a tassel of grass down his straight, proud nose. His eyes lifted.

"I thought you would pull back from me," he said.

"What do you mean?"

"When I refused to let you pleasure me unless you gave yourself completely, I thought you would keep your distance." He shifted onto his side to face her. "Since I met you, I have felt . . ."

Her heart beat a little faster. "As if you recognized me?"

His brow furrowed. "I don't think so. But I'd vowed that if I were chosen I would do what I had to do, but would take no pleasure in it." He smiled wryly and touched her cheek. "I wished to be miserable. I did not wish to like you."

"But you do."

He stroked her breast through her gown, his fingers making long sweeps over the peak, his expression shielded by his lashes. "You have your moments, Princess."

She judged he would offer no more compliments, so she turned the conversation to safer ground. "Tell me about the mail you loaned to Ian."

His mouth pursed. "My father discovered the secret to making this armor a decade ago."

"A decade. Why have I never seen its like before?"

He moved his fingers to her collarbone. "At the time, the king's cousin was the royal armorer. He was jealous of my father's skill. When my father refused to pretend this man was responsible for the invention, he had my father drummed out of the Armorer's Guild."

"I suppose your father was too proud to bend."

"It was more than pride." He stroked the hollow at the base of her throat, lost in memories. "The selling of the license would have made rich men of him and his heirs for many generations. Almost certainly, it would have meant our establishment among The Hundred, the families who rule in Ka'arkasba'ad. My father wanted us to be secure."

Lily rolled closer and nudged his knee with hers. "What did your mother think?"

His hand stilled. He spoke very carefully, as if the words were tripwires. "When my father was forced from the guild, he became angry and bitter."

"And sometimes he took it out on you?"

He shook his head, almost too forcefully. He must have realized she was thinking of the scars on his back. "No. That . . . that injury was different. Before that he never hit her, or me, never even shouted. But she couldn't bear his coldness." He drew a deep, slow breath. "When I was five, my mother left Ka'arkastan with my infant brother and returned to her people."

"What?" Lily went up on her elbow. "And left a five-year-old boy behind? Oh, Grae!"

His jaw tightened. He did not look at her. "It was not because she didn't love me. She must have believed my father needed me more than she did. That is how the Yskutians are."

"But what about what you needed?"

"I'm certain she took that into account."

"But if your father beat you—"

Grae threw himself off the cloak and stood over her, trembling with emotion. "He did not beat me but once, and he had cause. She loved me! She took my brother because he was too small. She did what she thought best." He covered his eyes. He was crying. Silent tears ran down his twisted face. She couldn't hold herself back. She did not know if it was what he wanted, but she rose and took him in her arms.

For a moment, he froze within her embrace. Then, like a glacier groaning with the spring, he cracked. His arms came round her and he held her so tightly she could barely breathe.

"Don't let go," he whispered, pressing desperate kisses to her cheek. "Don't let go."

"I won't," she promised.

"Never."

"Never," she agreed and he held her tighter yet. He was shaking like an aspen in a storm.

"I need you to love me," he said. "Someone has to."

She closed her eyes and hot tears spilled from the corners.

"I do," she said. "I will."

Chapter Seven

Explaining the night's events to her mother was not pleasant, but Lily was too exhausted to experience her usual anxiety. Lady Fortis had cleared the Audience room, then leaned forward on her black marble throne. She listened to the tale with pursed lips and shaking head.

"I don't know what's gotten into you," she said. "I'm not at all sure those slaves are a good influence."

Lily rubbed her aching temple. "It wasn't their fault, Mother. They rescued me."

"But they're not having their intended effect."

"And what is their intended effect?" she asked, too weary to guard her tongue. "To carve me into a precise copy of you?"

Her mother narrowed her icy blue eyes. "You could do worse."

Lily sighed and smoothed her bodice ribbons down the front of her rose pink gown. "You're right, Mother. My behavior was unforgivable and it won't happen again."

"I should think not!" said her mother.

Lily made her curtsy and turned before her expression could give her away.

"You need settling," her mother said by way of a parting shot.

Lily didn't want to ask what that might mean.

She trudged through the passage to her tower. The one bright spot in this day was the accord she'd reached with Grae. The thought of crawling into bed, with him to watch over her, was very appealing. He'd been so tender in the woods. They hadn't made love again, but she knew he'd wanted to. She smiled, recalling the way he'd held her, the way he'd kissed her hair. He didn't hate her after all. Her cheeks warmed and she touched her lips. Perhaps he loved her.

What had he said? She paused with her slipper on the first tower stair. *I've been starving for you.* A honeyed warmth swept her sex. Maybe she didn't need to rest right away . . .

But Grae wasn't waiting in her chamber, Col was. His nose was taped and two blood spots marred his pretty blue eyes. "Grae's off to sharpen his sword, Mistress. In a foul mood, too."

Lily's heart sank. She didn't know if she could bear more disappointment.

"Did he say what was wrong?" she asked, hoping against hope.

Col touched the tip of his nose as if to ensure it was still there. "No, Mistress. And with a mood as black as his, I'd lief as not ask."

She found him in the cutler's room off the East gatehouse. He sat alone on a stool, sharpening his sword against the lathe. The sureness of his movements betrayed his familiarity with the task. But that shouldn't have surprised her. He was an armorer's son.

"Col told me you were here," she said over the whine of the grinding wheel.

He didn't look up. "Have you need of my services, Princess?"

The words were coldly polite. They lodged in her heart like splinters of ice. What had happened to the man who had begged her to love him, who had held her like the world was ending? She swallowed and pulled her courage together.

"Is something wrong?" she asked, knowing that it was.

He flipped the blade and sent sparks skittering off the second edge. "Why would anything be wrong?"

"Because," she forced her hands to unclench from her gown, "you're acting as if you hate me. And this morning it was the opposite."

He stopped pumping the foot pedal and laid the sword across his knees. His eyes glittered like stones at the bottom of a stream, hard, inscrutable. He said nothing. Somehow this was crueler than any insult he might have uttered. She squared her shoulders.

"I see. I'm an idiot to have read anything into what you said or did this morning. You were overwrought. You don't need me. You don't need anyone."

Silence. His foot moved on the lathe pedal. Before he could set it spinning, she trapped his toe beneath her slipper. No more running away, she thought. For either of them. She put her hand on his shoulder and leaned towards his closed, angry face. His jaw tightened, but she did not quail.

"You know what I think, Grae? None of this was ever about honor. It was about fear. Fear of being vulnerable. Fear of needing. You know your father didn't love you and you don't really believe your mother did, or why would she leave you behind when she took your little brother? Now you're so hungry for love it scares you. And it scares you twice over that you want it from me."

His eyes held hers, hard as obsidian and twice as steady. "Believe what you like, Princess."

"Oh, I will," she said. "I will." But it wasn't easy to remember the man who'd hugged the breath from her this morning. She stepped back from him, burned by his chill, needing distance to restore her fragile faith.

"There's something else you should consider," he said, his thigh muscle working as he put the wheel in motion again. "Col and Ian deserve a reward for rescuing you." He lifted his sword but did not press it to the stone. "I think you know what they want most, Princess."

Her heart thumped once in shock. Of course, she did. They wanted to give her their virginity. She clenched her fists. Did he think this proved he didn't care? Because he was suggesting she explore that final intimacy with other men? She spun around before he could read the hurt in her face and strode so quickly from the room she was almost running. She knew he cared. She did. But that didn't make her heart feel any less battered.

When the worst of her turmoil had faded and she stood in the sanctuary of her chamber, trembling but rational, she realized he had asked no reward for himself. He, who had braved twelve armed men, alone, asked for nothing—which did not mean Col and Ian deserved nothing. Grae was suggesting she repay them for the wrong reasons, but he was right. Col and Ian had risked their lives for her, because of her stupidity. If they'd wanted riches, she'd have showered them with coin, but neither had shown any interest in wealth.

She put the matter to them after they'd all prepared for bed. As usual, Grae was taking the first watch. Once she'd explained what she proposed, the two men exchanged a speaking glance.

"That would be wonderful, Mistress," Col said. He started to unwrap his kalisari, but Ian leaned over and whispered in his ear. Col drew back in alarm. "No, Ian, don't ask her that."

"Don't ask me what?"

Ian folded his hands together beneath his smiling mouth. "Col and I would very much like to take you together."

"Together?"

"At the same time."

"At the same—" A picture formed of Grae's thumb filling her bottom while his manhood filled her sheath. "Oh, I see. But would that count? As a loss of virginity, I mean?"

Ian laughed. "We were hoping to switch places, assuming you enjoy the first go."

"We've heard it's very pleasurable," Col said.

"For the woman, too," Ian added.

"Oh, yes, Mistress. Otherwise, we wouldn't want to."

"And we'll be very careful." Ian cleared his throat. "I myself have, er, had a bit of experience."

Well, thought Lily, there were virgins and then there were virgins. She smiled at the two men, as eager as spaniels for a treat. How easy it was to please them.

"Very well," she said. "I put myself in your capable hands."

After so many nights together, they knew her well: her pleasures, her weaknesses. They stroked her slowly, waking each inch of skin, praising her beauty, her softness. They caressed each other as well. Now that she knew their secret, and had expressed no horror, they lost their shyness of touching each other openly. The sight of male hands on male bodies fascinated her. It seemed oddly natural to her. They were so beautiful, two strangers thrown together far from home, kept from the usual expression of their sexuality. How could they resist each other?

Except, Grae had resisted them. Grae had not even seemed tempted.

Men were different, she supposed. But she didn't want to think about Grae. She wanted to lose herself among the admiring hands, to writhe between these two hard males like snakes mating in a nest of silk.

"Enough," said Ian. His sex pressed her back like sun-baked stone. "I need to take her."

Col reached into the night table for a corked brown bottle.

"A gentle oil," Ian explained. "The court physician's personal recipe."

She pressed her lips together to contain her amusement. "I won't ask how you got that."

"It would be better not to know," he agreed, then jerked as Col reached over her body and began to apply the oil.

She turned onto her back so she could watch. With only the slightest hesitation, Col worked the oil over Ian's thick, upthrust sex, his grip so firm she thought it must be hurtful. Ian, however, clearly enjoyed his masculine strength. His grey eyes narrowed to gleaming slits. Every so often they flickered up her body to her face.

"More," he said, his voice roughened by lust. His erection shone with oil already, so he must have meant he wanted more caresses.

"You like doing this in front of me, don't you?" she said.

"Yes. Your eyes—" He shuddered and touched Col's wrist to halt him.

Without further explanation, he held out his palm. Col filled its cup with oil. Ian nudged her onto her side and began massaging the oil between her cheeks. His progress was slow. At first he merely teased the entrance to her secret passage, gradually working deeper until his longest finger was buried to the webbing. She could not suppress her moans of pleasure. Tingling ripples swept up her spine. She could hardly wait to feel that warmer, thicker intrusion.

"I think, Princess," said Ian, "that it would be easier if I went first. Then, when you are comfortable, Col can proceed."

She could only nod. The pressure built as he pressed slowly, lasciviously inside. It was frightening and wonderful. He coached her through the process, warning her what she might feel, urging her to relax. All these instructions were punctuated by ecstatic sighs and groans as he entered by increments.

"It's like silk," he said when he was fully home. "I wish you could feel it."

"You're like silk," she said, "like hot, pulsing silk."

They both shuddered. Ian gripped her hips and steadied himself.

"Now," he said, "I'm going to pull back a bit and Col will enter."

Lily trailed her fingers down Col's damp, heaving chest. He'd taken himself in hand already. She swept her thumb over the deep pink head, marveling at the tautness of his skin. Col whimpered softly in reaction. His fingers tightened on his shaft. Ian lifted her thigh over Col's hip. Together, she and Col positioned him at her gate.

"Oh, God," he said as the soft outer mouth closed over his glans. "You're so wet." He was trembling as he pushed inside, his eyes closed, his mouth slack with pleasure. He hilted with an endearing grunt, then shimmied a fraction deeper. "Oh, it's so marvelous. It's heaven. I don't think I ever want to leave."

Lily smiled and kissed him, gently, so as not to jar his poor nose.

"You're the best princess in the world," he declared.

Then they began to move. First Col thrust, then Ian. They rocked her between them, long alternating waves that inspired sensations so intense her throat tightened with sheer, physical joy. It was a dance of pleasure, perfectly timed. Neither man faltered. Neither missed his stroke. A thin wall separated their sexes. At the midpoint of each thrust she sensed a subtle increase in pressure as the rims of the heads passed each other. She noticed the men would slow each time they reached this point.

"You can feel each other, can't you?" she said.

The men shivered on either side of her. "Yes," they said in unison, then laughed.

Lily laughed, too, and stroked Col's thick red hair. "You are so

sweet." She kissed his cheek and reached behind her for Ian's head.
"Both of you."

"I can't last much longer," Col confessed.

"Neither can I," she whispered back, her laughter bubbling over. He
was so dear. She kissed his mouth this time, parting his lips with her
tongue. He sighed happily and joined her.

Some signal must have passed between the men because the pace
quickened. Flares of heat burst at the increase in friction, shooting up
her spine, melting her thighs. Her cry was lost in Col's kiss. It was too
sweet. She couldn't bear it. Her skin ached with pleasure, her bones,
her muscles. She could barely move between the two strong bodies that
buffeted hers, each straining separately and together to get deeper.
Arms twined around her. Legs. Someone kissed the back of her neck.
Someone fondled her breast.

She groaned. She didn't know whether to thrust forward or back.

Col heaved against her, up and oh-so-far in. He groaned even louder
than she. She wrenched her mouth free.

"Stay right there, Col." She reached behind her for Ian's hips.
"Don't pull out."

"Yes," Ian said, his breath hissing through his teeth. He pushed,
thick on thick, filling her, joining his eager, throbbing pulse to Col's,
and to hers.

She tilted her hips a fraction lower and rubbed her bud of pleasure
against the root of Col's shaft. That was all it took. She came like a
banshee wailing in the night, drums pounding with heavenly violence
through the tissues of her womb.

"Oh . . . my . . . God," she heard Col moan through her teeth-
chattering spasm.

As one, the men spilled inside her. Their groans singed her ears, and
their shudders set off another shower of spine-tingling sparks.

She wasn't sure when she noticed the shadow at the foot of the bed,
or how she knew it had been there for some time. He had opened the
hangings just wide enough to see. Beyond the reach of the bedlamps,
his eyes alone caught the light, glittering, unblinking.

How could she explain this to him? The pleasure Col and Ian had
showed her was sublime, but if it never happened again, she wouldn't
shed a tear. She had not felt what she'd felt when Grae entered her,
when Grae looked at her, as if her heart were being torn apart and
made new. She stared at the silent shadow. He didn't have to watch.
He had done it to hurt himself. To make himself hate her. He did not
deserve an explanation, but she ached to offer one just the same.

"Your turn," Col said to Ian, sounding as if he were catching his second wind.

Ian laughed and kissed her shoulder.

The shadow turned away.

Chapter Eight

The Yskutian delegation arrived at sunrise. As far as Lily knew they had not been expected nor invited. And yet, and yet, the three maids her mother sent to oversee her toilette were very bright of face for women who should have been yanked but recently from their beds in town.

"What do you need them for?" Col grumbled, annoyed by the women's recall to duty.

Lily hid her smile. The maids had tried to shoo her slaves from the room, but all proved resistant, even Grae. He stood now by the window, his bare muscular arms crossed over his bare muscular chest.

"Oh, la," said Lyn, the senior maid, her eyes avoiding the display of handsome male flesh. "Men can't do for a woman when it's really important. There's a prince in that delegation."

Lily's brows rose. *A prince.* She held up her shift and lifted her foot so that Lynn could slide a stocking up her leg. Unlike Srucia, which was divided into city-states such as Ammam, the country of Yskut had but one royal family, and only six royal princes.

Her eyes found Grae's. A wordless message passed between them. She realized that he, too, suspected her mother was up to something. But what? On the surface, matchmaking seemed the obvious conclusion. An alliance with an Yskutian prince would be a coup for proud little Ammam. But why would Lady Fortis assume her daughter could handle an Yskutian? She barely credited her with handling her slaves.

Indeed, her mother's waters ran too deep for her to fathom.

Lyn smoothed the second stocking up her leg, then reached for the gown the other maids had removed from the wardrobe.

"Not the green," said Ian, who had been watching them with interest, and considerably less resentment than Col or Grae. The maids were pretty, after all. "The blue is more flattering."

Lyn's chin went up. "The blue is too low cut for a morning reception."

"Nonsense," said another voice. For a second, Lily couldn't believe it was Grae's, but he strode to the wardrobe and removed a sapphire velvet gown.

Lyn spluttered as he eased it over her mistress's head. "Lady Fortis wishes to impress a prince," he said. "I assure you, the princes of Yskut are as impressed by a fine, fair bosom as any other men."

So. He thought she had a fair bosom. Bemused, Lily thrust her arms into the sleeves. The gown was closely fitted. Grae stepped behind her to fasten its tiny hooks, his fingers as deft as Lyn's had ever been. But then he did what the maid would never dream of doing. He reached into the bodice and resettled her breasts so that their curves swelled over the pearl-studded neckline.

The presence of the round-eyed maids could not quell Lily's reaction. Her nipples budded beneath his touch, lengthening, tightening. Her knees uncertain, she sagged into his embrace.

"You are ours," he whispered close to her ear. "This year is ours. If you think I'll entrust you to any man but those in this room, you are insane."

It was not something she had expected him to say. It was not something that, as his mistress, she should allow to pass uncontradicted. But she did not contradict him. She had too much pride to deny what she knew in her heart. Instead, she turned and stared. He was grinding his teeth in anger, but that look in his eyes might have been longing, or fear.

Either possibility gave her courage. How could she make him believe she loved him, that anyone loved him, if she wavered now? She stroked his whisker-roughened cheek. His eyelids quivered and she saw a fleeting shadow of the man-child who'd held her in the woods.

"I am yours," she said, and she didn't mean his and Col's and Ian's. She meant his. The truth had struck her the night before as she lay, limp with satisfaction, watching his lonely retreat from her pleasure bower.

He was her One True Love.

Nurse would have been proud. She had given her virginity to the man to whom it belonged, for all the good that did her now. Too bad the Yskutians couldn't give her Grae as a gift. Then she slapped both hands to her forehead. The gift! The blasted broken gift.

"Damnation," she said. Grae started back from her, his face stiff. "Oh, no, not you. I forgot to get the globe fixed, the one the ambassador gave my mother."

Frantically she dug through the chest where she thought she'd stowed it. "Oh, Lord, I hope the delegation doesn't notice it's missing. Ah! Here it is." She emerged, flushed but triumphant, and handed the broken halves to Ian. "Take this to my father and ask him, if he is able, to please repair it as quickly as he can."

"Wouldn't you prefer to speak to your father yourself?" Ian asked.

Lily blushed. It was a reasonable expectation, but surely one hurdle at a time was enough?

"I'll be too busy," she said. "You deliver and collect it, and then I'll sneak it back into my mother's office."

"Very good," Ian said, but she could tell he was perplexed.

From what Lily could see, the Yskutian prince was not the least bit impressed with her bosom. His eyes never left hers, not even when he bent over her hand to kiss it.

She, on the other hand, thought him the most perfect creature she had ever seen, even more beautiful than Col or Ian, even more exotic than Grae. His skin was smooth and creamy, his features as delicate as if they'd been carved in ivory. He was tall, well-formed, and wore the most sumptuous clothes: layered robes of heavily embroidered silk in varied jewel-bright hues, all gathered at the waist with a wide brocade sash. Set amongst all that glowing color was his silent, inscrutable essence, stillness amidst a fountain of noise.

His accent charmed her. His voice was as smooth and light as apple wine. He had such grace that the simplest of gestures, an adjustment of his robes, a tilting of his head, had the power to hypnotize her. She couldn't stop staring. But then, neither could he. They might have been alone at the official welcoming breakfast. They were alone for his tour of the castle grounds, Lady Fortis having dismissed her slaves for the afternoon.

Lily was not used to seeing a foreigner of his stature without bodyguard or armor. Of course, the men of Yskut did not wear armor into battle. And they used strange weapons, blades which never dulled and wicked black stars, *zhurim* they were called, which sliced like razors and returned to their owners after they were thrown.

When Lily questioned him about his current defenseless state, he paired the first two fingers of his right hand. "I could kill you with these, Princess, without you feeling a moment's pain."

"Science," her mother called it. Lily preferred "uncanny." She did not, however, sense any danger from the prince. He might not have ogled her bosom, but he clearly admired her. And there seemed to be no anger in him. He was a still pond on a windless day.

Now they stood atop the east watchtower, gazing out over farmland towards the harbor.

The prince waved his deadly hand over the view. "This is beautiful country."

"But not as beautiful as Yskut," she said, alerted by an undercurrent in his melodious voice.

Turning, he caught the amusement quivering on her lips. To her relief, he burst into a warm, infectious laugh. "You think I'm arrogant, don't you? No, don't lie. I can tell. In any case, I am arrogant." He caught the edge of the battlement in his hands and rocked back on his heels, a gesture many young men might make, but few Yskutians. As if aware of her thoughts, he looked at her sidelong and smiled. "I forget, you see. Until I travel abroad and see those puffed-up foreigners strutting about. How many years of history do they have to our thousands? A hundred? Perhaps two? 'How foolish they are to be proud of *that*,' I think. And then I am caught. 'How foolish you are,' I tell myself, 'to assume that anyone who sees the world differently is a fool.' Perhaps that is why my father sent me on this journey. Perhaps he thought I needed the reminder."

"You mean you don't know why he sent you?"

He shook his head. His queued hair shone blue-black in the noonday sun, the same color as Grae's, but not as thick. His eyes resembled Grae's as well, though they had not his shadows.

"My father is a deep soul. He merely said I was needed. But I have not met anyone I felt drawn to help yet, except for you and I cannot imagine why." He grinned. "Perhaps I was blinded by how pretty you are and merely wished you were the one I was sent to help."

Flattered, Lily smiled and scraped her slipper along the wall. "My mother would tell you I need a great deal of help. She fears I am not sufficiently masterful to rule as Ammam's queen."

"Ah." The prince nodded at the waving fields of wheat. "My father would say that the most important person to rule is yourself. And the most impossible person to rule is anyone besides yourself."

"I'm sure that's very wise," she said. "Although I don't know what good it does me."

"Your mother is formidable," the prince agreed with equal sobriety.

They turned to each other, eyes sparkling like naughty children. Lily was the first to giggle, but soon both were lost.

"Oh, dear," she said when she could speak again.

The prince caught her hand and carried it to his chest. "I don't know about you, Princess, but I think I have found something I needed."

"And what would that be?"

"A friend," he said. "A friend who is not my own kind."

Eyes stinging with emotion, Lily bowed to him in the stiff, formal fashion of his people. "I would be honored to have you call me friend." He smiled a serene Yskutian smile, then gave a little jump as if he'd just remembered something. "Oh!" he said. "So would I."

For once her mother did not make her stand on the carpet before her desk. They sat in the window in her jewel box of an office, each in her own chair. Lily stroked the carved arms and stared at the stained-glass roses while she waited for her mother to come to the point.

The prince had been in Ammam a week now, and his attentions to Lily had brought a smile to her mother's stern face. "He's so polite," she'd been saying since he arrived. "And so handsome. My goodness, I don't know how any woman could resist him." All of which was a thinly disguised attempt to find out whether Lily had.

She knew her mother was jumping to unwarranted conclusions. Or so she thought until her mother patted her arm and said, "Now. To the heart of the matter."

Lily turned from the window and prepared to listen.

"The prince has asked for your hand in marriage."

She squeezed her eyes shut, then opened them wide, as if her mother's words were a fever dream she could blink away.

Her mother laughed at her expression. "Yes, it's true. Rather precipitous, I admit, but for whatever reason you seem to have charmed him."

"But," Lily stammered and thought, how dare he? She did not feel flattered. She felt betrayed. The prince knew there was nothing but affection between them. After a week of intimate conversations, including a few on the topic of Grae, how could he not know? But perhaps Yskutians didn't believe in love matches. Perhaps he wished to live in a country that would perpetually remind him of his "arrogance."

"I cannot marry him," she said. "You must convey my regrets."

Her mother drew up in her chair. "I will not. He's just the sort of biddable fellow you need. Never forward. Never pushy."

"Unless he thinks someone *needs* him to push," Lily muttered.

Lady Fortis ignored the interruption. "And he's an Yskutian. Just imagine the potential for scholarly exchange."

Lily shook her head, startled to see how deeply her mother had misjudged the prince. She'd always considered her opinion on political matters to be infallible. But the Yskutians were anything but a "biddable" people. Nothing, not marriage, not money, not threat of war, could induce them to part with their secrets. If her mother could be so wrong about this, what else might she have misjudged? Perhaps Lily wasn't as hopeless as Lady Fortis thought.

Buoyed by that possibility, she gripped the arms of her chair. "I cannot marry him, Mother. And it isn't fair to lead him on. If you won't tell him, I will."

Her mother leaned back, her smile gone. "I could order you to marry him."

"Mother." Lily pressed her hands to her head. "You can't order me to marry. That would undermine everything this year is meant to achieve."

Her mother digested this reminder. She smoothed her cloth of gold gown over her knees. "Very well. I'll make you a deal. Marry within the month and I'll give the town their charter."

"Their charter!" Lily lost her breath at the scope of the offer. "You've been resisting that since you took the throne."

"So I have. I suppose my priorities are shifting."

Lily pushed from her chair, paced three steps towards her mother's desk and turned. "I can marry anyone I want?"

Her mother smiled, a small cat-in-the-creamery smile. "Let it not be said that I forced the heir to marry against her will. You may wed a serf for all I care." A dimple appeared in her smooth white cheek. "I'm betting you won't, though. I'm betting you care too much for the well-being of our people to marry anyone who will not enhance Ammam's position in the world. And in the meantime, you will not refuse the prince's offer."

Lily stared at her smug expression. Her heart was pounding against her ribs. "You assume I won't find a better candidate within a month."

Her mother spread her hands as if to say, *of course.*

Damn her. How had she known Lily wanted to see the town get their council? She'd never said a word. She'd been careful to relate the tale of her kidnaping with the utmost objectivity. But perhaps that was the problem. She should have been angrier. She should have hated them all for what a few had tried to do.

She shook her head. That was water under the bridge. What mattered was that she had an opportunity to change the shape of her world long before she expected to. She could not throw the chance away without at least considering it.

"I will take your month," she said. "But I make no promises."

Still smiling, her mother inclined her head. She knew when silence was golden.

Chapter Nine

"I have news," she said from her perch on the steps at the foot of her bed. Col's head rested on her knee, Ian leaned against the carved bedpost and Grae stood by the window, polishing the hilt of his sword. It was the same sword she'd given him on her birthday. She wondered at that. If his father's mail were any indication, he must own finer. Like the others, he'd been quiet this evening. Perhaps her mood was catching.

Col leaned into her knee like a pampered hunting dog. "Bad news?"

"I don't know that it's bad." She glanced at Grae, then Ian. She didn't want to tell them. She knew her mother would disapprove. But they had a right to know.

"Pull the thorn," Grae advised. "We're all big boys here."

She closed her eyes. "The prince has offered for my hand."

Silence greeted her announcement. She opened her eyes. Ian put one hand to his head. Grae merely froze.

"Od's bod," said Col. "He's only been here a week."

"I know." She stroked his russet hair as much for her comfort as his. "Apparently, the men of Yskut don't take long to make up their minds. The point is my year with the love guard is meant to prepare me for marriage. If I marry earlier—"

"We'll have to leave," Ian finished, his expression grim.

Grae looked out the window. The men still wore their public clothes. It had seemed better to tell them while they possessed that small barrier.

Col scratched the knee of his hose. "I guess even an Ammami husband can't be expected to tolerate three slaves in his wife's bed."

"No," Lily agreed.

His words repeated in her mind. *Even an Ammami husband.* She thought of Vizier, her mother's former slave, her long-time lover. Had her father minded? Would she want to marry a man who didn't? Most of all, could she treat her own husband that way, whether she loved him or not? She did not believe she could. It would be hard to live without love, but it would be harder to live without self-respect.

"What's the rush?" Grae asked, his voice scrupulously level. He stared at the hilt of his sword, his lips white, his fingers tense. Lily's heart went out to him. He was so proud. So full of love which he dared not offer anyone. He did not deserve this from her. But how could she deny what her people deserved? How could she put her and Grae's happiness first?

She swallowed against the tightness in her throat. "My mother has expressed some doubts about my ability to rule my future husband. She seems to think this prince is someone I could handle."

Grae snorted.

"I agree," she said. "And I told her as much. But she said if I marry within the month, she'll license the town's charter. She didn't say I had to marry the prince, but she's betting I won't find another suitable prospect in so short a time."

Col craned around to examine her face. "You can marry anyone?"

"Anyone my people could live with." She twisted her hands together. "I'm not saying I will marry the prince. Just that, in good conscience, I have to consider my mother's offer."

"We understand, Princess," Col said. "In fact—"

Ian cut him short. "No, Col."

"But"

"No. A man's word is his bond."

"I know, but—"

"No," Ian repeated, and this time he won Col's silence, not to mention a blush.

Before Lily could decide whether to probe further, Grae crossed the space between them and held out his hand. "Come with me, Princess. I need to speak to you privately."

The other men fell back. No doubt about it, Grae was king wolf here. Even she felt the pull to obey him. She put her hand in his and let him help her to her feet.

He led her down the stairs to the weaving room. The looms still sat against the walls and the prayer rug still covered the floor. She remembered how he'd lain there curled in sleep, a boy in sleep, a man whose heart could break as surely as her own. Her eyes stung. She prayed he wouldn't see the telltale glitter. When she turned to face him, he captured her hands in his. To her astonishment, his eyes shone as well.

"Princess." His voice throaty, he shook his head. "Just when I think I understand you, you surprise me."

She did not answer. She could not. His expression was for once unguarded. What it said made her throat close with emotion. His hands slid up her sleeves to her shoulders. His thumbs caressed the skin her neckline bared. He clasped her neck, then her jaw. His fingers fanned out behind her ears, the lightest, tenderest hold. Tendrils of heat unfurled in her breasts. He stepped closer.

"Princess," he whispered, the word ghosting over her lips.

"Lily," she said. "Call me Lily."

His smile brushed her mouth. "Lily then." He kissed her, soft as a breeze, skimming her mouth, her cheeks, her eyelids. "Beautiful Lily."

The kisses grew firmer, a gentle pressure, warm. Her arms rose, surrounding his back with the same light hold. He found a nerve on the side of her neck that made her shiver.

He laughed, low and soft. "Make love to me, Lily."

She stepped back and worked the sleeves of her gown over her shoulders. He unhooked the leather belt he wore wrapped thrice around his waist. The world fell away as they disrobed, each for the other, as if they had stepped into a dream. His eyes told her how lovely he found her, his eyes and the bold outward thrust of his sex. Her hands faltered when she saw it, shuddering and strong, in the last light of evening. He knelt before her. One by one, he undid the ribbons that rounded her thighs and peeled the hose down her legs.

He did not rise when she was naked. He kissed the gentle curve of her belly and turned his face from side to side. Arousal rolled through her in slow, liquid waves, a kind of drunkenness, one that heightened rather than dulled the nerves. She buried her fingers in his hair and stroked his scalp. Again she felt his smile against her skin, then her hair, then the secret purse of her sex. Here his kiss was deep and strong. He lifted the jewel of her pleasure and suckled it. She sighed, losing her strength, losing her breath.

He caught her before her knees could give way and lowered her to the rug.

"Simple," he said, as she opened to him. "You and me. Alone together."

"Yes," she said, and rubbed his hair-roughened legs with her smooth ones. He settled his elbows by her sides, the cap of his sex fitting neatly to her gate.

"You're wet," he said, his voice giving out a little.

"Yes," she said. "You made me that way."

He pushed inside. What a luxury this was, to feel this warm column of flesh sliding so smoothly into her body. She ran her hands down the wide sweep of his back and cupped his buttocks, lightly, the most polite of encouragements. He smiled and took her fully. She undulated beneath him, stretching into the wonderful sensations. He began to rock, long, slow strokes that lulled and aroused and dragged low, happy moans from her throat.

"That's it. Sing for me," he said and she knew her moans were music to him.

She sang until she could no longer hold him gently. Her hands fisted behind his shoulders, and her nails curled into her palms to avoid wounding him. Her legs she could not keep still. She stroked the soles of her feet over his calves, up his thighs. She locked her ankles behind his buttocks and dug her heels into the muscle there. Then she repeated the restless journey.

Through all this he was slow and steady. He caressed her with his sex, with his chest, with the hard clean line of his jaw. The end crept towards them, first with a quiver, then a tremor and finally a shudder that was weakness and strength and greed knotted together in a chain of gold.

"I can't wait," she gasped. "Bring me over. End it, Grae. End it."

His head dipped toward hers, his hair damp from their efforts, his breathing labored.

"I'll end it," he said, his strokes turning to angry hammer strikes. "I'll end it."

All his disappointments were in those thrusts, all his unrequited loves. Like a whirlwind, his passion caught her, disjointed her. She felt the thighs that pressed hers wider, the hand that tangled in her hair, the final swelling of his sex. His shoulders bunched beneath her hands. A drop of sweat fell to her breast. He licked it away and panted against her skin.

She gathered, arching, meeting his desperate blows with her own.

He broke a moment before she did. She felt his first hot burst, and his second and then she was lost with him, uttering cries that seemed to hold her heart. *I love you,* they said, wordless though they were. *I wish, I wish—*

She didn't know how long she lay with him sprawled atop her. She held him lightly, not wanting to cling but dreading the moment she'd have to let go.

"I need to tell you something," he said, and she remembered he'd had a reason for bringing her here, a reason beyond the pleasure they'd shared.

"Yes?"

He rose up on his elbow and his body slipped from hers. She winced.

"Col and Ian are princes," he said. "You could marry one of them."

She covered her forehead with her palm and stared at him, too shocked to speak.

"Yes," he said. "Ian is from Laravia and Col from Medellín. Col is a third son, but Medellín is a rich country. And he is very kind. I doubt even your mother would find him a bad match. Trust me, Princess. You don't want to marry the Yskutian. They have hearts, but they live by their heads. You wouldn't like that. You need to marry a man with a passion to match yours."

She could hardly take in what he was saying. She didn't know whether to be hurt that he could hand her so easily to another, or touched that he cared enough for her happiness to try. She squirmed out from under him and stood, needing distance to think.

"They're princes?" she said. "My slaves are princes?"

"All guard candidates swear an oath not to reveal their origins." He rolled onto his back and propped himself on his elbows. Lines scored the corners of his mouth. Perhaps this wasn't as easy for him as she'd thought. "Everyone knows that the best way to form alliances with Ammam is to send a slave. Ammam may be a small principality, but she is the Gateway to the South. The Choosing must be blind in order to be just."

"I don't understand. You told me your background."

"It doesn't matter if I break the rules. This was not my ambition. It was my father's, his way of redeeming the family after he was banished from the armorer's guild. Every coin he possessed went towards paying my entry tribute." His smile humorless, he touched the faint marks on his shoulder. "Do you know how I got these stripes? My father caught me behind a haystack with one of the village girls. I was thirteen. If he'd been a minute later, I would have been free today."

Her lips tightened at the bitterness in his voice. Did he honestly think of his time with her as imprisonment? Suddenly cold, she reached for her shift and pulled it over her head.

"Thirteen. That's young." She watched him from the side of her eye. "I suppose he locked you in a room after that, to make sure you didn't do it again."

He sat up, his glare more familiar than his kindness had ever been. "Are you saying I chose this? That I could have rebelled if I wanted to?"

"I'm saying it intrigues me that you care so much about your supposed oppressor's future happiness. That, having suffered so much, you risk disgrace by revealing the origins of your fellow slaves. A man who truly hated his position here would have asked for his freedom after he rescued me. You would have been sent home wreathed in glory. Perhaps you should ask yourself why you didn't."

She took no pleasure in his response, though it was no more than she'd expected. Immediately defensive, he got to his feet and grabbed his clothes. "Perhaps I didn't realize the woman who'd nearly raped me the night before would be so magnanimous. In any case, it doesn't matter now. Your efforts are better spent in deciding which of your slaves you'd like to marry."

"I've already decided," she said, for anger had made her reckless.

"Oh?"

She lifted her chin. "I've decided to marry you."

For a second his face went blank, eyes wide, jaw hanging, and then a look of pain crossed his features, a look such as she'd never seen on any man's face, and certainly not his. In that moment, she knew he loved her, truly loved her.

He soon recovered, or nearly. His laugh was harsh, but not as mocking as she was sure he wished to make it. "You can't marry me, Princess. I'm a poor man's poorer son."

It didn't matter what he said. That brief flash of longing had given her all the courage she needed. He was willing to sacrifice his happiness for hers. He had risked his life and his honor. A hundred times a day, he made serving her well a matter of pride, no matter how it galled him. And he had taught her some hard lessons about the true duties of a mistress. If those weren't princely actions, she didn't know what were. She closed the distance between them. She touched her heart. "You are a prince to me, the prince of my heart. When I rule you will stand beside me."

He stared at her as if she'd gone mad. She tried to smile but her lips quavered.

"Of course," she added, "we're not likely to rule for many years. By the time we wear the purple, you'll have lived here so long my people will have forgotten where you came from."

"You've lost your mind," he said, but his expression had softened. He wanted to believe it was possible. She could feel it.

"I can make it happen," she said, though in truth she didn't know how.

"You can't."

Again she heard the weakening, the longing. She rested her arms on his shoulders, clasped the back of his neck. "But if I could . . ."

"If you could." He shook his head. "I don't know, Princess. That's a lot to consider."

She tugged softly until his cheek brushed hers. "So long as you do consider it, my love."

He pushed back and looked into her face, his eyes once more naked. Tears sparkled in his lower lashes, more precious than diamonds.

"I do love you," he said. "God help me."

She laughed and hugged him close. Now she knew she could accomplish anything.

Lily sat up in bed as if a bolt of lightning had streaked through the window and pierced her chest. The armor was the answer. The bloody, blessed, Ka'arkish black armor. Her mother would move heaven and earth to outfit her garrison in the stuff. And Grae was the son of the man who'd invented it. All she had to do was tell her mother to offer his father a position as the royal armorer. Admittedly, this would make his father a traitor to his own people but after all this time, how much loyalty could he bear them? They'd betrayed him, spit on his genius. Surely he'd relish the chance to serve Lady Fortis. Especially if his son would one day reign as king.

She almost turned to wake him, to share her stroke of brilliance. Her hand stopped an inch from his shoulder. Would Grae approve? Grae wasn't sure he wanted to marry her. Grae was barely convinced she wanted to marry him. If she used his father as a bargaining chip, would he always wonder if she valued his father's skill more than she valued him?

Maybe she shouldn't tell him. Maybe only her mother needed to know. She could present marriage to Grae as an opportunity to make a useful alliance, not a promise, merely a chance. She sank back and pulled the covers to her chest. Yes, that would be easier all around. The cause was good. And she and Grae would be happy together.

One little secret couldn't change that.

Chapter Ten

Her mother rose from behind her desk, her face white with fury. "You want to marry your slave!"

The ornate crystal chandelier tinkled at the volume of her voice. Lily squeezed her hands together behind her back. Her fingers were icy, her palms damp.

"Yes," she said as steadily as she could. "I wish to marry Grae of Ka'arkasba'ad. He is a good man. He will rule well."

"Rule!" Her mother pressed both palms to her head. "No man will rule in Ammam while I have anything to say about it." She pointed at Lily, her finger trembling with passion. "No man will bring war to this country. No man will trod the women of Ammam beneath his heel."

"Grae isn't like that," she objected, even though saying he would rule had been a slip of the tongue. At least she thought it was. She shifted her weight. Last night, when she told him he was the prince of her heart, she had said he would rule beside her. Was that a slip as well?

"You cannot marry a slave," her mother said more reasonably. She smoothed her gown over the generous swell of her bosom. Today, she wore purple beneath her purple robes of state. The vivid hue made her eyes seem even paler. "I know we are not supposed to know such things but, whatever he may have told you, I assure you this slave's origins are humble."

"They are not as humble as you think," she said.

Her mother shot a skeptical look from beneath her brows. Lily's nails bit her palms. The queen could not know Grae's father had it within his means to grant one of her dearest wishes. The secret of the black mail would ransom a dozen princes. Once Lily told her about it, she'd be singing another tune. The words were in her throat, pressing on her tongue. Someone's hunting falcon flew past the window, screaming in triumph. Lily's chest burned with a desire to wipe the disapproval from her mother's face, to claim her own victory.

But she had not consulted Grae. And she suspected Grae would not approve, even assuming his father would. She could not induce a man to betray his country, no matter how strained his relationship with it.

They were not at war with Ka'arkastan. The only purpose this divulgence would serve was overcoming her mother's objection to the marriage.

It was the easy road.

If she stepped onto it, would Grae ever forgive her? Or would he believe she had once again set her will above his? She could not do it. With a quiet sigh, the words died unspoken. She raised her chin. "You said I might marry a serf. Do you mean to go back on your word?"

"Yes," said a voice from the door to the connecting chamber. "Do you?"

Lily expected to see Vizier, her trusty rescuer. Instead, she found her father dressed in his usual dusty black, his eyes lit with a fire she couldn't remember having seen there before. In his hand he cradled the Yskutian globe Ian had given to him to repair.

"William." Her mother sat, obviously shaken by his appearance.

"Yes, William it is." A faint smile played about his lips, more self-mocking than amused. "I bring you something you appear to need." He held out the hollow ivory sphere. Her mother looked at it, clearly confused. "I gather you broke it. Your daughter asked me to repair it so that its absence would not offend our visitors from Yskut."

"That's very considerate but I hardly think I need—"

Her father's laugh cut her short. What a strange sound it was, like the creaking of a door. "You don't know what it is, do you?"

"Of course, I do. It's a picture of the world. A trinket. Clever. But a trinket."

Her father leaned across the polished expanse of her desk, propping himself on one narrow hand. He held the globe before her face and turned it hypnotically from side to side. Lady Fortis watched him as a cat might eye an unexpectedly aggressive mouse.

"It is a meditation object," he said. "Years of work and thought go into making them. The creations of this particular artisan are highly prized. You see the tiny diamond chip set into the ivory? That is Ammam. Considering the recipient, I believe its message is that we inhabit a very small corner of a very small world. It is foolish to think that one man's perspective is the only perspective there is."

Her mother pushed her chair back from her desk. "One man's perspective, eh?"

Her father shrugged, his half-smile deepening. "Or one woman's."

Her mother's lips tightened. Vizier might have said *touché,* but Lady Fortis had too much pride for that.

"So," said her father, pressing his advantage home. "Did you or did you not tell our daughter she could marry any man she chose?"

"I did but—"

Her father touched his wife's lips. She started at the intimacy of the gesture, as did Lily. "And have you not taught our daughter that a woman is only as good as her word?"

"But she wants to marry a slave! Even *you* can see how impossible that is."

Her father dropped his hand and straightened. With a pang, Lily saw how gaunt he was, how her mother's scorn had tightened the skin above his beard. He stiffened his shoulders against the blow, but Lily saw his hurt. When he spoke, his voice was stiff as well.

"If my daughter admires this man, I suspect he is worthy. I have watched her over the years and she has demonstrated a great deal of sense. Fortis, please—" His voice broke but he did not pause. "If you love her, do not make her do as you did. Let her marry the choice of her heart. Then perhaps we can spare our citizens the spectacle of a queen who would rather sleep with her cabinet than speak to her king."

Lily knew then. She knew that he had minded all along. Theirs might have been a political marriage; her father might never have loved her mother, but insult by insult she had crushed his pride under her royal slipper, had made him the shadow man he was today. Lady Fortis did not know what she had lost, but now Lily did. Her father's mind was subtle and keen and under that silent black exterior a heart beat, a heart that was capable of courage and caring, even for a daughter who had shown him no more warmth or understanding than his wife.

But that was Lily's sin, one she would take care not to repeat. Who knew what he might have been, might still be, if someone he cared for treated him with respect, or love.

Never, she told herself. Never will I treat my husband that way. Never will I treat my people that way.

She curled her hands into fists and blinked back tears. All her life she had known she was different from her mother, that she did not, in her heart, even wish to be the same. She had bemoaned that difference, called it weakness, cowardice, when all along, in her own quiet way, she had been following her own path, because her conscience had not allowed her to do otherwise. Her father had called it good sense, Vizier, the ability to make her servants love her. She did not need to inspire fear in her people; she needed to inspire respect. And she could only do that if she ruled in a way that she herself could respect: a way that set love above fear. She would make mistakes, as her mother had, but her best would be sufficient. And she would have Grae's help, Grae's quiet strength, Grae's pride in a job well done.

With Grae at her side, her best might prove more than sufficient. She barely heard her mother's surrender, barely felt her tearful kiss, barely heard her whispered plea to reconsider. None of that mattered. Victory had been hers the moment she began to trust herself.

She straddled his belly, not taking him yet, merely enjoying the anticipation.

His eyes slid shut as she ran her hands over his powerful torso. His own hands spanned her waist, kneading and releasing in a hot, restless rhythm.

The prince had sailed that afternoon. He had taken her refusal philosophically, even promised to begin contemplating a useful wedding gift. She wondered when he would realize he'd already given it to her, by acting as the catalyst for her marriage to Grae.

Now they were alone in her chamber. Col and Ian stood guard at the base of the tower. She had not asked them to remove to this position. If Grae had, she had not heard him do it. Perhaps they sensed their relationship had changed.

She was Grae's now. She would always be Grae's. The knowledge warmed her face, her body. She leaned back until the hard rise of his sex brushed her buttocks, bent back by the division of warm, rounded flesh. His body quivered, the part she brushed and the part she rode.

"Princess." His hands tightened on her waist. He rolled her beneath him.

"Bully," she teased, but she lifted her knees in wanton invitation. He did not laugh.

"I need to take you," he said, the "take" a growl, his hands a pair of living manacles creeping up her arms, stretching them over her head. He notched her and pushed inside, one hard, quick thrust. He sighed with pleasure and pressed a fraction deeper. Their hands met palm to palm. Lily linked their fingers. Then they both were trapped.

"Mine," she said, with the most deliciously primitive satisfaction.

"Mine," he responded, and began the rhythm that would carry them both to completion.

But not without a satisfying struggle. She fought his rhythm. Pushed it faster with swiveling upward beats of her hips, with hidden tugs that massaged his pumping flesh and pulled him towards the very brink of pleasure.

"Too fast," he gasped, but he did not slow. Instead he pushed up on his arms, straighter, higher, until only his hips met hers.

Her hands freed, she caressed his taut, straining body. She teased the sweating cords of his neck and shoulders, the pinpoints at his breast, the small of his back, his buttocks.

"No," he rasped as she teased the hidden entrance. "Not this time. I'm too close."

She obeyed his request, though she smiled as if she might not. Her nails trailed lower, making him shiver. She cradled his swaying sac. Gently, she squeezed. Gently she pricked. It would hurt just a little, she thought, a sweet hurt, like a spanking.

His sex stiffened inside her. He groaned and closed his eyes. "Lily."

The world between the bed hangings spun. Sheets tangled and released her legs and then she was on top again, gazing into his beautiful face. His features were softened by the disarray of his long, thick hair, by the lust and love in his eyes. The sight made her clench inside, made her arch her back and press the thick, tensile strength of him against one wonderful, aching spot.

His lips curved in the subtlest, sweetest smile.

"Finish it," he said. "Finish us both."

She rode him, gracefully first, then with abandon. He squeezed her breasts, he stroked her hair, but those were dim sensations to the wild hard drive of his sex. She exulted in the greedy ramming in of him. She begrudged the reluctant pull. She clenched hard, struggling to keep him from going too far. Just to the rim of the swollen tip. No more. She enforced her will with a gripping tug, a gasp, and then down she flung again, taking him into her. Thick and smooth. His heat. His strength. Her liquid welcome.

She fed his shudders with her own and rode faster, losing control of her movements because the ache was so desperate, the fever so high. He held her hips. He slammed off the mattress to meet her. Sweating. Panting. A soft curse.

"Now," he said and pressed the point of gold with his thumbs.

Blindly they came, their hands locked together over the place their bodies met. She did not need her eyes. She felt their tremors, heard their tangled cries of relief. He pulsed inside her as she shook. The ease that followed, hers and his, warmed her like sunshine.

"Princess," he whispered. Had she fallen? She lay cradled in his arms. "Sweet Lily, I cannot marry you."

She laughed. She could not credit such foolishness when joy wrapped her so securely. In her heart, they were married already.

"Did you hear me?"

She kissed the hard, sweaty muscle of his shoulder. "I heard you."

"I love you, but I have thought carefully and I cannot live as your father lives. I would lose all respect for myself. And so would you. I could not bear that. I need your respect as much as I need your love."

The admission cost him. She could tell by the tension in his arms. So she did not laugh. She pushed up on his chest and smiled into his serious eyes.

"In some ways I am my mother's daughter," she said. "I can be stubborn. I do not like to admit I am wrong. And I hope I have a portion of her intelligence. But I am not my mother, Grae. I would never treat a man I loved as she treats my father. Nor would I deprive my people of the benefit of your wisdom, not to mention your sense of justice. I meant what I said to you before. When I rule, you will rule beside me."

To her surprise, he squirmed at that. "I don't know that I need to rule, precisely. I am only an armorer's son. I have no training for kingship. I cannot even sit a horse!"

Lily chuckled and snuggled back into his arms.

"Why are you laughing?" he said, endearingly aggrieved. "Kingship is a serious responsibility. I wasn't raised for this as you were. What if I—"

She silenced him with a soft kiss. "I laugh because I know you, Grae. You will not rest until you learn what is required. You are too proud not to do a job well, whether it is removing spots or making love or foiling an insurrectionist plot. If you have any doubts, Ian and Col can attest you are a natural leader, not to mention a cool head in a crisis. Trust me, you will learn to ride a horse and sit in judgment and remind your wife she has a responsibility not only to rule, but to serve."

A more flattering sort of man would have denied any necessity for the last. Grae merely scratched his jaw and looked doubtful. "You will help me?"

"Only if you will help me," she said.

That gave him pause. His arms tightened around her back.

"I will," he said with the seriousness of a solemn oath.

"Good," she said.

And they both smiled into the hush.

About the author:

Emma Holly started out writing fantasy, wandered into romance and then jumped, headfirst, into the murky waters of erotica where she was rewarded with (gasp!) real publishing contracts.

Red Sage gave her her first chance to combine all her literary loves. For those interested in her even-steamier side, Emma Holly also writes for Black Lace. Her fan mail occasionally embarrasses her, but so far she's bearing up!